The Decadent Short Story

The Decadent Short Story
An Annotated Anthology

Edited by Kostas Boyiopoulos, Yoonjoung Choi and
Matthew Brinton Tildesley

EDINBURGH
University Press

© editorial matter and organisation Kostas Boyiopoulos, Yoonjoung Choi and
Matthew Brinton Tildesley, 2015
© the chapters their several authors, 2015

Edinburgh University Press Ltd
The Tun - Holyrood Road
12(2f) Jackson's Entry
Edinburgh EH8 8PJ
www.euppublishing.com

Typeset in 11.5/14 Ehrhardt by
Servis Filmsetting Ltd, Stockport, Cheshire
and printed and bound in Great Britain by
CPI Group (UK) Ltd, Croydon CR0 4YY

A CIP record for this book is available from the British Library

ISBN 978 0 7486 9213 2 (hardback)
ISBN 978 0 7486 9215 6 (webready PDF)
ISBN 978 0 7486 9214 9 (paperback)
ISBN 978 0 7486 9216 3 (epub)

The right of Kostas Boyiopoulos, Yoonjoung Choi and Matthew Brinton Tildesley to be identified as
Editor of this work has been asserted in accordance with the Copyright, Designs and Patents Act 1988,
and the Copyright and Related Rights Regulations 2003 (SI No. 2498).

Contents

Acknowledgements viii
List of Illustrations x
Foreword, *Simon J. James* xi
Note on the Texts xiii

Introduction 1

I. Little Magazines 27
The Century Guild Hobby Horse
   Selwyn Image 'A Bundle of Letters: Giving a Selection from
      Three or Four of the Less Uninteresting of Them' (1888) 27
   Ernest Dowson 'A Case of Conscience' (1891) 38
   Ernest Dowson 'The Statute of Limitations' (1893) 48
The Dial
   Charles Ricketts 'The Cup of Happiness' (1889) 56
   Anon. [Charles Ricketts] 'Sensations' (1889) 65
   Charles Haslewood Shannon 'A Simple Story' (1889) 68
The Pagan Review
   W. S. Fanshawe [William Sharp] 'The Black Madonna' (1892) 71
The Chameleon
   Anon. [John Francis Bloxam] 'The Priest and the Acolyte' (1894) 86
The Yellow Book
   George Egerton 'A Lost Masterpiece: A City Mood, Aug. '93'
      (1894) 98
   Hubert Crackanthorpe 'Modern Melodrama' (1894) 104

Charlotte M. Mew 'Passed' (1894)	112
Lionel Johnson 'Tobacco Clouds' (1894)	126
'C. S.' [presumed Henry Harland] 'To Every Man a Damsel or Two' (1894)	134
Victoria Cross 'Theodora: A Fragment' (1895)	136
R. Murray Gilchrist 'The Crimson Weaver' (1895)	159
Mrs Ernest [Ada] Leverson 'The Quest of Sorrow' (1896)	166
Ella D'Arcy 'The Death Mask' (1896)	174

The Savoy

Rudolph Dircks 'Ellen' (1896)	181
Frederick Wedmore 'To Nancy' (1896)	186
Frederick Wedmore 'The Deterioration of Nancy' (1896)	196
Arthur Symons 'Pages from the Life of Lucy Newcome' (1896)	206
Theodore Wratislaw 'Mutability' (1896)	220
Joseph Conrad 'The Idiots' (1896)	233

The Pageant

John Gray 'Light' (1897)	253
Max Beerbohm 'Yai and the Moon' (1897)	272
Villiers de l'Isle-Adam 'Queen Ysabeau' (1897)	281

II. Other Sources — 299

Oscar Wilde 'The Nightingale and the Rose' (1888)	299
Vernon Lee 'The Legend of Madame Krasinska' (1890)	305
Oscar Wilde 'The Sphinx without a Secret' (1891)	327
E. Nesbit 'The Ebony Frame' (1891)	332
Eric Stenbock 'The True Story of a Vampire' (1894)	342
H. G. Wells 'The Flowering of the Strange Orchid' (1894, 1895)	350
Una Ashworth Taylor 'The Truce of God' (1896)	357
Vincent O'Sullivan 'Original Sin' (1896)	365
M. P. Shiel 'Xélucha' (1896)	370
Arthur Symons 'The Death of Peter Waydelin' (1905)	379

Appendices

1: Parodies

H. G. Wells 'A Misunderstood Artist' (1894)	392
Lionel Johnson 'Incurable' (1896)	396
2: Background Sources	400
3: Further Reading: a Timeline	420

Notes	427
Select Bibliography	459
Index	462

Acknowledgements

We wish to express our gratitude to Victoria Le Fevre for her fine eye for detail, and Ben Fletcher-Watson, Francesca M. Richards and Michael Shallcross for their sterling work tracking down archaic words, phrases and publications. We give special thanks to Simon J. James, Michael O'Neill and Mark Sandy, for their precious help and guidance. Our thanks also go to Laurel Brake, Kooenrad Claes, Stefano Cracolici, Nick Freeman, Angelique Richardson, Michael Mack, Glenda Norquay, Anthony Patterson, Talia Schaffer, Jonathan Wild and Sarah Wootton, for their advice and encouragement. We would also like to thank the librarians and archivists of Palace Green Library (Durham University), especially Mike Harkness, the Interlibrary Request Service Staff of Bill Bryson Library (Durham University), the staff of Bridgeman Art Library and York University Library, and from the Rare Books and Special Collections Department at Princeton University Library, Yvonne Crevier of the University of Massachusetts Press.

Our warm thanks go to Jackie Jones, Commissioning Editor of the Literary Studies Department of Edinburgh University Press, and Dhara Patel and Jenny Daly, Assistant Commissioning Editors. Our special thanks go to Nicola Wood, copy editor, for her dedication, thorough work and extraordinary attention to detail. We also thank James Dale, Managing Desk Editor, and Rebecca Mackenzie. This book would not be possible without their input and support.

Max Beerbohm's 'Yai and the Moom' is reproduced by permission of Berlin Associates Limited.

The excerpt ['The Amber Statuette'] from *The Hill of Dreams* by Arthur

Machen (Copyright © Arthur Machen, 1907) is reprinted by permission of A. M. Heath & Co. Ltd.

M. P. Shiel's 'Xélucha' from *Shapes in the Fire* (1896) is reprinted by permission of Copyright © Javier Marías (The Estate of M. P. Shiel).

Arthur Symons's 'Pages from the Life of Lucy Newcome' (1896) and 'The Death of Peter Waydelin' from *Spiritual Adventures* (1905) are reprinted by permission of Brian Read on behalf of the Literary Estate of Arthur Symons.

H. G. Wells's 'The Flowering of the Strange Orchid' (1894, 1895) and 'A Misunderstood Artist (1894) are reprinted by permission of United Agents on behalf of: The Literary Executors of the Estate of H. G. Wells.

'The Genesis of Spiritual Adventures' [pp. 20–1]. Corrected typescript; undated; Arthur Symons Papers, C0182, Box 9, Folder 7; Manuscripts Division, Department of Rare Books and Special Collections, Princeton University Library.

Will Rothenstein's drawing 'Mr. John Davidson' (Fig. 9) is reproduced by permission of the © Estate of Sir William Rothenstein / Bridgeman Images.

We would also like to thank Leonie Sturge-Moore and her sister Charmian O'Neil for kindly allowing us to reproduce textual and visual materials by Charles de Sousy Ricketts and Charles Haslewood Shannon. In addition our appreciation goes to Richard Underwood, Pennington Solicitors, for the reproduction of Joseph Conrad's 'The Idiots', as well as to Colby College Special Collections, Waterville, Maine, for the reproduction of Vernon Lee's 'The Legend of Madame Krasinska'.

The editors have made every attempt to secure permission for the texts and images included in this volume. If readers become aware of any missing information with regard to ownership rights for any material, the editors would be happy to hear from them.

List of Illustrations

All illustrations will be found between pages 287 and 298.

Figure 1. Charles Ricketts, front cover, *The Dial* 1 (1889).
Figure 2. C. H. Shannon, 'Return of the Prodigal', *The Dial* 1 (1889).
Figure 3. Charles Ricketts, illuminated initial piece to 'The Unwritten Book', *The Dial* 2 (1892).
Figure 4. *The Dial* 2 (1892), contents page.
Figure 5. Selwyn Image, title page, *The Century Guild Hobby Horse* Vol. 1 (1886).
Figure 6. Frederick Sandys, 'Danae in the Brazen Chamber', *The Century Guild Hobby Horse* 3.xii (1888).
Figure 7. C. H. Shannon, 'Umbilicus Tuus Crater Tornatilis, Numquam Indigens Poculis. Venter Tuus Sicut Acervus Tritici, Vallatus Liliis', drawing on stone, *The Century Guild Hobby Horse* 6.xxii (1891).
Figure 8. P. Wilson Steer, 'Skirt Dancing', *The Yellow Book* Vol. 3 (October 1894).
Figure 9. Will Rothenstein, 'Mr. John Davidson', *The Yellow Book* Vol. 4 (January 1895).
Figure 10. Patten Wilson, front cover, *The Yellow Book* Vol. 6 (July 1895).
Figure 11. Aubrey Beardsley, front cover, *The Savoy* 2 (April 1896).
Figure 12. Charles Ricketts, 'Oedipus, after a Pen Drawing', *The Pageant* 1 (1896).

Foreword

Simon J. James

The story of the British literary 'Decadence' of the 1880s and 1890s is an extraordinary one: that of a myth which its originators themselves had helped to create, whose afterlife quickly hardened into received opinion for much of the twentieth century before its being challenged, overturned and expanded by the scholarship of the last twenty years. This collection shows Decadence both to be what it is often imagined to be, but a great deal more besides.

The late nineteenth-century's explosion of reading material made possible as never before a vibrant *breadth* in the literary field, and the stories here demonstrate the freedom, a sense of permission, in the inhabitants of this newly broadened domain. Here are expanded possibilities of literary production and consumption, of experiments in literary form and the presentation of potential subject matter previously considered illicit. Decadent writing frequently seeks to extend the reach of the literary towards its boundaries with other art forms – to philosophy, especially ethics as well as aesthetics, music both high and low, to painting and sculpture; aesthetic response to an art form ekphrastically represented within the text is a commonly figured fictional theme. Perhaps the short story, however, is the quintessential Decadent art form. Many writers feature here heed Walter Pater's adjuration to value a moment's experience for that experience's own sake, and so dramatise moments less of epiphany (a term which implies the perception of a more lasting kind of achieved knowledge) but more of an intensively realised moment of living, of the inner life dramatised through sensory and bodily experience. Brief as these literary encounters may be, the hallucinatory of the fragmentary can yield the kind of truth possessed by a dream. The fantastic and the ghostly, the Gothic and the fable are present in a number of these stories, but often remain autonomously *un-allegorical*: these tropes do not translate as understood to be standing in for something else, but are imaginings of the variousness, of the potentialities of being. While the conventional short story usually displays 'a mania for a secret', in the words of Wilde's 'A Sphinx without a Secret', many of these stories refuse simply to unfold themselves at the tale's end, but merely evanesce, like tobacco smoke. Liberated both from a mimetic fidelity to real life, from the telos to mean or to be instructive, they can give voice to figures marginalised or ignored by Victorian fiction, or might demonstrate that the nature of human sexual experience is much wider than that of its literary representation hitherto. Decadence also often conflates the erotic with the deadly, and the frequent recurrence of death across these stories is a reminder of the transitory nature of human existence: E. Nesbit's 'The Ebony Frame' is one of only several deadly or vampiric works of art that recall Pater's undead La Gioconda or Dorian Gray's covert portrait. Simultaneously, the comic is never far away – the 'pose' of the Decadent identity is just that, and so is open to being suspended, reversed or ironised; the Decadence shown here is by no means utterly quiescent to the 'cult of beauty', (nor is exclusively male) as Ada Leverson's exquisitely funny 'The Quest of Sorrow' shows.

The self-consciously, even willingly, ephemeral nature of this material means that historically much of it has been hard to find – that the natural home of the Decadent short story is the Little Magazine means that the editors of this volume are much to be congratulated in having collated such a wealth of material. While there is certainly evidence of forms of proto-Modernism, a distinctive late Victorian sensibility is shown here, *The Decadent Short Story* successfully captures a discrete and distinctive literary moment.

Note on the Texts

The texts have been taken from their original, first publications. Only a couple of stories in the second section of this anthology have been taken from their second printings, as is evident in the 'Notes'. The texts have been standardised in order to comply with the same house style. Single quotation marks (with double quotation marks for an inner quote) have been applied throughout. Spelling variations have been adjusted: 'grey' instead of 'gray', and American spelling has been replaced with British spelling; for example '-ise' instead of '-ize', or 'labour' instead of 'labor'. Outdated hyphenation (or the lack of it) has been retained. Quite often terminal punctuation is not followed by capitalised words: this practice seems to be typical of the period and has been retained. There have been a very few alterations from colon to semi-colon, to suit the modern eye a little better, and also in the place they appear in the order of punctuation. Typographical and grammatical errors have been silently corrected.

Introduction

The 'short story' and 1890s 'Decadence': to date, these two terms have seldom been joined in academic discussion. One could surmise that when these two terms are paired, the result is a narrowed-down type of literature that yields a few lurid specimens of short fiction. This cannot be further from the truth. The aim of this anthology of thirty-six stories and two parodies from 1888 to 1905 is to show that the 'Decadent short story', more than the 'Decadent poem' in a way, proliferates as a phenomenon of immense cultural and aesthetic significance in Britain, as is manifest throughout the eclectic pages of the Little Magazines. It is a distinct category, yet it embodies a variety of styles and themes. As a sentinel of stylistic acuity, it evolves out of Aestheticism and feeds into twentieth-century Modernism. The literature of Decadence is epitomised by novelty, sensuousness and sensuality, morbid themes, a loss of Classical proportion, and excessive focus on style at the expense of content; it is 'a new and beautiful and interesting disease', as Arthur Symons famously phrased it.[1] Decadent writers were disillusioned by the stiff morality and hackneyed normality of the age and sought to upset it, both in life and in art. The short story with its emphasis on artistic delicacy and style at the expense of traditional moral clichés serves as the most suitable platform for this trend, *ipso facto*. Decadence and the short story form in Britain, as we will see, did not just overlap but were coterminous, interrelated and interdependent.

DECADENCE AND ITS CULTURAL BACKGROUND

Decadence as a cultural phenomenon, or as a way of behaving, by the last decade of the nineteenth century was readily identifiable in Britain. Unlike some literary distinctions named in hindsight, such as 'Early Modern Theatre', or even 'Romanticism', Decadence as an artistic and social trait was identified and named at the time of its manifestation. For some, Decadence was a flag to be waved brazenly, for others, the ultimate insult. So who or what may be termed Decadent in the late Victorian era?

'Decadence, decadence: you are all decadent nowadays.' Such was Hubert Crackanthorpe's lament in his article, 'Reticence in Literature: Some Roundabout Remarks' in the second volume of *The Yellow Book* in 1894. The problem for Crackanthorpe was one of perception:

> Ibsen, Degas, and the New English Art Club; Zola, Oscar Wilde, and the Second Mrs. Tanqueray. Mr. Richard Le Gallienne is hoist with his own petard; even the British playwright has not escaped the taint. Ah, what a hideous spectacle. All whirling along towards one common end.[2]

The bourgeois critics against whom Crackanthorpe was railing clearly perceived a broad swathe of modern artists as being Decadent, be they homegrown British, or continental imports. The pinnacle of such a conservative view of progressive art was Max Nordau's monolithic, and rabidly anti-modern treatise *Degeneration*, which appeared in English in early 1895. Indeed, Nordau's chosen examples of pathological degenerates follow Crackanthorpe's satirical list of Decadents quite closely. However the issue of Decadence as a perceived way of behaving was not a phenomenon born of, nor confined to the 1890s. British Decadence, as a mode of being, or as a set of preoccupations, began to form in the mid-1880s, and the evolution of this cultural movement was crystallised by Wilde in *The Picture of Dorian Gray*:

> Yes, there was to be, as Lord Henry had prophesied, a new hedonism that was to re-create life, and to save it from that harsh, uncomely puritanism that is having, in our own day, its curious revival. It was to have its service of the intellect, certainly; yet it was never to accept any theory or system that would involve the sacrifice of any mode of passionate experience. Its aim, indeed, was to be

experience itself, and not the fruits of experience, sweet or bitter as they might be. Of the asceticism that deadens the senses, as of the vulgar profligacy that dulls them, it was to know nothing. But it was to teach man to concentrate himself upon the moments of a life that is itself but a moment.[3]

Dorian's change in behaviour is a reaction; the 'new hedonism' is his defence against 'that harsh, uncomely puritanism'. Up until this moment in the novel, Dorian is a passive lover of beauty, largely unconcerned with the outside world, in terms of moral engagement. However, Lord Henry's hedonistic creed forces him to become active and morally engaged with this 'uncomely puritanism'. Dorian's socially detached Aestheticism thus morphs into socially engaged Decadence.

This moment in Wilde's novel is representative of a gradual cultural shift in Britain, as a reaction against the puritanism, which, as Wilde put it, 'is having, in our own day, its curious revival'. Evidence of such a revival of puritanism can be seen in the 'British Matron' letters which called for a ban on representations of the Nude in art, in *The Times* during May 1885. The 'British Matron' was in fact the treasurer of the Royal Academy, John Callcott Horsley, who decried the 'indecent pictures that disgrace our exhibitions'. This 'display of nudity at the . . . Academy' brought about in this unfortunate creature 'a burning sense of shame' as the gallery itself became, for her, transformed into a Bosch-like vision of Hell, forcing her

> to turn from them with disgust and cause only timid half glances to be cast at the paintings hanging close by . . . lest it should be supposed the spectator is looking at that which revolts his or her sense of decency.

Against this most vicious onslaught of indecency, the Matron announced that a 'noble crusade of purity . . . has been started to check the rank profligacy that abounds in our land'.[4] Indeed, several other voices followed the call. 'Senex' likened the artist's model to the prostitute, and 'Another British Matron' asked,

> What has the passion for the nude in art done for our neighbours across the Channel that we should view without fear and alarm its introduction and spread among ourselves? . . . Our honour for ourselves, our love for our daughters, and our regard for the future

welfare of our country, whose warriors, statesmen, and citizens are to be born of our daughters, compel us to decry and discountenance, with all our powers, these stealthy, steadfast advances of the cloven foot.[5]

Furthermore, these letters to *The Times* do not represent a few isolated outbursts. In the world of fine art, Purity societies disrupted the work of art schools, insisting upon segregation of the sexes as well as a ban on nude models. The wider Purity movement had developed out of a campaign to repeal the Contagious Diseases Acts of the 1860s, and by the mid-1880s had Art and Literature in its sights. A. S. Dyer's 1884 pamphlet, 'Facts for Men on Moral Purity and Health' stated,

> If you would keep yourself pure, you must set yourself against sensuous Literature and Art as resolutely as against foul tongued companions . . . An artist, or writer, whether in poetry or prose, who knowingly uses his talents to excite the animal passions, whatever the conventionalities of society may term him, is a mental prostitute.[6]

In 1889, the newly formed London County Council was petitioned by Purity campaigners, such as the notorious Mrs Ormiston Chant, to revoke the licences of London's music halls. Campaigners took offence at both the performers and their performance, claiming that there was little difference between them and the prostitutes that plied their trade on the music hall promenades. Popular haunts, such as the Empire, the Oxford and the Alhambra, were seriously hampered in their day-to-day running, and some were even closed, pending enquiries into the lyrical content of songs and the behaviour of performers. In the case of the Empire, structural alterations were made in an attempt to screen off the prostitutes from their clientele (the screen was, however, pulled down by the crowd as soon as the place reopened).[7] Hence, the Purity crusades, which Wilde referred to in 1890, were a powerful force in British society, and by the mid-1880s they were actively opposing and restricting artists, writers and performers. Those who worked in the Arts were therefore forced to react to such fierce opposition and interference; they could capitulate, refute or embrace this concept of transgression, which the puritans had foisted upon them.

Crackanthorpe's 1894 article is representative of many scholarly articles which opposed the Matron and her brood, and date back at least to Selwyn

Image's article 'On the Representation of the Nude in Art' which appeared in *The Century Guild Hobby Horse* in 1886. However, alongside the rhetoric, artists and writers also chose to engage in the moral debate by taking the same defiant path as Dorian Gray: if the nude and the sensuous were outlawed by the puritans, then the nude and the sensuous would become blazons for the defenders of Art. Alongside rhetorical arguments and the pictorial explorations of the body and sexuality, within the pages of the Little Magazines, patterns of preoccupations and themes emerge that form the Decadent short story.

Alongside preoccupations with sensuality and the body, and themes such as prostitution and the music halls, another typically Decadent trope was Roman Catholicism. Although the Catholic faith may not seem particularly subversive today, in 1880s and '90s Britain, it was a far more potent symbol of rebellion. For centuries, the Enemy of England had almost always been Catholic, be he Spanish, French or a champion of the Irish Free State. Practising Catholics in Victorian England had only recently been released from the shackles imposed on them after the English Civil War, which included heavy fines and total banishment from institutions such as the universities and government.

Wilde's naming of the 'new puritanism' is Protestant by definition, and the British Matron letters clearly link the ideas of Britishness and Protestant purity, and pit them in staunch opposition to all that is continental, and therefore Catholic. As George Moore, an Irish convert to both the Protestant faith and English national identity, declared, 'England is Protestantism, Protestantism is England.'[8] Mainstream Victorian culture was Protestant through and through. Taking up a Catholic pose in Victorian Britain was therefore a powerfully subversive statement. For some writers, such as Selwyn Image in the *Hobby Horse*, Catholicism was indeed merely a rhetorical pose. For others, such as the novelist Ronald Firbank, the ritualisation of sin embodied within the Catholic confessional appeared to be a major attraction. Others still, such as Ernest Dowson and John Gray, were quite sincere in their beliefs. Hence Catholicism, as a site of defiance, deviance, or indeed heartfelt solace, finds its way into Decadent writings.[9]

Another shaping influence on the literature of the time was the 1868 Amendment to the Obscene Publications Act of 1857. The original Act, drafted by Lord Chief Justice Campbell, stated that the definition of obscene or pornographic literature was 'works written for the single purpose of corrupting the morals of youth and of a nature calculated to shock the common feelings of decency in any well-regulated mind'.

However, in 1867, the Protestant Electoral Union republished an 1851 tract entitled *The Confessional Unmasked: Showing the Depravity of the Priesthood, Questions Put to Females in Confession, Perjury and Stealing Commanded and Encouraged, &C., &C.* Although eye-wateringly pornographic in content, the publishers defended themselves against the charge of obscenity by insisting that their *intent* was not to corrupt or deprave, but to show the depravity of the Catholic priesthood. This led Chief Justice Cockburn to amend the Act in 1868, stating that

> The test of obscenity is this, whether the tendency of the matter charged as obscenity is to deprave and corrupt those whose minds are open to such immoral influences and into whose hands a publication of this sort may fall.[10]

Hence the reader became a defining aspect of what was obscene or pornographic in the eyes of the Law. This resulted in the Victorian double standards of legend, whereby an upper-class gentlemen's club could circulate privately printed erotica of the highest order, whilst a lowly book seller, publicly distributing prints of the *Venus di Milo* or even Aristotle's writings on childbirth, would be prosecuted for trading in pornography.

However, the concept of reader involvement in a story proved singularly useful to creative writers of fiction. If the reader knows he or she is expected to read between the lines; saying nothing can become a substitute for saying the unsayable. Therefore, fragmented or expurgated texts could infer illicit content that is not technically present in the story. The 'letter' format and the expurgated story became popular ways of presenting half a story, where the reader is encouraged to provide certain details. Authors would often pepper their tales with instructions to read more into the work than is printed, or even include candid references to the 1868 Amendment's fussing over the hands into which a tale has fallen, to encourage this kind of reader involvement.[11] The Decadent writer had to navigate a singularly highly-strung tightrope, balancing titillation and rebellion in one hand, and compliance with the law in the other; a trick that became even more daring after Wilde's conviction in 1895.

THE 'LITTLE MAGAZINES'

The late Victorian age saw an explosion in the periodicals business, from daily newspapers to niche market magazines. The 1880s marked a highpoint in Britain's Imperial might, and the spoils of empire fuelled the booming British economy of the last two decades of Victoria's reign. The British middle classes found themselves with more money in their pockets and a concomitant array of consumer goods on which to spend it all. This included literature as a product, and discerning Victorians were offered the choice from an immense range of periodical literature. From *Woman's World* to *The Savoy*, one could seek to define oneself by the things one read. Another factor in the rise in literature was the universal Education Act 1870. By the last decade of Victoria's reign, more people than ever were literate. This resulted in more consumers *and* producers of literature; and the short story, as a literary form, was an ideal tool for both. There was a creative 'outburst' of short stories in the *fin de siècle* jostling for attention, as H. G. Wells recalls.[12] Magazines that included short stories were much cheaper to buy than the standard Victorian 'triple decker' novels. For the same economic motivations, a publisher would be far more likely to take on a new writer of short stories for the periodical market, than an untested novelist.

The Little Magazines were instrumental in allowing the audacious experiments of the Decadent short story.[13] As wider Decadent circles were fighting a defensive war over what may or may not be considered fit for artistic interpretation, the question of who has the 'right to define' art came to the fore. Some Decadent works display a definite remapping of artistic form to the point of deliberately alienating a wide readership, while others negotiate the aesthetic within more traditional bounds. This was also reflected in the policy spectrum of the magazines; from John Lane's diplomatically mild, all-inclusive policy of *The Yellow Book* to that of radical eclecticism and artistic isolationism in *The Dial*.

This dilemma was symptomatic of the paradoxical nature of the Decadent movement; that it is at once a voice for the democratisation of art, and yet in many ways inherently elitist. Two forms of commodification are revealed as Little Magazines were both trade market products and 'objects of luxury'.[14] The Little Magazine of the 1890s, as Ian Fletcher surmises, is 'the most forceful emblem of decadent anxiety, and its small and privatized character is itself elite'.[15] It liberated authors from the shackles of 'righteous' editorial policies of giant commercial periodicals such as George

Newnes's *The Strand Magazine*, whose glorification of Queen Victoria in the first pages of the first issue (January 1891) set an institutional, patriotic tone of middle-class values. Still, stories with Decadent elements sometimes made their way to popular magazines; Sherlock Holmes stories, laced as they are with drug and homoerotic allusions, also featured in *The Strand*. These exceptions were the result of a fluid culture that was growing out of Victorian tradition.

Apart from *The Yellow Book* and *The Savoy* which stamped the mien of the Yellow Nineties with Aubrey Beardsley's iconic, sinuous and tantalising drawings, magazines associated with Decadence were either part of a Pre-Raphaelite, Morrisian trajectory such as *The Century Guild Hobby Horse* (1884–94) or an imported French Symbolist aesthetic such as *The Dial* and *The Pageant* (1896–7). These magazines were partly inspired by French projects such as *Le Chat Noir* (1882–95), Anatole Baju's *Le Décadent* (1886–9) and the short-lived *La Décadence* (October 1886). These British and French magazines were then emulated in America, with the notable examples of *The Chap-Book* (1894–8) and *M'lle New York* (1895–6; 1898–9).[16]

These enterprises were part of a general *dernier cri* among avant-garde circles for which the art of editorship was as important as the vision it mediated through the magazine's coterie. The Little Magazine editor, like an orchestra conductor, put together contents that chimed and contrasted with one another; with care he selected the paper, the layout, the letterpress and the physical arrangement of the contents. The result is a momentous editorial event, an organic ensemble that conforms to the 'Wagnerian *Gesamtkunstwerk*' or 'total work of art'.[17] And yet, temporal fragmentation is inbuilt in this 'total work of art'; along these lines Fletcher suggests the link between the Little Magazine format and the Decadent short story: in the 'deconstruction of time, experience refin[es] itself into critical "moments"', rendering the present 'unpredictable, dangerous, open'.[18] The Little Magazine is an aesthetic artefact to be displayed and handled as a museum piece for the indulgent, selective, reflective reader, itself like an 'instant museum' as Jan Gordon has suggested,[19] containing assorted artefacts. Hence the Little Magazine and the short story are organised in space in a decorative and fragmented manner, an artefact nested within an artefact. As we will see below, Decadent short stories were often jigsaws of various genres; and likewise, the magazine 'was inter-generic, like decadence' itself.[20]

In many ways, *The Century Guild Hobby Horse* is the godfather of the late Victorian Little Magazines. Although its roots lie in the Pre-

Raphaelite and Morrisian Arts and Crafts movement, the *Hobby Horse*'s central coterie for most of its ten-year tenure, Herbert Horne, Selwyn Image, Arthur Galton and Lionel Johnson, soon reworked their stance in the wake of Walter Pater's writings and philosophy. By the mid-to-late-1880s, libertinism, Hellenic revivalism and the Paterian cult of the 'personality' became dominant themes, along with Catholic rhetoric and imagery. As the years progressed, a distinctly homoerotic edge became discernible within the *Hobby Horse*, and it is also memorable for being the only Little Magazine to which Oscar Wilde actually contributed. It was moreover the first magazine to become a self-conscious work of 'Total Art'. Handmade paper, carefully selected fonts and inks, wide margins and an almost fetishistic attention to print reproduction details made the *Hobby Horse* itself a work of art, as much as the fine art that it discussed and displayed. This aspect of the *Hobby Horse* is said to have inspired William Morris's Kelmscott Press.

The Dial, while certainly one of the Little Magazines, stretches the bounds of the term 'periodical', due to its *ad-hoc* and far from regular publication history. The five issues, in 1889, '92, '93, '96 and '97, were said to come out only when 'the sun of inspiration' shone on its makers, hence the name. Stridently anti-commercial, *The Dial* was ephemeral, excessive, expensive and exquisite. The *Hobby Horse*'s fixation with wide margins was taken to new heights in *The Dial*, with often the tiniest block of text, floating in the midst of a lavish ocean of costly, handmade paper. Almost exclusively the work of its central coterie, Charles Shannon, Charles Ricketts, Thomas Sturge Moore and John Gray, *The Dial* revelled in the sensual and even erotic in its artwork, prose and poetry, was steeped in classical imagery and allusion, and was bold to the point of aggression in its opinions over the right to define art. Proto-Modernist disruption of traditional form and deliberate reader-alienation are features of the prose, polemic and even physical form of the magazine.

The Chameleon, though often cited as one of the Little Magazines, was not a publicly available work, but a single-issue student magazine. It was to be a rebirth of the Oxford undergraduate journal, *The Spirit Lamp*, and very much inspired by Oscar Wilde, to whom it owes its infamy, as the publication was used by his accusers at the Old Bailey. Wilde and his lover, 'Bosie' Douglas, had both contributed to the magazine, and Douglas's homoerotic poem 'Two Loves', along with the editor, John Francis Bloxam's flagrantly homosexual and paederastic tale 'The Priest and the Acolyte' were publicly aired at Wilde's trials. Such a high profile scandal sent Bloxam into hiding and ensured the demise of the stillborn magazine, yet at the same time confirmed its place in Decadent history.

The Yellow Book was the most commercially successful Little Magazine, which has led to the assumption that it is therefore archetypal of the form. However, commercial success came at the price of exluding any of the elitist, or avant-garde manifestos which had been the foundations of the *Yellow Book*'s predecessors. Publisher John Lane and his editor, Henry Harland, advertised for unsolicited manuscripts in the magazine itself, and so this 'catch all' policy saw the Decadent lying down with the Conservative, traditional Protestant ethics stuck cheek-by-jowl with Modernist iconoclasm, and the young artistic *enfant terrible* that was Aubrey Beardsley was seen rubbing shoulders with elder statesmen of the Royal Academy. Along with its wide appeal, the *Yellow Book* was cheap, good quality and value for money. Much more of a 'book' than its predecessors, a typical volume of the *Yellow Book* was three-to-four hundred pages long, far outstripping even an annual volume of the *Hobby Horse*. Furthermore, its pages are dominated by the short story. Although not typically Decadent, Lane's open door policy led to the discovery of much in the way of new talent, and particularly new female writers, such as Victoria Cross and Ella D'Arcy who rose to become *de facto* co-editor alongside Harland.

Often seen as a direct descendant of the *Yellow Book* alone, *The Savoy* is in fact something of a return to Decadent form; it drew its inspiration much more from the *Hobby Horse* than the *Yellow Book*. Beardsley and the Decadent avant garde from the *Yellow Book* had been ousted by the conservatives within the periodical, after Wilde's arrest and conviction. In *The Savoy*, they teamed up with editor Arthur Symons and risqué publisher Leonard Smithers, alongside many survivors from the wreck of the *Hobby Horse*, which had foundered a little over a year before. One of the stories announced in the 'Prospectus' to the magazine in November 1895, before its launch, was H. Cranmer Byng's 'A Village Decadent'. However the story never appeared. This editorial backtracking perhaps is due to Symons's attempt to hoodwink the mainstream readership as to the relevance of the hot term 'Decadence'. This is also reflected in Symons's diplomatically reserved editorial note to the first issue.[21] In *The Savoy*, Zola, Nietzsche and Wagner are defended (by the likes of Havelock Ellis and George Bernard Shaw) against puritanical attackers such as Max Nordau. Beardsley's flamboyantly Decadent artwork reached its zenith in the magazine, and the *Savoy*'s short stories are a distillation of Decadent style and preoccupations. Symons and Ernest Dowson provide highlights in terms of Decadent poetry and prose. *The Savoy* is also notable for including W. B. Yeats's early short stories, such as 'Rosa Alchemica' with its Aesthetic mysticism. It was more ephemeral in its physical form than the *Yellow Book*, and its elitist, Decadent raison d'être ensured its commercial failure.

The Pageant was in many ways a sister publication to *The Dial*, but with a far wider group of contributors. Its two annual volumes of 1896 and '97 were edited by Charles Shannon and Joseph William Gleeson White, but were far more substantial and sumptuous than the ephemeral *Dial*. The more arch, elitist polemical edge to the *Dial* is not present in the *Pageant*, which leaves it a more serious and considered periodical, quite obviously made for posterity. In its appearance it looked more like an annual edition of the *Hobby Horse*; large format, wide margins and luxurious. Selwyn Image and Lucien Pissarro designed the outer illustrations, and like the early *Hobby Horse*, the Pre-Raphaelite brotherhood feature prominently in its artwork, directly or as an influence on the likes of Charles Ricketts. The letterpress includes work by the stalwarts of the *Hobby Horse*, *Dial* and *Savoy*, along with others such as Max Beerbohm (who had contributed to *The Yellow Book*). The short stories in the *Pageant* are weightier than those in many of the other Little Magazines, and are similar in vein to the more scholarly pieces in *The Dial* by Gray and Sturge Moore. Classical, oriental and religious themes dominate in the short stories of the *Pageant*, reflected in those stories chosen below.

The one and only issue of *The Pagan Review* is a remarkable literary and editorial oddity; its quirky contents were all the work of only one man, William Sharp, under various pseudonyms. Even the name of the editor, W. H. Brooks, was an alias. Whilst Symons contributed all the textual contents of the last issue of *The Savoy* out of necessity, Sharp did the same as an act of conscious mischief, pulling the strings behind imaginary authors' names, and even attracting subscriptions. In the highly idiosyncratic and formidable 'Foreword', the editor of *The Pagan Review* echoes Pater's 'Conclusion' and capitalises on the ideals of the literary 'new paganism' with the Latin slogan 'Sic transit gloria Grundi': 'thus passes the glory of Grundy'; Sharp whimsically replaces the word 'mundi' (world) with a reference to Mrs Grundy, the embodiment of conservative middle-class morality, stressing the iconoclasm of his magazine venture. By aiming 'at thorough-going unpopularity' and 'artistic inwardness', *The Pagan Review* emulates the elitist defiance of *The Dial* as it expresses total disregard for public opinion.[22]

THE DECADENT SHORT STORY: FORM AND GENRE

By 1895, bourgeois Victorian society perceived Decadence as a palpable threat to the social order, as may be seen in the runaway success of Nordau's *Degeneration* in English translation, and the trials of Oscar Wilde that followed only two months after its publication. Moreover, by the mid-1890s, the Decadent short story, as a distinctly British literary form, born of British culture, was fully formed, and identifiable in terms of its style, themes and preoccupations. Although it was partly influenced by its European counterparts (in France the short story was a popular genre from the beginning of the nineteenth century), in Britain the form had, at least in part, grown out of the legacy of Aestheticism.

Pater promoted the art of restrained and scintillating, euphuistic prose against the current of orthodox critics who still saw prose as a populist mode of expression. 'Prose,' Pater posits in 'Style' (*Fortnightly Review*, 1888), is 'as varied in its excellence as humanity itself reflecting on the facts of its latest experience – an instrument of many stops, meditative, observant, descriptive, eloquent, analytic, plaintive, fervid.'[23] The Decadent short story became self-conscious and self-reflexive as it responded to Pater's attention to style and its varieties. Reading anything that fostered stylistic or psychological complexity was 'a morbid fondness for mental gymnastics', as Ada Leverson writes in her story 'Suggestion',[24] and was dismissed by the Philistines as Decadent.

The germ of Aesthetic fiction is traced in Edgar Allan Poe (1809–49) who vindicates in 'The Philosophy of Composition' (1846) the brevity of the short story as it is experienced in a continuous reading session and strives for 'unity of effect'.[25] Along with defining the genre, Poe designates its 'Decadent' themes for treatment, such as 'the death of a beautiful woman'.[26] Hence, by a peculiar coincidence, Decadence and the short story were twin-born from the same cradle. Poe's tight definition resonates half a century later, despite Henry James who was a fervent advocate of the longer form of novella. For Frederick Wedmore the short story 'can never be a novel in a nutshell'. Hence, Decadent novels with their complex effects on the reader's sensibility, such as Huysmans's *À Rebours*, are like *long* 'short stories' if the oxymoron be allowed. For Henry Harland, whose vocation involved the endless and meticulous polishing of prose, the artist's 'difficulty will be, by distilling and purifying his impression, to present it to us in a phial'.[27]

In its interest in the atypical and the bizarre, often, the Decadent short story is partly inspired by the French *conte cruel* which was championed by Villiers de l'Isle-Adam, Barbey d'Aurevilly and Octave Mirbeau, themselves influenced by Poe. The cruel tale relies on narrative manipulation, suspense and often *grand-guignol* denouements – Murray Gilchrist's ultra-sadistic *The Stone Dragon and Other Romances* (1894) or Arthur Conan Doyle's medical chiller 'The Case of Lady Sannox' (1893) are atypical, British examples. The short story creates meaning by engaging the reader in a dynamic play of its formal elements and images. Plot gives way to 'situation' in what Frederick Wedmore describes as 'pregnant brevity'.[28] The emergent 'plotless' short story dominates *The Yellow Book* and *The Savoy*.[29] The boundaries between tale and story, however, are not clear. One might cautiously say that in the *conte cruel* Decadence is mostly a thematic concern whereas in the short story it gravitates towards workmanship and 'preciosity'. And yet, both share in a certain economy (even baroque economy) of style and in flashing the sizzling turn of phrase.

But how inclusive is the Decadent short story in terms of school and genre? Wendell V. Harris, a specialist on *fin-de-siècle* short fiction, provides an angle in a series of studies in the 1960s. By taking into account the magazines, the fiction produced by the coteries around them through the publishing ventures of John Lane, Leonard Smithers and Elkin Mathews, and the critical reaction to this fiction, Harris sees three types of short story under the 'Decadence' label:

> The 'new realism' which so scandalised the guardians of British morality, the sentimentally melancholy stories of love and romance such as were provided by Henry Harland and Ernest Dowson, and the stream of 'aesthetic' prose represented by Wilde and Beardsley and others.[30]

For Harris, the reasons these incongruent tendencies fall under the 'Decadent' umbrella are: either critical approval or condemnation. These categories are symptomatic of a 'single disorder' according to Nordau's *Degeneration*; they often appeared side-by-side in those eclectic Little Magazines.[31] Derek Stanford, writing at the same time as Harris, provides an extensive analysis of the 1890s short story, with an emphasis on the impact of art for art's sake and the intrinsic, thematic workings of the new, booming genre. As writers of the 1890s challenged Victorian institutions of morality by reckoning the irresistible forces of sensuality, the short story made the most of the 'new democracy of the touch' and 'egalitarianism of the erotic senses'.[32] With its iconoclasm it dramatised 'the debate on the claims of erotic attraction and the demands of a sexual morality geared to marriage and solely marital intercourse'.[33] The varied themes and shifting meanings in the Decadent short story are indeed shaped by the struggle and even productive *impasse* between the democracy of the senses and the constraints of stringent morality. By following a different trajectory, Stanford's idea indirectly agrees with Harris's; Decadence served as a vehicle that absorbed even 'Realism' to its ends.

Later critics shifted the focus to the unique formal aspects of the Decadent short story. John R. Reed focuses on fragmentation and reconfiguration of its traditional forms: 'The decadent style of details dissolve[s] a traditional form only to have it reassembled in a new and subtler manner.'[34] Jan Gordon puts emphasis on its 'paradox' in which nature 'sychronously disguises and reveals'; he is also interested in the intricate, counter-intuitive network of associations contrived both at the level of characters and language: 'If the tales themselves are often circular in structure, and the characters come to be reflective doubles of one another, so language often functions the same way.'[35]

These cultural and formalist readings lead to the conclusion that the Decadent short story is fraught with a tortuous self-contradiction: it can be both militantly iconoclastic against the conservative order and a free-floating, pretty jewel that is true only to itself, as Wilde would say, adhering to the principles of 'art for art's sake'. And yet this polarity enhances its complexity even further as it implies productive tensions and Hegelian syntheses between the two ends.

The present anthology attempts to break down further Wendell Harris's three categories of short stories with the 'Decadent' label into the full gamut of Aestheticism, Psychological or New Realism, Naturalism, New Woman fiction, fantasy, Gothic and parody. Our editorial choices reflect patterns, resonances and affinities between these trends as the stories speak to one another. They also suggest that these trends are pushed to new limits through the short-storyists's restive pursuit after new forms and genres. In 'The Philosophy of the Short Story' (1885), Brander Matthews suggests that the 'genera and species' of the short story melt into one another.[36] In line with Wilde's principle of the interchangeability of the arts, and like James Whistler's paintings arranged and titled as musical compositions, further species include pictorial, musical and sculptural traits: literary sketches, arabesques, etchings, fragments and studies. The generic pedigree can be further specialised: M. P. Shiel's 'shapes' (as well as 'pieces' comprising the 'concert' of *Shapes in the Fire*), Pater's 'imaginary portraits', Vincent O'Sullivan's 'bargains' (*A Book of Bargains*), Crackanthorpe's 'vignettes' – not dissimilar from even Baudelaire's urban micro-narratives of *Petits Poèmes en Prose* (1869) –, Ella D'Arcy's 'monochromes' and George Egerton's 'keynotes'. As if these were English collective nouns, they dispense into the Decadent short story an exquisite, idiosyncratic air.

These *précieux* tags also underpin the short story as a 'snapshot' of life, an 'Impressionist canvas because it leaves a sense of something complete yet unfinished'.[37] This idea by Valerie Shaw is intended for the short story at large. Nevertheless, the painterly qualities of Impressionism in particular, espoused by Whistler and Walter Sickert, were absorbed by the Decadents and expressed with periphrastic and elliptical language, subjective viewpoints, psychological tensions and such fragmented settings as the nocturnal metropolis and the boudoir. The Impressionist method fosters moral ambiguity and artifice with its static, sketch-like quality. And yet, these stories are also fleeting trifles, or 'mood pieces', proliferating in the pages of *The Yellow Book*. Egerton captures their slightness and fragility by calling them 'fancies' and 'toys of the brain, to write them down is to destroy them – as fancies! and yet –'.[38] Egerton's hesitancy suggests that the short story fixes a mental frame of psychological convolutedness with all its shades like a floodlit relief or a delicate origami. The short story seems to just about arrest the otherwise unpinnable state of mind which is continuously compelled to mutate in the flux of the thinking process, whether that be the mind-set of a murderer as in O'Sullivan's 'Original Sin' or that of the woman who has fatally confused dispassionate aestheticism with emotional engrossment as in Ella D'Arcy's 'The Pleasure-Pilgrim'.

On top of twiddling with different artistic media, the Decadent short story experiments with genres in a chimerical as well as a protean manner. The chimerical version yokes genres and types into a pastiche. Charles Ricketts's 'The Cup of Happiness' and William Sharp's 'The Black Madonna', featured in this anthology, blend drama script and prose. Protean expression is especially significant in the shape-shifting between story and essay. Victorian authors of erotica and curiosa circumvented censorship by dishing out their works in the guise of medical treatises and scientific textbooks. The short story refined this strategy as it adopted it for its own sake. Lionel Johnson's 'Tobacco Clouds', reprinted here, blurs the boundary between story and meditative analysis, for instance. Holbrook Jackson points out that Max Beerbohm's 'The Happy Hypocrite' (*The Yellow Book* 11, 1896), a frolicsome take on *Dorian Gray*, is 'an essay masquerading as a story'.[39] This is also inverted: Arthur Symons's travel memoirs and essays on culture can be easily read as Paterian short stories, in which the *flâneur*-narrator is flooded by sensuous impressions and renders them in exquisitely vivid, self-conscious language. Two compelling instances are 'The Gingerbread Fair at Vincennes: A Colour-Study' and 'At the Alhambra: Impressions and Sensations', in the fourth and fifth numbers of *The Savoy* respectively. Selwyn Image's 'A Bundle of Letters' epitomises and even dramatises the perfect intermarriage between scholasticism and fictional narrative.

Dangerously elusive, often with an erudite, formal aspect, learned and littered with names and allusions, the essay/story essentially performs a cross-dressing. Its roots are to be found in D. G. Rossetti's 'Hand and Soul' (1849), which appeared in the Pre-Raphaelite Little Magazine *The Germ*. 'Hand and Soul' revolutionised short fiction. Not only did it blend short fiction with biography and memoir; it was a story which triggered its Aesthetic and Decadent counterpart of the 1890s as it provided a manifesto in the potent metaphor of art being the sensuous and subjective embodiment of the Romantic artist's soul. This was the first 'imaginary portrait' that Pater adopted and systematised in the quasi-autobiographical portrayal of Florian Delial in 'The Child in the House' (1878). In his study of the Decadent short story, John Reed puts Pater's *Imaginary Portraits* (1887) alongside Dowson's *Dilemmas* (1895) and Symons's *Spiritual Adventures* (1905), contending that these works 'collapse from narrative form into scholarly discourse'.[40] Pater's innovative blending gives the short story a paced savour and drives the subject-matter to the sphere of connoisseurship. Vernon Lee, in following her mentor Walter Pater, notably wrote imaginary portraits of artists of the Italian Renaissance; one example is 'An Eighteenth Century Singer: An Imaginary Portrait' (1891). Stories by Symons such as 'Esther Kahn' and 'Christian Trevalga' resemble imaginary tales about artists. This crucial sub-genre is even exported to France as Marcel Schwob's literary faux-accounts of *Vies imaginaires* (1896) attest.

THE STORIES: THEMATIC GROUPINGS

As well as hybridising forms and genres, Decadence manifests itself through a range of themes. The most frequent themes of the Nineties' short story according to Derek Stanford are three: 'the life of sex, the life of art, bohemian and *déclassé* existence'.[41] These are certainly central thematic axes around which the Decadent short story in particular revolves. And their occurrence takes place not only within the full range between the extreme ends of fantasy and Naturalism, but also between prose of restrained suggestiveness and that of laden luxury. However, the stories in the present volume reflect a more varied and intertwined network beyond sexuality, art and bohemianism. They are often preoccupied with solipsistic narratives and the introspective self, the Wildean/Paterian cult of the personality, homoeroticism, unobtainable objects of desire, cross-gender images and voices, morbid psychology and obsession, *flâneurie* and sensuousness over action, tortuous paradoxes about artifice, fragmentation and degeneration, Roman Catholic constructions of ritualistic sinfulness, ennui and cosmopolitanism.

Stories about artists and their tussle against class and conventional morality fall under the category of the *Künstlerroman* (artist's novel), Decadent specimens of which are Arthur Machen's *The Hill of Dreams* (1897/1907) and even *À Rebours* since Des Esseintes is the artist of his own life. 'Hand and Soul', and the 'imaginary portrait' in general, is a peculiar variation of *Künstlerroman*. Egerton's 'A Lost Masterpiece' and Symons's 'The Death of Peter Waydelin' reproduced here are about artists. Although they present very different situations, they both probe in the inner workings of the artist's mind and dissect his/her Aesthetic ideas and impressions. Even Wilde's symbolist fairy tale 'The Nightingale and the Rose' conforms to this sub-genre with the nightingale-artist sacrificing itself in creating a frivolous masterpiece. The artist is a prominent theme in *fin-de-siècle* short fiction; notable examples outside of this book include the haunted Wagnerian composer Magnus in Vernon Lee's Gothic tale 'A Wicked Voice', and Antonio Antonelli's fixation with his violin in Dowson's 'Souvenirs of an Egoist'. These short stories entangle the artists' performances with themselves as they pivot around the realms of art and life.

Some of the short stories reduce, or elevate, the *theme* – depending on viewpoint – to *style*, to a cluster of images and effects. Such is the case with Shannon's 'A Simple Story' which prunes back plot, as its title suggests, in order to emphasise the sensuousness of experience. Ricketts's 'Sensations' and 'The Cup of Happiness' and Lionel Johnson's 'Tobacco Clouds' are also stories that register the acute Impressionist senses. Whilst 'Sensations' is about 'flashing' the impression, 'The Cup of Happiness' with its quirky, fragmented syntax and disjointedness of clauses is about flashing the turn of phrase itself, pointing to what Linda Dowling calls 'autonomy' of language.[42] These stories explore the senses above plot, disrupting conventional literary form, in a challenge to conformity. Stories that 'have no plot' are, according to Arthur Symons's later criticism of Joseph Conrad, quintessentially Decadent, and in the mould of French writers such as Huysmans, Verlaine and Balzac.[43] The text as a matrix of sensuous experience not interested in plot is always teasing with its possibilities or impossibilities.

The Decadent Short Story illustrates this, especially erotic, yearning after the unobtainable ideal. John Reed makes a distinction between the *in situ* perception of the world and that which is out of reach: 'Aestheticism seeks to achieve beauty here and now; Decadence purposely embraces the impossible quest of spiritual fulfilment.'[44] Beerbohm's 'Yai and the Moon' tells of a girl's infatuation with the mirage of the moon, echoing Guy de Maupassant's 'La Nuit' (1887). Dowson's 'A Case of Conscience' and 'The Statute of Limitations' deal with morbidly nursing the very lovesick desire for venerated, unobtainable girls. In John Gray's 'Light', a story that redefines female hysteria, a woman like Bernini's ecstatic Saint Teresa is in love with God and obsessed with fetishised pious texts. And in Ada Leverson's 'The Quest of Sorrow' a dandy seeks the ultimate Aesthetic experience in unhappiness. In all these stories the seekers of the extraordinary either die or just fail. The paradox is, as Reed contends, that 'the torture is grown a part of the pleasure'.[45]

Yearning after the impossible is akin to the Decadent mania for artifice, the love of artefacts and fetishistic worship. Sharp's 'The Black Madonna' is a tale of sacrilege and transgression as the young chief Bihr is lovestruck with the majestic statue of a sacred goddess. In Una Ashworth Taylor's neat tale 'The Truce of God', a remarkable variation on *Dorian Gray*, desire is triangulated in a sculptor, his statue of a beautiful woman and his fiancée; the line between life and artificiality here dissolves in this little hall of mirrors with dire consequences. Comparisons can be drawn between 'The Truce of God' and Richard le Gallienne's novella *The Worshipper of the Image* (1900). In E. Nesbit's supernatural or psychological story 'The Ebony Frame' the narrator is in love with a long dead woman's portrait. Similarly, Ella D'Arcy's 'The Death Mask,' another homage to Wilde's novel, tells of the ambiguously morbid contemplation on the corrected facial anatomy of a cadaver's cast. And Vernon Lee's 'Dionea', not included here, conflates the allure of a *femme fatale* with pygmalionism. Venerating artifice is also expressed in nature, which imitates artifice through seductive, monstrously exotic plants, a Huysmanian idea that H. G. Wells explores in his science fiction tale of 'The Flowering of a Strange Orchid'.

Constructions of Roman Catholic sin and sexual deviance are prominent themes of the Decadent story. As the opposition was clearly defined by its Englishness and Protestantism (and its pointedly anti-French stance), the Decadent writer aligned himself with Catholicism and was Francophile. Ernest Dowson's morbid reworkings of his own sexual frustrations are frequently set in Catholic France, and for John Gray, the Catholic faith itself became a channel for bodily sensations that border on the erotic. Bloxam's 'The Priest and the Acolyte' shocks by playing up sinfulness, transgression and priestly ritual as it nurses a Socratic, homosexual and pederastic physical relationship, not just within the ranks of the Holy Church but also within its inner sancta. Count Stenbock's 'The True Story of a Vampire' is about the same kind of relationship as in Bloxam's scandalous story but within a Gothic framework of vampirism and degeneration. O'Sullivan's 'Original Sin' is about urban sense of guilt as the twisted narrator is obsessed with a child to the point of murder. These stories are Decadent not only because they shock bourgeois morality, but also because they prop up and scrutinise conflicting cultural and psychological forces.

The selection of the stories in this book mirrors the complex constructions of gender identity and female sexuality. The Romantic Fatal Woman evolved in the 1890s to register both the sexual fascination of and misogynistic anxiety about the emancipated, aplomb cigarette-wielding New Woman. Villiers Adams's *conte cruel* of malevolence and political intrigue, 'Queen Ysabeau', Gilchrist's Gothic folktale 'The Crimson Weaver' and M. P. Shiel's urban Gothic and ultra-opulent 'Xélucha' – all appearing in the present volume – depict honey-trapping Swinburnian *femmes fatales*, similar to Helen Vaughan from Arthur Machen's novella *The Great God Pan* (1894) or Franz von Stuck's poisonous painting *The Sin* (1893). In contrast to these erotic horror fantasies, stories about fashionable mysterious ladies, the politics of flirtation and the telling hints of body language games, double or secret identities, and cross-dressing, are also loci that gravitate around the New Woman.[46] Victoria Cross's 'Theodora: A Fragment' is a seduction game in which the eponymous heroine plays up to the ambiguous sexuality of the dandy narrator. Theodore Wratislaw's 'Mutability' serves as an antagonistic counterpart to Cross's story in terms of gender with the calculated cruelty of dandy Algernon Deepdale. 'Theodora: A Fragment' is partly *marivaudage*, a type of fiction associated with nuance of feeling, exquisite *tête-à-têtes*, buoyant and suggestive dialogue; Henry Harland's 'The Invisible Prince' is also a great example of this technique. Vernon Lee's outstanding and complex 'The Legend of Madame Krasinska' is a doppelganger extravaganza about an aristocratic, cosmopolitan woman whose boredom drives her into isolation, identity confusion and hysteria. Madame Krasinska's ennui is symbolic of *fin-de-siècle* crisis at large. In many ways similar to Lee's story, Wilde's 'The Sphinx without a Secret' tracks a woman's unsettling pursuit of clandestine identity for its own sake. Both Lee's and Wilde's stories feature men acting as rationalising detectives who try to 'read' the unpredictable actions of creative, furtive women.

A third category of the New Woman is in the exploration of prostitution and sexual deviance; these became subjects for short stories such as Rudolph Dircks's 'Ellen', a tale of bold sexual deviation in a truly independent New Woman. Arthur Symons's tales of Lucy Newcome fictionalise a real-life woman's descent into prostitution, and draw attention to the hypocritical middle class who both create and exploit such creatures. Reading between the lines of Frederick Wedmore's fictional letters 'To Nancy', one may discern both the vices of the music halls and the sexual perversions of their clientele; while Henry Harland's 'To Every Man a Damsel or Two' casts a comic light on the theme of music hall prostitution.

Symons also identifies the themes of 'morbidity' and 'abnormality' as being Decadent, and this is certainly the case with Conrad's short story, 'The Idiots', included here. The tale is a morose meditation of biological degeneration, which may be read as a languid refutation of the call to 'Progress', voiced by the New Imperialists of the era, along with the puritans, typified by the outburst of 'Another British Matron' quoted above. Hubert Crackanthorpe's 'Modern Melodrama', dealing with the all-too-common theme of the death of a consumptive, may be seen in a similar light – the title suggestive of a society blighted by endemic disease.

Although the present selection aims at showcasing the tremendous diversity of the Decadent short story and the important role of the Little Magazines, there are conspicuous omissions partly due to space constraints and partly due to the fact that some of these stories have been much favoured by anthologists. These include first-rate stories by New Women writers of *The Yellow Book* set in their own time, namely Ella D'Arcy's 'The Pleasure-Pilgrim', Ada Leverson's 'Suggestion', Egerton's 'A Cross Line' and Netta Syrett's 'Thy Heart's Desire'. Most stories by Vernon Lee, some of which are 'Lady Tal', 'Prince Alberic and the Snake Lady' and especially 'Dionea', would sit comfortably in this anthology. Stories by Frederick Rolfe (Baron Corvo) are also of Decadent interest. Arthur Machen's fragmented, winding short fiction is essential Decadent reading; 'The White People' with its unsurpassable sense of unsettling atmosphere and 'The Novel of the White Powder' with its Gothic spectacle of degeneration are notable instances. An excerpt from Machen's *The Hill of Dreams* reprinted in Appendix 2 serves as a fictionalised anecdote, a little *Künstlerroman* showing the dismay of the Decadent short-storyist in the face of a narrow-minded, obdurate Victorian establishment.

One of the characteristics of Decadence is self-analysis which can lead to self-parody. The two parodies of Appendix 1, H. G. Wells's 'A Misunderstood Artist' and Lionel Johnson's 'Incurable', adopt paradox and points of view that are both detached and immersed. They demonstrate in their own way the extreme, self-undoing possibilities of Decadence when the artist follows the confusion of life, art and affectation to excess. 'The Quest of Sorrow' and 'The Sphinx without a Secret' cleverly tread the fine line between seriousness and self-parody; here parody is not demarcated but integrated with the very Decadent notion of overreaching from which it is spawned. Decadent parodies or satires were indeed quite common, with other notable examples, though not anthologised here, being Henry James's 'Death of a Lion' (from the *Yellow Book*, 1894) and Max Beerbohm's 'Enoch Soames' (1916).

THE ROAD TO MODERNISM

As stated above, periodicals such as *The Dial* dabbled in techniques and ideas that have a distinctly Modernist edge. Chapter 9 of James Joyce's *Ulysses* unites prose and drama, something that finds its presage in Charles Ricketts's fragmented, and possibly unfinished, 'The Cup of Happiness'. J. J. Duffy has referred to the 'naturalist-decadent prose' of Joyce's *Dubliners*,[47] and the experimental language of *Ulysses* and indeed *Finnegan's Wake* may owe something to the Decadent, linguistic japery of M. P. Shiel's stories like 'Xélucha'. Taking Huysmans as his benchmark in 1892, Arthur Symons wrote that 'the protagonist of every book is not so much a character as a bundle of impressions and sensations – the vague outline of a single consciousness, his own'.[48] This analysis of Decadent literature would be an excellent tool for exploring the works of Virginia Woolf as well as Joyce. Wolf's Lily Briscoe in *To the Lighthouse* is certainly a character who pieces together her own understanding of self through a series of fragmented experiences, artwork, memories and reflections upon and from others. Similarly, in her experimental stories of *Monday or Tuesday* (1921), especially 'Kew Gardens' (1919), Woolf describes the movement of characters in abstract, shifting colours and patterns – distinctly reminiscent of Ricketts's 'Sensations' in *The Dial*.

Furthermore, the Decadent themes of entropy and degeneration feed directly into Modernist texts such as *Heart of Darkness*, and as this anthology demonstrates, writers now hailed as icons of Modernism experimented in the Decadent short story, early in their careers. Conrad's 'The Idiots' begins in the realm of Victorian melodrama, but progresses through an entropic, emotional wasteland and ends in a proto-Modernist stream of consciousness. According to Martin Scofield, Ernest Hemingway's short stories depict 'snapshots of turmoil, precise delineations of individual fragments of disparate experience'.[49] Such criticism could be applied to many Decadent short stories, such as those of Symons, Wedmore, Dowson and Crackanthorpe, anthologised here. Indeed, Hemingway's fragmented and penetrating short story style could be traced back to Walter Pater's exhortation to become aware of the flame-like intensity of each individual moment; with *that* moment marking the genesis of British Decadence.

The connections between the Decadent short story and Modernist literature are myriad and multifarious. Ultimately, 'Romanticism', 'Aestheticism', 'Decadence' and 'Modernism' are not separate, mutually exclusive boxes, but one fluid evolution of culture and artistic expression, continuous and conterminous. Yet within this Heraclitian flow of culture, moments of profound cultural significance can crystallise, such as Dorian Gray's transition from passive Aesthete to active Decadent. Equally, certain modes of artistic expression become manifest, complete and unique. Such is the Decadent short story.

NOTES

1. Arthur Symons, 'The Decadent Movement in Literature', *Harper's New Monthly Magazine* 87 (1893): pp. 858–67; p. 859.
2. See Appendix 2, p. 412.
3. Oscar Wilde, *The Picture of Dorian Gray: The 1890 and 1891 Texts*, Joseph Bristow and Ian Small (eds), vol. 3 of *The Complete Works of Oscar Wilde* (Oxford: Oxford University Press, 2005), pp. 278–9.
4. A British Matron [John Callcott Horsley], 'A Woman's Plea: To the Editor of *The Times*', *The Times*, 20 May 1885: p. 10. *The Times Digital Archive*. Web. 31 Mar. 2014.
5. Another British Matron, 'Nude Studies: To the Editor of *The Times*', *The Times*, 23 May 1885: p. 10. *The Times Digital Archive*. Web. 31 Mar. 2014.

6. Alison Smith, *The Victorian Nude: Sexuality, Morality and Art* (Manchester: Manchester University Press, 1996), p. 218.
7. See London Metropolitan Archives, *Information Leaflet Number 47*. Available at <http://www.cityoflondon.gov.uk/things-to-do/visiting-the-city/archives-and-city-history/london-metropolitan-archives/Documents/visitor-information/47-theatre-and-music-hall-sources-at-lma.pdf> (last accessed 1 February 2014).
8. Michael Wheeler, *The Old Enemies: Catholic and Protestant in Nineteenth-Century English Culture* (Cambridge: Cambridge University Press, 2006), p. 290.
9. For details see Matthew Brinton Tildesley, '*The Century Guild Hobby Horse* and Oscar Wilde: A Study of British Little Magazines, 1884–1897', PhD Dissertation, Durham University, 2008, Chapters 2.1, 2.2 and 2.5.
10. For details, see Alec Craig, *The Banned Books of England*, foreword E. M. Forster (London: Allen, 1937), p. 23.
11. For example, Frederick Wedmore and Selwyn Image's works included here employ these techniques.
12. H. G. Wells, *The Country of the Blind and Other Stories* (London: Nelson, 1912), pp. iv–vii.
13. Peter Brooker and Andrew Thacker (eds), *The Oxford Critical and Cultural History of Modernist Magazines: Volume I: Britain and Ireland, 1880–1955* (Oxford: Oxford University Press, 2009), pp. 69–70.
14. Ibid., pp. 71–2.
15. Ian Fletcher, 'Decadence and the Little Magazines', in Ian Fletcher (ed.), *Decadence and the 1890s* (New York: Holmes, 1980), p. 202.
16. See Kirsten Macleod, '"Art for America's Sake": Decadence and the Making of American Literary Culture in the Little Magazines of the 1890s', *Prospects* 30 (October 2005): pp. 309–38.
17. Koenraad Claes and Marysa Demoor, 'The Little Magazine in the 1890s: Towards a "Total Work of Art"', *English Studies* 91:2 (2010): pp. 133–49; see esp. p. 138. See also Fletcher, 'Decadence', p. 174.
18. Fletcher, 'Decadence', p. 201.
19. Jan Gordon, '"Wilde's Child": Structure and Origin in the Fin-de-Siècle Short Story', *English Literature in Transition, 1880–1920* 15:4 (1972), pp. 277–90; p. 283.
20. Fletcher, 'Decadence', p. 173.
21. 'We have no formulas, and we desire no false unity of form or matter. We have not invented a new point of view. We are not Realists, or Romanticists, or Decadents. For us, all art is good which is good art.' Arthur Symons, 'Editorial Note', *The Savoy* 1 (1896).
22. See W. H. Brooks [William Sharp], 'Foreword', *The Pagan Review* 1 (August 1892), pp. 1–3.
23. Walter Pater, *Appreciations, with an Essay on Style* (London, Macmillan, 1889), p. 8.
24. Elaine Showalter (ed.), *Daughters of Decadence: Women Writers of the Fin-de-Siècle* (New Brunswick: Rutgers University Press, 1993), p. 40.
25. Edgar Allan Poe, 'The Philosophy of Composition', Richard Henry Stoddard (ed. and intro.), vol. 5 of *The Works of Edgar Allan Poe*, 6 vols (New York: Armstrong, 1884), p. 161.

26. Ibid., p. 166.
27. For Wedmore's and Harland's ideas see Appendix 2, pp. 418, 416. Harland's 'phial' image resonates with Anton Chekhov's 'filtering' of memory as method of writing short stories, in the same year (1897). S. S. Koteliansky and Philip Tomlinson (eds and trans.), *The Life and Letters of Anton Chekhov* (1925; London: Blom, 1965), p. 252.
28. Frederick Wedmore, 'The Short Story', *The Nineteenth Century: A Monthly Review* 43 (March 1898): pp. 406–16; p. 412.
29. See Adrian Hunter, *The Cambridge Introduction to the Short Story in English* (Cambridge; New York: Cambridge University Press, 2007), pp. 8, 32–42.
30. Wendell V. Harris, 'Identifying the Decadent Fiction of the Eighteen-Nineties', *English Literature in Transition, 1880–1920* 5:5 (1962): pp. 1–13; p. 4. See also Wendell V. Harris, 'Introductory: Distinguishing between Short Fiction and the Short Story', *Studies in Short Fiction* 6:1 (1968): pp. 58–84; p. 59.
31. Harris, 'Decadent Fiction', p. 4.
32. Derek Stanford, *Short Stories of the Nineties: A Biographical Anthology* (London: Baker, 1968), p. 29.
33. Ibid. See also p. 30.
34. John R. Reed, 'From Aestheticism to Decadence: Evidence from the Short Story', *Victorians Institute Journal* 11 (1982/3): pp. 1–12; p. 11.
35. Jan Gordon, 'Wilde's Child', pp. 283, 284.
36. See Appendix 2, p. 404.
37. Valerie Shaw, *The Short Story: A Critical Introduction* (New York: Longman, 1983), pp. 9, 13. See also pp. 13–15.
38. George Egerton, 'Fragment of a Letter, 1893' [epigraph], *Keynotes* (Boston: Roberts; London: Matthews and Lane, 1894).
39. Holbrook Jackson, *The Eighteen Nineties: A Review of Art and Ideas at the Close of the Nineteenth Century* (1913; London: Grant Richards, 1922), p. 123.
40. Reed, 'From Aestheticism to Decadence', p. 5.
41. Stanford, *Short Stories of the Nineties*, p. 35.
42. Linda Dowling, *Language and Decadence in the Victorian Fin de Siècle* (Princeton: Princeton University Press, 1986), pp. 164–5.
43. Arthur Symons, *Notes on Joseph Conrad: With Some Unpublished Letters* (London: Myers, 1925), pp. 8, 14, 23–7, 34.
44. Reed, 'From Aestheticism to Decadence', p. 2. See also p. 10.
45. Ibid., p. 11.
46. For connections between Decadence and the New Woman see Linda Dowling, 'The Decadent and the New Woman in the 1890s', *Nineteenth Century Fiction* 33 (1979): pp. 434–53; p. 436; and Joseph Stein, 'The New Woman and the Decadent Dandy', *Dalhousie Review* 55 (1975): pp. 54–62.
47. J. J. Duffy, 'The Stories of Frederick Wedmore: Some Correspondences with *Dubliners*', *James Joyce Quarterly* 5.2 (1968): pp. 144–9; p. 144.
48. Arthur Symons, *Figures of Several Centuries* (1916; London: Costanble, 1917), p. 299.
49. Martin Scofield, *The Cambridge Introduction to the American Short Story*, (Cambridge: Cambridge University Press, 2006), p. 139.

The Stories

I

Little Magazines

THE CENTURY GUILD HOBBY HORSE

A Bundle of Letters: Giving a Selection from Three or Four of the Less Uninteresting of Them

Selwyn Image

Selwyn Image (1849–1930), along with the architects Arthur Heygate Mackmurdo and Herbert Percy Home, was an originator, editor and chief contributor of articles to *The Century Guild Hobby Horse* (1884–94). Their communal home of 20 Fitzroy Street, Chelsea was a fixture of Decadent London throughout the 1880s and '90s. An Anglican vicar-turned artist, Image was a friend and outspoken supporter of Oscar Wilde, before and after his conviction; a defender, escort and, in one instance, husband to music-hall dancers; a passionate campaigner for the representation of the nude in fine art; and latterly Slade Professor of Fine Arts at Oxford University.

In this playful tale, he poses as the editor of a collection of letters, actually penned by Image himself. The necessarily partial format of letters was used by many writers at the time to suggest a more illicit subtext, and Image does indeed invite the reader to speculate as to possible extra-textual material. This is compounded by the text being presented as having been expurgated, along with his use of the word 'risk' in publishing the material. Beyond the innocuous opening letters lie several passages which take their details from Walter Pater's *The Renaissance: Studies in Art and Poetry*

(1873), particularly the incendiary 'Conclusion', whereby the letter writer subtly signals towards a life of Decadent libertinism, unstated in the text itself. In addition, this dialogue through which a gentleman Epicurean extols Paterian philosophy to a beautiful, untutored youth, pre-figures Lord Henry Wotton's relationship with Dorian Gray, and is indeed one of a brace of *Hobby Horse* pieces which may be considered direct influences on *The Picture of Dorian Gray*.

❧

There lies before me a packet of some five-and-twenty or thirty letters, tied across by a piece of red-tape, which a correspondent has sent to the Editor of the *Hobby Horse*, with the expression of his hope or fancy, that some things may be found in them of use for the Magazine. The Editor, unfortunately, has at this late moment more things on his hands than he knows how to conscientiously deal with: and upon me, therefore, who am his very humble servant to order, he has imposed the task of looking over these letters, and extracting from them any passages which seem to be worth publication. A troublesome and thankless task, I fear. Who is the writer of these commended epistles, and what are they about? Perhaps some sentimental youth, or young lady, writing to their 'dear friend' vague platitudes on 'things too high for them': perhaps an old gentleman moralising: or, worst of all, a tourist revelling in descriptions. The art of letter-writing, they assure us, like the art of prayer-writing, has died out. The penny-post, the rail-roads, telegrams, and, what on receiving one in the first days of their invention a dear old Scotch servant of ours, long since gone to the rest or the reward of a life-long faithfulness, indignantly called 'them nasty open things', the half-penny post-card, have ruined it. Mr. Ruskin has somewhere said about trains, that all we demand of them is that they shall carry us, like parcels, as quickly as may be from one place to another: the old, leisurely delight in the very travelling itself is no more. And all that we demand now-a-days of a letter is that it shall tell us as quickly as may be what our correspondent has to say: who has time, amid our increasingly important concerns, to linger over the delicate felicity with which he says it? upon my soul, the more I think of it the more I wish this preposterous packet had miscarried, or been stolen by a dishonest postman, as sometimes one hears of things happening. The sight of it makes me shudder at the fatal organisation of our postal arrangements. I wish I had been strong-minded enough to have told my editorial slave-driver to his face that I would have nothing to do with the thing. Well, anyhow I will have nothing to do with it to-night. To-morrow evening I will gird myself to the task. To-night I will seek refreshment, and a temporary forgetfulness of my burden, in a stroll abroad, a cigar, a glass of some crystal liquid, a chat with the fair bearer of it.

August 21st, midnight. I have had grace enough to keep to my resolve like a man. I have refused an invitation to dine at Kettner's, and another to go to the play-house; why is it that these rare enjoyments always offer themselves at infelicitous moments? At half-past seven o'clock, punctually, I sat down at my desk, and quietly untied the knot of pink tape. I have read the letters all through faithfully. They had one virtue at any rate to start with, they were not scrawled, but written. Why are most of us so rude to our friends, that we do not write but scribble to them? Surely it is nearly as impertinent a habit as mumbling out one's words, or talking with one's mouth full. What conceited people we are to fancy our utterances are worth *trouble* in deciphering them! my temper was certainly a little mollified by this writer's calligraphy; it put me in the mood to see virtues, not to damn vices; but perhaps the readers of the *Hobby Horse* will wish it had been otherwise. I do not pretend to be impartial, and above being influenced by the most trivial details; and a fairly written MS is at all events a compliment to your reader, which only pure ill-conditionedness will make him insensible to. As far as I can judge, these letters are written by a middle-aged man to a young friend of his, a lad or a youth, whose character and parts interest him, and suggest some strong hopes that they will develop one of these days to fine issues. The name of the boy is, I imagine, a playful nickname only; the name of the writer I must of course withhold. To-morrow I finally select the letters which seem to me most worth the risk of printing, three or four of them at most, probably. To-night I am too tired for anything else but to fall off asleep as fast as indulgent Nature will let me.

August 22nd. I have selected five letters out of the eight-and-twenty. I will omit their dates and addresses, which can be of no interest; and for the convenience of the readers of this Magazine, I will write at the commencement of each a short heading as to what they are mainly about. Here, then, they are.

Letter I. *Of the Art of Listening*. 'My dear Leonardo,.... I was out the other evening at an "At-Home". In old days people asked their friends to dine with them; but in London, and in our large towns, society has become a thing so vast and unmanageable, people have so long a list of friends and acquaintances, that neither their purses, nor their time, will allow them to offer the old-fashioned hospitality; and one of our modern institutions is by necessity the "At Home". And in palatial houses this method of entertainment may certainly be agreeable enough. In spacious and handsome rooms an able host and hostess may gather together their acquaintance with excellent opportunities for conversation, and, let us say, for hearing good music, or enjoying some other form of pleasing entertainment. But the facilities of Grosvenor House do not exist in our residences up such-and-such a street in Bloomsbury or in suburban Putney, where we have to thank our good fortune supposing the drawing-room is thirty feet by twenty. Yet here, and in even less commodious quarters, we imitate our more blessed fellow-mortals, and give our At-Homes. To such an entertainment I received an invitation last Friday; and, because my friends the M....s are really excellent good people, of whom I am sincerely fond, and I had no manageable excuse for getting off, I accepted it. The evening was drizzly, and the distance prodigious; so there was nothing left for it but to hail a hansom, with some not unnatural dissatisfaction at having to expend half-a-crown on so little alluring an entertainment — half-a-crown, you see, would have taken me nicely to the pit for "A Scrap of Paper", or made me the possessor of that charming old Catullus I was telling you about the other day, which now probably, forgive me my conceit, will fall into some much less appreciative hands — and drive off. Imagine an ordinary London house, with the narrow passage which we call the hall. A hired man-servant helps you to take off your overcoat, and when you have adjusted your white tie, precedes you to a room at the other end of the hall, through the open door of which you perceive a jammed mass of people, and hear a hubbub of voices. The grave hireling stridently proclaims your name; at the entrance stands your hostess, who warmly shakes you by the hand, assures you of your kindness in appearing, and keeps one eye the meanwhile fixed upon the next corner, who is following up behind you ready to be announced. And so you pass into the throng, gaze anxiously round for some familiar face, discover one, if you are in luck's way, thread carefully your passage up to it in and out between men's shoulders and over ladies' skirts, and add your voice to the general uproar. You start what one must call a conversation; but only with much ado can you catch what your friend says, and your own effort to get heard rasps your throat, till your voice is quickly as the raven's. The particular difficulty is to keep yourself attentively listening to what your friend is talking about. By some curious fate it is the surrounding chatter which strikes on you with greater distinctness. But the difficulty of listening is by no means confined to the infelicitous circumstances of an At-Home. After all it is an Art. A good listener is as rare a thing as a good talker.

'The perfect charm of Conversation is possible, I sometimes think, only between two, for it is then only that a man is absolutely at his ease. It is a fatal thing to try to be brilliant, or profound, or to show off one's learning, or what we used to call at College, to "score off" a man. When there is a third person in the circle the tendency to such things, perhaps inevitably, increases. Yet even, when the circumstances are most favourable, how rare is a good listener! To listen well you must give your friend the sense that you care for what he is saying, that you are not on the alert to catch him up, that you are not in the least hurry, that for the moment he is quietly in possession of you. There is no courtesy finer than this; and there are few things that make for the art of pleasant living more essentially than habits of courtesy. I am not thinking now merely of serious and set conversation. I can call to mind excellent acquaintances of mine, who lack too often that final touch of civility, of quite "good manners", which would make a man shrink from conveying any suspicion of indifference, impatience, of a desire to assert himself, when you happen to meet and are talking together. You see, we are all so full of our own business. We certainly make full use of any opportunity of pouring it forth on our friend, and sweeping him away in the flood of it. His own remarks are little other than impertinences, which we brush aside. We even go the length of asking him at intervals a question or so; but our vacant manner in receiving his answer to it, emphasised by a wandering eye, or a listless tone of voice, or an immediate outburst on some fresh topic, nettles him with the inevitable sense of how formal was the interrogation. I could bring you a dozen excellent talkers for one who possesses the complementary virtue of knowing how to listen.

'No At-Home is complete without a Recitation or two. Silence is proclaimed by the host for Mr So-and-So to "kindly favour us" with such-and-such a poem. These Recitations are often in many ways remarkable exhibitions of skilful elocution, and of passion. On Friday evening there arose a young gentleman, slim, thoughtfully attired, a trifle languid in the pose of him, with lank, jet locks. He gave us Lord Tennyson's Ballad of "The Revenge", and we all clapped our hands at the close of it. Lord Tennyson has written his poem, you will remember, in strongly-marked rhythmic cadences, and in rhyme. But on this occasion the rhythm was difficult to catch, and the rhymes impossible. I have often found this the case. A poem is recited with chief attention to its grammatical construction, to what would be called the common-sense of it. Is that the right method to proceed upon, I wonder? But this letter is already too long, and I must leave the question for another time. It interests me much, however: it interests me especially in reference to yourself, my boy; for the gods have given you a delicate, musical ear, and a delightful voice......

'P.S. When I left my friend's house somewhile after midnight, Nature was in her most tenderly consoling and reinvigorating mood. The rain had ceased; and from the deep, purified heavens shone down the whole company of stars. A gentle wind from the north-west bore with it, as in the early hours of the morning I have more than once experienced even in the heart of London, the sweet scents of the country, of hay-fields, of cottage-gardens, of wayside flowers. Amid this fragrant silence, under the immense and brilliant firmament, fatigue, petulance, regrets, criticism, vanished. Unconscious of the distance, I had reached home as if with magical celerity. And it was magical; for had not Nature herself bent down, and disencumbered me of all these impertinences?'

Letter II. *Of the Art of Reading Aloud.* 'My dear Leonardo,.... There is no doubt a difference between the Art of Reading and the Art of Reciting, yet in the main the same criticism applies to each. The gentleman I was telling you of, who recited for us the other evening Tennyson's "Revenge", set me pondering, as such performances always do, over the cognate and much wider Art of Reading Aloud. You will think me, I am afraid, difficult to please, and querulous. I have been complaining to you how hard a thing it is to come across a good Listener; it is an equally hard thing to come across a good Reader. We are taught Reading with about the same felicity in the result as we are taught the Classics: few of us can construe a Latin passage at sight, or read out a page of the new novel with intelligence and certainty enough to give pleasure. It is really astonishing how many of your friends, educated friends, educated gentlemen from the Universities, I have known, who, if you ask them what news there is in the morning's Paper, cannot give you a short paragraph without stutterings and corrections. Reading Aloud is no doubt largely a matter of practice; one's tongue needs to be loosed. But it is an Art worth the trouble of its practice; and one fancies that it must be within the grasp of most intelligent and well-educated people to obtain an acceptable skill therein.

'I would say that Reading Aloud, like Conversation, is not for a crowded assembly; it is for where two or three are gathered together in the name of peace. Under the shade of a tree upon a summer's lawn, in the warm, fragrant nook of some half-cut hay-stack; best of all, perhaps, where the curtains are drawn against the winter's desolation, and the room is mellow with soft lamplight, cheerful with the crackle of the fire: here are the occasions for exercising our accomplishment; when we ask not for an audience and applause, but for a friend only, or at most a few friends, with whom we may share the luxury of our literary sensations.

'The young gentleman, who recited for us the other evening, was, as I told you, so taken up with his grammatical constructions and dramatic passion, that the rhythmical cadence of the verses, and their rhymes, he let go to the winds. I take it that this is scarcely the way in which a poet would wish his work to be given us. To put the matter on a very low ground, the rhymes and the rhythm have cost him considerable trouble. Rhymes are not things which even poets hold at their beck and call; but rather, though at moments they come plentifully and unbidden, hovering round the inspired brain, waiting only to be arrested and summoned into its service, they are perpetually coy and difficult, and, when once arrived, have a trick of unpleasant masterfulness about them. It would be an interesting experience could one hear a true *Confessio Poetae*, and learn how often the necessities of a rhyme have changed his purpose, and settled by some mechanical requirement the final form of an expression, which strikes us as quite immediately inspired. To set the fine genius of a poet, then, on so difficult an exercise as rhyming, and yet, when we read his exercise out, to make of his rhymes, this painful solicitude of his for enchanting us, just nothing at all, seems a wrong-headed piece of business. I remember some years ago being called upon to review a class of children in one of our elementary schools, and amongst other performances to hear them recite their poetry. The subject of their study was the "Lay of the Last Minstrel"; and it is fixed indelibly on my memory in what a matter-of-fact way they gave poor Sir Walter's lines, curiously solicitous that at all events I should be under no mistake as to their understanding the grammatical analysis of them, in tones of the most prosaic emphasis sentence by sentence explaining the sequence of things, as it were a barrister unfolding to the court the entanglements of his case. The governess, careful and conscientious lady, was deaf to all I ventured afterwards to pour into her private ear in support of another method of reading verse: she called it "sing-song". I do not here enter upon the question, how far this criticism was justified by my bad reading. There is of course such a thing as "sing-song", and a distressing thing it is. Yet a poem after all is to my old-fashioned mind essentially a piece of music, the poet is a singer, his verses are something for us to chaunt. And this essential element in them, this element of musical sounds and cadences, is the first which a good reader would wish to impress on us.

The rhythm we *shall* hear, the rhymes, if there be rhymes, we *shall* hear, at any cost. The tones of the voice, the long-drawn lingering of the voice over certain syllables, shall tend towards the emphasisation of these things. I count the man, who reads me a passage of Homer, or Isaiah, or a love-song of Burns, without the sense of this principle, as lacking the primal justification for calling on me to listen to him. I will endure him, no not for all his dramatic force, his clear elocution, his indisputably evidenced capability of correctly analysing and parsing the passage.'

Letter III. '*Take us the foxes, the little foxes.*'...... 'Perhaps it is in a natural and healthy reaction from the frolic of our last night's entertainment, or perhaps it is because my work this afternoon has been sadly let and hindered by the visit of a charming little friend, whose prettiness robbed me of all heart to send her away, so that we sat chattering nonsense and sipping tea on and on; at any rate I feel this evening in a downright preacher's mood, an instructive, fervent, hortatory mood, that must have a congregation to expend itself on; and so, my dear Leonardo, you must play congregation to me, please, and imagine yourself sitting still and mute like a reverent member in his proper pew, and listen to my sermon.

'I have just been looking over a small portfolio of designs to the Song of Solomon by that famous king's living name-sake, Mr. Simeon Solomon. Their singular qualities of mystical significance and rich, sensuous decorativeness held me fascinated; they are exactly of a piece, that is, with the poem which they illustrate; and can one give much higher praise? When I had done looking at the drawings I took down my Bible to read a passage or two of this canonical scripture, and the first words my eyes lit upon were altogether consonant with my somewhat worried and depressed state; they are the cry of the Bridegroom fearful for his garden, "Take us the foxes, the little foxes, that spoil the vines: for our vines have tender grapes."

'The late Bishop of London wrote a book on the "Sinfulness of little sins", if I remember rightly, and put this quotation felicitously at the beginning of it as a motto. But it is by no means only the little sins that spoil life, but life's little experiences generally, those things which fret and fritter away our strength and performance, our use and enjoyment of life. If I may be forgiven an alliterative sentence, though I am not at all sure that I ought to be forgiven that catchpenny trick of which our modern *littérateurs* are so enamoured, I would say that life is spoiled not by its sins but by its silliness, not by its pains but by its paltriness. These are the foxes, the *little* foxes, that spoil our vines; that eat up the grapes, or leave only the sour ones to make but acid wine, and turn our stomachs. Life after all is a

Fine Art, or rather it is the Ars Artium itself; and how few of us have, I do not say a mastery over, but an initiation even into its secrets! In Art, you know, the great thing is to obtain breadth, to understand what is the proper proportion between the many elements of our subject, which of them to insist upon, which of them to press lightly upon, which of them to ignore. On the rock of details goes many a man to perdition. Is it not so with the details of every-day existence? To know how to treat them is the difficulty. This afternoon, for example, I had set myself with some scrupulosity to get through such and such work; but my charming little visitor, as I have told you, turned up unexpectedly, and the work by no means got done. Not being a skilled performer in the Art of Living, I was the whole time more or less wretched at having my intentions upset, with the result that I have ever since been in an irritable condition, extremely unpleasant and harmful to myself, and also unpleasant, it is probable, to my friends. A practical person will be likely enough to say, "But why did you not send the girl away, tell her you were busy, and so go on with your work?" Ah! but that supposes that my plans were of such unquestionable importance, that they had to be carried through. When a thing presents itself to you in that determined shape, all substantial difficulty vanishes; you may be too weak to do your duty, but it is at all events clear. The ordinary hours of life however are not determined enough to be dealt with by rigid, mechanical rules. How graceless and offensive are the slaves of such! I will pray for the instinct which knows what to do with each successive experience, which can tell me when to abandon things, when to abandon myself to them, without worry, without regret, without repentance..........'

Letter IV. *Of the Art of Enjoying Life*....... 'So our dear friend D... has gone. For me the loss is irreparable. He was a man naturally of great parts: he might have done much for himself, and for us all; yet now he lies in that crowded, desolate suburban cemetery, known, lamented by how few! His certainly was a pleasure-loving nature. I do not say so in any depreciatory tone. No one could be more generous, more courteous, more ready to do all that he could for you. But he longed passionately to come across whatever pleasures life had in store, to embrace these, to exhaust them; and on the whole how little pleasure he got! how greatly in excess were the long, dismal spaces of intolerable commonplace, of impotent rebellion, of pitiable repentance.

'For he, poor fellow, could not accept things sufficiently, he was always in pursuit of them. Like a child gathering flowers, the finer one for ever seemed ahead; and he rushed forward, dropping all that he had gathered, intent on that one, to be dropped too in its turn. How much of the secret of happiness, even of enjoyment, lies in a power of determined receptivity. I will take what the gods send me; but I will make of it what I choose. And it is astonishing how plastic experiences are. After all they are mere clay, to be left amorphous, or to be modelled into divine shapes, or into fiendish ones. So then, nothing is more fatal than to rush about hunting after opportunities. The Art of Enjoying Life is to be found in our own masterful personality, which determines to see of what fineness this and this moment is capable; what secret lies hid within it; what subtle sensation, intellectual or sensuous, it may be made to yield........'

Letter V. *Of the Art of Not Doing Too Much.* 'My dear Boy, I went down the other morning, as you asked me, to the National Gallery to look at the Turner. I feel very much on the whole as you do about it. The criticism of an intelligent, educated, sympathetic person, who is not professionally an artist, who has not even an amateur's familiarity with technical matters, is generally, I think, very much to the point. What he finds fault with is generally something with which we ought to find fault, if we are taking a well-balanced view of things. Of course I do not mean that such a critic, as I am supposing, should settle or unsettle for me my judgement upon a picture as a whole. In the nature of the case he will be unlikely to appreciate many points about it, the due appreciation of which comes only from wide study of Art, or practical familiarity with its methods. Yet, as no work of Art is absolutely perfect, it is likely enough that it is upon some one of its imperfections that our friend's fresh and unprejudiced intelligence fixes: he may give, certainly, too much weight to his objection; still that by no means prevents the objection being quite valid, so far as it goes. And, after all, there is a bias, a distortion, a blindness, which comes from habits too exclusively professional. We have to weigh the artist's judgement of a picture as well as the public's judgement. I think no wise man, who is also an honest and brave man, would ignore either. But all this is by the way, and must be forgiven me, please, in consideration of the garrulousness, which increasing years induce in one, and a certain accompanying inability not to run off, when tempting digressions present themselves.

'About the Turner. Yes, I quite feel with you, and could wish that it was not exhibited. Of course, there is much that is interesting in the picture, more probably than strikes you. The least scrawl or splash of so great a man as Turner remains always interesting: if it is a failure, it gives us some hint of what he was thinking of and trying after, and is at any rate, therefore, suggestive. Still, it may not for all that find its proper place in a public exhibition, whither come all sorts and conditions of men to stare and pass their judgements. Such experiments or failures, call them which you will, are calculated, I cannot help feeling, very often to prejudice our estimate of an artist, either in the way of making us unjustly depreciative of his talent, or, what is probably worse, affectedly undiscerning, ludicrously undiscerning in our wholesale laudation of it. And Turner's pictures are excellent ones for exemplifying the danger of which I am speaking. He worked prodigiously; but he did not always work, no human being possibly can, with unvarying success. His own jesting remark over one of his canvases, that it looked like a mess of mustard and oil, or something to that effect, shows his own realisation of this. Even in the National Gallery there is more than one painting of his that we could spare off the walls. They do not help, but hinder our judgement of him; they are in the way; and this is, of course, a more fatal objection to take against their presence there, than if one said that they were not up to his best standard, or that they were not in themselves particularly beautiful.

'Turner worked prodigiously: he was always producing, producing. If I did not know you, my dear fellow, to be the most industrious of youths, I should scarcely feel justified in uttering any protest against too much Industry, in preaching the Gospel of that exceedingly Fine Art, the Art of Not Doing Too Much. But this letter is not likely to meet other eyes than your own, so that I need not be under an apprehension of sowing seeds to add to the already too luxuriant crop of the world's Idleness. But is not one sometimes, in thinking over the past history of the Arts, driven into wishing that now and then these indefatigable workers had stayed their hands? Even with the very greatest of them, excepting, perhaps, Michelangelo and Leonardo, who have left so little finished in comparison with their many years, there are things that we could spare; rather, let me put it as I did just now, there are things of theirs in the way, impertinences which annoy us, and hinder our appreciation of them. I will give you only one instance, and it shall be from the Art of Literature: think of Milton's metrical version of the Psalms!

'A man's life, we are told upon the highest authority, consisteth not in the things that he possesseth; and an artist's life, we may say too, consisteth not in the things, certainly not in the number of things, that he produceth. Skill in production, and the desire of it, may become too imperative with a man. Surely the fine brain, the discerning eye, the unfaltering hand, are providentially bestowed on our more favoured brethren, not that they may turn every moment into an opportunity of adding so much and so much to our tangible possessions, but that at the end of their time they may have enriched us with the carefully-wrought expressions of their best experiences: what matter if these number but half-a-dozen? It may be, therefore, a real and proper self-denial in a man to keep from his canvases or his desk, to refuse to let himself go, to sit quiet, to drink in, to brood over Nature and the experiences she prepares for him, and by no means to allow himself, till the exact moment arrives, the luxury of turning them into Art. A genius for Rest and Idleness is not less admirable than a genius for Activity. The world is by this time very full, not only of human beings, but of their performances; and even the most valuable human beings should be on their guard against overburdening us with superfluous performances: by superfluous, I mean, such as they are not driven to by the necessity of circumstances or their proper genius.'....

Warned by such excellent reflections on the virtue of the old philosophic axiom Μηδὲν ἄγαν, let me here bring these extracts to a close. I hope the lad for whom the letters were written found profit in them: I hope on reading their last word he did not utter a sigh of relief, as I do now in transcribing my last extract, tying the bundle up again with its red tape, and dispatching it safely back into the Editorial hands.

A Case of Conscience

Ernest Dowson

Ernest Christopher Dowson (1867–1900), though noted today for his poetry, considered himself a prose writer in the first instance. During his short, tempestuous life, he translated several books, co-authored novels with Arthur Moore and wrote numerous short stories which may be considered jewels of Decadent literature. Dowson is one of the finest stylists of the period. This early story was first published in the *Hobby Horse* after he encountered his muse, the twelve-year-old Polish girl, Adelaide Foltinowicz ('Missie'), in 1891. Dowson's torment from his unrequited love of Adelaide haunted him and deeply affected his writing. The central themes of an impossible love, Catholicism and the image of an under-age girl were to recur throughout his creative work for the rest of his life.

In 1895, a perceptive reviewer in *The Athenaeum* wrote that 'A Case of Conscience' may give the impression that it is incomplete; but yet, it is a masterful, perfect jewel of literature, finished and polished, and drawn from only a few, scant narrative ingredients. The setting of the story is replete with Decadent imagery, from the autumnal opening in rural France, through the perceived corruption and morbidity of Catholic ritual, to the absinthe-fuelled conversations which uncover secret sins, ultimately dooming this still-born love affair. English (and therefore Protestant) modernity is posited as a destroyer of the near Edenic perfection of static, continental Catholic life, and the Catholic concept of confession is apparent on many levels, from the dramatic to the autobiographical. The open ending of the story, like a great many others of the time, focuses on a heightened sense of emotional crisis rather than any definitive culmination of plot.

I

It was in Brittany; and the apples were already acquiring a ruddier autumnal tint, amid their greens and yellows, though Autumn was not yet; and the country lay very still and fair, in the sunset, which had befallen, softly and suddenly, as is the fashion there. A man and a girl stood, looking down in silence at the village, Ploumariel, from their post of vantage, half way up the hill: at its lichened church spire, dotted with little gables, like dove-cotes; at the slated roof of its market; at its quiet, white houses. The man's eyes rested on it complacently, with the enjoyment of the painter, finding it charming; the girl's, a little absently, as one who had seen it very often before. She was pretty, and very young; but her grey serious eyes, the poise of her head, with its rebellious brown hair, braided plainly, gave her a little air of dignity, of reserve, which sat piquantly upon her youth. In one ungloved hand, that was brown from the sun, but very beautiful, she held an old parasol; the other played occasionally with a bit of purple heather. Presently, she began to speak; using English, just coloured by a foreign accent, that made her speech prettier.

'You make me afraid,' she said, turning her large, troubled eyes on her companion, 'you make me afraid; of myself, chiefly; but a little, of you. You suggest so much to me, that is new, strange, terrible. When you speak, I am troubled; all my old landmarks appear to vanish; I even hardly know right from wrong. I love you; my God, how I love you! but I want to go away from you, and pray, in the little, quiet church, where I made my first Communion. I will come to the world's end with you; but oh, Sebastian, do not ask me; let me go! You will forget me; I am a little girl to you, Sebastian! You cannot care very much for me.'

The man looked down at her, smiling masterfully, but very kindly. He took the mutinous hand, with its little sprig of heather, and held it between his own. He seemed to find her insistence adorable; mentally, he was contrasting her with all other women, whom he had known; frowning, at the memory of so many years, in which she had no part. He was a man of more than forty, built large; to an uniform, English pattern: there was a touch of military erectness in his carriage, which often deceived people, as to his vocation. Actually, he had never been anything but artist; though he came of a family of soldiers; and had once been War Correspondent of an illustrated paper. A certain distinction had always adhered to him; never more than now, when he was no longer young; was growing bald, had streaks of grey in his moustache. His face, without being handsome, possessed a certain charm: it was worn, and rather pale; the lines, about the firm mouth, were full of lassitude; the eyes, rather tired. He had the air of having tasted widely, curiously, of life in his day; prosperous, as he seemed now, that had left its mark upon him. His voice, which usually took an intonation, that his friends found supercilious, grew very tender, in addressing this little, French girl, with her quaint air of childish dignity.

'Marie-Yvonne, foolish child, I will not hear one word more. You are a little heretic; and I am sorely tempted to seal your lips from uttering heresy. You tell me that you love me; and you ask me, to let you go; in one breath. The impossible conjuncture! Marie-Yvonne,' he added, more seriously, 'trust yourself to me, my child! You know, I will never give you up. You know that these months that I have been at Ploumariel are worth all the rest of my life to me. It has been a difficult life, hitherto, little one: change it for me; make it worth while! You would let morbid fancies come between us. You have lived overmuch in that little church, with its worm-eaten benches, and its mildewed odour of dead people, and dead ideas. Take care, Marie-Yvonne; it has made you serious-eyed, before you have learnt to laugh; by and by, it will steal away your youth, before you have ever been young. I come to claim you, Marie-Yvonne, in the name of Life.' His words were half jesting; his eyes were profoundly in earnest. He drew her to him, gently; and when he bent down, and kissed her forehead, and then her shy lips, she made no resistance: only, a little tremor ran through her. Presently, with equal gentleness, he put her away from him. 'You have already given me your answer, Marie-Yvonne. Believe me, you will never regret it. Let us go down.'

They took their way in silence towards the village; presently, a bend of the road hid them from it, and he drew closer to her, helping her with his arm over the rough stones. Emerging, they had gone thirty yards so, before the scent of English tobacco drew their attention to a figure, seated by the road-side, under a hedge; they recognised it, and started apart, a little consciously.

'It is M. Tregellan,' said the young girl, flushing, 'and he must have seen us.'

Her companion, frowning, hardly suppressed a little, quick objurgation.

'It makes no matter,' he observed, after a moment: 'I shall see your uncle to-morrow, and we know, good man, how he wishes this; and, in any case, I would have told Tregellan.'

The figure rose, as they drew near; he shook the ashes out of his briar, and removed it to his pocket. He was a slight man, with an ugly, clever face; his voice, as he greeted them, was very low and pleasant.

'You must have had a charming walk, Mademoiselle. I have seldom seen Ploumariel look better.'

'Yes,' she said, gravely, 'it has been very pleasant. But I must not linger now,' she added, breaking a little silence, in which none of them seemed quite at ease. 'My uncle will be expecting me to supper.' She held out her hand, in the English fashion, to Tregellan, and then to Sebastian Murch; who gave the little fingers a private pressure.

They had come into the market-place, round which most of the houses in Ploumariel were grouped. They watched the young girl cross it briskly; saw her blue gown pass out of sight, down a bye street; then they turned to their own hotel. It was a low, white house, belted, half way down the front, with black stone; a pictorial object, as most Breton hostels. The ground floor was a *café*; and, outside it, a bench and long stained table enticed them to rest. They sat down, and ordered *absinthes*, as the hour suggested: these were brought to them presently by an old servant of the house; an admirable figure, with the white sleeves and apron relieving her linsey dress; with her good Breton face, and its effective wrinkles. For some time, they sat in silence, drinking and smoking. The artist appeared to be absorbed, in contemplation of his drink, considering its clouded green in various lights. After a while, the other looked up, and remarked, abruptly:

'I may as well tell you, that I happened to overlook you, just now, unintentionally.'

Sebastian Murch held up his glass, with absent eyes.

'Don't mention it, my dear fellow,' he remarked, at last, urbanely.

'I beg your pardon; but, I am afraid, I must.'

He spoke with an extreme deliberation, which suggested nervousness; with the air of a person, reciting a little, set speech, learnt imperfectly; and he looked very straight in front of him, out into the street, at two dogs quarrelling over some offal.

'I daresay you will be angry; I can't avoid that; at least, I have known you long enough to hazard it. I have had it on my mind to say something. If I have been silent, it hasn't been because I have been blind, or approved. I have seen how it was all along. I gathered it from your letters, when I was in England. Only, until this afternoon, I did not know how far it had gone; and now, I am sorry I did not speak before.'

He stopped short, as though he expected his friend's subtlety to come to his assistance; with admissions, or recriminations. But the other was still silent, absent: his face wore a look of annoyed indifference. After a while, as Tregellan still halted, he observed quietly:

'You must be a little more explicit. I confess, I miss your meaning.'

'Ah, don't be paltry,' cried the other, quickly. 'You know my meaning. To be very plain, Sebastian, are you quite justified in playing with that charming girl, in compromising her?'

The artist looked up at last, smiling; his expressive mouth was set, not angrily, but with singular determination.

'With Mademoiselle Mitouard?'

'Exactly; with the niece of a man whose guest you have recently been.'

'My dear fellow!' he stopped a little, considering his words: 'You are hasty, and uncharitable, for such a very moral person! you jump at conclusions, Tregellan. I don't, you know, admit your right to question me; still, as you have introduced the subject, I may as well satisfy you. I have asked Mademoiselle Mitouard to marry me, and she has consented, subject to her uncle's approval. And that her uncle, who happens to prefer the English method of courtship, is not likely to refuse.'

The other held his cigar between two fingers, a little away; his curiously anxious face suggested that the question had become to him one of increased nicety.

'I am sorry,' he said, after a moment. 'This is worse than I imagined; it's impossible.'

'It is you that are impossible, Tregellan,' said Sebastian Murch. He looked at him now quite frankly, absolutely; his eyes had a defiant light in them, as though he hoped to be criticised; wished nothing better than to stand on his defence, to argue the thing out. And Tregellan sat for a long time, without speaking; appreciating his purpose. It seemed more monstrous, the closer he considered it: natural enough withal, and so, harder to defeat; and yet he was sure that defeated it must be. He reflected how accidental it had all been; their presence there, in Ploumariel, and the rest! Touring in Brittany, as they had often done before, in their habit of old friends, they had fallen upon it by chance, a place unknown of Murray; and the merest chance had held them there. They had slept at the *Lion d'Or*, voted it magnificently picturesque, and would have gone away, and forgotten it; but the chance of travel had for once defeated them. Hard by, they heard of the little votive chapel of Saint Bernard; at the suggestion of their hostess, they set off to visit it. It was built steeply on an edge of rock, amongst odorous pines overhanging a ravine, at the bottom of which they could discern a brown torrent, purling tumidly along. For the convenience of devotees, iron rings, at short intervals, were driven into the wall; holding desperately to these, the pious pilgrim, at some peril, might compass the circuit; saying an oraison to Saint Bernard, and some ten *Aves*. Sebastian, who was charmed with the wild beauty of the scene, in a country ordinarily so placid, had been seized with a fit of emulation; not in any mood of devotion, but for the sake of a wider prospect. Tregellan had protested; and the Saint, resenting the purely aesthetic motive of the feat, had seemed to intervene. For, half way round, growing giddy may be, the artist had made a false step, lost his hold. Tregellan, with a little cry of horror, saw him disappear, amidst crumbling mortar and uprooted ferns. It was with a sensible relief, for the fall had the illusion of great depth, that, making his way rapidly down a winding path, he found him lying on a grass terrace, amidst *débris*, twenty feet lower; cursing his folly, and holding a lamentably sprained ankle; but, for the rest, uninjured! Tregellan had made off in haste to Ploumariel, in search of assistance; and, within the hour, he had returned, with two stalwart Bretons, and M. le Docteur Mitouard.

Their tour had been, naturally, drawing to its close. Tregellan, indeed, had an imperative need to be in London within the week. It seemed, therefore, a clear dispensation of Providence, that the amiable doctor should prove an hospitable person, and one inspiring confidence no less. Caring greatly for things foreign; and with an especial passion for England, a country whence his brother had brought back a wife; M. le Docteur Mitouard, insisted that the invalid could be cared for properly, at his house, alone. And there, in spite of protestations, earnest from Sebastian, from Tregellan half-hearted, he was installed. And there, two days later, Tregellan left him, with an easy mind; bearing away with him, half enviously, the recollection of the young, charming face of a girl, the Doctor's niece; as he had seen her, standing by his friend's sofa, when he paid his *adieux*; in the beginnings of an intimacy, in which, as he foresaw, the petulance of the invalid, his impatience at an enforced detention, might be considerably forgot. And all that had been two months ago.

II

'I am sorry you don't see it,' continued Tregellan, after a pause, 'to me, it seems impossible: considering your history, it takes me by surprise.'

The other frowned slightly; finding this persistence, perhaps, a trifle crude; he remarked, good humouredly enough:

'Will you be good enough to explain your opposition? Do you object to the girl? You have been back a week now, during which you have seen almost as much of her as I.'

'She is a child, to begin with; there is five and twenty years' disparity between you. But it's the relation I object to, not the girl. Do you intend to live in Ploumariel?'

Sebastian smiled, with a suggestion of irony.

'Not precisely. I think it would interfere a little with my career; why do you ask?'

'I imagined not. You will go back to London, with your little Breton wife, who is as charming here as the apple-blossom in her own garden. You will introduce her to your circle, who will receive her with open arms; all the clever bores, who write, and talk, and paint, and are talked about, between Bloomsbury and Kensington. Everybody who is emancipated, will know her; and everybody, who has a "fad"; and they will come in a body, and emancipate her, and teach her their "fads".'

'That is a caricature of my circle, as you call it, Tregellan! though I may remind you, it is also yours. I think she is being starved, in this corner; spiritually. She has a beautiful soul, and it has had no chance. I propose to give it one; and I am not afraid of the result.'

Tregellan threw away the stump of his cigar into the darkling street, with a little gesture of discouragement, of lassitude.

'She has had the chance to become what she is: a perfect thing.'

'My dear fellow,' exclaimed his friend, 'I could not have said more myself.'

The other continued, ignoring his interruption.

'She has had great luck. She has been brought up by an old eccentric, on the English system of growing up as she liked. And no harm has come of it; at least, until it gave you the occasion of making love to her.'

'You are candid, Tregellan!'

'Let her go, Sebastian, let her go,' he continued, with increasing gravity: 'Consider, what a transplantation: from this world of Ploumariel; where everything is fixed for her, by that venerable old *Curé*, where life is so easy, so ordered; to yours, ours; a world without definitions, where everything is an open question.'

'Exactly,' said the artist, 'why should she be so limited? I would give her scope, ideas. I can't see that I am wrong.'

'She will not accept them, your ideas. They will trouble her, terrify her; in the end, divide you. It is not an elastic nature; I have watched it.'

'At least, allow me to know her,' put in the artist, a little grimly.

Tregellan shook his head.

'The Breton blood; her English mother: passionate Catholicism! a touch of Puritan! Have you quite made up your mind, Sebastian?'

'I made it up, long ago, Tregellan!'

The other looked at him, curiously, compassionately; with a touch of resentment, at what he found his lack of subtlety. Then he said at last:

'I called it impossible; you force me to be very explicit, even cruel. I must remind you that you are, of all my friends, the one I value most, could least afford to lose.'

'You must be going to say something extremely disagreeable! something horrible,' said the artist, slowly.

'I am,' said Tregellan, 'but I must say it. Have you explained to Mademoiselle, or her uncle, your — your peculiar position?'

Sebastian was silent for a moment, frowning; the lines about his mouth grew a little sterner; at last, he said coldly:

'If I were to answer, Yes?'

'Then I should understand that there was no further question of your marriage.'

Presently, the other commenced in a hard, leaden voice.

'No, I have not told Marie-Yvonne that. I shall not tell her. I have suffered enough for a youthful folly; an act of mad generosity. I refuse to allow an infamous woman to wreck my future life, as she has disgraced my past. Legally, she has passed out of it; morally, legally, she is not my wife. For all I know, she may be, actually, dead.'

The other was watching his face, very grey and old now, with an anxious compassion.

'You know she is not dead, Sebastian,' he said simply. Then he added, very quietly, as one breaks supreme bad tidings. 'I must tell you something which, I fear, you have not realised. The Catholic Church does not recognise divorce. If she marry you, and find out; rightly or wrongly, she will believe that she has been living in sin; some day, she will find it out. No damnable secret, like that, keeps itself for ever: an old newspaper, a chance remark from one of your dear friends; and, the deluge. Do you see the tragedy, the misery of it? By God, Sebastian, to save you both, somebody shall tell her; and if it be not you, it must be I.'

There was extremest peace in the quiet square; the houses seemed sleepy at last, after a day of exhausting tranquillity, and the chestnuts, under which a few children, with tangled hair and fair, dirty faces, still played. The last glow of the sun fell on the grey roofs opposite; dying hard, it seemed, over the street in which the Mitouards lived; and they heard suddenly the tinkle of an *Angelus* bell. Very placid! the place, and the few peasants, in their pictorial hats and caps, who lingered. Only the two Englishmen sitting, their glasses empty, and their smoking over, looking out on it all with their anxious faces, brought in a contrasting note, of modern life; of the complex, aching life of cities, with its troubles, and its difficulties.

'Is that your final word, Tregellan?' asked the artist, at last, a little wearily.

'It must be, Sebastian! Believe me, I am infinitely sorry.'

'Yes, of course,' he answered, quickly, acidly: 'well, I will sleep on it.'

III

They made their first breakfast in an almost total silence; both wore the bruised, harassed air which tells of a night passed without benefit of sleep. Immediately afterwards, Murch went out alone. Tregellan could guess the direction of his visit, but not its object; he wondered if the artist was making his difficult confession. Presently, they brought him in a pencilled note; he recognised, with some surprise, his friend's tortuous hand.

'I have considered our conversation, and your unjustifiable interference. I am entirely in your hands; at the mercy of your extraordinary notions of duty. Tell her what you will, if you must; and pave the way to your own success. I shall say nothing; but I swear, you love the girl yourself; and are no right arbiter here. Sebastian Murch.'

He read the note through, twice, before he grasped its purport; then sat, holding it, in lax fingers, his face grown singularly grey.

'It's not true, it's not true,' he cried aloud; but a moment later knew himself for a self deceiver all along. Never had self-consciousness been more sudden, unexpected, or complete. There was no more to do, or say; this knowledge tied his hands: *Ite! missa est!* ...

He spent an hour painfully, invoking casuistry, tossed to and fro, irresolutely; but never, for a moment, disputing that plain fact, which Sebastian had so brutally illuminated. Yes! he loved her, had loved her all along: Marie-Yvonne! How the name expressed her! at once sweet and serious, arch and sad, as her nature. The little Breton wild flower! how cruel it seemed, to gather her! And he could do no more; Sebastian had tied his hands: things must be! He was a man, nicely conscientious; and now, all the elaborate devices of his honour, which had persuaded him to a disagreeable interference, were contraposed against him. This suspicion of an ulterior motive had altered it; and so, at last, he was left, to decide with a sigh, that, because he loved these two so well, he must let them go their own way, to misery.

Coming in, later in the day, Sebastian Murch found his friend packing.

'I have come to get your answer,' he said: 'I have been walking about the hills, like a madman, for hours. I have not been near her: I am afraid! Tell me what you mean to do?'

Tregellan rose; shrugged his shoulders; pointed to his valise.

'God help you both! I would have saved you, if you had let me. The Quimperlé *Courrier* passes, in half an hour. I am going by it. I shall catch a night train to Paris.'

As Sebastian said nothing; continued to regard him, with the same dull, anxious gaze; he went on, after a moment:

'You did me a grave injustice. You should have known me better than that. God knows, I meant nothing shameful; only the best; the least misery for you and her.'

'It was true then?' said Sebastian, curiously. His voice was very cold; Tregellan found him altered; he regarded the thing as it had been very remote, and outside them both.

'I did not know it, then,' said Tregellan, shortly.

He knelt down again, and resumed his packing; Sebastian, leaning against the bed, watched him with absent intensity, which was yet alive to trivial things; and he handed him, from time to time, a book, a brush, which the other packed mechanically, with elaborate care. There was no more to say; and presently, when the chambermaid entered for his luggage, they went down, and out into the splendid sunshine, silently. They had to cross the Square to reach the carriage; a dusty, ancient vehicle, hooded, with places for four, which waited outside the post office. A man in a blue blouse preceded them, carrying Tregellan's things. From the corner, they could look down the road to Quimperlé; and their eyes both sought the white house of Doctor Mitouard, standing back a little, in its trim garden, with its one incongruous apple tree; but there was no one visible.

Presently, Sebastian asked, suddenly:

'Is it true, that you said last night: divorce to a Catholic – ?'

Tregellan interrupted him.

'It is absolutely true, my poor friend.'

He had climbed into his place at the back, settled himself on the shiny leather cushion; he appeared to be the only passenger. Sebastian stood looking drearily in at the window, the glass of which had long perished.

'I wish I had never known, Tregellan! How could I ever tell her!'

Inside, Tregellan shrugged his shoulders; not impatiently, or angrily, but in sheer impotence; as one who gave it up.

'I can't help you,' he said, 'you must arrange it with your own conscience.'

'Ah, it's too difficult!' cried the other: 'I can't find my way.'

The driver cracked his whip, suggestively; Sebastian drew back a little further, from the off wheel.

'Well,' said the other, 'if you find it, write and tell me. I am very sorry, Sebastian.'

'Goodbye,' he replied. 'Yes! I will write.'

The carriage lumbered off, with a lurch to the right, as it turned the corner; it rattled down the hill, raising a cloud of white dust. As it passed the Mitouards' house, a young girl, in a large straw hat, came down the garden; too late to discover whom it contained. She watched it out of sight, indifferently, leaning on the little iron gate; then she turned, to recognise the long stooping figure of Sebastian Murch, who advanced to meet her.

The Statute of Limitations

Ernest Dowson

Dowson began writing the story in May 1892, and had planned to submit it to *Macmillan's Magazine*. However, Dowson was, by this time, a regular contributor to the Aesthetic enterprise of *The Hobby Horse* (his masterful poem known as 'Cynara' was first published therein the previous year). Dowson admired Herbert Horne's editorial audaciousness, and his letters to the magazine's editor show his eagerness to have the story found 'worthy to be shrined in the new Hobby' (16 November 1892). Although the setting of the story was probably inspired by the departure to Chile of a close friend, Charles Winstanley Tweedy, its subject-matter is consistent with Dowson's oeuvre.

'The Statute of Limitations', marked by Impressionist economy and precision, is arguably Dowson's finest short story, one which perfectly captures the spirit of Decadence, and one of the period's best. It plays on the imperial adventure theme and deconstructs Victorian melodrama, as its cynical title suggests. The story cleverly twists the basic premise of medieval romance in which the idealised lady is taken to the extreme by not being sought after, as it is insinuated in the story's use of Christina Rossetti's 'Prince's Progress'. The themes of futility, perversion, fetishism and artificiality are beautifully balanced, not only in the complex characterisation of the protagonist, Michael Garth, but also in the fragmented narrative style. This is a quasi-autobiographical story, disguising Dowson's tenacious idolisation of innocent little girls in general and his lifelong obsession with Adelaide Foltinowicz in particular. With its theme of morbid idealisation, it is attuned with many of Dowson's poems such as 'Amor Umbratilis', 'Flos Lunae' and 'A Lost Love'. 'The Statute of Limitations' is a proto-Modernist piece of fiction which, as it has been suggested, has led to the genesis of Joseph Conrad's *Heart of Darkness* (1899).

During five years of an almost daily association with Michael Garth, in a solitude of Chili, which threw us, men of common speech, though scarcely of common interests, largely on each other's tolerance, I had grown, if not into an intimacy with him, at least into a certain familiarity, through which the salient features of his history, his character, reached me. It was a singular character, and an history rich in instruction. So much I gathered from hints, which he let drop long before I had heard the end of it. Unsympathetic as the man was to me, it was impossible not to be interested by it. As our acquaintance advanced, it took (his character, I mean) more and more the aspect of a difficult problem in psychology, that

I was passionately interested in solving: to study it was my recreation, after watching the fluctuating course of nitrates. So that when I had achieved fortune, and might have started home immediately, my interest induced me to wait more than three months, and return in the same ship with him. It was through this delay, that I am enabled to transcribe the issue of my impressions; I found them edifying, if only for their singular irony. From his own mouth, indeed, I gleaned but little; although during our voyage home, in those long nights when we paced the deck together under the Southern Cross, his reticence occasionally gave way, and I obtained glimpses of a more intimate knowledge of him than the whole of our juxtaposition on the station had ever afforded me. I guessed more, however, than he told me; and what was lacking I pieced together later, from the talk of the girl to whom I broke the news of his death. He named her to me, for the first time, a day or two before that happened; a piece of confidence so unprecedented, that I must have been blind, indeed, not to have foreseen what it prefaced. I had seen her face the first time I entered his house, where her photograph hung on a conspicuous wall; the charming, oval face of a young girl, little more than a child, with great eyes, that one guessed, one knew not why, to be the colour of violets, looking out with singular wistfulness from a waving cloud of dark hair. Afterwards, he told me that it was the picture of his *fiancée*: but, before that, signs had not been wanting by which I had read a woman in his life.

Iquique is not Paris; it is not even Valparaiso; but it is a city of civilisation; and but two days' ride from the pestilential stew, where we nursed our lives doggedly on quinine and hope, the ultimate hope of evasion. The lives of most Englishmen yonder, who superintend works in the interior, are held on the same tenure: you know them by a certain savage, hungry look in their eyes. In the meantime, while they wait for their luck, most of them are glad enough, when business calls them down for a day or two to Iquique. There are shops and streets, lit streets through which blackeyed Señoritas pass in their lace mantillas; there are *cafés* too; and faro for those, who reck of it; and bull fights, and newspapers younger than six weeks; and in the harbour, taking in their fill of nitrates, many ships, not to be considered without envy, because they are coming, within a limit of days, to England. But Iquique had no charm for Michael Garth, and when one of us must go, it was usually I, his subordinate, who being delegated, congratulated myself on his indifference. Hard-earned dollars melted at Iquique; and to Garth, life in Chili had long been solely a matter of amassing them. So he stayed on, in the prickly heat of Agnas Blancas, and grimly counted the days, and the money (although his nature, I believe, was fundamentally generous, in his set concentration of purpose, he had grown morbidly avaricious) which should restore him to his beautiful mistress. Morose, reticent, unsociable as he had become, he had still, I discovered by degrees, a leaning towards the humanities, a nice taste, such as could only be the result of much knowledge, in the fine things of literature. His infinitesimal library, a few French novels, an Horace, and some well-thumbed volumes of the modern English poets, in the familiar edition of Tauchnitz, he put at my disposal, in return for a collection, somewhat similar, although a little larger, of my own. In his rare moments of amiability, he could talk on such matters with *verve* and originality; more usually, he preferred to pursue with the bitterest animosity an abstract fetish, which he called his 'luck'. He was by temperament, an enraged pessimist; and I could believe, that he seriously attributed to Providence, some quality inconceivably malignant, directed in all things personally against himself. His immense bitterness and his careful avarice, alike, I could explain, and in a measure justify, when I came to understand, that he had felt the sharpest stings of poverty, and, moreover, was passionately in love, in love *comme on ne l'est plus*. As to what his previous resources had been, I knew nothing, nor why they had failed him; but I gathered, that the crisis had come, just when his life was complicated by the sudden blossoming of an old friendship into love, in his case, at least, to be complete and final. The girl too was poor; they were poorer than most poor persons: how could he refuse the post, which, through the good offices of a friend, was, just then, unexpectedly offered him? Certainly, it was abroad; it implied five years' solitude in Equatorial America. Separation and change were to be accounted; perhaps, diseases and death, and certainly his 'luck', which seemed to include all these. But it also promised, when the term of his exile was up, and there were means of shortening it, a certain competence and, very likely, wealth; escaping those other contingencies, marriage. There seemed no other way. The girl was very young: there was no question of an early marriage; there was not, even, a definite engagement. Garth would take no promise from her; only for himself, he was her bound lover while he breathed; would keep himself free to claim her, when he came back, in five years, or ten, or twenty, if she had not chosen better. He would not bind her; but I can imagine how impressive his dark, bitter face must have made this renunciation to the little girl with the violet eyes; how tenderly she repudiated her freedom. She went out as a governess, and sat down to wait. And absence only riveted faster the chain of her affection: it set Garth more securely on the pedestal of her idea; for in love it is most usually the reverse of that social maxim, *les absents ont toujours tort*, which is true.

Garth, on his side, writing to her, month by month, while her picture smiled on him from the wall, if he was careful always to insist on her perfect freedom, added, in effect, so much more than this, that the renunciation lost its benefit. He lived in a dream of her; and the memory of her eyes and her hair was a perpetual presence with him, less ghostly than the real company among whom he mechanically transacted his daily business. Burnt away and consumed by desire of her living arms, he was counting the hours which still prevented him from them. Yet, when his five years were done, he delayed his return, although his economies had justified it; settled down for another term of five years, which was to be prolonged to seven. Actually, the memory of his old poverty, with its attendant dishonours, was grown a fury, pursuing him ceaselessly with whips. The lust of gain, always for the girl's sake, and so, as it were, sanctified, had become a second nature to him; an intimate madness, which left him no peace. His worst nightmare was to wake with a sudden shock, imagining that he had lost everything, that he was reduced to his former poverty; a cold sweat would break all over him before he had mastered the horror. The recurrence of it, time after time, made him vow grimly, that he would go home a rich man, rich enough to laugh at the fantasies of his luck. Latterly, indeed, this seemed to have changed; so that his vow was fortunately kept. He made money lavishly at last: all his operations were successful, even those, which seemed the wildest gambling; and the most forlorn speculations turned round, and shewed a pretty harvest, when Garth meddled with their stock.

And all the time he was waiting there, and scheming, at Agnas Blancas, in a feverish concentration of himself upon his ultimate reunion with the girl at home, the man was growing old; gradually at first, and insensibly; but towards the end, by leaps and starts, with an increasing consciousness of how he aged and altered, which did but feed his black melancholy. It was borne upon him, perhaps, a little brutally, and not by direct self-examination, when there came another photograph from England. A beautiful face still, but certainly the face of a woman, who had passed from the grace of girlhood (seven years now separated her from it), to a dignity touched with sadness; a face, upon which life had already written some of its cruelties. For many days after this arrival Garth was silent and moody, even beyond his wont; then he studiously concealed it. He threw himself again furiously into his economic battle; he had gone back to the inspiration of that other, older portrait: the charming, oval face of a young girl, almost a child, with great eyes, that one guessed, one knew not why, to be the colour of violets.

As the time of our departure approached, a week or two before we had gone down to Valparaiso, where Garth had business to wind up, I was enabled to study more intimately the morbid demon, which possessed him. It was the most singular thing in the world: no man had hated the country more, had been more passionately determined for a period of years to escape from it; and now that his chance was come, the emotion with which he viewed it was nearer akin to terror, than to the joy of a reasonable man, who is about to compass the desire of his life. He had kept the covenant, which he had made with himself: he was a rich man, richer than he had ever meant to be. Even now he was full of vigour, and not much past the threshold of middle age; and he was going home to the woman, whom for the best part of fifteen years, he had adored with an unexampled constancy; whose fidelity had been to him all through that exile, as the shadow of a rock in a desert land: he was going home to an honourable marriage. But withal he was a man with an incurable sadness; miserable and afraid. It seemed to me at times, that he would have been glad, if she had kept her troth less well; had only availed herself of that freedom, which he gave her, to disregard her promise. And this was the more strange, in that I never doubted the strength of his attachment: it remained engrossing and unchanged, the largest part of his life! No alien shadow had ever come between him, and the memory of the little girl with the violet eyes, to whom he, at least, was bound. But a shadow was there; fantastic it seemed to me at first, too grotesque to be met with argument; but in whose very lack of substance, as I came to see, lay its ultimate strength. The notion of the woman, which now she was, came between him and the girl whom he had loved, whom he still loved with passion, and separated them. It was only on our voyage home, when we walked the deck together interminably during the hot, sleepless nights, that he first revealed to me without subterfuge, the slow agony by which this phantom slew him. And his old, bitter conviction of the malignity of his luck, which had lain dormant in the first flush of his material prosperity, returned to him. The apparent change in it seemed to him, just then, the last irony of those hostile powers, which had pursued him.

'It came to me, suddenly,' he said, 'just before I left Agnas, when I had been adding up my pile, and saw there was nothing to keep me, that it was all wrong. I had been a blamed fool! I might have gone home years ago. Where is the best of my life? Burnt out, wasted, buried in that cursed oven!

Dollars? If I had all the metal in Chili, I couldn't buy one day of youth. Her youth too; that has gone with the rest: that's the worst part!'

Despite all my protests, his despondency increased as the steamer ploughed her way towards England, with the ceaseless throb of her screw, which was like the panting of a great beast. Once, when we had been talking of other matters, of certain living poets whom he favoured, he broke off with a quotation from the 'Prince's Progress' of Miss Rossetti:

> 'Ten years ago, five years ago,
>   One year ago,
> Even then you had arrived in time,
>   Though somewhat slow;
> Then you had known her living face,
>   Which now you cannot know.'

He stopped sharply, with a tone in his voice, which seemed to intend, in the lines, a personal instance.

'I beg your pardon!' I protested. 'I don't see the analogy. You haven't loitered; you don't come too late. A brave woman has waited for you; you have a fine felicity before you: it should be all the better, because you have won it laboriously. For Heaven's sake, be reasonable!' He shook his head sadly; then added, with a gesture of sudden passion, looking out, over the taffrail, at the heaving, grey waters: 'It's finished. I haven't any longer the courage.' 'Ah!' I exclaimed impatiently, 'say once for all, outright, that you are tired of her, that you want to back out of it.' 'No,' he said drearily, 'it isn't that. I can't reproach myself with the least wavering. I have had a single passion; I have given my life to it; it is there still, consuming me. Only the girl I loved; it's as if she had died. Yes, she is dead, as dead as Helen; and I have not the consolation of knowing, where they have laid her. Our marriage will be a ghastly mockery; a marriage of corpses. Her heart, how can she give it me? She gave it years ago to the man I was, the man who is dead. We, who are left, are nothing to one another, mere strangers.'

One could not argue with a perversity so infatuate: it was useless to point out, that in life a distinction so arbitrary as the one which haunted him does not exist. It was only left me to wait, hoping that, in the actual event of their meeting, his malady would be healed. But this meeting, would it ever be compassed? There were moments when his dread of it seemed to have grown so extreme, that he would be capable of any cowardice, any compromise, to postpone it, to render it impossible. He was afraid, that she would read his revulsion in his eyes, would suspect, how time and his very constancy had given her the one rival, with whom she could never compete; the memory of her old self, of her gracious girlhood, which was dead. Might not she too actually welcome a reprieve; however readily she would have submitted, out of honour or lassitude, to a marriage, which could only be a parody of what might have been?

At Lisbon, I hoped, that he had settled these questions, had grown reasonable and sane; for he wrote a long letter to her, which was subsequently a matter of much curiosity to me; and he wore, for a day or two afterwards, an air almost of assurance, which deceived me. I wondered what he had put in that epistle, how far he had explained himself, justified his curious attitude. Or was it simply a *résumé*, a conclusion to those many letters which he had written at Agnas Blancas, the last one which he would ever address to the little girl of the earlier photograph?

Later, I would have given much to decide this; but she herself, the woman, who read it, maintained unbroken silence. In return, I kept a secret from her, my private interpretation of the accident of his death. It seemed to me a knowledge tragical enough for her, that he should have died as he did, so nearly in English waters; within a few days of the home coming, which they had passionately expected for years. It would have been mere brutality to afflict her further, by lifting the veil of obscurity, which hangs over that calm, moonless night, by pointing to the note of intention in it. For it is in my experience, that accidents so opportune do not in real life occur; and I could not forget that, from Garth's point of view, death was certainly a solution. Was it not, moreover, precisely a solution, which so little time before he had the appearance of having found? Indeed, when the first shock of his death was past, I could feel that it was after all a solution: with his 'luck' to handicap him, he had perhaps avoided worse things than the death he met. For the luck of such a man, is it not his temperament, his character? Can any one escape from that? May it not have been an escape for the poor devil himself, an escape too for the woman, who loved him, that he chose to drop down, fathoms down, into the calm, irrecoverable depths of the Atlantic, when he did, bearing with him at least an unspoilt ideal, and leaving her a memory, that experience could never tarnish, nor custom stale?

THE DIAL

The Cup of Happiness

Charles Ricketts

Charles de Sousy Ricketts (1866–1931) and Charles Haslewood Shannon (1863–1937) were an artistic couple at the epicentre of fashionable, Decadent London in the 1880s and 1890s, and close friends of Oscar Wilde. They are also significant figures in the history of British Art Nouveau. The décor of Ricketts's Chelsea studio was used for Basil Hallward's studio in the opening chapter of *The Picture of Dorian Gray*, and both men have been cited as being the inspiration behind the character of Basil himself. The Anglo-French Ricketts was the dominant personality among their circle of talented artists, a 'natural aristocrat' according to George Bernard Shaw, and the principal voice within their first periodical, *The Dial*. This aggressively anti-commercial publication revelled in 'intelligent ostracism' and includes many literary works which can be read as proto-Modernist in their wilful disruption of literary form and subversion of Victorian tradition.

Ricketts's frankly bizarre tale, 'The Cup of Happiness', is woven around a typically Decadent, languorous Prince, and a female character, 'Fantasy' that fuses Aphrodite with Eve and the Lilith myth. This quasi-comic tale is notable for its kaleidoscopic content, ornately jewelled with classical allusion, and its fragmentary form, prefiguring Modernism's experimental techniques. It begins with a prose introduction which is then followed by a prologue, leading finally to theatrical script. The story is marked 'to be continued', but no sequel emerged. Ricketts's dizzying imagery is impressionistic, suggesting ideas and sensations, rather than the story relating any coherent message or plot. In the final play script, a Palm Tree, seeking to suppress 'thorns and snakes' apes the Victorian Purity societies that sought to outlaw sensuous literature.

※

The sound rolls through the reddening air, the muffled *thum!* the *dumb!* of a monotonous drum. Lamps flash ruddily on gaudy pictures of the promised piece, The Giant and Maiden. Again 'tis the chart of the human frame flaming by lamplight, with bright red veins, and liver a beautiful yellow.

Shouting clowns hoarsely proclaim the virtues and cures of an elixir, a magic goblet; or lift the curtain to show the careworn princess in her tinsel and spangles. And drums are rolled.

Come in! Come in!

'Tis a trick; a dear old-world trick; and in my quality of clown, I pray you, let me rattle my bells, show my happy cup, or make each weary puppet walk before the crowd, shout, declare the oldness of my piece; for it is a play, and not a medicine after all, my Cup of Happiness; not an elixir, a cure for the liver; it is a farce, an old farce; I vouch to its age, for it was begun by Madam Thalia, when the world was still young, still a delightful green, the beautiful green of a newly-painted cupboard; but the play lasted too long, and has changed considerably since; however, do not hesitate, I vow the play is old, old as Comedy herself.

In a bright garden, near a rail, stands a strange statue, but bitten to death is La Comédie Humaine, and writhes behind her stone-white mask.

The muse laughed on; so did the mask, grimly, growing heavy, too heavy. She danced with mad rapture, laughing shrilly, whilst her nervous hands, convulsed, clutched its grinning cheeks; but the mask of stone laughed the more at this, growing heavy, heavier still. Then her agonised hands could hold it no longer, the mask fell to the ground and broke its nose.

The muse? she vanished in a frenzied hiccup, for all the world like the snapping string of a violin.

Since this the white mask has been shown, with its sunken eyes, its broken nose, and its hollow awful eternal laugh, with castagnettes rattled to an ominous tune, with exaggerated tibias.

Schumann, like many, once saw this mask, this fatal mask, and has sung of it, a sob that is sobbed with clenched hands, accompanied by the throbs of a beating heart – Warum.

But this song is older than father Schumann's song; the swelling waves chant the older melody, a Warum more minor, but laugh ironically as they sweep from the beach, trimmed with rippling bubbles, inviting to their liquidness, to the secret of their song, Warum?

How the water splashes and spreads, in grinning circles, if you fling it a stone. Is it a laugh? No, – a sob; for though rimmed with golden sands it is not a cup of happiness after all; frankly, the water is sad.

You see it can think back for a considerable time, and since the breaking of the mask, so many things have changed.

Once the sweet and gracious lady Venus rose from its depths, through trails of these bright chiming bubbles, on dancing foam. The worlds of

Gods and men went mad; the stars danced, till they fell like drunken bees – hark! the trees still groan, and the rivers moan!

Oh beautiful Lady Aphrodite Anadyomene! mercifully wring the glittering drops from your flaming mane into my cup, my Cup of Happiness; and for the sake of your beauty, I beseech you do not be dumb, and in plaster, with your eyes fixed afar on desolate Cnydos.

Ah, if my fancy, with exquisite tints, could quicken your limbs into supple life! perhaps – who knows? – you might tell me you are not Venus after all, but Eve, a Jewess; and not wring balm from your splendid tresses.

Friends! you will see all I say is old, an old tune, with orthodox Princess and Prince; even an occasional, and quite accidental, virtue in the story is drawn as an initial. It was on a certain night when that virtue lost her head – but this is not quite true, as the play will show, for all virtues are Byzantine, and cannot bend their limbs.

As clown, I have shouted my talents, vaunted my magic goblet; and if my young fingers pull too nervously and obviously at my puppet strings, know I am only a pleasant amateur, and not a poor devil; let me laughingly rattle my fool's bells, my symbolical bells, shaped like happy cups reversed; for all plays want bells, or the Warum song would continue monotonously throughout, till the veiled god of comedy, like that mythical old man at the theatre door, puts out the lights one by one, and shrouds most things with dusty covers; for he is deaf to unlimited Warum songs, deaf even to the song of the crumbling and changing atoms, – so away with narrowing symbolism! laugh! and rattle the bells, not hung on a hyacinth sash as a prelude to a mystery – there is no mystery – I have pulled up the curtain.

BY WAY OF PROLOGUE.

The name of my prince is formed of the names of all the Cardinal Virtues, composed into an euphonic whole. The greatest care, the most loving pains, had been lavished on his education; his bon mots were printed on pink paper by public subscription, trimmed with lace designed by the best artists only – yet he was not happy! though the welfare of his kingdom could only be gauged by the literary degradation of his foreign neighbours, and public opinion had placed his portrait in the National Gallery as an old master – no, he was not happy.

He tossed, in his troubled sleep, on his orthodox and princely cushions, on a golden and orthodox couch; he sighed in his painted chamber, the walls politely re-echoing his sighs, for they were painted with virtues each overcoming a dragon, each holding a hall-marked Cup of Happiness in tapering hands, each daintily curving the little finger in so doing.

The Cup of Happiness! The Cup of Happiness! groaned the prince, in his attempts to recall gems of modern poetry; he suffered from insomnia, as should all well-bred and crowned heads, on cushions and couches of gold.

His princely eyes were dizzied with following the allegorical twist of the enamelled and painted dragons, mysterious in the moonlit room. Here glistened a gem, lighted by a gem, twinkling in the grey light that trickled down delicate tracings of incrusted silver, to flash in one vivid spot, where a virtue held an embossed cup beneath her face, wreathed with lingering light gliding round a contour. The faces smiled in the luminous gloom.

How his temples ached, as he clasped them with dissolving hands! how the obstinate smile of one virtue haunted his brain! Yea, in his very orthodox cushions.

She lingeringly moved her taper fingers round the rim of the cup, her eyes fixed on his, weaving circles of exquisite sound, distant, faint, but full of passion, like a bar from Lohengrin; round and round; slowly, caressingly; the web of visible melody floated from the golden rim. She poured a gummy liquid, opalescent at her touch; it glowed, bubbled, throbbed, and rose passionately towards her; now incandescent it sweeps through the prince's veins, dancing and seething there; it bubbles round him, blending his being with its dazzling liquidness. The prince staggered to his feet, the cold floor electrified him; he flung away his heavy wreath, heavy with a relentless and sickly scent.

The moonlight flowed on the veined pavement.

The breath of endless flowers was tossed towards him as from a censer, sickening him; sickly was the colour of his royal robes, sickly the pavement reflecting the sinuous yellow folds gliding languidly on the glassy surface of polished steps.

The moonlight flowed on moon-coloured jade, slept in a dreamy haze on steps of jet, in a copper basin it melted among strange dreaming water-plants with fat buds.

The Prince feared he loathed all flowers, as he bathed his head with wetted hands, then flung himself on a grassy bank.

There swarmed small tribes in worlds of mosses, in worlds of lichen on tree trunks; a moth flew by, brave with its symbols painted on its wings, its rainbows, its blood-coloured hearts.

The Cup of Happiness! The Cup of Happiness!

The grasses sighed, and rolled, to the night air, full of that passionate murmur, the pulsing of the sap, the yearning lisp of the whispering leaves and rustle of heavy petals.

Something tinkled and trilled, ecstatically kissing soft mosses, and chiming through pebbles, to swim through lush stalks, where pined some melancholy toad, gasping a mournful, monotonous croak that made the drooping poppies swoon on their stalks. A flower hung near, shaped like an amorous mouth, a flower with lips! He flung his slipper into a fragrant bush, and the rose petals fell in a mass, with the swish of a trailing robe.

The king felt sick, so he left his kingdom.

The orchestra rolls into a despairing wail. The curtain rises 'mid peals of thunder; twisted trees sway to and fro in agony. In the foreground, filled with trailing thorns, beneath which crawl wicked snakes, croaks a raven. The sun sets lurid in the distance with extended and poetical rays. Now and again a faint flash of lightning shines fitfully at a side wing, near a palm-tree.

PALM-TREE.

Colophium, away! you are singeing my leaves. I was painted by an Academician. You must strike that conceited Oak; 'tis your part. I am a symbol of virtue.

LIGHTNING.

I flash where I am told, pitiful canvas. Do you not believe in Providence? You have made me miss my thunder, which has rolled twice.

THUNDER (behind).

Silence there! how came you in this scene? Your place is in the next act. We are in an imaginative landscape.

Snakes hiss approvingly; carrion birds, flying across the sun, cry, Away! away! On the other hand some Oak-trees in the background blame the levity of the Lightning, for a palm-tree is a palm-tree, etc., ... after all. The Lightning flashes again.

PALM—TREE.

Ugh! it has singed my paint. The world has turned atheist since I was young.

Gnarled roots and brambles writhe and clutch. A bird is caught by thorny branches to be devoured by a snake gliding from a rose-bush on which hangs a spider web with a butterfly wing earnestly painted.

Enter MONSTER

who, fortunately for our story, has spent years in getting a regulation thorn quite thoroughly into his right paw, that a hero or saint passing his way might be the means to higher ends; for he felt himself worthy of higher things, longed to be fed on tipsy-cake, to own a pastrycook's shop, and saw the Cup of Happiness in a mincemeat bowl.

When? whither? where?

Takes out a pocket-book, eagerly notes this down to write verses on, and groans aloud. Trees, Orchestra, Thunder, all groan lugubriously. The Lightning flashes near Palm-tree; this excites universal indignation, and the snakes and thorns shout Away with both of them! Away! Away!

LIGHTNING (to Palm-tree).

We are misunderstood. I did not notice how beautifully you are drawn. Thorns and snakes are a great mistake in nature.

PALM-TREE.

Young friend! you are wise for your years; let us form a society to suppress them – and immodest literature.

MONSTER.

I swirled into Renaissance arabesques unnoticed. The world is without decorative instincts.

The limelight falls on the floor, flashes on the Palm-tree (who feels flattered), and settles itself on right entrance.

Enter PRINCE.

For three days I have wandered in a too uncongenial atmosphere; all strength lacks grace – how true! – all grace, of course, lacks strength – so I was offered a post on a review. There is an incompleteness about most things, if I may be allowed to say so. This spot, however, seems tuned to a nobler key, not so grossly realistic as most; I really think my higher nature will be touched presently, and my ominously swelling cloak makes, I feel, a nobly decorative mass against the setting sun.

Monster introduces himself with frank manliness. The thorn is extracted to the huge appreciation of pit and gallery. The situation is too literary – The Prince and Monster – the latter rubs his claws complacently; gives so full and fruity a sound to

'Your Highness', the honest scenery feels quite jealous; quotes a few well-chosen verses on Happiness, and remains in an ecstacy with tearful eyes before a vision of a mincemeat bowl floating through space to slow music.

PALM-TREE (sotto voce).

If you don't flash brightly against me, I'll break up the partnership.

BUTTERFLY-WING.

All is not gold that glitters.

Enter FANTASY.

Her form, sinuous as a willow, is swathed in some light exquisite material, and garlanded with dainty twigs of jessamine, and nodding columbine; her jewelled and braided hair knots round an opal; above her brow flutters a black butterfly, circled by her nimbus tinted like a dissolved topaz; she holds an iris twined with ivy, and looks at the Prince over her shoulder whilst she holds a red carnation to her parted lips.

Ah! sweet my love! sweet Prince, dear wretch! I love thee! The word lies softer than soft velvet tinged a deepening violet, not softer than my passion. The word is a poor counterfeit, and apes the truth; as a dark shadow, crawling from the sun, is image of the truth that gives it being. The word is lourd and gross, I would give sound to it, with a deep cello's note, or sigh of some flosh petal falling with scarce audible sound, on floor of ivory flooded with living sun.

How many, how many have been my lovers! They kissed my eyes, and passionately my neck, for I am, and was, beautiful. But look you on my face, my white face, how many have shed heavy tears; their tears circle my throat; for gently I gathered these, and they became bright pearls to place upon my bosom, my white breasts like to the domes of some fair silvered shrine.

At this she bares her bosom, a pale tea-rose nestles there, the butterfly flutters to her mouth.

List! the frightened birds have chirped themselves to drowsiness; the muffled sound of distant thunder gives but a deepening zest to the mad song of that fond silly bird, that lifts its voice to passion's utterance. Ah! I could love you thus, and trill a sweet linked text, to melt your senses into rapt delight, till dazed by throbbing notes, that dance so swiftly, your heart stops faint within you; and lo! the next notes drown all remembrance of what has passed – in full enjoyment.

PRINCE.

Bright spirit! your name? I do not know you.

FANTASY.

My name, my name? I have many names; men called me after some fair women. I was born of flowers in Adam's brain; the warm wind gave me breath; this I remember me; poor Adam damned! – They called me Lilith. But the blossoms still remember me, mimic the soft veinings of my skin, and glow with hidden passion they had not then confessed. Then angels fell, because that I was sweet to look upon, and brought from sleepy depths quaint coral wreaths that yet blush red with the remembrance. (She sighs.) My presence moved man to lovely song; it echoes still, and ever will resound; great cities grew, piled high like cliffs, fronted in image of my face, painted pink in reverence for my flesh. Soft lyres were turned to curvings of my waist, to tell how I was fed by doves. But that was not so royal, or so glad, as Solomon's idolatry; he kissed my footsteps and my dress, on polished floor of crystal that multiplied my image. Poor king! Poor kings! But no! My love, if death, is life!

She weaves garlands round her wrists; gradually her eyes close; she makes a vague gesture towards her head.

Ah me! list! list! I hear the tread, the growing dread re-echoes in my heart. Tread! tread! and dust in dark clouds as a sign. (She gives a scream.) The violet sea is stained with crow-black sails, and sets a bloody sun. The city is on flames! on flames! and blots with lurid red the circling heaven.

She pauses, dreamily looks for a wound near her bosom, but finds nothing. Slowly she takes a pearl from her throat and sadly drops it. The sound makes her start; but laughingly she loosens her hair; it falls round her in a golden cloud; she holds her face with both hands, and says:

Ah love! I had many, many, lovers, lovers! look at these amethysts and pomegranate blossoms; these opals that hold fallen and still passionate spirits, glowing in cells of milky crystal; faint beryls that have dreamt the dreams of the sea at noon; these sapphires like dying eyes; listen to the song of this splendid ruby, how full of glowing mirth and rich delight; it calls the damask rose sick and sentimental. All these, and much besides, have men found and devised, to my good pleasure.

She kisses her hand to the Prince, who leans against the Palm-tree. She beckons to him.

PALM-TREE (severely).

Madam, I am married!

Enter LIGHTNING.

with a pair of spectacles he has borrowed from a satirist.

Madam still possesses her illusions!

FANTASY.

Do you wish to appeal to the gallery? Away, poor fly-blown stage property; or I'll blow you out.

[Exit LIGHTNING.

The whole stage looks shocked, even the limelight blushes.

PALM-TREE.

When I was young, however . . . .

But Fantasy escapes from her clothes, and with her hair streaming behind her like a comet dances about the stage naked.

PRINCE and BACK SCENERY.

The play must stop if this goes on!

MONSTER,

though quite a freethinker, is even more shocked than the Palm-tree.

The Cup of Happiness will be compromised!

He pulls out an article on . . . . . But Fantasy, knotting her white arms behind her head, dissolves into space, leaving behind her only the glimmer of her feet.

[Exeunt.

A SEED.

I swell, I grow, I am growing, I shall be a beautiful tree.

A WORM (pulling at it).

Nonsense! a tree? We are worms! worms!

(*To be continued.*)

Sensations

Anon. [Charles Ricketts]

In a similar vein to 'A Cup of Happiness', 'Sensations' may be seen as being an experimental piece, revelling in sensation at the expense of plot. These stories, both taken from the first issue of *The Dial*, were branded 'rubbish' by 'Michael Field' but hailed as 'delightful' and 'perfect' by Oscar Wilde.

The idea of style over substance would have amused Wilde, no doubt, but 'Sensations' is also shot through with many Decadent ideas and motifs. Set in France, the tale's narrator is intensely sensitive, almost to the point of being sickly, rather akin to Huysmans's Des Esseintes. In the first scene, a thunderstorm batters his delicate senses, resulting in synaesthetic imagery, such as light that 'gave almost the impression of a blow'. Reminiscent of Thomas de Quincey's *The Affliction of Childhood* (1845), the narrator explores a morbid emotional intensity brought on by the thunderstorm, linked as it is for him, with the 'deathbed of a friend' years before. From there, the scene moves to an almost Zola-esque, malodorous Catholic Mass, where the bodily writhings of a paralytic both enthral and repulse the writer, and the tale ends in a confusion of Catholic symbolism, wreathed in scented tobacco smoke.

The 'Apology' which follows 'Sensations' marks an interesting development in the debate over who precisely has the right to define art. In the wake of the British Matron and her followers, Ricketts and Shannon strike a pose prescient of high Modernism, by distancing themselves from the 'paying public' altogether. For them, only the Artist has the right to define his Art. From this standpoint, the deliberate deconstruction of traditional prose in these stories becomes a conscious attempt to alienate general readers, demonstrating *The Dial*'s position as being a physical manifestation of *l'art pour l'art*.

Little by little the air grew thick and oily; the sky, colour of oil, was strangely streaked with slowly lengthening shafts of smoke, rising from the whitish houses. The window panes, instead of being cool and soothing, gave a harsh shock, almost painful, suggesting a shudder. The traffic on the stony road passed with a sound distinct without blare, almost veiled.

The morning was unpleasant, and a sudden forked flash was not altogether unexpected. Seen clearly, it seemed to descend slowly as if selecting a comfortable pinnacle on which to alight. — I must close the window. — The rictus of the thunder was decidedly nasty; the shudder suggested itself again, and the window was closed.

The room danced. Each repetition of vivid light gave almost the impression of a blow; the eye, puzzled, seemed to see from the back of the head — flash! flash! — blue, lilac, rose — flash! flash! Then other sensations rushed upon me, the consciousness of an awful tearing, crackling, and rolling round; something rolling wantonly in the glory of its strength, falling in key like a phrase of Bach; and still that awful sensation of dancing light — flash! flash! destroying all sense of touch, of space; all, save that of hearing, concentrated into one awful sense of sight. A friend in the room, naturally red-faced and florid, looked a pale grey almost like cigar ashes, while blue, rose, danced about the room, seemingly for minutes. While still realising my bodily presence, I felt myself rooted to the floor, my lips cold; my brain, flashing like the lightning, was becoming frenzied with the idea that my friend was as frightened as myself. I felt enraged, but powerless. I was panic-stricken.

Thank goodness it was over; what had happened?

A second endless flash lit up the room as I closed my eyes, conscious of each throb repeated at the back of my skull with the distinctness of a telegraph machine under nimble fingers. Then the roar of the thunder simultaneously, less awful, happily, than the dancing light.

The rain at last fallen, suddenly poured down the sloping street. I talked rapidly, my thoughts were galloping indiscriminately in the future and the past. The lightning was in the room. Or cramped in the corner of a railway carriage, the train was bearing me, three years ago, through the black night, to the certain deathbed of a friend (if it were not already too late), while the night was made awful by a thunderstorm that swept across England. My thoughts still rushed wildly; dreading the next flash, I chattered on in an altered voice. A few doors in the house slammed, feet ran up and down. The lightning flashed again as I closed my eyes. Somebody knocked at the door — Monsieur, vous est-t-il arrivé quelque chose? la maison a été frappée.

ET CUM SPIRITU TUO.

I enter the church for Solemn High Mass. I know I am pacing like a priest in procession and feel an irresistible desire to place my finger-tips together.

An old Irishman, late of the Horse Artillery, takes the red tickets, shows us to places, performs a slovenly genuflexion and returns to his station midway in the nave. I am trying to place my hat where I shall not compel some one else, or be myself obliged, to kneel upon it, for the church will be full, Father Somebody O. J. is going to preach. The air is oppressive from the earlier celebrations; the chattering girls and craped old women dotted with tottering octogenarians who have to bend both knees if at all, smell of vile soap and hidden dirt. The devout child at my side is ruminating Latin sentences which she approximates to the sound of English words. Two overfed young Englishwomen, vilely dressed, are planted just in front; one wears crimson plush, the other has constantly clipped the straggling hairs upon the nuque till now she has a festoon of bristles from ear to ear. The screen of light woodwork is overtrailed with ivy, and fairy lamps hang in each arcade. The weeping of the fiddles, the moans of the organ, warm the church. Without warning there is a loud Oh! oh! oh! . . . . on my right. I turn suddenly; the sight transfixes me; it is a Saint Jerome drawn all of wriggles, stretching his hands towards the altar, with his plaintive cries, as the procession enters the church; his body is gradually collapsing under the progress of a paralytic fit. We rise and the priests begin to murmur while a small crowd around the inert sufferer under the cramped seats are baring his chest and slapping the palms of his hands. He is carried away, one man at his knees, two at his shoulders; his arms are lifeless, his beard trails upon his chest where the shirt has been rudely torn open; only his eyes are full of strength, starting as though he had been strangled, wondering if it is purgatory or hell. Sally smiles, to show me she is not frightened. Breakfast delayed has unstrung my nerves; the drowsy smell of spiced cigarettes; it all passes like a dream where white and green and gold things dance a religious redowa before a flower-decked altar. The devout child tips out the contents of a purse made of a shell with a clatter. We pace, pace, pace; we worship the Saviour, the life-giving cross; we press unworthy lips to the feet bleeding scarlet, not less blessed that they are preposterously out of drawing and skewered with a gold nail.

APOLOGY.

The sole aim of this magazine is to gain sympathy with its views.

Intelligent ostracism meets one at every door for any view whatsoever, from choice of subject to choice of frame. If our entrance is not through an orthodox channel, it is not, therefore, entirely our fault; we are out of date in our belief that the artist's conscientiousness cannot be controlled by the paying public, and just as far as this notion is prevalent we hope we shall be pardoned our seeming aggressiveness.

A Simple Story

Charles Haslewood Shannon

Also from the first issue of *The Dial*, this piece by Shannon (his middle name has sometimes the variant spelling 'Hazelwood') takes for its theme the five-yearly visit of a Catholic bishop to a rural community. The frenzied preparations by the townsfolk and the near ecstatic response to the Holy Father's appearance depict an idolatrous and near-superstitious religion that is completely at odds with the Victorian Protestant norm. The setting is early Christian Greece, blending the Decadent preoccupations of Catholic ritual and ancient Greek sensuality.

'A Simple Story', like many writings in *The Dial*, may be viewed in a proto-Modernist light, in its challenge to traditional Victorian prose. Characters do not develop, and there is little in the way of dramatic tension. The visit of the Bishop merely maintains the status quo, giving the tale a cyclical, non-linear and unempirical quality. Catholicism is thus portrayed as an uncomplicated continuum, and a sensuous mode of being, flying in the face of a typically Protestant, empirical view of life, based upon actions, cause and effect.

Batilda had risen earlier than usual, for this was the long-expected day when the Holy Father Hilarion would stop and bless her hearth. With him her son Felix, whom it had pleased God to make a priest.

A wreath of polished ivy leaves made the door quite bright. The floor was fresh-strewn with rushes and sweet-smelling herbs; the roughly-hewn table stained red; a cross painted in red above the hearth, and by its foot a trimmed lamp placed. All this in honour of the Holy Father and her dear son, both now on their way to the Seven Isles, to bless and baptise there in the name of God.

Her eyes swelled with tears of pride, though she found so many matters to attend to. She bustled the two girls, Batilda and Basine, and her tearful face grew flushed over the wheaten cakes that would not bake. Those wheaten cakes still flat! and the Holy Father so near and probably so hungry!

The morning was radiant; something sang in the tangled hedge, something sang in the pale blue sky; these she did not heed, the cakes destroyed the smell of the fresh earth. Her wrath boiled over when Basine overset a precious earthen jar, and buried in her hands a crying head decked with yellow flowers. She had not noticed that before; yellow flowers in her yellow hair! and so much to do! She bustled the girls still more – sat down to moan with despair. She became still more tearful and active when the village people began to stir, to walk up to the hill-top and shade their eyes with their hands, waiting for the Holy Father. The sheep, still penned, thrust out perplexed and bleating heads, wondering when they would be led to pasture; the dogs were as active as Batilda. Young men congregated about the tall elm near the stream. Every one looked anxious, and their little brother ran backwards and forwards, distracting the two crazy girls with the news that the Holy Father had not yet come.

The sky grew paler, the pale green sea turned silver towards noon, and still no Holy Father. Everything had been ready some time, but Batilda still fretted, bustling the two girls for talking to everyone who came to see the wonderfully clean room, with the pretty ivy wreath, always with the question, Had the Holy Father come? so futile, since they knew as well as she did that he had not. The men put up with cold porridges without the usual lordly complaints, the excitement had been so great. Batilda stood robed in washed clothes, fretful but full of pride. The crowd on the hill-top stirred; her little boy ran down to say, There is a mule with brother Felix by it, and the Holy Father on top of the mule. Batilda wept with joy. People left their straw and clay covered huts. Radegond and her daughter ran past in blue robes, crying Batilda! Batilda! will you not come to meet the Holy Father? There were women who had time to think of blue gowns with fringes; they had not been up before the day to work for the Holy Father. The two crazy girls turned pale with excitement when Hilarion appeared, surrounded by the whole village out to welcome him; the aged dropped on their knees at their doors as he passed. After three hours suspense and despair, the cakes had baked as if by a miracle – how tall and handsome her boy Felix had grown! how like a saint he looked, supporting with his arm the Holy Father! how proud her husband would have been could he only have lived! She sank on her knees under the blessing of the Bishop, and her heart sang like the little black speck singing ecstatically, almost at the throne of God, lost in the pale blue sky.

The whole village of course flocked round. Some began to pray very audibly to make up for the five years since the Father last came. Little children were pushed forward; children with little square faces, pale blue eyes, hair almost the colour of their blonde flesh. Some hung back tearfully, frightened at their fathers beckoning solemnly to them; some kept their fists doubled in their eyes; but most looked frankly at the Bishop, with legs firmly apart and little bellies in dignified prominence.

The red table had been spread by active hands, with fresh porridge, baked fish, cakes, milk and tender herbs. Batilda almost wished to push the Bishop in at the door, so slow was he to enter, recognising this old man, that decrepit old woman, gutturally venting in holy exclamations. People now came forward with cheeses and shell-fish. The cows lowed as the frothing milk was brought from the stables by children who stopped obstinately at the door. As if she meant to starve the Holy Father! Stupid Basine was weeping for her sins, but Batilda laughed loudly as she sent people from the door, which grew more and more obstructed. Even the wicked Nazie, the one-eyed shepherd, was there, with his wicked dog, the terror of all the children. Young men pushed the children away, and stared sheepishly, their huge hands and arms hanging heavily at their sides. The Father would eat scarcely anything, nodding kindly to the crowd that looked almost alarmed each time he did so. Both the crazy girls now laughed loudly, pushing the people away. Batilda, shocked, wished to close the door; the very dogs would be coming in next! The Bishop, however, had finished with 'those excellent cakes' as he called them. – Could a man eat so little? – He motioned the foremost of the crowd to come forward. All swayed nervously, so he rose and spoke kindly to them. There were two couples to marry and their little children to baptise; three quarrels to arbitrate, and much kindliness to teach. Though it was broad daylight, Batilda lit the lamp and placed it near him. Felix stood solemnly by, like a bishop; he could not think of his mother only. The day advanced. People had come on mules from the hamlets. The Holy Father had stepped out on the common to speak to all; to console and chide. He spoke at length of a father in his home, told them that you must not move boundary stones in the night, nor strike a neighbour in a dark road because he had taken your corn from the big common granary (where the wheat stood in jars under a roof of rushes). He spoke of God's goodness in sending leaves and fruits every year, in putting fish in the waters. As he spoke he looked at the sky, becoming coloured with lovely clouds; some birds flew across it, and he almost wept, thinking if only the Holy Ghost might fly down to him with flaming wings.

Felix was to tarry the night with his mother, and join the Father next day in the Isles. The sea was becoming golden, golden as the sky. He still spoke to them, while Radegond in her blue robes sobbed audibly. Loic the sailor was ready; his boat looked black against the yellow sea; he would get the holy man across before sundown.

The crowd was dense around the Father; women holding dazed children to be blest; children dazed at seeing their parents weep, and smaller children washed by the Bishop. Radegond gave little moans, which the women took up with interest as the Father neared the beach, the sun shining in his eyes. When he turned towards them the sun flamed like a halo round his sparsely-locked head. Footsteps clattered on the beach, and the water gently lapped, lapped in golden ripples lined with green. The Father entered the boat, which had been bowing solemnly to him, and stood against the sun – Peace be with you – he bowed three times in the names of the three spirits. Men shoved away the boat. Some one came too late, rattling down the beach, to see the Bishop. The crowd, swaying with wistful faces, felt something was leaving them, – Peace be with you – he raised his hand and bent fingers. Some women went on their knees; the men still stood in the water. He blessed them again; they waded further, making large glittering circles, flashing with blue and green. – Peace be with you – they waded still further, while the oars beat rhythmically, slowly drowning his voice. He stood up, his arms outstretched like a cross, still blessing them, till he was lost against the sail. Two or three swam out a short distance. The boat now looked like a bird flying towards the violet horizon, where stood Seven Isles.

THE PAGAN REVIEW

The Black Madonna

W. S. Fanshawe [William Sharp]

W. S. Fanshawe is one of the numerous pseudonyms of Scottish novelist, poet and biographer William Sharp (1855–1905). His most well known pen-name was Fiona Macleod. Sharp was acquainted with Yeats during the 1890s and participated in the Celtic Revival Movement. He was also a member of the Hermetic Order of the Golden Dawn. Often in his works, paganism and nature-worship, inspired by Pater, is nurtured and matured into pagan Decadence. Sharp's novels and short stories mainly deal with fantastic and occult themes. He also edited works by such figures as Swinburne and Eugene Lee-Hamilton.

The Saturday Review (3 September 1892) dismissed the stories in *The Pagan Review* as 'gabble', particularly 'The Black Madonna'. This tale, set in Nubia (northern Sudan), is about savage beauty and archaic rituals, including human sacrifice. Prose morphs into ceremonial script. The story tells of the sacrilegious sexual union between a priest and the goddess-statue of the Black Madonna in what is a perfect conflation of paganism and Christianity. Incestuous allegorical undertones between the Virgin Mary and Christ are also present. 'The Black Madonna' has cryptic nods to Swinburne, such as the sexualised, pain-inflicting Madonna. It pays tribute to Swinburne's poem of the iconic Fatal Woman 'Dolores' (*Poems and Ballads*, 1866) which contains the hypnotic refrain 'Our Lady of Pain'. The allure of the latent goddess, despite the threat of everlasting damnation, also echoes 'Laus Veneris'. In addition, Sharp's penchant for the works of D. G. Rossetti is evident in the naming of the goddess Astarte, a reference to Dante Rossetti's poem 'Astarte Syriaca'.

The blood-red sunset turns the dark fringes of the forest into a wave of flame. A hot river of light streams through the aisles of the ancient trees, and, falling over the shoulder of a vast, smooth slab of stone that rises solitary in this wilderness of dark growth and sombre green, pours in a flood across an open glade and upon the broken columns and inchoate ruins of what in immemorial time had been a mighty temple, the fane of a perished god, or of many gods. As the sun rapidly descends, the stream of red light narrows, till, quivering and palpitating, it rests like a bloody sword upon a colossal statue of black marble, facing due westward. The statue is that of a woman, and is as of the Titans of old-time.

A great majesty is upon the mighty face, with its moveless yet seeing eyes, its faint inscrutable smile. Upon the triple-ledged pedestal, worn at the edges like swords ground again and again, lie masses of large white flowers, whose heavy fragrances rise in a faint blue vapour drawn forth with the sudden suspiration of the earth by the first twilight-chill.

In the great space betwixt the white slab of stone — hurled thither, or raised, none knoweth when or how — is gathered a dark multitude, silent, expectant. Many are Arab tribesmen, the remnant of a strange sect driven southward; but most are Nubians, or that unnamed swarthy race to whom both Arab and Negro are as children. All, save the priests, of whom the elder are clad in white robes and the younger girt about by scarlet sashes, are naked. Behind the men, at a short distance apart, are the women; each virgin with an ivory circlet round the neck, each mother or pregnant woman with a thin gold band round the left arm. Between the long double-line of the priests and the silent multitude stands a small group of five youths and five maidens; each crowned with heavy drooping white flowers; each motionless, morose; all with eyes fixt on the trodden earth at their feet.

The younger priests suddenly strike together square brazen cymbals, deeply chased with signs and letters of a perished tongue. A shrill screaming cry goes up from the people, followed by a prolonged silence. Not a man moves, not a woman sighs. Only a shiver contracts the skin of the foremost girl in the small central group. Then the elder priests advance slowly, chanting monotonously,

CHORUS OF THE PRIESTS:
We are thy children, O mighty Mother!
We are the slain of thy spoil, O Slayer!
We are thy thoughts that are fulfilled, O Thinker!
Have pity upon us!

And from all the multitude cometh as with one shrill screaming voice:
Have pity upon us! Have pity upon us! Have pity upon us!

THE PRIESTS:
Thou wast, before the first child came through the dark gate of the womb!
Thou wast, before ever woman knew man!
Thou wast, before the shadow of man moved athwart the grass!
Thou wast, and Thou art!

THE MULTITUDE:
Have pity upon us! Have pity upon us! Have pity upon us!

THE PRIESTS:
Hail, thou who art more fair than the dawn, more dark than night!
Hail thou, white as ivory or veiled in shadow!

Hail, thou of many names, and immortal!
Hail, Mother of God, Sister of the Christ, Bride of the Prophet!

THE MULTITUDE:

Have pity upon us? Have pity upon us! Have pity upon us!

THE PRIESTS:

O moon of night, O morning star! Consoler! Slayer!
Thou, who lovest shadow, and fear, and sudden death!
Who art the smile that looketh upon women and children!
Who hath the heart of man in thy grip as in a vice;
Who hath his pride and strength in thy sigh of yestereve;
Who hath his being in thy breath that goeth forth, and is not!

THE MULTITUDE:

Have pity upon us! Have pity upon us! Have pity upon us!

THE PRIESTS:

We knew thee not, nor the way of thee, O Queen!
But we bring thee what thou loved'st of old, and for ever!
The white flowers of our forests and the red flowers of our bodies!
Take them and slay not, O Slayer!
For we are thy slaves, O Mother of Life,
We are the dust of thy tired feet, O Mother of God!

As the white-robed priests advance slowly towards the Black Madonna, the younger tear off their scarlet sashes, and seizing the five maidens, bind them together, left arm to right, and hand to hand. Therewith the victims move slowly forward till they pass through the ranks of the priests, and stand upon the lowest edge of the pedestal of the great statue. Towards each steppeth, and behind each standeth, a naked priest, each holding a narrow irregular sword of antique fashion.

THE ELDER PRIESTS:

O Mother of God!

THE YOUNGER PRIESTS:

O Slayer, be pitiful!

THE VICTIMS:
O Mother of God! O Slayer! be merciful!

THE MULTITUDE (*in a loud screaming voice*):
Have pity upon us! Have pity upon us! Have pity upon us!

The last blood-red gleam fades from the Black Madonna, and flashes this way and that for a moment from the ten sword-knives that cut the air and plunge between the shoulders and to the heart of each victim. A wide spirt of blood rains upon the white flowers at the base of the colossal figure; where also speedily lie, dark amidst welling crimson, the swarthy bodies of the slain.

THE PRIESTS:
Behold, O Mother of God,
The white flowers of our forests and the red flowers of our bodies!
Have pity, O Compassionate,
Be merciful, O Queen!

THE MULTITUDE:
Have pity upon us! Have pity upon us! Have pity upon us!

But at the swift coming of the darkness, the priests hastily cover the dead with the masses of the white flowers; and one by one, and group by group, the multitude melteth away. When all are gone save the young chief, Bihr, and a few of his following, the priests prostrate themselves before the Black Madonna, and pray to her to vouchsafe a sign.

From the mouth of the carven figure cometh a hollow voice, sombre as the reverberation of thunder among barren hills.

THE BLACK MADONNA:
I hearken.

THE PRIESTS (*prostrate*):
Wilt thou slay, O Slayer?

THE BLACK MADONNA:
Yea, verily.

THE PRIESTS (*in a rising chant*):
Wilt thou save, O Mother of God?

THE BLACK MADONNA:
I save.

THE PRIESTS:
Can one see thee, and live?

THE BLACK MADONNA:
At the Gate of Death.

Whereafter, no sound cometh from the statue, already dim in the darkness that seems to have crept from the forest. The priests rise, and disappear in silent groups under the trees.

The thin crescent moon slowly rises. A phosphorescent glow from orchids and parasitic growths shimmers intermittently in the forest. A wavering beam of light falls upon the right breast of the Black Madonna; then slowly downward to her feet; then upon the motionless figure of Bihr, the warrior-chief. None saw him steal thither: none knoweth that he has braved the wrath of the Slayer; for it is the sacred time, when it is death to enter the glade.

BIHR (*in a low voice*):
Speak, Spirit that dwelleth here from of old . . .
Speak, for I would have speech with thee. I fear thee not, O Mother of God, for the priests of the Christ who is thy son say that thou wert but a woman . . . And it may be — it may be — what say the children of the Prophet: that there is but one God, and he is Allah.

(Deep silence. From the desert beyond the forest comes the hollow roaring of lions.)

BIHR (*in a loud chant*):
To the north and to the east I have seen many figures like unto thine, gods and goddesses: some mightier than thee — vast sphinxes by the flood of Nilus, gigantic faces rising out of the sands of the desert. And none spake, for silence is come upon them; and none slays, for the strength of the gods passes even as the strength of men.

(Deep silence. From the obscure waste of the forest come snarling cries, long-drawn howls, and the low moaning sigh of the wind.)

BIHR (*mockingly*):
For I will not be thrall to a woman, and the priests shall not bend me to their will as a slave unto the yoke. If thou thyself art God, speak, and I shall be thy slave to do thy will . . . . . Thrice have I come hither at the new moon, and thrice do I go hence uncomforted. . . . . What voice was that that spoke ere the victims died? I know not; but it hath reached mine ears never save when the priests are by. Nay (*laughing low*), O Mother of God, I ———

(Suddenly he trembles all over and falls on his knees, for from the blackness above him cometh a voice:)

THE BLACK MADONNA:
What would'st thou?

BIHR (*hoarsely*):
Have mercy upon me, O Queen!

THE BLACK MADONNA:
What would'st thou?

BIHR:
I worship thee, Mother of God! Slayer and Saver!

THE BLACK MADONNA:
What would'st thou?

BIHR (*tremulously*):
Show me thyself, thyself, even for this one time, O Strength and Wisdom!

Deep silence. The wind in the forest passes away with a faint wailing sound. The dull roaring of lions rises and falls in the distance. A soft yellow light illumes the statue, as though another moon were rising behind the temple.

A great terror comes upon Bihr the Chief, and he falls prostrate at the base of the Black Madonna.

His eyes are open, but they see not, save the burnt spikes of trodden grass, sere and stiff save where damp with newly-shed blood; and deaf are his ears, though he waits for he knoweth not what sound from above.

Suddenly he starts, and the sweat mats the hair on his forehead when he feels a touch on his right shoulder. Looking slowly round he sees beside him a woman, tall, and of a lithe and noble body. He seeth that her skin is dark, yet not of the blackness of the south. Two spheres of wrought gold cover her breasts, and from the serpentine zone round her waist is looped a dusky veil spangled with shining points. In her eyes, large as those of the desert-antelope, is the loveliness and the pathos and the pain of twilight.

BIHR (*trembling*):

Art thou — Art thou ———

THE BLACK MADONNA:

I am she whom thou worshippest.

BIHR:

(*Looking at the colossal statue, irradiated by the strange light that cometh he knows not whence; and then at the beautiful apparition by his side.*)
Thou art the Black Madonna, the Mother of God?

THE BLACK MADONNA:

Thou sayest it.

BIHR:

Thou hast heard my prayer, O Queen!

THE BLACK MADONNA:

Even so.

BIHR:

(*Taking heart because of the sweet and thrilling humanity of the goddess.*)
O Slayer and Saver, is the lightning thine and the fire that is in the earth? Canst thou whirl the stars as from a sling, and light the mountainous lands to the south with falling meteors? O Queen, destroy me not, for I am thy slave, and weaker than thy breath: but canst thou stretch forth thine hand and say yea to the lightning, and bid silence unto the thunder ere it breeds the bolts that smite? For if ———

THE BLACK MADONNA:
I make and I unmake. This cometh and that goeth, and I am ———

BIHR:
And thou art ———

THE BLACK MADONNA:
I was Ashtaroth of old. Men have called me many names. All things change, but I change not. Know me, O Slave! I am the Mother of God. I am the Sister of the Christ. I am the Bride of the Prophet.

BIHR (*with awe*):
And thou art the very Prophet, and the very Christ, and the very God! Each speaketh in thee, who art older than they ———

THE BLACK MADONNA:
I *am* the Prophet.

BIHR:
Hail, O Lord of Deliverance!

THE BLACK MADONNA:
I *am* the Christ, the Son of God.

BIHR:
Hail, O most Patient, most Merciful!

THE BLACK MADONNA:
I *am* the Lord thy God.

BIHR:
Hail, Giver of Life and Death!

THE BLACK MADONNA:
Yet here none is; for each goeth or each cometh as I will. I only am eternal.

BIHR:
(*Crawling forward, and kissing her feet.*)
Behold, I am thy slave to do thy will; thy sword to slay; thy spear to follow;

thy hound to track thine enemies. I am dust beneath thy feet. Do with me as thou wilt.

THE BLACK MADONNA:
(Slowly, and looking at him strangely.)
Thou shalt be my High Priest . . . . . Come back to-morrow an hour after the setting of the sun.

As Bihr the Chief rises and goeth away into the shadow she stareth steadily after him; and a deep fear dwells in the twilight of her eyes. Then, turning, she standeth awhile by the slain bodies of the victims of the sacrifice; and having lightly brushed away with her foot the flowers above each face, looketh long on the mystery of death. And when at last she glides by the great statue and passes into the ruins beyond, there is no longer any glow of light, and a deep darkness covereth the glade. From the deeper darkness beyond comes the howling of hyenas, the shrill screaming of a furious beast of prey, and the sudden bursting roar of lion answering lion.

When the dawn breaks, and a pale, wavering light glimmers athwart the great white slab of stone that, on the farther verge of the forest, faces the Black Madonna, there is nought upon the pedestal save a ruin of bloodied trampled flowers, though the sere yellow grass is stained in long trails across the open. The dawn withdraws again, but ere long suddenly wells forth, and it is as though the light wind were bearing over the forest a multitude of soft grey feathers from the breasts of doves. Then the dim concourse of feathers is as though innumerable leaves of wild-roses were falling, falling, petal by petal uncurling into a rosy flame that wafts upward and onward. The stars have grown suddenly pale, and the fires of Phosphor burn wanly green in the midst of a palpitating haze of pink. With a great rush, the sun swings through the gates of the East, tossing aside his golden, fiery mane as he fronts the new day.

And the going of the day is from morning silence unto noon silence, and from the silence of the afternoon unto the silence of the eve. Once more, towards the setting of the sun, the multitude cometh out of the forest, from the east and from the west, and from the north and from the south; once more the Priests sing the sacred hymns; once more the people supplicate as with one shrill screaming voice, *Have pity upon us! Have pity upon us! Have pity upon us!* Once more the victims are slain: of little children who might one day shake the spear and slay, five; and of little children who would one day bear and bring forth, five.

Yet again an hour passeth after the setting of the sun. There is no moon to lighten the darkness and the silence; but a soft glow falleth from the temple, and upon the man who kneels before the Black Madonna. But when Bihr, having no sign vouchsafed, and hearing no sound, and seeing nought upon the carven face, neither tremour of the lips nor life in the lifeless eyes, suddenly seeth the goddess, glorious in her beauty that is as of the night, coming towards him from out of the ruins, his heart leapeth within him in strange joy and dread. Scarce knowing what he doth, he springeth to his feet, trembling as a reed that leaneth against the flank of a lioness by the water-pool.

BIHR:
(*Yearningly, with supplicating arms:*)
Hail, God!.... Goddess, Most Beautiful!

She draws nigh to him, looking at him the while out of the deep twilight of her eyes.

THE BLACK MADONNA:
What would'st thou?

BIHR:
(*Wildly, stepping close, but halting in dread.*)
Thou art no Mother of God, O Goddess, Queen, Most Beautiful!

THE BLACK MADONNA:
What would'st thou, O blind fool that is so in love with death?

BIHR (*hoarsely*):
Make me like unto thyself, for I love you!

Deep silence. From afar, on the desert, comes the dull roaring of lions by the water-courses; from the forest a murmurous sound as of baffled winds snared among the thick-branched ancient trees.

BIHR:
(*Sobbing as one wounded in flight by an arrow.*)
For I love thee! I — love — thee! I ———

Deep silence. A shrill screaming of a bird fascinated by a snake comes from the forest. Beyond, from the desert, a long, desolate moaning and howling, where the hyenas prowl.

THE BLACK MADONNA:

When .. did .. thy folly .. this madness .. come upon thee .. O Fool?

BIHR (*passionately*):

O Most Beautiful! Most Beautiful! Thou — *Thou* — will I worship!

THE BLACK MADONNA:

Go hence, lest I slay thee!

BIHR:

Slay, O Slayer, for thou art Life and Death! . . . But I go not hence. I love thee! I love thee! I love thee!

THE BLACK MADONNA:

I am the Mother of God.

BIHR:

I love thee!

THE BLACK MADONNA:

God dwelleth in me. I am thy God.

BIHR:

I love thee!

THE BLACK MADONNA:

Go hence, lest I slay thee!

BIHR:

Thou tremblest, O Mother of God! Thy lips twitch, thy breasts heave, O thou who callest thyself God!

THE BLACK MADONNA:

(*Raising her right arm menacingly.*)

Go hence, thou dog, lest thou look upon my face no more.

Then suddenly, with bowed head and shaking limbs, Bihr the Chief turneth and passes into the forest. And as he fades into the darkness, the Black Madonna stareth a long while after him, and a deep fear broodeth in the twilight of her eyes. But by the bodies of the slain children she passes at last, and with a shudder looks not upon their faces, but strews the heavy white flowers more thickly upon them.

The darkness cometh out of the darkness, billow welling forth from spent billow on the tides of night. On the obscure waste of the glade nought moves, save the gaunt shadow of a hyena that crawls from column to column. From the blackness beyond swells the long thunderous howl of a lioness, echoing the hollow blasting roar of a lion standing, with eyes of yellow flame, on the summit of the great slab of smooth rock that faces the carven Madonna.

And when the dawn breaks, and long lines of pearl-grey wavelets ripple in a flood athwart the black-green sweep of the forest, there is nought upon the pedestal but red flowers that once were white, rent and scattered this way and that. The cool wind moving against the east ruffles the opaline flood into a flying foam of pink, wherefrom mists and vapours rise on wings like rosy flames, and as they rise their crests shine as with blazing gold, and they fare forth after the Morn that leaps towards the Sun.

And the going of the day is from morning silence unto noon silence, and from the silence of the afternoon unto the silence of eve. Once more towards the setting of the sun, the multitude cometh out of the forest, from the east and from the west, and from the north and from the south. Once more the priests sing the sacred hymns; once more the people supplicate as with one shrill screaming voice, *Have pity upon us! Have pity upon us! Have pity upon us!* Once more the victims are slain: five chiefs of captives taken in war; and unto each chief two warriors in the glory of youth.

Yet an hour after the setting of the sun. Moonless the silence and the dark, save for the soft yellow light that falleth from the temple, and upon the man who, crested with an ostrich-plume bound by a heavy circlet of gold, with a tiger-skin about his shoulders, and with a great spear in his hand, standeth beyond the statue and nigh unto the ruins, where no man hath ventured and lived.

BIHR (*with loud triumphant voice*):
Come forth, my Bride!

Deep silence, save for the sighing of the wind among the upper branches of the trees, and the panting of the flying deer beyond the glade.

BIHR:

(*Striking his spear against the marble steps.*)
Come forth, Glory of my eyes! Come forth, Body of my Body.

Deep silence. Then there is a faint sound, and the Black Madonna stands beside Bihr the Chief. And the man is wrought to madness by her beauty, and lusteth after her, and possesseth her with the passion of his eyes.

THE BLACK MADONNA:

(*Trembling, and strangely troubled.*)
What would'st thou?

BIHR:

Thou!

THE BLACK MADONNA (*slowly*):
Young art thou, Bihr, in thy comeliness and strength to be so in love with death.

BIHR:
Who giveth life, and who death? It is not thou, nor I.

THE BLACK MADONNA (*shuddering*):
It cometh. None can stay it.

BIHR:
Not thou? Thou can'st not stay it, even?

THE BLACK MADONNA (*whisperingly*):
Nay, Bihr; and this thing thou knowest in thy heart.

BIHR (*mockingly*):
O Mother of God! O Sister of Christ! O Bride of the Prophet!

THE BLACK MADONNA:
(*Putting her hand to her heart.*)
What would'st thou?

BIHR:
Thou!

THE BLACK MADONNA:
I am the Slayer, the Terrible, the Black Madonna.

BIHR:
And lo, thy God laugheth at thee, even as at me, and mine. And lo, I have come for thee; for I am become His Prophet, and thou art to be my Bride!

As he finisheth he turns towards the great Statue of the Black Madonna and, laughing, hurls his spear against its breast, whence the weapon rebounds with a loud clang. Then, ere the woman knows what he has done, he leaps to her and seizes her in his grasp, and kisses her upon the lips, and grips her with his hands till the veins sting in her arms. And all the sovereignty of her lonely godhood passeth from her like the dew before the hot breath of the sun, and her heart throbs against his side so that his ears ring as with the clang of the gongs of battle. He sobs low, as a man amidst baffling waves; and in the hunger of his desire she sinks as one who drowns.

Together they go up the long flat marble steps; together they pass into the darkness of the ruins. From the deeper darkness beyond cometh no sound, for the forest is strangely still. Not a beast of prey comes nigh unto the slain victims of the sacrifice, not a vulture falleth like a cloud through the night. Only, from afar, the dull roaring of the lions cometh up from the water-courses on the desert.

And the wind that bloweth in the night cometh with rain and storm, so that when the dawn breaks it is as a sea of sullen waves grey with sleet. But calm cometh out of the blood-red splendour of the east.

And on this, the morning of the fourth and last day of the Festival of the Black Madonna, the multitude of her worshippers come forth from the forest, singing a glad song. In front go the warriors, the young men brandishing spears, and with their knives in their left hands slicing the flesh upon their sides and upon their thighs: the men of the north clad in white garb and heavy burnous, the tribesmen of the south naked save for their loin-girths, but plumed as for war.

But as the priests defile beyond them upon the glade, a strange new song goeth up from their lips; and the people tremble, for they know that some dire thing hath happened.

THE PRIESTS (*chanting*):
Lo, when the law of the Queen is fulfilled, she passeth from her people awhile. For the Mother of God loveth the world, and would go in sacrifice. So loveth us the Mother of God that she passeth in sacrifice. Behold, she perisheth, who dieth not! Behold, she dieth, who is immortal!

Whereupon a great awe cometh on the multitude, as they behold smoke, whirling and fulgurant, issuing from the mouth and nostrils of the Black Madonna. But this awe passeth into horror, and horror into wild fear, when great tongues of flame shoot forth amidst the wreaths of smoke, and when from forth of the Black Madonna come strange and horrible cries, as though a mortal woman were perishing by the torture of fire.

With shrieks the women turn and fly; hurling their spears from them, the men dash wildly to the forest, heedless whither they flee.

But those that leap to the westward, where the great white rock standeth solitary, facing the Black Madonna, see for a moment, in the glare of sunrise, a swarthy, naked figure, with a tiger-skin about the shoulders, crucified against the smooth white slope. Down from the outspread hands of Bihr the Chief trickle two long wavering streamlets of blood; two long streamlets of blood drip, drip, down the white glaring face of the rock, from the pierced feet.

THE CHAMELEON

The Priest and the Acolyte

Anon. [John Francis Bloxam]

John Francis Bloxam (1873–1928) wrote this tale whilst at Exeter College, Oxford, and published it anonymously (signed 'X') in *The Chameleon*, an undergraduate magazine for which he also served as editor. He later became an Anglo-Catholic priest.

Although included in a privately produced magazine with an extremely small print-run, this story of a doomed homosexual and paederastic love affair gained notoriety through its erroneous connections with Oscar Wilde. After the story's use against Wilde at his trials, it was wrongly attributed to him for many years following his conviction, and appeared in several anthologies of Wilde's works. Although not of Wilde's literary calibre, the piece does indeed echo many of Wilde's preoccupations, from the angelic golden-haired boy himself (Wilde's 'type') to the transience of youthful beauty, and the notion of beautiful sins that take place under heady, incense-laden moonlight. The priest's argument, where he posits a noble, spiritual and pure love against the 'base motives' of his accusers is itself rather prescient of Wilde's own self-defence in court a few months later.

Decadent themes may also be found in the static, and even entropic opening, and the appeal of Catholic ritual, especially for the sexually deviant. The fact that the story was never intended to reach beyond a limited clique-readership led the author to be rather bold in both subject and detail. The child lover is an orphan, a mainstay of many pornographic works of the era, and although seen by many as a powerful 'Uranian' polemical work, the story still has the power to shock readers more than a century later.

Honi soit qui mal y pense.

PART ONE

'Pray, father, give me thy blessing, for I have sinned.'

The priest started; he was tired in mind and body, his soul was sad and his heart heavy as he sat in the terrible solitude of the confessional ever listening to the same dull round of oft-repeated sins. He was weary of the conventional tones and matter-of-fact expressions. Would the world always be the same? For nearly twenty centuries the Christian priests had sat in the confessional and listened to the same old tale. The world seemed to him no better; always the same, the same. The young priest sighed to himself, and for a moment almost wished people would be worse. Why could they not escape from these old wearily-made paths and be a little original in their vices, if sin they must? But the voice he now listened to aroused him from his reverie. It was so soft and gentle, so diffident and shy.

He gave the blessing and listened. Ah, yes! he recognised the voice now. It was the voice he had heard for the first time only that very morning: the voice of the little acolyte that had served his Mass.

He turned his head and peered through the grating at the little bowed head beyond; there was no mistaking those long soft curls. Suddenly for one moment the face was raised and the large moist blue eyes met his; he saw the little oval face flushed with shame at the simple boyish sins he was confessing, and a thrill shot through him, for he felt that here at least was something in the world that was beautiful, something that was really true. Would the day come when those soft scarlet lips would have grown hard and false? when the soft shy treble would have become careless and conventional? His eyes filled with tears, and in a voice that had lost its firmness he gave the absolution.

After a pause he heard the boy rise to his feet, and watched him wend his way across the little chapel and kneel before the altar while he said his penance. The priest hid his thin, tired face in his hands and sighed wearily.

The next morning, as he knelt before the altar and turned to say the words of confession to the little acolyte whose head was bent so reverently towards him, he bowed low till his hair just touched the golden halo that surrounded the little face, and he felt his veins burn and tingle with a strange new fascination.

When that most wonderful thing in the whole world, complete soul-absorbing love for another, suddenly strikes a man, that man knows what heaven means and he understands hell; but if the man be an ascetic, a priest whose whole heart is given to ecstatic devotion, it were better for that man if he had never been born.

When they reached the vestry and the boy stood before him reverently receiving the sacred vestments, he knew that henceforth the entire devotion of his religion, the whole ecstatic fervour of his prayers, would be connected with, nay, inspired by, one object alone. With the same reverence and humility as he would have felt in touching the consecrated elements he laid his hands on the curl-crowned head, he touched the small pale face, and, raising it slightly, he bent forward and gently touched the smooth white brow with his lips.

When the child felt the caress of his fingers, for one moment everything swam before his eyes; but when he felt the light touch of the tall priest's lips a wonderful assurance took possession of him: he understood. He raised his little arms, and, clasping his slim white fingers around the priest's neck, kissed him on the lips.

With a sharp cry the priest fell upon his knees, and, clasping the little figure clad in scarlet and lace to his heart, he covered the tender flushing face with burning kisses. Then suddenly there came upon them both a quick sense of fear; they parted hastily, with hot, trembling fingers folded the sacred vestments, and separated in silent shyness.

The priest returned to his poor rooms and tried to sit down and think, but all in vain; he tried to eat, but could only thrust away his plate in disgust;

he tried to pray, but instead of the calm figure on the cross, the calm, cold figure with the weary, weary face, he saw continually before him the flushed face of a lovely boy, the wide star-like eyes of his new-found love.

All that day the young priest went through the round of his various duties mechanically, but he could not eat nor sit quiet, for when alone strange shrill bursts of song kept thrilling through his brain, and he felt that he must flee out into the open air or go mad.

At length, when night came and the long, hot day had left him exhausted and worn out, he threw himself on his knees before his crucifix and compelled himself to think.

He called to mind his boyhood and his early youth; there returned to him the thought of the terrible struggles of the last five years. Here he knelt, Ronald Heatherington, priest of Holy Church, aged twenty-eight: what he had endured during these five years of fierce battling with those terrible passions he had fostered in his boyhood, was it all to be in vain? For the last year he had really felt that all passion was subdued, all those terrible outbursts of passionate love he had really believed to be stamped out for ever. He had worked so hard, so unceasingly, through all these five years since his ordination – he had given himself up solely and entirely to his sacred office; all the intensity of his nature had been concentrated, completely absorbed, in the beautiful mysteries of his religion. He had avoided all that could affect him, all that might call up any recollection of his early life. Then he had accepted this curacy, with sole charge of the little chapel that stood close beside the cottage where he was now living, the little mission-chapel that was the most distant of the several grouped round the old Parish Church of St. Anselm. He had arrived only two or three days before, and, going to call on the old couple who lived in the cottage the back of which formed the boundary of his own little garden, had been offered the services of their grandson as acolyte.

'My son was an artist fellow, sir,' the old man had said: 'he never was satisfied here, so we sent him off to London; he was made a lot of there, sir, and married a lady, but the cold weather carried him off one winter, and his poor young wife was left with the baby. She brought him up and taught him herself, sir, but last winter she was taken too, so the poor lad came to live with us – so delicate he is, sir, and not one of the likes of us; he's a gentleman born and bred, is Wilfred. His poor mother used to like him to go and serve at the church near them in London, and the boy was so fond of it himself that we thought, supposing you did not mind, sir, that it would be a treat for him to do the same here.'

'How old is the boy?' asked the young priest.

'Fourteen, sir,' replied the grandmother.

'Very well, let him come to the chapel to-morrow morning,' Ronald had agreed.

Entirely absorbed in his devotions, the young man had scarcely noticed the little acolyte who was serving for him, and it was not till he was hearing his confession later in the day that he had realised his wonderful loveliness.

'Ah, God! help me! pity me! After all this weary labour and toil, just when I am beginning to hope, is everything to be undone? am I to lose everything? Help me, help me, O God!'

Even while he prayed; even while his hands were stretched out in agonised supplication towards the feet of that crucifix before which his hardest battles had been fought and won; even while the tears of bitter contrition and miserable self-mistrust were dimming his eyes, – there came a soft tap on the glass of the window beside him. He rose to his feet and wonderingly drew back the dingy curtain. There in the moonlight before the open window stood a small white figure – there, with his bare feet on the moon-blanched turf, dressed only in his long white nightshirt, stood his little acolyte, the boy who held his whole future in his small childish hands.

'Wilfred, what are you doing here?' he asked in a trembling voice.

'I could not sleep, father, for thinking of you, and I saw a light in your room, so I got out through the window and came to see you. Are you angry with me, father?' he asked, his voice faltering as he saw the almost fierce expression in the thin, ascetic face.

'Why did you come to see me?' The priest hardly dared recognise the situation, and scarcely heard what the boy said.

'Because I love you, I love you – oh, so much! but you – you are angry with me – oh, why did I ever come! why did I ever come! – I never thought you would be angry!' and the little fellow sank on the grass and burst into tears.

The priest sprang through the open window, and seizing the slim little figure in his arms, he carried him into the room. He drew the curtain, and, sinking into the deep arm-chair, laid the little fair head upon his breast, kissing his curls again and again.

'O my darling! my own beautiful darling!' he whispered, 'how could I ever be angry with you? you are more to me than all the world. Ah, God! how I love you, my darling! my own sweet darling!'

For nearly an hour the boy nestled there in his arms, pressing his soft cheek against his; then the priest told him he must go. For one long last kiss their lips met, and then the small white-clad figure slipped through the window, sped across the little moonlit garden, and vanished through the opposite window.

When they met in the vestry next morning, the lad raised his beautiful flower-like face, and the priest, gently putting his arms round him, kissed him tenderly on the lips.

'My darling! my darling!' was all he said; but the lad returned his kiss with a smile of wonderful, almost heavenly love, in a silence that seemed to whisper something more than words.

'I wonder what was the matter with the father this morning?' said one old woman to another, as they were returning from the chapel; 'he didn't seem himself at all; he made more mistakes this morning than Father Thomas made in all the years he was here.'

'Seemed as if he had never said a Mass before!' replied her friend with something of contempt.

And that night, and for many nights after, the priest with the pale, tired-looking face drew the curtain over his crucifix, and waited at the window for the glimmer of the pale summer moonlight on a crown of golden curls, for the sight of slim boyish limbs clad in the long white night shirt that only emphasised the grace of every movement and the beautiful pallor of the little feet speeding across the grass. There at the window, night after night, he waited to feel tender loving arms thrown round his neck, and to feel the intoxicating delight of beautiful boyish lips raining kisses on his own.

Ronald Heatherington made no mistakes in the Mass now. He said the solemn words with a reverence and devotion that made the few poor people who happened to be there speak of him afterwards almost with awe; while the face of the little acolyte at his side shone with a fervour which made them ask each other what this strange light could mean. Surely the young priest must be a saint indeed, while the boy beside him looked more like an angel from heaven than any child of human birth.

PART TWO

The world is very stern with those that thwart her. She lays down her precepts, and woe to those who dare to think for themselves, who venture to exercise their own discretion as to whether they shall allow their individuality and natural characteristics to be stamped out, to be obliterated under the leaden fingers of convention.

Truly, convention is the stone that has become the head of the corner in the jerry-built temple of our superficial, self-assertive civilisation.

'And whosoever shall fall on this stone shall be broken: but on whomsoever it shall fall, it will grind him to powder.'

If the world sees anything she cannot understand, she assigns the basest motives to all concerned, supposing the presence of some secret shame, the idea of which, at least, her narrow-minded intelligence is able to grasp.

The people no longer regarded their priest as a saint and his acolyte as an angel. They still spoke of them with bated breath and with their fingers on their lips; they still drew back out of the way when they met either of them; but now they gathered together in groups of twos and threes and shook their heads.

The priest and his acolyte heeded not; they never even noticed the suspicious glances and half-suppressed murmurs. Each had found in the other perfect sympathy and perfect love: what could the outside world matter to them now? Each was to the other the perfect fulfilment of a scarcely preconceived ideal; neither heaven nor hell could offer more. But the stone of convention had been undermined; the time could not be far distant when it must fall.

. . . . .

The moonlight was very clear and very beautiful; the cool night air was heavy with the perfume of the old-fashioned flowers that bloomed so profusely in the little garden. But in the priest's little room the closely drawn curtains shut out all the beauty of the night. Entirely forgetful of all the world, absolutely oblivious of everything but one another, wrapped in the beautiful visions of a love that far outshone all the splendour of the summer night, the priest and the little acolyte were together.

The little lad sat on his knees with his arms closely pressed round his neck and his golden curls laid against the priest's close-cut hair; his white nightshirt contrasting strangely and beautifully with the dull black of the other's long cassock.

There was a step on the road outside – a step drawing nearer and nearer; a knock at the door. They heard it not; completely absorbed in each other, intoxicated with the sweetly poisonous draught that is the gift of love, they sat in silence. But the end had come; the blow had fallen at last. The door opened, and there before them in the doorway stood the tall figure of the rector.

Neither said anything; only the little boy clung closer to his beloved, and his eyes grew large with fear. Then the young priest rose slowly to his feet and put the lad from him.

'You had better go, Wilfred,' was all he said.

The two priests stood in silence watching the child as he slipped through the window, stole across the grass, and vanished into the opposite cottage.

Then the two turned and faced each other.

The young priest sank into his chair and clasped his hands, waiting for the other to speak.

'So it has come to this!' he said: 'the people were only too right in what they told me! Ah, God! that such a thing should have happened here! that it has fallen on me to expose your shame – our shame! that it is I who must give you up to justice, and see that you suffer the full penalty of your sin! Have you nothing to say?'

'Nothing - nothing,' he replied softly. 'I cannot ask for pity; I cannot explain; you would never understand. I do not ask you anything for myself, I do not ask you to spare me; but think of the terrible scandal to our dear Church.'

'It is better to expose these terrible scandals and see that they are cured. It is folly to conceal a sore; better show all our shame than let it fester.'

'Think of the child.'

'That was for you to do; you should have thought of him before. What has his shame to do with me? it was your business. Besides, I would not spare him if I could: what pity can I feel for such as he —— ?'

But the young man had risen, pale to the lips.

'Hush!' he said in a low voice; 'I forbid you to speak of him before me with anything but respect'; then softly to himself, 'with anything but reverence; with anything but devotion.'

The other was silent, awed for the moment. Then his anger rose.

'Dare you speak openly like that? Where is your penitence, your shame? have you no sense of the horror of your sin?'

'There is no sin for which I should feel shame,' he answered very quietly. 'God gave me my love for him, and He gave him also his love for me. Who is there that shall withstand God and the love that is His gift?'

'Dare you profane the name by calling such a passion as this "love"?'

'It was love, perfect love; it *is* perfect love.'

'I can say no more now; to-morrow all shall be known. Thank God, you shall pay dearly for all this disgrace,' he added in a sudden outburst of wrath.

'I am sorry you have no mercy; – not that I fear exposure and punishment for myself. But mercy can seldom be found from a Christian,' he added, as one that speaks from without.

The rector turned towards him suddenly, and stretched out his hands.

'Heaven forgive me my hardness of heart,' he said. 'I have been cruel; I have spoken cruelly in my distress. Ah, can you say nothing to defend your crime?'

'No: I do not think I can do any good by that. If I attempted to deny all guilt, you would only think I lied; though I should prove my innocence, yet my reputation, my career, my whole future, are ruined for ever. But will you listen to me for a little? I will tell you a little about myself.'

The rector sat down while his curate told him the story of his life, sitting by the empty grate with his chin resting on his clasped hands.

'I was at a big public school, as you know. I was always different from other boys. I never cared much for games. I took little interest in those things for which boys usually care so much. I was not very happy in my boyhood, I think. My one ambition was to find the ideal for which I longed. It has always been thus: I have always had an indefinite longing for something, a vague something that never quite took shape; that I could never quite understand. My great desire has always been to find something that would satisfy me. I was attracted at once by sin: my whole early life is stained and polluted with the taint of sin. Sometimes even now I think that there are sins more beautiful than anything else in the world. There are vices that are bound to attract almost irresistibly anyone who loves beauty above everything. I have always sought for love; again and again I have been the victim of fits of passionate affection; time after time I have seemed to have found my ideal at last; the whole object of my life has been, times without number, to gain the love of some particular person. Several times my efforts were successful; each time I woke to find that the success I had obtained was worthless after all; as I grasped the prize, it lost all its attraction – I no longer cared for what I had once desired with my whole heart. In vain I endeavoured to drown the yearnings of my heart with the ordinary pleasures and vices that usually attract the young. I had to choose a profession. I became a priest. The whole aesthetic tendency of my soul was intensely attracted by the wonderful mysteries of Christianity, the artistic beauty of our services. Ever since my ordination I have been striving to cheat myself into the belief that peace had come at last – at last my yearning was satisfied: but all in vain. Unceasingly I have struggled with the old cravings for excitement, and, above all, the weary, incessant thirst for a perfect love. I have found, and still find, an exquisite delight in religion: not in the regular duties of a religious life, not in the ordinary round of parish organisations; – against these I chafe incessantly; – no, my delight is in the aesthetic beauty of the services, the ecstasy of devotion, the passionate fervour that comes with long fasting and meditation.'

'Have you found no comfort in prayer?' asked the rector.

'Comfort? – no. But I have found in prayer pleasure, excitement, almost a fierce delight of sin.'

'You should have married. I think that would have saved you.'

Ronald Heatherington rose to his feet and laid his hand on the rector's arm.

'You do not understand me: I have never been attracted by a woman in my life. Can you not see that people are different, totally different, from one another? To think that we are all the same is impossible; our natures, our temperaments, are utterly unlike. But this is what people will never see; they found all their opinions on a wrong basis. How can their deductions be just if their premises are wrong? One law laid down by the majority, who happen to be of one disposition, is only binding on the minority *legally*, not *morally*. What right have you, or anyone, to tell me that such-and-such a thing is sinful for me? Oh, why can I not explain to you and force you to see?' and his grasp tightened on the other's arm. Then he continued, speaking fast and earnestly: –

'For me, with my nature, to have married, would have been sinful; it would have been a crime, a gross immorality, and my conscience would have revolted.' Then he added bitterly: 'Conscience should be that divine instinct which bids us seek after that which our natural disposition needs – we have forgotten that; to most of us, to the world, nay, even to Christians in general, conscience is merely another name for the cowardice that dreads to offend against convention. Ah, what a cursed thing convention is! I have committed no moral offence in this matter; in the sight of God my soul is blameless; but to you and to the world I am guilty of an abominable crime – abominable, because it is a sin against convention, forsooth! I met this boy; I loved him as I had never loved anyone or anything before; I had no need to labour to win his affection – he was mine by right; he loved me, even as I loved him, from the first; he was the necessary complement to my soul. How dare the world presume to judge us? What is convention to us? Nevertheless, although I really knew that such a love was beautiful and blameless, although from the bottom of my heart I despised the narrow judgement of the world, yet for his sake, and for the sake of our Church, I tried at first to resist. I struggled against the fascination he possessed for me. I would never have gone to him and asked his love; I would have struggled on till the end; but what could I do? It was he that came to me, and offered me the wealth of love his beautiful soul possessed. How could I tell to such a nature as his the hideous picture the world would paint? Even as you saw him this evening, he has come to me night by night, – how dare I disturb the sweet purity of his soul by hinting at the horrible suspicions his presence might arouse? I knew what I was doing. I have faced the world and set myself up against it. I have openly scoffed at its dictates. I do not ask you to sympathise with me, nor do I pray you to stay your hand. Your eyes are blinded with a mental cataract. You are bound, bound with those miserable ties that have held you body and soul from the cradle. You must do what you believe to be your duty. In God's eyes we are martyrs, and we shall not shrink even from death in this struggle against the idolatrous worship of convention.'

Ronald Heatherington sank into a chair, hiding his face in his hands, and the rector left the room in silence.

For some minutes the young priest sat with his face buried in his hands. Then with a sigh he rose and crept across the garden till he stood beneath the open window of his darling.

'Wilfred,' he called very softly.

The beautiful face, pale and wet with tears, appeared at the window.

'I want you, my darling; will you come?' he whispered.

'Yes, father,' the boy softly answered.

The priest led him back to his room; then, taking him very gently in his arms, he tried to warm the cold little feet with his hands.

'My darling, it is all over.' And he told him as gently as he could all that lay before them.

The boy hid his face on his shoulder, crying softly.

'Can I do nothing for you, dear father?'

He was silent for a moment. 'Yes, you can die for me; you can die with me.'

The loving arms were about his neck once more, and the warm, loving lips were kissing his own. 'I will do anything for you. O father, let us die together!'

'Yes, my darling, it is best: we will.'

Then very quietly and very tenderly he prepared the little fellow for his death; he heard his last confession and gave him his last absolution. Then they knelt together, hand in hand, before the crucifix.

'Pray for me, my darling.'

Then together their prayers silently ascended that the dear Lord would have pity on the priest who had fallen in the terrible battle of life. There they knelt till midnight, when Ronald took the lad in his arms and carried him to the little chapel.

'I will say mass for the repose of our souls,' he said.

Over his nightshirt the child arrayed himself in his little scarlet cassock and tiny lace cotta. He covered his naked feet with the scarlet sanctuary shoes; he lighted the tapers and reverently helped the priest to vest. Then before they left the vestry the priest took him in his arms and held him pressed closely to his breast; he stroked the soft hair and whispered cheeringly to him. The child was weeping quietly, his slender frame trembling with the sobs he could scarcely suppress. After a moment the tender embrace soothed him, and he raised his beautiful mouth to the priest's. Their lips were pressed together, and their arms wrapped one another closely.

'O my darling, my own sweet darling!' the priest whispered tenderly.

'We shall be together for ever soon; nothing shall separate us now,' the child said.

'Yes, it is far better so; far better to be together in death than apart in life.'

They knelt before the altar in the silent night, the glimmer of the tapers lighting up the features of the crucifix with strange distinctness. Never had the priest's voice trembled with such wonderful earnestness, never had the acolyte responded with such devotion, as at this midnight mass for the peace of their own departing souls.

Just before the consecration the priest took a tiny phial from the pocket of his cassock, blessed it, and poured the contents into the chalice.

When the time came for him to receive from the chalice, he raised it to his lips, but did not taste of it.

He administered the sacred wafer to the child, and then he took the beautiful gold chalice, set with precious stones, in his hand; he turned towards him; but when he saw the light in the beautiful face he turned again to the crucifix with a low moan. For one instant his courage failed him; then he turned to the little fellow again and held the chalice to his lips:

'*The Blood of our Lord Jesus Christ, which was shed for thee, preserve thy body and soul unto everlasting life.*'

Never had the priest beheld such perfect love, such perfect trust, in those dear eyes as shone from them now; now, as with face raised upwards he received his death from the loving hands of him that he loved best in the whole world.

The instant he had received Ronald fell on his knees beside him and drained the chalice to the last drop. He set it down and threw his arms round the beautiful figure of his dearly loved acolyte. Their lips met in one last kiss of perfect love, and all was over.

.   .   .   .   .

When the sun was rising in the heavens it cast one broad ray upon the altar of the little chapel. The tapers were burning still, scarcely half-burnt through. The sad-faced figure of the crucifix hung there in its majestic calm. On the steps of the altar was stretched the long, ascetic frame of the young priest, robed in the sacred vestments; close beside him, with his curly head pillowed on the gorgeous embroideries that covered his breast, lay the beautiful boy in scarlet and lace. Their arms were round each other; a strange hush lay like a shroud over all.

'And whosoever shall fall on this stone shall be broken: but on whomsoever it shall fall, it will grind him to powder.'

X.

THE YELLOW BOOK

A Lost Masterpiece: A City Mood, Aug. '93

George Egerton

George Egerton (1859–1945) is the *nom de plume* of Mary Chavelita Dunne Bright. Egerton was a notable New Woman writer. Her debut as an author was the short story collection *Keynotes* (1893), followed by *Discords* (1894), both published by John Lane and Elkin Mathews at the Bodley Head. Lane's famous Keynote Series – which included such Decadent classics as Arthur Machen's *The Great God Pan* (1894) and M. P. Shiel's *Prince Zaleski* (1895) – was initiated and inspired by Egerton's collection of the same title. The female protagonists populating Egerton's stories are culturally and socially conscious, steeped in sexual energies and reveries that bring together New Woman desires and the Decadent sensibility.

'A Lost Masterpiece' is a trifling sketch in which an author *flâneur* studies metropolitan London in a venture whose aim is to funnel the creative process. As such, the story is emblematic of a swathe of *Yellow Book* stories which take as their onanistic theme the New Writer writing about writers. The narrator (whose ambiguous gender identity adds further complexity) exhibits an acute nervous constitution and aesthetic taste akin to those of Huysmans's Des Esseintes. The narrative is emphatically subjective, and urban scenes parade before the reader with impressionistic verve. Egerton also showcases her interest in the contemporary fascination with the brain. Her metaphors of brain anatomy and aesthetic and artistic beauty combine sensory stimuli, subjectivity and art. The story's tone oscillates subtly between seriousness and self-parody, with the narrator's over-the-top egocentricity and agitation at the aesthetically disagreeable object. Egerton ingeniously develops the paradox in which Decadence is embraced through self-parody, psychological futility and excess.

I regret it, but what am I to do? It was not my fault – I can only regret it. It was thus it happened to me.

I had come to town straight from a hillside cottage in a lonely ploughland, with the smell of the turf in my nostrils, and the swish of the scythes in my ears; the scythes that flashed in the meadows where the upland hay, drought-parched, stretched thirstily up to the clouds that mustered upon the mountain-tops, and marched mockingly away, and held no rain.

The desire to mix with the crowd, to lay my ear once more to the heart of the world and listen to its life-throbs, had grown too strong for me; and so I had come back – but the sights and sounds of my late life clung to me – it is singular how the most opposite things often fill one with associative memory.

That *gamin* of the bird-tribe, the Cockney sparrow, recalled the swallows that built in the tumble-down shed; and I could almost see the gleam of their white bellies, as they circled in ever narrowing sweeps and clove the air with forked wings, uttering a shrill note, with a querulous grace-note in front of it.

The freshness of the country still lurked in me, unconsciously influencing my attitude towards the city.

One forenoon business drove me citywards, and following an inclination that always impels me to water-ways rather than road-ways, I elected to go by river steamer.

I left home in a glad mood, disposed to view the whole world with kindly eyes. I was filled with a happy-go-lucky *insouciance* that made walking the pavements a loafing in Elysian Fields. The coarser touches of street-life, the oddities of accent, the idiosyncrasies of that most eccentric of city-dwellers, the Londoner, did not jar as at other times – rather added a zest to enjoyment; impressions crowded in too quickly to admit of analysis, I was simply an interested spectator of a varied panorama.

I was conscious, too, of a peculiar dual action of brain and senses, for, though keenly alive to every unimportant detail of the life about me, I was yet able to follow a process by which delicate inner threads were being spun into a fanciful web that had nothing to do with my outer self.

At Chelsea I boarded a river steamer bound for London Bridge. The river was wrapped in a delicate grey haze with a golden sub-tone, like a beautiful bright thought struggling for utterance through a mist of obscure words. It glowed through the turbid waters under the arches, so that I feared to see a face or a hand wave through its dull amber – for I always think of drowned creatures washing wearily in its murky depths – it lit up the great warehouses, and warmed the brickwork of the monster chimneys in the background. No detail escaped my outer eyes – not the hideous green of the velveteen in the sleeves of the woman on my left, nor the supercilious giggle of the young ladies on my right, who made audible remarks about my personal appearance.

But what cared I? Was I not happy, absurdly happy? – because all the while my inner eyes saw undercurrents of beauty and pathos, quaint contrasts, whimsical details that tickled my sense of humour deliciously. The elf that lurks in some inner cell was very busy, now throwing out tender mimosa-like threads of creative fancy, now recording fleeting impressions with delicate sure brushwork for future use; touching a hundred vagrant things with the magic of imagination, making a running comment on the scenes we passed.

The warehouses told a tale of an up-to-date Soll und Haben, one of my very own, one that would thrust old Freytag out of the book-mart. The tall chimneys ceased to be giraffic throats belching soot and smoke over the blackening city. They were obelisks rearing granite heads heavenwards! Joints in the bricks, weather-stains? You are mistaken; they were hieroglyphics, setting down for posterity a tragic epic of man the conqueror, and fire his slave; and how they strangled beauty in the grip of gain. A theme for a Whitman!

And so it talks and I listen with my inner ear – and yet nothing outward escapes me – the slackening of the boat – the stepping on and off of folk – the lowering of the funnel – the name 'Stanley' on the little tug, with its self-sufficient puff-puff, fussing by with a line of grimy barges in tow;

freight-laden, for the water washes over them – and on the last a woman sits suckling her baby, and a terrier with badly cropped ears yaps at us as we pass . . . . .

And as this English river scene flashes by, lines of association form angles in my brain; and the point of each is a dot of light that expands into a background for forgotten canal scenes, with green-grey water, and leaning balconies, and strange crafts – Canaletti and Guadi seen long ago in picture galleries . . . . .

A delicate featured youth with gold-laced cap scrapes a prelude on a thin-toned violin, and his companion thrums an accompaniment on a harp.

I don't know what they play, some tuneful thing with an under-note of sadness and sentiment running through its commonplace – likely a music-hall ditty; for a lad with a cheap silk hat, and the hateful expression of knowingness that makes him a type of his kind, grins appreciatively and hums the words.

I turn from him to the harp. It is the wreck of a handsome instrument, its gold is tarnished, its white is smirched, its stucco rose-wreaths sadly battered. It has the air of an antique beauty in dirty ball finery; and is it fancy, or does not a shamed wail lurk in the tone of its strings?

The whimsical idea occurs to me that it has once belonged to a lady with drooping ringlets and an embroidered spencer; and that she touched its chords to the words of a song by Thomas Haynes Baily, and that Miss La Creevy transferred them both to ivory.

The youth played mechanically, without a trace of emotion; whilst the harpist, whose nose is a study in purples and whose bloodshot eyes have the glassy brightness of drink, felt every touch of beauty in the poor little tune, and drew it tenderly forth.

They added the musical note to my joyous mood; the poetry of the city dovetailed harmoniously with country scenes too recent to be treated as memories – and I stepped off the boat with the melody vibrating through the city sounds.

I swung from place to place in happy, lightsome mood, glad as a fairy prince in quest of adventures. The air of the city was exhilarating ether – and all mankind my brethren – in fact I felt effusively affectionate.

I smiled at a pretty anaemic city girl, and only remembered that she was a stranger when she flashed back an indignant look of affected affront.

But what cared I? Not a jot! I could afford to say pityingly: 'Go thy way, little city maid, get thee to thy typing.'

And all the while that these outward insignificant things occupied me, I knew that a precious little pearl of a thought was evolving slowly out of the inner chaos.

It was such an unique little gem, with the lustre of a tear, and the light of moonlight and streamlight and love smiles reflected in its pure sheen – and, best of all, it was all my own – a priceless possession, not to be bartered for the Jagersfontein diamond – a city childling with the prepotency of the country working in it – and I revelled in its fresh charm and dainty strength; it seemed original, it was so frankly natural.

And as I dodged through the great waggons laden with wares from outer continents, I listened and watched it forming inside, until my soul became filled with the light of its brightness; and a wild elation possessed me at the thought of this darling brain-child, this offspring of my fancy, this rare little creation, perhaps embryo of genius that was my very own.

I smiled benevolently at the passers-by, with their harassed business faces, and shiny black bags bulging with the weight of common every-day documents, as I thought of the treat I would give them later on; the delicate feast I held in store for them, when I would transfer this dainty elusive birthling of my brain to paper for their benefit.

It would make them dream of moonlit lanes and sweethearting; reveal to them the golden threads in the sober city woof; creep in close and whisper good cheer, and smooth out tired creases in heart and brain; a draught from the fountain of Jouvence could work no greater miracle than the tale I had to unfold.

Aye, they might pass me by now, not even give me the inside of the pavement, I would not blame them for it! – but later on, later on, they would flock to thank me. They just didn't realise, poor money-grubbers! How could they? But later on . . . . I grew perfectly radiant at the thought of what I would do for poor humanity, and absurdly self-satisfied as the conviction grew upon me that this would prove a work of genius – no mere glimmer of the spiritual afflatus – but a solid chunk of genius.

Meanwhile I took a 'bus and paid my penny. I leant back and chuckled to myself as each fresh thought-atom added to the precious quality of my pearl. Pearl? Not one any longer – a whole quarrelet of pearls, Oriental pearls of the greatest price! Ah, how happy I was as I fondled my conceit!

It was near Chancery Lane that a foreign element cropped up and disturbed the rich flow of my fancy.

I happened to glance at the side-walk. A woman, a little woman, was hurrying along in a most remarkable way. It annoyed me, for I could not help wondering why she was in such a desperate hurry. Bother the jade!

what business had she to thrust herself on my observation like that, and tangle the threads of a web of genius, undoubted genius?

I closed my eyes to avoid seeing her; I could see her through the lids. She had square shoulders and a high bust, and a white gauze tie, like a snowy feather in the breast of a pouter pigeon.

We stop – I look again – aye, there she is! Her black eyes stare boldly through her kohol-tinted lids, her face has a violet tint. She grips her gloves in one hand, her white-handled umbrella in the other, handle up, like a knobkerrie.

She has great feet, too, in pointed shoes, and the heels are under her insteps; and as we outdistance her I fancy I can hear their decisive tap-tap above the thousand sounds of the street.

I breathe a sigh of relief as I return to my pearl – my pearl that is to bring *me* kudos and make countless thousands rejoice. It is dimmed a little, I must nurse it tenderly.

Jerk, jerk, jangle – stop. – Bother the bell! We pull up to drop some passengers, the idiots! and, as I live, she overtakes us! How the men and women cede her the middle of the pavement! How her figure dominates it, and her great feet emphasise her ridiculous haste! Why should she disturb me? My nerves are quivering pitifully; the sweet inner light is waning, I am in mortal dread of losing my little masterpiece. Thank heaven, we are off again . . . . .

'Charing Cross, Army and Navy, V'toria!' – Stop!

Of course, naturally! Here she comes, elbows out, umbrella waning! How the steel in her bonnet glistens! She recalls something, what is it? – what is it? A-ah! I have it! – a strident voice, on the deck of a steamer in the glorious bay of Rio, singing:

> 'Je suis le vr-r-rai pompier,
> Le seul pompier . . . .'

and *la mióla* snaps her fingers gaily and trills her *r's*; and the Corcovado is outlined clearly on the purple background as if bending to listen; and the palms and the mosque-like buildings, and the fair islets bathed in the witchery of moonlight, and the star-gems twinned in the lap of the bay, intoxicate as a dream of the East.

> 'Je suis le vr-r-rai pompier,
> Le seul pompier . . . .'

What in the world is a *pompier*? What connection has the word with this creature who is murdering, deliberately murdering, a delicate creation of my brain, begotten by the fusion of country and town?

'Je suis le vr-r-rai pompier, ...'

I am convinced *pompier* expresses her in some subtle way – absurd word! I look back at her, I criticise her, I anathematise her, I *hate* her!

What is she hurrying for? We can't escape her – always we stop and let her overtake us with her elbowing gait, and tight skirt shortened to show her great splay feet – ugh!

My brain is void, all is dark within; the flowers are faded, the music stilled; the lovely illusive little being has flown, and yet she pounds along untiringly.

Is she a feminine presentment of the wandering Jew, a living embodiment of the ghoul-like spirit that haunts the city and murders fancy?

What business had she, I ask, to come and thrust her white-handled umbrella into the delicate network of my nerves and untune their harmony?

Does she realise what she has done? She has trampled a rare little mind-being unto death, destroyed a precious literary gem. Aye, one that, for aught I know, might have worked a revolution in modern thought; added a new human document to the archives of man; been the keystone to psychic investigations; solved problems that lurk in the depths of our natures and tantalise us with elusive gleams of truth; heralded in, perchance, the new era; when such simple problems as Home Rule, Bimetallism, or the Woman Question will be mere themes for schoolboard compositions – who can tell?

Well, it was not my fault. – No one regrets it more, no one – but what could I do?

Blame her, woman of the great feet and dominating gait, and waving umbrella-handle! – blame her! I can only regret it – regret it!

Modern Melodrama

Hubert Crackanthorpe

Hubert Montague Crackanthorpe (born Cookson) (1870–96) was a short-story writer and essayist. As such, he contributed to both *The Yellow Book* and *The Savoy*. In October–November 1896 he urged Grant Richards to save the ailing *Savoy*, positing Richards as the publisher in Leonard Smithers's stead, and Crackanthorpe himself as editor. However, he was drowned in the Seine just before Christmas that year, which was quite probably suicide, following on from marital traumas and infidelities. Crackanthorpe's stories are tight and carefully crafted, paying attention both to external objects and probing into the recesses of human behaviour, and were greatly admired by Henry James. He fused Naturalism with Decadence through 'the perverse, presentness of things' and the artificial framing of the objective world.

As the title suggests, 'Modern Melodrama' plays upon a theme that was, and remains, a cliché of the *fin-de-siècle* – the beautiful, young, yet doomed, consumptive. Hence, the Wildean preoccupations of youth, beauty and death are explored from a different angle in this emotionally intense, open-ended story. The 'wilted flowers' in the opening scene are emblematic of the tale that unfolds, as the golden-haired, blue-eyed and rose-lipped Daisy fights to discover the truth of her condition from the doctor and lover that would keep her ignorant. Daisy's near-Larkinesque musings over death in what was an early, post-Christian era, are distinctly modern; and this fragmented, desperate and emotionally intense story is a good example of New Realism – a genre for which Crackanthorpe is only now beginning to be recognised as an absolute master.

※

The pink shade of a single lamp supplied an air of subdued mystery; the fire burned red and still; in place of door and windows hung curtains, obscure, formless; the furniture, dainty, but sparse, stood detached and incoördinate like the furniture of a stage-scene; the atmosphere was heavy with heat, and a scent of stale tobacco; some cut flowers, half withered, tissue-paper still wrapping their stalks, lay on a gilt, cane-bottomed chair.

'Will you give me a sheet of paper, please?'

He had crossed the room, to seat himself before the principal table. He wore a fur-lined overcoat, and he was tall, and broad, and bald; a sleek face, made grave by gold-rimmed spectacles.

The other man was in evening dress; his back leaning against the mantel-piece, his hands in his pockets: he was moodily scraping the hearthrug with his toe. Clean-shaved; stolid and coarsely regular features; black, shiny hair, flattened on to his head; under-sized eyes, moist and glistening; the tint of his face uniform, the tint of discoloured ivory; he looked a man who ate well and lived hard.

'Certainly, sir, certainly,' and he started to hurry about the room.

'Daisy,' he exclaimed roughly, a moment later, 'where the deuce do you keep the note-paper?'

'I don't know if there is any, but the girl always has some.' She spoke in a slow tone — insolent and fatigued.

A couple of bed-pillows were supporting her head, and a scarlet plush cloak, trimmed with white down, was covering her feet, as she lay curled on the sofa. The fire-light glinted on the metallic gold of her hair, which clashed with the black of her eyebrows; and the full, blue eyes, wide-set, contradicted the hard line of her vivid-red lips. She drummed her fingers on the sofa-edge, nervously.

'Never mind,' said the bald man shortly, producing a notebook from his breast-pocket, and tearing a leaf from it.

He wrote, and the other two stayed silent; the man returned to the hearthrug, lifting his coat-tails under his arms; the girl went on drumming the sofa-edge.

'There,' sliding back his chair, and looking from the one to the other, evidently uncertain which of the two he should address. 'Here is the prescription. Get it made up to-night, a table-spoonful at a time, in a wine-glassful of water at lunch-time, at dinner-time and before going to bed. Go on with the port wine twice a day, and (to the girl, deliberately and distinctly) you must keep quite quiet; avoid all sort of excitement — that is extremely important. Of course you must on no account go out at night. Go to bed early, take regular meals, and keep always warm.'

'I say,' broke in the girl, 'tell us, it isn't bad — dangerous, I mean?'

'Dangerous! — no, not if you do what I tell you.'

He glanced at his watch, and rose, buttoning his coat.

'Good-evening,' he said gravely.

At first she paid no heed; she was vacantly staring before her: then, suddenly conscious that he was waiting, she looked up at him.

'Good-night, doctor.'

She held out her hand, and he took it.

'I'll get all right, won't I?' she asked, still looking up at him.

'All right — of course you will — of course. But remember you must do what I tell you.'

The other man handed him his hat and umbrella, opened the door for him, and it closed behind them.

* * *

The girl remained quiet, sharply blinking her eyes, her whole expression eager, intense.

A murmur of voices, a muffled tread of footsteps descending the stairs — the gentle shutting of a door — stillness.

She raised herself on her elbow, listening; the cloak slipped noiselessly to the floor. Quickly her arm shot out to the bell-rope: she pulled it violently; waited, expectant; and pulled again.

A slatternly figure appeared — a woman of middle-age — her arms, bared to the elbows, smeared with dirt; a grimy apron over her knees.

'What's up? — I was smashin' coal,' she explained.

'Come here,' hoarsely whispered the girl — 'here — no — nearer — quite close. Where's he gone?'

'Gone? 'oo?'

'That man that was here.'

'I s'ppose 'ee's in the downstairs room. I ain't 'eard the front door slam.'

'And Dick, where's he?'

'They're both in there together, I s'ppose.'

'I want you to go down — quietly — without making a noise — listen at the door — come up, and tell me what they're saying.'

'What? down there?' jerking her thumb over her shoulder.

'Yes, of course — at once,' answered the girl, impatiently.

'And if they catches me — a nice fool I looks. No, I'm jest blowed if I do!' she concluded. 'Whatever's up?'

'You must,' the girl broke out excitedly. 'I tell you, you must.'

'Must — must — an' if I do, what am I goin' to git out of it?' She paused, reflecting; then added: 'Look 'ere — I tell yer what — I'll do it for half a quid, there?'

'Yes — yes — all right — only make haste.'

'An' 'ow d' I know as I'll git it?' she objected doggedly. 'It's a jolly risk, yer know.'

The girl sprang up, flushed and feverish.

'Quick — or he'll be gone. I don't know where it is — but you shall have it — I promise — quick — please go — quick.'

The other hesitated, her lips pressed together; turned, and went out.

And the girl, catching at her breath, clutched a chair.

* * *

A flame flickered up in the fire, buzzing spasmodically. A creak outside. She had come up. But the curtains did not move. Why didn't she come in?

She was going past. The girl hastened across the room, the intensity of the impulse lending her strength.

'Come — come in,' she gasped. 'Quick — I'm slipping.'

She struck at the wall; but with the flat of her hand, for there was no grip. The woman bursting in, caught her, and led her back to the sofa.

'There, there, dearie,' tucking the cloak round her feet. 'Lift up the piller, my 'ands are that mucky. Will yer 'ave anythin'?'

She shook her head. 'It's gone,' she muttered. 'Now — tell me.'

'Tell yer? — tell yer what! Why — why — there ain't jest nothin' to tell yer.'

'What were they saying? Quick.'

'I didn't 'ear nothin'. They was talking about some ballet-woman.'

The girl began to cry, feebly, helplessly, like a child in pain.

'You might tell me, Liz. You might tell me. I've been a good sort to you.'

'That yer 'ave. I knows yer 'ave, dearie. There, there, don't yer take on like that. Yer'll only make yerself bad again.'

'Tell me — tell me,' she wailed. 'I've been a good sort to you, Liz.'

'Well, they wasn't talkin' of no ballet-woman — that's straight,' the woman blurted out savagely.

'What did he say? — tell me.' Her voice was weaker now.

'I can't tell yer — don't yer ask me — for God's sake, don't yer ask me.'

With a low crooning the girl cried again.

'Oh! for God's sake, don't yer take on like that — it's awful — I can't stand it. There, dearie, stop that cryin' an' I'll tell yer — I will indeed. It was jest this way — I slips my shoes off, an' I goes down as careful — jest as careful as a cat — an' when I gets to the door I crouches myself down, listenin' as 'ard as ever I could. The first things as I 'ears was Mr. Dick speakin' thick-like — like as if 'ee'd bin drinkin' — an t'other chap 'ee says somethin' about lungs, using some long word — I missed that — there was a van or somethin' rackettin' on the road. Then 'ee says "gallopin', gallopin'," jest like as 'ee was talkin' of a 'orse. An' Mr. Dick, 'ee says, "ain't there no chance — no'ow?" and 'ee give a sort of a grunt. I was awful sorry for 'im, that I was, 'ee must 'ave been crool bad, 'ee's mostly so quiet-like, ain't 'ee? An', in a minute, 'ee sort o' groans out somethin', an' t'other chap 'es answer 'im quite cool-like, that 'ee don't properly know; but, anyways, it 'ud be over afore the end of February. There I've done it. Oh! dearie, it's awful, awful, that's jest what it is. An' I 'ad no intention to tell yer — not a blessed word — that I didn't — may God strike me blind if I did!

Some'ow it all come out, seein' yer chokin' that 'ard an' feelin' at the wall there. Yer 'ad no right to ask me to do it — 'ow was I to know 'ee was a doctor?'

She put the two corners of her apron to her eyes, gurgling loudly.

'Look 'ere, don't yer b'lieve a word of it — I don't — I tell yer they're a 'umbuggin' lot, them doctors, all together. I know it. Yer take my word for that — yer'll git all right again. Yer'll be as well as I am, afore yer've done — Oh, Lord! — it's jest awful — I feel that upset — I'd like to cut my tongue out, for 'avin' told yer — but I jest couldn't 'elp myself.' She was retreating towards the door, wiping her eyes, and snorting out loud sobs — 'An', don't you offer me that half quid — I couldn't take it of yer — that I couldn't.'

* * *

She shivered, sat up, and dragged the cloak tight round her shoulders. In her desire to get warm she forgot what had happened. She extended the palms of her hands towards the grate: the grate was delicious. A smoking lump of coal clattered on to the fender; she lifted the tongs, but the sickening remembrance arrested her. The things in the room were receding, dancing round; the fire was growing taller and taller. The woollen scarf chafed her skin; she wrenched it off. Then hope, keen and bitter, shot up, hurting her. 'How could he know? Of course he couldn't know. She'd been a lot better this last fortnight — the other doctor said so — she didn't believe it — she didn't care ——— Anyway, it would be over before the end of February!'

Suddenly the crooning wail started again; next, spasms of weeping, harsh and gasping.

By-and-by she understood that she was crying noisily, and that she was alone in the room; like a light in a wind, the sobbing fit ceased.

'Let me live — let me live — I'll be straight — I'll go to church — I'll do anything! Take it away — it hurts — I can't bear it!'

Once more the sound of her own voice in the empty room calmed her. But the tension of emotion slackened, only to tighten again; immediately she was jeering at herself. What was she wasting her breath for? What had Jesus ever done for her? She'd had her fling, and it was no thanks to Him.

'"Dy-sy — Dy-sy ———"'

From the street below, boisterous and loud, the refrain came up. And, as the footsteps tramped away, the words reached her once more, indistinct in the distance:

'"I'm jest cryzy, all for the love o' you."'

She felt frightened. It was like a thing in a play. It was as if some one was there, in the room — hiding — watching her.

Then a coughing fit started, racking her. In the middle, she struggled to cry for help; she thought she was going to suffocate.

Afterwards she sank back, limp, tired, and sleepy.

The end of February — she was going to die — it was important, exciting — what would it be like? Everybody else died. Midge had died in the summer — but that was worry and going the pace. And they said that Annie Evans was going off too. Damn it! she wasn't going to be chicken-hearted. She'd face it. She'd had a jolly time. She'd be game till the end. Hell-fire — that was all stuff and nonsense — she knew that. It would be just nothing — like a sleep. Not even painful; she'd be just shut down in a coffin, and she wouldn't know that they were doing it. Ah! but they might do it before she was quite dead! It had happened sometimes. And she wouldn't be able to get out. The lid would be nailed, and there would be earth on the top. And if she called, no one would hear.

Ugh! what a fit of the blues she was getting! It was beastly, being alone. Why the devil didn't Dick come back?

That noise, what was that?

Bah! only some one in the street. What a fool she was!

She winced again as the fierce feeling of revolt swept through her, the wild longing to fight. It was damned rough — four months! A year, six months even, was a long time. The pain grew acute, different from anything she had felt before.

'Good Lord! what am I maundering on about? Four months — I'll go out with a fizzle like a firework. Why the devil doesn't Dick come? — or Liz — or somebody? What do they leave me alone like this for?'

She dragged at the bell-rope.

* * *

He came in, white and blear-eyed.

'Whatever have you been doing all this time?' she began angrily.

'I've been chatting with the doctor.' He was pretending to read a newspaper; there was something funny about his voice.

'It's ripping. He says you'll soon be fit again, as long as you don't get colds, or that sort of thing. Yes, he says you'll soon be fit again' — a quick, crackling noise — he had gripped the newspaper in his fist.

She looked at him, surprised, in spite of herself. She would never have thought he'd have done it like that. He was a good sort, after all. But — she didn't know why — she broke out furiously:

'You infernal liar! — I know. I shall be done for by the end of February — ha! ha!'

Seizing a vase of flowers, she flung it into the grate. The crash and the shrivelling of the leaves in the flames brought her an instant's relief. Then she said quietly:

'There — I've made an idiot of myself; but,' (weakly) 'I didn't know — I didn't know — I thought it was different.'

He hesitated, embarrassed by his own emotion. Presently he went up to her and put his hands round her cheeks.

'No,' she said, 'that's no good, I don't want that. Get me something to drink. I feel bad.'

He hurried to the cupboard and fumbled with the cork of a champagne bottle. It flew out with a bang. She started violently.

'You clumsy fool!' she exclaimed.

She drank off the wine at a gulp.

'Daisy,' he began.

She was staring stonily at the empty glass.

'Daisy,' he repeated.

She tapped her toe against the fender-rail.

At this sign, he went on:

'How did you know?'

'I sent Liz to listen,' she answered mechanically.

He looked about him, helpless.

'I think I'll smoke,' he said feebly.

She made no answer.

'Here, put the glass down,' she said.

He obeyed.

He lit a cigarette over the lamp, sat down opposite her, puffing dense clouds of smoke.

And, for a long while, neither spoke.

'Is that doctor a good man?'

'I don't know. People say so,' he answered.

Passed

Charlotte M. Mew

Charlotte Mew (1869–1928) was known more as a poet than a short-story writer. Her poems had an avant-garde quality that anticipated Modernism, and were highly admired by Thomas Hardy, Virginia Woolf and Siegfried Sassoon. However, it was her short story 'Passed', her debut into publishing, which made her name known in the world of literature. Mew was infatuated with Ella D'Arcy and later with May Sinclair but the feelings were never mutual and Mew's lesbian desires remained suppressed. After 'Passed', she published several short stories, mainly in *Temple Bar* and *Pall Mall Magazine*; arguably none of them had the thrust and distinctive flavour of her first story. She became depressed after her sister died and committed suicide by drinking disinfectant.

'Passed' is a dense story dealing with psychological confusion, prostitution, the allure of death, dream and insanity, and suggestions of lesbianism. As Joseph Bristow writes, the narrator is unable to 'find any aesthetic, spiritual, or sexual relief from the disaffecting conditions that characterise modern urban existence'. Henry Harland praised the psychology and sensuality of Mew's story but asked her to tone down its depiction of the dead by removing such phrases as 'starting eyeballs' and 'stiffening limbs' prior to publication. The unnamed narrator is again a *flâneuse*, intrigued by London's slums, its denizens and their plights. She sensationalises poverty, situating it in a Romance realm of frosty twilight which could also be associated with Nordau's 'dusk of nations'. The past tense of the title suggests the meditation of a swift, concluded experience, as well as Baudelairian chance encounters in the city and mortality. The story contrasts with the Naturalist depictions of poverty in George Gissing and Arthur Morrison, with its disconnected narrative and Impressionist tone, to the point where the city feels chimerical and artificial.

> 'Like souls that meeting pass,
> And passing never meet again.'

Let those who have missed a romantic view of London in its poorest quarters – and there will romance be found – wait for a sunset in early winter. They may turn North or South, towards Islington or Westminster, and encounter some fine pictures and more than one aspect of unique beauty. This hour of pink twilight has its monopoly of effects. Some of them may never be reached again.

On such an evening in mid-December, I put down my sewing and left tame glories of fire-light (discoverers of false charm) to welcome, as youth may, the contrast of keen air outdoors to the glow within.

My aim was the perfection of a latent appetite, for I had no mind to content myself with an apology for hunger, consequent on a warmly passive afternoon.

The splendid cold of fierce frost set my spirit dancing. The road rung hard underfoot, and through the lonely squares woke sharp echoes from behind. This stinging air assailed my cheeks with vigorous severity. It stirred my blood grandly, and brought thought back to me from the warm embers just forsaken, with an immeasurable sense of gain.

But after the first delirium of enchanting motion, destination became a question. The dim trees behind the dingy enclosures were beginning to be succeeded by rows of flaring gas jets, displaying shops of new aspect and evil smell. Then the heavy walls of a partially demolished prison reared themselves darkly against the pale sky.

By this landmark I recalled – alas that it should be possible – a church in the district, newly built by an infallible architect, which I had been directed to seek at leisure. I did so now. A row of cramped houses, with the unpardonable bow window, projecting squalor into prominence, came into view. Robbing these even of light, the portentous walls stood a silent curse before them. I think they were blasting the hopes of the sad dwellers beneath them – if hope they had – to despair. Through spattered panes faces of diseased and dirty children leered into the street. One room, as I passed, seemed full of them. The window was open; their wails and maddening requirements sent out the mother's cry. It was thrown back to her, mingled with her children's screams, from the pitiless prison walls.

These shelters struck my thought as travesties – perhaps they were not – of the grand place called home.

Leaving them I sought the essential of which they were bereft. What withheld from them, as poverty and sin could not, a title to the sacred name?

An answer came, but interpretation was delayed. Theirs was not the desolation of something lost, but of something that had never been. I thrust off speculation gladly here, and fronted Nature free.

Suddenly I emerged from the intolerable shadow of the brickwork, breathing easily once more. Before me lay a roomy space, nearly square, bounded by three-storey dwellings, and transformed, as if by quick mechanism, with colours of sunset. Red and golden spots wavered in the panes of the low scattered houses round the bewildering expanse. Overhead a faint crimson sky was hung with violet clouds, obscured by the smoke and nearing dusk.

In the centre, but towards the left, stood an old stone pump, and some few feet above it irregular lamps looked down. They were planted on a square of paving railed in by broken iron fences, whose paint, now discoloured, had once been white. Narrow streets cut in five directions from the open roadway. Their lines of light sank dimly into distance, mocking the stars' entrance into the fading sky. Everything was transfigured in the illuminated twilight. As I stood, the dying sun caught the rough edges of a girl's uncovered hair, and hung a faint nimbus round her poor desecrated face. The soft circle, as she glanced toward me, lent it the semblance of one of those mystically pictured faces of some mediaeval saint.

A stillness stole on, and about the square dim figures hurried along, leaving me stationary in existence (I was thinking fancifully), when my mediaeval saint demanded 'who I was a-shoving of?' and dismissed me, not unkindly, on my way. Hawkers in a neighbouring alley were calling, and the monotonous ting-ting of the muffin-bell made an audible background to the picture. I left it, and then the glamour was already passing. In a little while darkness possessing it, the place would reassume its aspect of sordid gloom.

There is a street not far from there, bearing a name that quickens life within one, by the vision it summons of a most peaceful country, where the broad roads are but pathways through green meadows, and your footstep keeps the time to a gentle music of pure streams. There the scent of roses, and the first pushing buds of spring, mark the seasons, and the birds call out faithfully the time and manner of the day. Here Easter is heralded by the advent in some squalid mart of air-balls on Good Friday; early summer and late may be known by observation of that unromantic yet authentic calendar in which alley-tors, tip-cat, whip- and peg-tops, hoops and suckers, in their courses mark the flight of time.

Perhaps attracted by the incongruity, I took this way. In such a thoroughfare it is remarkable that satisfied as are its public with transient substitutes for literature, they require permanent types (the term is so far misused it may hardly be further outraged) of Art. Pictures, so-called, are the sole departure from necessity and popular finery which the prominent wares display. The window exhibiting these aspirations was scarcely more inviting than the fishmonger's next door, but less odoriferous, and I stopped to see what the ill-reflecting lights would show. There was a typical selection. Prominently, a large chromo of a girl at prayer. Her eyes turned upwards, presumably to heaven, left the gazer in no state to dwell on the elaborately bared breasts below. These might rival, does wax-work attempt such beauties, any similar attraction of Marylebone's extensive show. This personification of pseudo-purity was sensually diverting, and consequently marketable.

My mind seized the ideal of such a picture, and turned from this prostitution of it sickly away. Hurriedly I proceeded, and did not stop again until I had passed the low gateway of the place I sought.

Its forbidding exterior was hidden in the deep twilight and invited no consideration. I entered and swung back the inner door. It was papered with memorial cards, recommending to mercy the unprotesting spirits of the dead. My prayers were requested for the 'repose of the soul of the Architect of that church, who passed away in the True Faith – December, – 1887'. Accepting the assertion, I counted him beyond them, and mentally entrusted mine to the priest for those who were still groping for it in the gloom.

Within the building, darkness again forbade examination. A few lamps hanging before the altar struggled with obscurity.

I tried to identify some ugly details with the great man's complacent eccentricity, and failing, turned toward the street again. Nearly an hour's walk lay between me and my home. This fact and the atmosphere of stuffy sanctity about the place, set me longing for space again, and woke a fine scorn for aught but air and sky. My appetite, too, was now an hour ahead of opportunity. I sent back a final glance into the darkness as my hand prepared to strike the door. There was no motion at the moment, and it was silent; but the magnetism of human presence reached me where I stood. I hesitated, and in a few moments found what sought me on a chair in the far corner, flung face downwards across the seat. The attitude arrested me. I went forward. The lines of the figure spoke unquestionable despair.

Does speech convey intensity of anguish? Its supreme expression is in form. Here was human agony set forth in meagre lines, voiceless, but articulate to the soul. At first the forcible portrayal of it assailed me with the importunate strength of beauty. Then the Thing stretched there in the obdurate darkness grew personal and banished delight. Neither sympathy nor its vulgar substitute, curiosity, induced my action as I drew near. I was eager indeed to be gone. I wanted to ignore the almost indistinguishable being. My will cried: Forsake it! – but I found myself powerless to obey. Perhaps it would have conquered had not the girl swiftly raised herself in quest of me. I stood still. Her eyes met mine. A wildly tossed spirit looked from those ill-lighted windows, beckoning me on. Mine pressed towards it, but whether my limbs actually moved I do not know, for the imperious summons robbed me of any consciousness save that of necessity to comply.

Did she reach me, or was our advance mutual? It cannot be told. I suppose we neither know. But we met, and her hand, grasping mine, imperatively dragged me into the cold and noisy street.

We went rapidly in and out of the flaring booths, hustling little staggering children in our unpitying speed, I listening dreamily to the concert of hoarse yells and haggling whines which struck against the silence of our flight. On and on she took me, breathless and without explanation. We said nothing. I had no care or impulse to ask our goal. The fierce pressure of my hand was not relaxed a breathing space; it would have borne me against resistance could I have offered any, but I was capable of none. The streets seemed to rush past us, peopled with despair.

Weirdly lighted faces sent blank negations to a spirit of question which finally began to stir in me. Here, I thought once vaguely, was the everlasting No!

We must have journeyed thus for more than half an hour and walked far. I did not detect it. In the eternity of supreme moments time is not. Thought, too, fears to be obtrusive and stands aside.

We gained a door at last, down some blind alley out of the deafening thoroughfare. She threw herself against it and pulled me up the unlighted stairs. They shook now and then with the violence of our ascent; with my free hand I tried to help myself up by the broad and greasy balustrade. There was little sound in the house. A light shone under the first door we passed, but all was quietness within.

At the very top, from the dense blackness of the passage, my guide thrust me suddenly into a dazzling room. My eyes rejected its array of brilliant light. On a small chest of drawers three candles were guttering, two more stood flaring in the high window ledge, and a lamp upon a table by the bed rendered these minor illuminations unnecessary by its diffusive glare. There were even some small Christmas candles dropping coloured grease down the wooden mantel-piece, and I noticed a fire had been made, built entirely of wood. There were bits of an inlaid work-box or desk, and a chair-rung, lying half burnt in the grate. Some peremptory demand for light had been, these signs denoted, unscrupulously met. A woman lay upon the bed, half clothed, asleep. As the door slammed behind me the flames wavered and my companion released my hand. She stood beside me, shuddering violently, but without utterance.

I looked around. Everywhere proofs of recent energy were visible. The bright panes reflecting back the low burnt candles, the wretched but shining furniture, and some odd bits of painted china, set before the spluttering lights upon the drawers, bore witness to a provincial intolerance of grime. The boards were bare, and marks of extreme poverty distinguished the whole room. The destitution of her surroundings accorded ill with the girl's spotless person and well-tended hands, which were hanging tremulously down.

Subsequently I realised that these deserted beings must have first fronted the world from a sumptuous stage. The details in proof of it I need not cite. It must have been so.

My previous apathy gave place to an exaggerated observation. Even some pieces of a torn letter, dropped off the quilt, I noticed, were of fine texture, and inscribed by a man's hand. One fragment bore an elaborate device in colours. It may have been a club crest or coat-of-arms. I was trying to decide which, when the girl at length gave a cry of exhaustion or relief, at the same time falling into a similar attitude to that she had taken in the dim church. Her entire frame became shaken with tearless agony or terror. It was sickening to watch. She began partly to call or moan, begging me, since I was beside her, wildly, and then with heart-breaking weariness, 'to stop, to stay'. She half rose and claimed me with distracted grace. All her movements were noticeably fine.

I pass no judgement on her features; suffering for the time assumed them, and they made no insistence of individual claim.

I tried to raise her, and kneeling, pulled her reluctantly towards me. The proximity was distasteful. An alien presence has ever repelled me. I should have pitied the girl keenly perhaps a few more feet away. She clung to me with ebbing force. Her heart throbbed painfully close to mine, and when I meet now in the dark streets others who have been robbed, as she has been, of their great possession, I have to remember that.

The magnetism of our meeting was already passing; and, reason asserting itself, I reviewed the incident dispassionately, as she lay like a broken piece of mechanism in my arms. Her dark hair had come unfastened and fell about my shoulder. A faint white streak of it stole through the brown.

A gleam of moonlight strays thus through a dusky room. I remember noticing, as it was swept with her involuntary motions across my face, a faint fragrance which kept recurring like a subtle and seductive sprite, hiding itself with fairy cunning in the tangled maze.

The poor girl's mind was clearly travelling a devious way. Broken and incoherent exclamations told of a recently wrung promise, made to whom, or of what nature, it was not my business to conjecture or inquire.

I record the passage of a few minutes. At the first opportunity I sought the slumberer on the bed. She slept well: hers was a long rest; there might be no awakening from it, for she was dead. Schooled in one short hour to all surprises, the knowledge made me simply richer by a fact. Nothing about the sternly set face invited horror. It had been, and was yet, a strong and, if beauty be not confined to youth and colour, a beautiful face.

Perhaps this quiet sharer of the convulsively broken silence was thirty years old. Death had set a firmness about the finely controlled features that might have shown her younger. The actual years are of little matter; existence, as we reckon time, must have lasted long. It was not death, but life that had planted the look of disillusion there. And romance being over, all good-byes to youth are said. By the bedside, on a roughly constructed table, was a dearly bought bunch of violets. They were set in a blue bordered tea-cup, and hung over in wistful challenge of their own diviner hue. They were foreign, and their scent probably unnatural, but it stole very sweetly round the room. A book lay face downwards beside them – alas for parochial energies, not of a religious type – and the torn fragments of the destroyed letter had fallen on the black binding.

A passionate movement of the girl's breast against mine directed my glance elsewhere. She was shivering, and her arms about my neck were stiffly cold. The possibility that she was starving missed my mind. It would have found my heart. I wondered if she slept, and dared not stir, though I was by this time cramped and chilled. The vehemence of her agitation ended, she breathed gently, and slipped finally to the floor.

I began to face the need of action and recalled the chances of the night. When and how I might get home was a necessary question, and I listened vainly for a friendly step outside. None since we left it had climbed the last flight of stairs. I could hear a momentary vibration of men's voices in the room below. Was it possible to leave these suddenly discovered children of peace and tumult? Was it possible to stay?

This was Saturday, and two days later I was bound for Scotland; a practical recollection of empty trunks was not lost in my survey of the situation. Then how, if I decided not to forsake the poor child, now certainly sleeping in my arms, were my anxious friends to learn my whereabouts, and understand the eccentricity of the scheme? Indisputably, I determined, something must be done for the half-frantic wanderer who was pressing a tiring weight against me. And there should be some kind hand to cover the cold limbs and close the wide eyes of the breathless sleeper, waiting a comrade's sanction to fitting rest.

Conclusion was hastening to impatient thought, when my eyes let fall a fatal glance upon the dead girl's face. I do not think it had changed its first aspect of dignified repose, and yet now it woke in me a sensation of cold dread. The dark eyes unwillingly open reached mine in an insistent stare. One hand lying out upon the coverlid, I could never again mistake for that of temporarily suspended life. My watch ticked loudly, but I dared not examine it, nor could I wrench my sight from the figure on the bed. For the first time the empty shell of being assailed my senses. I watched feverishly, knowing well the madness of the action, for a hint of breathing, almost stopping my own.

To-day, as memory summons it, I cannot dwell without reluctance on this hour of my realisation of the thing called Death.

A hundred fancies, clothed in mad intolerable terrors, possessed me, and had not my lips refused it outlet, I should have set free a cry, as the spent child beside me had doubtless longed to do, and failed, ere, desperate, she fled.

My gaze was chained; it could not get free. As the shapes of monsters of ever varying and increasing dreadfulness flit through one's dreams, the images of those I loved crept round me, with stark yet well-known features, their limbs borrowing death's rigid outline, as they mocked my recognition of them with soundless semblances of mirth. They began to wind their arms about me in fierce embraces of burning and supernatural life. Gradually the contact froze. They bound me in an icy prison. Their hold relaxed. These creatures of my heart were restless. The horribly familiar company began to dance at intervals in and out a ring of white gigantic bedsteads, set on end like tombstones, each of which framed a huge and fearful travesty of the sad set face that was all the while seeking vainly a pitiless stranger's care. They vanished. My heart went home. The dear place was desolate. No echo of its many voices on the threshold or stair. My footsteps made no sound as I went rapidly up to a well-known room. Here I besought the mirror for the reassurance of my own reflection. It denied me human portraiture and threw back cold glare. As I opened mechanically a treasured book, I noticed the leaves were blank, not even blurred by spot or line; and then I shivered – it was deadly cold. The fire that but an hour or two ago it seemed I had forsaken for the winter twilight, glowed with slow derision at my efforts to rekindle heat. My hands plunged savagely into its red embers, but I drew them out quickly, unscathed and clean. The things by which I had touched life were nothing. Here, as I called the dearest names, their echoes came back again with the sound of an unlearned language. I did not recognise, and yet I framed them. What was had never been!

My spirit summoned the being who claimed mine. He came, stretching out arms of deathless welcome. As he reached me my heart took flight. I called aloud to it, but my cries were lost in awful laughter that broke to my bewildered fancy from the hideously familiar shapes which had returned and now encircled the grand form of him I loved. But I had never known him. I beat my breast to wake there the wonted pain of tingling joy. I called past experience with unavailing importunity to bear witness the man was wildly dear to me. He was not. He left me with bent head a stranger, whom I would not if I could recall.

For one brief second, reason found me. I struggled to shake off the phantoms of despair. I tried to grasp while it yet lingered the teaching of this never-to-be-forgotten front of death. The homeless house with its indefensible bow window stood out from beneath the prison walls again. What had this to do with it? I questioned. And the answer it had evoked replied, 'Not the desolation of something lost, but of something that had never been.'

The half-clad girl of the wretched picture-shop came into view with waxen hands and senseless symbolism. I had grown calmer, but her doll-like lips hissed out the same half-meaningless but pregnant words. Then the nights of a short life when I could pray, years back in magical childhood, sought me. They found me past them – without the power.

Truly the body had been for me the manifestation of the thing called soul. Here was my embodiment bereft. My face was stiff with drying tears. Sickly I longed to beg of an unknown God a miracle. Would He but touch the passive body and breathe into it the breath even of transitory life.

I craved but a fleeting proof of its ever possible existence. For to me it was not, would never be, and had never been.

The partially relinquished horror was renewing dominance. Speech of any incoherence or futility would have brought mental power of resistance. My mind was fast losing landmarks amid the continued quiet of the living and the awful stillness of the dead. There was no sound, even of savage guidance, I should not then have welcomed with glad response.

'The realm of Silence,' says one of the world's great teachers, 'is large enough beyond the grave.'

I seemed to have passed life's portal, and my soul's small strength was beating back the noiseless gate. In my extremity, I cried, 'O God! for man's most bloody warshout, or Thy whisper!' It was useless. Not one dweller in the crowded tenements broke his slumber or relaxed his labour in answer to the involuntary prayer.

And may the 'Day of Account of Words' take note of this! Then, says the old fable, shall the soul of the departed be weighed against an image of Truth. I tried to construct in imagination the form of the dumb deity who should bear down the balances for me. Soundlessness was turning fear to madness. I could neither quit nor longer bear company the grim Presence in that room. But the supreme moment was very near.

Long since, the four low candles had burned out, and now the lamp was struggling fitfully to keep alight. The flame could last but a few moments. I saw it, and did not face the possibility or darkness. The sleeping girl, I concluded rapidly, had used all available weapons of defiant light.

As yet, since my entrance, I had hardly stirred, steadily supporting the burden on my breast. Now, without remembrance of it, I started up to escape. The violent suddenness of the action woke my companion. She staggered blindly to her feet and confronted me as I gained the door.

Scarcely able to stand, and dashing the dimness from her eyes, she clutched a corner of the drawers behind her for support. Her head thrown back, and her dark hair hanging round it, crowned a grandly tragic form. This was no poor pleader, and I was unarmed for fight. She seized my throbbing arm and cried in a whisper, low and hoarse, but strongly audible:

'For God's sake, stay here with me.'

My lips moved vainly. I shook my head.

'For God in heaven's sake' – she repeated, swaying, and turning her burning, reddened eyes on mine – 'don't leave me now.'

I stood irresolute, half stunned. Stepping back, she stooped and began piecing together the dismembered letter on the bed. A mute protest arrested her from a cold sister's face. She swept the action from her, crying, 'No!' and bending forward suddenly, gripped me with fierce force.

'Here! Here!' she prayed, dragging me passionately back into the room.

The piteous need and wild entreaty – no, the vision of dire anguish – was breaking my purpose of flight. A fragrance that was to haunt me stole between us. The poor little violets put in their plea. I moved to stay. Then a smile – the splendour of it may never be reached again – touched her pale lips and broke through them, transforming, with divine radiance, her young and blurred and never-to-be-forgotten face. It wavered, or was it the last uncertain flicker of the lamp that made me fancy it? The exquisite moment was barely over when darkness came. Then light indeed forsook me. Almost ignorant of my own intention, I resisted the now trembling figure, indistinguishable in the gloom, but it still clung. I thrust it off me with unnatural vigour.

    She fell heavily to the ground. Without a pause of thought I stumbled down the horrible unlighted stairs. A few steps before I reached the bottom my foot struck a splint off the thin edge of one of the rotten treads. I slipped, and heard a door above open and then shut. No other sound. At length I was at the door. It was ajar. I opened it and looked out. Since I passed through it first the place had become quite deserted. The inhabitants were, I suppose, all occupied elsewhere at such an hour on their holiday night. The lamps, if there were any, had not been lit. The outlook was dense blackness. Here too the hideous dark pursued me and silence held its sway. Even the children were screaming in more enticing haunts of gaudy squalor. Some, whose good angels perhaps had not forgotten them, had put themselves to sleep. Not many hours ago their shrieks were deafening. Were these too in conspiracy against me? I remembered vaguely hustling some of them with unmeant harshness in my hurried progress from the Church. Dumb the whole place seemed; and it was, but for the dim stars aloft, quite dark. I dared not venture across the threshold, bound by pitiable cowardice to the spot. Alas for the unconscious girl upstairs. A murmur from within the house might have sent me back to her. Certainly it would have sent me, rather than forth into the empty street. The faintest indication of humanity had recalled me. I waited the summons of a sound. It came.

    But from the deserted, yet not so shamefully deserted, street. A man staggering home by aid of friendly railings, set up a drunken song. At the first note I rushed towards him, pushing past him in wild departure, and on till I reached the noisome and flaring thoroughfare, a haven where sweet safety smiled. Here I breathed joy, and sped away without memory of the two lifeless beings lying alone in that shrouded chamber of desolation, and with no instinct to return.

    My sole impulse was flight; and the way, unmarked in the earlier evening, was unknown. It took me some minutes to find a cab; but the incongruous vehicle, rudely dispersing the haggling traders in the roadway, came at last, and carried me from the distorted crowd of faces and the claims of pity to peace.

I lay back shivering, and the wind crept through the rattling glass in front of me. I did not note the incalculable turnings that took me home.

My account of the night's adventure was abridged and un-sensational. I was pressed neither for detail nor comment, but accorded a somewhat humorous welcome which bade me say farewell to dying horror, and even let me mount boldly to the once death-haunted room.

Upon its threshold I stood and looked in, half believing possible the greeting pictured there under the dead girl's influence, and I could not enter. Again I fled, this time to kindly light, and heard my brothers laughing noisily with a friend in the bright hall.

A waltz struck up in the room above as I reached them. I joined the impromptu dance, and whirled the remainder of that evening gladly away.

Physically wearied, I slept. My slumber had no break in it. I woke only to the exquisite joys of morning, and lay watching the early shadows creep into the room. Presently the sun rose. His first smile greeted me from the glass before my bed. I sprang up disdainful of that majestic reflection, and flung the window wide to meet him face to face. His splendour fell too on one who had trusted me, but I forgot it. Not many days later the same sunlight that turned my life to laughter shone on the saddest scene of mortal ending, and, for one I had forsaken, lit the ways of death. I never dreamed it might. For the next morning the tragedy of the past night was a distant one, no longer intolerable.

At twelve o'clock, conscience suggested a search. I acquiesced, but did not move. At half-past, it insisted on one, and I obeyed. I set forth with a determination of success and no clue to promise it. At four o'clock, I admitted the task hopeless and abandoned it. Duty could ask no more of me, I decided, not wholly dissatisfied that failure forbade more difficult demands. As I passed it on my way home, some dramatic instinct impelled me to re-enter the unsightly church.

I must almost have expected to see the same prostrate figure, for my eyes instantly sought the corner it had occupied. The winter twilight showed it empty. A service was about to begin. One little lad in violet skirt and goffered linen was struggling to light the benediction tapers, and a troop of school children pushed past me as I stood facing the altar and blocking their way. A grey-clad sister of mercy was arresting each tiny figure, bidding it pause beside me, and with two firm hands on either shoulder, compelling a ludicrous curtsey, and at the same time whispering the injunction to each hurried little personage, – 'always make a reverence to the altar.' 'Ada, come back!' and behold another unwilling bob! Perhaps the good woman saw her Master's face behind the tinsel trappings and flaring lights. But she forgot His words. The saying to these little ones that has rung through centuries commanded liberty and not allegiance. I stood aside till they had shuffled into seats, and finally kneeling stayed till the brief spectacle of the afternoon was over.

Towards its close I looked away from the mumbling priest, whose attention, divided between inconvenient millinery and the holiest mysteries, was distracting mine.

Two girls holding each other's hands came in and stood in deep shadow behind the farthest rows of high-backed chairs by the door. The younger rolled her head from side to side; her shifting eyes and ceaseless imbecile grimaces chilled my blood. The other, who stood praying, turned suddenly (the place but for the flaring altar lights was dark) and kissed the dreadful creature by her side. I shuddered, and yet her face wore no look of loathing nor of pity. The expression was a divine one of habitual love.

She wiped the idiot's lips and stroked the shaking hand in hers, to quiet the sad hysterical caresses she would not check. It was a page of gospel which the old man with his back to it might never read. A sublime and ghastly scene.

Up in the little gallery the grey-habited nuns were singing a long Latin hymn of many verses, with the refrain 'Oh! Sacred Heart!' I buried my face till the last vibrating chord of the accompaniment was struck. The organist ventured a plagal cadence. It evoked no 'amen'. I whispered one, and an accidentally touched note shrieked disapproval. I repeated it. Then I spit upon the bloodless cheek of duty, and renewed my quest. This time it was for the satisfaction of my own tingling soul.

I retook my unknown way. The streets were almost empty and thinly strewn with snow. It was still falling. I shrank from marring the spotless page that seemed outspread to challenge and exhibit the defiling print of man. The quiet of the muffled streets soothed me. The neighbourhood seemed lulled into unwonted rest.

Black little figures lurched out of the white alleys in twos and threes. But their childish utterances sounded less shrill than usual, and sooner died away.

Now in desperate earnest I spared neither myself nor the incredulous and dishevelled people whose aid I sought.

Fate deals honestly with all. She will not compromise though she may delay. Hunger and weariness at length sent me home, with an assortment of embellished negatives ringing in my failing ears.

I had almost forgotten my strange experience, when, some months afterwards, in late spring, the wraith of that winter meeting appeared to me. It was past six o'clock, and I had reached, ignorant of the ill-chosen hour, a notorious thoroughfare in the western part of this glorious and guilty city. The place presented to my unfamiliar eyes a remarkable sight. Brilliantly lit windows, exhibiting dazzling wares, threw into prominence the human mart.

This was thronged. I pressed into the crowd. Its steady and opposite progress neither repelled nor sanctioned my admittance. However, I had determined on a purchase, and was not to be baulked by the unforeseen. I made it, and stood for a moment at the shop-door preparing to break again through the rapidly thickening throng.

Up and down, decked in frigid allurement, paced the insatiate daughters of an everlasting king. What fair messengers, with streaming eyes and impotently craving arms, did they send afar off ere they thus 'increased their perfumes and debased themselves even unto hell'? This was my question. I asked not who forsook them, speaking in farewell the 'hideous English of their fate'.

I watched coldly, yet not inapprehensive of a certain grandeur in the scene. It was Virtue's very splendid Dance of Death.

A sickening confusion of odours assailed my senses; each essence a vile enticement, outraging Nature by a perversion of her own pure spell.

A timidly protesting fragrance stole strangely by. I started at its approach. It summoned a stinging memory. I stepped forward to escape it, but stopped, confronted by the being who had shared, by the flickering lamp-light and in the presence of that silent witness, the poor little violet's prayer.

The man beside her was decorated with a bunch of sister flowers to those which had taken part against him, months ago, in vain. He could have borne no better badge of victory. He was looking at some extravagant trifle in the window next the entry I had just crossed. They spoke, comparing it with a silver case he turned over in his hand. In the centre I noticed a tiny enamelled shield. The detail seemed familiar, but beyond identity. They entered the shop. I stood motionless, challenging memory, till it produced from some dim corner of my brain a hoarded 'No'.

The device now headed a poor strip of paper on a dead girl's bed. I saw a figure set by death, facing starvation, and with ruin in torn fragments in her hand. But what place in the scene had I? A brief discussion next me made swift answer.

They were once more beside me. The man was speaking: his companion raised her face; I recognised its outline, – its true aspect I shall not know. Four months since it wore the mask of sorrow; it was now but one of the pages of man's immortal book. I was conscious of the matchless motions which in the dim church had first attracted me.

She was clothed, save for a large scarf of vehemently brilliant crimson, entirely in dull vermilion. The two shades might serve as symbols of divine and earthly passion. Yet does one ask the martyr's colour, you name it 'Red' (and briefly thus her garment): no distinctive hue. The murderer and the prelate too may wear such robes of office. Both are empowered to bless and ban.

My mood was reckless. I held my hands out, craving mercy. It was my bitter lot to beg. My warring nature became unanimously suppliant, heedless of the debt this soul might owe me – of the throes to which I left it, and of the discreditable marks of mine it bore. Failure to exact regard I did not entertain. I waited, with exhaustless fortitude, the response to my appeal. Whence it came I know not. The man and woman met my gaze with a void incorporate stare. The two faces were merged into one avenging visage – so it seemed. I was excited. As they turned towards the carriage waiting them, I heard a laugh, mounting to a cry. It rang me to an outraged Temple. Sabbath bells peal sweeter calls, as once this might have done.

I knew my part then in the despoiled body, with its soul's tapers long blown out.

Wheels hastened to assail that sound, but it clanged on. Did it proceed from some defeated angel? or the woman's mouth? or mine? God knows!

Tobacco Clouds

Lionel Johnson

Lionel Pigot Johnson (1867–1902) was a poet, essayist and critic, and the cousin of Lord Alfred Douglas. Indeed, it was Johnson who introduced Wilde to Douglas, an act he regretted later, as is evident in his poem, 'The Destroyer of a Soul' (1892). A repressed homosexual and devout Catholic convert, Johnson's poetry remains his most significant legacy, particularly the poem 'The Dark Angel' (1893), often seen as an exploration of his own sexuality. He was a central figure in the *Hobby Horse* coterie (becoming co-editor at one point) and contributed works to *The Savoy* as well as *The Yellow Book*, from which this story is taken.

Although a languorous air of indulgence bookends this reflective piece, the detail and philosophy contained within is quite studiously crafted. Johnson's poetic imagery of the fleetingness of cigarette smoke interweaves with classical theories of Epicureanism, and most notably, those classical notions of the intensity of life that are distilled into the 'Conclusion' of Walter Pater's *Renaissance*. As such, 'Tobacco Clouds' could be read as a response to Selwyn Image's 'Bundle of Letters', whereby the diligent student of the elder mentor has taken up his challenge to 'live in the moment'. The many allusions to Latin literature and philosophy, and the precious attention to antiquarian book details contained in the tale seem to pay homage to several of Image's works, and also paint a portrait of the author akin to Dorian Gray's aesthetic sensibilities in the earlier chapters of Wilde's novel.

❧

Cloud upon cloud: and, if I were to think that an image of life can lie in wreathing, blue tobacco smoke, pleasant were the life so fancied. Its fair changes in air, its gentle motions, its quiet dying out and away at last, should symbolise something more than perfect idleness. Cloud upon cloud: and I will think, as I have said; it is amusing to think so.

It is that death, out and away upon the air, which charms me; charms more than the manner of the blown red rose, full of dew at morning, upon the grass at sunset. The clouds' end, their death in air, fills me with a very beauty of desire; it has no violence in it, and it is almost invisible. Think of it! While the cloud lived, it was seemly and various; and with a graceful change it passed away: the image of a reasonable life is there, hanging among tobacco clouds. An image and a test: an image, because elaborated by fancy; a true and appealing image, and so, to my present way of life, a test.

That way is, to walk about the old city, with 'a spirit in my feet', as Shelley and Catullus have it, of joyous aims and energies; and to speed home to my solitary room over the steep High Street; in an arm-chair, to read Milton and Lucretius, with others. There is nothing unworthy in all this: there is open air, an ancient city, a lonely chamber, perfect poets. Those should make up a passing life well; for death! I can watch tobacco clouds, exploring the secret of their beautiful conclusion. And, indeed, I think that already this life has something of their manner, those wheeling clouds! It has their light touch upon the world, and certainly their harmlessness. Early morning, when the dew sparkles red; honey, and coffee, and eggs for a breakfast; the quick, eager walk between the limes, through the Close of fine grass, to the river fields; then the blithe return to my poets; all that, together, comes to resemble the pleasant spheres of tobacco cloud; I mean, the circling hours, in their passage, and in their change, have something of a dreamy order and progression. Such little incidents! Now, grey air and whistling leaves; now, a marketing crowd of country folk round the Cross; and presently, clear candles; with Milton, in rich Baskerville type, or Lucretius, in the exquisite print of early Italy.

Such little incidents, in a world of battles and of plagues; of violent death by sea and land! Yet this quiet life, too, has difficulties and needs; its changes must be gone through with a ready pleasure and a mind unhesitating. For, trivial though they be in aspect and amount, yet the consecration of them, to be an holy discipline of experience, is so much the greater an attempt: it is an art. Each thing, be it man, or book, or place, should have its rights, when it encounters me; each has its proper quality, its peculiar spirit, not to be misinterpreted by me in carelessness, nor overlooked with impatience. That is clear; but neither must I vaunt my just view of common life. Meditation, at twilight, by the window looking toward the bare downs, is very different from that anxious examination of motives, dear to sedulous souls. My meditation is only still life: the clouds of smoke go up, grey and blue; the earlier stars come out, above the sunset and the melancholy downs; and deep, mournful bells ring slowly among the valley trees. Then, if my day have been successful, what peace follows, and how profound a charm! The little things of the day, sudden glances of light upon grey stone, pleasant snatches of organ music from the church, quaint rustic sights in some near village: they come back upon me, gentle touches of happiness, airs of repose. And when the mysteries come about me, the fearfulness of life, and the shadow of night; then, have I not still the blue, grey clouds, *occultis de rebus quo referam?* So I escape the tribulations of doubt, those gloomy tribulations; and I live in the strength of dreams, which never doubt.

Is it all a delusion? But that is a foolish wonder; nothing is a delusion, except the extremes of pleasure and of pain. Take what you will of the world; its crowds, or its calms; there is nothing altogether wrong to every one. Lucretius, upon his watch-tower, deny it as he may, found some exultation and delight in the lamentable prospect below; it filled him with a magnificent darkness of soul, a princely compassion at heart. And Milton, in his evil days, felt himself to be tragic and austere; he knew it, not as a proud boast, but as a proud fact. No! life is never wrong, altogether, to every one: you and I, he and she, priest and penitent, master and slave; one with another, we compose a very glory of existence before the unseen Powers. Therefore, I believe in my measured way of life; its careful felicities, fashioned out of little things: to you, the change of Ministries, and the accomplishment of conquests, bring their wealth of rich emotion; to me, who am apart from the louder concerns of life, the flowering of the limes, and the warm autumn rains, bring their pensive beauty and a store of memories.

Is it I, am indolent? Is it you, are clamorous? Why should it be either? Let us say, I am the lover of quiet things, and you are enamoured of mighty events. Each, without undue absorption in his taste, relishes the savour of a different experience.

But I think, I am no egoist; no melancholy spectator of things, cultivating his intellect with old poetry, nourishing his senses upon rural nature. There are times, when the swarms of men press hard upon a solitary; he hears the noise of the streets, the heavy vans of merchandise, the cry of the railway whistle; and in a moment, his thoughts travel away, to London, to Liverpool; to great docks and to great ships; and away, till he is watching the dissimilar bustle of Eastern harbours, and hearing the discordant sounds of Chinese workmen. The blue smoke curls and glides away, with blue pagodas, and snowy almond bloom, and cherry flowers, circling and gleaming in it, like a narcotic vision. O magic of tobacco! Dreams are there, and superb images, and a somnolent paradise. Sometimes, the swarms of humanity press wearily and hardly; with a cruel insistence, crushing out my right to happiness. I think, rather I brood, upon the fingers that deftly rolled the cigarette, upon the people in tobacco plantations, upon all the various commerce involved in its history: how do they all fare, those many workers? Strolling up and down, devouring my books through their lettered backs; remembering the workers with leather, paper, ink, who toiled at them, they frighten me from the peace. What a full world it is! What endless activities there are! And, oh, Nicomachean Ethics! how much conscious pleasure is in them all! Things, mere tangible things, have a terrible power of education; of calling out from the mind innumerable thoughts and sympathies. Like childish catechisms and categories – *Whence have we sago?* – plain substances introduce me to swarms of men, before unrealised. And they all lived and died, and cared for their children, or not, and led reasonable lives, or not; and, without any alternative, had casual thoughts and constant passions. Did each one of them ever stop in his work, and think that the world revolved about him alone; and all was his, and for him? Most men may have thought so, and shivered a little afterwards; and worked on steadily. Or did each one of them ever think that he was always beset with companions, hordes of men and women, necessary and inevitable? Then, he must have struggled a little in his mind, as a man fights for air, and worked on steadily. It does not do, this interrogation of mysteries, which are also facts. Nor am I called upon, from without or from within, to write an Essay upon the Problem of Economic Distribution. *Proesentia temnis!* Nature says to me: it is the stir of the world, and the great play of forces, that I am wailing, to no end. Let the great life continue, and the sun shine upon bright palaces; and geraniums, red geraniums, glow at the windows of dingy courts; death and sorrow come upon both, and upon me. And on all sides there is infinite tenderness; the invincible good-will, which says kind and cheerful things to every one sometimes, by a friend's mouth; the humane pieties of the world, which make glad the *Civitas Dei*, and make endurable the *Regnum Hominis*. I need not make myself miserable.

Full night at last; the dead of night, as dull folk have it; ignorant persons, who know nothing of nocturnal beauty, of night's lively magic. It was a good thought, to come out of my lonely room, to look at the cloisters by moonlight, and to wander round the Close, under the black shadows of the buttresses, while the moon is white upon their strange pinnacles. There is no noise, but only a silence, which seems very old; old, as the grey monuments and the weathered arches. The wreathing, blue tobacco clouds look thin and pale, like breath upon a dark frosty night; they drift about these old precincts, with a kind of uncertainty and discomfort; one would think, they wanted a rich Mediterranean night, heavy odours of roses, and very fiery stars. Instead, they break upon mouldering traceries, and doleful cherubs of the last century; upon sunken headstones, and black oak doors with ironwork over them. Perhaps the cigarette is southern and Latin, southern and Oriental, after all; and I am a dreamer, out of place in this northern grey antiquity. If it be so, I can taste the subtle pleasures of contrast; and, dwelling upon the singular features of this old town, I can make myself a place in it, as its conscious critic and adopted alien. There is a curious apprehension of enjoyment, a genuine touch of luxury, in this nocturnal visit to these old northern things! I consider, with satisfaction, how the Stuart king, who spurned tobacco contumeliously, put a devoted faith in witches, those northern daughters of the devil; northern, and very different from the dames of Thessaly; from the crones of Propertius, and of Horace, and of Apuleius the Golden. Who knows, but I may hear strange voices in the near aisle before cockcrow? By night, night in the north, happen cold and dismal things; and then, what a night is this! Chilly stars, and wild, grey clouds, flying over a misty moon.

At last, here comes a great and solemn sound; the commanding bells of the cathedral tower, in their iron, midnight toll. Through the sombre strokes, and striking into their long echoes, pierce the thin cries of bats, that wheel in air, like lost creatures who hate themselves; the uncanny flitter-mice! They trace superb, invisible circles on the night; crying out faintly and plaintively, with no sort of delight in their voices: things of keen teeth, furry bodies, and skeleton wings covered scantily in leather. The big moths, too: they blunder against my face, and dash red trails of fire off my cigarette; so busily they spin about the darkness. *Sadducismus triumphatus!* Yes, truly: here are little, white spirits awake and at some faery work; white, as heather upon the Cornish cliffs is white, and all innocent, rare things in heaven and earth. There is nothing dreadful, it seems, about this night, and this place; no glorious fury of evil spirits, doing foul and ugly things; only the quiet town asleep under a wild sky, and gentle creatures of the night moving about ancient places. And the wind rises, with a sound of the sea, murmuring over the earth and sighing away to the sea; the trembling sea, beyond the downs, which steals into the land by great creeks and glimmering channels; with swaying, taper masts along them, and lantern lights upon black barges. Certainly, this is no Lucretian night: not that tremendous

> *Nox, et noctis signa severa*
> *Noctivagoeque faces coeli, flammoeque volantes.*

Rather, it reminds me of the Miltonic night, which is peopled alluringly with

> 'faery elves,
> Whose midnight revels by a forest side
> Or fountain, some belated peasant sees,
> Or dreams he sees, while overhead the moon
> Sits arbitress:'

a Miltonic night, and a Shakespearean dawn; for the white morning has just peered along the horizon, white morning, with dusky flames behind it; and the spirits, the visions, vanish away, 'following darkness, like a dream'.

The streets are very still, with that silence of sleeping cities, which seems ready to start into confused cries; as though the Smiter of the Firstborn were travelling through the households. There is the Catholic chapel, in its Georgian, quaint humility; recalling an age of beautiful, despised simplicity; the age of French emigrant old priests and vicars-apostolic, who stood for the Supreme Pontiff, in grey wigs. The sweet limes are swaying against its singular, umbered windows, with their holy saints and prophets in last-century design; ruffled, querulous persons looking very bluff and blown. I wonder, how it would be inside; I suppose, night has a little weakened that lingering smell of daily incense, which seems so immemorial and so sad. Wonderful grace of the mighty Roman Church! This low square place, where the sanctuary is poor and open, without any mystical touch of retirement and of loftiness, has yet the unfailing charm, the venerable mystery, which attend the footsteps of the Church; the same air of command, the same look of pleading, fill this homely, comfortable shrine, which simple country gentlemen set up for the ministrations of harassed priests, in an age of no enthusiasm. I like to think that this quiet chapel, in the obedience of Rome, in communion with that supreme apostolate, is always open to me upon this winding little by-street; it fills me with perfect memories, and it seems to bless me.

But here is a benediction of light! the quick sun, reddening half the heavens, and rising gloriously. In the valley, clusters of elm rock and swing with the breeze, quivering for joy; far away, the bare uplands roll against the sunrise, calm and pastoral; *otia dia* of the morning. Surely the hours have gone well, and according to my preference; one dying into another, as the tobacco clouds die. My meditations, too, have been peaceful enough; and, though solitary, I have had fine companions. What would the moral philosophers, those puzzled sages, think of me? An harmless hedonist? An amateur in morals, who means well, though meaning very little? Nay! let the moralist by profession give, to whom he will, *sa musique, sa flamme*; to any practical person, who is a wise shareholder and zealous vestryman. For myself, my limited and dreamy self, I eschew these upright businesses; upright memories and meditations please me more, and to live with as little action as may be. Action: why do they talk of action? Match me, for pure activity, one evening of my dreams, when life and death fill my mind with their messengers, and the days of old come back to me. And now, homewards, for a little sleep; that profound and rich slumber at early dawn which is my choice delight. A sleep, bathed in musical impressions, and filled with fresh dreams, all impossible and happy; four hours, and five, and six perhaps; then the cathedral matin bell will chime in with my fancies, and I shall wake harmoniously. I shall feel infinitely cheerful, after the spirit of the *Compleat Angler*; I shall remember that I was once at Ware, and at Amwell, those placid haunts of Walton. A conviction of beauty, and contentment in life will lay hold on me, more than commonly; it is probable that I shall read *The Spectator*, and Addison, rather than Steele, at breakfast. And I know which paper it will be: it will be about *Will Wimble* coming up to the house, with two or three hazel twigs in his hand, fresh cut in *Sir Roger*'s woods. Or, if I prove faithful to my great Lucretius; the man, not the book, for I read him in the Giuntine; I will read that marvellous *It ver et Venus*; that dancing masque of beauty. For *L'Allegro*, I do not read that; it is read aloud to me by the morning, with exquisite, bright cadences. After my honey from the flowers of a very rustic farm, and my coffee, from some wonderful Eastern place; and my eggs, marked by the careful housewife as she took them from her henhouse, covered with stonecrop over its old tiles; after all these delicates, now comes the first cigarette, pungent and exhilarating. As the grey blue clouds go up, the ruddy sunlight glows through them, straight as an arrow through the gold. Away they wander, out of the window, flung back upon the air, against the roses, and disappear in the buoyant morning.

My thoughts go with them, into the morning, into all the mornings over the world. They travel through the lands, and across the seas, and are everywhere at home, enjoying the presence of life. And past things, old histories, are turned to pleasant recollections; a *pot-pourri*, justly seasoned, and subtly scented; the evil humours and the monstrous tyrannies pass away, and leave only the happiness and the peace.

Call me, my dear friend, what reproachful name you please; but, by your leave, the world is better for my cheerfulness. True, should the terrible issues come upon me, demanding high courage, and finding but good temper, then give me your prayers, for I have my misdoubts. Till then, let me cultivate my place in life, nurturing its comelier flowers; taking the little things of time with a grateful relish and a mind at rest. So hours and years pass into hours and years, gently, and surely, and orderly; as these clouds, grey and blue clouds, of tobacco smoke, pass up to the air, and away upon the wind; incense of a goodly savour, cheering the thoughts of my heart, before passing away, to disappear at last.

To Every Man a Damsel or Two

'C. S.' [presumed Henry Harland]

Henry Harland (1861–1905) was an American novelist who travelled to London in 1889 and eventually became the literary editor of the *Yellow Book*. His policy for the magazine was to make the short story the 'backbone' of the publication, attesting to the popularity of the genre among both writers and readers at the time. Harland was central to the *Yellow Book*, and it has been said that his failing health was to blame for the periodical's eventual demise in 1897. Harland converted to Roman Catholicism in the same year.

This fleeting tale gives an insight into the atmosphere of the late Victorian music halls, being as they were, far more than simply places of theatrical entertainment. Defending the Empire music hall against those seeking to close its promenade, on account of the prostitutes who habitually plied their trade there, Arthur Symons wrote that the beauty of the music halls was that one was not 'obliged to sit through a whole evening's performance' but could pick and choose what to see from the night's bill. Harland's comic tale gives us a glimpse into the other spaces within music halls, apart from the stage, and the rare beasts that inhabited them.

He wandered up the carpeted steps, rather afraid all the while of the two tall men in uniform who opened the great doors wide to let him into the soft warm light and babble of voices within. At the top he paused, and slowly unbuttoned his overcoat, not knowing which way to turn; but the crowd swept him up, and carried him round, until he found himself leaning against a padded wall of plush, looking over a sea of heads at the stage far beneath. He turned round, and stood watching the happy crowd, which laughed, and talked, and nodded ceaselessly to itself. Near him, on a sofa, with a table before her, was a woman spreading herself out like some great beautiful butterfly on a bed of velvet pansies. He stood admiring her half unconsciously for some time, and at last, remembering that he was tired and sleepy, and seeing that there was still plenty of room, he threaded his way across and sat down.

The butterfly began tossing a wonderful little brown satin shoe, and tapping it against the leg of the table. Then the parasol slipped across him, and fell to the ground. He hastened to pick it up, lifting his hat as he did so. She seemed surprised, and glancing at a man leaning against the wall, caught his eye, and they both laughed. He blushed a good deal, and wondered what he had done wrong. She spread herself out still further in his direction, and cast side glances at him from under her Gainsborough.

'What were you laughing at just now?' he said impulsively.

'My dear boy, when?'

'With that man.'

'Which man?'

'It doesn't matter,' he said, blushing again.

She looked up, and winked at the man leaning against the wall.

'Have I offended you by speaking to you?' he said, looking with much concern into her eyes.

She put a little scented net of a handkerchief up to her mouth, and went into uncontrollable fits of laughter.

'What a funny boy you are!' she gasped. 'Do do it again.'

He looked at her in amazement, and moved a little further away.

'I'm going to tell the waiter to bring me a port – after that last bit of business.'

'I don't understand all this,' he said desperately: 'I wish I had never spoken to you; I wish I had never come in here at all.'

'You're very rude all of a sudden. Now don't be troublesome and say you're too broke to pay for drinks,' she added as the waiter put the port down with great deliberation opposite her, and held out the empty tray respectfully to him. He stared.

'Why don't you pay, you cuckoo?'

Mechanically he put down a florin, and the waiter counted out the change.

There was a pause. She fingered the stem of her wine-glass, taking little sips, and watching him all the while.

'How often have you been here before?' she said, suddenly catching at his sleeve. 'You must tell me. I fancy I know your face: surely I've met you before somewhere?'

'This is the first time I have ever been to a music-hall,' he said doggedly.

She drank off her port directly.

'Come – come away at once. Yes, all right – I'm coming with you; so go along.'

'But I've only just paid to come in,' he said hesitatingly.

'Never mind the paying,' and she stamped her little satin foot, 'but do as I tell you, and go.' And taking his arm, she led him through the doors down to the steps, where the wind blew cold, and the gas jets roared fitfully above.

'Go,' she said, pushing him out, 'and never come here again; stick to the theatres, you will like them best.' And she ran up the steps and was gone.

He rushed after her. The two tall men in uniform stepped before the doors.

'No re-admission, sir,' said one, bowing respectfully and touching his cap.

'But that lady,' he said, bewildered, and looking from one to the other.

The men laughed, and one of them, shrugging his shoulders, pointed to the box-office.

He turned, and walked down the steps. Was it all a dream? He glanced at his coat. The flower in his buttonhole had gone.

Theodora: A Fragment

Victoria Cross

Victoria Cross, the pen-name of Annie Sophie Cory (1868–1952), was the writer of twenty-three novels and three short-story collections. Like other emerging New Women writers, her talent was spotted by the *Yellow Book*'s editor, Henry Harland. In fact, this short story was part of a novel, *The Refiner's Fire*, which she had completed in 1894. Cross sent the manuscript of her novel to John Lane who deemed it unpublishable due to its ultra-radical, provocative treatment of sexuality. Harland considered it a 'work of genius' and after a heated dispute with Lane, he managed to persuade him to publish one chapter, under the title 'Theodora: A Fragment', in the *Yellow Book*. In the same year (1895) Lane published Cross's *The Woman Who Didn't* in his Keynote Series. Cross finally published the full novel from which this tale is taken, retitled *Six Chapters of a Man's Life*, in 1903.

The story tells of the flirtatious game between a Decadent New Woman, Theodora Dudley, and dandy-explorer Cecil Ray. Theodora is androgynous and experiments with her sexual identity. Cecil's character evokes Sir Richard Burton, the sexually adventurous, yet ambiguous, translator of *The Book of the Thousand Nights and a Night* (1885), the *Kama Sutra* (1883), and collaborator with Leonard Smithers, publisher of *The Savoy*. The story's theme of cross-dressing presents readers with the issues of ambiguous sexual identity and gender transference, echoing Théophile Gautier's scandalous 'bible of transvestism' *Mademoiselle de Maupin* (1835–6). The atmosphere is heavy with haschisch and opium, the setting is bursting with Huysmanian *objets d'art* and oriental curios, and desire is presented in prurient and sensual detail. Because of its unmistakable Decadence and defiant transgression of Victorian moral and social norms, the story was attacked most viciously by contemporary critics. Ada Leverson also burlesqued the story in 'Tooraloora: A Fragment' (1895), a carefully crafted satire that acknowledged the original's literary merit. In the 1903 novel version Theodora commits suicide.

・　・　・　・　・　・　・　・　・　・
　・　・　・　・　・　・　・　・　・　・

I did not turn out of bed till ten o'clock the next morning, and I was still in dressing-gown and slippers, sitting by the fire, looking over a map, when Digby came in upon me.

'Hullo, Ray, only just up, eh? as usual?' was his first exclamation as he entered, his ulster buttoned to his chin, and the snow thick upon his boots. 'What a fellow you are! I can't understand anybody lying in bed till ten o'clock in the morning.'

'And I can't understand anybody driving up at seven,' I said, smiling, and stirring my coffee idly. I had laid down the map with resignation. I knew Digby had come round to jaw for the next hour at least. 'Can I offer you some breakfast?'

'Breakfast!' returned Digby contemptuously. 'No, thanks. I had mine hours ago. Well, what do you think of her?'

'Of whom? – this Theodora?'

'Oh, it's Theodora already, is it?' said Digby, looking at me. 'Well, never mind: go on. Yes, what do you think of her?'

'She seems rather clever, I think.'

'Do you?' returned Digby, with a distinct accent of regret, as if I had told him I thought she squinted. 'I never noticed it. But her looks, I mean?'

'She is very peculiar,' I said, merely.

'But you like everything extraordinary. I should have thought her very peculiarity was just what would have attracted you.'

'So it does,' I admitted; 'so much so, that I am going to take the trouble of calling this afternoon expressly to see her again.'

Digby stared hard at me for a minute, and then burst out laughing. 'By Jove! You've made good use of your time. Did she ask you?'

'She did,' I said.

'This looks as if it would be a case,' remarked Digby lightly, and then added, 'I'd have given anything to have had her myself. But if it's not to be for me, I'd rather you should be the lucky man than any one else.'

'Don't you think all that is a little "previous"?' I asked satirically, looking at him over the coffee, which stood on the map of Mesopotamia.

'Well, I don't know. You must marry some time, Cecil.'

'Really!' I said, raising my eyebrows and regarding him with increased amusement. 'I think I have heard of men remaining celibates before now, especially men with my tastes.'

'Yes,' said Digby, becoming suddenly as serious and thoughtful as if he were being called upon to consider some weighty problem, and of which the solution must be found in the next ten minutes. 'I don't know how you would agree. She is an awfully religious girl.'

'Indeed?' I said with a laugh. 'How do you know?'

Digby thought hard.

'She is,' he said with conviction, at last. 'I see her at church every Sunday.'

'Oh then, of course she must be – proof conclusive,' I answered.

Digby looked at me and then grumbled, 'Confounded sneering fellow you are. Has she been telling you she is not?'

I remembered suddenly that I had promised Theodora not to repeat her opinions, so I only said, 'I really don't know what she is; she may be most devout for all I know – or care.'

'Of course you can profess to be quite indifferent,' said Digby ungraciously. 'But all I can say is, it doesn't look like it – your going there this afternoon; and anyway, she is not indifferent to you. She said all sorts of flattering things about you.'

'Very kind, I am sure,' I murmured derisively.

'And she sent round to my rooms this morning a thundering box of Havannahs in recognition of my having won the bet about your looks.'

I laughed outright. 'That's rather good biz for you! The least you can do is to let me help in the smoking of them, I think.'

'Of course I will. But it shows what she thinks of you, doesn't it?'

'Oh, most convincingly,' I said with mock earnestness. 'Havannahs are expensive things.'

'But you know how awfully rich she is, don't you?' asked Digby, looking at me as if he wanted to find out whether I were really ignorant or affecting to be so.

'My dear Charlie, you know I know nothing whatever about her except what you tell me – or do you suppose she showed me her banking account between the dances?'

'Don't know, I am sure,' Digby grumbled back. 'You sat in that passage long enough to be going through a banking account, and balancing it too, for that matter! However, the point is, she is rich – tons of money, over six thousand a year.'

'Really?' I said, to say something.

'Yes, but she loses every penny on her marriage. Seems such a funny way to leave money to a girl, doesn't it? Some old pig of a maiden aunt tied it up in that way. Nasty thing to do, I think; don't you?'

'Very immoral of the old lady, it seems. A girl like that, if she can't marry, will probably forego nothing but the ceremony.'

'She runs the risk of losing her money, though, if anything were known. She only has it *dum casta manet*, just like a separation allowance.'

'Hard lines,' I murmured sympathetically.

'And so of course her people are anxious she should make a good match – take some man, I mean, with an income equal to what she has now of her own, so that she would not feel any loss. Otherwise, you see, if she married a poor man, it would be rather a severe drop for her.'

'Conditions calculated to prevent any fellow but a millionaire proposing to her, I should think,' I said.

'Yes, except that she is a girl who does not care about money. She has been out now three seasons, and had one or two good chances and not taken them. Now myself, for instance, if she wanted money and position and so on, she could hardly do better, could she? And my family and the rest of it are all right; but she couldn't get over my red hair – I know it was that. She's mad upon looks – I know she is; she let it out to me once, and I bet you anything, she'd take you and chuck over her money and everything else, if you gave her the chance.'

'I am certainly not likely to,' I answered. 'All this you've just told me alone would be enough to choke me off. I have always thought I could never love a decent woman unselfishly enough, even if she gave up nothing for me; and, great heavens! I should be sorry to value myself, at – what do you say she has? – six thousand a year?'

'Leave the woman who falls in love with the cut of your nose to do the valuation. You'll be surprised at the figure! said Digby with a touch of resentful bitterness, and getting up abruptly. 'I'll look round in the evening,' he added, buttoning up his overcoat. 'Going to be in?'

'As far as I know,' I answered, and he left.

I got up and dressed leisurely, thinking over what he had said, and those words 'six thousand' repeating themselves unpleasantly in my brain.

The time was in accordance with strict formality when I found myself on her steps. The room I was shown into was large, much too large to be comfortable on such a day; and I had to thread my way through a perfect maze of gilt-legged tables and statuette-bearing tripods before I reached the hearth. Here burnt a small, quiet, chaste-looking fire, a sort of Vestal flame, whose heat was lost upon the tessellated tiles, white marble, and polished brass about it. I stood looking down at it absently for a few minutes, and then Theodora came in.

She was very simply dressed in some dark stuff that fitted closely to her, and let me see the harmonious lines of her figure as she came up to me. The plain, small collar of the dress opened at the neck, and a delicious, solid, white throat rose from the dull stuff like an almond bursting from its husk. On the pale, well-cut face and small head great care had evidently been bestowed. The eyes were darkened, as last night, and the hair arranged with infinite pains on the forehead and rolled into one massive coil at the back of her neck.

She shook hands with a smile – a smile that failed to dispel the air of fatigue and fashionable dissipation that seemed to cling to her; and then wheeled a chair as near to the fender as she could get it.

As she sat down, I thought I had never seen such splendid shoulders combined with so slight a hip before.

'Now I hope no one else will come to interrupt us,' she said simply. 'And don't let's bother to exchange comments on the weather nor last night's dance. I have done that six times over this morning with other callers. Don't let's talk for the sake of getting through a certain number of words. Let us talk because we are interested in what we are saying.'

'I should be interested in anything if you said it,' I answered.

Theodora laughed. 'Tell me something about the East, will you? That is a nice warm subject, and I feel so cold.'

And she shot out towards the blaze two well-made feet and ankles.

'Yes, in three weeks' time I shall be in a considerably warmer climate than this,' I answered, drawing my chair as close to hers as fashion permits.

Theodora looked at me with a perceptibly startled expression as I spoke.

'Are you really going out so soon?' she said.

'I am, really,' I said with a smile.

'Oh, I am so sorry!'

'Why?' I asked merely.

'Because I was thinking I should have the pleasure of meeting you lots more times at different functions.'

'And would that be a pleasure?'

'Yes, very great,' said Theodora, with a smile lighting her eyes and parting faintly the soft scarlet lips.

She looked at me, a seducing softness melting all her face and swimming in the liquid darkness of the eyes she raised to mine. A delicious intimacy seemed established between us by that smile. We seemed nearer to each other after it than before, by many degrees. A month or two of time and ordinary intercourse may be balanced against the seconds of such a smile as this.

A faint feeling of surprise mingled with my thoughts, that she should show her own attitude of mind so clearly, but I believe she felt instinctively my attraction towards her, and also undoubtedly she belonged, and had always been accustomed, to a fast set. I was not the sort of man to find fault with her for that, and probably she had already been conscious of this, and felt all the more at ease with me. The opening-primrose type of woman, the girl who does or wishes to suggest the modest violet unfolding beneath the rural hedge, had never had a charm for me. I do not profess to admire the simple violet; I infinitely prefer a well-trained hothouse gardenia. And this girl, about whom there was nothing of the humble, crooked-neck violet – in whom there was a dash of virility, a hint at dissipation, a suggestion of a certain decorous looseness of morals and fastness of manners – could stimulate me with a keen sense of pleasure, as our eyes or hands met.

'Why would it be a pleasure to meet me?' I asked, holding her eyes with mine, and wondering whether things would so turn out that I should ever kiss those parting lips before me.

Theodora laughed gently.

'For a good many reasons that it would make you too conceited to hear,' she answered. 'But one is because you are more interesting to talk to than the majority of people I meet every day. The castor of your chair has come upon my dress. Will you move it back a little, please?'

I pushed my chair back immediately and apologised.

'Are you going alone?' resumed Theodora.

'Quite alone.'

'Is that nice?'

'No. I should have been very glad to find some fellow to go with me, but it's rather difficult. It is not everybody that one meets whom one would care to make such an exclusive companion of, as a life like that out there necessitates. Still, there's no doubt I shall be dull unless I can find some chum there.'

'Some Englishman, I suppose?'

'Possibly; but they are mostly snobs who are out there.'

Theodora made a faint sign of assent, and we both sat silent, staring into the fire.

'Does the heat suit you?' Theodora asked, after a pause.

'Yes, I like it.'

'So do I.'

'I don't think any woman would like the climate I am going to now, or could stand it,' I said.

Theodora said nothing, but I had my eyes on her face, which was turned towards the light of the fire, and I saw a tinge of mockery come over it.

We had neither said anything farther, when the sound of a knock reached us, muffled, owing to the distance the sound had to travel to reach us by the drawing-room fire at all, but distinct in the silence between us.

Theodora looked at me sharply.

'There is somebody else. Do you want to leave yet?' she asked, and then added in a persuasive tone, 'Come into my own study, where we shan't be disturbed, and stay and have tea with me, will you?'

She got up as she spoke.

The room had darkened considerably while we had been sitting there, and only a dull light came from the leaden, snow-laden sky beyond the panes, but the firelight fell strongly across her figure as she stood, glancing and playing up it towards the slight waist, and throwing scarlet upon the white throat and under-part of the full chin. In the strong shadow on her face I could see merely the two seducing eyes. Easily excitable where once a usually hypercritical or rather hyperfanciful eye has been attracted, I felt a keen sense of pleasure stir me as I watched her rise and stand, that sense of pleasure which is nothing more than an assurance to the roused and unquiet instincts within one, of future satisfaction or gratification, with, from, or at the expense of the object creating the sensation. Unconsciously a certainty of possession of Theodora to-day, to-morrow, or next year, filled me for the moment as completely as if I had just made her my wife. The instinct that demanded her was immediately answered by a mechanical process of the brain, not with doubt or fear, but simple confidence. 'This is a pleasant and delightful object to you – as others have been. Later it will be a source of enjoyment to you – as others have been.' And the lulling of this painful instinct is what we know as pleasure. And this instinct and its answer are exactly that which we should not feel within us for any beloved object. It is this that tends inevitably to degrade the loved one, and to debase our own passion. If the object is worthy and lovely in any sense, we should be ready to love it as being such, for itself, as moralists preach to us of Virtue, as theologians preach to us of the Deity. To love or at least to strive to love an object for the object's sake, and not our own sake, to love it in its relation to *its* pleasure and not in its relation to our own pleasure, is to feel the only love which is worthy of offering to a fellow human being, the one which elevates – and the only one – both giver and receiver. If we ever learn this lesson, we learn it late. I had not learnt it yet.

I murmured a prescribed 'I shall be delighted,' and followed Theodora behind a huge red tapestry screen that reached half-way up to the ceiling.

We were then face to face with a door which she opened, and we both passed over the threshold together.

She had called the room her own, so I glanced round it with a certain curiosity. A room is always some faint index to the character of its occupier, and as I looked a smile came to my face. This room suggested everywhere, as I should have expected, an intellectual but careless and independent spirit. There were two or three tables, in the window, heaped up with books and strewn over with papers. The centre-table had been pushed away, to leave a clearer space by the grate, and an armchair, seemingly of unfathomable depths, and a sofa, dragged forward in its place. Within the grate roared a tremendous fire, banked up half-way to the chimney, and a short poker was thrust into it between the bars. The red light leapt over the whole room and made it brilliant, and glanced over a rug, and some tumbled cushions on the floor in front of the fender, evidently where she had been lying. Now, however, she picked up the cushions, and tossed them into the corner of the couch, and sat down herself in the other corner.

'Do you prefer the floor generally?' I asked, taking the armchair as she indicated it to me.

'Yes, one feels quite free and at ease lying on the floor, whereas on a couch its limits are narrow, and one has the constraint and bother of taking care one does not go to sleep and roll off.'

'But suppose you did, you would then but be upon the floor.'

'Quite so; but I should have the pain of falling.'

Our eyes met across the red flare of the firelight.

Theodora went on jestingly: 'Now, these are the ethics of the couch and the floor. I lay myself voluntarily on the floor, knowing it thoroughly as a trifle low, but undeceptive and favourable to the condition of sleep which will probably arise, and suitable to my requirements of ease and space. I avoid the restricted and uncertain couch, recognising that if I fall to sleep on that raised level, and the desire to stretch myself should come, I shall awake with pain and shock to feel the ground, and see above me the couch from which I fell – do you see?'

She spoke lightly, and with a smile, and I listened with one. But her eyes told me that these ethics of the couch and floor covered the ethics of life.

'No, you must accept the necessity of the floor, I think, unless you like to forego your sleep and have the trouble of taking care to stick upon your couch; and for me the difference of level between the two is not worth the additional bother.'

She laughed, and I joined her.

'What do you think?' she asked.

I looked at her as she sat opposite me, the firelight playing all over her, from the turn of her knee just marked beneath her skirt to her splendid shoulders, and the smooth soft hand and wrist supporting the distinguished little head. I did not tell her what I was thinking; what I said was: 'You are very logical. I am quite convinced there's no place like the ground for a siesta.'

Theodora laughed, and laid her hand on the bell.

A second or two after, a door, other than the one we had entered by, opened, and a maid appeared.

'Bring tea and pegs,' said Theodora, and the door shut again.

'I ordered pegs for you because I know men hate tea,' she said. 'That's my own maid. I never let any of the servants answer this bell except her; she has my confidence, as far as one ever gives confidence to a servant. I think she likes me. I like making myself loved,' she added impulsively.

'You've never found the least difficulty in it, I should think,' I answered, perhaps a shade more warmly than I ought, for the colour came into her cheek and a slight confusion into her eyes.

The servant's re-entry saved her from replying.

'Now tell me how you like your peg made, and I'll make it,' said Theodora, getting up and crossing to the table when the servant had gone.

I got up, too, and protested against this arrangement.

Theodora turned round and looked up at me, leaning one hand on the table.

'Now, how ridiculous and conventional you are!' she said. 'You would think nothing of letting me make you a cup of tea, and yet I must by no means mix you a peg!'

She looked so like a young fellow of nineteen as she spoke that half the sense of informality between us was lost, and there was a keen, subtle pleasure in this superficial familiarity with her that I had never felt with far prettier women. The half of nearly every desire is curiosity, a vague, undefined curiosity, of which we are hardly conscious; and it was this that Theodora so violently stimulated, while her beauty was sufficient to nurse the other half. This feeling of curiosity arises, of course, for any woman who may be new to us, and who has the power to move us at all. But generally, if it cannot be gratified for the particular one, it is more or less satisfied by the general knowledge applying to them all; but here, as Theodora differed so much from the ordinary feminine type, even this instinctive sort of consolation was denied me. I looked down at her with a smile.

'We shan't be able to reconcile Fashion and Logic, so it's no use,' I said. 'Make the peg, then, and I'll try and remain in the fashion by assuming it's tea.'

'Great Scott! I hope you won't fancy it's tea while you are drinking it!' returned Theodora laughing.

She handed me the glass, and I declared nectar wasn't in it with that peg, and then she made her own tea and came and sat down to drink it, in not at all an indecorous, but still informal proximity.

'Did you collect anything in the East?' she asked me, after a minute or two.

'Yes; a good many idols and relics and curiosities of sorts,' I answered. 'Would you like to see them?'

'Very much,' Theodora answered. 'Where are they?'

'Well, not in my pocket,' I said smiling. 'At my chambers. Could you and Mrs. Long spare an afternoon and honour me with a visit there?'

'I should like it immensely. I know Helen will come if I ask her.'

'When you have seen them I must pack them up, and send them to my agents. One can't travel about with those things.'

A sort of tremor passed over Theodora's face as I spoke, and her glance met mine, full of demands and questionings, and a very distinct assertion of distress. It said distinctly, 'I am so sorry you are going.' The sorrow in her eyes touched my vanity deeply, which is the most responsive quality we have. It is difficult to reach our hearts or our sympathies, but our vanity is always available. I felt inclined to throw my arm round that supple-looking waist – and it was close to me – and say, 'Don't be sorry; come too.' I don't know whether my looks were as plain as hers, but Theodora rose carelessly, apparently to set her teacup down, and then did not resume her seat by me, but went back to the sofa on the other side of the rug. This, in the state of feeling into which I had drifted, produced an irritated sensation, and I was rather pleased than not when a gong sounded somewhere in the house and gave me a graceful opening to rise.

'May I hope to hear from you, then, which day you will like to come?' I asked, as I held out my hand.

Now this was the moment I had been expecting, practically, ever since her hand had left mine last night, the moment when it should touch it again. I do not mean consciously, but there are a million slight, vague physical experiences and sensations within us of which the mind remains unconscious. Theodora's white right hand rested on her hip, the light from above struck upon it, and I noted that all the rings had been stripped from it; her left was crowded with them, so that the hand sparkled at each movement, but not one remained on her right. I coloured violently for the minute as I recollected my last night's pressure, and the idea flashed upon me at once that she had removed them expressly to avoid the pain of having them ground into her flesh.

The next second Theodora had laid her hand confidently in mine. My mind, annoyed at the thought that had just shot through it, bade me take her hand loosely and let it go, but Theodora raised her eyes to me, full of a soft disappointment which seemed to say, 'Are you not going to press it, then, after all, when I have taken off all the rings entirely that you may?' That look seemed to push away, walk over, ignore my reason, and appeal directly to the eager physical nerves and muscles. Spontaneously, whether I would or not, they responded to it, and my fingers laced themselves tightly round this morsel of velvet-covered fire.

We forgot in those few seconds to say the orthodox good-byes; she forgot to answer my question. That which we were both saying to each other, though our lips did not open, was, 'So I should like to hold and embrace you;' and she, 'So I should like to be held and embraced.'

Then she withdrew her hand, and I went out by way of the drawing-room where we had entered.

In the hall her footman showed me out with extra obsequiousness. My three-hours' stay raised me, I suppose, to the rank of more than an ordinary caller.

It was dark now in the streets, and the temperature must have been somewhere about zero. I turned my collar up and started to walk sharply in the direction of my chambers. Walking always induces in me a tendency to reflection and retrospection, and now, removed from the excitement of Theodora's actual presence, my thoughts lapped quietly over the whole interview, going through it backwards, like the calming waves of a receding tide, leaving lingeringly the sand. There was no doubt that this girl attracted me very strongly, that the passion born yesterday was nearing adolescence; and there was no doubt, either, that I ought to strangle it now before it reached maturity. My thoughts, however, turned impatiently from this question, and kept closing and centring round the object itself, with maddening persistency. I laughed to myself as Schopenhauer's theory shot across me that all impulse to love is merely the impulse of the genius of the genus to select a fitting object which will help in producing a Third Life. Certainly the genius of the genus in me was weaker than the genius of my own individuality, in this instance, for Theodora was as unfitted, according to the philosopher's views, to become a co-worker with me in carrying out Nature's aim, as she was fitted to give me as an individual the strongest personal pleasure.

I remember Schopenhauer does admit that this instinct in man to choose some object which will best fulfil the duty of the race, is apt to be led astray, and it is fortunate he did not forget to make this admission, if his theory is to be generally applied, considering how very particularly often we are led astray, and that our strongest, fiercest passions and keenest pleasures are constantly not those suitable to, nor in accordance with, the ends of Nature. The sharpest, most violent stimulus, we may say, the true essence of pleasure, lies in some gratification which has no claim whatever, in any sense, to be beneficial or useful, or to have any ulterior motive, conscious or instinctive, or any lasting result, or any fulfilment of any object, but which is simple gratification and dies naturally in its own excess.

As we admit of works of pure genius that they cannot claim utility, or motive, or purpose, but simply that they exist as joy-giving and beautiful objects of delight, so must we have done with utility, motive, purpose, and the aims of Nature, before we can reach the most absolute degree of positive pleasure. To choose an admissible instance, a naturally hungry man, given a slice of bread, will he or will he not devour it with as great a pleasure as the craving drunkard feels in swallowing a draught of raw brandy?

In the first case a simple natural desire is gratified, and the aim of Nature satisfied; but the individual's longing and subsequent pleasure cannot be said to equal the furious craving of the drunkard, and his delirious sense of gratification as the brandy burns his throat.

My inclination towards Theodora could hardly be the simple, natural instinct, guided by natural selection, for then surely I should have been swayed towards some more womanly individual, some more vigorous and at the same time more feminine physique. In me, it was the mind that had first suggested to the senses, and the senses that had answered in a dizzy pleasure, that this passionate, sensitive frame, with its tensely-strung nerves and excitable pulses, promised the height of satisfaction to a lover. Surely to Nature it promised a poor if possible mother, and a still poorer nurse. And these desires and passions that spring from that border-land between mind and sense, and are nourished by the suggestions of the one and the stimulus of the other, have a stronger grip upon our organisation, because they offer an acuter pleasure, than those simple and purely physical ones in which Nature is striving after her own ends and using us simply as her instruments.

I thought on in a desultory sort of way, more or less about Theodora, and mostly about the state of my own feelings, until I reached my chambers. There I found Digby, and in his society, with his chaff and gabble in my ears, all reflection and philosophy fled, without leaving me any definite decision made.

The next afternoon but one found myself and Digby standing at the windows of my chambers awaiting Theodora's arrival. I had invited him to help me entertain the two women, and also to help me unearth and dust my store of idols and curiosities, and range them on the tables for inspection. There were crowds of knick-knacks picked up in the crooked streets and odd corners of Benares, presents made to me, trifles bought in the Cairo bazaars, and vases and coins discovered below the soil in the regions of the Tigris. Concerning several of the most typical objects Digby and I had had considerable difference of opinion. One highly interesting bronze model of the monkey-god at Benares he had declared I could not exhibit on account of its too pronounced realism and insufficient attention to the sartorial art. I had insisted that the god's deficiencies in this respect were not more striking than the objects in flesh-tints, hung at the Academy, that Theodora viewed every season.

'Perhaps not,' he answered. 'But this is *not* in pink and white, and hung on the Academy walls for the public to stare at, and therefore you can't let her see it.'

This was unanswerable. I yielded, and the monkey-god was wheeled under a side-table out of view.

Every shelf and stand and table had been pressed into the service, and my rooms had the appearance of a corner in an Egyptian bazaar, now when we had finished our preparations.

'There they are,' said Digby, as Mrs. Long's victoria came in sight.

Theodora was leaning back beside her sister, and it struck me then how representative she looked, as it were, of herself and her position. From where we stood we could see down into the victoria, as it drew up at our door. Her knees were crossed under the blue carriage-rug, on the edge of which rested her two small pale-gloved hands. A velvet jacket, that fitted her as its skin fits the grape, showed us her magnificent shoulders, and the long easy slope of her figure to the small waist. On her head, in the least turn of which lay the acme of distinction, amongst the black glossy masses of her hair, sat a small hat in vermilion velvet, made to resemble the Turkish fez. As the carriage stopped, she glanced up; and a brilliant smile swept over her face, as she bowed slightly to us at the window. The handsome painted eyes, the naturally scarlet lips, the pallor of the oval face, and each well-trained movement of the distinguished figure, as she rose and stepped from the carriage, were noted and watched by our four critical eyes.

'A typical product of our nineteenth-century civilisation,' I said, with a faint smile, as Theodora let her fur-edged skirt draw over the snowy pavement, and we heard her clear cultivated tones, with the fashionable drag in them, ordering the coachman not to let the horses get cold.

'But she's a splendid sort of creature, don't you think?' asked Digby. 'Happy the man who —— eh?'

I nodded. 'Yes,' I assented. 'But how much that man should have to offer, old chap, that's the point; that six thousand of hers seems an invulnerable protection.'

'I suppose so,' said Digby with a nervous yawn. 'And to think I have more than double that and yet —— It's a pity. Funny it will be if my looks and your poverty prevent either of us having her.'

'My own case is settled,' I said decisively. 'My position and hers decide it for me.'

'I'd change places with you this minute if I could,' muttered Digby moodily, as steps came down to our door, and we went forward to meet the women as they entered.

It seemed to arrange itself naturally that Digby should be occupied in the first few seconds with Mrs. Long, and that I should be free to receive Theodora.

Of all the lesser emotions, there is hardly any one greater than that subtle sense of pleasure felt when a woman we love crosses for the first time our own threshold. We may have met her a hundred times in her house, or on public ground, but the sensation her presence then creates is altogether different from that instinctive, involuntary, momentary and delightful sense of ownership that rises when she enters any room essentially our own.

It is the very illusion of possession.

With this hatefully egoistic satisfaction infused through me, I drew forward for her my own favourite chair, and Theodora sank into it, and her tiny, exquisitely-formed feet sought my fender-rail. At a murmured invitation from me, she unfastened and laid aside her jacket. Beneath, she revealed some purplish, silk-like material, that seemed shot with different colours as the firelight fell upon it. It was strained tight and smooth upon her, and the swell of a low bosom was distinctly defined below it. There was no excessive development, quite the contrary, but in the very slightness there was an indescribably sensuous curve, and a depression, rising and falling, that seemed as if it might be the very home itself of passion. It was a breast with little suggestion of the duties or powers of Nature, but with infinite seduction for a lover.

'What a marvellous collection you have here,' she said throwing her glance round the room. 'What made you bring home all these things?'

'The majority were gifts to me – presents made by the different natives whom I visited or came into connection with in various ways. A native is never happy, if he likes you at all, until he has made you some valuable present.'

'You must be very popular with them indeed,' returned Theodora, glancing from a brilliant Persian carpet, suspended on the wall, to a gold and ivory model of a temple, on the console by her side.

'Well, when one stays with a fellow as his guest, as I have done with some of these small rajahs and people, of course one tries to make oneself amiable.'

'The fact is, Miss Dudley,' interrupted Digby, 'Ray admires these fellows, and that is why they like him. Just look at this sketch-book of his – what trouble he has taken to make portraits of them.'

And he stretched out a limp-covered pocket-album of mine.

I reddened slightly and tried to intercept his hand.

'Nonsense, Digby. Give the book to me,' I said; but Theodora had already taken it, and she looked at me as I spoke with one of those delicious looks of hers that could speak so clearly. Now it seemed to say, 'If you are going to love me, you must have no secrets from me.' She opened the book and I was subdued and let her. I did not much care, except that it was some time now since I had looked at it, and I did not know what she might find in it. However, Theodora was so different from girls generally, that it did not greatly matter.

'Perhaps these are portraits of your different conquests amongst the Ranees, are they?' she said. 'I don't see "my victims", though, written across the outside as the Frenchmen write on their albums.'

'No,' I said, with a smile, 'I think these are only portraits of men whose appearance struck me. The great difficulty is to persuade any Mohammedan to let you draw him.'

The very first leaf she turned seemed to give the lie to my words. Against a background of yellow sand and blue sky, stood out a slight figure in white, bending a little backward, and holding in its hands, extended on either side, the masses of its black hair that fell through them, till they touched the sand by its feet. Theodora threw a side-glance full of derision on me, as she raised her eyes from the page.

'I swear it isn't,' I said hastily, colouring, for I saw she thought it was a woman. 'It's a young Sikh I bribed to let me paint him.'

'Oh, a young Sikh, is it?' said Theodora, bending over the book again. 'Well it's a lovely face; and what beautiful hair!'

'Yes, almost as beautiful as yours,' I murmured, in safety, for the others were wholly occupied in testing the limits of the flexibility of the soapstone.

Not for any consideration in this world could I have restrained the irresistible desire to say the words, looking at her sitting sideways to me, noting that shining weight of hair lying on the white neck, and that curious masculine shade upon the upper lip. A faint liquid smile came to her face.

'Mine is not so long as that when you see it undone,' she said, looking at me.

'How long is it?' I asked mechanically, turning over the leaves of the sketch-book, and thinking in a crazy sort of way what I would not give to see her with that hair unloosed, and have the right to lift a single strand of it.

'It would not touch the ground,' she answered, 'it must be about eight inches off it, I think.'

'A marvellous length for a European,' I answered in a conventional tone, though it was a difficulty to summon it.

Within my brain all the dizzy thoughts seemed reeling together till they left me hardly conscious of anything but an acute painful sense of her proximity.

'Find me the head of a Persian, will you?' came her voice next.

'A Persian?' I repeated mechanically.

Theodora looked at me wonderingly and I recalled myself.

'Oh, yes,' I answered, 'I'll find you one. Give me the book.'

I took the book and turned over the leaves towards the end. As I did so, some of the intermediate pages caught her eye, and she tried to arrest the turning leaves.

'What is that? Let me see.'

'It is nothing,' I said, passing them over. 'Allow me to find you the one you want.'

Theodora did not insist, but her glance said: 'I will be revenged for this resistance to my wishes!'

When I had found her the portrait, I laid the open book back upon her knees. Theodora bent over it with an unaffected exclamation of delight. 'How exquisite! and how well you have done it! What a talent you must have!'

'Oh no, no talent,' I said hastily. 'It's easy to do a thing like that when your heart is in it.'

Theodora looked up at me and said simply, 'This is a woman.'

And I looked back in her eyes and said as simply, 'Yes, it is a woman.'

Theodora was silent, gazing at the open leaf, absorbed. And half-unconsciously my eyes followed hers and rested with hers on the page.

Many months had gone by since I had opened the book; and many, many cigars, that according to Tolstoi deaden every mental feeling, and many, many pints of brandy that do the same thing, only more so, had been consumed, since I had last looked upon that face. And now I saw it over the shoulder of this woman. And the old pain revived and surged through me, but it was dull – dull as every emotion must be in the near neighbourhood of a new object of desire – every emotion except one.

'Really it is a very beautiful face, isn't it?' she said at last, with a tender and sympathetic accent, and as she raised her head our eyes met.

I looked at her and answered, 'I should say yes, if we were not looking at it together, but you know beauty is entirely a question of comparison.'

Her face was really not one-tenth so handsome as the mere shadowed, inanimate representation of the Persian girl, beneath our hands. I knew it and so did she. Theodora herself would have been the first to admit it. But nevertheless the words were ethically true. True in the sense that underlay the society compliment, for no beauty of the dead can compare with that of the living. Such are we, that as we love all objects in their relation to our own pleasure from them, so even in our admiration, the greatest beauty, when absolutely useless to us, cannot move us as a far lesser degree has power to do, from which it is possible to hope, however vaguely, for some personal gratification. And to this my words would come if translated. And I think Theodora understood the translation rather than the conventional form of them, for she did not take the trouble to deprecate the flattery.

I got up, and, to change the subject, said, 'Let me wheel up that little table of idols. Some of them are rather curious.'

I moved the tripod up to the arm of her chair.

Theodora closed the sketch-book and put it beside her, and looked over the miniature bronze gods with interest. Then she stretched out her arm to lift and move several of them, and her soft fingers seemed to lie caressingly – as they did on everything they touched – on the heads and shoulders of the images. I watched her, envying those senseless little blocks of brass.

'This is the Hindu equivalent of the Greek Aphrodite,' I said, lifting forward a small, unutterably hideous, squat female figure, with the face of a monkey, and two closed wings of a dragon on its shoulders.

'Oh, Venus,' said Theodora. 'We must certainly crown her amongst them, though hardly, I think, in this particular case, for her beauty!'

And she laughingly slipped off a diamond half-hoop from her middle finger, and slipped the ring on to the model's head. It fitted exactly round the repulsive brows of the deformed and stunted image, and the goddess stood crowned in the centre of the table, amongst the other figures, with the circlet of brilliants, flashing brightly in the firelight, on her head. As Theodora passed the ring from her own warm white finger on to the forehead of the misshapen idol, she looked at me. The look, coupled with the action, in my state, went home to those very inner cells of the brain where are the springs themselves of passion. At the same instant the laughter and irresponsible gaiety and light pleasure on the face before me, the contrast between the delicate hand and the repellent monstrosity it had crowned – the sinister, allegorical significance – struck me like a blow. An unexplained feeling of rage filled me. Was it against her, myself, her action, or my own desires? It seemed for the moment to burn against them all. On the spur of it, I dragged forward to myself another of the images from behind the Astarte, slipped off my own signet-ring, and put it on the head of the idol.

'This is the only one for me to crown,' I said bitterly, with a laugh, feeling myself whiten with the stress and strain of a host of inexplicable sensations that crowded in upon me, as I met Theodora's lovely inquiring glance.

There was a shade of apprehensiveness in her voice as she said, 'What is that one?'

'Shiva,' I said curtly, looking her straight in the eyes. 'The god of self-denial.'

I saw the colour die suddenly out of her face, and I knew I had hurt her. But I could not help it. With her glance she had summoned me to approve or second her jesting act. It was a challenge I could not pass over. I must in some correspondingly joking way either accept or reject her coronation. And to reject it was all I could do, since this woman must be nothing to me. There was a second's blank pause of strained silence. But, superficially, we had not strayed off the legitimate ground of mere society nothings, whatever we might feel lay beneath them. And Theodora was trained thoroughly in the ways of fashion.

The next second she leant back in her chair, saying lightly, 'A false, absurd, and unnatural god; it is the greatest error to strive after the impossible; it merely prevents you accomplishing the possible. Gods like these,' and she indicated the abominable squint-eyed Venus, 'are merely natural instincts personified, and one may well call them gods since they are invincible. Don't you remember the fearful punishments that the Greeks represented as overtaking mortals who dared to resist Nature's laws, that they chose to individualise as their gods? You remember the fate of Hippolytus who tried to disdain Venus, of Pentheus who tried to subdue Bacchus? These two plays teach the immortal lesson that if you have the presumption to try to be greater than Nature she will in the end take a terrible revenge. The most we can do is to guide her. You can never be her conqueror. Consider yourself fortunate if she allows you to be her charioteer.'

It was all said very lightly and jestingly, but at the last phrase there was a flash in her eye, directed upon me – yes, me – as if she read down into my inner soul, and it sent the blood to my face.

As the last word left her lips, she stretched out her hand and deliberately took my ring from the head of Shiva, put it above her own diamonds on the other idol, and laid the god I had chosen, the god of austerity and mortification, prostrate on its face, at the feet of the leering Venus.

Then, without troubling to find a transition phrase, she got up and said, 'I am going to look at that Persian carpet.'

It had all taken but a few seconds; the next minute we were over by the carpet, standing in front of it and admiring its hues in the most orthodox terms. The images were left as she had placed them. I could do nothing less, of course, than yield to a woman and my guest. The jest had not gone towards calming my feelings, nor had those two glances of hers – the first so tender and appealing as she had crowned the Venus, the second so virile and mocking as she had discrowned the Shiva. There was a strange mingling of extremes in her. At one moment she seemed will-less, deliciously weak, a thing only made to be taken in one's arms and kissed. The next, she was full of independent uncontrollable determination and opinion. Most men would have found it hard to be indifferent to her. When beside her you must either have been attracted or repelled. For me, she was the very worst woman that could have crossed my path.

As I stood beside her now, her shoulder only a little below my own, her neck and the line of her breast just visible to the side vision of my eye, and heard her talking of the carpet, I felt there was no price I would not have paid to have stood for one half-hour in intimate confidence with her, and been able to tear the veils from this irritating character.

From the carpet we passed on to a table of Cashmere work and next to a pile of Mohammedan garments. These had been packed with my own personal luggage, and I should not have thought of bringing them forth for inspection. It was Digby who, having seen them by chance in my portmanteau, had insisted that they would add interest to the general collection of Eastern trifles. 'Clothes, my dear fellow, clothes; why, they will probably please her more than anything else.'

Theodora advanced to the heap of stuffs and lifted them.

'What is the history of these?' she said laughing. 'These were not presents to you!'

'No,' I murmured. 'Bought in the native bazaars.'

'Some perhaps,' returned Theodora, throwing her glance over them. 'But a great many are not new.'

It struck me that she would not be a woman very easy to deceive. Some men value a woman in proportion to the ease with which they can impose upon her, but to me it is too much trouble to deceive at all, so that the absence of that amiable quality did not disquiet me. On the contrary, the comprehensive, cynical, and at the same time indulgent smile that came so readily to Theodora's lips charmed me more, because it was the promise of even less trouble than a real or professed obtuseness.

'No,' I assented merely.

'Well, then?' asked Theodora, but without troubling to seek a reply. 'How pretty they are and how curious! this one, for instance.' And she took up a blue silk zouave, covered with gold embroidery, and worth perhaps about thirty pounds. 'This has been a good deal worn. It is a souvenir, I suppose?'

I nodded. With any other woman I was similarly anxious to please I should have denied it, but with her I felt it did not matter.

'Too sacred perhaps, then, for me to put on?' she asked with her hand in the collar, and smiling derisively.

'Oh dear no!' I said, 'not at all. Put it on by all means.'

'Nothing is sacred to you, eh? I see. Hold it then.'

She gave me the zouave and turned for me to put it on her. A glimpse of the back of her white neck, as she bent her head forward, a convulsion of her adorable shoulders as she drew on the jacket, and the zouave was fitted on. Two seconds perhaps, but my self-control wrapped round me had lost one of its skins.

'Now I must find a turban or fez,' she said, turning over gently, but without any ceremony, the pile. 'Oh, here's one!' She drew out a white fez, also embroidered in gold, and, removing her hat, put it on very much to one side, amongst her black hair, with evident care lest one of those silken inflected waves should be disturbed; and then affecting an undulating gait, she walked over to the fire.

'How do you like me in Eastern dress, Helen?' she said, addressing her sister, for whom Digby was deciphering some old coins. Digby and I confessed afterwards to each other the impulse that moved us both to suggest it was not at all complete without the trousers. I did offer her a cigarette, to enhance the effect.

'Quite passable, really,' said Mrs. Long, leaning back and surveying her languidly.

Theodora took the cigarette with a laugh, lighted and smoked it, and it was then, as she leant against the mantel-piece with her eyes full of laughter, a glow on her pale skin, and an indolent relaxation in the long, supple figure, that I first said, or rather an involuntary, unrecognised voice within me said, 'It is no good; whatever happens I must have you.'

'Do you know that it is past six, Theo?' said Mrs. Long.

'You will let me give you a cup of tea before you go?' I said.

'Tea!' repeated Theodora. 'I thought you were going to say haschisch or opium, at the least, after such an Indian afternoon.'

'I have both,' I answered, 'would you like some?' thinking, 'By Jove, I should like to see you after the haschisch.'

'No,' replied Theodora, 'I make it a rule not to get intoxicated in public.'

When the women rose to go, Theodora, to my regret, divested herself of the zouave without my aid, and declined it also for putting on her own cloak. As they stood drawing on their gloves I asked if they thought there was anything worthy of their acceptance amongst these curiosities. Mrs. Long chose from the table near her an ivory model of the Taj, and Digby took it up to carry for her to the door. As he did so his eye caught the table of images.

'This is your ring, Miss Dudley, I believe,' he said.

I saw him grin horridly as he noted the arrangement of the figures. Doubtless he thought it was mine.

I took up my signet-ring again, and Theodora said carelessly, without the faintest tinge of colour rising in her cheek, 'Oh, yes, I had forgotten it. Thanks.'

She took it from him and replaced it.

I asked her if she would honour me as her sister had done.

'There is one thing in this room that I covet immensely,' she said, meeting my gaze.

'It is yours, of course, then,' I answered. 'What is it?'

Theodora stretched out her open hand. 'Your sketch-book.'

For a second I felt the blood dye suddenly all my face. The request took me by surprise, for one thing; and immediately after the surprise followed the vexatious and embarrassing thought that she had asked for the one thing in the room that I certainly did not wish her to have. The book contained a hundred thousand memories, embodied in writing, sketching, and painting, of those years in the East. There was not a page in it that did not reflect the emotions of the time when it had been filled in, and give a chronicle of the life lived at the date inscribed on it. It was a sort of diary in cipher, and to turn over its leaves was to re-live the hours they represented. For my own personal pleasure I liked the book and wanted to keep it, but there were other reasons too why I disliked the idea of surrendering it. It flashed through me, the question as to what her object was in possessing herself of it. Was it jealousy of the faces or any face within it that prompted her, and would she amuse herself, when she had it, by tearing out the leaves or burning it? To give over these portraits merely to be sacrificed to a petty feminine spite and malice, jarred upon me. Involuntarily I looked hard into her eyes to try and read her intentions, and I felt I had wronged her. The eyes were full of the softest, tenderest light. It was impossible to imagine them vindictive. She had seen my hesitation and she smiled faintly.

'Poor Herod with your daughter of Herodias,' she said, softly. 'Never mind, I will not take it.'

The others who had been standing with her saw there was some embarrassment that they did not understand, and Mrs. Long turned to go slowly down the corridor. Digby had to follow. Theodora was left standing alone before me, her seductive figure framed in the open doorway. Of course she was irresistible. Was she not the new object of my desires?

I seized the sketch-book from the chair. What did anything matter?

'Yes,' I said hastily, putting it into that soft, small hand before it could draw back. 'Forgive me the hesitation. You know I would give you anything.'

If she answered or thanked me, I forget it. I was sensible of nothing at the moment but that the blood seemed flowing to my brain, and thundering through it, in ponderous waves. Then I knew we were walking down the passage, and in a few minutes more we should have said good-bye, and she would be gone.

An acute and yet vague realisation came upon me that the corridor was dark, and that the others had gone on in front, a confused recollection of the way she had lauded Nature and its domination a short time back, and then all these were lost again in the eddying torrent of an overwhelming desire to take her in my arms and hold her, control her, assert my will over hers, this exasperating object who had been pleasing and seducing every sense for the last three hours, and now was leaving them all unsatisfied. That impulse towards some physical demonstration, that craving for physical contact, which attacks us suddenly with its terrific impetus, and chokes and stifles us, ourselves, beneath it, blinding us to all except itself, rushed upon me then, walking beside her in the dark passage; and at that instant Theodora sighed.

'I am tired,' she said languidly. 'May I take your arm?' and her hand touched me.

I did not offer her my arm, I flung it round her neck, bending back her head upon it, so that her lips were just beneath my own as I leant over her, and I pressed mine on them in a delirium of passion.

Everything that should have been remembered I forgot.

Knowledge was lost of all, except those passive, burning lips under my own. As I touched them, a current of madness seemed to mingle with my blood, and pass flaming through all my veins.

I heard her moan, but for that instant I was beyond the reach of pity or reason, I only leant harder on her lips in a wild, unheeding, unsparing frenzy. It was a moment of ecstasy that I would have bought with years of my life. One moment, the next I released her, and so suddenly, that she reeled against the wall of the passage. I caught her wrist to steady her. We dared neither of us speak, for the others were but little ahead of us; but I sought her eyes in the dusk.

They met mine, and rested on them, gleaming through the darkness. There was no confusion nor embarrassment in them, they were full of the hot, clear, blinding light of passion; and I knew there would be no need to crave forgiveness.

The next moment had brought us up to the others, and to the end of the passage.

Mrs. Long turned round, and held out her hand to me.

'Good-bye,' she said. 'We have had a most interesting afternoon.'

It was with an effort that I made some conventional remark.

Theodora, with perfect outward calm, shook hands with myself and Digby, with her sweetest smile, and passed out.

I lingered some few minutes with Digby, talking; and then he went off to his own diggings, and I returned slowly down the passage to my rooms.

My blood and pulses seemed beating as they do in fever, my ears seemed full of sounds, and that kiss burnt like the brand of hot iron on my lips. When I reached my rooms, I locked the door and flung both the windows open to the snowy night. The white powder on the ledge crumbled and drifted in.

. . . .
. . . .

The Crimson Weaver

R. Murray Gilchrist

Robert Murray Gilchrist (1867–1917) was a prolific novelist and short-story writer who spent the 1890s in the English countryside, mostly the Peak District. His short stories embody what might be called Decadent horror, with elements of Gothic and historical fantasy being prominent. In the early 1890s he published most of his Decadent tales in W. E. Henley's *National Observer*. These were collected in *The Stone Dragon and Other Tragic Romances* (1894). This disturbing literary landmark is packed with perfervid, gruesome and ensanguined images of sexuality that play around themes of gender and undermine patriarchy. *The Academy* praised the authenticity of the collection and hailed it as 'Decadent', aligning Gilchrist with Poe, de l'Isle-Adam and Baudelaire's *Les Fleurs du Mal*.

Despite Lane's desperate efforts to purify the *Yellow Book* in the July volume following Wilde's conviction, 'The Crimson Weaver' is steeped in morbid otherworldliness; even the cover image by Patten Wilson, Beardsley's successor, is an allusion to this story. It is a tale of the monstrous and the erotic that challenges Christian, Puritan values, pitting spiritual orthodoxy and fortitude against irresistible erotic desires. Employing a highly aesthetic style, and set in a liminal landscape of voluptuous yet eerie dilapidation, the story tells of a fatally beautiful witch, an extreme Keatsian 'dame sans merci', who weaves her robes with the flesh and blood of those who surrender to her beauty. The dying men's faces woven into the fabric are grotesque, and the story's arsenal of Decadent images is comparable to those of M. P. Shiel. The story serves as its own allegory, in which the Decadent storyteller weaves a tale out of thickening blood itself.

My Master and I had wandered from our track and lost ourselves on the side of a great 'edge'. It was a two-days' journey from the Valley of the Willow Brakes, and we had roamed aimlessly; eating at hollow-echoing inns where grey-haired hostesses ministered, and sleeping side by side through the dewless midsummer nights on beds of fresh-gathered heather.

Beyond a single-arched wall-less bridge that crossed a brown stream whose waters leaped straight from the upland, we reached the Domain of the Crimson Weaver. No sooner had we reached the keystone when a beldam, wrinkled as a walnut and bald as an egg, crept from a cabin of turf and osier and held out her hands as a warning.

'Enter not the Domain of the Crimson Weaver!' she shrieked. 'One I loved entered. – I am here to warn men. Behold, I was beautiful once!'

She tore her ragged smock apart and discovered the foulness of her bosom, where the heart pulsed behind a curtain of livid skin. My Master drew money from his wallet and scattered it on the ground.

'She is mad,' he said. 'The evil she hints cannot exist. There is no fiend.'

So we passed on, but the bridge-keeper took no heed of the coins. For awhile we heard her bellowed sighs issuing from the openings of her den.

Strangely enough, the tenour of our talk changed from the moment that we left the bridge. He had been telling me of the Platonists, but when our feet pressed the sun-dried grass I was impelled to question him of love. It was the first time I had thought of the matter.

'How does passion first touch a man's life?' I asked, laying my hand on his arm.

His ruddy colour faded, he smiled wryly.

'You divine what passes in my brain,' he replied. 'I also had begun to meditate. . . . . But I may not tell you. . . . . In my boyhood — I was scarce older than you at the time — I loved the true paragon. 'Twere sacrilege to speak of the birth of passion. Let it suffice that ere I tasted of wedlock the woman died, and her death sealed for ever the door of that chamber of my heart. . . . . Yet, if one might see therein, there is an altar crowned with ever-burning tapers and with wreaths of unwithering asphodels.'

By this time we had reached the skirt of a yew-forest, traversed in every direction by narrow paths. The air was moist and heavy, but ever and anon a light wind touched the tree-tops and bowed them, so that the pollen sank in golden veils to the ground.

Everywhere we saw half-ruined fountains, satyrs vomiting senilely, nymphs emptying wine upon the lambent flames of dying phoenixes, creatures that were neither satyrs nor nymphs, nor gryphins, but grotesque adminglings of all, slain by one another, with water gushing from wounds in belly and thigh.

At length the path we had chosen terminated beside an oval mere that was surrounded by a colonnade of moss-grown arches. Huge pike quivered on the muddy bed, crayfish moved sluggishly amongst the weeds.

There was an island in the middle, where a leaden Diana, more compassionate than a crocodile, caressed Actaeon's horns ere delivering him to his hounds. The huntress' head and shoulders were white with the excrement of a crowd of culvers that moved as if entangled in a snare.

Northwards an avenue rose for the space of a mile, to fall abruptly before an azure sky. For many years the yew-mast on the pathway had been undisturbed by human foot; it was covered with a crust of greenish lichen.

My Master pressed my fingers. 'There is some evil in the air of this place,' he said. 'I am strong, but you — you may not endure. We will return.'

''Tis an enchanted country,' I made answer, feverishly. 'At the end of yonder avenue stands the palace of the sleeping maiden who awaits the kiss.

Nay, since we have pierced the country thus far, let us not draw back. You are strong, Master — no evil can touch us.'

So we fared to the place where the avenue sank, and then our eyes fell on the wondrous sight of a palace, lying in a concave pleasaunce, all treeless, but so bestarred with fainting flowers, that neither blade of grass nor grain of earth was visible.

Then came a rustling of wings above our heads, and looking skywards I saw flying towards the house a flock of culvers like unto those that had drawn themselves over Diana's head. The hindmost bird dropped its neck, and behold it gazed upon us with the face of a mannikin!

'They are charmed birds, made thus by the whim of the Princess,' I said.

As the birds passed through the portals of a columbary that crowned a western tower, their white wings beat against a silver bell that glistened there, and the whole valley was filled with music.

My Master trembled and crossed himself. 'In the name of our Mother,' he exclaimed, 'let us return. I dare not trust your life here.'

But a great door in front of the palace swung open, and a woman with a swaying walk came out to the terrace. She wore a robe of crimson worn into tatters at skirt-hem and shoulders. She had been forewarned of our presence, for her face turned instantly in our direction. She smiled subtly, and her smile died away into a most tempting sadness.

She caught up such remnants of her skirt as trailed behind, and strutted about with the gait of a peacock. As the sun touched the glossy fabric I saw eyes inwrought in deeper hue.

My Master still trembled, but he did not move, for the gaze of the woman was fixed upon him. His brows twisted and his white hair rose and stood erect, as if he viewed some unspeakable horror.

Stooping, with sidelong motions of the head, she approached; bringing with her the smell of such an incense as when amidst Eastern herbs burns the corse. . . . . She was perfect of feature as the Diana, but her skin was deathly white and her lips fretted with pain.

She took no heed of me, but knelt at my Master's feet — a Magdalene before an impregnable priest.

'Prince and Lord, Tower of Chastity, hear!' she murmured. 'For lack of love I perish. See my robe in tatters!'

He strove to avert his face, but his eyes still dwelt upon her. She half rose and shook nut-brown tresses over his knees.

Youth came back in a flood to my Master. His shrivelled skin filled out;

the dying sunlight turned to gold the whiteness of his hair. He would have raised her had I not caught his hands. The anguish of foreboding made me cry:

'One forces roughly the door of your heart's chamber. The wreaths wither, the tapers bend and fall.'

He grew old again. The Crimson Weaver turned to me.

'O marplot!' she said laughingly, 'think not to vanquish me with folly. I am too powerful. Once that a man enter my domain he is mine.'

But I drew my Master away.

''Tis I who am strong,' I whispered. 'We will go hence at once. Surely we may find our way back to the bridge. The journey is easy.'

The woman, seeing that the remembrance of an old love was strong within him, sighed heavily, and returned to the palace. As she reached the doorway the valves opened, and I saw in a distant chamber beyond the hall an ivory loom with a golden stool.

My Master and I walked again on the track we had made in the yew-mast. But twilight was falling, and ere we could reach the pool of Diana all was in utter darkness; so at the foot of a tree, where no anthill rose, we lay down and slept.

Dreams came to me — gorgeous visions from the romances of eld. Everywhere I sought vainly for a beloved. There was the Castle of the Ebony Dwarf, where a young queen reposed in the innermost casket of the seventh crystal cabinet; there was the Chamber of Gloom, where Lenore danced, and where I groped for ages around columns of living flesh; there was the White Minaret, where twenty-one princesses poised themselves on balls of burnished bronze; there was Melisandra's arbour, where the sacred toads crawled over the enchanted cloak.

Unrest fretted me; I woke in spiritual pain. Dawn was breaking — a bright yellow dawn, and the glades were full of vapours.

I turned to the place where my Master had lain. He was not there. I felt with my hands over his bed: it was key-cold. Terror of my loneliness overcame me, and I sat with covered face.

On the ground near my feet lay a broken riband, whereon was strung a heart of chrysolite. It enclosed a knot of ash-coloured hair — hair of the girl my Master had loved.

The mists gathered together and passed sunwards in one long many-cornered veil. When the last shred had been drawn into the great light, I gazed along the avenue, and saw the topmost bartizan of the Crimson Weaver's palace.

It was midday ere I dared start on my search. The culvers beat about my head. I walked in pain, as though giant spiders had woven about my body.

On the terrace strange beasts — dogs and pigs with human limbs, — tore ravenously at something that lay beside the balustrade. At sight of me they paused and lifted their snouts and bayed. Awhile afterwards the culvers rang the silver bell, and the monsters dispersed hurriedly amongst the drooping blossoms of the pleasaunce, and where they swarmed I saw naught but a steaming sanguine pool.

I approached the house and the door fell open, admitting me to a chamber adorned with embellishments beyond the witchery of art. There I lifted my voice and cried eagerly: 'My Master, my Master, where is my Master?' The alcoves sent out a babble of echoes, blended together like a harp-cord on a dulcimer: 'My Master, my Master, where is my Master? For the love of Christ, where is my Master?' The echo replied only, 'Where is my Master?'

Above, swung a globe of topaz, where a hundred suns gambolled. From its centre a convoluted horn, held by a crimson cord, sank lower and lower. It stayed before my lips and I blew therein, and heard the sweet voices of youth chant with one accord.

'Fall open, oh doors: fall open and show the way to the princess!'

Ere the last of the echoes had died a vista opened, and at the end of an alabaster gallery I saw the Crimson Weaver at her loom. She had doffed her tattered robe for one new and lustrous as freshly drawn blood. And marvellous as her beauty had seemed before, its wonder was now increased a hundredfold.

She came towards me with the same stately walk, but there was now a lightness in her demeanour that suggested the growth of wings.

Within arm's length she curtseyed, and curtseying showed me the firmness of her shoulders, the fullness of her breast. The sight brought no pleasure; my cracking tongue appealed in agony:

'My Master, where is my Master?'

She smiled happily. 'Nay, do not trouble. He is not here. His soul talks with the culvers in the cote. He has forgotten you. In the night we supped, and I gave him of Nepenthe.'

'Where is my Master? Yesterday he told me of the shrine in his heart — of ever-fresh flowers — of a love dead yet living.'

Her eyebrows curved mirthfully.

''Tis foolish boys' talk,' she said. 'If you sought till the end of time you would never find him — unless I chose. Yet — if you buy of me — myself to name the price.'

I looked around hopelessly at the unimaginable riches of her home. All that I have is this Manor of the Willow Brakes — a moorish park, an ancient house where the thatch gapes and the casements swing loose.

'My possessions are pitiable,' I said, 'but they are all yours. I give all to save him.'

'Fool, fool!' she cried. 'I have no need of gear. If I but raise my hand, all the riches of the world fall to me. 'Tis not what I wish for.'

Into her eyes came such a glitter as the moon makes on the moist skin of a sleeping snake. The firmness of her lips relaxed; they grew child-like in their softness. The atmosphere became almost tangible: I could scarce breathe.

'What is it? All that I can do, if it be no sin.'

'Come with me to my loom,' she said, 'and if you do the thing I desire you shall see him. There is no evil in't — in past times kings have sighed for the same.'

So I followed slowly to the loom, before which she had seated herself, and watched her deftly passing crimson thread over crimson thread.

She was silent for a space, and in that space her beauty fascinated me, so that I was no longer master of myself.

'What you wish for I will give, even if it be life.'

The loom ceased. 'A kiss of the mouth, and you shall see him who passed in the night.'

She clasped her arms around my neck and pressed my lips. For one moment heaven and earth ceased to be; but there was one paradise, where we were sole governours. . . . .

Then she moved back and drew aside the web and showed me the head of my Master, and the bleeding heart whence a crimson cord unravelled into many threads.

'I wear men's lives,' the woman said. 'Life is necessary to me, or even I — who have existed from the beginning — must die. But yesterday I feared the end, and he came. His soul is not dead — 'tis truth that it plays with my culvers.'

I fell back.

'Another kiss,' she said. 'Unless I wish, there is no escape for you. Yet you may return to your home, though my power over you shall never wane. Once more — lip to lip.'

I crouched against the wall like a terrified dog. She grew angry; her eyes darted fire.

'A kiss,' she cried, 'for the penalty!'

My poor Master's head, ugly and cadaverous, glared from the loom. I could not move.

The Crimson Weaver lifted her skirt, uncovering feet shapen as those of a vulture. I fell prostrate. With her claws she fumbled about the flesh of my breast. Moving away she bade me pass from her sight. . . . .

So, half-dead, I lie here at the Manor of the Willow Brakes, watching hour by hour the bloody clew ever unwinding from my heart and passing over the western hills to the Palace of the Siren.

The Quest of Sorrow

Mrs. Ernest [Ada] Leverson

Ada Leverson (née Beddington; 1862–1933) was a novelist, satirist and wit. She parodied and satirised Aesthetic posturing in the work of such writers and friends as Max Beerbohm, George Moore, Beardsley, Symons and Wilde. Her parody of *Dorian Gray*, 'An Afternoon Party' in *Punch* (1893) delighted Wilde, with whom she had a lifelong friendship. Leverson's parodies are not vicious attacks but playful and effervescent criticisms. They are ambiguously close to the Decadent/Aesthetic spirit, the object of her parody. Self-parody is one of the key features of the Decadence: Leverson's 'Suggestion' (1895) and 'The Quest of Sorrow' acknowledge the anxieties and moral/aesthetic dilemmas of works by the Decadents and Aesthetes, reshaping 'their positions more effectively to address the changing social-political concerns of the era'.

'The Quest of Sorrow' is a humorous mockery of a young dandy whose sole aim is to experience the ultimate thrill, the sensation of sorrow and sadness. Clearly emulating the theme of longing for the unachievable, the story questions the futility of Decadent desire, though sympathetically. It ends with an ingenious and mind-bogglingly paradoxical twist, by suggesting that Cecil Carington feels the ultimate sorrow after all his attempts at experiencing failure, rejection and grief have failed. Along with 'Suggestion', 'The Quest of Sorrow' offers tantalising reflections of the Wildean Aesthetes. In its self-conscious affectation, the story itself morphs into the very Decadent text it parodies. It presents the ironic situation in which the protagonist's mediocre poetry is accepted as an 'amusing parody on a certain modern school of verse'.

※

I

It is rather strange, in a man of my temperament, that I did not discover the void in my life until I was eighteen years old. And then I found out that I had missed a beautiful and wonderful experience.

I had never known grief. Sadness had shunned me, pain had left me untouched; I could hardly imagine the sensation of being unhappy. And the desire arose in me to have this experience; without which, it seemed to me, that I was not complete. I wanted to be miserable, despairing: a Pessimist! I craved to feel that gnawing fox, Anxiety, at my heart; I wanted my friends (most of whom had been, at some time or other, more or less heartbroken) to press my hand with sympathetic looks, to avoid the subject of my trouble, from delicacy; or, better still, to have long, hopeless talks with me about it, at midnight. I thirsted for salt tears; I longed to clasp Sorrow in my arms and press her pale lips to mine.

Now this wish was not so easily fulfilled as might be supposed, for I was born with those natural and accidental advantages that militate most against failure and depression. There was my appearance. I have a face that rarely passes unnoticed (I suppose a man may admit, without conceit, that he is not repulsive), and the exclamation, 'What a beautiful boy!' is one that I have been accustomed to hear from my earliest childhood to the present time.

I might, indeed, have known the sordid and wearing cares connected with financial matters, for my father was morbidly economical with regard to me. But, when I was only seventeen, my uncle died, leaving me all his property, when I instantly left my father's house (I am bound to say, in justice to him, that he made not the smallest objection) and took the rooms I now occupy, which I was able to arrange in harmony with my temperament. In their resolute effort to be neither uninterestingly commonplace nor conventionally bizarre (I detest – do not you? – the ready-made exotic) but at once simple and elaborate, severe and florid, they are an interesting result of my complex aspirations, and the astonishing patience of a bewildered decorator. (I think everything in a room should not be entirely correct; and I had some trouble to get a marble mantel-piece of a sufficiently debased design.) Here I was able to lead that life of leisure and contemplation for which I was formed and had those successes – social and artistic – that now began to pall upon me.

The religious doubts, from which I am told the youth of the middle classes often suffers, were, again, denied me. I might have had some mental conflicts, have revelled in the sense of rebellion, have shed bitter tears when my faiths crumbled to ashes. But I can never be insensible to incense; and there must, I feel, be something organically wrong about the man who is not impressed by the organ. I love religious rites and ceremonies, and on the other hand, I was an agnostic at five years old. Also, I don't think it matters. So here there is no chance for me.

To be miserable one must desire the unattainable. And of the fair women who, from time to time, have appealed to my heart, my imagination, etc., every one, *without a single exception*, has been kindness itself to me. Many others, indeed, for whom I have no time, or perhaps no inclination, write me those letters which are so difficult to answer. How can one sit down and write, 'My dear lady – I am so sorry, but I am really too busy?'

And with, perhaps, two appointments in one day – a light comedy one, say, in the Park, and serious sentiment coming to see one at one's rooms – to say nothing of the thread of a flirtation to be taken up at dinner and having perhaps to make a jealous scene of reproaches to some one of whom one has grown tired, in the evening – you must admit I had a sufficiently occupied life.

I had heard much of the pangs of disappointed ambition, and I now turned my thoughts in that direction. A failure in literature would be excellent. I had no time to write a play bad enough to be refused by every manager in London, or to be hissed off the stage; but I sometimes wrote verses. If I arranged to have a poem rejected I might get a glimpse of the feelings of the unsuccessful. So I wrote a poem. It was beautiful, but that I couldn't help, and I carefully refrained from sending it to any of the more literary reviews or magazines, for there it would have stood no chance of rejection. I therefore sent it to a commonplace, barbarous periodical, that appealed only to the masses; feeling sure it would not be understood, and that I should taste the bitterness of Philistine scorn.

Here is the little poem – if you care to look at it. I called it

FOAM-FLOWERS

Among the blue of Hyacinth's golden bells
(Sad is the Spring, more sad the new-mown hay),

Thou art most surely less than least divine,
Like a white Poppy, or a Sea-shell grey.
I dream in joy that thou art nearly mine;
Love's gift and grace, pale as this golden day,
Outlasting Hollyhocks, and Heliotrope
(Sad is the Spring, bitter the new-mown hay).
The wandering wild west wind, in salt-sweet hope,
With glad red roses, gems the woodland way.

Envoi

A bird sings, twittering in the dim air's shine,
Amid the mad Mimosa's scented spray,
Among the Asphodel, and Eglantine,
'Sad is the Spring, but sweet the new-mown hay.'

I had not heard from the editor, and was anticipating the return of my poem, accompanied by some expressions of ignorant contempt that would harrow my feelings, when it happened that I took up the frivolous periodical. Fancy my surprise when there, on the front page, was my poem – signed, as my things are always signed, '*Lys de la Vallée*'. Of course I could not repress the immediate exhilaration produced by seeing oneself in print; and when I went home I found a letter, thanking me for the *amusing parody on a certain modern school of verse* – and enclosing ten-and-six!

A parody! And I had written it in all seriousness!

Evidently literary failure was not for me. After all, what I wanted most was an affair of the heart, a disappointment in love, an unrequited affection. And these, for some reason or other, never seemed to come my way.

One morning I was engaged with Collins, my servant, in putting some slight final touches to my toilette, when my two friends, Freddy Thompson and Claude de Verney, walked into my room.

They were at school with me, and I am fond of them both, for different reasons. Freddy is in the Army; he is two-and-twenty, brusque, slangy, tender-hearted, and devoted to me. De Verney has nothing to do with this story at all, but I may mention that he was noted for his rosy cheeks, his collection of jewels, his reputation for having formerly taken morphia, his epicurism, his passion for private theatricals, and his extraordinary touchiness. One never knew what he would take offence at. He was always being hurt, and writing letters beginning: 'Dear Mr. Carington' or 'Dear Sir'

– (he usually called me Cecil), 'I believe it is customary when a gentleman dines at your table', etc.

I never took the slightest notice, and then he would apologise. He was always begging my pardon and always thanking me, though I never did anything at all to deserve either his anger or gratitude.

'Hallo, old chap,' Freddy exclaimed, 'you look rather down in the mouth. What's the row?'

'I am enamoured of Sorrow,' I said, with a sigh.

'Got the hump – eh? Poor old boy. Well, I can't help being cheery, all the same. I've got some ripping news to tell you.'

'Collins,' I said, 'take away this eau-de-cologne. It's corked. Now, Freddy,' as the servant left the room, 'your news.'

'I'm engaged to Miss Sinclair. Her governor has given in at last. What price that? . . . I'm tremendously pleased, don't you know, because it's been going on for some time, and I'm awfully mashed, and all that.'

Miss Sinclair! I remembered her – a romantic, fluffy blonde, improbably pretty, with dreamy eyes and golden hair, all poetry and idealism.

Such a contrast to Freddy! One associated her with pink chiffon, Chopin's nocturnes, and photographs by Mendelssohn.

'I congratulate you, my dear child,' I was just saying, when an idea occurred to me. Why shouldn't I fall in love with Miss Sinclair? What could be more tragic than a hopeless attachment to the woman who was engaged to my dearest friend? It seemed the very thing I had been waiting for.

'I have met her. You must take me to see her, to offer my congratulations,' I said.

Freddy accepted with enthusiasm.

A day or two after, we called. Alice Sinclair was looking perfectly charming, and it seemed no difficult task that I had set myself. She was sweet to me as Freddy's great friend – and we spoke of him while Freddy talked to her mother.

'How fortunate some men are!' I said, with a deep sigh.

'Why do you say that?'

'Because you're so beautiful,' I answered, in a low voice, and in my *earlier manner* – that is to say, as though the exclamation had broken from me involuntarily.

She laughed, blushed, I think, and turned to Freddy. The rest of the visit I sat silent and as though abstracted, gazing at her. Her mother tried, with well-meaning platitudes, to rouse me from what she supposed to be my boyish shyness . . . .

II

What happened in the next few weeks is rather difficult to describe. I saw Miss Sinclair again and again, and lost no opportunity of expressing my admiration; for I have a theory that if you make love to a woman long enough, and ardently enough, you are sure to get rather fond of her at last. I was progressing splendidly; I often felt almost sad, and very nearly succeeded at times in being a little jealous of Freddy.

On one occasion – it was a warm day at the end of the season, I remember – we had gone to skate at that absurd modern place where the ice is as artificial as the people, and much more polished. Freddy, who was an excellent skater, had undertaken to teach Alice's little sister, and I was guiding her own graceful movements. She had just remarked that I seemed very fond of skating, and I had answered that I was – on thin ice – when she stumbled and fell. . . . She hurt her ankle a little – a very little, she said.

'Oh, Miss Sinclair – "Alice" – I am sure you are hurt!' I cried, with tears of anxiety in my voice. 'You ought to rest – I am sure you ought to go home and rest.'

Freddy came up, there was some discussion, some demur, and finally it was decided that, as the injury was indeed very slight, Freddy should remain and finish his lesson. And I was allowed to take her home.

We were in a little brougham; delightfully near together. She leaned her pretty head, I thought, a little on one side – *my* side. I was wearing violets in my button-hole. Perhaps she was tired, or faint.

'How are you feeling now, dear Miss Sinclair?'

'Much better – thanks!'

'I am afraid you are suffering. . . . I shall never forgot what I felt when you fell! – My heart ceased beating!'

'It's very sweet of you. But, it's really nothing.'

'How precious these few moments with you are! I should like to drive with you for ever! Through life – to eternity!'

'Really! What a funny boy you are!' she said softly.

'Ah, if you only knew, Miss Sinclair, how – how I envy Freddy.'

'Oh, Mr. Carington!'

'Don't call me Mr. Carington. It's so cold – so ceremonious. Call me Cecil. Won't you?'

'Very well, Cecil.'

'Do you think it treacherous to Freddy for me to envy him – to tell you so?'

'Yes, I am afraid it is; a little.'

'Oh no. I don't think it is. – How are you feeling now, Alice?'

'Much better, thanks very much.' . . .

Suddenly, to my own surprise and entirely without pre-meditation, I kissed her – as it were, accidentally. It seemed so shocking, that we both pretended I hadn't, and entirely ignored the fact; continuing to argue as to whether or not it was treacherous to say I envied Freddy. . . . I insisted on treating her as an invalid, and lifted her out of the carriage, while she laughed nervously. It struck me that I was not unhappy yet. But that would come.

The next evening we met at a dance. She was wearing flowers that Freddy had sent her; but among them she had fastened one or two of the violets I had worn in my button-hole. I smiled, amused at the coquetry. No doubt she would laugh at me when she thought she had completely turned my head. She fancied me a child! Perhaps, on her wedding-day, I should be miserable at last.

. . . 'How tragic, how terrible it is to long for the impossible!'

We were sitting out, on the balcony. Freddy was in the ballroom, dancing. He was an excellent dancer.

'*Impossible!*' she said; and I thought she looked at me rather strangely. 'But you don't really, really ——'

'Love you?' I exclaimed, lyrically. 'But with all my soul! My life is blighted for ever, but don't think of me. It doesn't matter in the least. It may kill me, of course; but never mind. Sometimes, I believe, people *do* live on with a broken heart, and——'

'My dance, I think,' and a tiresome partner claimed her.

Even that night, I couldn't believe, try as I would, that life held for me no further possibilities of joy . . . .

About half-past one the next day, just as I was getting up, I received a thunderbolt in the form of a letter from Alice.

Would it be believed that this absurd, romantic, literal, beautiful person wrote to say she had actually broken off her engagement with Freddy? She could not bear to blight my young life; she returned my affection; she was waiting to hear from me.

Much agitated, I hid my face in my hands. What! was I never to get away from success – never to know the luxury of an unrequited attachment? Of course, I realised, now, that I had been deceiving myself; that I had only liked her enough to wish to make her care for me; that I had striven, unconsciously, to that end. The instant I knew she loved me all my interest was gone. My passion had been entirely imaginary. I cared nothing, absolutely nothing, for her. It was impossible to exceed my indifference. And Freddy! Because *I* yearned for sorrow, was that a reason that I should plunge others into it? Because I wished to weep, were my friends not to rejoice? How terrible to have wrecked Freddy's life, by taking away from him something that I didn't want myself!

The only course was to tell her the whole truth, and implore her to make it up with poor Freddy. It was extremely complicated. How was I to make her see that I had been *trying* for a broken heart; that I *wanted* my life blighted?

I wrote, endeavouring to explain, and be frank. It was a most touching letter, but the inevitable, uncontrollable desire for the *beau rôle* crept, I fear, into it and I fancy I represented myself, in my firm resolve not to marry her whatever happened – as rather generous and self-denying. It was a heartbreaking letter, and moved me to tears when I read it.

This is how it ended:

. . . . 'You have my fervent prayers for your happiness, and it may be that some day you and Freddy, walking in the daisied fields together, under God's beautiful sunlight, may speak not unkindly of the lonely exile.

'Yes, exile. For to-morrow I leave England. To-morrow I go to bury myself in some remote spot – perhaps to Trouville – where I can hide my heart and pray unceasingly for your welfare and that of the dear, dear friend of my youth and manhood.

'Yours and his, devotedly, till death and after,

'Cecil Carington.'

It was not a bit like my style. But how difficult it is not to fall into the tone that accords best with the temperament of the person to whom one is writing!

I was rather dreading an interview with poor Freddy. To be misunderstood by him would have been really rather tragic. But even here, good fortune pursued me. Alice's letter breaking off the engagement had been written in such mysterious terms, that it was quite impossible for the simple Freddy to make head or tail of it. So that when he appeared, just after my letter (which had infuriated her) – Alice threw herself into his arms, begging him to forgive her; pretending – women have these subtleties – that it had been a *boutade* about some trifle.

But I think Freddy had a suspicion that I had been 'mashed', as he would say, on his *fiancée*, and thought vaguely that I had done something rather splendid in going away.

If he had only stopped to think, he would have realised that there was nothing very extraordinary in 'leaving England' in the beginning of August; and he knew I had arranged to spend the summer holidays in France with De Verney. Still, he fancies I acted nobly. Alice doesn't.

And so I resigned myself, seeing, indeed, that Grief was the one thing life meant to deny me. And on the golden sands, with the gay striped bathers of Trouville, I was content to linger with laughter on my lips, seeking for Sorrow no more.

The Death Mask

Ella D'Arcy

Ella D'Arcy (Constance Eleanor Mary Byrne) (1857?–1937) was a short-story writer and prolific contributor to the *Yellow Book*, throughout much of its publication history. She rose to the position of de facto assistant editor to Henry Harland. Her stories are mainly concerned with the New Woman, and in particular problematic and loveless marriages. Her bold, unconventional treatment of marriage was recognised by Harland in her story 'Irremediable' which appeared in the first volume of the *Yellow Book*, after having been rejected by numerous conservative magazines. Of note is her shocking masterpiece 'The Pleasure-Pilgrim', a study of the psychology of a nymphomaniac. Her collection *Monochromes* (1895) was part of Lane's Keynote series.

'The Death Mask' is the first of 'Two Stories'; the other being 'The Villa Lucienne'. The two stories are unrelated. 'The Death Mask' is a psychological foray into Aestheticism and the paradoxical relationship between art and life, offering a distilled variation on Dorian Gray's portrait. The reviewer of her collection of stories *Modern Instances* (1898) recognised 'The Death Mask' as the 'triumph' of the book, surmising that it is a study of Paul Verlaine, 'half-satyr, half-divine'. The story begins with the death of a notorious absinthe-drinking Master whose talents are much admired, and ends in the bizarre beauty of the mask which obliterates the ugliness and vice of the Master's real life. The word pun of Mask and Master suggests that there is no difference between real life and the artefact.

The Master was dead; and Peschi, who had come round to the studio to see about some repairs – part of the ceiling had fallen owing to the too-lively proceedings of Dubourg and his eternal visitors overhead – displayed a natural pride that it was he who had been selected from among the many *mouleurs* of the Quarter, to take a mask of the dead man.

All Paris was talking of the Master, although not, assuredly, under that title. All Paris was talking of his life, of his genius, of his misery, and of his death. Peschi, for the moment, was sole possessor of valuable unedited details, to the narration of which Hiram P. Corner, who had dropped in to pass the evening with me, listened with keenly attentive ears.

Corner was a recent addition to the American Art Colony; ingenuous as befitted his eighteen years, and of a more than improbable innocence. Paris, to him, represented the Holiest of Holies; the dead Master, by the adorable impeccability of his writings, figuring therein as one of the High Priests. Needless to say, he had never come in contact with that High Priest, had never even seen him; while the Simian caricatures which so frequently embellished the newspapers, made as little impression on the lad's mind as did the unequivocal allusions, jests, and epigrams, for ever flung up like sea-spray against the rock of his unrevered name.

The absorbing interest Corner felt glowed visibly on his fresh young western face, and it was this, I imagine, which led Peschi to propose that we should go back with him to his *atelier* and see the mask for ourselves.

Peschi is a Genoese; small, lithe, very handsome; a skilled workman, a little demon of industry; full of enthusiasms, with the real artist-soul. He works for Felon the sculptor, and it was Felon who had been commissioned to do the bust for which the death mask would serve as model.

It is always pleasant to hear Peschi talk; and to-night, as we walked from the Rue Fleurus to the Rue Notre-Dame-des-Champs he told us something of mask-taking in general, with illustrations from this particular case.

On the preceding day, barely two hours after death had taken place, Rivereau, one of the dead man's intimates, had rushed into Peschi's workroom, and carried him off, with the necessary materials, to the Rue Monsieur, in a cab. Rivereau, though barely twenty, is perhaps the most notorious of the *bande*. Peschi described him to Corner as having dark, evil, narrow eyes set too close together in a perfectly white face, framed by falling, lustreless black hair; and with the stooping shoulders, the troubled walk, the attenuated hands common to his class.

Arrived at the house, Rivereau led the way up the dark and dirty staircase to the topmost landing, and as they paused there an instant, Peschi could hear the long-drawn, hopeless sobs of a woman within the door.

On being admitted he found himself in an apartment consisting of two small, inconceivably squalid rooms, opening one from the other.

In the outer room, five or six figures, the disciples, friends, and lovers of the dead poet, conversed together; a curious group in a medley of costumes. One in an opera-hat, shirt-sleeves, and soiled grey trousers tied up with a bit of stout string; another in a black coat buttoned high to conceal the fact that he wore no shirt at all; a third in clothes crisp from the tailor, with an immense bunch of Parma violets in his buttonhole. But all were alike in the strangeness of their eyes, their voices, their gestures.

Seen through the open door of the further room, lay the corpse under a sheet, and by the bedside knelt the stout, middle-aged mistress, whose sobs had reached the stairs.

Madame Germaine, as she was called in the Quarter, had loved the Master with that complete, self-abnegating, sublime love of which certain women are capable – a love uniting that of the mother, the wife, and the nurse all in one. For years she had cooked for him, washed for him, mended for him; had watched through whole nights by his bedside when he was ill; had suffered passively his blows, his reproaches, and his neglect, when, thanks to her care, he was well again. She adored him dumbly, closed her eyes to his vices, and magnified his gifts, without in the least comprehending them. She belonged to the *ouvrière* class, could not read, could not write her own name; but with a characteristic which is as French as it is un-British, she paid her homage to intellect, where an Englishwoman only gives it to inches and muscle. Madame Germaine was prouder perhaps of the Master's greatness, worshipped him more devoutly, than any one of the super-cultivated, ultra-corrupt group, who by their flatteries and complaisances had assisted him to his ruin.

It was with the utmost difficulty, Peschi said, that Rivereau and the rest had succeeded in persuading the poor creature to leave the bedside and go into the other room while the mask was being taken.

The operation, it seems, is a sufficiently horrible one, and no relative is permitted to be present. As you cover the dead face over with the plaster, a little air is necessarily forced back again into the lungs, and this air as it passes along the windpipe causes strange rattlings, sinister noises, so that you might swear that the corpse was returned to life. Then, as the mould is removed, the muscles of the face drag and twitch, the mouth opens, the tongue lolls out; and Peschi declared that this always remains for him a gruesome moment. He has never accustomed himself to it; on every recurring occasion it fills him with the same repugnance; and this, although he has taken so many masks, is so deservedly celebrated for them, that *la bande* had instantly selected him to perpetuate the Master's lineaments.

'But it's an excellent likeness,' said Peschi; 'you see they sent for me so promptly that he had not changed at all. He does not look as though he were dead, but just asleep.'

Meanwhile we had reached the unshuttered shop-front, where Peschi displays, on Sundays and week-days alike, his finished works of plastic art to the *gamins* and *filles* of the Quarter.

Looking past the statuary, we could see into the living-room beyond, it being separated from the shop only by a glass partition. It was lighted by a lamp set in the centre of the table, and in the circle of light thrown from beneath its green shade, we saw a charming picture: the young head of Madame Peschi bent over her baby, whom she was feeding at the breast. She is eighteen, pretty as a rose, and her story and Peschi's is an idyllic one; to be told, perhaps, another time. She greeted us with the smiling, cordial, unaffected kindliness which in France warms your blood with the constant sense of brotherhood; and, giving the boy to his father – a delicious opalescent trace of milk hanging about the little mouth – she got up to see about another lamp which Peschi had asked for.

Holding this lamp to guide our steps, he preceded us now across a dark yard to his workshop at the further end, and while we went we heard the young mother's exquisite nonsense-talk addressed to the child, as she settled back in her place again to her nursing.

Peschi, unlocking a door, flashed the light down a long room, the walls of which, the trestle-tables, the very floor, were hung, laden, and encumbered with a thousand heterogeneous objects. Casts of every description and dimension, finished, unfinished, broken; scrolls for ceilings; caryatides for chimney-pieces; cornucopias for the entablatures of buildings; chubby Cupids jostling emaciated Christs; broken columns for Père Lachaise, or consolatory upward-pointing angels; hands, feet, and noses for the Schools of Art; a pensively posed *échorché* contemplating a Venus of Milo fallen upon her back; these, and a crowd of nameless, formless things, seemed to spring at our eyes, as Peschi raised or lowered the lamp, moved it this way or the other.

'There it is,' said he, pointing forwards; and I saw lying flat upon a modelling-board, with upturned features, a grey, immobile simulacrum of the curiously mobile face I remembered so well.

'Of course you must understand,' said Peschi, 'it's only in the rough, just exactly as it came from the *creux*. Fifty copies are to be cast altogether, and this is the first one. But I must prop it up for you. You can't judge of it as it is.'

He looked about him for a free place on which to set the lamp. Not finding any, he put it down on the floor. For a few moments he stood busied over the mask with his back to us.

'Now you can see it properly,' said he, and stepped aside.

The lamp threw its rays upwards, illuminating strongly the lower portion of the cast, throwing the upper portion into deepest shadow, with the effect that the inanimate mask was become suddenly a living face, but a face so unutterably repulsive, so hideously bestial, that I grew cold to the roots of my hair . . . . . A fat, loose throat, a retreating chinless chin, smeared and bleared with the impressions of the meagre beard; a vile mouth, lustful, flaccid, the lower lip disproportionately great; ignoble lines; hateful puffinesses; something inhuman and yet worse than inhuman in its travesty of humanity; something that made you hate the world and your fellows, that made you hate yourself for being ever so little in *this* image. A more abhorrent spectacle I have never seen . . . . .

So soon as I could turn my eyes from the ghastly thing, I looked at Corner. He was white as the plaster faces about him. His immensely opened eyes showed his astonishment and his terror. For what I experienced was intensified in his case by the unexpected and complete disillusionment. He had opened the door of the tabernacle, and out had crawled a noisome spider; he had lifted to his lips the communion cup, and therein squatted a toad. A sort of murmur of frantic protestation began to rise in his throat; but Peschi, unconscious of our agitation, now lifted the lamp, passed round with it behind the mask, held it high, and let the rays stream downwards from above.

The astounding way the face changed must have been seen to be believed in. It was exactly as though, by some cunning sleight of hand, the mask of a god had been substituted for that of a satyr . . . . . You saw a splendid dome-like head, Shakespearean in contour; a broad, smooth, finely-modelled brow; thick, regular, horizontal eyebrows, casting a shadow which diminished the too great distance separating them from the eyes; while the deeper shadow thrown below the nose altered its character entirely. Its snout-like appearance was gone, its deep, wide-open, upturned nostrils were hidden, but you noticed the well-marked transition from forehead to nose-base, the broad ridge denoting extraordinary mental power. Over the eyeballs the lids had slidden down smooth and creaseless; the little tell-tale palpebral wrinkles which had given such libidinous lassitude to the eye had vanished away. The lips no longer looked gross, and they closed together in a beautiful, sinuous line, now first revealed by the shadow on the upper one. The prominence of the jaws, the muscularity of the lower part of the face, which gave it so painfully microcephalous an appearance, were now unnoticeable; on the contrary, the whole face looked small beneath the noble head and brow. You remarked the medium-sized and well-formed ears, with the 'swan' distinct in each, the gently-swelling breadth of head above them, the full development of the forehead over the orbits of the eyes. You discerned the presence of those higher qualities which might have rendered him an ascetic or a saint; which led him to understand the beauty of self-denial, to appreciate the wisdom of self-restraint; and you did not see how these qualities remained inoperative in him, being completely overbalanced by the size of the lower brain, the thick, bull throat, and the immense length from the ear to the base of the skull at the back.

I had often seen the Master in life: I had seen him sipping *absinthe* at the d'Harcourt; reeling, a Silemus-like figure, among the nocturnal Bacchantes of the Boul' Miche; lying in the gutter outside his house, until his mistress should come to pick him up and take him in. I had seen in the living man more traces than a few of the bestiality which the death-mask had completely verified; but never in the living man had I suspected anything of the beauty, of the splendour, that I now saw.

For that the Master had somewhere a beautiful soul you divined from his works; from the exquisite melody of all of them, from the pure, the ecstatic, the religious altitude of some few. But in actual daily life, his loose and violent will-power, his insane passions, held that soul bound down so close a captive, that those who knew him best were the last to admit its existence.

And here, a mere accident of lighting displayed not only that existence, but its visible, outward expression as well. In these magnificent lines and arches of head and brow, you saw what the man might have been, what God had intended him to be; what his mother had foreseen in him, when, a tiny infant like Peschi's yonder, she had cradled the warm, downy, sweet-smelling little head upon her bosom, and dreamed day-dreams of all the high, the great, the wonderful things her boy later on was to do. You saw what the poor, purblind, middle-aged mistress was the only one to see in the seamed and ravaged face she kissed so tenderly for the last time before the coffin-lid was closed.

You saw the head of gold; you could forget the feet of clay, or, remembering them, you found for the first time some explanation of the anomalies of his career.

You understood how he who could pour out passionate protestations of love and devotion to God in the morning, offering up body and soul, flesh and blood in his service; dedicating his brow as a footstool for the Sacred Feet; his hands as censers for the glowing coals, the precious incense; condemning his eyes, misleading lights, to be extinguished by the tears of prayer; you understood how, nevertheless, before evening was come, he would set every law of God and decency at defiance, use every member, every faculty, in the service of sin.

It was given to him, as it is given to few, to see the Best, to reverence it, to love it; and the blind, groping hesitatingly forward in the darkness, do not stray as far as he strayed.

He knew the value of work, its imperative necessity; that in the sweat of his brow the artist, like the day-labourer, must produce, must produce; and he spent his slothful days shambling from café to café.

He never denied his vices; he recognised them and found excuses for them, high moral reasons even, as the intellectual man can always do. To indulge them was but to follow out the dictates of Nature, who in herself is holy; cynically to expose them to the world was but to be absolutely sincere.

And his disciples, going further, taught with a vague poetic mysticism that he was a fresh Incarnation of the Godhead; that what was called his immorality was merely his scorn of truckling to the base conventions of the world. But in his saner moments he described himself more accurately as a man blown hither and thither by the winds of evil chance, just as a withered leaf is blown in autumn; and having received great and exceptional gifts, with Shakespeare's length of years in which to turn them to account, he had chosen instead to wallow in such vileness that his very name was anathema among honourable men.

Chosen? Did he choose? Can one say after all that he chose to resemble the leaf rather than the tree? The gates of gifts close on the child with the womb, and all we possess comes to us from afar, and is collected from a thousand diverging sources.

If that splendid head and brow were contained in the seed, so also were the retreating chin, the debased jaw, the animal mouth. One as much as the other was the direct inheritance of former generations. Considered in a certain aspect, it seems that a man by taking thought, may as little hope to thwart the implanted propensities of his character, as to alter the shape of his skull or the size of his jawbone.

I lost myself in mazes of predestination and free-will. Life appeared to me as a huge kaleidoscope turned by the hand of Fate. The atoms of glass coalesce into patterns, fall apart, unite together again, are always the same, but always different, and, shake the glass never so slightly, the precise combination you have just been looking at is broken up for ever. It can never be repeated. This particular man, with his faults and his virtues, his unconscious brutalities, his unexpected gentlenesses, his furies of remorse; this man with the lofty brain, the perverted tastes, the weak, irresolute, indulgent heart, will never again be met with to the end of time; in all the endless combinations to come, this precise combination will never be found. Just as of all the faces the world will see, a face like the mask there will never again exchange glances with it . . . . .

I looked at Corner, and saw his countenance once more aglow with the joy of a recovered Ideal; while Peschi's voice broke in on my reverie, speaking with the happy pride of the artist in a good and conscientious piece of work.

'Eh bien, how do you find it?' said he; 'it is beautiful, is it not?'

THE SAVOY

Ellen

Rudolph Dircks

Rudolf Dircks (dates unknown) was an author, playwright, editor and art historian. 'Ellen', his only contribution to *The Savoy*, is one of several New

Woman fictions of the era. Seen by some critics of *The Savoy* as mere masculine titillation, the work can be read as a strident rejection of the dominant, bourgeois sexual mores of the period, with a distinctly proto-feminist edge.

The story revolves around a young woman's choice for social, financial and sexual independence, as defined against the contemporary norms of marriage and female subjugation. The careful delineation of Ellen's social and intellectual status marks her out as quite distinct from the typical 'ruined maid' of Victorian melodrama: hers is an informed choice and one which both fulfils and empowers her as an individual, independent woman. The anonymity of her chosen, would-be partner only serves to accentuate the female-centric nature of the tale. 'Ellen' does, however, conform to certain stereotypes. Ellen is once more an orphan, linking the tale to the wider world of pornography, and this rebellious character is plagued by a typically Decadent, morbid self-absorption. Yet Dircks's carefully crafted ending suspends any moral judgement.

※

She had now been a waitress at the little *café* off Cheapside for something over two years; her circumstances had not changed during that time; she herself had scarcely changed; her features had, perhaps, developed a little and become more defined, her manner less hesitating — and that was all. That was all, at least, that was noticeable. A great change, however, had occurred in her between then and now that was not noticeable; that silent, miraculous change, so imperceptible, so profound, which works in a woman between the ages of eighteen and twenty.

She had come during those two years to have an exaggerated, almost a morbid idea of her own want of good looks; she had observed that regular frequenters of the *café* — young city-clerks, journalists and the rest — avoided the series of marble-topped tables at which she served for those which were attended by other girls smarter and prettier; she rarely received the little attentions which the other girls among themselves proclaimed. It was the stray customer, the bird of passage, who kept her busy. But, as a matter of fact, it was not her want of good looks that kept the younger men aloof; it was something in her manner, an absence, perhaps, of that fictitious spirit of gaiety, of that alert responsiveness, which men find so arresting in women. Really, she was not at all bad-looking.

Still, this neglect ate into her heart a little. She regretted her want of adaptability, of the faculty of being able to assume all those charming (as they seemed to her) little airs and graces, partly natural, partly cultivated, which so became the other girls; she, it is true, rather despised these coquetries of her companions, but her own deficiencies of the sort made her feel at times particularly dull and stupid and angry with herself. One or two of the girls at the *café* had, during her time, married one or two of the young men who came there, and would afterwards pay an occasional visit to the place, certainly in pretty frocks, and, to all appearance, radiant and happy. But these girls were fortunate. Others, again, had suddenly disappeared, and none knew whither; but as their disappearance happened to be simultaneous with a break in the regular attendance of certain customers, dark stories were whispered to which the non-appearance of the missing ones seemed to lend colour.

After a while, Ellen did not mind so much being neglected; the smart of the sting became less and less painful, till finally, she rather, if anything, preferred escaping the attentions which fell to the share of the other girls. This may have been partly owing to the view which she came to take of men; her position had provided her with opportunities for arriving at a generalisation, and she came to think of men as either silly or wicked — silly, when they were attracted by the trivial insincerities of the girls in the *café*; wicked, when they took advantage of their rarer simplicity. She did not conceive, now, that she would ever fall in love, that anyone would ever fall in love with her.

All the same, as the two years advanced, Ellen began to feel a curious isolation of the heart, an emptiness which she never attributed to the absence of a lover. Besides, she had an intuitive suspicion that she possessed qualities which would be fatal to her retaining the affections of a husband, that there would be little joy for her in the companionship which would place her in the position of a wife. Not that she thought anything very clearly about these things; the vague emotions and sensations which moved her, the detached things which floated in her mind had not yet found the relief which comes with realisation; her impulses were not remotely guided by self-consciousness. A sense of loneliness oppressed her, which was not diminished by the companionship of her fellow servants at the *café*, and she wanted companionship of some sort. It was dreadful for her at times to feel so much alone, to feel that there was nothing in the world, in this great London, which she really cared for; that there was no one, since the death of her father and mother, who really cared for her.

She had this sense of loneliness even in the busiest time of the day, when an enormous wave of traffic swept by outside the *café*, and, inside, all was stir and movement. Even amid all this stir and din, when she was occupied in flitting from one table to another, in taking orders and attending to them, even at such moments her thoughts would be playing to another tune, her soul would be filled with unrest and impatience. Life, indeed, became a great struggle for her. Sometimes she said to herself that she would run away — from she knew not what, where she knew not to; and sometimes she wished very sincerely that she were dead.

. . . . She had seen many strange faces during those two years; at last it began to dawn upon her that one of these faces which had been strange was becoming familiar: a face with a fair, pointed beard and blue eyes. Beyond, however, merely ordering what he wanted, he had not spoken to her; it was improbable that he had noticed her; but his regular attendance at the tables at which she served began to attract the attention of the other girls, who derived some entertainment from hinting to Ellen that she was carrying on a flirtation, a suggestion which happened to be sufficiently inappropriate to appeal to their sense of humour. It was in keeping with Ellen's temperament that no romantic ideas entered her head at this point, where, possibly, the least susceptible of her companions would — as women will — have woven a complete fabric of foolish sentiment. Still, as he continued to come regularly, she began involuntarily to feel a certain liking for him; the fact of his never attempting to enter into any sort of conversation with her had its not unpleasant side for her. So, by-and-by, they both seemed to begin to know each other in this silent way. And yet there came moments when Ellen felt somehow that she would like to talk to him, like to tell him all about herself, and what she felt. His presence accentuated a dimly-realised need for self-expression, of pouring into some ear the flood of vague sentiments which possessed her. She could not talk to the other girls; they would not understand, or they would laugh at her; but she could, she felt, talk to this fair-bearded man with the blue eyes. But not at the *café*; she would rather remain silent for ever than do that. Then, how?

This idea of speaking to him, of sharing with him her whole confidence, seized upon her, and developed with an intensity which caused her ceaseless perturbation and pain.

After a little time, indeed, they drifted, naturally enough, into a conventional intercourse, almost monosyllabic, uninteresting, which seemed to her hopelessly trivial — but how to advance beyond it! Once or twice she thought she observed a look of interrogation in the blue eyes, a look which invited her confidence, and, at the same time, occasioned her a poignant feeling of self-consciousness — there, at the *café*, while meeting the significant glances, the partly ironical, partly suggestive, glances of her companions. No! she could not speak to him there; she had nothing to say to him there. Yet it was hard to resist the appeal of his eyes.

'You are looking pale. Do you go out much?' he said to her one day.

'No; only home and back.'

'Ah! you should.'

'We don't close till seven,' she said. Then, their eyes meeting, she continued irresistibly: 'Will you meet me to-night?'

It was not till an hour or so later that she realised that she was to meet him that evening at the principal entrance to St. Paul's; that she realised that she herself had made the appointment. She had leapt the barrier, and was shocked at the extent of her daring, a little humiliated even; yet, above everything, singularly elated and careless. She had never breathed so freely.

But when they met, the need for self-expression was no longer apparent; she only felt stupid and shy. He suggested that they should go to a theatre or to an exhibition at Earl's Court, but she would not go to either place. Then they walked along the Embankment, between Blackfriars' Bridge and Charing Cross. He talked a good deal, but she hardly caught or understood what he said, and was quietly irresponsive. There was in his manner an air of familiarity which slightly repelled her; she began to wish that she had not, after all, asked him to meet her; to think of abruptly leaving him. Once he put his arm through hers, and was surprised at the startled expression which sprang to her face as she quickly drew apart from him. After this his manner changed, and she felt more at ease. The incident had defined her attitude.

Reaching the gardens on the Embankment, near Charing Cross, they entered a gate and sat on one of the seats. There were some children playing about on the path whose antics amused her, and led her to talk about her own childhood, to tell him of those dear, half-forgotten things which everyone remembers so well, of that dim world of curious fancies which all of us at one time inhabited. He was sympathetic, and they talked on so in the fading light until it was time for the gates of the garden to be closed. As they passed through them, their intimacy had become as natural and easy as she could have dared to hope.

They crossed the Strand and penetrated the maze of streets which lead in the direction of King's Cross, where she had her lodging. And now all the things that had lain in her mind, all the incoherent emotions that had possessed her, became coherent and simple, derived shape and form in the attempt to express them. She told him all about her present life, about the other girls in the *café* and their sentimental episodes. She told him of the feeling of loneliness, of abstraction, of the vague itching at her heart which never ceased.

At last they reached a house in one of the outlying streets of Regent Square.

'I don't know why I asked you to meet me to-night,' she said, stopping at the door of this house; 'I don't know what is the matter with me. But I wanted to speak to someone. And I couldn't speak to the other girls; they would only have made fun of me, I think. I feel happier now that I have had a nice long talk with someone — still — there is something — something ─────' She paused a moment, and then proceeded, rather abruptly: 'I don't want to be married, the same as most girls do; I don't like men, as a rule — at least, not in that way . . . besides, I think I should always be happier remaining as I am at present, working for myself, independent.'

She gave a little shriek of delight at a thought which suddenly occurred to her, a flash of mental illumination, which enabled her to divine the source of all her perplexities, which instantly enabled her to solve the problem of her happiness; a thought which filled her poor, empty heart. 'I think,' she said, softly, 'if I had a baby, my very own, I should want nothing — nothing in this world more than that!' Her lips quivered and tears came into her eyes, exquisitely tender tears.

She then turned to the door and opened it with a latch-key.

'Are you living alone?' he asked.

'Yes, quite alone,' she said, retreating into the passage without turning.

He followed her a couple of paces, and then stood with one foot on the doorstep. He looked into the passage, but could not make out whether she were standing there in the dark or not. He wondered if she were standing there. Then taking the handle of the door he drew it gently to, and went down the street.

To Nancy

Frederick Wedmore

Sir Frederick Wedmore (1844–1921; knighted in 1912) was a respected art critic, editor and author, and both his criticism and fiction display a marked French influence. The tale of Nancy Nanson was a source of pride for Wedmore; in his *Memories* (1912), he recalled the story's positive reception, citing the opinion of 'a sometime Acting Manager' of the Empire theatre, who 'knew familiarly the subject'. Indeed the central relationship of a fashionable artist taking a young dancer for his muse was a common coupling, as may be gleaned from artwork included in The Yellow Book.

The story charts the progress, or decline, of the young Nancy from provincial theatre to the London music halls. Like Selwyn Image's 'Bundle of Letters' it takes the partial form of letters between the elder Clement Ashton R. A. and the girl. Similarly, the initial tone is one of bland advice coupled with avuncular concern. However, as the tale develops, the girl's blossoming sexual maturity causes problems on both sides of the correspondence. Wedmore draws attention to the one-sidedness of letters, and Ashton's repeated concern over the disparity between the public and private Nancy all encourage the reader to theorise as to the true nature of the 'whole' story. His descriptions of Nancy, from her 'monstrously refined' form to her erotically charged dance, coupled with his own fevered dreams about the girl, feelings of jealousy and confession of 'hidden thoughts', all reveal a more lurid picture than the one Ashton is consciously revealing in his letters.

Weymouth, 29th September.

It happens that I have seen much of you, Nancy, at an eventful moment — eventful for yourself I mean, in your life and your career — and here, because I like you, and like to think of and reflect on you, there is written down, straight and full, the record of my impression; concealing nothing, though written to yourself: a letter absolutely frank, looking all facts in the face; for, young though you are, you are intelligent enough to bear them. My letter you may find tedious, perhaps, but at all events unusual; for letters, even when detailed, generally omit much, hide some part of a thought — put the thing in a way that pleases the writer, or is intended to please the receiver. Here am I at the end of my first page, Nancy, and all preface! Well, I shall recall, to begin with, how it was that I met you.

Acquit me, please, of any general love of your over-praised Music Hall. Neither it nor the Theatre counts for much in my life. I like you personally: I imagine a Future for you; but I am not anxious for 'the status of the profession'. Life, it is just possible, has other goals than that of being received in smart drawing-rooms — whatever art you practise, its practice is your reward. Society, my dear, has bestowed of late upon the stage 'lover' an attention that is misplaced. We are getting near the end of it: the *cabotin*, in a frock coat, no longer dominates the situation at afternoon teas. Youths from the green-room have, in the Past, over the luncheon-table, imparted to me, with patronage, their views about Painting; to me, Nancy, to your old friend, who has painted for thirty years — a full Academician one year since, with but few honours (as men call them) left to gain: few years, alas! in which to live to gain them. Child as you are, your common sense — that neatly-balanced little mind of yours, so unusually clear — that neatly-balanced mind assures you that it is not the profession you follow, but what you have been able to do in it, and what you really are, that gives you — I mean, of course, gives any one — legitimate claim to be in privileged places, to be motioned to the velvet of the social sward. 'Artist', indeed! As well expect to be received with welcome for having had sufficient capital to buy a camp stool and a few feet of German moulding with which to frame a canvas sent to the Dudley Gallery, as to be suffered to dictate and to dogmatise in virtue of a well-worn coat and an appearance at a London theatre!

You have read so far, and yet I have not reminded you how it was that you and I came to know each other. It was just two years ago, in this same town from which I write to you. I saw a photograph that struck me, at the door of your place of entertainment — at the door of the 'People's Delight'. The face was young — but I have known youth. Pretty, it was — but a fashionable portrait-painter lives with prettiness. It was so monstrously refined!

At three o'clock, they said, there would be an entertainment — Miss Nancy Nanson would certainly be seen. And in I went, with a companion — old Sir James Purchas, of Came Manor — my host more than once in these parts. Sir James, you know, is not a prey to the exactions of conventionality, and there was no reason why the humble entertainment your lounge and shelter offered to the tripper should not afford us half an hour's amusement.

The blazing September afternoon you recollect – September with the glare of the dog days. The 'people', it seemed, were not profiting that day by the 'People's Delight', for the place was all but empty — everyone out of doors — and we wandered, not aimlessly indeed, but not successfully, among those cavernous, half-darkened regions, among the stalls for fruits and sweets and cheap jewellery, in search of a show. A turn, and we came suddenly on rows of empty chairs placed in front of a small stage, with drawn curtain; and, at a money-taker's box (for reserved seats, as I supposed) — leaning over the money-taker's counter, in talk with someone who came, it may be, from a selling-stall — there was a child, a little girl. Sir James touched my arm, directing my attention to her, and I took the initiative — said to the little girl: 'We came to see Miss Nancy Nanson. You can tell us, perhaps, when is the show going to begin?' 'There won't be any entertainment this afternoon,' the girl answered; 'because, you see, there isn't any audience. I am Miss Nancy Nanson.' The dignity of the child!

The fact was, you remember, that photograph at the entrance gave the impression of a girl of seventeen; and I did not at all connect it with the figure of the well-spoken, silver-voiced, elegant child, who proved to be yourself — since then my model and my youthful friend. But the moment you spoke, and when my eyes, still not quite used to the obscurity, took in your real face and those refined expressions, the identity was established, though the photograph, with its dexterous concealment, showed more the Nancy Nanson you were going to be, than the Nancy Nanson you were. I was pleased, nevertheless; and we talked about yourself for a few minutes; and when you said (because I asked you) that there would be an entertainment next day, I told you we would come to see it, certainly. And Sir James was indulgent. And I am a man of my word.

And now there is a bit we can afford to hurry over; for the next stage of our acquaintance does not advance, appreciably, the action of your story. We came; we saw your entertainment: your three turns; singing, dancing; and pretty enough it was; but yet, so-so. You were such a pleasant child, of course we applauded you — so refined, yet singing, tolerably, such nonsense. Even then, it was your charming little personality, you know — it was not your performance that had in it attractiveness. Next day, I left the neighbourhood.

For two years after that, I never saw Miss Nancy Nanson, 'vocalist and dancer'; only once heard of and read of you — only once, perhaps, thought of you. The once was last Christmas — your name I saw was advertised in a pantomime played by 'juveniles'. I might, it is just possible, have gone to see it. But the average 'juvenile!' — think! — and then, the influenza and the weather!

Well! this present glowing September, Nancy — glowing and golden as it was two years ago — brought me again, and very differently, into touch with you. The Past is over. Now I fix your attention — for you are still patient with me — I fix your attention on the Present, and I point out to you, in detail — I realise to myself — how the time is critical, eventful;

how you stand, Nancy, upon a certain brink. I am not going to prophesy what you may be; but I tell you what you are. The real You, you know: something better and deeper than that which those seven pastels, any or all of them together, show you — my delighted notes of your external beauty; touched, I think, with some charm of grace that answers well to your own; and mimicking, not badly, the colours and contours of your stage presence. Nothing more. Chance gleams — an artist's 'snap-shots' at Miss Nancy Nanson, vocalist and dancer, at sixteen. (Sixteen yesterday.) But *you* — No!

This present September — a fortnight since — I came again to Weymouth; this time alone; putting up at the old 'Gloucester' (it was George the Third's house) from which I write to you; and not at Came Manor in the neighbourhood. In the Weymouth of to-day one is obliged, in nearly every walk, to pass the 'People's Delight' — your cheap vulgarity, my dear, that the great Georgian time would have resented. I passed it soon, and the two names biggest upon the bills were, 'Achilles, the Strong Man' — there are things in which even a decayed watering place cannot afford to be behind the fashion — 'Achilles, the Strong Man', then, and 'Miss Nancy Nanson'. Again did I go in; took the seat, exactly, that I had taken two years since, in the third row of chairs; and while a band of three made casual, lifeless, introductory music, I waited for the show.

The curtain rose presently on a great, living, breathing, over-energetic statue — a late Renaissance bronze, by John of Bologna, he seemed — that muscular piece of colour and firm form, that nigger, posed effectively, and of prodigious force. 'John of Bologna' — but you never heard of him! Then he began his operations — Achilles, the Strong Man — holding, and only by his teeth, enormous weights; and rushing round with one, two, hundredweight, as if it were a feather; lifting, with that jaw of his, masses of iron; crashing them on the stage again, and standing afterwards with quivering muscles, heaving chest. Applause — I joined in it myself in common courtesy — and then the curtain fell.

A wait. The band struck up again — it was your first turn. A slim and dainty figure, so very slight, so very young, in a lad's evening dress, advanced with swiftness towards the footlights, and bowed in a wide sweep that embraced everyone. Then you began to sing — and not too well, you know — a song of pretty-enough sentiment; the song of a stripling whose sweetheart was his mother. His mother, she sufficed for him. It suited your young years. A tender touch or two, and with a boy's manliness. Applause! You vanished.

You vanished to return. In a girl's dress this time, with movements now more swift and now more graceful. Another song, and this time dancing with it. It was dancing you were born for. 'She has grown another being — and yet with the old pleasantness — in these two years,' I thought. 'A child no longer.' In colour and agility you were a brilliant show. I have told you since, in talking, what I thought of you. You were not a Sylvia Grey, my dear; still less that other Sylvia Voltaire praised, contrasting her with the Camargo. The Graces danced like Sylvia, Voltaire said — like the Camargo, the wild nymphs. No! you were not Voltaire's Sylvia, any more than you were Sylvia Grey. Sylvia Grey's dance is perfect, from the waist upwards — as an observant actress pointed out to me, with whom I saw it. Swan-like in the holding and slow movement of the head and neck; exquisite in the undulations of the torso. Where Sylvia Grey ends — I mean where her remarkableness ends (for she has legs like another, I take it) — you, my dear, begin. But you want an Ingres to do you justice. The slimness of the girl, and what a fineness, as of race; and then, the agility of infinite practice, and sixteen young years!

A third turn — then it was that you were agile most of all. The flying feet went skyward. Black shoes rushed, comet-like, so far above your head, and clattered on the floor again; whilst against the sober crimson of the background curtain — a dull, thin stuff, stretched straightly — gleamed the white of moving skirts, and blazed the boss of brightest scarlet that nestled somewhere in the brown gold of your head. Then, flushed and panting, it was over.

Next day, in a gaunt ante-room, or extra chamber, its wooden floor quite bare, and the place furnished only with a couple of benches and a half-voiceless semi-grand piano — the wreck of an Erard that was great once — in that big, bare room, Nancy, where my pastels since have caught your pose in lilac, rose and orange, but never your grave character, I came upon, and closely noted, and, for a quarter of an hour, talked to, a sedate young girl in black — a lady who, in all her bearing, ways, gesture, silver voice, was as refined as any, young or old, that I have been in contact with in my long life — and I have lived abundantly amongst great ladies, from stately, restful Quakeress to the descendant of the 'hundred Earls'. No one is more refined than you. This thing may not last with you. Whether it lasts depends, in great measure, upon the life you lead, in the strange world opening to you. Your little craft, Nancy, your slender skiff, will have some day to labour over voluminous seas.

You remember what you told me, in the great ante-room, standing by the wreck of the Erard, that your fingers touched. All your life to that time. You were frankness absolutely; standing there in your dull, black frock that became you to perfection; standing with hat of broad, black straw — the clear-cut nose, the faultless mouth, the bright-brown hair curled short about your head, and the limpid look of your serene eyes, steadily grey. It was interesting, and amusing too, your story. I told you, you remember, how much you had got on, how changed you were, what progress I had noticed. And you said a pretty 'Thank you'. It was clear that you meant it. We were friends. I asked who taught you — so far as anything *can* be taught in this world, where, at bottom, one's way is, after all, one's own. You said, your mother. And I told you I'd seen your name in some London Christmas play-bill. 'I had a big success,' you said. What a theatrical moment it was! — the one occasion in all my little dealings with you in which I found the traditions of 'the profession' stronger with you than your own personal character. Now, your own personal instinct is to be modest and natural; the traditions of 'the profession' are to boast. You did boast, Nancy! You had a big success, had you? Perhaps, for yourself; I do not say you failed. But the piece — my dear, you know it was a frost. Did it run three weeks? Come now! And someone, out of jealousy, paid four guineas — she or her friends did — to get you a bad notice somewhere in back-stairs journalism. And they got it, and then repented of it. You were friends with them afterwards. But what a world, Nancy! — a world in which, for four guineas, a scoundrel contributes his part towards damning your career!

You remember, before I asked if I might make some sketches of you, you were turning over a song that had been sent you by 'a gentleman at Birmingham'. He had had it 'ruled' for you, and wanted you to buy it for three pounds. It was 'rather a silly song', you thought. I settled myself quietly to master the sense, or, as was more probable, the nonsense, of it. My dear, it was blank rubbish! But you were not going to have it, you said, 'Mamma would never buy a song I didn't like and take to.' That was well, I thought. And then you slowly closed the ruined Erard, and were going away. But on the road down-stairs, remember, I persuaded you to ask your mother that you might give me sittings. I told you who I was. And in the gaunt ante-room, lit well from above, I had a sitting next day. It was the first of several. And your mother trusted me, and trusted you, as you deserve to be trusted. And we worked hard together, didn't we? — you posing, and I drawing. And there are seven pastels which record — *tant bien que mal*, my dear — the delightful outside of you, the side the public might itself see, if it had eyes to really see — the flash of you in the dance, snow-white or carmine; and I got all that with alacrity — 'swift means' I took, to 'radiant ends' — the poise of the slim figure, the white frock slashed with gold, the lifted foot, and that gleam of vivid scarlet in your hair against the background of most sober crimson.

This tranquil Sunday I devote to writing to you, is the day after your last appearance at the 'People's Delight'. You and your mother, very soon, you tell me, leave Weymouth and your old associations — it is your home, you know — and you leave it for ever. The country, you admit, is beautiful, but you are tired of the place. I don't much wonder. And you leave it — the great bay, the noble chalk downs, the peace of Dorset and its gleaming quiet — you leave it for lodgings in the Waterloo Road. For you must be among the agents for the Halls. Though you have been upon the Stage since you were very little, you have but lately, so you say, put your heart into it. Well! it is not unnatural. But no more Sunday drives into the lovely country, recollect, with your brother, who is twenty-one and has his trade; and your uncle, who is in a good way of business here, you said — your uncle, the plumber.

And so, last night being your last night, Nancy, it was almost like a Benefit. As for your dancing, you meant, I knew, to give us the cup filled — yes, filled and running over. I had noticed that, on some earlier evening, when Little Lily Somebody — a dumpling child, light of foot, but with not one 'line' in all her meaningless, fat form — when Little Lily Somebody had capered her infantile foolishness, to the satisfaction of those who rejoice in mere babyhood, someone presented her with a bouquet. And you danced, excellently, just after her — you, height and grace, slimness and soul — and someone, with much effusion, handed you up a box of chocolates. And you smiled pleasantly. I saw there was a little conflict in your mind, however, between the gracious recognition of what was well-enough meant, and the resentment — well, the resentment we can hardly call it; the regret, at all events — at being treated so very visibly as a child — and yesterday you were to be sixteen! So I myself — who, if this small indignity had not been offered you, might conceivably have given you, in private, at all events, a basket of fine fruit — I meant to offer you flowers. It might have been fruit, I say, if smuggled into the ante-room where I had done my pastels; for I had seen you once there, crunching, quite happily, imperfect apples between perfect teeth — your perfect teeth, almost the only perfect things, Nancy, in an imperfect world.

But it had to be flowers. So I sent round to the dressing-room, just as you were getting ready, two button-holes merely — wired button-holes — of striped carnations, red or wine-coloured. They were not worn in your first turn. They were not worn in your second. In your third turn, I espied them at your neck's side, in the fury of your dance. Already there are people, I suppose, who would have thought those striped carnations happy — tossed, tossed to pieces, in the warmth of your throat.

Your second turn, last night, you know, was in flowing white, slashed with gold — old-gold velvet — with pale stockings. The third — when the flowers died happy in your riot — in pure white alone, with stockings black. You remember the foot held in your hand, as you swing round upon the other toe — and one uplifted leg seen horizontal, in its straight and modelled slimness.

My dear — what were my little flowers? Who could have known — when you had finished — the great things still to come? When the applause seemed over, and the enthusiasm of some lieutenant from Dorchester was, as I take it, abated and suppressed — when the applause was over, a certain elocutionist (Mr. Paris Brown, wasn't it?) brought you again upon the stage, and saying it was your last appearance, made you some presentation: a brooch from himself, 'of no intrinsic value' he informed us — I willingly believed him — a bracelet from I don't know who — that *had* an 'intrinsic value', I surmise — and a bouquet, exquisite. It was 'From an admirer', Mr. Paris Brown, the elocutionist, read out, from an accompanying card. Then he congratulated you upon your Past; prophesied as to your Future; and, in regard to the presents to you, he said, in words that were quite happily chosen — because, Nancy, they were reticent while they were expressive — 'She is but a — *girl*; and she has done her duty by the management. Long may she be a credit to her father and mother!' Your mother I was well aware of — your mother I respect; and you, you love her. But your father — he was invented, I think, for the occasion, as an additional protection, should the designs upon you of the admirer from Dorchester prove to be not altogether such as they ought to be. The precaution was unnecessary; it was taking Time by the forelock. Our young friend looked ingenuous, and smitten grievously — you seem so big upon the stage, Nancy — so grown up, I mean. I could, I think, have toned down his emotions, had I told him you were a bare sixteen.

Nancy, there is — for me — a certain pathos in this passage of yours from childhood into ripening girlhood; a book closed, as it were; a phase completed; an ending of the way. 'What chapter is to open? Nancy Nanson

— what phase or facet of her life,' I ask myself, 'is now so soon to be presented? What other way, what unfamiliar one, is to follow her blameless and dutiful childhood?' I had a restless night, Nancy. Thinking of this, one saw — ridiculously perhaps — a presage in the first bouquet, a threat in the first bracelet — in the admirer's card. Would she be like the rest? — at least, too many. Besmirched, too?

Remember, Nancy, I am no Puritan at all. I recognise Humanity's instincts. There is little I do not tolerate. I recognise the gulf that separates the accidentally impolitic from the essentially wrong. But we owe things to other people — to the World's laws. We have responsibilities. *Noblesse oblige*; and all superiority is *Noblesse*. 'She must not be like the rest,' I said, last night, in broken dreams; 'dining, winking, leering even, since sold at last and made common.' In broken dreams, last night — or in wakeful hours — your feet tossed higher; your gay blood passed into the place — electrical, overpowering. You can be so grave and sweet, you know; and you can be so mad.

Have you ever lain awake, in the great, long darkness, and watched in the darkness a procession — the people of your Past and all your Future? But you have no Past. For myself, I have watched them. My mother, who is long gone; those who were good to me, and whom I slighted; the relations who failed me; the friend I lost. And the uncertain figures of the Future! But the line of the Future is short enough for me — for you, it is all yours. Last night, it seemed to me, the dark was peopled with your enemies; with your false friends, who were coming — always coming — the unavoidable crowd of the egotistic destroyers of youth. Their dark hearts, I thought, look upon her as a prey; some of them cruel, some of them cynical, yet some of them only careless. And I wished that last night had not come — your sixteenth birthday — with the applause and gifts and menacing triumph.

There are women, perhaps, men cannot wrong — since they have wronged themselves too much. 'This is a good girl,' I said; and my over-anxious mind — in real affection for her — cries out to all the horrid forces of the world: 'Leave Nancy!'

Nancy, when you read this, you smile — and naturally — at your most sombre friend. You think, of course, with all the reckless trust, courageous confidence, of girlhood, 'So superfluous! So unnecessary!'

Go the straight way! . . . Whatever way you go, I shall always be your friend.

The Deterioration of Nancy

Frederick Wedmore

In this second part of the tale, Wedmore's repeated, and pointed instructions to read far more into the story than is actually printed, reveal a somewhat typical tale of a young music-hall performer's fall from grace; yet what is far more intriguing is the suggestion of Ashton's own sexual perversions. Clearly horrified by Nancy's maturing body and personality, his emotions swing between sexual attraction and revulsion. In an example of what Ronald Pearsall has called the late-Victorian 'cult of the little girl', Ashton attempts to overcome these unruly emotions with a forced, grandfatherly concern, coupled with a wish for her to remain forever a child. His repeated desire that she not be like 'the others' suggests the Freudian notion of recurrent behavioural patterns stemming from the repression, and attempted sublimation of natural sexual instincts.

[I have obtained access to the remaining portion of the Correspondence between a distinguished member of the Royal Academy and Miss Nancy Nanson, of the Variety Stage. I see that the young lady's are the more numerous and the shorter letters; and in them, as they proceed, I seem to discern some change of tone — a rather quick transition or development (call it what you will) which, if it is really there, is unlikely to have escaped the eye of her correspondent, and may perhaps even have prepared him in a certain measure for a *dénouement* which, nevertheless, when it arrived, disturbed him seriously. That, at least, is my own reading of Miss Nanson's notes. But I am possibly wrong.]

WEYMOUTH:
September 25th.

DEAR MR. ASHTON.

As I suppose you leave Weymouth to-day I will send this to London. It is only to thank you very much for your long letter and your kindness to me, in which Mother joins. I hope you are well.

I remain yours very sincerely
NANCY NANSON.

MR. CLEMENT ASHTON.

100 YORK ROAD, WATERLOO ROAD.
Oct. 20.

DEAR MR. ASHTON

I thought I should like to let you know that I have come to London. I have not an engagement yet, but I have a pantomime engagement in view.

With best wishes I remain yours sincerely

NANCY NANSON.

CLEMENT ASHTON, ESQ: R.A.

100 YORK ROAD, WATERLOO ROAD.
Nov. 5.

DEAR MR. ASHTON

I was so sorry I was out when you called. If I had known you were coming I would have stayed at home. We are all right here. The landlady is awfully nice. I would come and see you if you appointed a time.

I think you will be glad to hear that I'm engaged for principal girl for the Pantomime at the Theatre Royal, Hoxton, by R. Solomon, Esq. In about a month we shall begin rehearsing. I am engaged for eight weeks.

We hope you are well.

Hoping to see you soon, with my best wishes, in which Mother unites, I am yours very sincerely,

NANCY NANSON.

100 YORK ROAD, WATERLOO ROAD,
November 20.

DEAR MR. ASHTON

It was so kind of you to take me to the theatre yesterday afternoon. I must write to tell you so. How nice Miss Annie Hughes was! She makes you laugh and cry. I like her more than any actress I have ever seen. The man was funny, wasn't he!

Thanking you again, and with best regards from Mother, believe me yours very sincerely

NANCY NANSON.

P.S. I am to do an extra on Saturday nights at the Bedford Camden Town, and at Gatti's, Westminster Bridge Road. I am very pleased, as I am tired of 'resting'. When we go to Hoxton we shall take lodgings where there is a piano. I have been practising an acrobatic trick for the pantomime. The public likes them. The Theatre Royal, Hoxton, is more for the masses than the classes.

THE WALK, HOXTON,
Christmas Day.

DEAR MR. ASHTON

O! thank you for remembering us on Christmas Day. I was so pleased. We hope you will come to see the Panto. It went very well last night. I go very well so far. My voice sounds splendid here. It is not lost in the glass roof, as at the 'People's Delight'.

I have been so very, very busy rehearsing, I have seen very little of Hoxton yet, so I do not know how I shall like it. I shall know better soon; now that we have started the Panto.

With best wishes for a happy Christmas from Mother and from me, I am yours sincerely and gratefully, in haste,

NANCY NANSON.

THE WALK, HOXTON,
6th January.

I am glad you came to see me yesterday afternoon. How did you like me? But it was so flat. I am sorry you came to a matinée. Half the house are mere *children*, then. In the evening it is different. And they cut out part of my song yesterday. It made me cry — I was so cross. I generally jump about much more. I am much merrier. Mother and I shall be so pleased if you have time to come again.

Sincerely yours in haste,
N. NANSON.

P.S. Mr. Solomon wants to engage me for next year, I think. And for *better money*.

THE STUDIOS, WESTMINSTER,
7th January.

DEAR NANCY,

No, I did *not* think you were up to the mark yesterday. It was a ragged performance. I write, of course, frankly. First then, as to your singing, — I never very much believed in that. But you would sing much better if you knew that you sang badly. You would then understand that I was serious when I told you, what you really wanted was singing lessons. Voice *production*, my dear. And your speaking voice is excellent. You used it well upon the whole, yesterday. A little careless, I thought — a mistake sometimes, in the emphasis. But what is pantomime dialogue! I will come again, if you like me to see you, and you will do all that better. For agility in dancing, for vivacity in action, you seemed as good as it is possible to be. And you take in every point — even yesterday I noticed, you believed in every bit of the story. To do so, and to live in it, is the foundation of an actress. Yes, with your intelligence, with your alertness, your quick life, actress just as much as dancer you may very well be.

You come to Westminster, next week, any morning except Wednesday. I must make one more drawing of you. Not a pastel this time. I have long since done with the pastels of you. They are good as far as they go. Your colour and your dress, your movement and your pose, they record not at all unhappily. But I want a careful drawing — a drawing in line — and shall make it perhaps in pencil; perhaps even in silver-point. You are such a strange, variable child, you see — there is not one subject in you, but a hundred; and I shall not be contented till I have, somewhere else than in my memory, the eyebrow's line, the delicate low forehead, the fine nose, half Greek (and it gains so in character as you throw your mind into your work) — all that and the curve of the open nostril. This moment, they are at my fingers' ends. And your grave sweetness!

Frank, is it not? Yet I am not a foolish person, making up to you. I am not a vulgar flatterer of the first prettiness in the street. You know how much I am an artist — heart and soul, my dear — by which I mean that unlike too many of my brethren, I am not only a painter.

Your 'notices' are good, I see. Very good. I congratulate you. The time is coming perhaps when you will *patronise* me — when you will even be so very great that you will quite 'cut' me. 'No, no,' I hear you say — indeed you said it when I saw you last — 'No, no, Mr. Ashton, I should never do *that.*' You say it with your voice — and with your steady eyes you say it even more.

Until next week, then!

I am sincerely yours,
CLEMENT ASHTON.

THE WALK, HOXTON:
10*th February.*

DEAR MR. ASHTON.

Mother says, How long since we have seen you! You said you would come again to our Panto. Since that, remember, I have been twice to

Westminster, to sit to you. They are going to publish one of the drawings, are they? You will put my name to it, won't you?

Saturday is my last night. Mother says, Can you come then? I shall have all my admirers. And the boys in the gallery — though you say I sing so badly — all the boys in the gallery taking up my song. After Saturday, I am booked for the Halls.

Yesterday I was taken a long drive to Hagley Wood. It is near Barnet. I have had a great deal of attention here.

I am yours very sincerely,
NANCY NANSON.

P.S. Mr. Ashton, I allow you to say anything. Be sure and tell me what you think, if you come Saturday.

THE STUDIOS, WESTMINSTER:
Sunday, 16th Feb:

MY DEAR NANCY:

Yes, you allow me to say any thing — for a lifetime divides us — and because I am a friend of yours I shall say the bare hard truth. I saw you yesterday, as you know, for you espied me from the stage. From the point of view of a theatrical success, the thing was quite undoubted. You were a mass of nerves. You came across the house to us. The footlights ceased to be. Your effect was extraordinary. Shylock's 'How much more elder art thou than thy years!' — the thing he said to Portia — is a question which may be put, no doubt, with reasonableness, to many little ladies at the theatre. There is nothing like the theatre for ageing you. You, Nancy, are now, not five months, but two years older than you were last autumn. At first I was afraid of it, physically. That last time that you came to me, to the studio, your face was quite drawn: not only its expressions, its very lines, had aged. You were pale; you were worn. And sixteen!

But yesterday that was all right, again; and, Nancy, it was the deeper *You* that had altered. I — I was always an idealist, remember, and so you will forgive me. I go down to the grave, when my time comes, poet, after all, far more than craftsman. Those changes, more or less, that I notice in you — those changes not for the better, I mean — I was never blind to the possibility of them. Idealist though I am, I foresaw them — I foresaw them, with forebodings.

There was my first long letter to you. It will be well, perhaps, that I should not say anything more in detail. But read that again — the last part of it, I mean — and be warned.

But no — the detail shan't be spared you, though what it really comes to — I tell it you from my heart, and you will keep this letter to yourself — all that it really comes to is that you will be 'spoilt'. 'Spoilt' or 'ruined'. You are so sensible in many things. Clever I don't know that you are, except in your profession. It all runs into that one channel with you. Quickness of 'study', closeness of observation, immediate faultless power of mimicry, vivacity, agility in the dance — all *that* we know; and then at home your sensitiveness, your quickness, and your helpful tact. But as to books, as to pictures, as to music beyond your showy music of the theatre, as to the things that happen in the world, and that interest people — these things are all nothing to you. Who can wonder! Your whole little eager heart is in your work. Your work is your play too — and the whole of your play. But a thirst for admiration, my dear, and vanity, vanity! Will you split, like the others, on that rock?

Last night, your face had new expressions. There were things I never saw in it, before. In that palace-scene, the slim young thing — how queenly you were, in the white silk, spangled with silver; how queenly, and withal a little contemptuous, a little scornful! I watched you, Nancy, with a keenness horribly inconvenient for you — or the scornful look, the bored look, the *blasé* look (I have said the worst that I can say) would have passed perhaps unperceived. They were there.

Again, you acted to the house too much. I am not finding fault with you technically for that, — though you did, I think, overdo it. I am talking to the girl, and not to the stage character. There was one look at the Boxes: at a private Box rather — but I spare you.

Who the dickens are the people who have had this influence upon you? — hour by hour; drop by drop, I suppose: here a little and there a little — in the life I begin to hate for you . . . . But it is no use hating it. I suppose that I could take you from it, if I liked. I have the money to — no overwhelming claims on me. But you would leave all this unwillingly; and, in the end, *ought* you to leave it?

My dear Nancy, I will spare you any more. But read much more than I have actually written. Imagine yourself talked to, very gravely: fancy yourself receiving a *good long, serious* talking to. Think! Think! I have finished.

My dear child, you are a good girl at heart, you know — and such an eager little fiery one — when you are not grave and sober. The stuff is in you out of which they make Sisters of Charity. The stuff is in you out of which ———— But No! Why?

> I am your old and fatherly, your *grand*-fatherly friend, if you prefer it —
>
> CLEMENT ASHTON.

Tuesday, Feb. 18th.

MY DEAR MR. ASHTON.

I cried so much when I got your letter. For you have been very kind to me. I suppose I deserved it.

> NANCY.

GREAT CORAM STREET,
Thursday, Feb. 20th.

DEAR MR. ASHTON,

We have moved. Until I get into a burlesque at Easter, I am working two of the Halls. On Monday I have a new song at the Metropolitan — the 'Met' — Edgware Road, nine o'clock. New dresses, and I do a new dance. Also at Gatti's, Westminster Bridge Road, at 10.15.

> Sincerely yours and gratefully,
> NANCY NANSON.

GREAT CORAM STREET,
Tuesday, Feb. 25.

THE engagement only lasts a week, Mr. Ashton. Am I not going to be a favourite, then? I have tried for that music-hall kept by that faddy lady, the philanthropist. She is very *severe*. Why, she won't let you take up your skirts, even. I say, and *Mother* says, she ought to keep a *chapel* — not a music-hall.

> In haste,
> NANCY.

GREAT CORAM STREET.

You were always kind to me. Mother is wild. And you, *you will never forgive me.*

> From
> NANCY.

WESTMINSTER,
18th April.

MY DEAR NANCY.

At least I hurried to make the matter smoother for you at home, though, sooner or later that would have been effected anyhow; for you and your mother are at one, generally. She is really fond of you, and you of her. I have not done much for you.

And now what *can* I do? My business — if I have any — is to wait. 'Did I,' I ask myself, 'lose any opportunity of action?' Could I have stepped in, to stop you? Nancy, I talk brutally, though I would not know, with definiteness, any detail — but the valuation set by me on mere physical chastity — were it that that was in question — might be perhaps three half-pence. One friend at all events you have, between whom and yourself no mad outrageous freak of yours, raises insuperable barriers. And you feel that. Then why was I concerned for your Future, months ago? The deterioration, the slow change in you, that must be coming or have come; the undermining and deterioration, it may be — I say, that is the deep injury — but the very words draw round you like a curse. I haven't the heart left to sketch in words a sure decline. And, if I had, why should I overdo it?

Was it done by you for gain, for sudden greed, for ambition, for vanity? Answer yourself — not me. If it had been done for love — well then at all events I might have thought of your Future differently. Nancy, I must make excuses for you — excuses in any case. Once in your short life at least, you have been near to want — that winter you and your Mother came out into the Strand, from the empty treasury of a bogus management, with sixpence in your pockets, instead of a salary. Yes, sixpence it was — that was your salary. You told me so yourself. And your voice 'went' in that cruel winter weather, as the little figure, with its slender grace, slid through the fog and blackened rain and reeking river mists of December in London. After that, Money, which seems to some people a small thing in the distance — so sure, so unimportant — must have loomed large and of *immense* importance, in the near foreground, to you. Again, of course, we have our moods. We may be taken unawares. Judgement goes — principle. All your life, Nancy — with only trivial exceptions, after all — your life is good to this hour. And in all our lives, every day has its own difficulties: every hour is a choice. Good and diligent, and sweet and bright, wise too and helpful — week after week, month after month, you answer to your helm; and then there comes one hour which leaves you rudderless. I should be hard on you indeed, if I remembered only that hour — if I forgot the ninety and nine. My dear Nancy, I am *not* hard on you!

It is late at night when I write this. And, in my thoughts, you have been with me the whole of the day. The story can't be an unusual story — and I am a man of the world, or ought to be. No, the story can't be an unusual story; but the girl is an unusual girl.

Well, you must live it down, my dear — must have done with it — must forget it. But then there is the deterioration — *some* deterioration at least — that made the thing possible. And what more may be possible — mend and patch and cobble as we will?

All day you have been in my thoughts. When I was setting my palette in the morning; arranging the light; screwing up the easel; waiting for the sitter, who was late — they are always late — I thought 'She has made a mess of it — poor little Nancy — foolish minx!' I was very silent with my sitter. I was scarcely even polite. She noticed it; and it affected her. The sitting was a failure. I bowed the lady out. Nancy Nanson in my thoughts. The luncheon table was all wrong: not a thing as it ought to have been. 'Nancy Nanson, at the Devil, poor girl!' A walk in the streets, afterwards. The omnibuses rattling past me in Victoria Street. 'Nancy Nanson — is it all up with her?' Nothing else. The bell of Christ Church, Westminster, a tinkle for Evensong. The day goes on, then! 'Nancy Nanson!' Afterwards, in the quiet of St. James's Park, near Birdcage Walk, the clear sound of the bugle — the recall to barracks. 'Nancy Nanson!' And then, the space of the Park water, calm, as I saw it from the foot-bridge, by the five poplars — and the April evening sky, clear and serene. 'Nancy Nanson at the Devil! Poor girl! The Devil perhaps. The dear and clever irresponsible child!'

Nancy, I've no more blame for you. The vials of my anger are poured out. Months ago I said 'I shall always be your friend.' 'Go the straight way!' I said. And I believed you would. What a collapse if I must say to you, to-night, only this word — the very sound of it, connected with you, is vulgar and repulsive — 'If you should get into any scrape, you know, and I can help you, come to me. I *will* help you. Right and left I will help you. I will see you through.' . . .

But only to say — *that*!

Nancy! — with deep regard and real affection,

CLEMENT ASHTON.

Post-script. But I can't end like this. Just when you want to be reproached the least, some of my sentences sound hard. Be hopeful! For, as it seems to me, whatever happened, the quite irreparable has *not* happened. Surely, surely, you can forget, for ever, one mad hour! And, from whatever point, you can begin 'the journey homeward' — to yourself. You can be the real You again; the real Nancy — your very characteristic, the perfection of the contrast between the wildness of the theatre and your happy quietude.

So at home I must think of you. With that golden wig, that adds — piquantly perhaps and yet abominably — to your years, the maddening dancer is put off. The brown-haired child, in the plain dress, is in her place — the short brown hair, the quiet eyes, the tender, sensitive mouth. Your lodging-house parlour is ornamented with a play-bill, and photographs are stuck about the mantelpiece — Miss Marie Dainton, is it? and your uncle, the plumber; and, again, a celebrity of the Halls; and somebody else, who was nice to you, a year ago, at Weymouth; some comrade you were fond of: 'She's a dear girl,' you said. In the lodging-house parlour your mother sits beside the fireplace, combing out the golden wig, after its last night's service. The kettle, in preparation for tea-time, not far off, is at the side of the fire. It begins to sing. You, Nancy, sit beyond the table, on a cane-bottomed chair; with your knees crossed — as I saw you that first time I called on you in London — your hands, so young, so nervous, and so highly bred, smooth out upon your lap a bit of wool-work that you — whose instinct is to please and to be pleasant — are doing for your landlady. And, in the glow of the fender, lies curled up, warm and sleeping, that grey kitten rescued from misery, four days before, by you; won to you by your magnetism, or your kindness — they are both the same. In the morning, when your mother leaves your bed — leaves the tired child, worn out by the theatre, to an hour's extra resting — the soft grey thing, that you bewitched and cared for, creeps to your side — is happy.

Did they ever teach you, at your school, I wonder, verses of Wordsworth on the Stock-dove? What did the stock-dove sing?

> He sang of love with quiet blending,
> Slow to begin, and never ending;
> Of serious faith, and inward glee.
> That was the song — the song for me!

Nancy! — the spirit of the stock-dove's song lies in the deepest heart of Nancy Nanson.

C. A.

[There was reason to apprehend that the Correspondence closed with this letter. One other note, however — in the round hand of Miss Nanson — has been discovered, and is therefore appended.]

GREAT CORAM STREET.

Thank you so very, *very* much — and for not asking any exact questions, too. I was a fool. Some one behaved badly to me. No doubt I 'compromised' myself. I was on deep waters. But I did *not* go under. No, Mr. Ashton.

You *have* been rather cross with me — but I was *very* troublesome. You understand the curious mixture that signs herself — and is —

Your grateful
NANCY.

Pages from the Life of Lucy Newcome

Arthur Symons

Arthur Symons (1865–1945) was a prolific writer, principally a poet and critic, whose body of work chronicles the Decadent movement in *fin-de-siècle* London. He was editor of *The Savoy*, where this story first appeared in April 1896. December of that year saw the publication of 'The Childhood of Lucy Newcome' in the same periodical, and Symons completed 'The Life and Adventures of Lucy Newcome' in 1898, though it was never published during his lifetime. The whole story is based upon the life of Muriel Broadbent, a celebrated prostitute whom Symons met at the Alhambra music hall in the early 1890s, when she was the mistress of Symons's friend, Herbert Horne, editor of the *Hobby Horse*. Selwyn Image of the *Hobby Horse* and Symons both provided character references as surety for her rented rooms. The publication of the 'Lucy' stories was probably the major factor in a most acrimonious split between Horne and Symons, which resulted in a lifetime of insults, traded in letters and memoirs. The whole story was intended to be published as 'A Novel à la Goncourt', being an impressionistic series of fragmented images depicting a young woman's descent into prostitution. As such, specific sensations were to be the focus of the tale, rather than characters or plot. Symons's unpublished letters display the fact that, after several failed attempts, he was still trying to publish the whole story as a novel in the early 1930s.

'Pages' is the second section of the tale (temporally), where we see the orphaned Lucy in transition from ruined maid to fallen woman. As such, the plot is never far from melodrama, however, the tale may be read as a sustained attack on middle-class hypocrisy and prudery. In 'Childhood' we learn that Lucy's sense of reputation and shame were instilled in her by an emotionally frigid guardian aunt, whose son provided the fatherless child.

In 'Pages', every middle-class male views the distraught and desperate Lucy as sexual prey, underneath the pose of care and concern. Equally, Lucy is ostracised from the camaraderie of the working classes, a victim of their inverted snobbery. This leaves her isolated in a manner that is reminiscent of Thomas Hardy's Jude, or Tess. The final image of 'Pages' encapsulates quite wonderfully the notions of doubles and secrets which resonate throughout *fin-de-siècle* literature, and indeed, culture.

I

As Lucy Newcome walked down the street, with the baby in her arms, her first sensation was one of thankfulness, to be out of the long, blank, monotonous hospital, where she had suffered obscurely; to be once more free, and in the open air. How refreshing it is to be out of doors again! she said to herself. But she had not walked many steps before the unfamiliar morning air made her feel quite light-headed; for a moment she fancied she was going to faint; and she leant against the wall, closing her eyes, until the feeling had passed. As she walked on again, things still seemed a little dizzy before her eyes, and she had to draw in long breaths, for fear that curious cloudy sensation should come into her brain once more. She held the baby carefully, drawing the edges of the cloak around its face, so that it should not feel cold and wake up. It was the first time she had carried the baby out of doors, and it seemed to her that everyone must be looking at her. She was not much afraid of being recognised, for she knew that she had altered so much since her confinement; and for that reason she was glad to be looking so thin and white and ill. But she felt sure that people would wonder who she was, and why such a young girl was carrying a baby; perhaps they would not think it was hers; she might be only carrying it for some married woman. And she let her left hand, on which there was no wedding-ring, show from under the shawl in which it had been her first instinct to envelop it. Many thoughts came into her mind, but in a dull confused way, as she walked slowly along, feeling the weight of the baby dragging at her arms. At last they began to ache so much that she looked around for somewhere to sit down. She had not noticed where she had been going; why should she? where was there for her to go? and she found herself in one of the side streets, at the end of which, she remembered, was the park. There, at all events, she could sit down; and when she had found a seat, she took the baby on her knees, and lay back in the corner with a sense of relief.

At first she did not try to think of plans for the future. She merely resigned herself, unconsciously enough, to the vague, peaceful, autumn sadness of the place and the hour. The damp smell of the earth, sharp and comforting, came to her nostrils; the leaves, smelling a little musty, dropped now and then past her face on to the shawl in which the baby was wrapt. There was only enough breeze to make a gentle sighing among the branches overhead; and she looked up at the leafy roof above her, as she had looked up so often when a child, and felt better for being there. Gradually her mind began to concentrate itself: what am I to do, she thought, what am I to do?

Just then the little creature lying on her knees stirred a little, and opened its blue eyes. She caught it to her breast with kiss after kiss, and began to rock it to and fro, with a passionate fondness. 'Mammy's little one,' she said; 'all Mammy's, Mammy's own'; and began to croon over it, with a sort of fierce insistence. Yes, she must do something, and at once, for the child's sake.

But the more she tried to find some plan for the future, the more hopeless did the task seem to become. There was her aunt, whom she would never go back to, whom she would never see again; never. There was her cousin, who had cast her off; and she said to herself that she hated her cousin. All her aunt's friends were so respectable: they would never look at her; and she could never go to them. Her cousin's friends were like himself, only worse, much worse. No, there was nowhere for her to look for help; and how was she to help herself? She knew nothing of any sort of business, she had no showy accomplishments to put to use; and besides, with a baby, who would give her employment? Oh, why had she ever listened to her cousin, why had she been such a fool as to have a baby? she said to herself, furiously; and then, feeling the bundle stir in her arms, she fell to hugging and kissing it again.

As she lifted up her face, a woman who was passing half paused, looking at her in a puzzled way, and then, after walking on a little distance, turned and came back, hesitatingly. Lucy knew her well: it was Mrs. Graham, her aunt's laundress, with whom she had had to settle accounts every week. She had never liked the woman, but now she was overjoyed at meeting her; and as Mrs. Graham said, questioningly, 'Miss Lucy? Lord, now, it isn't you?' she answered, 'Yes, it's me; don't you know me, Mrs. Graham?'

'Well,' the woman said, 'I wasn't sure; how you have changed, Miss!

I asked Mrs. Newcome where you was, and she said you was gone abroad.'

The woman stopped and looked curiously at the baby. She had taken in the situation at a glance; and though she was rather surprised, she was not nearly so much surprised as Lucy had expected, and she seemed more interested than shocked.

'Pretty baby, Miss,' she said, stooping down to have a closer look.

'Yes,' said Lucy, in a matter of fact way, 'it's my baby. I've been very unhappy.'

'Have you now, Miss?' said Mrs. Graham, sitting down by her side, and looking at her more curiously than ever. 'Well, you do look ill. But where have you been all this time, and where are you living now?'

'I'm not living anywhere,' said Lucy; 'I only came out of hospital to-day and I've nowhere to go.'

'You don't mean to say that!' said Mrs. Graham; 'but,' she added, looking at the baby, 'his father . . .'

'He has left me,' said Lucy, as quietly as she could.

At this Mrs. Graham glanced at her in a somewhat less favourable way. She did not disapprove of people running away from home and getting children as irregularly as they liked; but she very much disapproved of their being left.

'I haven't a penny in the world,' Lucy went on; 'at least, I have only a little more than two shillings; and I don't know what I am going to do.'

'Oh dear now, oh dear!' said Mrs. Graham, rather coldly, 'that's very sad, it is. I do say that's hard lines. And so you was left without anything. That's very hard lines.'

'I'm so glad I met you, Mrs. Graham,' said Lucy. 'Perhaps you can help me. Oh, do try to help me if you can! I haven't anybody, really, to look to, and I haven't a roof to shelter me. I can't stay in the streets all day. I'm so afraid the baby will take cold, or something. It isn't for myself I mind so much. What shall I do?'

While Lucy spoke, Mrs. Graham was considering matters. Without being exactly hard-hearted, she was not naturally sympathetic, and, while she felt sorry for the poor girl, she was not at all carried away by her feelings. But she did not like to leave her there as she was, and an idea had occurred to her which made her all the more ready to act kindly towards a creature in distress. So she said, after a moment's pause, 'Well, you'd better come along with me, Miss, and have a rest, anyway. Shan't I carry the baby?'

'Oh, you are good!' cried Lucy, seizing her hand, and almost crying as she tried to thank her. 'No, no, I'll carry the baby! And may I really come in with you? You don't mind? You don't mind being seen?'

'Oh, no, *I* don't mind!' said Mrs. Graham, a little loftily. 'It's this way, Miss.'

And they began to walk across the park. Lucy felt so immensely relieved that she was almost gay. She gave up thinking of what was going to happen, and trudged along contentedly by the side of the older woman. After they had left the park and had reached the poorer quarter of the town, she suddenly stopped outside a sweet-shop. 'It won't be very extravagant if I get a pennyworth of acid-drops, will it?' she said, with almost her old smile; and Mrs. Graham had to wait while she went in and bought them. Then they went on together through street after street, till at last Mrs. Graham said, 'It's here, come in.'

As the door opened Lucy heard the barking of a dog; and next moment she found herself in a room such as she had never been in in her life, but which seemed to her, at that moment, the most delightful place in the world. It was a kitchen, horribly dirty, with a dog-kennel in one corner, and a rabbit-hutch on the top of the kennel; there was a patchwork rug on the floor, and a deal table in the middle, with a piece of paper on one end of it as a tablecloth, and a loaf of bread, without a plate, standing in the middle of the table.

'Have something to eat, Miss,' said Mrs. Graham, and Lucy sank into an old stuffed armchair, which stood by the side of the fire-place, the springs broken and protruding, and the flock coming through the horse-hair in great grey handfuls.

The baby was still asleep, and lay quietly on her lap as she munched ravenously at the thick slice of bread and butter which Mrs. Graham cut for her. All at once she heard a little cry, and, looking round in the corner behind her, she saw a baby lying in a clothes-basket.

'You'll have to sleep with the children to-night,' said Mrs. Graham. 'We've only two rooms besides this, and the children has one of them. When you've had a bit of a meal, you'd better lie down and rest yourself.'

When Lucy went into the room which was to be her bedroom for the night, she could not at first distinguish the bed. There were no bedclothes, but some old coats and petticoats had been heaped up over a mattress on a little iron bedstead in the corner.

'Now just lie down for a bit,' said Mrs. Graham, 'and you give me the baby. I know the ways of them.'

Lucy threw herself on the bed. She could at least rest there; and she put a couple of acid-drops into her mouth, and then, almost before she knew it, she was asleep, in her old baby-fashion, sucking her thumb.

II

Lucy slept at Mrs. Graham's two nights. She had been told that she would have to work; and she would do anything, she said, anything. Mrs. Graham had a cousin, Mrs. Marsh, who had a large laundry; and Mrs. Marsh happened to be just then in want of a shirt and collar hand. Lucy knew nothing about ironing, but she was sure she could learn it without the least difficulty. So the two women set out for Mrs. Marsh's. It was not very far off, and when they got there Mr. and Mrs. Marsh were standing at the big side-gate, where the things were brought in and out, watching one of their vans being unloaded. The shop-door was open, and inside, in the midst of the faint steam, rising from piles of white linen, smoking under the crisp hiss of the hot irons, Lucy saw four young women, wearing loose blouses, their sleeves rolled up above their elbows, their faces flushed with the heat, bending over their work. Mrs. Marsh looked at her amiably enough, and she led the way into the laundry. Besides the four girls, the two shirt and collar hands, the gauferer and the plain ironer, there was a man ramming clothes into a boiler with a long pole, and a youth, Mrs. Marsh's son, turning a queer, new-fangled instrument like a barrel, which dollied the clothes by means of some mechanical contrivance. Clothes were hanging all around on clothes-horses; and overhead, on lines; the shirts were piled up in neat heaps at the end of the ironing-boards; some of the things lay in baskets on the ground. As Lucy looked around, her eye suddenly caught a white embroidered dress which was hanging up to dry; and for the moment she felt quite sick; it was exactly like a dress of her mother's.

And the heat, too, was overpowering; she scarcely knew what was being said, as the two women discussed her to her face, and bargained between themselves as to the price of her labour. She realised that she was to come there next day; that she was to learn to iron cuffs and collars and shirt-fronts like the young woman nearest to her, whom they called Polly; and, as a special favour, she was to be paid eight shillings a-week, the full price at once instead of only six shillings, which was generally given to beginners. That she realised, she realised it acutely; for she was already beginning to find out that money means something very definite when you are poor, and that a shilling more or less may mean all the difference between everything and nothing.

That day it was arranged that she should rent a little attic in a house not far from Mrs. Graham's, a house where a carpenter and his wife lived: they had no children, and she could have a room to herself. She was to pay five shillings a-week for her room and what they called her keep, that is to say, breakfast and supper, which, she soon found out, meant bread and cheese one day, bread and dripping another, and bread and lard a third, always with some very weak tea, water just coloured. Then there was the baby; she could not look after the baby while she was out at work, so the carpenter's wife, who was called Mrs. Marsh, like the laundress, though she was no relation, promised to take charge of the baby during the day for half-a-crown extra. Five shillings and half-a-crown made seven-and-six, and that left her only sixpence a week to live on: could one say to live on? At all events, she had now a roof over her head; she would scarcely starve, not quite starve; and she sat in her attic, the first night she found herself there, and wondered what was going to happen; if she would have strength to do the work, strength to live on, day after day, strength to nurse her baby, whose little life depended on hers. She sat on the edge of the bed, looking out at the clear, starry sky, visible above the roofs, and she sent up a prayer, up into that placid, unresponsive sky, hanging over her like the peace that passeth understanding, and has no comfort in it for mere mortals, a prayer for strength, only for the strength of day by day, one day at a time.

Next morning she took up her place at the ironing-board, next to Polly, between her and the head ironer, whom she was told to watch. They were all Lancashire girls, not bad-hearted, but coarse and ignorant, always swearing and using foul language. Lucy had never heard people who talked like that; it wounded her horribly, and her pale face went crimson at every one of their coarse jokes. They had no sort of ill-will to her, but they knew she had a child, and was not married, and they could not help reminding her of the fact, which indeed seemed to them no less scandalous than their language seemed to her. They really believed that a woman who had been seduced was exactly the same as a prostitute; they talked of people who led a gay life: 'Ah, my wench, it's a gay life, but a short one'; and they were convinced that every-one who led a gay life came to a deplorable end before she was five-and-twenty. To have had a child, without having been married, was the first step, so they held, in an inevitably downward course; indeed, they believed that all kinds of horrible things came of it, and they talked to one another of the ghastly stories they had 'heerd tell'. Lucy had never heard of such things, and she half believed them. 'Can all this really be true?' she said to herself sometimes, in a paroxysm of terror; and she tried not to think of it, as of something that might possibly be true, but must certainly be kept out of sight and out of mind.

One of the girls, Polly, was always very nice to her, and would come round sometimes to her little room and hold the baby for her; but the others called her 'Miss Stuck-up', 'Miss Fine-airs', and when she blushed, cried, even, at the ribaldries which seemed to them so natural and matter-of-course, they would taunt her with her bastard, and ask her if she didn't know how a baby was made, she who pretended to be such an innocent. She never tried to answer them; she did her work (after three days she could do it almost as well as the most practised of them), and she got through day after day as best she could. 'It was for baby's sake,' she whispered to herself, 'all for baby's sake.'

In the middle of the day they had a dinner-hour, and the girls brought their dinner with them, which they generally ate out of doors, in the drying-ground at the back, glad to be out of the steam and heat for a few minutes. That hour was Lucy's terror. She had no dinner to bring with her: how could she, out of sixpence a week? and every day she pretended to go out and get her meal at an eating-house, scared lest one of them should come round the corner, and see her walking up and down the road, filling up the time until she could venture to go back again. She knew that if any one of them had guessed the truth, had known that she could never afford even the cheapest price of a dinner, they would one and all have shared with her their sandwiches, and bread and cheese, and meat pies, and apple dumplings. But she would not have let them know for worlds; and the aching suspense, lest she should be found out, was almost as bad to bear as the actual pang of hunger. She grew thinner and paler, and every day it seemed to her that the baby grew thinner and paler too. How could she nourish it, when she had no nourishment herself? She wept over it, and prayed God in agony not to visit her sin on the child. All this while the poor little thing lay and wailed, a feeble, fretful, continual wail, ceasing and going on, ceasing and going on again. It seemed to her that the sound would lodge itself in her brain, and drive her mad, quite mad. She heard it when she was in the laundry, bending over the steaming linen; it pierced through the crisp hiss of the irons as they passed shiningly over the surface; she heard it keeping time to her footsteps as she walked hungrily up and down that road in the dinner-hour; she dreamt of it even, and woke up to hear the little wail break out in the stillness of the night, in her attic bed. And the wail was getting feebler and feebler; the baby was dying, oh! she knew that it was dying, and she could not save it; there was no way, absolutely no way to save it.

III

She had now been eight weeks at the laundry, and she seemed to get thinner every day. As she looked at her face in the glass, she was quite frightened at the long hollows she saw in her white cheeks, the dark lines under her eyes: her own face seemed to fade away from her as she looked at it, away into a mist; and through the mist she heard the small persistent crying of the baby, as if from a great way off. 'Am I going to be ill?' she wondered, looking down at her fingers helplessly. Certainly both she and the child were in need of the doctor; but who was to pay for a doctor? It was impossible.

That day, for the first time since she had been at the laundry, she had a half-holiday, and she put on her hat and went out into the streets, merely to walk about, and so think the less. 'I can at least look at the shops,' she said to herself, and she made her way to the more fashionable part of the town, where the milliners' and jewellers' shops were, and as she looked at the rings and bracelets, the smart hats and stylish jackets, it seemed to her worse than ever, to see all these things, and to know that none of them would ever be hers. It was now three o'clock; she had had nothing since her early breakfast, and the long walk, the loitering about, had tired her; it seemed to her, once more, as if a mist came floating up about her, through which the sound of voices was deadened before it reached her ears, and the ground felt a little uncertain under her feet, as if it were slightly elastic as she trod upon it. She turned aside out of the main street, into the big arcade, where she thought it would be quieter, and she found herself staring at a row of photographs of actresses, quite blankly, hardly seeing them. As she put her hand to her forehead, to press down her eyelids for a moment, she heard some one speaking to her, and looking round she saw a middle-aged gentleman standing by her side, and saying in a very kind voice: 'My child, are you ill?' Was she then looking so ill? she wondered, or was she really ill? She did not think so, only hungry and faint. How hungry and faint she was! And as she shook her head, and said, 'No, thank you,' she felt certain that the old gentleman, who looked so kind, would not believe her. Evidently he did not believe her, for he continued to look at her, and to say . . . what was it? she only knew that he told her, quite decidedly, that she must come and have some tea. 'Thank you,' she said again: how was she to say no? and she walked along beside the gentleman in silence. He did not say anything more, but before she quite knew it, they were sitting at a little table in a tea-shop, and she had a cup of tea before her, real tea (how well she remembered, from what a distance, the taste of real tea!), and she was buttering a huge scone that made her mouth water, only to look at it.

When she had eaten her scone and drunk her tea, she saw that the gentleman was looking at her more kindly than ever, but with a certain expression which she could not help understanding. He was a man of about fifty, somewhat tall, with broad shoulders and a powerful head, on which the iron-grey hair was cut close. His face was bronzed, he had a thick, closely-cut beard, and his eyes were large, grey, luminous, curiously sympathetic eyes, very kind, but a little puzzling in their expression. And he began to talk to her, asking her questions, feeling his way. She blushed furiously: how he had misunderstood her! She was not angry, only frightened and disturbed; and of course such a thing could never be, never. He seemed quite grieved when she told him hurriedly that she must go; and when they were outside the shop he insisted on walking a few steps with her; if not then, would she not come and see him some other day? He would be so glad to do anything he could to help her; that is, if she would come and see him. But she blushed again, and shook her head, and told him how impossible it was; but as he insisted on her taking his card, she took it. What was the harm? He had been kind to her. And of course she would never use it.

That night, as she ate her supper of bread and dripping, washing it down with what Mrs. Marsh called tea, she thought of the tea-shop and the meal she had had there, the pleasantness of the place, the bright little tables, the waitresses gliding about, the well-dressed people who had been in there. And the life she was living seemed more unbearable than ever. At first she had been so glad to be anywhere, to find any sort of refuge, where there was a roof over her head, and some sort of bed to lie on, that the actual sordidness of her surroundings had seemed of little moment; but now it seemed more and more impossible to go on living among such people, without an educated person to speak to, without a book to read, without any of the little pleasantnesses of comfortable life. No, I cannot go on with this for ever, she said to herself; and she began to muse, thinking vague things, vaguely; thinking of what the girls at the laundry said to her, what they thought of her, and how to them it would be no difference at all, no difference at all; for was she not (they all said it) a fallen creature? When she went upstairs, and heard the feeble wail of her child, she almost wondered that she could have refused to take the man's money, which would have paid for a doctor. Oh, yes, she was a fallen creature, no doubt; and when you are once fallen you go on falling. But of course, all the same, it was impossible: she *could* not; and there was an end of it.

But such thoughts as these, once set wandering through her brain, came back, and brought others with them. They came especially when she was very hungry; they seemed to float to her on the steam of that tea which she had drunk in the tea-shop; they whispered to her from the small, prim letters of the card which she still kept, with its sober, respectable-looking name, 'Mr. Reginald Barfoot', and the address of a huge, handsome building which she had often seen, mostly laid out in bachelors' flats, very expensive flats. But of course, all the same, it was impossible.

IV

On the Saturday of that week, while she was working at the laundry, she had a message from Mrs. Marsh to say that her child was very ill. She hurried back, and found the little thing in convulsions. The poor little wasted body shook as if every moment would be its last. She held it in her arms, and crooned over it, and cried over it, and with her lips and fingers seemed to soothe the pain out of it. Presently it dropped into a quiet slumber. Lucy sat on the chair by the bedside, and thought. She had never seen an attack like that; she was terribly frightened; would it not come on again? and if so, what was to be done? A doctor, certainly a doctor must be called. But she had no money, and doctors (she remembered her aunt's doctor) were so expensive. The money must be got, and at once. She looked at the card, at the address. Was it not a matter of life or death? She would go.

Then she felt that it was impossible; that she could never do it. Was it really a matter of life or death? The baby slept quietly. She would wait till to-morrow.

Through that night, and half-way through Sunday, the child seemed much better; but about three the convulsions came on again. Lucy was frantic with terror, and when the little thing, now growing feebler and feebler, had got over a worse paroxysm than ever, and had quieted down again, she called Mrs. Marsh, and begged her to look after the child while she went and fetched the doctor. 'I may be a little while,' she said; 'but baby is quiet now; you'll be very careful, won't you?' She gave the child one big kiss on both his little eyes; then she put on her hat and went out.

She went straight to the address on the card, without hesitation now, rang at the door, and a man-servant showed her into a room which seemed to her filled with books and photographs and pretty things. There was a fire in the grate, which shed a warm, comfortable glow over everything. She held out her hands to it; she was shivering a little. How nice it is here, she could not help thinking, or, rather, the sensation of its comfort flashed through her unconsciously, as she stood there looking at the photographs above the mantel-piece, as blankly as she had looked at those photographs, that other day, in the arcade. And then the door opened, and Mr. Barfoot came in, smiling, as he had smiled at her before. He did not say anything, only smiled; and as he came quite close, and took her hand, a sudden terror came into her eyes, she drew back violently, and covering her face with her hands, sobbed out, 'I can't, I can't!'

For a moment the man looked at her wonderingly; then the expression of his face changed, he took her hands very gently, saying, 'My poor child!' Something in the voice and touch reassured her; she let him draw away her hands from before her eyes, in which the tears were beginning to creep over the lower eyelids. She looked straight into his face; there was no smile there now, and she almost wondered why she had been so frightened a moment before. He led her to a chair. 'Sit down, now,' he said, 'and let us have a talk.' She sat down, already with a sense of relief, and he drew up a chair beside her, and took her hand again, soothingly, as one might take the hand of a timid child. 'Now,' he said, 'tell me all about it. How ill you look, my poor girl. You are in trouble. Tell me all about it.'

At first she was silent, looking into his face with a sort of hesitating confidence. Then, looking down again, she said, 'May I?'

'I want you to,' he said. 'I want you to let me help you.'

'Oh, will you?' she said impulsively, pressing the hand he held. 'I haven't a friend in the world. I am all alone. I have been very unhappy. It was all my fault. Will you really help me? It isn't for myself, it . . . it's my baby. I am afraid he's dying, he's so very ill, and to-day he had convulsions, and I thought . . . I thought he would really have died. And I haven't a penny to get a doctor. And that's why I came.'

She broke off, and the hesitation came into her eyes again. She let her hand rest quite still; he felt the fingers turning cold as she waited for what he would say.

'Why didn't you tell me before?' was all he said, but the voice and the eyes were kinder than ever. She almost smiled, she was so grateful; and he went on, 'Now we must see about the doctor at once. There's a doctor who lives only three doors from here. If he's in, you must take him back with you. Here, do you see, you'll give him this card; or, no, I'll see him about that. Just get him to come with you. And now I'm going to give you a sovereign, for anything you want, and to-morrow . . . but first of all, the doctor. Would you like me to come with you?'

'No, please,' said Lucy.

'Well, you had better go there at once. And mind you get anything you want, and for yourself, too. Why, you don't know how ill you look yourself! And then to-morrow I shall come and see how you are getting on, and then you must tell me all about yourself. Not now. You go straight to the doctor. By the way, what is your address?'

Lucy told him, hardly able to speak; she could not quite understand how it was that things had turned out so differently from what she had expected, or how everything seemed to be coming right without any trouble at all. She was bewildered, grateful, quiescent; and as she got up, and closed her hand mechanically over the sovereign he slipped into it, she was already thinking of the next thing to do, to find the doctor, to take the doctor back with her at once, to save her child.

'Now I shall come in to-morrow at eleven,' she heard him saying, 'and then I'll see if you want anything more. Now good-bye. Dr. Hedges, the third door from here, on the same side.'

He opened the door for her himself, and as she went downstairs she felt the sovereign in her hand, pressing into her flesh, in a little round circle. She wrapped up the sovereign in her handkerchief, and thrust it into her bodice. She was repeating, 'Dr. Hedges, the third door from here, on the same side,' over and over again, without knowing it, so mechanically, that she would have passed the door had she not seen a brougham standing outside. It was the doctor's brougham, and as she went up the steps in front of the house, the door opened and the doctor himself came out. 'I want you, please, to come with me at once,' she said; 'my baby . . . I'm afraid he'll die if you don't. Can you come at once?'

The doctor looked at her critically; he liked pretty women, and this one was so young too. 'Yes, my dear,' he said, 'I'll come at once, if you like. Where is it? All right; jump in; we'll be there in a minute.'

The doctor talked cheerfully, and without expecting any answer, all the way to the house. 'It's the mother,' he thought to himself, 'who wants the doctor.' Lucy sat by his side white and motionless, putting up her hand sometimes to her bodice, to feel if the gold was there. 'Heart wrong,' thought the doctor.

When they reached the house, Lucy opened the door. 'Come in,' she said, and began to fly up the stairs; then, suddenly checking herself, 'No, come quietly, perhaps baby is sleeping.' They went up quietly, and Lucy opened the attic door with infinite precaution. As she held open the door for the doctor to come in, she saw Mrs. Marsh move towards her, she saw the bed, and on the bed a little body lying motionless, its white face on the pillow; she saw it all at a glance, and, as the doctor came cheerfully into the room, she realised that everything had been in vain, that (she said to herself) she had waited just too long.

She sat down by the side of the bed, and looked straight in front of her, not saying a word, nor crying; she seemed to herself to have been stunned. The doctor examined the child, and then, taking Mrs. Marsh into a corner of the room, began to question her. 'Poor little thing,' said Mrs. Marsh, 'he just went off like you might have snuffed out a candle. He was always weakly, like; and she, you know, sir, she ain't by no means strong, not fit to have the charge of a baby, sir. I'm that thankful she takes it so quiet like. Did you say, sir, there'll have to be a crowner's quest? Well, I do hope not; it do look so bad.'

At this moment they heard a wild cry behind them; both turned, and saw Lucy fling herself full length upon the bed, clasping the little body in her arms, sobbing convulsively. The tears streamed down her cheeks, the sobs forced themselves out in great bursts, almost in shouts. 'It will do her good to have a good cry,' said the doctor. 'I'll leave you now; rely on me to see after things.' And he went out quietly.

Lucy never remembered quite how she got through the rest of that day. It always seemed to her afterwards like a bad dream, through which she had found her way vaguely, in a thick darkness. Early in the evening she undressed and went to bed, and then, lying awake in the little room where the dead baby lay folded in white things and covered up for its long sleep, her mind seemed to soak in, unconsciously, all the discomfortable impressions that had made up her life since she had been living in that miserable little room. Through all the hopeless sordidness of that life she lived again, enduring the insults of the laundry, the labour of long days, starvation almost, and the loneliness of forced companionship with such people as Mrs. Marsh and Polly the ironer. She had borne it for her child's sake, and now there was no longer any reason for bearing it. Her life had come to a full stop; the past was irrevocably past, folded away like the little dead body; her mind had not the courage to look a single step before her into the future; she closed her eyes, and tried to shut down the darkness upon her brain.

When she awoke in the morning it was nearly nine o'clock. She got up and dressed slowly, carefully, and when she had had her breakfast she went out to an undertaker's, from whom she ordered a baby's coffin. Remembering that she had a sovereign, she asked him to make it very nicely, and chose the particular kind of wood. She stayed in the shop some time, looking at inscriptions on the coffin lids, and asking questions about the ages of the people who were going to be buried. When she got back it was nearly eleven. She had taken off her hat, and was tidying her hair, quite mechanically, in front of the glass, when she heard a clock strike. Then she remembered that Mr. Barfoot was coming to see her about eleven. She stood there, lifting the hair back from her forehead with her two thin hands, and her eyes met their reflection in the glass, very seriously and meditatively.

Mutability

Theodore Wratislaw

Theodore Wratislaw (1871–1933) was a civil servant and minor poet of the 1890s, who contributed several poems to *The Yellow Book* and *The Savoy*. His poetry has been compared with both Arthur Symons's and Ernest Dowson's; his poems in *Caprices* (1893) and *Orchids* (1896) follow Symons's ephemeral, sexual escapades, intoxicating perfumes and urban images quite closely. His only published prose fiction, 'Mutability', could be seen in a similar light. However, the greatest parallels in terms of Decadent tropes are to be found with J. K. Huysmans's seminal study of Decadent behaviour *À Rebours*.

Akin to Huysmans's anti-hero, Des Esseintes, Wratislaw's ironically named 'Algernon Deepdale' has a 'nervous temperament', and is the very definition of mutability or capriciousness (this theme is suggested in the title of Wratislaw's *Caprices*; also the poems therein deal with ephemeral romantic interludes). Deepdale's emotional engagement with people, places and sensations is only ever fleeting and superficial. Hence the city of London is by turns an entropic wasteland and an enticing, if temporary, 'most perfect flower'. Equally, in his dealings with women, feelings of love, desire, loathing, guilt and remorse are experienced in the moment, and then casually cast aside, as, too often, are the women themselves. The only lasting characteristic in Deepdale is therefore narcissism coupled with a singularly brutal misogyny, that is distinctly reminiscent of Des Esseintes's more famous progeny, Dorian Gray. The conceit of interchanging the serious with the trivial is also a common thread between 'Mutability' and

Wilde's play *The Importance of Being Earnest* (1895), along with the name 'Algernon'.

I

The strong sweet south-wester, fresh and vigorous as a god, after its journey across the Channel which flashed blue and white to the horizon and broke in chalky waves at the foot of the down, flung the girl's hair, loose and wet from the sea, across her chin and throat, fluttering its straggling gold into her eyes. The man who lay at her feet watched her with admiration and desire as she stood sideways to the wind that threatened to blow the sailor-cap on her head, a hundred yards down the grassy slope into the discoloured breakers. They had been together a good deal since the day when Algernon Deepdale — a young man well known to exist only on his expectations and an aunt — came to the hotel at which the Grays had been staying, and had recognised her as the partner of a dance some weeks back. Her friendship had made the time go rapidly, and he had thrown up an invitation in order to stay longer in the seaside town which her presence alone made endurable. Hers was an exceptional beauty, but it was not her only charm. She was possessed of an intelligence not very common among women, nor was ever at a loss for ideas or words. She talked with her eyes and hands as well as her lips, as if the momentary thought that she expressed moved her body to the cadence of her words, her gestures giving strength to the phrase. She was a living being, thought Deepdale, contrasting her mentally with the lack of animation and ideas which is the portion of the majority. Moreover, she was fond of being well dressed, as even the French muslin blouse tied at throat and waist with an unobtainable vieux-rose-colour ribbon attested. His eyes followed her every movement, and a little tempest of desire went through him, as his gaze at last unconsciously attracted her and she turned with a smile.

'The wind is too strong,' she said, as she sat down, throwing her hair from her face and pulling her skirts over her ankles.

'Helen, will you marry me?' he said, taking his cigarette out of his mouth, and looking up into her eyes.

'*Apropos* of what? How dreadfully abrupt you are!' she replied.

'*Apropos* of my thoughts and in logical sequence. May I have an answer?'

'Why do you ask me that?' she answered, somewhat awkwardly.

'For several reasons,' he replied. 'First, because I am going away this afternoon; then because I should like you to be my wife; and the third reason I think you have known for some time.'

'I am so sorry,' she said, gently. 'It is quite impossible.'

'I don't see why,' he answered.

'It is quite impossible,' she continued. 'My people would be dead against it, and I am much too extravagant for you. Besides, I don't want to marry anyone.'

'Do you not care for me at all, Helen?' he asked.

'I like you very well,' she replied, 'but how long have I known you? Three months? In another three you will have forgotten me.'

'You mean you don't like me enough to marry me? Is that it?'

She was silent. Then suddenly she said:

'Why cannot you be patient? You have only known me for this little time and yet you want everything or nothing, at once.'

'Oh no, not at once. I would wait for you, if there was any chance. Is there, Helen?'

She shook her head.

'How can I tell? There is none now,' she said.

'But if there was?' he persisted.

'I can't say. Forget me. It will be much better. There can be no use in looking forward for a year.'

'I think there would be — for me,' he answered.

She laughed lightly.

'How long have you thought of me like this?' she asked.

'Since the first time I saw you,' he said, 'that afternoon, when it was so dark I could barely make out your face, but I fell in love with your mouth, the loveliest mouth in the world.'

A smile came back to her face. The flag on the coastguard's cottage flapped in the wind, and, far below, the blue waves curled silently into innumerable points of foam. A steamer, infinitesimal though it seemed, left a track of pale smoke behind it, and the sun shone joyously over all.

'How sweet it is,' he said, yielding himself up to the sensuous delight of summer centring in the beauty of the girl at his side. 'Let me look at it all once more, since I must leave it all to-day. How you are to be envied, you who remain. And I have to go back to that intolerable, dusty, sultry, horrible town!'

He turned to look at the downs behind, and turned back again.

'No, there is nothing like the sea,' he continued. 'Oh, Helen, if I could take back some hope of you!'

'You are so impatient!' she said. 'You must wait and see if there is a chance. I don't suppose there will be. You had better forget me altogether. You can easily.'

'Will you decide which I shall do?' he asked.

'No, it is for you to decide.'

'I shall wait then,' he answered. 'You will not promise, Helen?'

'No,' she said, shaking her head. 'We must go back,' she added, abruptly. 'Are you ready?'

'Yes,' he said, springing up and stretching his hands to her. She took them and rose.

'We are good friends,' he asked, still holding her hands. She smiled in his eyes with a 'Yes.'

'You are not angry?' she asked. 'You won't be bitter against me, will you? I should be so sorry.'

'Bitter?' he repeated. 'No, certainly not. How could I be?'

'Don't be bitter about it,' she continued. 'I should hate to think that you could be angry with me.'

'I can well promise you that,' he said, bending his face towards hers. How beautiful she was, with her little round face, her exquisite mouth and her eyes! 'And I shall not forget you. I shall wait.'

She smiled, and then added more seriously:

'Don't wait for me. It would be foolish of you to give up anything for my sake. I can promise you nothing.'

'You cannot prevent my hoping, can you?' he asked.

'I suppose not,' she answered, as they turned down the hillside and rejoined their party without more delay.

II

The chalky downs faded behind the train, and Deepdale found himself back again in the town which he imagined that he hated so much. In fact, it was desolate — with that lamentably seedy desolation which London wears for three months out of the twelve. Piccadilly without a well-dressed man or woman is not a pleasant sight, and Deepdale reached his rooms near that thoroughfare in an exceedingly bad temper. His letters — including several bills and a note from Mrs. Westham to warn him that she was coming to see him immediately on his arrival — also displeased him.

Mrs. Westham was the only woman out of the innumerable women with whom he had had relations of some kind who was utterly devoted to him, and who therefore bored him beyond all others. Though their relationship was of long standing he hesitated to break it off, partly from the vanity of being so able to dominate her, and partly from the desire of causing her as little pain as possible. So long as he could keep her at a distance he was content, but when a meeting became inevitable it was for him an unpleasant experience. Fortunately she had her house to attend to, and he managed to arrange that his spare hours as a rule should not coincide with hers. Her husband was abroad for six months out of the year or her movements would have been even more restrained. But at last he found himself at the end of his patience. Let come what would, with the receipt of her note he determined to break off the affair altogether.

With his return to the everyday world of London, on the other hand, his attraction towards Helen Gray had speedily faded. He had almost forgotten the incident of the morning. At the bottom, he had been insincere in professing love for her. She was certainly beautiful, she would in all probability, as an only child, be fairly rich, and she was a woman he would be proud to have for his wife, for purposes of display at Ascot or the opera. Moreover, the gracious beauty of her form and face were a promise of deeper happiness to the man whom she could love. But he was not very deeply hurt, he thought, by her refusal, which, after all, was extremely sensible. His income of nine hundred a year would be mere poverty in marriage, and it was doubtful if he would have more for several years.

His man announcing Mrs. Westham disturbed his thoughts.

She came in hesitatingly. When the door had closed he kissed her, and drew a chair to the window. She turned up her veil.

'Good God!' he exclaimed, 'how ill you look! What is the matter?'

Her face, which once had had a certain charm for him, was drawn and yellow. He would hardly have recognised her.

'I am ill,' she said, 'but never mind that now. Are you glad to see me?' she asked, kissing his hands.

'Of course I am,' he answered.

'How changed you are, Algy,' she answered. 'But you can't help not being as fond of me now as you were a year ago! I wonder why you have changed?'

It was the same scene he had been through before, over and over again.

She always asked the same questions and he always made the same replies. She had very little tact, he thought! He was prepared for another unpleasant quarter of an hour, but he hoped that it would result in his being able to prevent its recurrence in the future.

'Who were the people you saw so much of while you were away?' she asked. 'You never told me their names.'

'The Grays,' he answered, briefly.

'Oh!' she said. 'It was that Gray girl who was talked about in connection with you. To think that I didn't know. I suppose you are engaged to her now?'

'I am not,' he replied, coldly.

'Did you propose to her?'

'No.'

'I don't believe you,' she said. 'Well, I am going, you don't want me. I will not bore you again.' She choked a little. 'You are not worth my love. I wonder if you will ever find a woman to love you as I have done. But I won't bore you again.'

'Don't be a fool, Milly,' he said. 'Sit down.'

'I told you that I would give you up when you found another woman,' she continued, standing. 'When I heard you talked about with that Gray girl I did not even feel jealous. I was so sure of you. But you are quite changed. Oh, God help me! Algy, how can I live without you?' she cried, as she sank back into the chair.

He leaned forward and stroked her hand.

'You don't even kiss me now!' she exclaimed, passionately, throwing back his caress. 'And I had so much to tell you! Are you tired of me? Is that the truth?'

'No,' he said, indifferently.

'It is,' she retorted. 'Yet even now I cannot see it. I love you too much to believe it. Tell me and let me know. Are you tired of me?'

At all events, it was his duty to hurt her as little as possible. 'Of course, I am not,' he answered. Then a thought struck him which made him look curiously at her. The same thought at that moment came uppermost in her mind, crushing out her misery for the time. She lay back in the chair and half closed her eyelids.

'There is one thing I wanted to tell you,' she said, 'I have a child!'

The announcement was not unforeseen, but it was a shock. To conceal the fact he flicked the end of his cigarette carefully into the grate before answering. Then he said:

'Are you quite sure now?'

She nodded. Her heart was beating a tattoo and she could barely speak.

'What an infernal complication!' he exclaimed, frowning, although a vague feeling of pride which appeared to him to be wholly stupid, but which he could not check, rose in him. 'What are you going to do?'

'I shall have to kill myself,' she replied. Why did he not throw himself at her feet, she thought, beseeching her not to do such a thing? He did not answer, but stared hard at the end of the cigarette, still frowning.

'I believe you would be glad if I did!' she exclaimed. Then as her excitement grew, she continued, 'Algy, you are not so brutal as to wish that, are you?'

'Don't be absurd. I was thinking what on earth is to be done. When is he coming back?'

'Not for three months.'

Abruptly and without tangible cause, the whole story of their relationship unfolded itself before him, bare of the imagined beauty with which his thought had once bedecked it, in its plain and squalid ugliness. He was filled in spite of himself with horror of the woman before him. It seemed — in this crisis of his nerves — as if he could not tolerate her presence for a moment longer. Though his face did not show his feeling, she seemed to grasp his thought. She felt that there was no mercy to be expected from him, no hope for her to cling to. She rose bravely.

'Good-bye, Algy,' she said. 'We shall not meet again. Don't speak to me. Let me go. Good-bye.'

He took her hand for a moment and then opened the door. As she went out he called his servant to open the street door for her and returned to his room.

'Thank God that is finished,' he muttered, as he moved about, nervously touching things on the tables or the mantelpiece. Then, after a time, he went out. At his club he found the only man he looked on as a friend, Lord Reggie Cork, a philosophical young man whose eternal tranquillity of temper was extremely pleasing to the nervous temperament of Deepdale.

'Hullo, Deepdale,' he said, 'come and dine with me. What are you doing in town at this time? Do you feel inclined to go to Norway?'

'Norway? Are you going?'

'To-morrow, ten-thirty. Come with me, there's a good chap!'

Deepdale thought for a moment. Then he answered:

'Right! I will come with you. I shall not come back here till next year. I am sick of town and of England too. I have been getting into trouble.'

Deepdale proceeded to expound matters to his friend and to ask his advice.

Whatever Lord Reggie's opinion may have been, the two men left England on the morrow, Deepdale having arranged to let his chambers during his absence.

III

He kept his word and did not return till the following year. When he did the season was well under weigh. It was an exceptionally beautiful spring, and London was — in Deepdale's eyes at least — its central and most perfect flower. To one who had been away from it so long, the city seemed to give a promise of new life, and, as his cab flashed down Piccadilly, the sight of the crush of carriages, the crowd at Hyde Park Corner, lifted his heart like a draught of wine. Lady Audley, on whom he called, was delighted to see him. She reproached him for his long disappearance and his tardy return.

'You haven't seen the new beauty,' she said, laughing. In answer to his inquiry, she continued —

'She's an old friend of yours, I hear. In society? No; she used not to be, but Lady Rivers, people say, met her somewhere or other in the winter, and was so fascinated that she has had her under her wing for the last three weeks. We are all raving about her.'

'You say I know her?' he asked.

'If that isn't like you men!' she laughed. 'You have met this girl, fallen in love with her, I believe, and have forgotten all about it. Well, you will fall in love with her again. That is my prophecy.'

'When am I likely to see her?' he asked.

'If you like to bore yourself by coming here to-night you are sure to see her. Come any time after eleven.'

'Won't you tell me who she is?' he said.

'No. She will surprise you; and you will have to be grateful to me for giving you an emotion.'

He took his leave presently, and made his way into the Park. The subject slipped out of his mind, and he did not mention it to any of the numberless acquaintances he met. Most of them seemed glad to see him, but a few appeared to his sensitive egoism to be somewhat strange in manner. He was wondering at this, a little annoyed, when he ran up against Lord Reggie, whom he had not seen for several months.

'Hullo, Deepdale!' he exclaimed. 'Just back? I say, you've come at a bad time.'

'How's that?' asked Deepdale.

'Haven't you heard, or are you trying to play deep?' he answered.

'I have heard nothing,' was the answer.

'Good Lord! I'll have to tell you then. Come and sit down.'

Deepdale obeyed.

'It's pretty serious, old chap,' Cork continued. 'It's all over the place, or it wouldn't matter so much. You remember a woman I saw at your place once or twice — Mrs. Westham — the woman you told me about?'

Deepdale nodded.

'Well, she poisoned herself a month ago,' said the other, lowering his voice. 'But that isn't all. These women are so confoundedly theatrical. She couldn't make her exit from this world without letting people know why. I dare say she didn't mean to harm you, but it looks as if she wanted a little revenge at the last moment. She wrote a letter to you and left it on her table before drinking the stuff. It came out at the inquest; I've a paper at my rooms, but I daresay you can guess what it was.'

Deepdale, with his head bent, was gazing at the point of his stick in the gravel.

'Damn her,' he said, in a low voice, choking with anger, yet stunned with the shock. He had nearly forgotten her, but the news of her death was like a violent blow. 'How far has it gone?'

'Everywhere, naturally. You can't prevent people reading newspapers.'

'I saw Lady Audley just now,' he muttered. 'She said nothing.'

'Very likely she hadn't heard. But she won't be nice when she does.'

'Let us go to your rooms,' he said, standing up a little shakily. It cost him an effort not to break down altogether. His knees seemed to have lost all sensation; he could hardly steady himself, his hands shook, and his face had gone suddenly white.

Lord Reggie drew his arm through his own.

'Steady, old man,' said he, as they crossed the Row. 'It's no good showing 'em how you've been hit. Get into this cab,' he added as they emerged from the archway.

'No, we'll walk!' exclaimed Deepdale, with an oath. 'Damn the woman! I thought I was going to have a good time of it this season. You know my aunt is dead? No? she died a week ago and left me nearly everything. I've been scraping along all this time on a few beggarly hundreds a year, and now that it's thousands, this infernal woman steps in and spoils all my hand! Damn her!'

'You needn't swear,' said Cork. 'You were pretty well gone on her once, weren't you?'

Deepdale made no answer as his thoughts went back into the past. He walked with his head bent down. Suddenly he exclaimed:

'My God, what a thing to happen to a man!'

His first feeling of anger had passed. He was overwhelmed now with remorse. Why had he not stayed and helped her? He forgot how weary of her presence he had been, and reproached himself only for his leaving her to her trouble. What misery she must have endured! What a beast he was! Would he have to go through life with the consciousness of having committed the most callous of murders, of having caused the death of the one woman who had really loved him, wearisome though she was!

'What am I to do, Reggie?' he asked, to break the silence.

'Wait and see what happens,' replied Cork philosophically. He was a believer in Fate.

'What an infernal scandal it will be,' Deepdale murmured under his breath. He was too fond of society to be as unconventional as he wished, and he by no means wished to give up his season.

When they reached Lord Reggie's chambers, he sank into a chair.

'Give me the paper and get me a drink — brandy and soda,' he said.

The lines were a misty blur, and he could not read at first. After a time some of the sentences became legible. He was reading her letter; the letter that was meant only for him, and yet was printed for everyone's eyes; trying to skip the details of her death, though they forced themselves under his notice and burnt themselves on his mind. It was a much saner and less effusive letter than he expected, and was both dignified and pathetic.

Lord Reggie sat opposite his friend, dreading an outburst of frantic grief. He was relieved when Deepdale lifted his head and merely remarked,

'I don't believe the thing has gone or will go as far as you try to make out. Haven't you exaggerated?'

A sudden revulsion of feeling had come upon him. The sober sentences had calmed him, and he had recovered his nerve. After all, what did it matter? He was not responsible for her death. He had tired of her and left her. That was nothing unusual. Her foolishness was no fault of his. So far he satisfied himself; and as to the scandal, he would have to live it down or go away if it became necessary.

Deepdale's temperament was one that is not rare. He could take things easily or badly, almost as he chose. Though the catastrophe might, if he had allowed it to do so, have broken him down, yet by an effort of will he managed to throw it on one side. The shock remained, like a wound that annoys when the first pain has gone by, but he had determined to let it gain no ascendancy over him. He was able to forget very easily, and he relied on this ability to preserve him from any future outbreaks of conscience.

Instead of answering, Lord Reggie, relieved to find that there was to be no scene, proceeded to discourse with some warmth to his friend on his callousness and brutality. Deepdale listened meekly, and when Lord Reggie had come to the end of his disquisition, they arranged to dine and pass the evening together. It was not far from midnight when they appeared at Lady Audley's party. Deepdale was relieved to find that there was no change towards him in any of the people to whom he spoke. A weight seemed lifted from his heart.

'Where is your new beauty?' he asked his hostess, when there was a momentary cessation of arrivals.

'She's here. That is all I know,' she answered, glancing with pretended dismay into the hopelessly crowded room. 'Oh, there she is,' she exclaimed, as some movement opened a momentary space in the crush. His eyes followed the direction of hers, and lighted on a tall fair girl with blonde hair and enormous pale yellow sleeves.

'What? Miss Gray?' he asked.

'Go and talk to her,' she replied. 'I am a confirmed match-maker, you know,' she added, good humouredly, as she turned to smile on some new guests.

Deepdale edged his way towards his old acquaintance. He made slow progress, but at last he succeeded in reaching her. Her welcome was more cordial than he could have hoped, and the man to whom she had been speaking moved away unwillingly.

'Where have you been all this time?' she said. 'You ought to be punished. You look ever so much older, and you don't look well.'

'No,' he answered, 'I'm rather seedy. But you are more beautiful than ever,' he added, lowering his voice.

She laughed. 'You have not forgotten your old sin of paying untrue compliments!'

'Untrue?' he replied. 'Will you never believe me? Can't we get out of this crowd? Shall we go on the balcony?'

The balcony was large, and by good luck they found two chairs.

'Tell me all about yourself,' she said as she sat down. He obeyed as far as he could, and did not omit to mention the death of his aunt and his consequent increase of fortune.

'How delightful for you,' she said. 'And now you are perfectly happy, I suppose.'

'Do you think I am so inconstant?' he asked. 'Or have you forgotten the downs?'

'No, I don't forget. It is you who forget, and go away for three-quarters of a year without a word.'

'It was an unpardonable sin,' he replied; 'but will you forgive me? It was really very necessary, and perhaps, perhaps you remember why it was of no use for me to come back sooner?'

'I forgive you,' she said softly.

'Are you any happier now that you have achieved success?' he asked. 'You used to long for success.'

'No, I think not,' she answered. 'It seems only natural. And then everything appears just as stupid as before. There is always something wanting to my life. I don't know what.'

'It is the same with me,' he said, 'with a difference. I know what I want.'

'I should have thought you had everything you wanted,' she answered.

'No, there is always one thing,' he said, touching her hand. She withdrew it gently, and stood up.

'Let us go in,' she said; 'I am cooler now, and I am afraid of catching cold.'

'When may I come and see you?' he asked, as he rose.

She thought for a moment.

'On Friday,' she answered.

'And to-day is Monday!' he exclaimed.

'Friday is the only possible day this week. I am staying with Lady Rivers, you know, and I have to go out with her. But I can be in on Friday, about four, if you like.'

'On Friday, then,' he answered. 'I want to ask you a question I asked you once before,' he added, as they re-entered the room, and further talk became impossible.

She turned away with a smile.

'Who was that you were on the balcony with?' asked Lady Rivers an hour later, as they were driving home.

'A Mr. Deepdale,' Helen answered, 'an old friend. I have asked him to come on Friday to tea.'

'My dear Helen!' exclaimed Lady Rivers, 'he is quite impossible. You ought not to know such a man.'

'Why not?' she queried.

'Haven't you heard about his wickedness? It is really too dreadful.'

'No, I have heard nothing against him,' she answered frigidly, while some strange fear made her tremble. 'I believe he is going to ask me to marry him.'

'Helen! You must not think of it,' said Lady Rivers in an agonising tone. 'It would be very wrong of you. I don't know the whole tale, but my husband told me a good deal of it.'

'I wish to hear nothing,' she replied, coldly.

'Oh, yes, you must, and I shall tell you.'

IV

The three following days were like nightmares to Helen. She had listened to the story without the least change of expression, but in her own room she had broken into a passion of tears. Until that moment she had scarcely realised that she loved the man at all. She knew it at last, conquered by jealousy of the woman he had killed. To her own despair, she was not overwhelmed with horror for his crime. It did not seem unnatural. She only hated the woman who had come between them. But her own state of mind seemed like dishonour, and she suffered all the tortures of remorse for what she could not help.

Before Friday, however, she had regained some tranquillity. She would refuse, if he proposed to her, and would forget him. When Deepdale called, she therefore welcomed him very frigidly. But she was alone, and he had determined not to let the opportunity slip.

'Why are you so changed, so cold?' he asked, after a time. The truth suddenly flashed upon him, and he swiftly decided on his course of action. 'Have people been telling you tales about me?' he added.

'Tales that are true, I am afraid,' she answered.

'I would have told you myself,' he said, gently. 'It is too dreadful for words, isn't it? You should pity me, rather than blame me; my life is quite ruined. I have nothing left me now on earth.'

'Don't say that,' she murmured. 'You will forget, and so will others. But it is very sad.'

'It is much more; it is my ruin. But you, at least, may pity me. My life is hard enough to bear, without losing you even as a friend — for you were my friend once, were you not?'

She did not answer, but her lips moved inaudibly.

'You know now why I went away. Can you not guess what I suffered all the time, knowing that I had lost you, you who were ever like a star in my dark heaven? Think now what my life will be, without the one hope that filled me for so long, the one thing that made me live. I have lost that — and I have lost everything. It is my own fault — and yet not so much my fault as perhaps you think. It was my sin, and I must pay for it. In these days there is no Elizabeth to forgive Tannhauser.'

She listened immovably, but her eyes were moist, and her lips parted, as she breathed rapidly.

'I will go,' he said, rising. 'Shall I ever see you again, I wonder? Oh, Helen,' he cried, taking her hands as she stood before him, 'I could have loved you so well!'

She did not move away, and he bent his head to cover her hands with kisses.

'Helen,' he said, looking into her eyes, 'is it all over? Will not your forgiveness cover even me? Cannot the past be the past? I am brokenhearted for my crime. You and you only can give me new life. Will you forgive me? Will you not love me as I love you?'

He placed his arm round her neck, tentatively. She did not resist, and as he drew nearer, her head sank on his shoulder, and she uttered a little sigh of content.

He smiled to himself in triumph; then he bent his head and kissed her on the mouth.

The Idiots

Joseph Conrad

Joseph Conrad (1857–1924) was one of the leading writers of novels in English at the turn of the last century. 'The Idiots' is his only contribution to *The Savoy*, to whom he submitted the story after it was rejected by *Cosmopolis*. Although he did not consider himself part of Decadent circles during the 1890s, he very much admired the poetry of Arthur Symons, and was almost certainly influenced by the short stories of Ernest Dowson. Furthermore, Symons (a friend to Conrad in his later years) sought to link him, posthumously, with Decadent styles and techniques in his book, *Notes on Joseph Conrad* (1925).

'The Idiots' certainly stands testament to Symons's analysis, being a tale of the unnatural or abnormal offspring of a French farm worker. The idiot children bear no connection with their parents, literally looking like 'other people's children'; and statements like 'Ah! There's another' and 'there are more of them' in the frame narration add to the feeling of a lack of human individuality among this morbid brood. The Victorian virtues of hard work and devotion to the family are here turned on their head, and only result in the protagonists' descent into madness, murder and suicide. Contemporary concerns over degeneration are reflected in the themes of biological entropy and a concomitant insanity, and are in this respect reminiscent of Robert Louis Stevenson's post-Darwinian Gothic tale of vampirism, 'Olalla' (1885). French Decadent literary techniques may be seen in such descriptions as the Zola-esque 'opal-tinted and odorous' mist over the manure heap on the farm.

We were driving along the road from Treguier to Kervanda. We passed at a smart trot between the hedges topping an earth wall on each side of the road; then at the foot of the steep ascent before Ploumar the horse dropped into a walk, and the driver jumped down heavily from the box. He flicked his whip and climbed the incline, stepping clumsily uphill by the side of the carriage, one hand on the footboard, his eyes on the ground. After a while he lifted his head, pointed up the road with the end of the whip, and said –

'The idiot!'

The sun was shining violently upon the undulating surface of the land. The rises were topped by clumps of meagre trees, with their branches showing high on the sky as if they had been perched upon stilts. The small fields, cut up by hedges and stone walls that zigzagged over the slopes, lay in rectangular patches of vivid greens and yellows, resembling the unskilful daubs of a naive picture. And the landscape was divided in two by the white streak of a road stretching in long loops far away, like a river of dust crawling out of the hills on its way to the sea.

'Here he is,' said the driver, again.

In the long grass bordering the road a face glided past the carriage at the level of the wheels as we drove slowly by. The imbecile face was red, and the bullet head with close-cropped hair seemed to lie alone, its chin in the dust. The body was lost in the bushes growing thick along the bottom of the deep ditch.

It was a boy's face. He might have been sixteen, judging from the size – perhaps less, perhaps more. Such creatures are forgotten by time, and live untouched by years till death gathers them up into its compassionate bosom; the faithful death that never forgets in the press of work the most insignificant of its children.

'Ah! There's another,' said the man, with a certain satisfaction in his tone, as if he had caught sight of something expected.

There was another. That one stood nearly in the middle of the road in the blaze of sunshine at the end of his own short shadow. And he stood with hands pushed into the opposite sleeves of his long coat, his head sunk between the shoulders, all hunched up in the flood of heat. From a distance he had the aspect of one suffering from intense cold.

'Those are twins,' explained the driver.

The idiot shuffled two paces out of the way and looked at us over his shoulder when we brushed past him. The glance was unseeing and staring, a fascinated glance; but he did not turn to look after us. Probably the image passed before the eyes without leaving any trace on the misshapen brain of the creature. When we had topped the ascent I looked over the hood. He stood in the road just where we had left him.

The driver clambered into his seat, clicked his tongue, and we went downhill. The brake squeaked horribly from time to time. At the foot he eased off the noisy mechanism and said, turning half round on his box:

'We shall see some more of them by-and-by.'

'More idiots? How many of them are there, then?' I asked.

'There's four of them – children of a farmer near Ploumar here . . . . The parents are dead now,' he added, after a while. 'The grandmother lives on the farm. In the daytime they knock about on this road, and they come home at dusk along with the cattle . . . . It's a good farm.'

We saw the other two: a boy and a girl, as the driver said. They were dressed exactly alike, in shapeless garments with petticoat-like skirts. The imperfect thing that lived within them moved those beings to howl at us from the top of the bank, where they sprawled amongst the tough stalks of furze. Their cropped black heads stuck out from the bright yellow wall of countless small blossoms. The faces were purple with the strain of yelling; the voices sounded blank and cracked like a mechanical imitation of old people's voices; and suddenly ceased when we turned into a lane.

I saw them many times in my wandering about the country. They lived on that road, drifting along its length here and there, according to the inexplicable impulses of their monstrous darkness. They were an offence to the sunshine, a reproach to empty heaven, a blight on the concentrated and purposeful vigour of the wild landscape. In time the story of their parents shaped itself before me out of the listless answers to my questions, out of the indifferent words heard in wayside inns or on the very road those idiots haunted. Some of it was told by an emaciated and sceptical old fellow with a tremendous whip, while we trudged together over the sands by the side of a two-wheeled cart loaded with dripping seaweed. Then at other times other people confirmed and completed the story; till it stood at last before me, a tale formidable and simple, as they always are, those disclosures of obscure trials endured by ignorant hearts.

When he returned from his military service Jean Pierre Bacadou found the old people very much aged. He remarked with pain that the work of the farm was not satisfactorily done. The father had not the energy of old days. The hands did not feel over them the eye of the master. Jean-Pierre noted with sorrow that the heap of manure in the courtyard before the only entrance to the house was not so large as it should have been. The fences were out of repair, and the cattle suffered from neglect. At home the mother was practically bedridden, and the girls chattered loudly in the big kitchen, unrebuked, from morning to night. He said to himself: 'We must change all this.' He talked the matter over with his father one evening when the rays of the setting sun entering the yard between the outhouses ruled the heavy shadows with luminous streaks. Over the manure heap floated a mist, opal-tinted and odorous, and the marauding hens would stop in their scratching to examine with a sudden glance of their round eye the two men, both lean and tall, talking together in hoarse tones. The old man, all twisted with rheumatism and bowed with years of work, the younger bony and straight, spoke without gestures in the indifferent manner of peasants, grave and slow. But before the sun had set the father had submitted to the sensible arguments of the son. 'It is not for me that I am speaking,' insisted Jean-Pierre. 'It is for the land. It's a pity to see it badly used. I am not impatient for myself.' The old fellow nodded over his stick. 'I dare say; I dare say,' he muttered. 'You may be right. Do what you like. It's the mother that will be pleased.'

The mother was pleased with her daughter-in-law. Jean-Pierre brought the two-wheeled spring-cart with a rush into the yard. The grey horse galloped clumsily, and the bride and bridegroom, sitting side by side, were jerked backwards and forwards by the up and down motion of the shafts, in a manner regular and brusque. On the road the distanced wedding guests straggled in pairs and groups. The men advanced with heavy steps, swinging their idle arms. They were clad in town clothes: jackets cut with clumsy smartness, hard black hats, immense boots, polished highly. Their women all in simple black, with white caps and shawls of faded tints folded triangularly on the back, strolled lightly by their side. In front the violin sang a strident tune, and the biniou snored and hummed, while the player capered solemnly, lifting high his heavy clogs. The sombre procession drifted in and out of the narrow lanes, through sunshine and through shade, between fields and hedgerows, scaring the little birds that darted away in troops right and left. In the yard of Bacadou's farm the dark ribbon wound itself up into a mass of men and women pushing at the door with cries and greetings. The wedding dinner was remembered for months. It was a splendid feast in the orchard. Farmers of considerable means and excellent repute were to be found sleeping in ditches, all along the road to Treguier, even as late as the afternoon of the next day. All the countryside participated in the happiness of Jean-Pierre. He remained sober, and, together with his quiet wife, kept out of the way, letting father and mother reap their due of honour and thanks. But the next day he took hold strongly, and the old folks felt a shadow – precursor of the grave – fall upon them finally. The world is to the young.

When the twins were born there was plenty of room in the house, for the mother of Jean-Pierre had gone away to dwell under a heavy stone in the cemetery of Ploumar. On that day, for the first time since his son's marriage, the elder Bacadou, neglected by the cackling lot of strange women who thronged the kitchen, left in the morning his seat under the mantel of the fireplace, and went into the empty cow-house, shaking his white locks dismally. Grandsons were all very well, but he wanted his soup at midday. When shown the babies, he stared at them with a fixed gaze, and muttered something like: 'It's too much.' Whether he meant too much happiness, or simply commented upon the number of his descendants, it is impossible to say. He looked offended – as far as his old wooden face could express anything; and for days afterwards could be seen, almost any time of the day, sitting at the gate, with his nose over his knees, a pipe between his gums, and gathered up into a kind of raging concentrated sulkiness. Once he spoke to his son, alluding to the newcomers with a groan: 'They will quarrel over the land.' 'Don't bother about that, father,' answered Jean-Pierre, stolidly, and passed, bent double, towing a recalcitrant cow over his shoulder.

He was happy, and so was Susan, his wife. It was not an ethereal joy welcoming new souls to struggle, perchance to victory. In fourteen years both boys would be a help; and, later on, Jean-Pierre pictured two big sons striding over the land from patch to patch, wringing tribute from the earth beloved and fruitful. Susan was happy too, for she did not want to be spoken of as the unfortunate woman, and now she had children no one could call her that. Both herself and her husband had seen something of the larger world – he during the time of his service; while she had spent a year or so in Paris with a Breton family, but had been too home-sick to remain longer away from the hilly and green country, set in a barren circle of rocks and sands, where she had been born. She thought that one of the boys ought perhaps to be a priest, but said nothing to her husband, who was a republican, and hated the 'crows', as he called the ministers of religion. The christening was a splendid affair. All the commune came to it, for the Bacadous were rich and influential, and, now and then, did not mind the expense. The grandfather had a new coat.

Some months afterwards, one evening when the kitchen had been swept, and the door locked, Jean-Pierre, looking at the cot, asked his wife: 'What's the matter with those children?' And, as if these words, spoken calmly, had been the portent of misfortune, she answered with a loud wail that must have been heard across the yard in the pig-sty; for the pigs (the Bacadous had the finest pigs in the country), stirred and grunted complainingly in the night. The husband went on grinding his bread and butter slowly, gazing at the wall, the soup-plate smoking under his chin. He had returned late from the market, where he had overheard (not for the first time) whispers behind his back. He revolved the words in his mind as he drove back. 'Simple! Both of them.... Never any use!... Well! May be, may be. One must see. Would ask his wife.' This was her answer. He felt like a blow on his chest, but said only: 'Go, draw me some cider. I am thirsty!'

She went out moaning, an empty jug in her hand. Then he arose, took up the light, and moved slowly towards the cradle. They slept. He looked at them sideways, finished his mouthful there, went back heavily, and sat down before his plate. When his wife returned he never looked up, but swallowed a couple of spoonfuls noisily, and remarked, in a dull manner:

'When they sleep they are like other people's children.'

She sat down suddenly on a stool near by, and shook with a silent tempest of sobs, unable to speak. He finished his meal, and remained idly thrown back in his chair, his eyes lost amongst the black rafters of the ceiling. Before him the tallow candle flared red and straight, sending up a slender thread of smoke. The light lay on the rough, sunburnt skin of his throat; the sunk cheeks were like patches of darkness, and his aspect was mournfully stolid, as if he had ruminated with difficulty endless ideas. Then he said, deliberately:

'We must see . . . consult people. Don't cry . . . . They won't be all like that . . . surely! We must sleep now.'

After the third child, also a boy, was born, Jean-Pierre went about his work with tense hopefulness. His lips seemed more narrow, more tightly compressed than before; as if for fear of letting the earth he tilled hear the voice of hope that murmured within his breast. He watched the child, stepping up to the cot with a heavy clang of sabots on the stone floor, and glanced in, along his shoulder, with that indifference which is like a deformity of peasant humanity. Like the earth they master and serve, those men, slow of eye and speech, do not show the inner fire; so that, at last, it becomes a question with them as with the earth, what there is in the core: heat, violence, a force mysterious and terrible – or nothing but a clod, a mass fertile and inert, cold and unfeeling, ready to bear a crop of plants that sustain life or give death.

The mother watched with other eyes; listened with otherwise expectant ears. Under the high hanging shelves supporting great sides of bacon overhead, her body was busy by the great fireplace, attentive to the pot swinging on iron gallows, scrubbing the long table where the field hands would sit down directly to their evening meal. Her mind remained by the cradle, night and day on the watch, to hope and suffer. That child, like the other two, never smiled, never stretched its hands to her, never spoke; never had a glance of recognition for her in its big black eyes, which could only stare fixedly at any glitter, but failed hopelessly to follow the brilliance of a sun-ray slipping slowly along the floor. When the men were at work she spent long days between her three idiot children and the childish grandfather, who sat grim, angular, and immovable, with his feet near the warm ashes of the fire. The feeble old fellow seemed to suspect that there was something wrong with his grandsons. Only once, moved either by affection or by the sense of proprieties, he attempted to nurse the youngest. He took the boy up from the floor, clicked his tongue at him, and essayed a shaky gallop of his bony knees. Then he looked closely with his misty eyes at the child's face and deposited him down gently on the floor again. And he sat, his lean shanks crossed, nodding at the steam escaping from the cooking-pot with a gaze senile and worried.

Then mute affliction dwelt in Bacadou's farmhouse, sharing the breath and the bread of its inhabitants; and the priest of the Ploumar parish had great cause for congratulation. He called upon the rich landowner, the Marquis de Chavanes, on purpose to deliver himself with joyful unction of solemn platitudes about the inscrutable ways of Providence. In the vast dimness of the curtained drawing-room, the little man, resembling a black bolster, leaned towards a couch, his hat on his knees, and gesticulated with a fat hand at the elongated, gracefully-flowing lines of the clear Parisian toilette from which the half-amused, half-bored marquise listened with gracious languor. He was exulting and humble, proud and awed. The impossible had come to pass. Jean-Pierre Bacadou, the enraged republican farmer, had been to mass last Sunday – had proposed to entertain the visiting priests at the next festival of Ploumar! It was a triumph for the Church and for the good cause. 'I thought I would come at once to tell Monsieur le Marquis. I know how anxious he is for the welfare of our country,' declared the priest, wiping his face. He was asked to stay to dinner.

The Chavanes returning that evening, after seeing their guest to the main gate of the park, discussed the matter while they strolled in the moonlight, trailing their elongated shadows up the straight avenue of chestnuts. The marquis, a royalist of course, had been mayor of the commune which includes Ploumar, the scattered hamlets of the coast, and the stony islands that fringe the yellow flatness of the sands. He had felt his position insecure, for there was a strong republican element in that part of the country; but now the conversion of Jean-Pierre made him safe. He was very pleased. 'You have no idea how influential those people are,' he explained to his wife. 'Now, I am sure, the next communal election will go all right. I shall be re-elected.' 'Your ambition is perfectly insatiable, Charles,' exclaimed the marquise, gaily. 'But, ma chère amie,' argued the husband, seriously, 'it's most important that the right man should be mayor this year, because of the elections to the Chamber. If you think it amuses me . . . .'

Jean-Pierre had surrendered to his wife's mother. Madame Levaille was a woman of business known and respected within a radius of at least fifteen miles. Thickset and stout, she was seen about the country, on foot or in an acquaintance's cart, perpetually moving, in spite of her fifty-eight years, in steady pursuit of business. She had houses in all the hamlets, she worked quarries of granite, she freighted coasters with stone – even traded with the Channel Islands. She was broad-cheeked, wide-eyed, persuasive in speech: carrying her point with the placid and invincible obstinacy of an old woman who knows her own mind. She very seldom slept for two nights together in the same house; and the wayside inns were the best places to inquire in as to her whereabouts. She had either passed, or was expected to pass there at six; or somebody, coming in, had seen her in the morning, or expected to meet her that evening. After the inns that command the roads, the churches were the buildings she frequented most. Men of liberal opinions would induce small children to run into sacred edifices to see whether Madame Levaille was there, and to tell her that so-and-so was in the road waiting to speak to her – about potatoes, or flour, or stones, or houses; and she would curtail her devotions, come out blinking and crossing herself into the sunshine; ready to discuss business matters in a calm sensible way across a table in the kitchen of the inn opposite. Latterly she had stayed for a few days several times with her son-in-law; arguing against sorrow and misfortune with composed face and gentle tones. Jean-Pierre felt the convictions imbibed in the regiment torn out of his breast – not by arguments, but by facts. Striding over his fields he thought it over. There were three of them. Three! All alike! Why? Such things did not happen to everybody – to nobody he ever heard of. One yet – it might pass. But three! All three. For ever useless, to be fed while he lived and . . . . What would become of the land when he died? This must be seen to. He would sacrifice his convictions. One day he told his wife:

'See what your God will do for us. Pay for some masses.'

Susan embraced her man. He stood unbending, then turned on his heels and went out. But afterwards when a black *soutane* darkened his doorway he did not object; even offered some cider himself to the priest. He listened to the talk meekly; went to mass between the two women; accomplished what the priest called 'his religious duties' at Easter. That morning he felt like a man who had sold his soul. In the afternoon he fought ferociously with an old friend and neighbour who had remarked that the priests had the best of it and were now going to eat the priest-eater. He came home dishevelled and bleeding, and happening to catch sight of his children (they were kept generally out of the way), cursed and swore incoherently, banging the table. Susan wept. Madame Levaille sat serenely unmoved. She assured her daughter that 'It will pass'; and taking up her thick umbrella, departed in haste to see after a schooner she was going to load with granite from her quarry.

A year or so afterwards the girl was born. A girl! Jean-Pierre heard of it in the fields, and was so upset by the news that he sat down on the boundary wall and remained there till the evening, instead of going home as he was urged to do. A girl! He felt half cheated. However, when he got home he was partly reconciled to his fate. One could marry her to a good fellow

– not to a good for nothing, but to a fellow with some understanding and a good pair of arms. Besides, the next may be a boy, he thought. Of course they would be all right. His new credulity knew of no doubt. The ill luck was broken. He spoke cheerily to his wife. She was also hopeful. Three priests came to that christening, and Madame Levaille was godmother. The child turned out an idiot too.

Then on market days Jean-Pierre was seen bargaining bitterly, quarrelsome and greedy; then getting drunk with taciturn earnestness; then driving home in the dusk at a rate fit for a wedding, but with a face gloomy enough for a funeral. Sometimes he would insist on his wife coming with him; and they would drive in the early morning, shaking side by side on the narrow seat above the helpless pig, that, with tied legs, grunted a melancholy sigh at every rut. The morning drives were silent; but in the evening, coming home, Jean-Pierre, tipsy, was viciously muttering, and growled at the confounded woman who could not rear children that were like anybody else's. Susan, holding on against the erratic swayings of the cart, pretended not to hear. Once, as they were driving through Ploumar, some obscure and drunken impulse caused him to pull up sharply opposite the church. The moon swam amongst light white clouds. The tombstones gleamed pale under the fretted shadows of the trees in the churchyard. Even the village dogs slept. Only the nightingales, awake, spun out the thrill of their song above the silence of graves. Jean-Pierre said thickly to his wife:

'What do you think is there?'

He pointed his whip at the tower – in which the big dial of the clock appeared high in the moonlight like a pallid face without eyes – and getting out carefully, fell down at once by the wheel. He picked himself up and climbed one by one the few steps to the iron gate of the churchyard. He put his face to the bars and called out indistinctly:

'Hey there! Come out!'

'Jean! Return! Return!' entreated his wife in low tones.

He took no notice, and seemed to wait there. The song of nightingales beat on all sides against the high walls of the church, and flowed back between stone crosses and flat grey slabs, engraved with words of hope and sorrow.

'Hey! Come out!' shouted Jean-Pierre loudly.

The nightingales ceased to sing.

'Nobody?' went on Jean-Pierre. 'Nobody there. A swindle of the crows. That's what this is. Nobody anywhere. I despise it. Allez! Houp!'

He shook the gate with all his strength, and the iron bars rattled with a frightful clanging, like a chain dragged over stone steps. A dog near-by barked hurriedly. Jean-Pierre staggered back, and after three successive dashes got into his cart. Susan sat very quiet and still. He said to her with drunken severity:

'See? Nobody. I've been made a fool! Malheur! Somebody will pay for it. The next one I see near the house I will lay my whip on . . . on the black spine . . . I will. I don't want him in there . . . he only helps the carrion crows to rob poor folk. I am a man . . . . We will see if I can't have children like anybody else . . . now you mind . . . . They won't be all . . . all . . . we see . . . .'

She burst out through the fingers that hid her face:

'Don't say that, Jean; don't say that, my man!'

He struck her a swinging blow on the head with the back of his hand and knocked her into the bottom of the cart, where she crouched, thrown about lamentably by every jolt. He drove furiously, standing up, brandishing his whip, shaking the reins over the grey horse that galloped ponderously, making the heavy harness leap upon his broad quarters. The country rang clamorous in the night with the irritated barking of farm dogs, that followed the rattle of wheels all along the road. A couple of belated wayfarers had only just time to step into the ditch. At his own gate he caught the post and was shot out of the cart head first. The horse went on slowly to the door. At Susan's piercing cries the farm hands rushed out. She thought him dead, but he was only sleeping where he fell, and cursed his men who hastened to him for disturbing his slumbers.

Autumn came. The clouded sky descended low upon the black contours of the hills; and the dead leaves danced in spiral whirls under naked trees till the wind, sighing profoundly, laid them to rest in the hollows of bare valleys. And from morning till night one could see all over the land black denuded boughs, the boughs gnarled and twisted, as if contorted with pain, swaying sadly between the wet clouds and the soaked earth. The clear and gentle streams of summer days rushed discoloured and raging at the stones that barred the way to the sea, with the fury of madness bent upon suicide. From horizon to horizon the great road to the sands lay between the hills in a dull glitter of empty curves, resembling an unnavigable river of mud.

Jean-Pierre went from field to field, moving blurred and tall in the drizzle, or striding on the crests of rises, lonely and high upon the grey curtain of drifting clouds, as if he had been pacing along the very edge of the universe. He looked at the black earth, at the earth mute and promising, at the mysterious earth doing its work of life in death-like stillness under the veiled sorrow of the sky. And it seemed to him that to a man worse than childless there was no promise in the fertility of fields, that from him the earth escaped, defied him, frowned at him like the clouds, sombre and hurried above his head. Having to face alone his own fields, he felt the inferiority of man who passes away before the clod that remains. Must he give up the hope of having by his side a son who would look at the turned-up sods with a master's eye? A man that would think as he thought, that would feel as he felt; a man who would be part of himself, and yet remain to trample masterfully on that earth when he was gone? He thought of some distant relations, and felt savage enough to curse them aloud. They! Never! He turned homewards, going straight at the roof of his dwelling, visible between the enlaced skeletons of trees. As he swung his legs over the stile a cawing flock of birds settled slowly on the field; dropped down, behind his back, noiseless and fluttering, like flakes of soot.

That day Madame Levaille had gone early in the afternoon to the house she had near Kervanion. She had to pay some of the men who worked in her granite quarry there, and she went in good time because her little house contained a shop where the workmen could spend their wages without the trouble of going to town. The house stood alone amongst rocks. A lane of mud and stones ended at the door. The sea-winds coming ashore on Stonecutter's Point, fresh from the fierce turmoil of the waves, howled violently at the unmoved heaps of black boulders holding up steadily short-armed, high crosses against the tremendous rush of the invisible. In the sweep of gales the sheltered dwelling stood in a calm resonant and disquieting, like the calm in the centre of a hurricane. On stormy nights, when the tide was out, the bay of Fougère, fifty feet below the house, resembled an immense black pit, from which ascended mutterings and sighs as if the sands down there had been alive and complaining. At high tide the returning water assaulted the ledges of rock in short rushes, ending in bursts of livid light and columns of spray, that flew inland, stinging to death the grass of pastures.

The darkness came from the hills, flowed over the coast, put out the red fires of sunset, and went on to seaward pursuing the retiring tide. The wind dropped with the sun, leaving a maddened sea and a devastated sky. The heavens above the house seemed to be draped in black rags, held up here and there by pins of fire. Madame Levaille, for this evening the servant of her own workmen, tried to induce them to depart. 'An old woman like me ought to be in bed at this late hour,' she good-humouredly repeated. The quarrymen drank, asked for more. They shouted over the table as if they had been talking across a field. At one end four of them played cards, banging the wood with their hard knuckles, and swearing at every lead. One sat with a lost gaze, humming a bar of some song, which he repeated endlessly. Two others, in a corner, were quarrelling confidentially and fiercely over some woman, looking close into one another's eyes as if they had wanted to tear them out, but speaking in whispers that promised violence and murder discreetly, in a venomous sibillation of subdued words. The atmosphere in there was thick enough to slice with a knife. Three candles burning about the long room glowed red and dull like sparks expiring in ashes.

The slight click of the iron latch was at that late hour as unexpected and startling as a thunder-clap. Madame Levaille put down a bottle she held above a liqueur glass; the players turned their heads; the whispered quarrel ceased; only the singer, after darting a glance at the door, went on humming with a stolid face. Susan appeared in the doorway, stepped in, flung the door to, and put her back against it, saying, half aloud:

'Mother!'

Madame Levaille, taking up the bottle again, said calmly: 'Here you are, my girl. What a state you are in!' The neck of the bottle rang on the rim of the glass, for the old woman was startled, and the idea that the farm had caught fire had entered her head. She could think of no other cause for her daughter's appearance.

Susan, soaked and muddy, stared the whole length of the room towards the men at the far end. Her mother asked:

'What has happened? God guard us from misfortune!'

Susan moved her lips. No sound came. Madame Levaille stepped up to her daughter, took her by the arm, looked into her face.

'In God's name,' she said shakily, 'what's the matter? You have been rolling in mud . . . . Why did you come? . . . Where's Jean?'

The men had all got up and approached slowly, staring with dull surprise. Madame Levaille jerked her daughter away from the door, swung her round upon a seat close to the wall. Then she turned fiercely to the men:

'Enough of this! Out you go – you others! I close.'

One of them observed, looking down at Susan collapsed on the seat: 'She is – one may say – half dead.'

Madame Levaille flung the door open.

'Get out! March!' she cried, shaking nervously.

They dropped out into the night, laughing stupidly. Outside, the two Lotharios broke out into loud shouts. The others tried to soothe them, all talking at once. The noise went away up the lane with the men, who staggered together in a tight knot, remonstrating with one another foolishly.

'Speak, Susan. What is it? Speak!' entreated Madame Levaille, as soon as the door was shut.

Susan pronounced some incomprehensible words, glaring at the table. The old woman clapped her hands above her head, let them drop, and stood looking at her daughter with disconsolate eyes. Her husband had been 'deranged in his head' for a few years before he died, and now she began to suspect her daughter was going mad. She asked, pressingly:

'Does Jean know where you are? Where is Jean?'

Susan pronounced with difficulty:

'He knows . . . he is dead.'

'What!' cried the old woman. She came up near, and peering at her daughter, repeated three times: 'What do you say? What do you say? What do you say?'

Susan sat dry-eyed and stony before Madame Levaille, who contemplated her, feeling a strange sense of inexplicable horror creep into the silence of the house. She had hardly realised the news, further than to understand that she had been brought in one short moment face to face with something unexpected and final. It did not even occur to her to ask for any explanation. She thought: accident – terrible accident – blood to the head – fell down a trap door in the loft . . . . . She remained there, distracted and mute, blinking her old eyes.

Suddenly, Susan said:

'I have killed him.'

For a moment the mother stood still, almost unbreathing, but with composed face. The next second, she burst out into a shout:

'You miserable madwoman . . . they will cut your neck . . . .'

She fancied the gendarmes entering the house, saying to her: 'We want your daughter; give her up': the gendarmes with the severe, hard faces of men on duty. She knew the brigadier well – an old friend, familiar and respectful, saying heartily, 'To your good health, Madame!' before lifting to his lips the small glass of cognac – out of the special bottle she kept for friends. And now! . . . . She was losing her head. She rushed here and there, as if looking for something urgently needed – gave that up, stood stock still in the middle of the room, and screamed at her daughter:

'Why? Say! Say! Why?'

The other seemed to leap out of her strange apathy.

'Do you think I am made of stone?' she shouted back, striding towards her mother.

'No! It's impossible . . . . .' said Madame Levaille, in a convinced tone.

'You go and see, mother,' retorted Susan, looking at her with blazing eyes. 'There's no mercy in heaven – no justice. No! . . . . I did not know . . . . Do you think I have no heart? Do you think I have never heard people jeering at me, pitying me, wondering at me? Do you know how some of them were calling me? The mother of idiots – that was my nickname! And my children never would know me, never speak to me. They would know nothing; neither men – nor God. Haven't I prayed! But the Mother of God herself would not hear me. A mother! . . . . Who is accursed – I, or the man who is dead? Eh? Tell me. I took care of myself. Do you think I would defy the anger of God and have my house full of those things – that are worse than animals who know the hand that feeds them? Who blasphemed in the night at the very church door? Was it I? . . . . I only wept and prayed for mercy . . . . and I feel the curse at every moment of the day – I see it round me from morning to night . . . I've got to keep them alive – to take care of my misfortune and shame. And he would come. I begged him and Heaven for mercy . . . . No! . . . Then we shall see . . . . He came this evening. I thought to myself: "Ah! again!" . . . I had my long scissors. I heard him shouting . . . . I saw him near . . . . I must – must I? . . . Then take! . . . And I struck him in the throat above the breast-bone . . . . I never heard him even sigh . . . . I left him standing . . . . It was a minute ago . . . . How did I come here?'

Madame Levaille shivered. A wave of cold ran down her back, down her fat arms under her tight sleeves, made her stamp gently where she stood. Quivers ran over the broad cheeks, across the thin lips, ran amongst the wrinkles at the corners of her steady old eyes. She stammered:

'You wicked woman – you disgrace me. But there! You always resembled your father. What do you think will become of you . . . in the other world? In this . . . Oh misery!'

She was very hot now. She felt burning inside. She wrung her perspiring hands – and suddenly, starting in great haste, began to look for her big shawl and umbrella, feverishly, never once glancing at her daughter, who stood in the middle of the room following her with a gaze distracted and cold.

'Nothing worse than in this,' said Susan.

Her mother, umbrella in hand and trailing the shawl over the floor, groaned profoundly.

'I must go to the priest,' she burst out passionately. 'I do not know whether you even speak the truth! You are a horrible woman. They will find you anywhere. You may stay here – or go. There is no room for you in this world.'

Ready now to depart, she yet wandered aimlessly about the room, putting the bottles on the shelf, trying to fit with trembling hands the covers on cardboard boxes. Whenever the real sense of what she had heard emerged for a second from the haze of her thoughts she would fancy that something had exploded in her brain without, unfortunately, bursting her head to pieces – which would have been a relief. She blew the candles out one by one without knowing it, and was horribly startled by the darkness. She fell on a bench and began to whimper. After a while she ceased, and sat listening to the breathing of her daughter, whom she could hardly see, still and upright, giving no other sign of life. She was becoming old rapidly at last, during those minutes. She spoke in tones unsteady, cut about by the rattle of teeth, like one shaken by a deadly cold fit of ague.

'I wish you had died little. I will never dare to show my old head in the sunshine again. There are worse misfortunes than idiot children. I wish you had been born to me simple – like your own . . . .'

She saw the figure of her daughter pass before the faint and livid clearness of a window. Then it appeared in the doorway for a second, and the door swung to with a clang. Madame Levaille, as if awakened by the noise from a long nightmare, rushed out.

'Susan!' she shouted from the doorstep.

She heard a stone roll a long time down the declivity of the rocky beach above the sands. She stepped forward cautiously, one hand on the wall of the house, and peered down into the smooth darkness of the empty bay. Once again she cried:

'Susan! You will kill yourself there.'

The stone had taken its last leap in the dark, and she heard nothing now. A sudden thought seemed to strangle her, and she called no more. She turned her back upon the black silence of the pit and went up the lane towards Ploumar, stumbling along with sombre determination, as if she had started on a desperate journey that would last, perhaps, to the end of her life. A sullen and periodic clamour of waves rolling over reefs followed her far inland between the high hedges sheltering the gloomy solitude of the fields.

Susan had run out, swerving sharp to the left at the door, and on the edge of the slope crouched down behind a boulder. A dislodged stone went on downwards, rattling as it leaped. When Madame Levaille called out, Susan could have, by stretching her hand, touched her mother's skirt, had she had the courage to move a limb. She saw the old woman go away, and she remained still, closing her eyes and pressing her side to the hard and rugged surface of the rock. After a while a familiar face with fixed eyes and an open mouth became visible in the intense obscurity amongst the boulders. She uttered a low cry and stood up. The face vanished, leaving her to gasp and shiver alone in the wilderness of stone heaps. But as soon as she had crouched down again to rest, with her head against the rock, the face returned, came very near, appeared eager to finish the speech that had been cut short by death, only a moment ago. She scrambled quickly to her feet and said: 'Go away, or I will do it again.' The thing wavered, swung to the right, to the left. She moved this way and that, stepped back, fancied herself screaming at it, and was appalled by the unbroken stillness of the night. She tottered on the brink, felt the steep declivity under her feet, and rushed down blindly to save herself from a headlong fall. The shingle seemed to wake up; the pebbles began to roll before her, pursued her from above, raced down with her on both sides, rolling past with an increasing clatter. In the peace of the night the noise grew, deepening to a rumour, continuous and violent, as if the whole semicircle of the stony beach had started to tumble down into the bay. Susan's feet hardly touched the slope that seemed to run down with her. At the bottom she stumbled, shot forward, throwing her arms out, and fell heavily. She jumped up at once and turned swiftly to look back, her clenched hands full of sand she had clutched in her fall. The face was there, keeping its distance, visible in its own sheen that made a pale stain in the night. She shouted, 'Go away' – she shouted at it with pain, with fear, with all the rage of that useless stab that could not keep him quiet, keep him out of her sight. What did he want now? He was dead. Dead men have no children. Would he never leave her alone? She shrieked at it – waved her outstretched hands. She seemed to feel the breath of parted lips, and, with a long cry of discouragement, fled across the level bottom of the bay.

She ran lightly, unaware of any effort of her body. High sharp rocks that, when the bay is full, show above the glittering plain of blue water like pointed towers of submerged churches, glided past her, rushing to the land at a tremendous pace. To the left, in the distance, she could see something shining: a broad disc of light in which narrow shadows pivoted round the centre like the spokes of a wheel. She heard a voice calling, 'Hey! There!' and answered with a wild scream. So, he could call yet! He was calling after her to stop. Never! . . . She tore through the night, past the startled group of seaweed-gatherers who stood round their lantern paralysed with fear at the unearthly screech coming from that fleeing shadow. The men leaned on their pitchforks staring fearfully. A woman fell on her knees, and, crossing herself, began to pray aloud. A little girl with her ragged skirt full of slimy seaweed began to sob despairingly, lugging her soaked burden close to the man who carried the light. Somebody said: 'The thing ran out towards the sea.' Another voice exclaimed: 'And the sea is coming back! Look at the spreading puddles. Do you hear – you woman – there! Get up!' Several voices cried together. 'Yes, let us be off! Let the accursed thing go to the sea!' They moved on, keeping close round the light. Suddenly a man swore loudly. He would go and see what was the matter. It had been a woman's voice. He would go. There were shrill protests from women – but his high form detached itself from the group and went off running. They sent an unanimous call of scared voices after him. A word, insulting and mocking, came back, thrown at them through the darkness. A woman moaned. An old man said gravely: 'Such things ought to be left alone.' They went on slower, now shuffling in the yielding sand and whispering to one another that Millot feared nothing, having no religion, but that it would end badly some day.

Susan met the incoming tide by the Raven islet and stopped, panting, with her feet in the water. She heard the murmur and felt the cold caress of the sea, and, calmer now, could see the sombre and confused mass of the Raven on one side and on the other the long white streak of Molène sands that are left high above the dry bottom of Fougère Bay at every ebb. She turned round and saw far away, along the starred background of the sky, the ragged outline of the coast. Above it, nearly facing her, appeared the tower of Ploumar church; a slender and tall pyramid shooting up dark and pointed into the clustered glitter of the stars. She felt strangely calm. She knew where she was, and began to remember how she came there – and why. She peered into the smooth obscurity near her. She was alone. There was nothing there; nothing near her, either living or dead.

The tide was creeping in quietly, putting out long impatient arms of strange rivulets that ran towards the land between ridges of sand. Under the night the pools grew bigger with mysterious rapidity, while the great sea, yet far off, thundered in a regular rhythm along the indistinct line of the horizon. Susan splashed her way back for a few yards without being able to get clear of the water that murmured tenderly all around and, suddenly, with a spiteful gurgle, nearly took her off her feet. Her heart thumped with fear. This place was too big and too empty to die in. To-morrow they would do with her what they liked. But before she died she must tell them

– tell the gentlemen in black clothes that there are things no woman can bear. She must explain how it happened . . . . She splashed through a pool, getting wet to the waist, too preoccupied to care . . . . She must explain. 'He came in the same way as ever and said, just so: "Do you think I am going to leave the land to those people from Morbihan that I do not know? Do you? We shall see! Come along, you creature of mischance!" And he put his arms out. Then, Messieurs, I said: "Before God – never!" And he said, striding at me with open palms: "There is no God to hold me! Do you understand, you useless carcase. I will do what I like." And he took me by the shoulders. Then I, Messieurs, called to God for help, and next minute, while he was shaking me, I felt my long scissors in my hand. His shirt was unbuttoned, and, by the candle-light, I saw the hollow of his throat. I cried: "Let go!" He was crushing my shoulders. He was strong, my man was! Then I thought: No! . . . Must I? . . . Then take! – and I struck in the hollow place. I never saw him fall. Never! Never! . . . Never saw him fall . . . . The old father never turned his head. He is deaf and childish, gentlemen . . . . Nobody saw him fall. I ran out . . . . Nobody saw . . . .'

She had been scrambling amongst the boulders of the Raven and now found herself, all out of breath, standing amongst the heavy shadows of the rocky islet. The Raven is connected with the main land by a natural pier of immense and slippery stones. She intended to return home that way. Was he still standing there? At home. Home! Four idiots and a corpse. She must go back and explain. Anybody would understand . . . .

Below her the night or the sea seemed to pronounce distinctly:

'Aha! I see you at last!'

She started, slipped, fell; and without attempting to rise, listened, terrified. She heard heavy breathing, a clatter of wooden clogs. It stopped.

'Where the devil did you pass?' said an invisible man, hoarsely.

She held her breath. She recognised the voice. She had not seen him fall. Was he pursuing her there dead, or perhaps . . . alive?

She lost her head. She cried from the crevice where she lay huddled, 'Never, never!'

'Ah! You are still there. You led me a fine dance. Wait, my beauty, I must see how you look after all this. You wait . . . .'

Millot was stumbling, laughing, swearing meaninglessly out of pure satisfaction, pleased with himself for having run down that fly-by-night. 'As if there were such things as ghosts! Bah! It took an old African soldier to show those clodhoppers . . . . But it was curious. Who the devil was she?'

Susan listened, crouching. He was coming for her, this dead man. There was no escape. What a noise he made amongst the stones.... She saw his head rise up, then the shoulders. He was tall – her own man! His long arms waved about, and it was his own voice sounding a little strange... because of the scissors. She scrambled out quickly, rushed to the edge of the causeway, and turned round. The man stood still on a high stone, detaching himself in dead black on the glitter of the sky.

'Where are you going to?' he called roughly.

She answered, 'Home!' and watched him intensely. He made a striding, clumsy leap on to another boulder, and stopped again, balancing himself, then said:

'Ha! ha! Well, I am going with you. It's the least I can do. Ha! ha! ha!'

She stared at him till her eyes seemed to become glowing coals that burned deep into her brain, and yet she was in mortal fear of making out the well-known features. Below her the sea lapped softly against the rock with a splash, continuous and gentle.

The man said, advancing another step:

'I am coming for you. What do you think?'

She trembled. Coming for her! There was no escape, no peace, no hope. She looked round despairingly. Suddenly the whole shadowy coast, the blurred islets, the heaven itself, swayed about twice, then came to a rest. She closed her eyes and shouted:

'Can't you wait till I am dead!'

She was shaken by a furious hate for that shade that pursued her in this world, unappeased even by death in its longing for an heir that would be like other people's children.

'Hey! What?' said Millot, keeping his distance prudently. He was saying to himself: 'Look out! Some lunatic. An accident happens soon.'

She went on, wildly:

'I want to live. To live alone – for a week – for a day. I must explain to them.... I would tear you to pieces, I would kill you twenty times over rather than let you touch me while I live. How many times must I kill you – you blasphemer! Satan sends you here. I am damned too!'

'Come,' said Millot, alarmed and conciliating. 'I am perfectly alive!... Oh, my God!'

She had screamed, 'Alive!' and at once vanished before his eyes, as if the islet itself had swerved aside from under her feet. Millot rushed forward, and fell flat with his chin over the edge. Far below he saw the water whitened by her struggles, and heard one shrill cry for help that seemed to dart upwards along the perpendicular face of the rock, and soar past, straight into the high and impassive heaven.

Madame Levaille sat, dry-eyed, on the short grass of the hill side, with her thick legs stretched out, and her old feet turned up in their black cloth shoes. Her clogs stood near by, and further off the umbrella lay on the withered sward like a weapon dropped from the grasp of a vanquished warrior. The Marquis of Chavanes, on horseback, one gloved hand on thigh, looked down at her as she got up laboriously, with groans. On the narrow track of the seaweed-carts four men were carrying inland Susan's body on a hand-barrow, while several others straggled listlessly behind. Madame Levaille looked after the procession. 'Yes, Monsieur le Marquis,' she said dispassionately, in her usual calm tone of a reasonable old woman. 'There are unfortunate people on this earth. I had only one child. Only one! And they won't bury her in consecrated ground!'

Her eyes filled suddenly, and a short shower of tears rolled down the broad cheeks. She pulled the shawl close about her. The marquis leaned slightly over in his saddle, and said:

'It is very sad. You have all my sympathy. I shall speak to the Curé. She was unquestionably insane, and the fall was accidental. Millot says so distinctly. Good-day, Madame.'

And he trotted off, thinking to himself: 'I must get this old woman appointed guardian of those idiots, and administrator of the farm. It would be much better than having here one of those other Bacadous, probably a red republican, corrupting my commune.'

THE PAGEANT

Light

John Gray

John Gray (1866–1934) was born into a working-class Methodist family but died a highly revered canon of the Roman Catholic Church. In his youth he was famed for his beauty and was part of Wilde's intimate circle in the very late 1880s. Dorian Gray was said to have been named after him, and for a while, Gray signed himself 'Dorian' in letters to Wilde. However, as Wilde's notoriety morphed into infamy following the novel's publication, Gray took pains to distance himself from his former friend. He enjoyed cult status as the author of *Silverpoints* (1893), a collection of finely wrought, delicate poetry and a publishing milestone in 1890s Decadence.

Gray was a central figure in *The Dial* where he contributed prose fiction, critical essays and singularly homoerotic poetry, all infused with Catholic themes and imagery. 'Light', published in *The Pageant*, continues in this vein, being a sensual and mysterious tale of a simple smith's wife's conversion to Catholicism, in the mid-Victorian era. Hers is a bodily conversion, where art and physical ecstasy convey religious truth, rather than any reasoned, intellectual debate. Protestant logic is shunned, and even mocked, in this tale of dreams and visions, sumptuous *belles lettres*, fetishism, magic, mystery and a divine madness with its 'terrible bliss' and 'ecstatic terror'. The poetry included appears to be a mix of Gray's own creations and genuine medieval devotional verse.

This is the whole story, though it range over no more than a few months. The first forty odd years of this life are pure preliminary, obscurely and fatally composed, to the passage which marches nobly and passionately to an ecstatic end. Until this ecstasy broke across its decline, the heroine's life had so little to be revealed, even through the medium of most powerful lenses! She had lived her life in a neglected mode; to her, *sentiment* of life was only supplemented by *knowledge* of life, never supplanted by it. Like children, she derived support from accepting things as they are; trees which she had always remembered were to her as enduring as the sky; a fallen tree was something tragic. When she was a child, during the night of a terrible storm, a young man had been struck blind by lightning, and four old trees had been blown down. The blind man still desolated to her ear a certain stone passage with his 'Buy of the blind!' and she still called the two remaining elms the Seven Sisters. Here she had a group of impressions: on the one hand she was acquainted with the long-past facts, like anybody else of her age; on the other hand she had a *sentiment* of the thing, not fantastic, nor in any way connected with fear of lightning, in which it was at once ordinary and extraordinary. The government of the country, the queen, the town council, to her sentiment were like facts of nature; while her intelligence knew well enough why the sovereign reigns, that there might have been another sovereign or no sovereign, whence the members of Parliament and the Cabinet come, and the different applications of revenue and parochial taxes. So also with, say, printed books and pictures. The author writes, the printer prints, the binder binds; but in that part of her where lay the undefined, but undisputed, convictions, a book as a determined object had an authority beyond any combination of the elements which produce it. In like manner a certain engraving she possessed of one of the Martin biblical subjects, while it filled her with awe and admiration, had no value as a product of human invention, skill, and patience; the feeblest pencil drawing of a flower stood for more on this footing; perfect knowledge that the engraving was the result of thousands of dexterous scratches made no difference; even if she had seen the engraver bending over the plate with his goggle and gravers, she would not have connected his work permanently with a picture which had hung in the same place time out of memory. May this insistence upon the lifelong rivalry of simple heart and simple brain tend to indulgent appreciation of the heroine's conception of God, comparable to her sentimental notion of any settled fact; for though at this grave point her attitude approached that of most uneducated people, in her case it was in no way answerable to neglect or laziness.

Her husband was a smith; his daily work had been at the same factory ever since their marriage; his weekly wages had varied only within familiar limits. These conditions, in conjunction with her husband's meek disposition, would have secured the evenness of her married life, apart from her sanguine fatalism. The smith went to his work at an early hour of the morning. His dressing was finished completely in the bedroom, even to his top hat. Before starting he took a cup of coffee, which in summer was prepared by his wife, in winter by himself. When the smell of the pipe he lighted in the doorway reached her nostrils, his wife got up. This had been the strange signal all the time, which she had never happened to mention to him. She only heard him leave the house on days when he was a little poorly or the weather was bad, when she was fully awake and listening; for, with an oiled lock, and by holding the knocker with one hand, he left with scarcely perceptible noise.

Until she took her breakfast she busied herself heartily with rougher work; after breakfast the bedroom was set in order, as also the part of the house through which her husband passed when he returned, from the door-handle to the kitchen stove. Next she prepared dinner, and while this was cooking she made her first toilette, rather tidying of her person. The smith came in at a quarter-past one, ate in silence for half an hour, and went away. After dinner her house work for the day was soon finished;

she made her real toilette, and settled to needle work or reading, or went out. At a quarter-past six tea was eaten in the sitting-room, where husband and wife passed the evening until supper, for which meal they went to the kitchen again. Then the smith smoked his pipe, drowsed, his wife prepared his breakfast for the morrow, and the house was shut up for the night.

This was the outline of a typical ordinary day, as days had passed for twenty years. Sunday showed an important variation; it differed from the week-day in every one of its outward details.

On Sunday they rose later, breakfasted later; not only was breakfast different in character, but different plates, cups, and forks were used. The smith was pompous, reflective, in broadcloth and clean shirt, in the wearing of his oiled hair and embellishments struggling to realise the daguerreotype portrait of himself young. His wife also was contained, formal. The pair preserved on Sunday the attitude of courting days, stripped of tenderness. The smith left the house first, making for the distant Lemon Street Baptist Chapel. Another chapel of the same body was very much nearer, quite close in fact, in the opposite direction; he was a 'steward' of the chapel which took tithes of all his being. When he was gone (he banged the street-door on Sunday) his wife cleared breakfast away, as sedately as if her husband were still present; then she went to the poorer but more aristocratic Bible Christian Chapel in Chapel Street, also very distant from the house, but the only colony of the sect in the town. Returning, she had reached home, and put the potatoes to simmer, before the smith reappeared; he stopped to gad on the way home; you could see it in the grimace of recognition, which his wrinkles were slow to relinquish.

After dinner the husband went again to his chapel; while his wife first did what was absolutely necessary to be done in the house, then read a little, then laid tea long before the time. (Almost every Sunday some one came to tea.) Lastly, with folded hands, she chaffered for her husband's return; real yearning for his presence possessed her. At tea, if strangers were present, the pair called each other Mrs. and Mr. Smith.

The Sunday evening was a notable weekly event with them; it offered so much strictly ordered variety. In their religious world, by a rough delimitation, the morning is applied to worship, the afternoon to the instruction of children, while the evening is a forlorn crumb for the need of the whole world outside the particular sect. (Sometimes a week-day evening is given up to projects of enlightenment of Parsees, Tierra del Fuegians, Buddhist monks — heathen generally.) But that crumb, the Sunday evening service, gritty enough to the damned, is sweet in the tooth of the judges. In the morning man speaks to God; in the evening God, richly commented [upon], to express it cautiously, speaks to man.

The smith's wife adored the Sunday evening service, partly from habit and training, partly in a childlike way; for it was narrative, anecdotal, variable. In addition it meant the occasional company of her husband. Every third Sunday evening he was free, and the two went together where they liked; on one of the two intervening Sundays they went to the husband's chapel and came back together, almost always much edified, in a mechanical way, by the warnings to the wicked which they had heard.

On a certain Sunday when the wife, in the order of things, was spending the evening alone, her husband said to her suddenly, not as usual, 'Where are you going this evening?' but:

'Why don't you go to . . .'

'Newbury Park?' A voice inside her finished the sentence. It was very distinct, and, strangely, the reverberation seemed to come from her chest rather than from her head. The husband's question was:

'Why don't you go to Winter Street?' They called all the chapels by familiar names, like 'the iron chapel', or by the name of a street.

'I was thinking of going to Newbury Park.'

'It is so far,' he persisted; 'why don't you go to Winter Street? Captain Stocker (an inspired engineer officer with no chin) is going to preach. You like him . . .'

'I am inclined to go to Newbury Park.' He did not answer, and she repeated:

'I want to go to Newbury Park.' She was ashamed to explain her choice more narrowly.

'Oh, very well.' They could get no nearer to a quarrel on such a subject, and to Newbury Park she went.

Not at all easy in her mind though. It was a dismal night, and the distance was so great. And then to have had words with her husband on a Sunday evening. Fatigued, and almost tearful, she came into the hot room she thought of as Newbury Park. Preliminaries of consecration of the proceedings past, the speaker, standing behind a little rostrum with his hands behind him, said, 'Verily, verily, I say unto thee: Except a man be born again, he cannot see the kingdom of God.'

She knew these words just as well as the 'Our Father' or 'There is a green hill.' . . . She had heard sermons, discourses, upon them beyond recollection. At another time she would have nodded the cadences of the phrase, her lips anticipating each word. Now the words loomed great and unfamiliar, as if memory or hearing were out of focus; in a darkness, the negation of a stunning light, which yet seemed near. She saw the speaker grasp the front of the rostrum with both hands, stretch his arms stiff; she heard him repeat:

'Our Lord speaks: Verily, verily; truth of truth, unanswerable absolute truth; He says, I say unto *you*.' He raised his right hand and dropped a threatening index, as a bravo might a revolver, straight at her. 'Except a man be born again, he cannot see the kingdom of God.'

A ray fell from distant heaven. Alighting in her, it exploded her soul into radiant, conscious being. In an instant, before the speaker had punctuated the sentence, so to speak, herself and the visible and invisible world were created anew. The flood was overpowering; a thousand biblical reminiscences; the creation of the world, sacrifices, voices and fire from heaven, whole psalms with every word and letter distinct in idea, were present in a flash. She was afraid and consoled at once. With the desire to scream came the comfortable words: *I* am here. She had seen women swoon, have hysterics, in chapel. It had never happened to herself. There was no danger now; the body had no time to exclaim as it went down under the victory of spirit. Panorama veiled panorama with incredible rapidity, and side issues came and went too at the same time, scraps of conversation years and years ago, visions of streets, forgotten faces, trivial occasions and incidents; a great deduction emanating all the time, the life of our Lord in minute detail, from babyhood with all its incidents (of which she had no practical knowledge) to the terrors of Calvary. Not stopping here, for the new creature she was for the moment knew no fear or hesitation; she followed His being boldly from the lips of His wounded, tortured body to the ecstatic arms of His Father.

Such was the preliminary trial of the course she had now to run.

She began immediately to foot the glorious path. She began to pray; but her prayer had no words, no known aim; she prayed for things she had never heard of, and in a language she did not know. The light she threw round her gave visible objects an unaccustomed, alluring interest: a sin at the first step, which was followed instantly by forgiveness and reconciliation. The Light within her was the object, the object of objects.

The Light said, in words of music and light, 'He giveth His beloved sleep,' and a veil was drawn across the ecstasy.

When she reached home she had not the faintest excuse to make any confidence to her husband of what had taken place. Indeed, how could she possibly communicate it? She had no terms in which to express the new birth even to herself.

The Monday morning rose as pale as any other. There seemed no prospect of a return of the ecstasy. The repetition of the words which had induced it was unavailing. Only the universe was still rational to her, as in the moment of revelation; it stood no longer simply a fact, dull, uniform, unexplained; the living parts of it were very much alive, the dead not worth a thought. And the Lord of Life lived in her; she knew that; there could be no mistake about that.

She began to pray; a long communion with the Light by faith; for it was not evident. But now her prayer was in mortal phrases of human speech; a tempestuous, chaotic prayer, though with no movement of the lips, no activity of the brain; it throbbed, as before, from her chest. It was a long narrative, with supposed rejoinders, interruptions. It often repeated itself; it was full of cross purposes. Some parts of it were in a lower tone, parts so low as to be next to silence; at last, in a dead hush, the request escaped her: 'Speak to me.' Then a full swell ensued, gigantic soliloquy, in a small degree comparable to incidents of the great interview, a half memory that, in the mystic prayer, the soul to soul speech, a desperate entreaty had been made; that she might know the bliss of faith, never again receive revelation or smallest encouragement; that she might live like Him, die like Him, forsaken by Him, with no sight of His face, no sound of His voice. Had He put in her heart a prayer so exalted? She knew, with angelic perception, how great this prayer was. She framed such a prayer instantly; she knew that He looked for courage in her: 'Try me, test me, give me suffering, neglect me; give me grace to love in absence, for present, how could I do else?'

She shook through all her body like some one awakened from sleep, saw the visible objects of the kitchen, the work which engaged her hands; she found, with a light surprise, that she had been busy all the time.

The dinner was excellent. The smith almost overstayed the twenty-five minutes he had; his wife was so cheerful, so smiling, so clean personally. He took for granted, as well he might, that this was a favourable combination of ordinary circumstances. Not at all; it was an ordinary aspect of a new order of things. Those who know even a little of heaven usually know a great deal about earth; and here was no exception. To see the world with washed eyes, everyday matters and objects, to distinguish their classes, means to handle the matter which concerns one with dignity and discretion.

This woman had been, let us say, from the point of view of a high standard, fairly cheerful, demure, restful to the working man, who was nearly always tired when he saw her. But why should duty to a husband in this sense depend upon accidents of nature and circumstances? She put and answered this question. Also in the preparation of food and the cleansing of crockery and accessories. *Intention* can add something to perfect mechanical execution. An utensil cleansed in the highest name must be abundantly clean, lavishly brilliant. To scour potatoes as though they were all alike and little different from other roots, to leave them in hot water so long, steam them so long, and then fling them at the eater; slaves for slaves might act thus. Coming to conclusions such as these under the image of incensing the Divine, who Himself swung the censer, an unlearned woman, who had handled very few books in her life, was primed to confound many a doctor.

For something more than two weeks a state of being showed little variation from one day to another. Exalted faith in the Divine Presence hourly renewed, either at the occasion of reconciliation after slips, neglects, moments in which something stood before the Light; or by simple, formal pact. She agreed to ask nothing but at the Divine dictation, to expect nothing, not to be inquisitive or impatient; above all, to keep the union a secret, to hold infinite stability as jealously as though it were a bubble. So, while every day changed from point to point like the colours of an opal, an infinity of differently coloured sparks, though storm and hush succeeded, contrition and ecstasy, before his very eyes, the smith saw not the weakest ripple in his wife's placid and perfect demeanour.

To return a moment to her everyday conduct of life, she was scrupulous to dress, to keep herself, as the warden of an idea, as the shell in which it lay active and sleepless, hidden.

One morning the interminable conversation had dropped to an even mildness; the answers to her whispered confidences seemed to grow faint — almost inaudible. An alarm came upon her, and under the strange condition, in the language she did not know. It would not be beaten away. Calm retreated into the depths of a distance such as she had never before beheld, and a rough voice bellowed through all the vacuum:

'Halt!' She held her breath, firm amidst immensity of loneliness unknown to sand, or sea, or sky.

'Doubt!' added the voice, with long-drawn insistence; and a hail of questions rushed vertical upon her, driving her down, down. What was she? whence? who? where were her titles? The Light she housed, what was it? it? it? Why *it*? What was its form? Was it a person? What person? Did it really speak? Did it speak truth? Descent must be arrested before she could answer, but that was impossible, till faith spread arms beneath her, and in seas of down and spice, in a world of light fluttering into song hushed at the moment of utterance, all her being melted into those conditions, and the familiar voice said with unfamiliar tenderness, 'My Beloved is mine, and I am His.'

'No, no,' she cried, 'I am afraid.' The sound of her voice brought her within the narrow walls of the kitchen with a jar. She sat down and wept for a long time without thought.

The paroxysm coincided with the smith's return to dinner. His wife stared at the clock until her face was as candid as its own, and the key sounded in the latch. She had a severe cold at this time, hence her husband took little heed of her swollen appearance. He, for his part, was sullen, unsympathetic. The perfection of material surroundings had begun to prey upon him. His ideal of life was of a balance of give and take; he knew so well in his work how a good job foreshadows a bad; and while he relished new comfort, he already smarted under a deprivation. Ah, man, man; the lentils of captivity were sweet in his memory at the table of joy!

He finished his dinner and went away, but the darkness of his presence remained behind, filling all the part of the house through which he had passed. She cleared the meal. The platters returned noiselessly to the dresser, brighter than they had left it. 'Give me sorrow,' she prayed; 'give me desertion, longing. Ah, I have longing; I long, I long.' She went to the bedroom, dressed herself, came down, and went out. She took no note of the direction: the invisible Guide had all the care of that. Her way lay across the adjoining heath; then by a turn she retraced her steps. Her eye rested here and there on scrub and struggling growth, always in the name with which every leaf was signed. It came into her fancy that she would like to see the sea which He had made. Instantly, like a child to be humoured, she saw the great expanse of the water with noble vision, shoreward and seaward at once, and the delicate contact of its rim with the fringe of the sky. Then, changing a little, the horizon was more distant; it seemed the same sea, but there was so much more of it; it was the face of waters clinging to the confines of a larger planet. The stars too, for these appeared, fell into unusual patterns. Occupied with the vision, she gradually descended into the town. She went on, absorbed in her prayer, crestfallen and timid, delighted to take a low place before Him; when she turned her head, as though she had heard her name, and saw in a stationer's window the words emblazoned: 'Except a man be born again, he cannot see the kingdom of God.' The sight of the words certainly awoke a profusion of memories; not so many but that she noted clearly the position of the card, the manner in which it was entrenched among piles of book backs. The card reminded her that she wished to buy something of the linendraper a few shops on. It is difficult to see how it should have reminded her, unless it was the denial of the wish to buy this card. How can you hang up your birth? or whilst you live in it, why should you write up in your room the information that you were once born?

For some time communion, though tender, delicious, uninterrupted, took place on a lower level. It was the expression on her part of deep contrition; ever a new wound meekly, weakly, presented for healing. With the consciousness that the subject was less exalted than sometimes, there was no notion in her mind of comparison, for deepest anguish was ecstasy beyond thought. The very vagueness of her attitude was soothing, a reward, delight that she was permitted to know the divine union by faith. On a certain night she dreamed (it is fit to state that she never dreamed of the Divine Lover, and little at any time). She dreamed that she arrived in a square in a large town. A garden was in the midst of it, and it was enclosed by large, gaudy buildings lighted up, though it was day. She made her way to one corner of the square where there was a book shop, over which was a poem written in gold letters. The poem had eight lines; four which rhymed correctly, and in continuation four others, not rhymed, which seemed to dwindle away. In her dream this had a deep meaning, but she only retained the concluding words:

> . . . it was a wondrous thing
> To be so loved.

In the window of the shop was the card she had seen in the stationer's window, bearing the words, 'Except a man' . . . at least so she took for granted, for she did not distinguish them. Turning round she saw that the square had an Oriental aspect; then the dream became stupid, then unpleasant; a pungent smell pervaded it. She woke suddenly to the fact that it was tobacco; she heard the soft click of the street door. Running over the circumstances of the vivid dream, she had the staunchness to reject it as of no consequence. She looked upon the time it took to examine it as time wasted, and turned joyfully to address Him who never sleeps. It was He who began:

'If I should not be who you think I am, would you love Me?'

'That I would,' she answered fervently and without hesitation.

'And if you make a mistake, and were to be damned?'

'I should still be grateful.'

'You do not know.'

'You have given me knowledge above all knowledge.' And the silent utterance of her soul grew voluble, universal, a torrent of reckless thanks and prayer. Thanks for what she had never possessed, prayers for what she already enjoyed. She offered thanks for her existence, that she was her very self, that she was a *woman*. The Lord had been born of a *woman*. She could understand a little what it must have been to be the holy mother of God. This notion was very new to her, quite new; but that caused her no surprise, for everything was new.

There was a peculiar bliss in the thought. She came to it again and again. When she had pursued it to the end of one set of considerations it returned afresh and afresh. The morning passed with astounding rapidity — the contrary phenomenon was commoner — but nothing was belated. The dinner was as punctually served to the minute as though she had watched the clock anxiously all the time.

The habit of divine communication had long since become continual. She was able to maintain it through the most complicated demands upon her attention. Her ordinary life presented few alterations to view, her ordinary manner, her ordinary appearance. A greater solicitude might have been noted. Her clothing was really very different from what it had been, but the changes were so dexterous as to be scarcely perceptible. It cannot be denied, too, that as soon as the traces of dinner had been removed she hastened to put on the best clothes she allowed herself to wear on a weekday.

It had become necessary that she should go to a London shop, one of those warehouses where everything is to be bought. This periodical visit was always made in the same way. She hurried off immediately after dinner. From Charing Cross, which she reached by rail, she walked across Charing Cross Road and Leicester Square to Piccadilly Circus, whence she took an omnibus to her destination. Her shopping over, she came back by a different omnibus to the railway station. On the present occasion she laughed to recognise in Leicester Square the scene of her dream, in the Alhambra Theatre the Oriental colouring of it. Sure enough, too, in the north-west corner of it, was the book-shop, but the name of the proprietor stood where the poem had been cramped in her dream. In the window, by a coincidence, a white card was visible in exactly the position which the text had occupied. Rejection of the dream gave way to this extent, that she crossed the road to find out what it was. The back and side of a book were exposed, and before it was a written label: 'Just published: *The Excellent Way*', and some further particulars. She wanted the book, though the idea was preposterous; she had never in her life paid even two shillings for a book; this one surely cost more. There was no time for dallying; her errand pressed. She went into the shop, and the book lay dazzling on the dark counter before her. The shopman, amused at her shyness, her unwillingness to touch it, exposed the back, the sides, opened at the title-page. She saw there was a picture. The desire to possess the book grew. The shopman dropped the leaves casually through his fingers. She saw the words: 'Lord, if thou art not present.' ... 'Ten-and-six,' said the man; 'it is beautifully printed, beautifully got up.' She thought that did not prove much, but she repeated with alarm 'Ten-and-six!' The leaves splashed over each other. Seeing again the words she had seen before, she hurriedly closed, gave gold and silver for brown paper, string, and a possibility. In the omnibus she opened the parcel and peeped into the book.

Popery! and she wrapped it up again as well as she could.

At the store, in the tea-room where she went, according to her custom, to get breath and take a little refreshment, she could not resist taking another look at the book she carried. This time she patiently sought out the poem which had first arrested her eye.

> Lord, if thou art not present, where shall I
> Seek thee the absent ...

It was very disheartening; it did not speak to her at all. She could not find words in which to reproach herself with her folly. After a few moments of such reflection, ill at ease with her conclusion, she took yet another dip and alighted on a page where a sonnet began:

> Before myself I tremble, all my members quake
> When lips and nose I mark, and both the hollow caves ...

It was hopeless; she shut the book resolutely with the sudden determination to return it. With this intention she took her departure and hurried to the book-shop, which, when she reached it, was closed.

The train had little comfort for her. Only when she was some few minutes on the road did she remember that the loved communion had been interrupted just as long as this unfortunate book had been in her possession. She hastened to repair the deprivation; and though her wish did not remain entirely without response, the book beside her was a drag by its presence. She had thoughts at one moment of throwing it out of the window.

Reaching home, the book had to be smuggled into the house. The difficulty of this accomplishment, not to mention the danger, was something very like a blow to the poor owner. There was no possible question as to whether her husband could be let see it or not; accordingly it was necessary to enter the house quickly and noiselessly, to deposit the book nimbly upon one of the dark stairs while she went into the sitting-room to give an account of her journey and soothe the anger of the smith, which she could count upon — anger at her forced absence, though it was surely as much upon his account as upon her own; then she must snatch the packet dexterously as she went up to take off her coat and bonnet, and hide it effectually before she could be followed. It had to be done and she did it. She was very weak next morning through lying awake devouring her tears.

To allay the agony of her doubt, the difficulty of return to the divine communion, her first determination was to put the book out of sight and leave it there. This turned out so little satisfactory as a salve that she changed tactic, and, withdrawing it from its lurking-place, she cut the leaves and began to read it straight through, disregarding the shocks to her accustomed beliefs which occurred ten times on every page. Her determination was so strong still when she had penetrated a few pages that she found herself spelling out the name of she did not know whom: Blessed Jacopone da Todi, not skipping this, to her, unnecessary preliminary to the perusal of the poem following it, which answered her unconscious glance with better promise than any of the preceding had vouchsafed. Ah! dear Lord, Light in dark places indeed. The first line she read set all her doubts at rest. Joy filled all her being, she did not know why; but such was the perfection of joy to her, when she could not trace it to any earthly origin. She could not have declared that she understood fifty per cent of the words under her eye, but she was sure in the awakened part of her that here was something for her. What did she care now about the origin of the book, for what petty or even wicked purpose it might have been put together? She knew enough to be certain that He uses all things, all means, for His good pleasure. Until she could look into His face, follow with her own eyes the moving lines of His lips as they move in speech, she must be content to hear His voice where it is to be heard.

> O Love, all love above!
> Why hast thou struck me so?
> All my heart broke atwo,
> Consumed with flames of love,
> Burning and flaming cannot find solace;

> It cannot fly from torment, being bound;
> Like wax amid live coal it melts apace.
> It languishes alive, no help being found.

And so forth. The words had no special reference to her own condition at the time, probably none at all; yet such was the force of this unlooked-for revelation, she knew once for all and at the first glance that these words were meant for her. Even had she been told that Blessed Jacopone was a minor brother, and had she been told at the same time what a minor brother was, it would have made no difference to her. From the afternoon when she was made free of the ancient Italian poem, the father of so much of the best that has followed it, she gave it her attention until she knew it all by heart, and could again put away the book containing it, for she cut no more pages.

With no more power to define a symbol than a baby, she knew very well from the outset, and practically, that all visible nature, and more especially the Word of God (that is the Bible) are intelligible only in the manner of symbol; that all appearances, all divine utterances, portray something beyond, which in turn is the emblem of some remoter truth – reality. She was fully convinced that the various recorded and unrecorded acts of Christ, the incidents of the life He passed on earth, are continually re-enacted for the furtherance of His kingdom, and the nourishment of the souls of His. This belief, perhaps it is proper to add, was held only on the authority of Christ; it had no further support. She knew that the way of illumination has either to be trod without fear or left alone. There must be courage to meet and face Apollyon, but how much more courage does it need to listen to the voice of the Beloved!

Let it then be stated categorically (where the smith's wife had been convinced in one point of time) that she had not shunned a conclusion which had been forced upon her: Christ had once been born of woman miraculously; that momentous event had had its direct value, the physical redemption of man and fallen nature; but beyond this was there not something else? It is a matter of vulgar knowledge that the great sacrifice is infinitely more far-reaching in its effect. As our Lord then was born of His mortal mother in mortal flesh, so is He conceived mystically in every one of His chosen, and born spiritually, but not less truly. The act too is reciprocal, and the ramifications of the mystery extend no doubt till limitless space is filled with the glory of God.

On an afternoon, at the accustomed hour, the smith reached his house, and hearing no sound to indicate the presence of his wife within doors, walked into the sitting-room to verify her absence. She was sitting in the usual chair, with her head bowed and her hands crossed in a strange attitude upon her breast. He asked her what she was doing, but all the answer he received was a deprecating wave of her hand. He placed himself before her, intercepting the light of the window, and there stood stock still. Presently she lifted her hands with the palms towards him, and then stooped the whole upper part of her frame until her forehead almost touched her knees. Raising her face then, her lips, which were very white, moved rapidly without sound, presently breaking into cadences:

> Against me let no blame henceforth be held
> If such a love confoundeth all my wit . . .

She brushed her hands across her eyes, shook her head, and smiled recognition to her husband.

The following day their doctor called in the afternoon, quite accidentally. He explained his visit as accident, adding some professional jest. He stayed almost an hour, and then, a strange request, asked for some tea. The smith's wife, quietly flattered, prepared a cup of tea, and they resumed their conversation. The doctor snatched greedily at any seeming opportunity of talking upon religious subjects; but she would not be enticed, and at length he went away. When the smith returned, his wife told him of the visit; he affected surprise, though he had just seen the doctor, and heard from him the following opinion on the health of his wife: 'Take care of your wife, you will not have her much longer; I cannot discover anything wrong with her!'

There was a great peace over life for a day or two, a rest from ecstasy as sweet or sweeter. Then, sweeter yet, suddenly the renewal, the 'light without pause or bound', of the poem. To light the world from one's own body, to bear the Light within one, to be the genetrix — it surpassed reason.

> Not iron nor the fire can separate
> Or sunder those whom love doth so unite;
> Not suffering nor death can reach the state
> To which my soul is ravished; from its height
> Beneath it, lo! it sees all things create;
> It dominates the range of dimmest sight . . .

She gave way completely to the fact. The conviction that she truly bore within her her august Familiar was so profound that she grew to the pain of regret that the course of nature must obtain, and that, the day and hour accomplished, she must part with the mystical burden and enter into a new relationship. So jealous did she become that a notion one would think she could not escape did not enter her thought; that, namely, of comparing her legal husband to Saint Joseph. The truth is that her grasp of the existing situation was on a very high level of mystery. As to her part in it, she held it almost as a person without sex, the necessary condition of her entering it once overpast.

> Transformed in Him, almost the very Christ;
> One with her God, she is almost divine;
> Riches above all riches to be priced,
> All that is Christ's is hers, and she is queen.
> How can I still be sad, despair-enticed,
> Or ask for medicine to cure my spleen?
> The fetid sweet from sin,
> With sweetness overspread,
> The old forgot and dead
> In the new reign of Love.

The tone of complaint in the poem of Jacopone, though it had no meaning in her experience, did not raise the smallest question in her. She knew the treasure of sense within the terms employed. The joy was so intense that it seemed to her quite natural that another should express it, or try to express it, in the language of pain and dismay. In her prayers she was just as likely to pour out volumes of expostulation and injury, frantic and unseemly tenderness, sheer incoherency. In one passage the poem runs:

> Thou canst not shield Thyself from love, love brought
> Thee captive by the road from heaven to earth;
> Love brought Thee down to lowness, to be naught,
> To roam rejected from Thy humble birth.
> No house nor field enhanced Thy lowly lot;
> Poor, Thou hast given riches and great worth.
> In life, in death, no dearth
> Of love hast Thou declared;
> Thy heart hath flamed and flared
> With nothing else but love.

This was strong food, and it was devoured greedily. The aliment must be nothing but love:

'Thou wast not flesh,' Jacopone makes Saint Francis break out at the Divine Lover in the passion of his rebuke:

> Thou wast not flesh, but love, in frame and brain;
> Love made Thee man to bear our sins reward.
> Thy love required the cross, the world's disdain . . . .

All through, the phrases of the great Italian song filled her with terrible bliss, ecstatic terror. When an anxiety did not of itself come into her mind, the poem readily suggested it. Her own temper would have been most likely to have sucked the present sweetness, but the untractable companion of Saint Francis would not have it thus. He is full of apprehension. If this little love which, now, at the outset, is vouchsafed to me, so fills all my being, taxes all my strength, how shall I possibly endure the distention when it grows great, as grow it must? The smith's wife saw the force of this question in a manner outside Jacopone's anticipation.

Disregarding dates, hours, lapses of time (she gave little heed; the Lover dictated season to her and time of day; it was day or night for her at His bidding, spring or autumn), the time was nigh for the mysterious birth. It rushed upon her suddenly; there seemed only a few minutes given her in which to prepare the setting of the astounding miracle. The historical circumstances were present to her in a flash, she knew not whence; but the whole incident, the actual details, had to be animated. She moved about quietly under the sorest stress she had ever known, while the agitated soul of her seemed to be traversing space in all directions in the fervour of the moment; she was muttering to herself over and over again:

> In such a deadly swound,
> Alas! where am I brought?

Johann Scheffler has shown the nativity in sentences of tenderness which human speech has poor hope ever to excel, so frail that they cannot be stirred from the tongue in which they were first set; Friedrich Spe has expressed physical contact with Christ in words which swoon upon his lips; the English language holds the pomp and glory of song in Crashaw's poem on the circumcision. If these three masters could be distilled into one and their concentrated sweetness impinged direct upon a sensitive heart, the victim might present a parallel to the overwhelmed blacksmith's wife, fallen the most pitiable heap of flesh. The lamentable workman, the words of the doctor fresh in his brain (they had gnawed through into every fibre of it) lifted his wife in his grimed arms; lifted her, a strange contradiction of terms, into depths. It cannot be told from what vision he aroused her.

It was frightening to a poor man like the blacksmith to see his wife consent to be put to bed without a murmur of protest. Even had she been evidently suffering he would have expected her to deny that anything was the matter with her, and certainly to refuse to go to bed. To every inquiry she returned the same blissful smile, of such candid reassurance that those about her could not believe that she suffered. The news of the mysterious ailment (which was to end in death) ran down the street, and unaccustomed women gathered at the clean bedside, and there remained.

She now lived in the heights. She had now, as she thought, transcended all; it had been a long fight to break with such clearly justifiable habit as that which kept her the slave of the calls of her house. But love, great love had made wreck of all; love, tyrannical, had broken down the flesh, even in its purest strongholds:

> I have no longer eyes for forms of creatures,
> I cry to Him Who doth alone endure;
> Though earth and heaven exhaust their varied natures,
> Through love their forms are thin and nowise sure;
> When I had looked upon His splendid features,
> Light of the sun itself was grown obscure.
> Cherubim, rare and pure
> By knowledge and high thought,
> The seraphin, are naught
> To him who looks on love.

She no longer waked and slept; night and day alike passed in calm ecstasy. The Beloved could not leave her any more. Seen by none of the busybodies at her bedside, she held at will and laid aside within easy reach the divine Presence come to her with the loving confidence He had Himself taught her. Locality had ceased to have that vital importance which it once had; great sense of her individuality remained, and stronger still was the personality of the divine Lover. She knew (for ecstasy brought with it supreme knowledge) that her body lay in sheets, supposed to be lingering and ailing; that it was given over to the care of hands she knew, to which she gave no heed. She knew that her kitchen stood untended by its proper guardian; but love was grown terrible now, she dared not deny it lest it should crush the universe in despite. The officious woman in the room would bend her ear to the smiling lips when they moved, to hear, low and sweet and distinct:

> Love, Love, how Thou hast dealt a bitter wound!
> I cry for nothing now but love alone.
> Love, Love, to Thee I am securely bound;
> I can embrace none other than my own.
> Love, Love, so strongly hast Thou wrapt me round,
> My heart by love for ever overthrown,
> For love I am full prone.
> Love, but to be with Thee!
> O Love, in mercy be
> My death, my death of love!

'She is raving!' But no change of expression answered the opinion, though it was distinctly heard and understood.

On a given day the number of people passing to and fro began to increase. The fire was kept more brisk. There was noiseless hurry going on. She knew quite well that they were preparing for her death. An extra pillow was put behind her, and not half-an-hour elapsed before another was added. Then one beckoned another outside the room, and she supposed that the smith had been sent for. Not long afterwards, in fact, he arrived. As he came into the room her lips began to move again.

'She is raving!' the leading attendant volunteered, not for the first time that morning. Though the smith had not heard it before, he rejected the hypothesis with a gesture of disdain. The fact was, that the dignity of his wife's appearance filled him with vanity. Not those, he thought of the women who stood round like birds of prey, none of those is my wife, but the serene woman propped up with pillows, who is already half in heaven, on whom I shall set my eyes only once or twice more. He bent to her face, and heard here and there as a syllable was accented:

> To Love for ever wed,
> Love hath united both
> Our hearts in perfect troth
> Of everlasting love.

'Her head is as clear as mine,' he said scornfully; 'she's no more raving than you are.'

'What's she say?' asked the woman, awed.

'I can't say it like her.'

'She's going.'

'Lower her head,' whispered one. The smith looked savage, as though he would defend her from molestation with violence. The women continued to mutter what ought to be done.

She motioned to raise her hands; the smith took one of them; her lips moved:

> Love, Love, O Jesus, I have reached the port;
> Love, Love, O Jesus, whither . . .

Yai and the Moon

Max Beerbohm

Max Beerbohm (1872–1956) was a well-known essayist, short story writer, satirist, and caricaturist. His talent was first recognised whilst he was an undergraduate at Merton College, Oxford, when he published his essay on Decadent artifice titled 'A Defence of Cosmetics' in the first volume of *The Yellow Book* (1894). This essay, one of the most important documents of British Decadence, echoes Baudelaire's 'Éloge du maquillage' (1863). Beerbohm was somewhat hesitant in his dealings with Wilde and his circle, and his later attitude towards Decadence was playful, lampooning it without attacking it. Wilde praised Beerbohm's 'The Happy Hypocrite' (1897), a satire of *The Picture of Dorian Gray* (1890–1) and its Aestheticist ideology.

'Yai and the Moon' concerns a girl's futile love for a masculinised Moon. It reads like a dainty oriental folktale, but is also akin to an evocative Wildean fairy tale. The tale subscribes to the contemporary cult of Japanophilia, a fascination for artists James McNeill Whistler and Aubrey Beardsley. With the hypnotic rhythm of its prose, the leitmotif of the moon, and its Symbolist images, it is particularly influenced by Wilde's *Salomé* (1891 in French; 1894 in English), which was first published with Beardsley's sensational illustrations. The story is unique for contrasting dreamy Aestheticism with scientific intellectualism. Sanza, Yai's bridegroom-to-be, is akin to Keats's Apollonius, with a penchant for analysing the moon with his cold scientific facts. Sanza's criticism of Yai's erotic fixation with the moon (a clever pun on 'lunacy') as a symptom of hysteria is reminiscent of Max Nordau's notorious diagnosing of Decadent artists as 'degenerate'.

※

The Bay of Yedo is all blue and yellow. The village of Haokami is pink. And Umanosuké, who ruled the village worthily, was a widower. And Yai, his daughter, was wayward. The death of his wife had grieved Umanosuké. 'She was more dear to me,' he had cried over her tomb, 'than the plum-tree in my garden, more dear than the half of all my pied chrysanthemums. And now she is dead. The jewelled honeycomb is taken from me. Void is the pavilion of my desire. As an untrod island, as a little island in a sea of tears, so am I. My wife is dead. What is left to me?' Yai, not more then than a baby, had sidled up to him, cooing, 'I, O father!' And the villagers had murmured in reverent unison, 'We, O sir!' And so the widower had straightway put from him his hempen weeds and all the thistles of his despair, had lifted his laughing child upon his shoulder, and touched with his hand the bowed heads of the villagers, saying, 'Bliss, of all things most wonderful, is fled from me. But Authority remains, and therefore will I make no more lamentation.' Henceforth Umanosuké lived for Authority. Full of wisdom were his precepts, and of necessity his decrees. Whenever the villagers quarrelled, as villagers will, among themselves, and struck each other with their paper-fans and parasols, at his coming they would lie flat upon the green ground, eager of his arbitrage. With the villagers he had not any trouble. With Yai, alas! he had.

'Five years are gone,' he said sternly to her, one morning, 'since the sun glanced upon that sugared waterfall, your mother. Nor ever once have you sought to please me, since the day when you delivered yourself into my charge. The toys that I fashioned for your fingers you have not heeded, and from the little pictures that I painted for your pleasure you have idly turned your eyes. When I would awe you to obedience, you do but flout me. When I make myself even as a child and would be your playmate, you drive me from your presence. You will soon be eight years old. Behave, I beseech you, better!'

Yai ran into the garden, laughing.

On the morning of her thirteenth birthday, Umanosuké resumed his warning. 'Ten years ago,' he said, 'there flew from me that fair heron's wing that was your mother. I would she were here that she might assuage the bitter sorrow you are always to me. You break the figured tablets from which I would teach you wisdom. Strewn with unfingered dust are the books you should have long learnt utterly. Your feet fly always over the sand or through the flowers and feather-grasses. I see you from my window bend your attentive ear to the vain music of the seashell. I often hear you in foolish parley with the birds. Me, your father, you do dishonour. Reflect! You are growing old. You will never see twelve again. Behave, I beseech you, better!'

Yai ran into the garden, pouting.

On the morning of the day before her wedding-day, Umanosuké called her to him and said, once and for all, 'Since faded and fell that fair treillage of convolvulus, than which I can find no better simile for your mother, it is already fifteen round years. And, lo! in nothing but dreams and errantry have you spent your girlhood. I, who begat you, have grown sad in contemplating all your faults. Had I not, knowing the wisdom of the philosophers, believed that in the span of every life there is good and evil equally distributed, and that your evil girlhood was surely the preamble of a most perfect prime, your faults had been intolerable. But I was comforted in my belief, and when I betrothed you to young Sanza, the son of Oiyâro, my heart was filled with fair hopes. Only illusions!'

'But, father,' said Yai, 'I do not love Sanza.'

'How can you tell that you do not love him,' her father demanded, 'seeing that you hardly know him?'

'He is ugly, father,' said Yai. 'He wears strange garments. His voice is harsh. Twice we have walked together by the side of the sea, and when he praised my beauty and talked of all he had learnt at the university, and of all he wished me to learn also, I knew that I did not love him. His thoughts are not like mine.'

'That may well be,' Umanosuké answered, 'seeing that *he* was held to be the finest student of his year, and *you* are a most ignorant maid. As for his face, it is topped with the highest forehead in Haokami. As for his garments, they are symbols of advancement. In fourteen languages he can lift his voice. I am an old man now, a man of the former fashion, and many of Sanza's thoughts seem strange to me, as to you. But when I am in his presence I bow humbly before his intellect. He is a marvellous young man, indeed. He understands all things. If you mean that *you* are unworthy of *him*, I certainly agree with you.'

'Then, it is that I am unworthy of him, father,' faltered Yai, with downcast eyes.

'Sanza does not think so,' said her father, more gently. 'He told me, yesterday, that he thought you were quite worthy of him. And as I look at you, little daughter, and see how fair a maid you are, I think he was right. It is because I love you that I would you were without fault. I have never been able to rule you. It is therefore that I give you gladly to Sanza, who will understand you, as he understands all other things.'

'Perhaps,' said Yai, 'Sanza is too wise to understand me, and I am not wise enough to love him. I do not know how it is — but, oh, father! indulge me in one whim, and I will never be graceless nor unfilial again! Tell Sanza you will not let him be my bridegroom!'

'To-morrow you will be his wife,' said Umanosuké. 'That you think yourself indifferent to him, is nothing to me. You are betrothed to him. He has given to you, in due form, a robe of silken tissue, a robe incomparably broidered with moons and lilac. When once, the lover has given to the maiden the robe of silken tissue, his betrothal is sacred in the eyes of our God.'

'Father,' said Yai, 'the robe has been given to me indeed. It lies in my room, and over all its tissue are moons and lilac. But lilac is said to be the flower of unfaith, and moons are but images of him whom I love. Ever since I was little, I have loved the Moon. As a little child I loved him, and now my heart is not childish, but I love him still. From my window, father, I watch him as he rises in silver from the edge of the sea. I watch him as he climbs up the hollow sky. For love of him I forgo sleep, and when he sinks into the sea he leaves me desolate. Of no man but him can I be the bride.'

Umanosuké raised his hand. 'The Moon,' he said, 'is the sacred lantern that our God has given us. We must not think of it but as of a lantern. I do not know the meaning of your thoughts. There is mischief in them and impiety. I pray you, put them from you, lest they fall as a curse upon your nuptials. I did but send for you that I might counsel you to bear yourself this afternoon, in Sanza's presence, as a bride should, with deference and love, not with unmaidenly aversion. It is not well that the bridegroom, when he comes duly on the eve of his wedding to kiss the hand of his bride, and to sprinkle her chamber with rose-leaves, should be treated ungraciously and put to shame. Little daughter, I will not argue with you. Know only that this wedding is well devised for your happiness. If you love me but a little, try to please me with obedience. I am older than you, and I know more. Behave, I beseech you, better!'

Yai ran into the garden, weeping.

She paced up and down the long path of porcelain. She beat her hands against the bark of her father's favourite uce-tree, whose branches were always spangled with fandangles, and cursed the name of her bridegroom. For hours she wandered among the flower-beds, calling upon the name of her love.

The gardeners watched her furtively from their work, and murmured, smiling one to another, 'This evening we need not carry forth our water-jars, for Yai has watered all the flowers with her tears.'

When the hour came for her bridegroom's visit, though, Yai had bathed her eyes in orange-water, and sat waiting at her window. She saw him, a tiny puppet in the far distance, start from the pavilion that was his home. As he came nearer, she noted his brisk tread, and how the sun shone upon his European hat. What a complacent smile curved his lips! How foolish he looked, for all his learning! In one hand he swung a black umbrella, in the other a small parcel of brown paper. 'He will release me,' whispered Yai; but her heart misgave her, and she shrank away from the window.

When her nurse ushered Sanza into the room, Yai hardly turned her head.

'Well,' he said cheerily, as he placed his hat on the floor, 'here I am, you see! Quite punctual, I think? Brought my rose-leaves along with me. Really, my dear Yai,' he said, after a pause, 'I do think you might rise to meet me when I come into the room. You know I don't stickle for sentiment — far from it, — but surely, on such an occasion, a little display of affection wouldn't be amiss. Personally, you know, I object to all this rose-leaf business; but I'm not going to offend your father's religious views, and it's really rather a quaint old ceremony in its way; and I *do* think that you might — what shall I say? — meet me half-way.'

Yai came forward listlessly.

'You'll excuse the suggestion,' he laughed, shaking her hand. 'Now, I had better undo my parcel, I suppose? I expect you know more about these little Japanese customs than I do'; and he began to loosen the string.

'What have you in there?' asked Yai.

'Why, the rose-leaves, to be sure!' Sanza replied, producing a tin that had once held cocoa.

'Most lovers bring their rose-leaves in a bowl, I fancy,' said Yai, with a faint smile. 'But it is no matter. Please do not sprinkle them yet.'

'How stupid of me!' exclaimed Sanza, throwing back his handful of rose-leaves into the tin. 'If one does a thing at all, let it be done correctly. I have to kiss your hand first, of course.'

'Please do not kiss my hand, Sanza,' the girl said simply. 'I do not love you. I do not wish to be your bride.'

Sanza whistled.

'What about that silk material I sent you the other day?' he asked sharply. 'I understood that your failure to return it was *ipso facto* an acceptance of my proposal?'

'I kept the silken robe that was broidered with moons and lilac,' Yai murmured, 'because I wished to please my father, whom I have often grieved. I thought then that I could be your bride. Now I know that I cannot.'

'Why this change of front?' gasped her lover.

'I have no good reason,' she said, 'that I can give you; only that I thought I was stronger than I am — stronger than my love.'

'If you will excuse me,' muttered Sanza, with momentary irrelevance, 'I will sit down.' And he squatted upon the floor, disposing the tails of his frock-coat around him. 'May I ask,' he said at length, 'to what love you refer?'

'My love for the Moon,' Yai answered.

'The — the *what?*' cried Sanza.

'The Moon,' she repeated, adding rather foolishly, 'I — I thought perhaps you had guessed.'

Sanza laughed heartily.

'Well, really,' he said, 'you quite took me in. I should suggest your becoming an actress, if it weren't for native prejudices. You'd go far. Oh, very good! Ha, ha!'

'I am not jesting, Sanza,' said Yai sadly. 'I am very earnest. Ever since I was little, I have loved the Moon. As a little child I loved him, and now my heart is not childish, but I love him still. My heart grows glad, as he rises in silver from the edge of the sea and climbs up the hollow sky. When he climbs quickly, I shudder lest he fall; when he lingers, I try to fancy it is for love of me; when he sinks at length into the sea, I weep bitterly.'

Sanza began to humour her.

'Oh yes,' he said, 'the Moon's a wonderful climber. I've noticed that. And a very good fellow, too, from all accounts. I don't happen to know him personally. He was senior to me at the university. I must get you to introduce us.'

'You jest poorly,' said Yai.

Sanza frowned.

'Come, come,' he resumed presently, 'you know as well as I do that the Moon is just an extinct planet, 237,000 miles distant from the Earth.

Perhaps you didn't know? Well, selenography is rather a hobby of mine, and I'll give you one or two little facts. The Moon is a subject which has attracted a great many physiologists in all ages. Thanks to the invention of photography, we moderns have accumulated a considerable amount of knowledge regarding it. The negatives obtained at the Lick Observatory, for example, prove conclusively that the immense craters and mountainous ridges visible upon its surface, so far from being surrounded with an atmosphere similar in density to our own, are, in fact, enclosed only by a gaseous envelope, not less than 200 times thinner than the most rarefied atmosphere obtainable on the Earth.'

But Yai had shut her ears.

'Sanza,' she said, when he ceased, 'will you release me? If you think me mad, you cannot wish me to be your bride.'

For a moment Sanza hesitated — but for a moment.

'Madness,' he said, 'is a question of degree. We are all potentially mad. If you were left to indulge in these absurd notions, you would certainly become mad, in time. As it is, I fancy you have a touch of Neuromania. And, when you speak, I have noticed a slight tendency to Echolalia. But these are trifles, my dear. Any sudden change of life is apt to dispel far more serious symptoms. Your very defects, small though they are, will make me all the more watchful and tender towards you when I am your husband.'

'You are very cruel and very cowardly,' sobbed Yai, 'and I hate you!'

'Nonsense!' said Sanza, snatching one of her hands and kissing it loudly.

In another minute the room had been sprinkled with rose-leaves and Yai was alone.

At sunset her father came to the room and bent over her and kissed her. 'Do not weep, little daughter,' he said. 'It is well that you should be wed, though you are so unwilling. Sleep happily now, little daughter. To-morrow, all in your honour, the way will be strewn with anemones and golden grain. Little lanterns will waver in the almond trees.'

Yai spoke not a word.

But when her father had reached the threshold of her room, she ran swiftly to him and flung her arms around his neck, and whispered to him through tears, 'Forgive me for being always an evil daughter.'

Umanosuké caressed her and spoke gentle words. And when he left her, at length, he barred the door of her room. For in that land there is an old custom, which ordains that the bride's room be sealed on the wedding-eve, lest the bride be stolen away in the night.

Umanosuké's footsteps grew faint in the distance. So soon as she could hear them no more, Yaï shook the door, noiselessly, if peradventure it were not rightly barred. It did not yield. Noiselessly she crept across the floor, the rose-leaves brushing her bare and tiny feet. Noiselessly she slid back the wickered grill from her window. She wrapped her skirt very tightly round her, and raised herself on to the ledge. Down a trellis that covered the outer wall she climbed lightly. No one saw her.

Darting swiftly from shadow to shadow, she passed down the long garden, and dragged from its shed the little, reeded skiff that her father had once given to her. She did not dare drag it down the beach, lest the noise of the rustling shingle should betray her. Easily (for it was light as a toy) she lifted it on her shoulder, and carried it down, so, to the darkening waters, launched it, and stepped in.

She knew at what point on the edge of the great sea her lover would rise. She knew by the aspect of the stars that he would rise before the end of another hour. Could she reach the edge of the great sea so soon? Crouching low in the skiff, a little figure scrupulously balanced, she brushed the water with her paddle. Strong and supple was her wrist, and sure were her eyes, and swiftly the frail craft sped on over the waters. Never once did the maid flag nor falter, though her hands grew cold and stiff in their strenuous exercise. Though darkness closed in around her, and the waters rushed past her, on either side, with a shrill sound as of weeping, she had no fear, but only love in her heart. Gazing steadfastly before her at that glimmering, white line, where the sky curves down upon the sea, and ever whispering through her lips the name of her love, she held her swift course over the waters.

Clearer, clearer to her gaze, grew the white line and the arched purple that rested on it. Another minute, and she could hear the waves lapping its surface, a sweet monotony of music, seeming to call her on. A few more strokes of her paddle, swept with a final impulse, and the boat bore her with a yet swifter speed. Soon she suffered it to glide on obliquely, till it grazed the white line with its prow. She had reached the tryst of her devotion. Faint and quivering, she lay back and waited there.

After a while, she leant over the side of the boat and peered down into the sea. Far, far under the surface she seemed to descry a little patch of silver, of silver that was moving. She clasped her hands to her eyes and gazed down again. The silver was spreading, wider and wider, under the water, till the water's surface became even as a carpet of dazzling silver.

The Moon rose through the sea, and paused under the canopy of the sky.

So great, so fair was he, of countenance so illustrious, that little Yai did but hide her head in the folds of her garment, daring not to look up at him.

She heard a voice, that was softer and more melancholy than the west wind, saying to her, 'Child of the Ruler of Haokami, why sought you to waylay me?' And again the voice said, 'Why sought you to waylay me?'

'Because,' Yai answered faintly, 'because I have long loved you.'

And as she crouched before him, the Moon covered her with silver, insomuch that she was able to look up into his eyes, being herself radiant, even as he was. And she stretched out her arms to him and besought him that she might sail over the sky with him that night.

'Nay,' said the Moon, 'but you know not what you ask. Over the sky you might sail in my embrace, and love me, and be my darling. I would bear you among the stars and lie with you in the shadows of the clouds. The tiny world would lie outspread beneath us, and in the wonder of our joy we would not heed it. We would mingle the cold silver of our lips, and in the wreath of our arms our love-dreams would come true. But soon I should sink into the sea yonder. On the grey surface of the sea I should leave you to drown.'

'Take me in your arms!' cried the girl.

And the Moon bent down to her and took her gently in his arms.

Next morning, the Sun, as he was rising from the sea, saw a little pale body floating over the waves.

'Why!' he exclaimed, 'there is the child of the ruler of Haokami. She was always wayward. I knew she would come to a bad end. And this was to have been her wedding-day too! I suppose she was really in love with me and swam to meet me. How very sad!' And he covered her with gold.

'After all,' he muttered, rising a little higher, 'it does not do for these human beings to have ideas above their station. It always leads to unhappiness. The dead child down there would soon have forgotten her unfortunate attachment to me, if she had only stayed ashore and married that impertinent little fellow, who is always spying at me through his confounded telescope. And there he is, to be sure! up betimes and strutting about his garden, with a fine new suit on! Quite the bridegroom!'

Queen Ysabeau

Villiers de l'Isle-Adam
translated by *A. Texeira de Mattos*

Auguste Villiers de l'Isle-Adam (1838–89) was a count and a French Symbolist writer of short stories, novels, plays and poetry. He was a close friend of Stéphane Mallarmé and was also acquainted with Gautier and Baudelaire. His most famous works are the collection of short stories *Contes Cruels* (*Cruel Tales*) (1883), the novel *L'Ève Future* (1886) and the posthumously published Symbolist play *Axël* (1890). *Contes Cruels*, of which 'Queen Ysabeau' is part, was instrumental in popularising the cruel tale genre. The book, immortalised in Des Esseintes's Decadent library, treats themes of Gothic horror and the fantastic, and was influenced by Baudelaire's translations of Poe. Alexander Texeira de Mattos (1865–1921) was a prolific Dutch translator of French literature and a dandy. He was a close friend of and travelling companion to Arthur Symons. In 1900 he married Lily Wilde, Oscar's widowed sister-in-law.

'Queen Ysabeau' is a historical romance story based on Queen of France Isabeau of Bavaria (Elisabeth of Bavaria-Ingolstadt; c.1370–1435) who has come to be seen as notorious for her scheming personality, fatal beauty and profligacy. The Marquis de Sade even wrote a historical novel about Isabeau (1813). In Villiers's story, set in a dissolute French Court, Ysabeau is the epitome of frivolity and monstrous intrigue. Her calculated, elaborate revenge plot on her lover is gradually revealed in their tantalisingly languorous and sensual bedroom scene. The ending twist accentuates Ysabeau's vacuous insatiability and corruption for its own sake to maximum effect. Cruelty and eroticism are deftly juxtaposed, anticipating Wilde's devious beauty Salomé, and even echoing Gautier's 'One of Cleopatra's Nights' (1838). Symons, who wrote about Villiers in *The Symbolist Movement in Literature* (1899), also translated 'Queen Ysabeau'.

The Keeper of the Palace of Books said: 'Queen Nitocris, the Fair One with the Rosy Cheeks, widow of Papi I. of the Tenth Dynasty, to avenge the murder of her brother, invited the conspirators to sup with her in an underground hall of her Palace of Aznac. Then, leaving the hall, she suddenly caused it to be flooded with the waters of the Nile.' – Manethon.

In or about the year 1404 — I go back so far lest I should distress my contemporaries — Ysabeau, wife to King Charles VI. and Regent of France, abode in Paris at the old Hôtel Montagu, a royal residence better known as the Hôtel Barbette.

There they planned the famous torchlight jousting-parties on the Seine — gala nights, concerts, banquets, made marvellous by the beauty of the women and the young nobles, and by the unequalled luxury displayed by the Court.

The Queen had introduced those gowns *à la gore* in which the bosom glanced through a network of ribands enriched with precious stones, and those tall head-dresses which required that the centre-pieces of the feudal gates should be raised by several cubits. In the daytime the meeting-place of the courtiers was near the Louvre, in the great hall and upon the terrace of orange-trees of Messire Escabala, the King's steward. Play ran high there, and at times the dice were cast for stakes large enough to starve a province. They dissipated the wealth of treasure which the thrifty Charles V. had been at such pains to amass. As the coffers diminished, the tithes, tolls, statute-tasks, aids, subsidies, seizures, exactions, and gabels were increased at will. Joy reigned in every heart.

It was in those days, also, that John of Nevers, sullen, standing aloof, making ready to abolish all those hateful taxes in his own States — John of Nevers, Knight, Lord of Salines, Count of Flanders and Artois, Count of Nevers, Baron of Réthel, Palatine of Mechlin, twice Peer of France and Premier Peer, cousin to the King, a soldier destined to be named by the Council of Constance the *sole* leader of armies who might be obeyed blindly without fear of excommunication, Premier Grand Feudatory of the Realm, first subject of the King (who himself is but the first subject of the nation), Hereditary Duke of Burgundy, the future hero of Nicopolis and of the victory of Hesbaie, in which, deserted by the Flemings, he gained the heroic title of *The Fearless* in presence of the whole army by delivering France from her principal enemy — it was in those days, I was saying, that the son of Philip the Bold and Margaret II., that John the Fearless, in a word, first began to think of saving the country and of defying with fire and sword Henry of Derby, Earl of Hereford and Lancaster, fifth of the name, King of England — he who, when a price was put upon his head by that King, was declared a traitor by France, by way of all thanks.

Awkward attempts were for the first time made to play at cards, which had since a few days been imported by Odette de Champ-d'Hiver. Wagers of all kinds were made. They drank wines that came from the finest slopes of the Duchy of Burgundy. The ring was heard of the Tenzons, the Virelays of the Duke of Orleans, one of the Knights of the Fleurs-de-Lys who doted most upon beautiful rhymes. They discussed fashions and armour; often sang dissolute couplets.

Bérénice Escabala, the daughter of that man of wealth, was a charming child, and exceeding fair to look upon. Her virgin smile attracted the most brilliant of the swarm of noblemen. It was notorious that she extended to all indifferently the same gracious reception.

One day it happened that a young lord, the Vidame of Maulle, who was then Queen Ysabeau's favourite, rashly pledged his word (after drinking, assuredly!) that he would triumph over the inflexible innocence of this daughter of Master Escabala; in short, that she should be his within an approximate time.

This boast was hazarded in the midst of a group of courtiers. Around them stirred the laughter and the refrains of the time; but the hubbub did not drown the young man's reckless phrase. The wager was accepted to the clinking of wine-cups, and came to the ears of Louis of Orleans.

Louis of Orleans, brother-in-law to the Queen, had been distinguished by her, in the early days of the Regency, with a passionate affection. He was a brilliant and frivolous prince, but of most evil omen. Between him and Ysabeau of Bavaria were certain parities of nature which likened their adultery to incest. Beside the capricious aftermath of a withered love, he was still able to command in the Queen's heart a sort of bastard attachment more of the nature of a compact than of sympathy.

The Duke kept a watch upon the favourites of his sister-in-law. When the lovers' intimacy seemed to threaten the influence which he was determined to retain over the Queen, he showed little scruple in the means he employed to produce between them a rupture which was nearly always tragic. He would even stoop to play the informer.

And thus he took care that the observation aforesaid was carried to the Vidame of Maulle's royal paramour.

Ysabeau smiled, jested at the remark, and seemed to give it no further thought.

The Queen had her seers, who sold her the secrets of the East, potent to feed the flame of the desires she inspired. A new Cleopatra, she was a tall, listless woman, fashioned to preside over courts of love in some remote manor, or to set the mode to a province, rather than to plan how to free the soil of the country from the English. On this occasion, however, she consulted none of her seers — not even Arnaut Guilhem, her alchemist.

One night, not long after, the Lord of Maulle was with the Queen at the Hôtel Barbette. The hour was late; the fatigue of their pleasure was lulling the two lovers to sleep.

Suddenly Monsieur de Maulle seemed to hear, within Paris, the sound of bells tolled with infrequent and solemn strokes.

He started.

'What is that?' he asked.

'Nothing . . . . Let it be! . . .' replied Ysabeau playfully, and without opening her eyes.

'Nothing, my fair Queen? . . . Is it not the tocsin?'

'Yes . . . perhaps . . . . Well, my love, and then?'

'There must be a house on fire.'

'I was just dreaming of it,' said Ysabeau.

The fair sleeper's lips parted in a smile of pearls.

'And more,' she continued; 'in my dream, it was you who had lighted it. I saw you fling a torch into the oil and fodder cellars, sweet heart.'

'Me?'

'Yes! . . .' (She drawled the syllables languidly.) 'You were burning the house of Messire Escabala, my steward, you know, to win your wager of the other day.'

The Lord of Maulle half opened his eyes, seized with vague distrust.

'What wager? Are you not asleep yet, beautiful angel mine?'

'Why, your wager that you would be the lover of his daughter, little Bérénice, who has such beautiful eyes! . . . Oh! what a sweet and pretty child, is she not?'

'What are you saying, dear Ysabeau?'

'Do you not understand me, my lord? I was dreaming, I said, that you had set fire to my steward's house to carry off his daughter during the conflagration, and make her your mistress, and win your wager.'

The Vidame looked about him in silence.

The glare from a lowering distance lighted up the window-panes of the chamber; purple reflections tinged with blood the ermine of the royal bed; the lilies on the escutcheons and those breathing their last in vases of enamel blushed red! And red, also, were the two goblets, upon a credence-table laden with wines and fruits.

'Ah! I remember . . .' murmured the young man. 'It is true; I wished to draw the attention of the courtiers towards that little one in order to divert them from our happiness! . . . But see, Ysabeau; it is really a great fire . . . and the flames rise from the direction of the Louvre!'

At these words the Queen raised herself upon her elbow, silently and very fixedly contemplated the Vidame of Maulle, shook her head; then, lazily smiling, pressed a long kiss upon the young man's lips.

'You shall tell these things to Master Cappeluche when presently he breaks you upon the wheel on the Place de Grève! . . . You are a wicked incendiary, my love!'

And as the perfumes which issued from her eastern body bewildered and scorched the senses till the power to think had fled, she nestled up against him.

The tocsin continued; they distinguished afar the shouts of the crowd.

He replied, jesting:

'They would first have to prove the crime.'

And he returned the kiss.

'Prove it, naughty one?'

'Surely!'

'Could you prove the number of kisses I have given you? As well try to count the butterflies that flit on a summer's night!'

He contemplated this fiery mistress — and yet how pale! — who had just lavished upon him delights and raptures of most marvellous voluptuousness.

He took her hand.

'Besides, it will be very easy,' continued she. 'To whose interest was it to profit by a fire in order to carry off the daughter of Messire Escabala? Yours alone. Your word is pledged in the wager! . . . And as you would never be able to say where you were when the fire broke out! . . . You see, that is quite sufficient, at the Châtelet, to put you upon your trial. The inquiry comes first, and then . . . (she gently yawned) the torture does the rest.'

'I should not be able to say where I was?' asked Monsieur de Maulle.

'Of course not; for, King Charles VI. then living, in that hour you lay in the arms of the Queen of France, child that you are!'

Death, in fact, arose stark and erect on either side of the charge.

'That is true,' said the Lord of Maulle, under the enchantment of the gentle gaze of his love.

He grew drunk with joy; he threw his arm about the young waist enfolded in her lukewarm hair, red as burnt gold.

'These are dreams,' said he. 'Oh, my sweet life! . . .'

They had made music that evening; his dulcimer lay flung upon a cushion; a cord snapped all alone.

'Sleep, sleep, my angel! You need sleep!' said Ysabeau, languidly drawing the young man's forehead upon her bosom.

The sound of the instrument had made him start; the enamoured are superstitious.

On the morrow the Vidame of Maulle was arrested and thrown into a dungeon of the Grand Châtelet. The trial commenced on the charge foretold. All happened exactly as predicted by the august enchantress, 'whose beauty was so great that it was destined to outlive her passions'.

It was impossible for the Vidame of Maulle to find what lawyers call an *alibi*.

After the preliminary investigation, ordinary and extraordinary, he was cross-examined and sentenced to be broken on the wheel.

The punishment of incendiaries, the black veil, and so forth . . . nothing was omitted.

Only, a strange incident took place at the Grand Châtelet.

The young man's counsel had become deeply attached to him; and his client had confessed everything to him.

Knowing the innocence of Monsieur de Maulle, his defender was guilty of an act of heroism.

On the eve of the execution, he came to the condemned man's dungeon and helped him to escape beneath the shelter of his gown. In short, he put himself in his place.

Was his the noblest of hearts? or was he an ambitious man playing a terrible part? Who shall ever tell?

Broken and burnt by the torture, the Vidame of Maulle crossed the frontier and died in exile.

But the counsel was detained in his place.

The paramour of the Vidame of Maulle, when she learnt of the young man's escape, experienced only a feeling of exceeding vexation.

She refused to recognise the defender of her lover.

So that the name of Monsieur de Maulle might be erased from the list of the living, she ordered the execution of the sentence *even so*.

Whence came that the counsel was broken on the wheel upon the Place de Grève, in the place and instead of the Lord of Maulle.

Pray for their souls.

Figure 1 *The Dial* 1 (1889), front cover by Charles Ricketts.

Figure 2 C. H. Shannon, 'Return of the Prodigal', *The Dial* 1 (1889), AB. An example of using Biblical subjects in order to excuse the depiction of an illicit act, in this case a homosexual kiss. Such techniques can also be found in textual form in Pierre Louÿs's *Aphrodite* (1896).

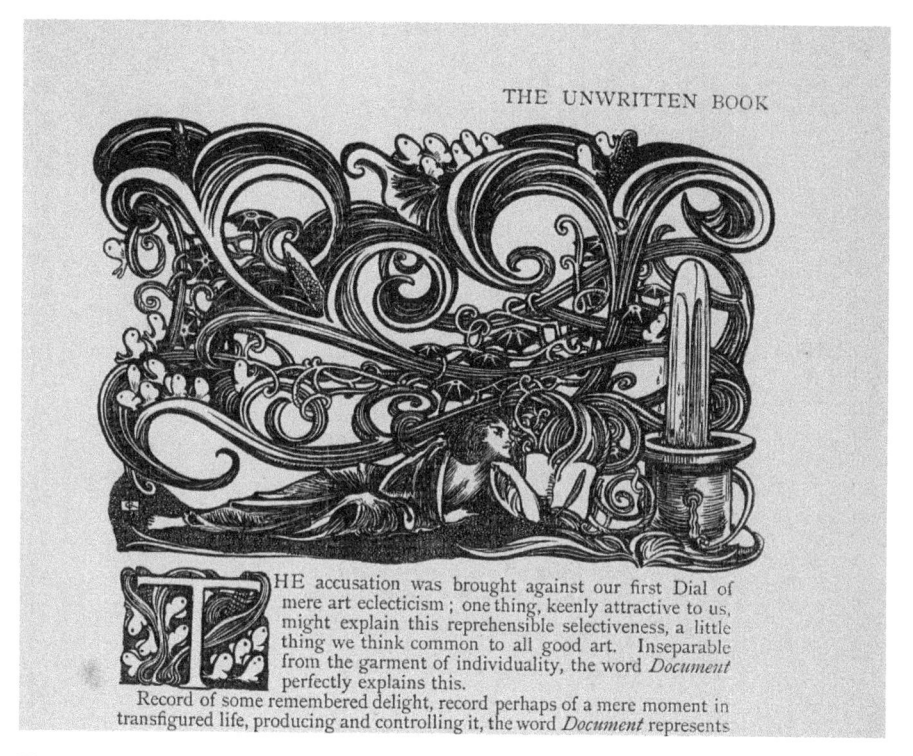

Figure 3 Charles Ricketts, illuminated initial piece to 'The Unwritten Book', *The Dial* 2 (1892), p. 25. Within this intricate web of vegetative flourishes, the phallic object, with its suggestive seminal emissions, oscillates between implicitness and explicitness.

Figure 4 *The Dial* 2 (1892), contents page. The margin in extremis.

Figure 5 *The Century Guild Hobby Horse* Vol. 1 (1886), title page by Selwyn Image. This illustration was also used as the cover art for the individual numbers of the *Hobby Horse*.

Figure 6 Frederick Sandys, 'Danae in the Brazen Chamber', *The Century Guild Hobby Horse* 3.xii (1888), facing p. 147. Another way of legitimising erotic artwork was by using a Classical theme, in this case a scene from the life of Danae, mother of Perseus.

Figure 7 C. H. Shannon, 'Umbilicus Tuus Crater Tornatilis, Numquam Indigens Poculis. Venter Tuus Sicut Acervus Tritici, Vallatus Liliis', drawing on stone, *The Century Guild Hobby Horse* 6.xxii (1891), facing p. 41. Once again, a Biblical reference, this time to the Song of Solomon, 7:2.

Figure 8 P. Wilson Steer, 'Skirt Dancing', *The Yellow Book* Vol. 3 (October 1894), p. [173]. Wilson Steer's paintings on this subject – evocative of Edgar Degas's dancers – could work as illustrations to Frederick Wedmore's letters 'To Nancy' in *The Savoy*.

Figure 9 Will Rothenstein, 'Mr. John Davidson', *The Yellow Book* Vol. 4 (January 1895), p. [205]. Not every sensuous illustration had to feature a nude, or a female subject.

Figure 10 *The Yellow Book* Vol. 6 (July 1895), front cover by Patten Wilson. The second cover image of the magazine's post-Beardsley period. This is suggestive of Gilchrist's 'The Crimson Weaver' featured therein: the Japanese art nouveau patterns on the figure's robe allude to the knitted flesh-and-blood veins of her male victims.

Figure 11 *The Savoy* 2 (April 1896), front cover by Aubrey Beardsley. Beardsley's drawing done in his flamboyant, florid manner seems to mock Victorian middle-class morality and hypocrisy. The scene of the lady with her chaperon in a respectable looking Baroque setting is undermined by the fact that she is receiving a milliner in her dressing room instead of the drawing room, thereby implying a kept woman or courtesan.

Figure 12 Charles Ricketts, 'Oedipus, after a Pen Drawing', *The Pageant* 1 (1896), p. 65. Exuding an air of opulent decay, this luxurious drawing is similar to Gustave Moreau's paintings on the Sphinx, whilst resembling the Pre-Raphaelite manner of expressiveness and vividness.

II

Other Sources

The Nightingale and the Rose

Oscar Wilde

Oscar Fingal O'Flahertie Wills Wilde (1854–1900) was popularly perceived as the 'High Priest' of Decadence in England, particularly after the publication of his single, yet monumental novel, *The Picture of Dorian Gray*. Although an acclaimed playwright, poet, critic, journalist and raconteur, as well as novelist and short-story writer, it was Wilde's life that left the largest impression on the last years of Victoria's reign. Famous as a dandy whilst an undergraduate at Oxford, Wilde courted publicity throughout his life in a truly modern fashion. Although his sensational works caused a good deal of public outrage (particularly *The Portrait of Mr. W. H.* in 1889, followed swiftly by *Dorian Gray*), his flagrantly homosexual lifestyle led to his downfall. Wilde's works, and especially his letters display a life-long fascination with Roman Catholicism, and he is said to have been received into the Catholic faith on his deathbed, at the age of forty-six, whilst in exile in France.

'The Nightingale and the Rose' is at once a children's fairy-tale, yet even more, a Symbolist fantasy in a shimmering and sparing style with extensive use of simile, generic repetition, anthropomorphism and inter-textual literary echoes. Here the dramatisation of the contrast between artistic idealism and opportunist materialism heightens and maximises the effect of frivolity. The story also weaves in Decadent images of futility, vampirism, phallic penetration and prostitution. As critics have pointed out, Catholicism is also present in the story, with the Nightingale as the Crucified Christ and the rose as the Virgin Mary (*Pietà*). The story is a paean to 'style' and higher artifice with the Artist-Nightingale pouring forth her aria, her soul, to create the unnatural rose.

'She said that she would dance with me if I brought her red roses,' cried the young Student; 'but in all my garden there is no red rose.'

From her nest in the holm-oak tree the Nightingale heard him, and she looked out through the leaves, and wondered.

'No red rose in all my garden!' he cried, and his beautiful eyes filled with tears. 'Ah, on what little things does happiness depend! I have read all that the wise men have written, and all the secrets of philosophy are mine, yet for want of a red rose is my life made wretched.'

'Here at last is a true lover,' said the Nightingale. 'Night after night have I sung of him, though I knew him not; night after night have I told his story to the stars, and now I see him. His hair is dark as the hyacinth-blossom, and his lips are red as the rose of his desire; but passion has made his face like pale ivory, and sorrow has set her seal upon his brow.'

'The Prince gives a ball to-morrow night,' murmured the young Student, 'and my love will be of the company. If I bring her a red rose she will dance with me till dawn. If I bring her a red rose, I shall hold her in my arms, and she will lean her head upon my shoulder, and her hand will be clasped in mine. But there is no red rose in my garden, so I shall sit lonely, and she will pass me by. She will have no heed of me, and my heart will break.'

'Here indeed is the true lover,' said the Nightingale. 'What I sing of, he suffers; what is joy to me, to him is pain. Surely Love is a wonderful thing. It is more precious than emeralds, and dearer than fine opals. Pearls and pomegranates cannot buy it, nor is it set forth in the market-place. It may not be purchased of the merchants, nor can it be weighed out in the balance for gold.'

'The musicians will sit in their gallery,' said the young Student, 'and play upon their stringed instruments, and my love will dance to the sound of the harp and the violin. She will dance so lightly that her feet will not touch the floor, and the courtiers in their gay dresses will throng round her. But with me she will not dance, for I have no red rose to give her'; and he flung himself down on the grass, and buried his face in his hands, and wept.

'Why is he weeping?' asked a little Green Lizard, as he ran past him with his tail in the air.

'Why, indeed?' said a Butterfly, who was fluttering about after a sunbeam.
'Why, indeed?' whispered a Daisy to his neighbour, in a soft, low voice.
'He is weeping for a red rose,' said the Nightingale.
'For a red rose!' they cried; 'how very ridiculous!' and the little Lizard, who was something of a cynic, laughed outright.

But the Nightingale understood the secret of the Student's sorrow, and she sat silent in the oak-tree, and thought about the mystery of Love.

Suddenly she spread her brown wings for flight, and soared into the air. She passed through the grove like a shadow, and like a shadow she sailed across the garden.

In the centre of the grass-plot was standing a beautiful Rose-tree, and when she saw it, she flew over to it, and lit upon a spray.

'Give me a red rose,' she cried, 'and I will sing you my sweetest song.'
But the Tree shook its head.

'My roses are white,' it answered; 'as white as the foam of the sea, and whiter than the snow upon the mountain. But go to my brother who grows round the old sun-dial, and perhaps he will give you what you want.'

So the Nightingale flew over to the Rose-tree that was growing round the old sun-dial.

'Give me a red rose,' she cried, 'and I will sing you my sweetest song.'
But the Tree shook its head.

'My roses are yellow,' it answered; 'as yellow as the hair of the mermaiden who sits upon an amber throne, and yellower than the daffodil that blooms in the meadow before the mower comes with his scythe. But go to my brother who grows beneath the Student's window, and perhaps he will give you what you want.'

So the Nightingale flew over to the Rose-tree that was growing beneath the Student's window.

'Give me a red rose,' she cried, 'and I will sing you my sweetest song.'
But the Tree shook its head.

'My roses are red,' it answered, 'as red as the feet of the dove, and redder than the great fans of coral that wave and wave in the ocean-cavern. But the winter has chilled my veins, and the frost has nipped my buds, and the storm has broken my branches, and I shall have no roses at all this year.'

'One red rose is all I want,' cried the Nightingale, 'only one red rose! Is there no way by which I can get it?'

'There is a way,' answered the Tree; 'but it is so terrible that I dare not tell it to you.'

'Tell it to me,' said the Nightingale, 'I am not afraid.'

'If you want a red rose,' said the Tree, 'you must build it out of music by moonlight, and stain it with your own heart's-blood. You must sing to me with your breast against a thorn. All night long you must sing to me, and the thorn must pierce your heart, and your life-blood must flow into my veins, and become mine.'

'Death is a great price to pay for a red rose,' cried the Nightingale, 'and Life is very dear to all. It is pleasant to sit in the green wood, and to watch the Sun in his chariot of gold, and the Moon in her chariot of pearl. Sweet is the scent of the hawthorn, and sweet are the bluebells that hide in the valley, and the heather that blows on the hill. Yet Love is better than Life, and what is the heart of a bird compared to the heart of a man?'

So she spread her brown wings for flight, and soared into the air. She swept over the garden like a shadow, and like a shadow she sailed through the grove.

The young Student was still lying on the grass, where she had left him, and the tears were not yet dry in his beautiful eyes.

'Be happy,' cried the Nightingale, 'be happy; you shall have your red rose. I will build it out of music by moonlight, and stain it with my own heart's-blood. All that I ask of you in return is that you will be a true lover, for Love is wiser than Philosophy, though she is wise, and mightier than Power, though he is mighty. Flame-coloured are his wings, and coloured like flame is his body. His lips are sweet as honey, and his breath is like frankincense.'

The Student looked up from the grass, and listened, but he could not understand what the Nightingale was saying to him, for he only knew the things that are written down in books.

But the Oak-tree understood, and felt sad, for he was very fond of the little Nightingale who had built her nest in his branches.

'Sing me one last song,' he whispered; 'I shall feel very lonely when you are gone.'

So the Nightingale sang to the Oak-tree, and her voice was like water bubbling from a silver jar.

When she had finished her song the Student got up, and pulled a notebook and a lead-pencil out of his pocket.

'She has form,' he said to himself, as he walked away through the grove – 'that cannot be denied to her; but has she got feeling? I am afraid not. In fact, she is like most artists; she is all style, without any sincerity. She would not sacrifice herself for others. She thinks merely of music, and everybody knows that the arts are selfish. Still, it must be admitted that she has some beautiful notes in her voice. What a pity it is that they do not mean anything, or do any practical good.' And he went into his room, and lay down on his little pallet-bed, and began to think of his love; and, after a time, he fell asleep.

And when the Moon shone in the heavens the Nightingale flew to the Rose-tree, and set her breast against the thorn. All night long she sang with her breast against the thorn, and the cold crystal Moon leaned down and listened. All night long she sang, and the thorn went deeper and deeper into her breast, and her life-blood ebbed away from her.

She sang first of the birth of love in the heart of a boy and a girl. And on the topmost spray of the Rose-tree there blossomed a marvellous rose, petal following petal, as song followed song. Pale was it, at first, as the mist that hangs over the river – pale as the feet of the morning, and silver as the wings of the dawn. As the shadow of a rose in a mirror of silver, as the shadow of a rose in a water-pool, so was the rose that blossomed on the topmost spray of the Tree.

But the Tree cried to the Nightingale to press closer against the thorn. 'Press closer, little Nightingale,' cried the Tree, 'or the Day will come before the rose is finished.'

So the Nightingale pressed closer against the thorn, and louder and louder grew her song, for she sang of the birth of passion in the soul of a man and a maid.

And a delicate flush of pink came into the leaves of the rose, like the flush in the face of the bridegroom when he kisses the lips of the bride. But the thorn had not yet reached her heart, so the rose's heart remained white, for only a Nightingale's heart's-blood can crimson the heart of a rose.

And the Tree cried to the Nightingale to press closer against the thorn. 'Press closer, little Nightingale,' cried the Tree, 'or the Day will come before the rose is finished.'

So the Nightingale pressed closer against the thorn, and the thorn touched her heart, and a fierce pang of pain shot through her. Bitter, bitter was the pain, and wilder and wilder grew her song, for she sang of the Love that is perfected by Death, of the Love that dies not in the tomb.

And the marvellous rose became crimson, like the rose of the eastern sky. Crimson was the girdle of petals, and crimson as a ruby was the heart.

But the Nightingale's voice grew fainter, and her little wings began to beat, and a film came over her eyes. Fainter and fainter grew her song, and she felt something choking her in her throat.

Then she gave one last burst of music. The white Moon heard it, and she forgot the dawn, and lingered on in the sky. The red rose heard it, and it trembled all over with ecstasy, and opened its petals to the cold morning air. Echo bore it to her purple cavern in the hills, and woke the sleeping shepherds from their dreams. It floated through the reeds of the river, and they carried its message to the sea.

'Look, look!' cried the Tree, 'the rose is finished now'; but the Nightingale made no answer, for she was lying dead in the long grass, with the thorn in her heart.

And at noon the Student opened his window and looked out.

'Why, what a wonderful piece of luck!' he cried; 'here is a red rose! I have never seen any rose like it in all my life. It is so beautiful that I am sure it has a long Latin name'; and he leaned down and plucked it.

Then he put on his hat, and ran up to the Professor's house with the rose in his hand.

The daughter of the Professor was sitting in the doorway winding blue silk on a reel, and her little dog was lying at her feet.

'You said that you would dance with me if I brought you a red rose,' cried the Student. 'Here is the reddest rose in all the world. You will wear it to-night next your heart, and as we dance together it will tell you how I love you.'

But the girl frowned.

'I am afraid it will not go with my dress,' she answered; 'and, besides, the Chamberlain's nephew has sent me some real jewels, and everybody knows that jewels cost far more than flowers.'

'Well, upon my word, you are very ungrateful,' said the Student angrily; and he threw the rose into the street, where it fell into the gutter, and a cart-wheel went over it.

'Ungrateful!' said the girl. 'I tell you what, you are very rude; and, after all, who are you? Only a Student. Why, I don't believe you have even got silver buckles to your shoes as the Chamberlain's nephew has'; and she got up from her chair and went into the house.

'What a silly thing Love is,' said the Student as he walked away. 'It is not half as useful as Logic, for it does not prove anything, and it is always telling one of things that are not going to happen, and making one believe things that are not true. In fact, it is quite unpractical, and, as in this age to be practical is everything, I shall go back to Philosophy and study Metaphysics.'

So he returned to his room and pulled out a great dusty book, and began to read.

The Legend of Madame Krasinska

Vernon Lee

Born Violet Paget in Boulogne, northern France, Vernon Lee (1856–1935) was an erudite author and an Italophile, who wrote essays on Italian culture, and set many of her stories in Italy. She was an early feminist, and a lesbian (her lovers included the British poet and novelist Amy Levy). Although she had an uneasy relationship with Decadence – parodying it in her novel *Miss Brown* (1884) – she is firmly classed within Aestheticism. Lee was a loyal disciple of Walter Pater and his formulations of Aesthetic Beauty. Her contributions to *The Yellow Book* in the post-Beardsley period ensured the magazine's continued links with Decadence. Her story collections, including *Hauntings* (1890) and *Vanitas* (1892), are paced, learned and refined, dealing with such themes as elegant femininity, the supernatural and artistic performance.

'The Legend of Madame Krasinska' is an exemplar of stylistic richness and craftsmanship. Akin to other stories of Lee's, such as 'Lady Tal', it is a sketch of a 'frivolous' woman peering into 'the great waste of precious things', as Lee wrote in her foreword to *Vanitas*. With its themes of split personality, confused identity and hysteria, the story is centred on the eponymous heroine who imitates an old, pauper woman, initially in a mocking way, but gradually takes up that woman's identity. This leads Madame Krasinska into the shadowy and dangerous recesses of the labyrinthine city. The story adopts the trope of the *flâneuse*, creating a female dandy who suffers from boredom and stifling social convention. Her artificial identity replaces her natural self in a manner reminiscent of Dorian Gray's portrait taking over the man's life. The writing style is 'exquisite' (a favourite epithet of Lee's) and the kaleidoscopic, opulent depiction of the masked ball even alludes to Poe's 'The Mask of the Red Death' (1842). The male narrator acts like a detective who strives to decipher female identity, fantasy and desire with his inquisitive eyes.

It is a necessary part of this story to explain how I have come by it, or, rather, how it has chanced to have me for its writer.

I was very much impressed one day by a certain nun of the order who call themselves Little Sisters of the Poor. My friend Cecco Bandini (that is not his real name, of course) had taken me to these sisters to support his recommendation of a certain old lady, the former door-keeper of his studio, whom he wished to place in the asylum. It turned out, of course, that Cecchino was perfectly able to plead his case without my assistance; so I left him blandishing the Mother Superior in the big, cheerful kitchen, and begged to be shown over the rest of the establishment. The sister who was told off to accompany me was the one of whom I wish to speak.

This lady was tall and slight; her figure, as she preceded me up the narrow stairs and through the whitewashed wards, was uncommonly elegant and charming, and she had a girlish rapidity of movement, which caused me to experience a little shock at the first real sight which I caught of her face. It was young and remarkably pretty, with a kind of refinement peculiar to American women; but it was inexpressibly, solemnly tragic; and one felt that under her tight linen cap, the hair must be snow white. The tragedy, whatever it might have been, was now over; and the lady's expression, as she spoke to the old creatures scraping the ground in the garden, ironing the sheets in the laundry, or merely huddling over their braziers in the chill winter sunshine, was pathetic only by virtue of its strange present tenderness, and by that trace of terrible past suffering.

She answered my questions very briefly, and was as taciturn as ladies of religious communities are usually loquacious. Only, when I expressed my admiration for the institution which contrived to feed scores of old paupers on broken victuals begged from private houses and inns, she turned her eyes full upon me and said, with an earnestness which was almost passionate, 'Ah, the old! The old! It is so much, much worse for them than for any others. Have you ever tried to imagine what it is to be poor and forsaken and old?'

These words and the strange ring in the sister's voice, the strange light in her eyes, remained in my memory. What was not, therefore, my surprise when, on returning to the kitchen, I saw her start and lay hold of the back of the chair as soon as she caught sight of Cecco Bandini. Cecco, on his side also, was visibly startled, but only after a moment; it was clear that she recognised him long before he identified her. What little romance could there exist in common between my eccentric painter and that serene, but tragic Sister of the Poor?

A week later, it became evident that Cecco Bandini had come to explain the mystery, but to explain it (as I judged by the embarrassment of his manner) by one of those astonishingly elaborate lies occasionally attempted by perfectly frank persons. It was not the case. Cecchino had come indeed to explain that little dumb scene which had passed between him and the Little Sister of the Poor. He had come, however, not to satisfy my curiosity, or to overcome my suspicions, but to execute a commission which he had greatly at heart; to help, as he expressed it, in the accomplishment of a good work by a real saint.

Of course, he explained, smiling that good smile under his black eyebrows and white moustache, he did not expect me to believe very literally the story which he had undertaken to get me to write. He only asked, and the lady only wished, me, to write down her narrative without any comments, and leave to the heart of the reader the decision about its truth or falsehood.

For this reason, and the better to attain the object of appealing to the profane, rather than to the religious reader, I have abandoned the order of narrative of the Little Sister of the Poor; and attempted to turn her pious legend into a worldly story, as follows: —

I

Cecco Bandini had just returned from the Maremma, to whose solitary marshes and jungles he had fled in one of his fits of fury at the stupidity and wickedness of the civilised world. A great many months spent among buffaloes and wild boars, conversing only with those wild cherry-trees, of whom he used whimsically to say, 'they are such good little folk', had sent him back with an extraordinary zest for civilisation, and a comic tendency to find its products, human and otherwise, extraordinary, picturesque, and suggestive. He was in this frame of mind when there came a light rap on his door-slate; and two ladies appeared on the threshold of his studio, with the shaven face and cockaded hat of a tall footman overtopping them from behind. One of them was unknown to our painter; the other was numbered among Cecchino's very few grand acquaintances.

'Why haven't you been round to me yet, you savage?' she asked, advancing quickly with a brusque hand-shake and a brusque bright gleam of eyes and teeth, well-bred but audacious and a trifle ferocious. And dropping on to a divan she added, nodding first at her companion and then at the pictures all round, 'I have brought my friend, Madame Krasinska, to see your things,' and she began poking with her parasol at the contents of a gaping portfolio.

The Baroness Fosca — for such was her name — was one of the cleverest, fastest, and slangiest ladies of the place, with a taste for art and ferociously frank conversation. To Cecco Bandini, as she lay back among her furs on that shabby divan of his, she appeared in the light of the modern Lucretia Borgia, the tamed panther of fashionable life. 'What an interesting thing civilisation is!' he thought, watching her every movement with the eyes of the imagination; 'why, you might spend years among the wild folk of the Maremma without meeting such a tremendous, terrible, picturesque, powerful creature as this!'

Cecchino was so absorbed in the Baroness Fosca, who was in reality not at all a Lucretia Borgia, but merely a remarkably rough-and-ready piece of frivolity, that he was scarcely conscious of the presence of her companion. He knew that she was very young, very pretty, and very smart, and that he had made her his best bow, and offered her his least rickety chair; for the rest, he sat opposite to his Lucretia Borgia of modern life, who had meanwhile found a cigarette, and was puffing away and explaining that she was about to give a fancy ball, which should be the most *crâne*, the only amusing thing, of the year.

'Oh,' he exclaimed, kindling at the thought, 'do let me design you a dress all black and white and wicked green — you shall go as Deadly Nightshade, as Belladonna Atropa ———'

'Belladonna Atropa! fiddle-sticks! I've got something much better than that' .... The Baroness was answering contemptuously, when Cecchino's attention was suddenly called to the other end of the studio by an exclamation on the part of his other visitor.

'Do tell me all about her; — has she a name? Is she really a lunatic?' asked the young lady who had been introduced as Madame Krasinska, keeping a portfolio open with one hand, and holding up in the other a coloured sketch she had taken from it.

'What have you got there? Oh, only the Sora Lena!' and Madame Fosca reverted to the contemplation of the smoke-rings she was making.

'Tell me about her — Sora Lena, did you say?' asked the younger lady eagerly.

She spoke French, but with a pretty little American accent, despite her Polish name. 'She was very charming,' Cecchino said to himself, a radiant impersonation of youthful brightness and elegance as she stood there in her long silvery furs, holding the drawing with tiny, tight-gloved hands, and shedding around her a vague exquisite fragrance — no, not a mere literal perfume, that would be far too coarse, but something personal akin to it.

'I have noticed her so often,' she went on, with that silvery young voice of hers, 'she's mad, isn't she? And what did you say her name was? Please tell me again.'

Cecchino was delighted. 'How true it is,' he reflected, 'that only refinement, high-breeding, luxury can give people certain kinds of sensitiveness, of rapid intuition. No woman of another class would have picked out just that drawing, or would have been interested in it without stupid laughter.'

'Do you want to know the story of poor old Sora Lena?' asked Cecchino, taking the sketch from Madame Krasinska's hand, and looking over it at the charming, eager young face.

The sketch might have passed for a caricature; but anyone who had spent so little as a week in Florence those six or seven years ago would have recognised at once that it was merely a faithful portrait. For Sora Lena — more correctly Signora Maddalena — had been for years and years one of the most conspicuous sights of the town. In all weathers you might have seen that hulking old woman, with her vague, staring, reddish face, trudging through the streets or standing before shops, in her extraordinary costume of thirty years ago, her enormous crinoline, on which the silk skirt and ragged petticoat hung limply, her gigantic coal-scuttle bonnet, shawl, prunella boots, and great muff or parasol — one of several outfits, all alike, of that distant period; all alike inexpressibly dirty and tattered. In all weathers you might have seen her stolidly going her way, indifferent to stares and jibes, of which, indeed, there were by this time comparatively few, so familiar had she grown to staring, jibing Florence. In all weathers, but most noticeably in the worst, as if the squalor of mud and rain had an affinity with that sad, draggled, soiled, battered piece of human squalor, that lamentable rag of half-witted misery.

'Do you want to know about Sora Lena?' repeated Cecco Bandini, meditatively. They formed a strange, strange contrast, these two women, the one in the sketch and the one standing before him. And there was to him a pathetic whimsicalness in the interest which the one had excited in the other. 'How long has she been wandering about here? Why, as long as I can remember the streets of Florence, and that,' added Cecchino sorrowfully, 'is a longer while than I care to count up. It seems to me as if she must always have been there, like the olive-trees and the paving stones; for after all, Giotto's tower wasn't there before Giotto, whereas poor old Sora Lena — But, by the way, there is a limit even to her. There is a legend about her; they say that she was once sane, and had two sons, who went as Volunteers in '59, and were killed at Solferino, and ever since then she has sallied forth, every day, winter or summer, in her best clothes, to meet the young fellows at the Station. May be. To my mind it doesn't matter much whether the story be true or false: it is fitting,' and Cecco Bandini set about dusting some canvases which had attracted the Baroness Fosca's attention. When Cecchino was helping that lady into her furs, she gave one of her little brutal smiles, and nodded in the direction of her companion.

'Madame Krasinska,' she said laughing, 'is very desirous of possessing one of your sketches, but she is too polite to ask you the price of it. That's what comes of our not knowing how to earn a penny for ourselves, doesn't it, Signor Cecchino?' Madame Krasinska blushed, and looked more young, and delicate, and charming.

'I did not know whether you would consent to part with one of your drawings,' she said in her silvery, child-like voice, — 'it is — this one — which I should so much have liked to have — .... to have .... bought.' Cecchino smiled at the embarrassment which the word 'bought' produced in his exquisite visitor. Poor charming young creature, he thought; the only thing she thinks people one knows can sell is themselves, and that's called getting married. 'You must explain to your friend,' said Cecchino to the Baroness Fosca, as he hunted in a drawer for a piece of clean paper, 'that such rubbish as this is neither bought nor sold; it is not even possible for a poor devil of a painter to offer it as a gift to a lady — but,' — and he handed the little roll to Madame Krasinska, making his very best bow as he did so — 'it is possible for a lady graciously to accept it.'

'Thank you so much,' answered Madame Krasinska, slipping the drawing into her muff; 'it is very good of you to give me such a .... such a very interesting sketch,' and she pressed his big, brown fingers in her little grey gloved hand.

'Poor Sora Lena!' exclaimed Cecchino, when there remained of the visit only a faint perfume of exquisiteness; and he thought of the hideous old draggle-tailed mad woman, reposing, rolled up in effigy, in the delicious daintiness of that delicate grey muff.

II

A fortnight later, the great event was Madame Fosca's fancy ball, to which the guests were bidden to come in what was described as comic costume. Some, however, craved leave to appear in their ordinary apparel, and among these was Cecchino Bandini, who was persuaded, moreover, that his old-fashioned swallow tails, which he donned only at weddings, constituted quite comic costume enough.

This knowledge did not interfere at all with his enjoyment. There was even, to his whimsical mind, a certain charm in being in a crowd among which he knew no one; unnoticed or confused, perhaps, with the waiters, as he hung about the stairs and strolled through the big palace rooms. It was as good as wearing an invisible cloak, one saw so much just because one was not seen; indeed, one was momentarily endowed (it seemed at least to his fanciful apprehension) with a faculty akin to that of understanding the talk of birds; and, as he watched and listened he became aware of innumerable charming little romances, which were concealed from more notable but less privileged persons.

Little by little the big white and gold rooms began to fill. The ladies, who had moved in gorgeous isolation, their skirts displayed as finely as a peacock's train, became gradually visible only from the waist upwards; and only the branches of the palm-trees and tree ferns detached themselves against the shining walls. Instead of wandering among variegated brocades and iridescent silks and astonishing arrangements of feathers and flowers, Cecchino's eye was forced to a higher level by the thickening crowd; it was now the constellated sparkle of diamonds on neck and head that dazzled him, and the strange, unaccustomed splendour of white arms and shoulders. And, as the room filled, the invisible cloak was also drawn closer round our friend Cecchino, and the extraordinary faculty of perceiving romantic and delicious secrets in other folks' bosoms became more and more developed. They seemed to him like exquisite children, these creatures rustling about in fantastic dresses, powdered shepherds and shepherdesses with diamonds spirting fire among their ribbons and top-knots; Japanese and Chinese embroidered with sprays of flowers; mediaeval and antique beings, and beings hidden in the plumage of birds, or the petals of flowers; children, but children somehow matured, transfigured by the touch of luxury and good-breeding, children full of courtesy and kindness. There were, of course, a few costumes which might have been better conceived or better carried out, or better — not to say best — omitted altogether. One grew bored, after a little while, with people dressed as marionettes, champagne bottles, sticks of sealing wax, or captive balloons; a young man arrayed as a female ballet dancer, and another got up as a wet nurse with baby *obligato*, might certainly have been dispensed with. Also, Cecchino could not help wincing a little at the daughter of the house being mummed and painted to represent her own grandmother, a respectable old lady whose picture hung in the dining-room, and whose spectacles he had frequently picked up in his boyhood. But these were mere trifling details. And, as a whole, it was beautiful, fantastic. So Cecchino moved backward and forward, invisible in his shabby black suit, and borne hither and thither by the well-bred pressure of the many-coloured crowd; pleasantly blinded by the innumerable lights, the sparkle of chandelier pendants, and the shooting flames of jewels; gently deafened by the confused murmur of innumerable voices, of crackling stuffs and soothing fans, of distant dance music; and inhaling the vague fragrance which seemed less the decoction of cunning perfumers than the exquisite and expressive emanation of this exquisite bloom of personality. Certainly, he said to himself, there is no pleasure so delicious as seeing people amusing themselves with refinement: there is a transfiguring magic, almost a moralising power, in wealth and elegance and good-breeding.

Just as he was making this reflection, a little burst of voices came from the landing. The multi-coloured costumes fluttered like butterflies toward a given spot, there was a little heaping together of brilliant colours and flashing jewels. Then the crowd fell aside on either side of the doorway, not without much craning of delicate, fluffy, young necks and heads, and shuffle on tiptoe. A little gangway was cleared; and there walked into the middle of the white and gold drawing-room, a lumbering, hideous figure, with reddish, vacant face, sunk in an immense tarnished satin bonnet, and draggled, faded, lilac silk skirts spread over a vast dislocated crinoline. The feet dabbed along in the broken prunella boots; the mangy rabbit-skin muff bobbed loosely with the shambling gait; and then, under the big chandelier, there came a sudden pause, and the thing looked slowly round, a gaping, mooning, blear-eyed stare.

It was the Sora Lena.

There was a perfect storm of applause.

III

Cecchino Bandini did not slacken his pace till he found himself, with his thin overcoat and opera hat all drenched, among the gas reflections and puddles before his studio door; that shout of applause and that burst of clapping pursuing him down the stairs of the palace and all through the rainy streets. There were a few embers in his stove; he threw a faggot on them, lit a cigarette, and proceeded to make reflections, the wet opera hat still on his head. He had been a fool, a savage. He had behaved like a child, rushing past his hostess with that ridiculous speech in answer to her inquiries; 'I am running away because bad luck has entered your house.'

Why had he not guessed it at once? What on earth else could she have wanted his sketch for?

He determined to forget the matter, and, as he imagined, he forgot it. Only, when the next day's evening paper displayed two columns describing Madame Fosca's ball, and more particularly 'that mask', as the reporter had it, 'which among so many that were graceful and ingenious, bore off in triumph the palm for witty novelty', he threw the paper down and gave it a kick towards the wood box. But he felt ashamed of himself, picked it up, smoothed it out and read it all — foreign news and home news, and even the description of Madame Fosca's masked ball, conscientiously through. Last of all he perused, with dogged resolution, the column of petty casualties; a boy bit in the calf by a dog who was not mad; the frustrated burgling of a baker's shop; even to the bunches of keys and the umbrella and two cigar cases picked up by the police, and consigned to the appropriate municipal limbo, until he came to the following lines: 'This morning the *Guardians of Public Safety*, having been called by the neighbouring inhabitants, penetrated into a room on the top floor of a house situate in the little street of the gravedigger (Viccolo del Beccamorto), and discovered, hanging from a rafter, the dead body of Maddalena X. Y. Z. The deceased had long been noted throughout Florence for her eccentric habits and apparel.' The paragraph was headed, in somewhat larger type: 'Suicide of a female lunatic'.

Cecchino's cigarette had gone out, but he continued blowing at it all the same. He could see in his mind's eye a tall, slender figure, draped in silvery plush and silvery furs, standing by the side of an open portfolio, and holding a drawing in her tiny hand, with the slender solitary gold bangle over the grey glove.

IV

Madame Krasinska was in a very bad humour. The old Chanoiness, her late husband's aunt, noticed it; her guests noticed it; her maid noticed it: and she noticed it herself. For, of all human beings, Madame Krasinska — Netta, as smart folk familiarly called her — was the least subject to bad humour. She was as uniformly cheerful as birds are supposed to be, and she certainly had none of the causes for anxiety or sorrow which even the most proverbial bird must occasionally have. She had always had money, health, good looks; and people had always told her — in New York, in London, in Paris, Rome, and St. Petersburg — from her very earliest childhood, that her one business in life was to amuse herself. The old gentleman whom she had simply and cheerfully accepted as a husband, because he had given her quantities of bonbons, and was going to give her quantities of diamonds, had been kind, and had been kindest of all in dying of sudden bronchitis when away for a month, leaving his young widow with an affectionately indifferent recollection of him, no remorse of any kind, and a great deal of money, not to speak of the excellent Chanoiness, who constituted an invaluable *chaperon*. And, since his happy demise, no cloud had disturbed the cheerful life or feelings of Madame Krasinska. Other women, she knew, had innumerable subjects of wretchedness; or if they had none, they were wretched from the want of them. Some had children who made them unhappy, others were unhappy for lack of children, and similarly as to lovers; but she had never had a child and never had a lover, and never experienced the smallest desire for either. Other women suffered from sleeplessness, or from sleepiness, and took morphia or abstained from morphia with equal inconvenience; other women also grew weary of amusement. But Madame Krasinska always slept beautifully, and always stayed awake cheerfully; and Madame Krasinska was never tired of amusing herself. Perhaps it was all this which culminated in the fact that Madame Krasinska had never in all her life envied or disliked anybody; and that no one, apparently, had ever envied or disliked her. She did not wish to outshine or supplant any one; she did not want to be richer, younger, more beautiful, or more adored than they. She only wanted to amuse herself, and she succeeded in so doing.

This particular day — the day after Madame Fosca's ball — Madame Krasinska was not amusing herself. She was not at all tired: she never was; besides, she had remained in bed till mid-day; neither was she unwell, for that also she never was; nor had any one done the slightest thing to vex her. But there it was. She was not amusing herself at all. She could not tell why; and she could not tell why, also, she was vaguely miserable. When the first batch of afternoon callers had taken leave, and the following batches had been sent away from the door, she threw down her volume of Gyp, and walked to the window. It was raining: a thin, continuous spring drizzle. Only a few cabs, with wet, shining backs, an occasional lumbering omnibus or cart, passed by with wheezing, straining, downcast horses. In one or two shops a light was appearing, looking tiny, blear, and absurd in the grey afternoon. Madame Krasinska looked out for a few minutes, then, suddenly turning round, she brushed past the big palms and azaleas, and rang the bell.

'Order the brougham at once,' she said.

She could by no means have explained what earthly reason had impelled her to go out. When the footman had inquired for orders she felt at a loss: certainly she did not want to go to see any one, nor to buy anything, nor to inquire about anything.

What *did* she want? Madame Krasinska was not in the habit of driving out in the rain for her pleasure; still less to drive out without knowing whither. What did she want? She sat muffled in her furs, looking out on the wet, grey streets as the brougham rolled aimlessly along. She wanted — she wanted — she couldn't tell what. But she wanted it very much. That much she knew very well — she wanted. — The rain, the wet streets, the muddy crossings — oh, how dismal they were! and still she wished to go on.

Instinctively, her polite coachman made for the politer streets, for the polite Lung' Arno. The river quay was deserted, and a warm, wet wind swept lazily along its muddy flags. Madame Krasinska let down the glass. How dreary! The foundry, on the other side, let fly a few red sparks from its tall chimney into the grey sky; the water droned over the weir; a lamp-lighter hurried along.

Madame Krasinska pulled the check-string.

'I want to walk,' she said.

The polite footman followed behind along the messy flags, muddy and full of pools; the brougham followed behind him. Madame Krasinska was not at all in the habit of walking on the embankment, still less walking in the rain.

After some minutes she got in again, and bade the carriage drive home. When she got into the lit streets she again pulled the check-string and ordered the brougham to proceed at a foot's pace. At a certain spot she remembered something, and bade the coachman draw up before a shop. It was the big chemist's.

'What does the Signora Contessa command?' and the footman raised his hat over his ear. Somehow she had forgotten. 'Oh,' she answered, 'wait a minute. Now I remember, it's the next shop, the florist's. Tell them to send fresh azaleas to-morrow and fetch away the old ones.'

Now the azaleas had been changed only that morning. But the polite footman obeyed. And Madame Krasinska remained for a minute, nestled in her fur rug, looking on to the wet, yellow, lit pavement, and into the big chemist's window. There were the red heart-shaped chest protectors, the frictioning gloves, the bath towels, all hanging in their place. Then boxes of eau de Cologne, lots of bottles of all sizes, and boxes, large and small, and variosities of indescribable nature and use, and the great glass jars, yellow, blue, lilac, and ruby red, with a spark from the gas lamp behind in their heart. She stared at it all, very intently, and without a notion about any of these objects. Only she knew that the glass jars were uncommonly bright, and that each had a ruby, or topaz, or amethyst of gigantic size, in its heart. The footman returned.

'Drive home,' ordered Madame Krasinska. As her maid was taking her out of her dress a thought — the first since so long — flashed across her mind, at the sight of certain skirts, and an uncouth cardboard mask, lying in a corner of her dressing-room. How odd that she had not seen the Sora Lena that evening . . . . She used always to be walking in the lit streets at that hour.

V

The next morning Madame Krasinska woke up quite cheerful and happy. But she began, nevertheless, to suffer, ever since the day after the Fosca ball, from the return of that quite unprecedented and inexplicable depression. Her days became streaked, as it were, with moments during which it was quite impossible to amuse herself; and these moments grew gradually into hours. People bored her for no accountable reason, and things which she had expected as pleasures brought with them a sense of vague or more distinct wretchedness. Thus she would find herself suddenly in the midst of a ball or a dinner-party, invaded suddenly by a confused sadness or boding of evil, she did not know which. And once, when a box of new clothes had arrived from Paris, she was overcome, while putting on one of the frocks, with such a fit of tears that she had to be put to bed instead of going to the Tornabuoni's party.

Of course, people began to notice this change; indeed, Madame Krasinska had ingenuously complained of the strange alteration in herself. Some persons suggested that she might be suffering from slow blood-poisoning, and urged an inquiry into the state of the drains. Others recommended arsenic, morphia, or antipyrine. One kind friend brought her a box of peculiar cigarettes; another forwarded a parcel of still more peculiar novels; most people had some pet doctor to cry up to the skies; and one or two suggested her changing her confessor, not to mention an attempt being made to mesmerise her into cheerfulness.

When her back was turned, meanwhile, all the kind friends discussed the probability of an unhappy love affair, loss of money on the Stock Exchange, and similar other explanations. And while one devoted lady tried to worm out of her the name of her unfaithful lover and of the rival for whom he had forsaken her, another assured her that she was suffering from a lack of personal affections. It was a fine opportunity for the display of pietism, materialism, idealism, realism, psychological lore, and esoteric theosophy.

Oddly enough, all this zeal about herself did not worry Madame Krasinska, as she would certainly have expected it to worry any other woman. She took a little of each of the tonic or soporific drugs; and read a little of each of those sickly, sentimental, brutal, realistic, or politely improper novels. She also let herself be accompanied to various doctors, and she got up early in the morning and stood for an hour on a chair in a crowd in order to benefit by the preaching of the famous Father Agostino. She was quite patient even with the friends who condoled about the lover or absence of such. For all these things became, more and more, completely indifferent to Madame Krasinska — unrealities which had no weight in the presence of the painful reality.

This reality was that she was rapidly losing all power of amusing herself, and that when she did occasionally amuse herself she had to pay for what she called this *good time* by an increase of listlessness and melancholy.

It was not melancholy or listlessness such as other women complained of. They seemed, in their fits of blues, to feel that the world around them had got all wrong, or at least was going out of its way to annoy them. But Madame Krasinska saw the world quite plainly, proceeding in the usual manner, and being quite as good a world as before. It was she who was all wrong. It was, in the literal sense of the words, what she supposed people might mean when they said that So-and-so was *not himself;* only that So-and-so, on examination, appeared to be very much himself — only himself in a worse temper than usual. Whereas she . . . Why, in her case, she really did not seem to be herself any longer. Once, at a grand dinner, she suddenly ceased eating and talking to her neighbour, and surprised herself wondering who the people all were and what they had come for. Her mind would become, every now and then, a blank; a blank at least full of vague images, misty and muddled, which she was unable to grasp, but of which she knew that they were painful, weighing on her as a heavy load must weigh on the head or back. Something had happened, or was going to happen, she could not remember which, but she burst into tears none the less. In the midst of such a state of things, if visitors or a servant entered, she would ask sometimes who they were. Once a man came to call, during one of these fits; by an effort, she was able to receive him and answer his small talk more or less at random, feeling the whole time as if someone else were speaking in her place. The visitor at length rose to depart, and they both stood for a moment in the midst of the drawing-room.

'This is a very pretty house; it must belong to some rich person. Do you know to whom it belongs?' suddenly remarked Madame Krasinska, looking slowly round her at the furniture, the pictures, statues, nicknacks, the screens and plants. 'Do you know to whom it belongs?' she repeated.

'It belongs to the most charming lady in Florence,' stammered out the visitor politely, and fled.

'My darling Netta,' exclaimed the Chanoiness from where she was seated crocheting benevolently futile garments by the fire; 'you should not joke in that way. That poor young man was placed in a painful, in a very painful position by your nonsense.'

Madame Krasinska leaned her arms on a screen, and stared her respectable relation long in the face.

'You seem a kind woman,' she said at length. 'You are old, but then you aren't poor, and they don't all call you a mad woman. That makes all the difference.'

Then she set to singing — drumming out the tune on the screen — the soldier song of '59, *Addio, mia bella, addio.*

'Netta!' cried the Chanoiness, dropping one ball of worsted after another. 'Netta!'

But Madame Krasinska passed her hand over her brow and heaved a great sigh. Then she took a cigarette off a cloisonné tray, dipped a spill in the fire, and remarked,

'Would you like to have the brougham to go to see your friend at the Sacré Coeur, Aunt Thérèse? I have promised to wait in for Molly Wolkonsky and Bice Forteguerra. We are going to dine at Doney's with young Pomfret.'

VI

Madame Krasinska had repeated her evening drives in the rain. Indeed she began also to walk about regardless of weather. Her maid asked her whether she had been ordered exercise by the doctor, and she answered, yes. But why she should not walk in the Cascine or along the Lung' Arno, and why she should always choose the muddiest thoroughfares, the maid did not inquire. As it was, Madame Krasinska never showed any repugnance or seemly contrition for the state of draggle in which she used to return home; sometimes when the woman was unbuttoning her boots, she would remain in contemplation of their muddiness, murmuring things which Jefferies could not understand. The servants, indeed, declared that the Countess must have gone out of her mind. The footman related that she used to stop the brougham, get out and look into the lit shops, and that he had to stand behind, in order to prevent lady-killing youths of a caddish description from whispering expressions of admiration in her ear. And once, he affirmed with horror, she had stopped in front of a certain cheap eating-house, and looked in at the bundles of asparagus, at the uncooked chops displayed in the window. And then, added the footman, she had turned round to him slowly and said,

'They have good food in there.'

And meanwhile, Madame Krasinska went to dinners and parties, and gave them, and organised picnics, as much as was decently possible in Lent, and indeed a great deal more.

She no longer complained of the blues; she assured every one that she had completely got rid of them, that she had never been in such spirits in all her life. She said it so often, and in so excited a way, that judicious people declared that now that lover must really have jilted her, or gambling on the Stock Exchange have brought her to the verge of ruin.

Nay, Madame Krasinska's spirits became so obstreperous as to change her in sundry ways. Although living in the fastest set, Madame Krasinska had never been a fast woman. There was something childlike in her nature which made her modest and decorous. She had never learned to talk slang, or to take up vulgar attitudes, or to tell impossible stories; and she had never lost a silly habit of blushing at expressions and anecdotes which she did not reprove other women for using and relating. Her amusements had never been flavoured with that spice of impropriety, of curiosity of evil, which was common in her set. She liked putting on pretty frocks, arranging pretty furniture, driving in well got up carriages, eating good dinners, laughing a great deal, and dancing a great deal, and that was all.

But now Madame Krasinska suddenly altered. She became, all of a sudden, anxious for those exotic sensations which honest women may get by studying the ways, and frequenting the haunts, of women by no means honest. She made up parties to go to the low theatres and music-halls; she proposed dressing up and going, in company with sundry adventurous spirits, for evening strolls in the more dubious portions of the town. Moreover, she, who had never touched a card, began to gamble for large sums, and to surprise people by producing a folded green roulette cloth and miniature roulette rakes out of her pocket. And she became so outrageously conspicuous in her flirtations (she who had never flirted before), and so outrageously loud in her manners and remarks, that her good friends began to venture a little remonstrance . . . .

But remonstrance was all in vain; and she would toss her head and laugh cynically, and answer in a brazen, jarring voice.

For Madame Krasinska felt that she must live, live noisily, live scandalously, live her own life of wealth and dissipation, because . . .

She used to wake up at night with the horror of that suspicion. And in the middle of the day, pull at her clothes, tear down her hair, and rush to the mirror and stare at herself, and look for every feature, and clutch for every end of silk, or bit of lace, or wisp of hair, which proved that she was really herself. For gradually, slowly, she had come to understand that she was herself no longer.

Herself — Well, yes, of course she was herself. Was it not herself who rushed about in such a riot of amusement; herself whose flushed cheeks and over-bright eyes, and cynically flaunted neck and bosom she saw in the glass; whose mocking loud voice and shrill laugh she listened to? Besides, did not her servants, her visitors, know her as Netta Krasinska; and did she not know how to wear her clothes, dance, make jokes, and encourage men, afterwards to discourage them? This, she often said to herself, as she lay awake the long nights, as she sat out the longer nights gambling and chaffing, distinctly proved that she really was herself. And she repeated it all mentally when she returned, muddy, worn out, and as awakened from a ghastly dream, after one of her long rambles through the streets, her daily walks towards the station.

But still . . . What of those strange forebodings of evil, those muddled fears of some dreadful calamity . . . something which had happened, or was going to happen . . . poverty, starvation, death — whose death, her own? or some one else's? That knowledge that it was all, all over; that blinding, felling blow which used every now and then to crush her . . . Yes, she had felt that first at the railway station. At the station? but what had happened at the station? Or was it going to happen still? Since to the station her feet seemed unconsciously to carry her every day. What was it all? Ah!

she knew. There was a woman, an old woman, walking to the station to meet . . . Yes, to meet a regiment on its way back. They came back, those soldiers, among a mob yelling triumph. She remembered the illuminations, the red, green, and white lanterns, and those garlands all over the waiting-rooms. And quantities of flags. The bands played. So gaily! They played Garibaldi's hymn, and *Addio, Mia Bella*. Those pieces always made her cry now. The station was crammed, and all the boys, in tattered, soiled uniforms, rushed into the arms of parents, wives, friends. Then there was like a blinding light, a crash . . . An officer led the old woman gently out of the place, mopping his eyes. And she, of all the crowd, was the only one to go home alone. Had it really all happened? and to whom? Had it really happened to her, had her boys . . . . But Madame Krasinska had never had any boys.

It was dreadful how much it rained in Florence, and stuff boots do wear out so quick in mud. There was such a lot of mud on the way to the station; but of course it was necessary to go to the station in order to meet the train from Lombardy — the boys must be met.

There was a place on the other side of the river where you went in and handed your watch and your brooch over the counter, and they gave you some money and a paper. Once the paper got lost. Then there was a mattress, too. But there was a kind man — a man who sold hardware — who went and fetched it back. It was dreadfully cold in winter, but the worst was the rain. And having no watch one was afraid of being late for that train, and had to dawdle so long in the muddy streets. Of course one could look in at the pretty shops. But the little boys were so rude. Oh, no, no, not that — anything rather than be shut up in a hospital. The poor old woman did no one any harm — why shut her up?

'*Faites votre jeu, messieurs*,' cried Madame Krasinska, raking up the counters with the little rake she had had made of tortoiseshell, with a gold dragon's head for a handle —'*Rien ne va plus — vingt-trois — Rouge, impair et manque.*'

VII

How did she come to know about this woman? She had never been inside that house over the tobacconist's, up three pairs of stairs to the left; and yet she knew exactly the pattern of the wall-paper. It was green with a pinkish trellis-work in the grand sitting-room, the one which was opened only on

Sunday evenings, when the friends used to drop in and discuss the news, and have a game of *tresette*. You passed through the dining-room to get through it. The dining-room had no window, and was lit from a skylight; there was always a little smell of dinner in it, but that was appetising. The boys' rooms were to the back. There was a plaster Joan of Arc in the hall, close to the clothes-peg. She was painted to look like silver, and one of the boys had broken her arm, so that it looked like a gas-pipe. It was Momino who had done it, jumping on to the table when they were playing. Momino was always the scapegrace; he wore out so many pairs of trousers at the knees, but he was so warm-hearted! and after all, he had got all the prizes at school, and they all said he would be a first-rate engineer. Those dear boys! They never cost their mother a farthing, once they were sixteen; and Momino bought her a big, beautiful muff out of his own earnings as a pupil-teacher. Here it is! Such a comfort in the cold weather, you can't think, especially when gloves are too dear. Yes, it is rabbit-skin, but it is made to look like ermine, quite a handsome article. Assunta, the maid of all work, never would clean out that kitchen of hers — servants are such sluts! and she tore the moreen sofa-cover, too, against a nail in the wall. She ought to have seen that nail! But one mustn't be too hard on a poor creature, who is an orphan into the bargain. Oh, God! oh, God! and they lie in the big trench at S. Martino, without even a cross over them, or a bit of wood with their name. But the white coats of the Austrians were soaked red, I warrant you! And the new dye they call magenta is made of pipe-clay — the pipe-clay the dogs clean their white coats with — and the blood of Austrians. It's a grand dye, I tell you!

Lord, Lord, how wet the poor old woman's feet are! And no fire to warm them by. The best is to go to bed when one can't dry one's clothes; and it saves lamp-oil. That was very good oil the parish priest made her a present of . . . Aï, aï, how one's bones ache on the mere boards, even with a blanket over them! That good, good mattress at the pawn-shop! It's nonsense about the Italians having been beaten. The Austrians were beaten into bits, made cats'-meat of; and the volunteers are returning to-morrow. Temistocle and Momina — Momino is Girolamo, you know — will be back to-morrow; their rooms have been cleaned, and they shall have a flask of real Montepulciano . . . The big bottles in the chemist's window are very beautiful, particularly the green one. The shop where they sell gloves and scarves is also very pretty; but the English chemist's is the prettiest, because of those bottles. But they say the contents of them is all rubbish, and no real medicine . . . Don't speak of S. Bonifazio! I have seen it. It is where they keep the mad folk and the wretched, dirty, wicked, wicked old women .... There was a handsome book bound in red, with gold edges, on the best sitting-room table; the *Aeneid*, translated by Caro. It was one of Temistocle's prizes, and that Berlin-wool cushion .... yes, the little dog with the cherries looked quite real ....

'I have been thinking I should like to go to Sicily, to see Etna, and Palermo, and all those places,' said Madame Krasinska, leaning on the balcony by the side of Prince Mongibello, smoking her fifth or sixth cigarette.

She could see the hateful hooked nose, like a nasty hawk's beak, over the big black beard, and the creature's leering, languishing black eyes, as he looked up into the twilight. She knew quite well what sort of man Mongibello was. No woman could approach him, or allow him to approach her; and there she was on that balcony alone with him in the dark, far from the rest of the party, who were dancing and talking within. And to talk of Sicily to him, who was a Sicilian too! But that was what she wanted — a scandal, a horror, anything that might deaden those thoughts which would go on inside her.... The thought of that strange, lofty whitewashed place, which she had never seen, but which she knew so well, with an altar in the middle, and rows and rows of beds, each with its set-out of bottles and baskets, and horrid slobbering and gibbering old women in them. Oh ... she could hear them!

'I should like to go to Sicily,' she said in a tone that was now common to her, adding slowly and with emphasis, 'but I should like to have someone to show me all the sights ....'

'Countess!' and the black beard of the creature bent over her — close to her neck — 'how strange — I also feel a great longing to see Sicily once more, but not alone — those lovely, lonely valleys ...'

Ah! — there was one of the creatures who had sat up in her bed and was singing, singing 'Casta Diva!' 'No, not alone' — she went on hurriedly, a sort of fury of satisfaction, of the satisfaction of destroying something, destroying her own fame, her own life, filling her as she felt the man's hand on her arm — 'not alone, Prince — with someone to explain things — someone who knows all about it — and in this lovely spring weather. You see, I am a bad traveller — and I am afraid ... of being alone ...' The last words came out of her throat loud, hoarse, and yet cracked and shrill — and just as the Prince's arm was going to clasp her, she rushed wildly into the room, exclaiming —

'Ah, I am she — I am she — I am mad!'

For in that sudden voice, so different from her own, Madame Krasinska had recognised the voice that should have issued from the cardboard mask she had worn, the voice of Sora Lena.

VIII

Yes, Cecchino certainly recognised her now. Strolling about in that damp May twilight among the old, tortuous streets, he had mechanically watched the big black horses draw up at the posts which closed that labyrinth of black narrow alleys, the servant in his white waterproof opened the door, and the tall, slender woman got out and walked quickly along. And mechanically, in his woolgathering way, he had followed the lady, enjoying the charming note of delicate pink and grey which her little frock made against those black houses, and under that wet grey sky, streaked pink with the sunset. She walked quickly along, quite alone, having left the footman with the carriage at the entrance of that condemned old heart of Florence; and she took no notice of the stares and words of the boys playing in the gutters, the pedlars housing their barrows under the black archways, and the women leaning out of windows. Yes; there was no doubt. It had struck him suddenly as he watched her pass under a double arch and into a kind of large court, not unlike that of a castle, between the frowning tall houses of the old Jews' quarters; houses escutcheoned and stanchioned, once the abode of Ghibelline nobles, now given over to rag pickers, scavengers and unspeakable trades.

As soon as he recognised her he stopped, and was about to turn: what business has a man following a lady, prying into her doings when she goes out at twilight, with carriage and footman left several streets back, quite alone through unlikely streets? And Cecchino, who by this time was on the point of returning to the Maremma, and had come to the conclusion that civilisation was a boring and loathsome thing, reflected upon the errands which French novels described ladies as performing, when they left their carriage and footman round the corner . . . But the thought was disgraceful to Cecchino, and disgraceful to this lady — no, no. And at this moment he stopped, for the lady had stopped a few paces before him, and was staring fixedly into the grey evening sky. There was something strange in that stare; it was not that of a woman who is hiding disgraceful proceedings. And in staring round, she must have seen him; yet she stood still, like one wrapped in wild thoughts. Then suddenly she passed under the next archway, and disappeared in the dark passage of a house. Somehow Cecco Bandini could not make up his mind, as he ought to have done long ago, to turn back. He slowly passed through the oozy ill-smelling archway, and stood before that house. It was very tall, narrow and black as ink, with a jagged roof against the wet, pinkish sky. From the iron hook, made to hold brocades and Persian carpets on gala days of old, fluttered some rags, obscene and ill-omened in the wind. Many of the window panes were broken. It was evidently one of the houses which the municipality had condemned to destruction for sanitary reasons, and whence the inmates were gradually being evicted.

'That's a house they're going to pull down, isn't it?' he inquired in a casual tone of the man at the corner, who kept a sort of cookshop, where chestnut pudding and boiled beans steamed on a brazier in a den. Then his eye caught a half-effaced name close to the lamp-post, 'Little Street of the Grave-digger'. 'Ah,' he added quickly, 'this is the street where old Sora Lena committed suicide — and — is — is that the house?'

Then, trying to extricate some reasonable idea out of the extraordinary tangle of absurdities, which had all of a sudden filled his mind, he fumbled in his pocket for a silver coin, and said hurriedly to the man with the cooking brazier,

'See here, that house, I'm sure, isn't well inhabited. That lady has gone there for a charity — but — but one doesn't know that she mayn't be annoyed in there. Here's fifty centimes for your trouble. If that lady doesn't come out again in three-quarters of an hour — there! it's striking seven — just you go round to the stone posts — you'll find her carriage there — black horses and grey liveries — and tell the footman to run upstairs to his mistress — understand?' And Cecchino Bandini fled, overwhelmed at the thought of the indiscretion he was committing, but seeing, as he turned round, those rags waving an ominous salute from the black, gaunt house with its irregular roof against the wet twilight sky.

IX

Madame Krasinska hurried though the long black corridor, with its slippery bricks and typhoid smell, and went slowly but resolutely up the black staircase. Its steps, constructed perhaps in the days of Dante's grandfather, when a horn buckle and leathern belt formed the only ornaments of Florentine dames, were extraordinarily high, and worn off at the edges by innumerable generations of successive nobles and paupers. And as it twisted sharply on itself, the staircase was lighted at rare intervals by barred windows, overlooking alternately the black square outside, with its jags of overhanging roof, and a black yard, where a broken well was surrounded by a heap of half-sorted chicken's feathers and unpicked rags. On the first landing was an open door, partly screened by a line of drying tattered clothes; and whence issued shrill sounds of altercation and snatches of tipsy song. Madame Krasinska passed on heedless of it all, the front of her delicate frock brushing the unseen filth of those black steps, in whose crypt-like cold and gloom there was an ever-growing breath of charnel. Higher and higher, flight after flight, steps and steps. Nor did she look to the right or to the left, nor ever stop to take breath, but climbed upward, slowly, steadily. At length she reached the topmost landing, on to which fell a flickering beam of the setting sun. It issued from a room, whose door was standing wide open. Madame Krasinska entered. The room was completely empty, and comparatively light. There was no furniture in it, except a chair, pushed into a dark corner, and an empty birdcage at the window. The panes were broken, and here and there had been mended with paper. Paper also hung, in blackened rags, upon the walls.

Madame Krasinska walked to the window and looked out over the neighbouring roofs, to where the bell in an old black belfry swung tolling the Ave Maria. There was a porticoed gallery on the top of a house some way off; it had a few plants growing in pipkins, and a drying line. She knew it all so well. On the window sill was a cracked basin, in which stood a dead basil plant, dry, grey. She looked at it some time, moving the hardened earth with her fingers. Then she turned to the empty bird-cage. 'Poor solitary starling! how he had whistled to the poor old woman!' Then she began to cry.

But after a few moments she roused herself. Mechanically, she went to the door and closed it carefully. Then she went straight to the dark corner, where she knew that the stoved-in straw chair stood. She dragged it into the middle of the room, where the hook was in the big rafter. She stood on the chair, and measured the height of the ceiling. It was so low that she could graze it with the palm of her hand. She took off her gloves, and then her bonnet — it was in the way of the hook. Then she unclasped her girdle, one of those narrow Russian ribbons of silver woven stuff, studded with niello. She buckled one end firmly to the big hook. Then she unwound the strip of muslin from under her collar. She was standing on the broken chair, just under the rafter. 'Pater noster qui es in caelo,' she mumbled, as she still childishly did when putting her head on the pillow every night.

The door creaked and opened slowly. The big, hulking woman, with the vague, red face and blear stare, and the rabbit-skin muff, bobbing on her huge crinolined skirts, shambled slowly into the room. It was the Sora Lena.

When the man from the cook-shop under the archway and the footman entered the room, it was pitch dark. Madame Krasinska was lying in the middle of the floor, by the side of an overturned chair, and under a hook in the rafter whence hung her Russian girdle. When she awoke from her swoon, she looked slowly round the room; then rose, fastened her collar and murmured, crossing herself, 'O God, thy mercy is infinite.' The men said that she smiled.

Such is the legend of Madame Krasinska, known as Mother Angélique-Marie among the Little Sisters of the Poor.

The Sphinx without a Secret
An etching

Oscar Wilde

Wilde first published 'The Sphinx without a Secret' under the title 'Lady Alroy' in *The Court and Society Review* (1887). The revised title directs attention to the crowning paradox around which the story is built: that the mysterious woman's secret is that there is no secret. This paradox, flirting with self-parody, operates in a way similar to Ada Leverson's 'The Quest of Sorrow'; Wilde also nicknamed Leverson the 'Sphinx of modern life'. Wilde elaborates on a phrasal witticism in the same manner as, for instance, in 'A Modern Millionaire'. The Parnassian subtitle 'An etching' designates the lapidary precision of the chiseller short-storyist.

Here Wilde employs art-for-art's sake rhetoric and pushes it to another level. The mastery of the story lies in the fact that not only does Lady Alroy harbour a secret for its own sake, but the man who is attracted to her mystery also nurtures the very same mystery in what could be perceived as interactive pretence, an artifice fed by itself. The story plays with Victorian conceptions of the double life, futility, the clandestine world, public image and particularly male constructions of gender – Lord Henry says to Gladys in *Dorian Gray* that women are 'sphinxes without secrets'. The story revels in appearance at the expense of content, where deception is more real than truth.

※

One afternoon I was sitting outside the Café de la Paix, watching the splendour and shabbiness of Parisian life, and wondering over my vermouth at the strange panorama of pride and poverty that was passing before me, when I heard some one call my name. I turned round, and saw Lord Murchison. We had not met since we had been at college together, nearly ten years before, so I was delighted to come across him again, and we shook hands warmly. At Oxford we had been great friends. I had liked him immensely, he was so handsome, so high-spirited, and so honourable. We used to say of him that he would be the best of fellows, if he did not always speak the truth, but I think we really admired him all the more for his frankness. I found him a good deal changed. He looked anxious and puzzled, and seemed to be in doubt about something. I felt it could not be modern scepticism, for Murchison was the stoutest of Tories, and believed in the Pentateuch as firmly as he believed in the House of Peers; so I concluded that it was a woman, and asked him if he was married yet.

'I don't understand women well enough,' he answered.

'My dear Gerald,' I said, 'women are meant to be loved, not to be understood.'

'I cannot love where I cannot trust,' he replied.

'I believe you have a mystery in your life, Gerald,' I exclaimed; 'tell me about it.'

'Let us go for a drive,' he answered, 'it is too crowded here. No, not a yellow carriage, any other colour – there, that dark-green one will do'; and in a few moments we were trotting down the boulevard in the direction of the Madeleine.

'Where shall we go to?' I said.

'Oh, anywhere you like!' he answered – 'to the restaurant in the Bois; we will dine there, and you shall tell me all about yourself.'

'I want to hear about you first,' I said. 'Tell me your mystery.'

He took from his pocket a little silver-clasped morocco case, and handed it to me. I opened it. Inside there was the photograph of a woman. She was tall and slight, and strangely picturesque with her large vague eyes and loosened hair. She looked like a *clairvoyante*, and was wrapped in rich furs.

'What do you think of that face?' he said; 'is it truthful?'

I examined it carefully. It seemed to me the face of some one who had a secret, but whether that secret was good or evil I could not say. Its beauty was a beauty moulded out of many mysteries – the beauty, in fact, which is psychological, not plastic – and the faint smile that just played across the lips was far too subtle to be really sweet.

'Well,' he cried impatiently, 'what do you say?'

'She is the Gioconda in sables,' I answered. 'Let me know all about her.'

'Not now,' he said; 'after dinner'; and began to talk of other things.

When the waiter brought us our coffee and cigarettes I reminded Gerald of his promise. He rose from his seat, walked two or three times up and down the room, and, sinking into an armchair, told me the following story: –

'One evening,' he said, 'I was walking down Bond Street about five o'clock. There was a terrific crush of carriages, and the traffic was almost stopped. Close to the pavement was standing a little yellow brougham, which, for some reason or other, attracted my attention. As I passed by there looked out from it the face I showed you this afternoon. It fascinated me immediately. All that night I kept thinking of it, and all the next day. I wandered up and down that wretched Row, peering into every carriage, and waiting for the yellow brougham; but I could not find *ma belle inconnue*, and at last I began to think she was merely a dream. About a week afterwards I was dining with Madame de Rastail. Dinner was for eight o'clock; but at half-past eight we were still waiting in the drawing-room. Finally the servant threw open the door, and announced Lady Alroy. It was the woman I had been looking for. She came in very slowly, looking like a moonbeam in grey lace, and, to my intense delight, I was asked to take her in to dinner. After we had sat down I remarked quite innocently, "I think I caught sight of you in Bond Street some time ago, Lady Alroy." She grew very pale, and said to me in a low voice, "Pray do not talk so loud; you may be overheard." I felt miserable at having made such a bad beginning, and plunged recklessly into the subject of French plays. She spoke very little, always in the same low musical voice, and seemed as if she was afraid of some one listening. I fell passionately, stupidly in love, and the indefinable atmosphere of mystery that surrounded her excited my most ardent curiosity. When she was going away, which she did very soon after dinner, I asked her if I might call and see her. She hesitated for a moment, glanced round to see if any one was near us, and then said, "Yes; to-morrow at a quarter to five." I begged Madame de Rastail to tell me about her; but all that I could learn was that she was a widow with a beautiful house in Park Lane, and as some scientific bore began a dissertation on widows, as exemplifying the survival of the matrimonially fittest, I left and went home.

'The next day I arrived at Park Lane punctual to the moment, but was told by the butler that Lady Alroy had just gone out. I went down to the club quite unhappy and very much puzzled, and after long consideration wrote her a letter, asking if I might be allowed to try my chance some other afternoon. I had no answer for several days, but at last I got a little note saying she would be at home on Sunday at four, and with this extraordinary postscript: "Please do not write to me here again; I will explain when I see you." On Sunday she received me, and was perfectly charming; but when I was going away she begged of me, if I ever had occasion to write to her again, to address my letter to "Mrs. Knox, care of Whittaker's Library, Green Street." "There are reasons," she said, "why I cannot receive letters in my own house."

'All through the season I saw a great deal of her, and the atmosphere of mystery never left her. Sometimes I thought that she was in the power of some man, but she looked so unapproachable that I could not believe it. It was really very difficult for me to come to any conclusion, for she was like one of those strange crystals that one sees in museums, which are at one moment clear, and at another clouded. At last I determined to ask her to be my wife: I was sick and tired of the incessant secrecy that she imposed on all my visits, and on the few letters I sent her. I wrote to her at the library to ask her if she could see me the following Monday at six. She answered yes, and I was in the seventh heaven of delight. I was infatuated with her: in spite of the mystery, I thought then – in consequence of it, I see now. No; it was the woman herself I loved. The mystery troubled me, maddened me. Why did chance put me in its track?'

'You discovered it, then?' I cried.

'I fear so,' he answered. 'You can judge for yourself.

'When Monday came round I went to lunch with my uncle, and about four o'clock found myself in the Marylebone Road. My uncle, you know, lives in Regent's Park. I wanted to get to Piccadilly, and took a short cut through a lot of shabby little streets. Suddenly I saw in front of me Lady Alroy, deeply veiled and walking very fast. On coming to the last house in the street, she went up the steps, took out a latch-key, and let herself in. "Here is the mystery," I said to myself; and I hurried on and examined the house. It seemed a sort of place for letting lodgings. On the doorstep lay her handkerchief, which she had dropped. I picked it up and put it in my pocket. Then I began to consider what I should do. I came to the conclusion that I had no right to spy on her, and I drove down to the club. At six I called to see her. She was lying on a sofa, in a tea-gown of silver tissue looped up by some strange moonstones that she always wore. She was looking quite lovely. "I am so glad to see you," she said; "I have not been out all day." I stared at her in amazement, and pulling the handkerchief out of my pocket, handed it to her. "You dropped this in Cumnor Street this afternoon, Lady Alroy," I said very calmly. She looked at me in terror, but made no attempt to take the handkerchief. "What were you doing there?" I asked. "What right have you to question me?" she answered. "The right of a man who loves you," I replied; "I came here to ask you to be my wife." She hid her face in her hands, and burst into floods of tears. "You must tell me," I continued. She stood up, and, looking me straight in the face, said, "Lord Murchison, there is nothing to tell you." – "You went to meet some one," I cried; "this is your mystery." She grew dreadfully white, and said, "I went to meet no one." – "Can't you tell the truth?" I exclaimed. "I have told it," she replied. I was mad, frantic; I don't know what I said, but I said terrible things to her. Finally I rushed out of the house. She wrote me a letter the next day; I sent it back unopened, and started for Norway with Alan Colville. After a month I came back, and the first thing I saw in the *Morning Post* was the death of Lady Alroy. She had caught a chill at the Opera, and had died in five days of congestion of the lungs. I shut myself up and saw no one. I had loved her so much, I had loved her so madly. Good God! how I had loved that woman!'

'You went to the street, to the house in it?' I said.

'Yes,' he answered.

'One day I went to Cumnor Street. I could not help it; I was tortured with doubt. I knocked at the door, and a respectable-looking woman opened it to me. I asked her if she had any rooms to let. "Well, sir," she replied, "the drawing-rooms are supposed to be let; but I have not seen the lady for three months, and as rent is owing on them, you can have them." – "Is this the lady?" I said, showing the photograph. "That's her, sure enough," she exclaimed; "and when is she coming back, sir?" – "The lady is dead," I replied. "Oh, sir, I hope not!" said the woman; "she was my best lodger. She paid me three guineas a week merely to sit in my drawing-rooms now and then." – "She met some one here?" I said; but the woman assured me that it was not so, that she always came alone, and saw no one. "What on earth did she do here?" I cried. "She simply sat in the drawing-room, sir, reading books, and sometimes had tea," the woman answered. I did not know what to say, so I gave her a sovereign and went away. Now, what do you think it all meant? You don't believe the woman was telling the truth?'

'I do.'

'Then why did Lady Alroy go there?'

'My dear Gerald,' I answered, 'Lady Alroy was simply a woman with a mania for mystery. She took these rooms for the pleasure of going there with her veil down, and imagining she was a heroine. She had a passion for secrecy, but she herself was merely a Sphinx without a secret.'

'Do you really think so?'

'I am sure of it,' I replied.

He took out the morocco case, opened it, and looked at the photograph. 'I wonder?' he said at last.

The Ebony Frame

E. Nesbit

Edith Nesbit (1858–1924) was a prolific short-story writer, novelist and poet. Even though she was better known as a writer of children's literature, she wrote many atmospheric and claustrophobic tales of terror and supernatural fantasies. She was a friend of male writers with strong political and social opinions, such as H. G. Wells, Havelock Ellis and Bernard Shaw. She became a founding member of the Fabian Society, and a political activist. *Grim Tales* (1893) is her first ghost story collection; the often anthologised 'Man-Size in Marble' has been considered as her most chilling Gothic tale, suggestive of Nesbit's 'criticism of the dangerous pretensions of her purportedly radical male contemporaries'.

'The Ebony Frame' is a supernatural tale of obsession. While it invites comparison with Poe's 'The Oval Portrait', it is more similar to some of Théophile Gautier's *contes fantastiques*. The story's male narrator is ambiguously in love with either a ghost or a Pre-Raphaelite portrait. The 'ebony frame' by definition divides the real and the supernatural realms; but here not only does it tether them but also blurs the boundaries between art and life. The erotic encounter with the seductive ghost framed in the ancient portrait epitomises the theme of both male and female supressed sexual desire hidden under 'the sterility and boredom of marriage/social convention'. Adhering to typical Gothic techniques, the story ends with the elimination of the dangerous sexual desire through the house fire, an allusion to the historic burning of witches. Yet, far from feeling safe, readers are left with an unsettling feeling of disquiet and confusion as the narrator destabilises any sense of reality in the final sentence.

To be rich is a luxurious sensation — the more so when you have plumbed the depths of hard-up-ness as a Fleet Street hack, a picker-up of unconsidered pars, a reporter, an unappreciated journalist — all callings utterly inconsistent with one's family feeling and one's direct descent from the Dukes of Picardy.

When my Aunt Dorcas died and left me five hundred a year and a furnished house in Chelsea, I felt that life had nothing left to offer except immediate possession of the legacy. Even Mildred Mayhew, whom I had hitherto regarded as my life's light, became less luminous. I was not engaged to Mildred, but I lodged with her mother, and I sang duets with Mildred, and gave her gloves when it would run to it, which was seldom. She was a dear good girl, and I meant to marry her some day. It is very nice to feel that a good little woman is thinking of you — it helps you in your work — and it is pleasant to know she will say 'Yes' when you say 'Will you?'

But, as I say, my legacy almost put Mildred out of my head, especially as she was staying with friends in the country just then.

Before the first gloss was off my new mourning I was seated in my aunt's own armchair in front of the fire in the dining-room of my own house. My own house! It was grand, but rather lonely. I *did* think of Mildred just then.

The room was comfortably furnished with oak and leather. On the walls hung a few fairly good oil-paintings, but the space above the mantel-piece was disfigured by an exceedingly bad print, 'The Trial of Lord William Russell', framed in a dark frame. I got up to look at it. I had visited my aunt with dutiful regularity, but I never remembered seeing this frame before. It was not intended for a print, but for an oil-painting. It was of fine ebony, beautifully and curiously carved.

I looked at it with growing interest, and when my aunt's housemaid — I had retained her modest staff of servants — came in with the lamp, I asked her how long the print had been there.

'Mistress only bought it two days afore she was took ill,' she said; 'but the frame — she didn't want to buy a new one — so she got this out of the attic. There's lots of curious old things there, sir.'

'Had my aunt had this frame long?'

'Oh, yes, sir. It come long afore I did, and I've been here seven years come Christmas. There was a picture in it — that's upstairs too — but it's that black and ugly it might as well be a chimley-back.'

I felt a desire to see this picture. What if it were some priceless old master in which my aunt's eyes had only seen rubbish?

Directly after breakfast next morning I paid a visit to the lumber-room.

It was crammed with old furniture enough to stock a curiosity shop. All the house was furnished solidly in the early Victorian style, and in this room everything not in keeping with the 'drawing-room suite' ideal was stowed away. Tables of papier-mâché and mother-of-pearl, straight-backed chairs with twisted feet and faded needlework cushions, firescreens of old-world design, old bureaux with brass handles, a little work-table with its faded moth-eaten silk flutings hanging in disconsolate shreds: on these and the dust that covered them blazed the full daylight as I drew up the blinds. I promised myself a good time in re-enshrining these household gods in my parlour, and promoting the Victorian suite to the attic. But at present my business was to find the picture as 'black as the chimney-back'; and presently, behind a heap of hideous still-life studies, I found it.

Jane the housemaid identified it at once. I took it downstairs carefully and examined it. No subject, no colour were distinguishable. There was a splodge of a darker tint in the middle, but whether it was figure or tree or house no man could have told. It seemed to be painted on a very thick panel bound with leather. I decided to send it to one of those persons who pour the waters of eternal youth on rotting family portraits — mere soap and water Mr. Besant tells us it is; but even as I did so the thought occurred to me to try my own restorative hand at a corner of it.

My bath-sponge, soap, and nailbrush vigorously applied for a few seconds showed me that there was no picture to clean! Bare oak presented itself to my persevering brush. I tried the other side, Jane watching me with indulgent interest. Same result. Then the truth dawned on me. Why was the panel so thick? I tore off the leather binding, and the panel divided and fell to the ground in a cloud of dust. There were two pictures — they had been nailed face to face. I leaned them against the wall, and next moment I was leaning against it myself.

For one of the pictures was myself — a perfect portrait — no shade of expression or turn of feature wanting. Myself — in a cavalier dress, 'love-locks and all!' When had this been done? And how, without my knowledge? Was this some whim of my aunt's?

'Lor', sir!' the shrill surprise of Jane at my elbow; 'what a lovely photo it is! Was it for a fancy ball, sir?'

'Yes,' I stammered. 'I — I don't think I want anything more now. You can go.'

She went; and I turned, still with my heart beating violently, to the other picture. This was a woman of the type of beauty beloved of Burne Jones and Rossetti — straight nose, low brows, full lips, thin hands, large deep luminous eyes. She wore a black velvet gown. It was a full-length portrait. Her arms rested on a table beside her, and her head on her hands; but her face was turned full forward, and her eyes met those of the spectator bewilderingly. On the table by her were compasses and instruments whose uses I did not know, books, a goblet, and a miscellaneous heap of papers and pens. I saw all this afterwards. I believe it was a quarter of an hour before I could turn my eyes away from hers. I have never seen any other eyes like hers. They appealed, as a child's or a dog's do; they commanded, as might those of an empress.

'Shall I sweep up the dust, sir?' Curiosity had brought Jane back. I acceded. I turned from her my portrait. I kept between her and the woman in the black velvet. When I was alone again I tore down 'The Trial of Lord William Russell', and I put the picture of the woman in its strong ebony frame.

Then I wrote to a frame-maker for a frame for my portrait. It had so long lived face to face with this beautiful witch that I had not the heart to banish it from her presence; from which it will be perceived that I am by nature a somewhat sentimental person.

The new frame came home, and I hung it opposite the fireplace. An exhaustive search among my aunt's papers showed no explanation of the portrait of myself, no history of the portrait of the woman with the wonderful eyes. I only learned that all the old furniture together had come to my aunt at the death of my great-uncle, the head of the family; and I should have concluded that the resemblance was only a family one, if everyone who came in had not exclaimed at the 'speaking likeness'. I adopted the 'fancy ball' explanation.

And there, one might suppose, the matter of the portraits ended. One might suppose it, that is, if there were not evidently a good deal more written here about it. However, to me, then, the matter seemed ended.

I went to see Mildred; invited her and her mother to come and stay with me. I rather avoided glancing at the picture in the ebony frame. I could not forget, nor remember without singular emotion, the look in the eyes of that woman when mine first met them. I shrank from repeating that look.

I reorganised the house somewhat, preparing for Mildred's visit. I turned the dining-room into a drawing-room. I brought down much of the old-fashioned furniture, and, after a long day of arranging and re-arranging, I sat down before the fire, and, lying back in a pleasant languor, I idly raised my eyes to the picture. I met her dark, deep, hazel eyes, and once more my gaze was held fixed as by a strong magic — the kind of fascination that keeps one sometimes staring for whole minutes into one's own eyes in the glass. I gazed into her eyes, and felt my own dilate, pricked with a smart like the smart of tears.

'I wish,' I said, 'oh, how I wish you were a woman, and not a picture! Come down! Ah, come down!'

I laughed at myself as I spoke; but even as I laughed I held out my arms.

I was not sleepy; I was not drunk. I was as wide awake and as sober as ever was a man in this world. And yet, as I held out my arms, I saw the eyes of the picture dilate, her lips tremble — if I were to be hanged for saying it, it is true. Her hands moved slightly, and a sort of flicker of a smile passed over her face.

I sprang to my feet. 'This won't do,' I said, still aloud. 'Firelight does play strange tricks. I'll have the lamp.'

I pulled myself together and made for the bell. My hand was on it, when I heard a sound behind me, and turned — the bell still unrung. The fire had burned low, and the corners of the room were deeply shadowed; but, surely, there — behind the tall worked chair — was something darker than a shadow.

'I must face this out,' I said, 'or I shall never be able to face myself again.' I left the bell, I seized the poker, and battered the dull coals to a blaze. Then I stepped back resolutely, and looked up at the picture. The ebony frame was empty! From the shadow of the chair came a silken rustle, and out of the shadow the woman of the picture was coming — coming towards me.

I hope I shall never again know a moment of such blank and absolute terror as that. I could not have moved or spoken to save my life. Either all the known laws of nature were nothing, or I was mad. I stood trembling, but, I am thankful to remember, I stood still, while the black velvet gown swept across the hearthrug towards me.

Next moment a hand touched me — a hand soft, warm, and human — and a low voice said, 'You called me. I am here.'

At that touch and that voice the world seemed to give a sort of bewildering half-turn. I hardly know how to express it, but at once it seemed not awful — not even unusual — for portraits to become flesh — only most natural, most right, most unspeakably fortunate.

I laid my hand on hers. I looked from her to my portrait. I could not see it in the firelight.

'We are not strangers,' I said.

'Oh, no, not strangers.' Those luminous eyes were looking up into mine — those red lips were near me. With a passionate cry — a sense of having suddenly recovered life's one great good, that had seemed wholly lost — I clasped her in my arms. She was no ghost — she was a woman — the only woman in the world.

'How long,' I said, 'O love — how long since I lost you?'

She leaned back, hanging her full weight on the hands that were clasped behind my head.

'How can I tell how long? There is no time in hell,' she answered.

It was not a dream. Ah, no — there are no such dreams. I wish to God there could be. When in dreams do I see her eyes, hear her voice, feel her lips against my cheek, hold her hands to my lips, as I did that night — the supreme night of my life? At first we hardly spoke. It seemed enough,

> after long grief and pain,
> To feel the arms of my true love
> Round me once again.

. . . .

It is very difficult to tell this story. There are no words to express the sense of glad reunion, the complete realisation of every hope and dream of a life, that came upon me as I sat with my hand in hers and looked into her eyes.

How could it have been a dream, when I left her sitting in the straight-backed chair, and went down to the kitchen to tell the maids I should want nothing more — that I was busy, and did not wish to be disturbed; when I fetched wood for the fire with my own hands, and, bringing it in, found her still sitting there — saw the little brown head turn as I entered, saw the love in her dear eyes; when I threw myself at her feet and blessed the day I was born, since life had given me this?

Not a thought of Mildred: all the other things in my life were a dream — this, its one splendid reality.

'I am wondering,' she said after awhile, when we had made such cheer each of the other as true lovers may after long parting — 'I am wondering how much you remember of our past.'

'I remember nothing,' I said. 'Oh, my dear lady, my dear sweetheart — I remember nothing but that I love you — that I have loved you all my life.'

'You remember nothing — really nothing?'

'Only that I am yours; that we have both suffered; that ———— Tell me, my mistress dear, all that you remember. Explain it all to me. Make me understand. And yet ———— No, I don't want to understand. It is enough that we are together.'

If it was a dream, why have I never dreamed it again?

She leaned down towards me, her arm lay on my neck and drew my head till it rested on her shoulder. 'I am a ghost, I suppose,' she said, laughing softly; and her laughter stirred memories which I just grasped at, and just missed. 'But you and I know better, don't we? I will tell you everything you have forgotten. We loved each other — ah! no, you have not forgotten that — and when you came back from the war we were to be married. Our pictures were painted before you went away. You know I was more learned than women of that day. Dear one, when you were gone they said I was a witch. They tried me. They said I should be burned. Just because I had looked at the stars and had gained more knowledge than they, they must needs bind me to a stake and let me be eaten by the fire. And you far away!'

Her whole body trembled and shrank. O love, what dream would have told me that my kisses would soothe even that memory?

'The night before,' she went on, 'the devil did come to me. I was innocent before — you know it, don't you? And even then my sin was for you — for you — because of the exceeding love I bore you. The devil came, and I sold my soul to eternal flame. But I got a good price. I got the right to come back, through my picture (if anyone looking at it wished for me), as long as my picture stayed in its ebony frame. That frame was not carved by man's hand. I got the right to come back to you. Oh, my heart's heart, and another thing I won, which you shall hear anon. They burned me for a witch, they made me suffer hell on earth. Those faces, all crowding round, the crackling wood and the smell of the smoke ————'

'Oh, love! no more — no more.'

'When my mother sat that night before my picture she wept, and cried, "Come back, my poor lost child!" And I went to her, with glad leaps of heart. Dear, she shrank from me, she fled, she shrieked and moaned of ghosts. She had our pictures covered from sight and put again in the ebony frame. She had promised me my picture should stay always there. Ah, through all these years your face was against mine.'

She paused.

'But the man you loved?'

'You came home. My picture was gone. They lied to you, and you married another woman; but some day I knew you would walk the world again and that I should find you.'

'The other gain?' I asked.

'The other gain,' she answered slowly, 'I gave my soul for. It is this. If you also will give up your hopes of heaven I can remain a woman, I can move in your world — I can be your wife. Oh, my dear, after all these years, at last — at last.'

'If I sacrifice my soul,' I said slowly, with no thought of the imbecility of such talk in our 'so-called nineteenth century' – 'if I sacrifice my soul, I win you? Why, love, it's a contradiction in terms. You *are* my soul.'

Her eyes looked straight into mine. Whatever might happen, whatever did happen, whatever may happen, our two souls in that moment met, and became one.

'Then you choose — you deliberately choose — to give up your hopes of heaven for me, as I gave up mine for you?'

'I decline,' I said, 'to give up my hope of heaven on any terms. Tell me what I must do, that you and I may make our own heaven here — as now, my dear love.'

'I will tell you to-morrow,' she said. 'Be alone here to-morrow night — twelve is ghost's time, isn't it? — and then I will come out of the picture and never go back to it. I shall live with you, and die, and be buried, and there will be an end of me. But we shall live first, my heart's heart.'

I laid my head on her knee. A strange drowsiness overcame me. Holding her hand against my cheek, I lost consciousness. When I awoke the grey November dawn was glimmering, ghost-like, through the uncurtained window. My head was pillowed on my arm, which rested — I raised my head quickly – ah! not on my lady's knee, but on the needleworked cushion of the straight-backed chair. I sprang to my feet. I was stiff with cold, and dazed with dreams, but I turned my eyes on the picture. There she sat, my lady, my dear love. I held out my arms, but the passionate cry I would have uttered died on my lips. She had said twelve o'clock. Her lightest word was my law. So I only stood in front of the picture and gazed into those grey-green eyes till tears of passionate happiness filled my own.

'Oh, my dear, my dear, how shall I pass the hours till I hold you again?'

No thought, then, of my whole life's completion and consummation being a dream.

I staggered up to my room, fell across my bed, and slept heavily and dreamlessly. When I awoke it was high noon. Mildred and her mother were coming to lunch.

I remembered, at one shock, Mildred's coming and her existence.

Now, indeed, the dream began.

With a penetrating sense of the futility of any action apart from *her*, I gave the necessary orders for the reception of my guests. When Mildred and her mother came I received them with cordiality; but my genial phrases all seemed to be some one else's. My voice sounded like an echo; my heart was other where.

Still, the situation was not intolerable until the hour when afternoon tea was served in the drawing-room. Mildred and her mother kept the conversational pot boiling with a profusion of genteel commonplaces, and I bore it, as one can bear mild purgatories when one is in sight of heaven. I looked up at my sweetheart in the ebony frame, and I felt that anything that might happen, any irresponsible imbecility, any bathos of boredom, was nothing, if, after it all, *she* came to me again.

And yet, when Mildred, too, looked at the portrait, and said, 'What a fine lady! One of your flames, Mr. Devigne?' I had a sickening sense of impotent irritation, which became absolute torture when Mildred — how could I ever have admired that chocolate-box barmaid style of prettiness? — threw herself into the high-backed chair, covering the needlework with her ridiculous flounces, and added, 'Silence gives consent! Who is it, Mr. Devigne? Tell us all about her: I am sure she has a story.'

Poor little Mildred, sitting there smiling, serene in her confidence that her every word charmed me — sitting there with her rather pinched waist, her rather tight boots, her rather vulgar voice — sitting in the chair where my dear lady had sat when she told me her story! I could not bear it.

'Don't sit there,' I said; 'it's not comfortable!'

But the girl would not be warned. With a laugh that set every nerve in my body vibrating with annoyance, she said, 'Oh, dear! mustn't I even sit in the same chair as your black-velvet woman?'

I looked at the chair in the picture. It *was* the same; and in her chair Mildred was sitting. Then a horrible sense of the reality of Mildred came upon me. Was all this a reality after all? But for fortunate chance might Mildred have occupied, not only her chair, but her place in my life? I rose.

'I hope you won't think me very rude,' I said; 'but I am obliged to go out.'

I forget what appointment I alleged. The lie came readily enough.

I faced Mildred's pouts with the hope that she and her mother would not wait dinner for me. I fled. In another minute I was safe, alone, under the chill, cloudy autumn sky — free to think, think, think of my dear lady.

I walked for hours along streets and squares; I lived over again and again every look, word, and hand-touch — every kiss; I was completely, unspeakably happy.

Mildred was utterly forgotten: my lady of the ebony frame filled my heart and soul and spirits.

As I heard eleven boom through the fog, I turned, and went home.

When I got to my street, I found a crowd surging through it, a strong red light filling the air.

A house was on fire! Mine!

I elbowed my way through the crowd.

The picture of my lady — that, at least, I could save!

As I sprang up the steps, I saw, as in a dream — yes, all this was *really* dream-like — I saw Mildred leaning out of the first-floor window, wringing her hands,

'Come back, sir,' cried a fireman; we'll get the young lady out right enough.'

But *my* lady? I went on up the stairs, cracking, smoking, and as hot as hell, to the room where her picture was. Strange to say, I only felt that the picture was a thing we should like to look on through the long glad wedded life that was to be ours. I never thought of it as being one with her.

As I reached the first floor I felt arms round my neck. The smoke was too thick for me to distinguish features.

'Save me!' a voice whispered. I clasped a figure in my arms, and, with a strange dis-ease, bore it down the shaking stairs and out into safety. It was Mildred. I knew *that* directly I clasped her.

'Stand back,' cried the crowd.

'Everyone's safe,' cried a fireman.

The flames leaped from every window. The sky grew redder and redder. I sprang from the hands that would have held me. I leaped up the steps. I crawled up the stairs. Suddenly the whole horror of the situation came on me. '*As long as my picture remains in the ebony frame.*' What if picture and frame perished together?

I fought with the fire, and with my own choking inability to fight with it. I pushed on. I must save my picture. I reached the drawing-room.

As I sprang in I saw my lady — I swear it — through the smoke and the flames, hold out her arms to me — to me — who came too late to save her, and to save my own life's joy. I never saw her again.

Before I could reach her, or cry out to her, I felt the floor yield beneath my feet, and fell into the fiery hell below.

. . . .

How did they save me? What does that matter? They saved me somehow — curse them. Every stick of my aunt's furniture was destroyed. My friends pointed out that, as the furniture was heavily insured, the carelessness of a nightly-studious housemaid had done me no harm.

No harm!

That was how I won and lost my only love.

I deny, with all my soul in the denial, that it was a dream. There are no such dreams. Dreams of longing and pain there are in plenty, but dreams of complete, of unspeakable happiness — ah, no — it is the rest of life that is the dream.

But if I think that, why have I married Mildred, and grown stout and dull and prosperous?

I tell you it is all *this* that is the dream; my dear lady only is the reality. And what does it matter what one does in a dream?

The True Story of a Vampire

Eric Stenbock

Count Eric Stanislaus Stenbock (1860–95) was an aristocrat poet from Estonia, who also wrote fantastic stories. He was a flamboyant Decadent, with homosexual tendencies, notorious for his eccentricity, such as his penchant for keeping exotic animals in his house, as well as for his alcohol and drug abuse. Symons admiringly referred to him as 'inhuman', 'abnormal', 'degenerate' and 'reptilian'. Yeats called him 'scholar, connoisseur, drunkard, poet, pervert, most charming of men'. Stenbock's poetry volume *The Shadow of Death* (1894) was ridiculed by a reviewer of *Pall Mall Gazette* as a parody of 'that latterday literary abortion, the youthful *decadent*'. His short stories in *Studies of Death* (1894) are inundated with bizarre and macabre themes: morbid love and death; Socratic homoeroticism; fetishised Catholicism and chastity; exquisite violins made out of human tissue; all told within an atmosphere reminiscent of a Wildean fairy tale.

For Symons, 'The True Story of a Vampire' exerts an 'unholy fascination'. The story sits alongside more famous *fin-de-siècle* vampire texts, most notably Bram Stoker's *Dracula*, but with heightened Decadent imagery: it turns Stoker's heterosexual predator into a homosexual/paederastic charmer who saps young boys' lifeblood. Indeed, the story is uncannily similar to the homosexual love depicted in 'The Priest and the Acolyte', which was published in the same year (1894). Stenbock reworks several vampire clichés, even turning them on their head: the vampiric tale is rendered without the presence of blood imagery, and the female narrator is ignored utterly by the vampire, thus becoming the sole survivor. The final line, 'People do not, as a rule, believe in Vampires!' hauls the readers' attention back to the beginning, and, with a wry, self-parodic twist, casts doubt on the veracity of the tale just told.

Vampire stories are generally located in Styria; mine is also. Styria is by no means the romantic kind of place described by those who have certainly never been there. It is a flat, uninteresting country, only celebrated by its turkeys, its capons, and the stupidity of its inhabitants. Vampires generally arrive at night, in carriages drawn by two black horses.

Our Vampire arrived by the commonplace means of the railway train, and in the afternoon. You must think I am joking, or perhaps that by the word 'Vampire' I mean a financial vampire. No, I am quite serious. The Vampire of whom I am speaking, who laid waste our hearth and home, was a *real* vampire.

Vampires are generally described as dark, sinister-looking, and singularly handsome. Our Vampire was, on the contrary, rather fair, and certainly was not at first sight sinister-looking, and though decidedly attractive in appearance, not what one would call singularly handsome.

Yes, he desolated our home, killed my brother – the one object of my adoration – also my dear father. Yet, at the same time, I must say that I myself came under the spell of his fascination, and, in spite of all, have no ill-will towards him now.

Doubtless you have read in the papers *passim* of 'the Baroness and her beasts'. It is to tell how I came to spend most of my useless wealth on an asylum for stray animals that I am writing this.

I am old now; what happened then was when I was a little girl of about thirteen. I will begin by describing our household. We were Poles; our name was Wronski; we lived in Styria, where we had a castle. Our household was very limited. It consisted, with the exclusion of domestics, of only my father, our governess – a worthy Belgian named Mademoiselle Vonnaert – my brother, and myself. Let me begin with my father: he was old, and both my brother and I were children of his old age. Of my mother I remember nothing: she died in giving birth to my brother, who is only one year, or not as much, younger than myself. Our father was studious, continually occupied in reading books, chiefly on recondite subjects and in all kinds of unknown languages. He had a long white beard, and wore habitually a black velvet skull-cap.

How kind he was to us! It was more than I could tell. Still it was not I who was the favourite. His whole heart went out to Gabriel – Gabryel as we spelt it in Polish. He was always called by the Russian abbreviation Gavril – I mean, of course, my brother, who had a resemblance to the only portrait of my mother, a slight chalk sketch which hung in my father's study. But I was by no means jealous: my brother was and has been the only love of my life. It is for his sake that I am now keeping in Westbourne Park a home for stray cats and dogs.

I was at that time, as I said before, a little girl; my name was Carmela. My long tangled hair was always all over the place, and never would be combed straight. I was not pretty – at least, looking at a photograph of me at that time, I do not think I could describe myself as such. Yet at the same time, when I look at the photograph, I think my expression may have been pleasing to some people: irregular features, large mouth, and large wild eyes.

I was by way of being naughty – not so naughty as Gabriel in the opinion of Mlle Vonnaert. Mlle Vonnaert, I may intercalate, was a wholly excellent person, middle-aged, who really *did* speak good French, although she was a Belgian, and could also make herself understood in German, which, as you may or may not know, is the current language of Styria.

I find it difficult to describe my brother Gabriel; there was something about him strange and superhuman, or perhaps I should rather say praeterhuman, something between the animal and the divine. Perhaps the Greek idea of the Faun might illustrate what I mean; but that will not do either. He had large, wild, gazelle-like eyes; his hair, like mine, was in a perpetual tangle – that point he had in common with me, and indeed, as I afterwards heard, our mother having been of gipsy race, it will account for much of the innate wildness there was in our natures. I was wild enough, but Gabriel was much wilder. Nothing would induce him to put on shoes and stockings, except on Sundays – when he also allowed his hair to be combed, but only by me. How shall I describe the grace of that lovely mouth, shaped verily 'en arc d'amour'. I always think of the text in the Psalm, 'Grace is shed forth on thy lips, therefore has God blessed thee eternally' – lips that seemed to exhale the very breath of life. Then that beautiful, lithe, living, elastic form!

He could run faster than any deer; spring like a squirrel to the topmost branch of a tree: he might have stood for the sign and symbol of vitality itself. But seldom could he be induced by Mlle Vonnaert to learn lessons; but when he did so, he learnt with extraordinary quickness. He would play upon every conceivable instrument, holding a violin here, there, and everywhere except the right place; manufacturing instruments for himself out of reeds – even sticks. Mlle Vonnaert made futile efforts to induce him to learn to play the piano. I suppose he was what was called spoilt, though merely in the superficial sense of the word. Our father allowed him to indulge in every caprice.

One of his peculiarities, when quite a little child, was horror at the sight of meat. Nothing on earth would induce him to taste it. Another thing which was particularly remarkable about him was his extraordinary power over animals. Everything seemed to come tame to his hand. Birds would sit on his shoulder. Then sometimes Mlle Vonnaert and I would lose him in the woods – he would suddenly dart away. Then we would find him singing softly or whistling to himself, with all manner of woodland creatures around him, – hedgehogs, little foxes, wild rabbits, marmots, squirrels, and such like. He would frequently bring these things home with him and insist on keeping them. This strange menagerie was the terror of poor Mlle Vonnaert's heart. He chose to live in a little room at the top of a turret; but which, instead of going upstairs, he chose to reach by means of a very tall chestnut-tree, through the window. But in contradiction of all this, it was his custom to serve every Sunday Mass in the parish church, with hair nicely combed and with white surplice and red cassock. He looked as demure and tamed as possible. Then came the element of the divine. What an expression of ecstasy there was in those glorious eyes!

Thus far I have not been speaking about the Vampire. However, let me begin with my narrative at last. One day my father had to go to the neighbouring town – as he frequently had. This time he returned accompanied by a guest. The gentleman, he said, had missed his train, through the late arrival of another at our station, which was a junction, and he would therefore, as trains were not frequent in our parts, have had to wait there all night. He had joined in conversation with my father in the too-late-arriving train from the town: and had consequently accepted my father's invitation to stay the night at our house. But of course, you know, in those out-of-the-way parts we are almost patriarchal in our hospitality.

He was announced under the name of Count Vardalek – the name being Hungarian. But he spoke German well enough: not with the monotonous accentuation of Hungarians, but rather, if anything, with a slight Slavonic intonation. His voice was peculiarly soft and insinuating. We soon afterwards found that he could talk Polish, and Mlle Vonnaert vouched for his good French. Indeed he seemed to know all languages. But let me give my first impressions. He was rather tall, with fair wavy hair, rather long, which accentuated a certain effeminacy about his smooth face. His figure had something – I cannot say what – serpentine about it. The features were refined; and he had long, slender, subtle, magnetic-looking hands, a somewhat long sinuous nose, a graceful mouth, and an attractive smile, which belied the intense sadness of the expression of the eyes. When he arrived his eyes were half closed – indeed they were habitually so – so that I could not decide their colour. He looked worn and wearied. I could not possibly guess his age.

Suddenly Gabriel burst into the room: a yellow butterfly was clinging to his hair. He was carrying in his arms a little squirrel. Of course he was bare-legged as usual. The stranger looked up at his approach; then I noticed his eyes. They were green: they seemed to dilate and grow larger. Gabriel stood stock-still, with a startled look, like that of a bird fascinated by a serpent. But nevertheless he held out his hand to the newcomer. Vardalek, taking his hand – I don't know why I noticed this trivial thing, – pressed the pulse with his forefinger. Suddenly Gabriel darted from the room and rushed upstairs, going to his turret-room this time by the staircase instead of the tree. I was in terror what the Count might think of him. Great was my relief when he came down in his velvet Sunday suit, and shoes and stockings. I combed his hair, and set him generally right.

When the stranger came down to dinner his appearance had somewhat altered; he looked much younger. There was an elasticity of the skin, combined with a delicate complexion, rarely to be found in a man. Before, he had struck me as being very pale.

Well, at dinner we were all charmed with him, especially my father. He seemed to be thoroughly acquainted with all my father's particular hobbies. Once, when my father was relating some of his military experiences, he said something about a drummer-boy who was wounded in battle. His eyes opened completely again and dilated; this time with a particularly disagreeable expression, dull and dead, yet at the same time animated by some horrible excitement. But this was only momentary.

The chief subject of his conversation with my father was about certain curious mystical books which my father had just lately picked up, and which he could not make out, but Vardalek seemed completely to understand. At dessert-time my father asked him if he were in a great hurry to reach his destination; if not, would he not stay with us a little while: though our place was out of the way, he would find much that would interest him in his library.

He answered, 'I am in no hurry. I have no particular reason for going to that place at all, and if I can be of service to you in deciphering these books, I shall be only too glad.' He added with a smile which was bitter, very very bitter: 'You see I am a cosmopolitan, a wanderer on the face of the earth.'

After dinner my father asked him if he played the piano. He said, 'Yes, I can a little,' and he sat down at the piano. Then he played a Hungarian csardas – wild, rhapsodic, wonderful.

That is the music which makes men mad. He went on in the same strain.

Gabriel stood stock-still by the piano, his eyes dilated and fixed, his form quivering. At last he said very slowly, at one particular motive – for want of a better word you may call it the *relâche* of a csardas, by which I mean that point where the original quasi-slow movement begins again – 'Yes, I think I could play that.'

Then he quickly fetched his fiddle and self-made xylophone, and did actually, alternating the instruments, render the same very well indeed.

Vardalek looked at him, and said in a very sad voice, 'Poor child! you have the soul of music within you.'

I could not understand why he should seem to commiserate instead of congratulate Gabriel on what certainly showed an extraordinary talent.

. . . . .

Gabriel was shy even as the wild animals who were tame to him. Never before had he taken to a stranger. Indeed, as a rule, if any stranger came to the house by any chance, he would hide himself, and I had to bring him up his food to the turret chamber. You may imagine what was my surprise when I saw him walking about hand in hand with Vardalek the next morning, in the garden, talking lively with him, and showing his collection of pet animals, which he had gathered from the woods, and for which we had had to fit up a regular zoological gardens. He seemed utterly under the domination of Vardalek. What surprised us was (for otherwise we liked the stranger, especially for being kind to him) that he seemed, though not noticeably at first – except perhaps to me, who noticed everything with regard to him – to be gradually losing his general health and vitality. He did not become pale as yet; but there was a certain languor about his movements which certainly there was by no means before.

My father got more and more devoted to Count Vardalek. He helped him in his studies; and my father would hardly allow him to go away, which he did sometimes – to Trieste, he said: he always came back, bringing us presents of strange Oriental jewellery or textures.

I knew all kinds of people came to Trieste, Orientals included. Still, there was a strangeness and magnificence about these things which I was sure even then could not possibly have come from such a place as Trieste, memorable to me chiefly for its necktie shops.

When Vardalek was away, Gabriel was continually asking for him and talking about him. Then at the same time he seemed to regain his old vitality and spirits. Vardalek always returned looking much older, wan, and weary. Gabriel would rush to meet him, and kiss him on the mouth. Then he gave a slight shiver; and after a little while began to look quite young again.

Things continued like this for some time. My father would not hear of Vardalek's going away permanently. He came to be an inmate of our house. I indeed, and Mlle Vonnaert also, could not help noticing what a difference there was altogether about Gabriel. But my father seemed totally blind to it.

One night I had gone downstairs to fetch something which I had left in the drawing-room. As I was going up again I passed Vardalek's room. He was playing on a piano, which had been specially put there for him, one of Chopin's nocturnes, very beautifully: I stopped, leaning on the banisters to listen.

Something white appeared on the dark staircase. We believed in ghosts in our part. I was transfixed with terror, and clung to the banisters. What was my astonishment to see Gabriel walking slowly down the staircase, his eyes fixed as though in a trance! This terrified me even more than a ghost would. Could I believe my senses? Could that be Gabriel?

I simply could not move. Gabriel, clad in his long white night-shirt, came downstairs and opened the door. He left it open. Vardalek still continued playing, but talked as he played.

He said – this time speaking in Polish – *Nie umiem wyrazic jak ciehie kocham*, – 'My darling, I fain would spare thee; but thy life is my life, and I must live, I who would rather die. Will God not have *any* mercy on me? Oh! oh! life; oh, the torture of life!' Here he struck one agonised and strange chord, then continued playing softly, 'O Gabriel, my beloved! my life, yes *life* – oh, why life? I am sure this is but a little that I demand of thee. Surely thy superabundance of life can spare a little to one who is already dead. No, stay,' he said now almost harshly, 'what must be, must be!'

Gabriel stood there quite still, with the same fixed vacant expression, in the room. He was evidently walking in his sleep. Vardalek played on; then said, 'Ah!' with a sign of terrible agony. Then very gently, 'Go now, Gabriel; it is enough.' And Gabriel went out of the room and ascended the staircase at the same slow pace, with the same unconscious stare. Vardalek struck the piano, and although he did not play loudly, it seemed as though the strings would break. You never heard music so strange and so heart-rending!

I only know I was found by Mlle Vonnaert in the morning, in an unconscious state, at the foot of the stairs. Was it a dream after all? I am sure now that it was not. I thought then it might be, and said nothing to anyone about it. Indeed, what could I say?

Well, to let me cut a long story short, Gabriel, who had never known a moment's sickness in his life, grew ill; and we had to send to Gratz for a doctor, who could give no explanation of Gabriel's strange illness. Gradual wasting away, he said; absolutely no organic complaint. What could this mean?

My father at last became conscious of the fact that Gabriel was ill. His anxiety was fearful. The last trace of grey faded from his hair, and it became quite white. We sent to Vienna for doctors. But all with the same result.

Gabriel was generally unconscious, and when conscious, only seemed to recognise Vardalek, who sat continually by his bedside, nursing him with the utmost tenderness.

One day I was alone in the room; and Vardalek cried suddenly, almost fiercely, 'Send for a priest at once, at once,' he repeated. 'It is now almost too late!'

Gabriel stretched out his arms spasmodically, and put them round Vardalek's neck. This was the only movement he had made for some time. Vardalek bent down and kissed him on the lips. I rushed downstairs; and the priest was sent for. When I came back Vardalek was not there. The priest administered extreme unction. I think Gabriel was already dead, although we did not think so at the time.

Vardalek had utterly disappeared; and when we looked for him he was nowhere to be found; nor have I seen or heard of him since.

My father died very soon afterwards; suddenly aged, and bent down with grief. And so the whole of the Wronski property came into my sole possession. And here I am, an old woman, generally laughed at for keeping, in memory of Gabriel, an asylum for stray animals – and – people do not, as a rule, believe in Vampires!

The Flowering of the Strange Orchid

H. G. Wells

Herbert George Wells (1866–1946) was novelist, short story writer, futurist, historian, political and social thinker, and teacher. He is best known for his science fiction, or Scientific Romance as he put it, especially his early works *The Time Machine* (1895), *The Island of Doctor Moreau* (1896) *and The War of the Worlds* (1898). Launching his career as a drama critic for the *Pall Mall Gazette* and a literary reviewer for *The Saturday Review*, Wells was fully conscious of the Aesthetic and Decadent movements of the time, from Huysmans to Beardsley and Wilde. Wells himself had some sympathy for Aesthetic sensibilities, and Decadent leitmotifs make their way into many of his works. The themes of entropy and degeneration in *The Time Machine*, the Wildean angel in *The Wonderful Visit* (1895) and the Jekylite, amoral scientist Dr Moreau are all indicators of the cultural presence of Decadence.

'The Flowering of the Strange Orchid' is a neat scientific tale in which Wells combines the Darwinian idea of ruthless struggle for survival with the fantastic theme of seductive vampirism. The bachelor protagonist, Wedderburn, experiments in the artificial propagation of hothouse orchids with an almost fanatical zeal, reminiscent of Doctor Moreau's maniac desire to create artificial humans. Orchids are a stock image of Decadence, from Huysmans's *À Rebours* to Theodore Wratislaw's poems *Orchids* (1896). This is arguably Wells's most Decadent short story, and it brings to mind Des Esseintes's attraction to the artificial, unnatural and feminine beauty of orchids. Like an Oriental femme fatale, the flower in Wells's tale is a narcotic, enticing and incapacitating its victims with its 'intensely sweet scent'. Like an exotic Venus Flytrap, the orchid drains the blood of its prey, in a deadly, leech-like embrace.

The buying of orchids always has in it a certain speculative flavour. You have before you the brown shrivelled lump of tissue, and for the rest you must trust your judgement, or the auctioneer, or your good-luck, as your taste may incline. The plant may be moribund or dead, or it may be just a respectable purchase, fair value for your money, or perhaps – for the thing has happened again and again – there slowly unfolds before the delighted eyes of the happy purchaser, day after day, some new variety, some novel richness, a strange twist of the labellum, or some subtler colouration or unexpected mimicry. Pride, beauty, and profit blossom together on one delicate green spike, and, it may be, even immortality. For the new miracle of Nature may stand in need of a new specific name, and what so convenient as that of its discoverer? 'Johnsmithia'! There have been worse names.

It was perhaps the hope of some such happy discovery that made Winter-Wedderburn such a frequent attendant at these sales – that hope, and also, maybe, the fact that he had nothing else of the slightest interest to do in the world. He was a shy, lonely, rather ineffectual man, provided with just enough income to keep off the spur of necessity, and not enough nervous energy to make him seek any exacting employments. He might have collected stamps or coins, or translated Horace, or bound books, or invented new species of diatoms. But, as it happened, he grew orchids, and had one ambitious little hothouse.

'I have a fancy,' he said over his coffee, 'that something is going to happen to me to-day.' He spoke – as he moved and thought – slowly.

'Oh, don't say *that*!' said his housekeeper – who was also his remote cousin. For 'something happening' was a euphemism that meant only one thing to her.

'You misunderstand me. I mean nothing unpleasant . . . though what I do mean I scarcely know.

'To-day,' he continued, after a pause, 'Peters' are going to sell a batch of plants from the Andamans and the Indies. I shall go up and see what they have. It may be I shall buy something good, unawares. That may be it.'

He passed his cup for his second cupful of coffee.

'Are these the things collected by that poor young fellow you told me of the other day?' asked his cousin as she filled his cup.

'Yes,' he said, and became meditative over a piece of toast.

'Nothing ever does happen to me,' he remarked presently, beginning to think aloud. 'I wonder why? Things enough happen to other people. There is Harvey. Only the other week; on Monday he picked up sixpence, on Wednesday his chicks all had the staggers, on Friday his cousin came home from Australia, and on Saturday he broke his ankle. What a whirl of excitement! – compared to me.'

'I think I would rather be without so much excitement,' said his housekeeper. 'It can't be good for you.'

'I suppose it's troublesome. Still... you see, nothing ever happens to me. When I was a little boy I never had accidents. I never fell in love as I grew up. Never married.... I wonder how it feels to have something happen to you, something really remarkable.

'That orchid-collector was only thirty-six – twenty years younger than myself – when he died. And he had been married twice and divorced once; he had had malarial fever four times, and once he broke his thigh. He killed a Malay once, and once he was wounded by a poisoned dart. And in the end he was killed by jungle-leeches. It must have all been very troublesome, but then it must have been very interesting, you know – except, perhaps, the leeches.'

'I am sure it was not good for him,' said the lady, with conviction.

'Perhaps not.' And then Wedderburn looked at his watch. 'Twenty-three minutes past eight. I am going up by the quarter to twelve train, so that there is plenty of time. I think I shall wear my alpaca jacket – it is quite warm enough – and my grey felt hat and brown shoes. I suppose ——'

He glanced out of the window at the serene sky and sunlit garden, and then nervously at his cousin's face.

'I think you had better take an umbrella if you are going to London,' she said in a voice that admitted of no denial. 'There's all between here and the station coming back.'

When he returned he was in a state of mild excitement. He had made a purchase. It was rare that he could make up his mind quickly enough to buy, but this time he had done so.

'These are Vandas,' he said, 'and a Dendrobe and some Palaeonophis.' He surveyed his purchases lovingly as he consumed his soup. They were laid out on the spotless tablecloth before him, and he was telling his cousin all about them as he slowly meandered through his dinner. It was his custom to live all his visits to London over again in the evening for her and his own entertainment.

'I knew something would happen to-day. And I have bought all these. Some of them – some of them – I feel sure, do you know, that some of them will be remarkable. I don't know how it is, but I feel just as sure as if someone had told me that some of these will turn out remarkable.

'That one' – he pointed to a shrivelled rhizome – 'was not identified. It may be a Palaeonophis – or it may not. It may be a new species, or even a new genus. And it was the last that poor Batten ever collected.'

'I don't like the look of it,' said his housekeeper. 'It's such an ugly shape.'

'To me it scarcely seems to have a shape.'

'I don't like those things that stick out,' said his housekeeper.

'It shall be put away in a pot to-morrow.'

'It looks,' said the housekeeper, 'like a spider shamming dead.'

Wedderburn smiled and surveyed the root with his head on one side. 'It is certainly not a pretty lump of stuff. But you can never judge of these things from their dry appearance. It may turn out to be a very beautiful orchid indeed. How busy I shall be to-morrow! I must see to-night just exactly what to do with these things, and to-morrow I shall set to work.'

'They found poor Batten lying dead, or dying, in a mangrove swamp – I forget which,' he began again presently, 'with one of these very orchids crushed up under his body. He had been unwell for some days with some kind of native fever, and I suppose he fainted. These mangrove swamps are very unwholesome. Every drop of blood, they say, was taken out of him by the jungle-leeches. It may be that very plant that cost him his life to obtain.'

'I think none the better of it for that.'

'Men must work though women may weep,' said Wedderburn with profound gravity.

'Fancy dying away from every comfort in a nasty swamp! Fancy being ill of fever with nothing to take but chlorodyne and quinine – if men were left to themselves they would live on chlorodyne and quinine – and no one round you but horrible natives! They say the Andaman islanders are most disgusting wretches – and, anyhow, they can scarcely make good nurses, not having the necessary training. And just for people in England to have orchids!'

'I don't suppose it was comfortable, but some men seem to enjoy that kind of thing,' said Wedderburn. 'Anyhow, the natives of his party were sufficiently civilised to take care of all his collection until his colleague, who was an ornithologist, came back again from the interior; though they could not tell the species of the orchid and had let it wither. And it makes these things more interesting.'

'It makes them disgusting. I should be afraid of some of the malaria clinging to them. And just think, there has been a dead body lying across that ugly thing! I never thought of that before. There! I declare I cannot eat another mouthful of dinner.'

'I will take them off the table if you like, and put them in the window-seat. I can see them just as well there.'

The next few days he was indeed singularly busy in his steamy little hothouse, fussing about with charcoal, lumps of teak, moss, and all the other mysteries of the orchid cultivator. He considered he was having a wonderfully eventful time. In the evening he would talk about these new orchids to his friends, and over and over again he reverted to his expectation of something strange.

Several of the Vandas and the Dendrobium died under his care, but presently the strange orchid began to show signs of life. He was delighted and took his housekeeper right away from jam-making to see it at once, directly he made the discovery.

'That is a bud,' he said, 'and presently there will be a lot of leaves there, and those little things coming out here are aërial rootlets.'

'They look to me like little white fingers poking out of the brown,' said his housekeeper. 'I don't like them.'

'Why not?'

'I don't know. They look like fingers trying to get at you. I can't help my likes and dislikes.'

'I don't know for certain, but I don't *think* there are any orchids I know that have aërial rootlets quite like that. It may be my fancy, of course. You see they are a little flattened at the ends.'

'I don't like 'em,' said his housekeeper, suddenly shivering and turning away. 'I know it's very silly of me – and I'm very sorry, particularly as you like the thing so much. But I can't help thinking of that corpse.'

'But it may not be that particular plant. That was merely a guess of mine.'

His housekeeper shrugged her shoulders. 'Anyhow I don't like it,' she said.

Wedderburn felt a little hurt at her dislike to the plant. But that did not prevent his talking to her about orchids generally, and this orchid in particular, whenever he felt inclined.

'There are such queer things about orchids,' he said one day; 'such possibilities of surprises. You know, Darwin studied their fertilisation, and showed that the whole structure of an ordinary orchid-flower was contrived in order that moths might carry the pollen from plant to plant. Well, it seems that there are lots of orchids known the flower of which cannot possibly be used for fertilisation in that way. Some of the Cypripediums, for instance; there are no insects known that can possibly fertilise them, and some of them have never been found with seed.'

'But how do they form new plants?'

'By runners and tubers, and that kind of outgrowth. That is easily explained. The puzzle is, what are the flowers for?

'Very likely,' he added, '*my* orchid may be something extraordinary in that way. If so I shall study it. I have often thought of making researches as Darwin did. But hitherto I have not found the time, or something else has happened to prevent it. The leaves are beginning to unfold now. I do wish you would come and see them!'

But she said that the orchid-house was so hot it gave her the headache. She had seen the plant once again, and the aërial rootlets, which were now some of them more than a foot long, had unfortunately reminded her of tentacles reaching out after something; and they got into her dreams, growing after her with incredible rapidity. So that she had settled to her entire satisfaction that she would not see that plant again, and Wedderburn had to admire its leaves alone. They were of the ordinary broad form, and a deep glossy green, with splashes and dots of deep red towards the base. He knew of no other leaves quite like them. The plant was placed on a low bench near the thermometer, and close by was a simple arrangement by which a tap dripped on the hot-water pipes and kept the air steamy. And he spent his afternoons now with some regularity meditating on the approaching flowering of this strange plant.

And at last the great thing happened. Directly he entered the little glass-house he knew that the spike had burst out, although his great *Palaeonophis Lowii* hid the corner where his new darling stood. There was a new odour in the air, a rich, intensely sweet scent, that overpowered every other in that crowded, steaming little greenhouse.

Directly he noticed this he hurried down to the strange orchid. And, behold! The trailing green spikes bore now three great splashes of blossom, from which this overpowering sweetness proceeded. He stopped before them in an ecstasy of admiration.

The flowers were white, with streaks of golden orange upon the petals; the heavy labellum was coiled into an intricate projection, and a wonderful bluish purple mingled there with the gold. He could see at once that the genus was altogether a new one. And the insufferable scent! How hot the place was! The blossoms swam before his eyes.

He would see if the temperature was right. He made a step towards the thermometer. Suddenly everything appeared unsteady. The bricks on the floor were dancing up and down. Then the white blossoms, the green leaves behind them, the whole greenhouse, seemed to sweep sideways, and then in a curve upward.

* * * * *

At half-past four his cousin made the tea, according to their invariable custom. But Wedderburn did not come in for his tea.

'He is worshipping that horrid orchid,' she told herself, and waited ten minutes. 'His watch must have stopped. I will go and call him.'

She went straight to the hothouse, and, opening the door, called his name. There was no reply. She noticed that the air was very close, and loaded with an intense perfume. Then she saw something lying on the bricks between the hot-water pipes.

For a minute, perhaps, she stood motionless.

He was lying, face upward, at the foot of the strange orchid. The tentacle-like aërial rootlets no longer swayed freely in the air, but were crowded together, a tangle of grey ropes, and stretched tight with their ends closely applied to his chin and neck and hands.

She did not understand. Then she saw from one of the exultant tentacles upon his cheek there trickled a little thread of blood.

With an inarticulate cry she ran towards him, and tried to pull him away from the leech-like suckers. She snapped two of these tentacles, and their sap dripped red.

Then the overpowering scent of the blossom began to make her head reel. How they clung to him! She tore at the tough ropes, and he and the white inflorescence swam about her. She felt she was fainting, knew she must not. She left him and hastily opened the nearest door, and, after she had panted for a moment in the fresh air, she had a brilliant inspiration. She caught up a flower-pot and smashed in the windows at the end of the greenhouse. Then she re-entered. She tugged now with renewed strength at Wedderburn's motionless body, and brought the strange orchid crashing to the floor. It still clung with the grimmest tenacity to its victim. In a frenzy, she lugged it and him into the open air.

Then she thought of tearing through the sucker rootlets one by one, and in another minute she had released him and was dragging him away from the horror.

He was white and bleeding from a dozen circular patches.

The odd-job man was coming up the garden, amazed at the smashing of glass, and saw her emerge, hauling the inanimate body with red-stained hands. For a moment he thought impossible things.

'Bring some water!' she cried, and her voice dispelled his fancies. When, with unnatural alacrity, he returned with the water, he found her weeping with excitement, and with Wedderburn's head upon her knee, wiping the blood from his face.

'What's the matter?' said Wedderburn, opening his eyes feebly, and closing them again at once.

'Go and tell Annie to come out here to me, and then go for Doctor Haddon at once,' she said to the odd-job man so soon as he had brought the water; and added, seeing he hesitated, 'I will tell you all about it when you come back.'

Presently Wedderburn opened his eyes again, and, seeing that he was troubled by the puzzle of his position, she explained to him, 'You fainted in the hothouse.'

'And the orchid?'

'I will see to that,' she said.

Wedderburn had lost a good deal of blood, but beyond that he had suffered no very great injury. They gave him brandy mixed with some pink extract of meat, and carried him upstairs to bed. His housekeeper told her incredible story in fragments to Dr Haddon. 'Come to the orchid-house and see,' she said.

The cold outer air was blowing in through the open door, and the sickly perfume was almost dispelled. Most of the torn aërial rootlets lay already withered amidst a number of dark stains upon the bricks. The stem of the inflorescence was broken by the fall of the plant, and the flowers were growing limp and brown at the edges of the petals. The doctor stooped towards it, then saw that one of the aërial rootlets still stirred feebly, and hesitated.

The next morning the strange orchid still lay there, black now and putrescent. The door banged intermittently in the morning breeze, and all the array of Wedderburn's orchids was shrivelled and prostrate. But Wedderburn himself was bright and garrulous upstairs in the glory of his strange adventure.

The Truce of God

Una Ashworth Taylor

Una Ashworth Taylor (1857–1922) was a novelist born into a literary household, a focal point for artists and writers of the day, among them Thomas Carlyle, Robert Louis Stevenson and Tennyson. After her mother's death she moved to London in 1891 with her older sister Ida, a prolific biographer and novelist, where Taylor hosted a successful salon for the London intelligentsia. Her fiction is steeped in fantasy modes and adheres to Paterian and Wildean Aestheticism. Unlike the work of many New Women authors, Taylor's is free from socio-political messages. Of note is her novel *The City of Sarras* (1887) whose themes anticipate *Dorian Gray*.

'The Truce of God' is part of the collection *Nets for the Wind* (1896), tales of Aesthetic, fantasy landscapes conjured up by jewelled, ostentatious prose. One of these stories, 'The Seed of the Sun', deals with the erotic fixation of a woman with a plant. 'The Truce of God' is an intentional rewriting of *Dorian Gray*, as Talia Schaffer points out, unfolding 'a terrifying vision of the interchangeability of life and art'. This pygmalionic, entropic story deals with the tragedy of indulging in artifice and the poetics of the body. In a montage of elliptical fragmented scenes, it tells of the sculptor Hermas and his obsession with his statue which gradually drains the life of his lover Mèril, making her statuesque. Sculptural frigidity interchanges with biological vitality and the icy stasis of art is confounded with the living body.

Hermas stood beside the statue and Mèril stood by him. The statue was the figure of a youth; in the hand of the youth was a sword, and upon his head a crown of laurel leaves; his eyes were closed. Hermas had made the statue, its temples had the wings of sleep.

'The statue is stronger than I,' said the sculptor. 'It has no needs. Without bread it will not starve, without water it will not thirst. Pain, before which man is powerless, before it is impotent.'

Across the sunlight which flooded the great bare room, the shadow of a flying swallow passed in a swift curve. Hermas paused to watch the bird's flight through the summer air. Then he went on:

'Men and beasts agonise, plants have their health and their maladies, flower gives birth to flower, and bird mates with bird. But spring-time and harvest time, winter and summer, stone remains stone, and marble marble. The statue is stronger than I.'

He expected no reply, – how should Mèril answer him?

'Of old,' he continued, after a brief pause, 'we are told men made gods of stone; was it in truth that they in stone discerned a God?'

Mèril laughed softly. She loved Hermas; she had his hands to kiss, his face to look on, his voice to hear, she knew no more. Of what lay beyond Hermas she questioned nothing. She had neither past nor future, for her yesterday and to-morrow were not. What signified to her those eternal interrogations of eternal mysteries, what mattered it to her those vulnerabilities of humanity, or that sterile inviolability of stone? Even while he spoke Hermas had raised his hand once more to the marble, indenting a wound mark above the heart.

'Nor when I strike does it suffer,' he said moodily.

Mèril laughed again; thrusting her scarlet-tinged face between the sculptor and his work, she twined her arms round the statue, and with her feet poised on the stone base she reached the eyelids of the youth with her soft lips.

'Nor, if I cherish it, will it love,' she cried gayly. 'Its loss is infinite.'

Her touch was the touch of a flower, her face in its sensitive uncertainty was like a reflection, vivid in sunlight, pale in shadow.

'Take heed, Mèril.' Hermas set her on the ground. 'There is a legend that once, playing heedlessly, a youth set his marriage ring upon the open hand of a stone Venus. She shut her fingers on the gift and held him bondsman.'

Mèril kissed the hand in which hers lay.

'Ah, Hermas,' she said, 'you, like that old lost world, think that because marble is not mortal it is God; that to be less than human is to be half divine.'

They were the haphazard words of an intelligence that only mirrored the images of life upon its surface, but they turned the current of his thoughts.

'And to be less than woman,' he jested, 'is to be – Mèril.'

'Am I less than woman?' she asked, a little cloud of trouble overcasting her face.

His speculative eyes rested upon her evasive loveliness; and the speculation died out of them. 'You are the soul of a rose, – if roses have souls,' he answered her caressingly; 'where others feel needs you only follow impulses, where they pursue aims you only obey instincts.'

'What is the distinction?' she persisted.

'How should you understand!' he said. 'Want is the consciousness of a void, it is the pang of hunger and the torture of thirst. Impulse is to the joy of bread without hunger, to the joy of dew without fever's parching.'

For a moment a faint gleam of comprehension lay in her eyes, then lifting his hand she laid it on her hair.

'What is it to me, what is anything to me without or within?' she cried. 'Love is enough!'

She loved so much. She had a genius for love; it is a genius which demands great things of those to whom it is given. Further, it has the sacrificial quality of all genius; it produces no works even for the merchandise of the heart. Likewise Hermas loved her, but with a difference. Mèril needed her whole self – Hermas had to be only part of himself – to love. Mèril, by reason of her love, could do many things; Hermas had to put aside many things to love.

When Hermas made the statue he was poor, the great house which was their home was beautiful as a palace and bare as a prison. Mèril loved its bareness, it was so white and still. There is a restlessness to some women in the presence even of things inanimate.

But after the winged statue was made, Hermas became famous and he became rich. Men and women came and went in the rooms which once were solitary. The world entered Mèril's paradise. At its hands she demanded nothing; to Hermas it gave all that he demanded. Soon there remained nothing for him to strive for save the unattainable; he suffered the supreme defeat of victory. When a man has won all that is winnable, he can hereafter only draw blanks. It is an inevitable penalty of success – Hermas grew hardened to it; as it became a custom it ceased to be a sensation, but the accent of life was lost.

Often he left Mèril. When he left her she lived alone in the great echoing house. She needed no companionship. Hermas was present or Hermas was absent, and when he was absent her life lay between a memory and an expectation. She was not unhappy, for her memories and her expectations were both of joy. Only in the stillness and the solitude she grew like a shadow; waiting, she wasted away with her heart's homesickness for his arms.

Once he came back to her suddenly. She had not known his return, she had not heard his footsteps. She had fallen asleep in the white room where the winged statue stood upon his pedestal with his closed eyelids and parted lips. There Hermas found her. The sunshine of the late afternoon flooded the room with dusty radiance, the cobweb threads of her hair had caught both the radiance and the dustiness; they shone as if powdered with gold, like the feathers of a gold-moth's wings, but her face was very white, and in the full summer heat she lay as if the chill of winter encompassed her. A dumb terror held Hermas for a moment speechless, then kneeling beside her he wakened her with kisses. He saw the colour spring back to her face, the lagging pulses beat swiftly, and still his kisses touched her lips as never before they had touched them. Under those kisses her eyes shone like mad stars.

'You are my life,' she whispered. 'Life of my life!' Then with a swift recoil of terror she shrank from him.

'See!' she cried, 'the statue bleeds!'

He turned. By some freak of reflected light a sun-ray, dyed red as blood by the ruby crystal of a great cup set on a high shelf above, struck its stain upon the breast of the statue – and on the breast of the statue, above its heart, was the wound mark Hermas had cut in the marble.

He saw and laughed.

'It bleeds because of my kisses,' he said. 'Stone is a jealous god.' Then his laughter died away. 'Jealous and strong,' he added, as if compelled by some afterthought of indefinite distrust.

Again his gaze reverted to Mèril. He saw once more her face as he had seen it in sleep, white and still. Even now it seemed to him as if the crimson flush, new-born with his coming, was fading and giving place to that former pallor. It was like the contagion of marble.

Mèril had risen; she was standing close beside the statue, her eyes were drowsily raised towards it, as if she half expected to see the flow of the wound and the drip of the life-blood from its cleft heart. But the red stain was gone; the sunlight had shifted; the sun sank fast in throbbing colours behind the walls and roofs of the city streets, and as it sank it left behind it a sky of amber and orange, flecked with rose-red clouds. Presently these too faded, and a clear twilight which was like white fire filled the room.

Neither of the two had spoken for many minutes, but Hermas was watching Mèril with a sharpening sense of disquietude. At last he broke the silence.

'Why were you sleeping?' he demanded, with a certain urgency.

Mèril crept back to him; she leant against him, and drew his passive hand softly over her eyelids.

'I wanted it,' she said. Then after a short pause, 'I want it still,' she murmured, with a gesture of profoundest languor. He let her sleep, but the slumber seemed to him like the invasion of an enemy – it had the remoteness of death.

The next day, and the next, something of that shadowy drowsiness clung to her; her life lay beneath it as the muted strings of a violin. Then by slow degrees its muffled stillness was broken; beneath his hands the film which overspread her vitality dispersed; warmth, and colour, and movement revived. In those days his love changed. Before, he had loved her, now he became her lover. She was aware of some change, with a vague, indefinite consciousness. The perception brought with it an unaccustomed burden; a sense of inadequacy to respond to some new demand oppressed her. Her joy was gone. The unfamiliarities of life's relations are like estrangements to women; a new nearness is like a separation.

'I have a grief, Hermas,' she said.

'I see no tears,' he answered lightly, yet wondering.

'To you I gave all,' she continued, paying no heed to his words, 'I gave all, and more than all can no woman give. Now, you who were once content, need more.'

He made no response. She moved restlessly, striving to disentangle the thread of her thoughts.

'To give more, I must be more,' she went on.

'More than Mèril?' he said, smiling. But he could not dispel that troubled sense of incompleteness.

She lifted wistful eyes to his; their wistfulness was like a passion.

'Ah, Hermas,' she cried, 'I cannot, cannot understand; it is like lying between a waking and a sleep, between a life and a death – and neither are mine. But the sleep is stronger than the waking and the death than the life.'

'Death is not stronger than life,' he asserted, stirred to denial by some sense of contest. His own fantastic imaginings had found utterance in her words.

'It is stronger, it is stronger,' she reiterated. 'Its expression is in impotence, the helplessness of dead lips, the weakness of dead hands, but behind the dead is the death-giver, and he is stronger than all.'

Mèril clasped her arms round Hermas.

'Give me life,' she said, 'give me life, that I may give back to you all you demand.'

. . . . .

It was evening. A gay crowd thronged hall and stairs and corridors. Mèril passed among the guests with the face of a woman to whom a crowd is a solitude. Once her lips trembled and her colour came and went, as Hermas for a moment lingered at her side.

A woman near by laughed.

'You are his bondwoman,' she said.

'To be bondwoman of one is to be freedwoman of many,' Mèril answered.

The woman who jeered paused. She had fought with the world and won, yet confronted by Mèril's eyes with their remote enfranchisement, her triumphs shrank into littleness. What were they but tributes to the world's empire? To conquer a world is to proclaim that the world is worth conquest. She was a thrall to her victories.

Yet – she knew Hermas – once she had loved him. She looked from him to Mèril; from the god who was dust, to the worship which was infinite, – looked and was silent, and turned away, lest in place of pity she should envy the emancipation of the bondage she derided.

The hours wore on to midnight. But for Mèril the lassitude of the summer night had no fatigue, and the turmoil of laughter and jests had no unrest. Her heart waited, enclosed in its own quietude, for the hour when no voice save the voice of Hermas should sound in her ears, when no eyes save her eyes should look upon his face. And yet, even as she waited, she was conscious of coming change – the ear of some spiritual sense caught as it were the whirr of fortune's wheel which turned. Something was coming, – coming that very night. It would come, as day comes after a dream, reality after an image, – the same yet not the same.

She stole from the crowd, away from the voices, away from the lights and the glitter, and the movement – they oppressed her like a narrowed horizon. The grey night was in the summer-garden, – its hand lay upon the eyes of the flowers. The air was like the breath of the earth's fever, but it was silent. She was not tired, but she would rest; without weariness she craved for repose in that dumb greyness. In a niche, beneath a high stone wall, was a seat of stone, shadowed from the twilight; she sought it. The soft dark plumes of the cypresses against the sky were motionless; there were star-shadows on the grass, and something was calling her to sleep, and she was sinking, sinking into the utmost recess of slumber, where even dreams are forgotten and out of mind.

Within the house the lights burnt lower and lower. Men and women came from it in twos and threes, singly, or in loitering companies. Presently they came no more. All was still, – the last footstep had died away, and the windows one by one darkened in the wall.

Hermas waited. Soon Mèril would come to him, – come with words or with silence, with the grace of unashamed caresses, or with the half-fear of her heart's surrendering worship. He was patient for her coming, with the patience bred of security, the decoy which ensnares men to inaction until joy's hour has passed by beyond recall, uncaptured and unpossessed.

Without Mèril slept. From time to time, in that leaden slumber, she stirred with some fret of restless awakening; once with wide-open eyes she looked upon the night, then again sleep re-entangled her in its meshes, and her weighted lids re-closed.

Within, Hermas passed from room to room. He had waited, and Mèril had not come. He sought her. He would find her somewhere sleeping, as once before in the afternoon sunlight he had found her, and she would waken, as then she had wakened. But he sought in vain. Each room was tenantless and forlorn, as solitude assumes to itself forlornness when once it has been peopled. He called her name. No answer came. Then all the darkness and the vacancy became vitalised with fears – on every threshold a terror stood sentinel – the very silence became a menace.

He relinquished his unavailing search, – he fled from the empty house, and unsought he found her. The fire of his kisses was on her lips and her eyelids and her hands, but no least quiver of response, the answer of life to life, came from the quiet figure, wrapped in that inanimate repose. He lifted her in his arms and retraced his steps; he laid her on the low window-seat where before he had found her on the first day of his home-coming. When day came, day would waken her, he told his despair, and his despair answered him. He waited and watched and waited; and the statue, with its winged brows, stood near by in sinister whiteness, with the mark of the bloodless scar, and the muteness of its passive secrecy. Over Hermas the old fantasy regained ascendency. The marble lived, lived with an evasive vitality, which, like the breath of a malignant herb, poisoned the air with unknown malady; and the statue was stronger than he, in that strange half-life which eluded his grasp. And he, Hermas, had given to the marble a form, had endowed that passive, dormant life within it with the fashioning of a man's shape, had set a weapon in its hands, and, under the image of a death-wound, had ascribed to the senseless figure a heart.

He left Mèril and drew near the statue.

. . . . .

And Mèril still slept, held in the soft prison of that tenacious slumber.

Without, the early dawn radiated in silver tints across the sky, the steel glimmers of light caught the dew-drenched grass, and, penetrating the windows, struck here and there upon a glass cup or a bright metal. Then sudden shafts of opal fires shot across the silver, and flakes of scarlet flame drifted like burning spray upon the wide expanse of the morning's blueness.

With the shock of a cry, Mèril wakened. The cry still rang in her ears, – the cry of a dream. For a moment she lay confused, doubting, wondering, until memory's balance readjusted itself, and life the substantial divided itself from life the unsubstantial, and wakefulness, with which all wakefulness she had ever known became as a blurred phantom, swept over her senses with a vividness that pierced and stung.

'Hermas,' she cried, and she repeated, 'Hermas.' Against the pedestal, where once the statue had stood, Hermas was leaning. At his feet the statue lay shattered upon the marble floor. The shaft of its weapon was broken, the hilt severed from the hand which had held it, and in the hand of Hermas lay the point of the splintered blade.

'The statue is dead,' said Hermas.

Mèril came swiftly towards him; her eyes saw him alone, her heart beat for the captivity of his hand.

'I slept,' she said, 'but I have wakened.'

Her eyes shone; the whole joy of the summer daybreak, its strength and its fullness, was in the beating of her pulses, its rose-colour on her lips.

Hermas stirred; he moved as if to meet her – then he fell back to the same posture.

'The statue is dead,' he repeated. She was beside him, she clasped her arms round his neck – his words had no significance to her ears.

'Life has come to me,' she whispered. 'It has come that I may give it back to you – give all that you demand. My grief is gone.'

Hermas raised himself erect. He held her to him and with blind lips sought hers. When he released her, her eyes fell upon the sword point. It lay where it had fallen from his hand, – the sword point which he had drawn from his breast.

'Hermas,' Mèril cried with sudden terror, 'the blade is wet.'

Original Sin

Vincent O'Sullivan

American poet, short-story writer and critic, Vincent O'Sullivan (1868–1940) spent most of his life in Paris and London, mingling with the likes of Beardsley, Dowson, Symons, Leonard Smithers and John Davidson. He also contributed works to *The Savoy*. In the mid-nineties he became a loyal friend to Oscar Wilde, assisting him financially and publicly defending him in the aftermath of his conviction. As Holbrook Jackson comments, O'Sullivan was one of the chief players of the *fin-de-siècle* Decadent scene, 'a modern of the moderns'. His literary works include the poetry volumes *Poems* (1896) and *The Houses of Sin* (1897), the collection of prose poems

The Green Window (1899) and the novellas collected in *A Dissertation upon Second Fiddles* (1902).

'Original Sin' appears in O'Sullivan's short-story collection *A Book of Bargains: Stories of the Weird and the Fantastic* (1896) published by Smithers with a frontispiece by Aubrey Beardsley, and was advertised in the last number of *The Savoy*. The book shocked with its explorations of misanthropy and aberrance; The *Yorkshire Post* condemned it as 'offal' and called for the author's and publisher's prosecution. As with 'A Study of Murder', this tale reveals O'Sullivan's obsession with morbid psychology, perversion and murder – themes that intertwine with the feelings of sinfulness and guilt that suffuse his poetry. In this harrowing version of the Victorian cult of the child, the protagonist, Alphonse D'Aubert, fits the doppelgänger trope, thereby evoking Stevenson's *Dr Jekyll and Mr Hyde*. O'Sullivan's airtight story is a masterful and nuanced study of criminal psychology, degeneration and destructive desire, tinged with sexual undertones.

Sans cesse à mes côtes s'agite le Démon,
Il nage autour de moi comme un air impalpable;
Je l'avale, et le sens qui brûle mon poumon
Et l'emplit d'un désir éternel et coupable.

— *Les Fleurs du Mal.*

When Alphonse D'Aubert had laid down his book for the fifth time, having taken it up five times in his wrestle with his thoughts, he decided that even *L'Ennemi des Lois* could not distract him, and so, at four o'clock in the morning, he went into the streets. As he crossed the deserted *Boulevard*, a little boy drew near with a plaintive cry: '*Charité, Monsieur!*' and Alphonse, who was almost morbidly good-natured, gave him an alms, and paused for a few minutes of pleasant talk. When he fell to his walk again, he began to consider, with a sort of sick wonder, why the child who lived in his mind to such fell purpose, could not become to him as this child he had just left: as all other children, — exquisite, helpless, piteous things, craving for love and protection. Thus it was always with him: after his blackest nights he was ever in the morning at his penitentials; and when the dawn was creeping over the roofs of the houses, he forgot how feverishly he had yearned in the darkness to press his long fingers on the soft throat of a child.

Whether Alphonse was in love with Madame Dantonel or not, it may be said that she was the creature he cared most for on earth. Certainly, on her side, she looked for nothing more tender than a friendship with this somewhat strange young man, whom, in a way of motherly tenderness, she regarded, with his *bizarreries*, his exclusiveness, his superior silences, as a rather terrible child, spoilt by his excellent fortune in the world. At her house in the *Champs-Elysées* he found himself most readily at his ease; and this fact led him by the hand to the opinion, that he was never in the least happy when he was not there. She was the widow of a man who had been engaged with politics: Alphonse never troubled to inquire how engaged; only recognised the death of the political person as a relief, and as a period to the slight embarrassment with which he was wont to listen to the patriotics — an embarrassment which all forms of activity brought to his contemplative and somewhat melancholy spirit. And after that, he was never so serene, so nearly joyous, as when he was in the company of Madame Dantonel and the little Clotilde, her only child, who was now four years old.

It was on a day when he was most delightful, when he was taking life gaily, that, looking at the little girl as she played on the floor, the stunning desire came to him to take her by the throat and squeeze out her life. He took his leave in manifest disturbance; and fled into the street. He was shaking with horror: of a truth he loved this child, next to its mother, supremely; and yet, amid his disgust, he could not stifle a lust to murder her, — a thrilling satisfaction, as he thought of the life ebbing from her face while he crushed her soft round throat with his fingers. That was the first bad night of the many bad nights to come. On the following afternoon he went to the house again, to try himself — to see how he would 'get on'; but within five minutes he departed, grinding his teeth and biting at nails to keep down his passion, which was driving him to rush back to the house and slay the child before its mother's face. But after a ghastly night of torture, and sweat, and weeping, he found himself, in the morning, suddenly recovered! All his old affection for the child once more lived in his heart: the devil, it seemed, had been worsted; and it was in this glad condition that he lived for a few weeks. He had given Clotilde many presents before; but now he spent hours in the toy-shops, finding a certain piety in thus eagerly buying, as though he were making good a case with his conscience. Ah, those few excellent days! How brilliant he was; how he dealt with the sunshine; how airily he tossed a salute to the passengers in the street!

But it was on a dreary afternoon, when the rain was whipping through the court-yard, as Alphonse stood talking lightly to Madame Dantonel and the child, that he suddenly knew himself to be the slave of his old passion. Oh, to crush that satin throat! He made one tremendous, straining effort, and so beat himself; but the effort was too much for his physical strength, and he fell on the floor as if dead.

When he began to get his senses, he found Madame Dantonel bending over him with a look of sharp anxiety.

'Ah, my poor friend!' she exclaimed, 'but you have been very ill!'

'I have been ill, but now I am well,' says Alphonse, in a thick voice. 'I am going away — far away from Paris.'

'Going away!' And when she got over her surprise: 'But why?'

'Because I do no good here,' he said, getting on his feet. 'Because I find my life too narrow. I go to the *café*, I chat, I smoke cigarettes. Good. I dine, I go to the opera, to a *soirée*. My God!' he cries out, 'do you call that a life? Please, my dearest friend, do not prevent me. I am going away.'

She took his hand very kindly. 'Go, if you wish it,' she said; 'but remember that you have always two friends here. Is it not so, Clotilde?'

Alphonse was taken with a hard shudder as he went out.

He decided to go to England; with an ultimate thought, perhaps, of America. He crossed the channel in wintry and boisterous weather, and when he came to Dover he was well content to lie there; postponing, gratefully enough, his arrival at London till the next day. Tired with his tossing journey, he took to his bed early; and at once fell into the profound sleep of fatigue, from which he awoke, about two o'clock, hot and trembling. The figure of the child was before him in the darkness of the room; the full throat, above all! was apparent and particular. He rolled on the bed, and tore and bit the pillows: not before had he longed with this violent frenzy to see the child stretched at his feet, looking solidly white and dead. Damp and shaking, he put on his clothes and went down to talk with the night-porter — a desperate chance under the best conditions; for a foreigner, hopeless! as he found. So he returned to his room, and opened his windows to the raining night. A strong salt wind was singing up channel; and Alphonse let it get into his hair and eyes, finding respite in this way, and a certain peace. Thus he spent the night, till the dawn came to shew the grey, uneasy sea, and the grey sky. He departed, when morning had come, on board the earliest packet-boat, and that evening he found himself again in Paris.

Things having come to this point, you may ask fairly: Why did he not turn to the obvious remedy — self-destruction? Yes! But upon reflection it does not seem so likely. Indeed, upon reflection it would appear, that when a man has a desire, a fierce lust to satisfy, he prefers, however the powers of his soul may rebel, to live for the gratification of that desire, that fierce lust. Be that as it will, the man I am writing about did not contemplate suicide; did not, for a moment, glance along that road of escape. But he gave a dainty supper, to which he invited some of his male acquaintance, and a few ladies of generous virtue. There sat by him a superb creature, with gleaming shoulders and snapping black eyes; and as the mirth grew more disordered, he laid his hand on her swelling throat and tried to tempt himself to kill her in the sight of the revellers. Any one rather than the child! But even as he thought it, the child floated before his eyes; the remembrance of the strange satiety he would feel when he had choked out her life, which he would not feel at all were he to kill this woman, caused his hand to fall listlessly to his side; and pleading a sudden dizziness, he left the merry-makers to themselves.

So on the next afternoon, we find him once more repairing to the *Champs-Elysées* and the house of Madame Dantonel. He was feeling easier to-day; and he discovered at Madame Dantonel's, one visitor who helped to soothe his irritated nerves. This was an old military officer; and Alphonse found his cheerfulness and honest geniality of character very pleasant. He had sat for about twenty minutes, when Madame Dantonel exclaimed: —

'My poor little Clotilde! She has a cold, a slight sore throat, and this is the time when the *bonne* goes down-stairs, so she will be quite alone. Forgive me if I go to her.'

The time had come. 'Permit me!' said Alphonse, on his feet in an instant. It was as though a stranger were talking: he could no more help the words than he could help breathing. 'Pray do not deprive *Monsieur* of your company. I will go to Clotilde; it will delight me to see her, and I know the room quite well.'

He hardly waited for the murmured pleasure, but ran, trembling with eagerness, up the stairs. The little girl was in bed playing with her doll, and she greeted him with a smile and a glad cry. He clenched his teeth, and squeezed and crushed her throat till the pretty tiny face became black and swollen, and the poor little frame, after a shake and a quiver, lay quite still.

As he came down, he heard Madame Dantonel say good-bye to the visitor, and the hush of her dress as she passed through the hall.

'*Mon Dieu!* how pale you look!' she cried, raising both hands. 'Is anything the matter with Clotilde?'

'Clotilde is very well,' says Alphonse. 'But I think the room was too hot for me, and I am going away now.'

'Really! so soon?' she said, genuinely sorry. And she held out her hand.

'No! please don't shake hands with me, I am not worthy!' cries Alphonse, with a wan smile, passing the matter off as a jest. 'You will find Clotilde very well,' he said again.

The door closed behind him. As the mother went upstairs to her child, he took his way to a chymist's shop which he knew of in the neighbourhood.

Xélucha

M. P. Shiel

Matthew Phipps Shiell (1865–1947), born in the West Indies, was a prolific writer, mostly of novels and short stories. Famously, in his teens, with the blessing of the authorities of the British Empire, as legend has it, Shiel was crowned by his father King of Redonda, an uninhabited, volcanic islet in the vicinity of Montserrat, and since a quasi-serious 'micronation' or virtual kingdom. Together with the work of such British authors as Machen, Gilchrist and Robert W. Chambers, Shiel's oeuvre is eclectic, arcane and has an exotic and bizarre beauty. Shiel's fiction exhibits a grandiose, visionary power that is unique in English literature, tackling such themes of racialism, colonialism, Nietzschean vitality and warfare. Selections from his early publications, especially the detective stories collected in *Prince Zaleski* (1895), the stories of *Shapes in the Fire* (1896) and his scientific romance *The Purple Cloud* (1901), feature some of the most Decadent, dazzlingly laden and bejewelled prose of the era.

'Xélucha' is a supernatural, urban Gothic fantasia which explores male hysteria, anxiety and a simultaneous erotic fascination with the inscrutable other that is embodied in the feminine. The story confirms Shiel as a master stylist, whose heavily ornamented prose tops even Gautier, Huysmans and Wilde. The baroque, ostentatious use of language and scholasticism, the web of erudite vocabulary, arcana, obscurities, allusions and echoes is so extreme that English almost morphs into an alien medium. It is as if the seductive yet revolting *femme fatale* Xélucha transmutes into the very purple textual surface itself. As Susan Navarette claims, the story facilitates 'the reader's covertly lecherous experience with the Decadent text'. This is a story of artifice, of efflorescent decay and morbid anatomy. Like an extreme Paterian Mona Lisa, Xélucha possesses a dangerous level of scientific knowledge; and with her condescending attitude towards Mérimée's ignorance, Shiel upsets Victorian gender stereotypes.

※

> He goeth after her ... and knoweth not ...

[FROM A DIARY]

Three days ago! by heaven, it seems an age. But I am shaken — my reason is debauched. A while since, I fell into a momentary coma precisely resembling an attack of *petit mal*. 'Tombs, and worms, and epitaphs' — that is my dream. At my age, with my physique, to walk staggery, like a man stricken! But all that will pass: I must collect myself — my reason is debauched. Three days ago! it seems an age! I sat on the floor before an old cista full of letters. I lighted upon a packet of Cosmo's. Why, I had forgotten them! they are turning sere! Truly, I can no more call myself a young man. I sat reading, listlessly, rapt back by memory. To muse is to be lost! of *that* evil habit I must wring the neck, or look to perish. Once more I threaded the mazy sphere-harmony of the minuet, reeled in the waltz, long pomps of candelabra, the noonday of the bacchanal, about me. Cosmo was the very tsar and maharajah of the Sybarites! the Priap of the *détraqués!* In every unexpected alcove of the Roman Villa was a couch, raised high, with necessary foot-stool, flanked and canopied with *mirrors* of clarified gold. Consumption fastened upon him; reclining at last at table, he could, till warmed, scarce lift the wine! his eyes were like two fat glow-worms, coiled together! they seemed haloed with vaporous emanations of phosphorus! Desperate, one could see, was the secret struggle with the Devourer. But to the end the princely smile persisted calm; to the end — to the last day — he continued among that comic crew unchallenged choragus of all the rites, I will not say of Paphos, but of Chemos! and Baal-Peor! Warmed, he did not refuse the revel, the dance, the darkened chamber. It was utterly black, rayless; approached by a secret passage; in shape circular; the air hot, haunted always by odours of balms, bdellium, hints of dulcimer and flute; and radiated round with a hundred thick-strewn ottomans of Morocco. Here Lucy Hill stabbed to the heart Caccofogo, mistaking the scar on his back for the scar of Soriac. In a bath of malachite the Princess Egla, waking late one morning, found Cosmo lying stiffly dead, the water covering him wholly.

'But in God's name, Mérimée!' (so he wrote), 'to think of Xélucha dead!

Xélucha! Can a moon-beam, then, perish of suppurations? Can the rainbow be eaten by worms? Ha! ha! ha! laugh with me, my friend: "*elle dérangera l'Enfer*"! She will introduce the *pas de tarantule* into Tophet! Xélucha, the feminine! Xélucha recalling the splendid harlots of history! Weep with me — manat rara meas lacrima per genas! expert as Thargelia; cultured as Aspatia; purple as Semiramis. She comprehended the human tabernacle, my friend, its secret springs and tempers, more intimately than any *savant* of Salamanca who breathes. *Tarare* — but Xélucha is not dead! Vitality is not mortal; you cannot wrap flame in a shroud. Xélucha! where then is she? Translated, perhaps — rapt to a constellation like the daughter of Leda. She journeyed to Hindostan, accompanied by the train and appurtenance of a Begum, threatening descent upon the Emperor of Tartary. I spoke of the desolation of the West; she kissed me, and promised return. Mentioned you, too, Mérimée — "her Conqueror" — "Mérimée, Destroyer of Woman". A breath from the conservatory rioted among the ambery whiffs of her forelocks, sending it singly a-wave over that thulite tint you know. Costumed cap-à-pie, she had, my friend, the dainty little completeness of a daisy mirrored bright in the eye of the browsing ox. A simile of Milton had for years, she said, inflamed the lust of her Eye: "The barren plains of Sericana, where Chineses drive with sails and wind their cany wagons light." I, and the Sabaeans, she assured me, wrongly considered Flame the whole of being; the other half of things being Aristotle's quintessential light. In the Ourania Hierarchia and the Faust-book you meet a completeness: burning Seraph, Cherûb full of eyes. Xélucha combined them. She would reconquer the Orient for Dionysius, and return. I heard of her blazing at Delhi; drawn in a chariot by lions. Then this rumour — probably false. Indeed, it comes from a source somewhat turgid. Like Odin, Arthur, and the rest, Xélucha — will reappear.'

Soon subsequently, Cosmo lay down in his balneum of malachite, and slept, having drawn over him the water as a coverlet. I, in England, heard little of Xélucha: first that she was alive, then dead, then alighted at old Tadmor in the Wilderness, Palmyra now. Nor did I greatly care, Xélucha having long since turned to apples of Sodom in my mouth. Till I sat by the cista of letters and re-read Cosmo, she had for some years passed from my active memories.

The habit is now confirmed in me of spending the greater part of the day in sleep, while by night I wander far and wide through the city under the sedative influence of a tincture which has become necessary to my life. Such an existence of shadow is not without charm; nor, I think, could many minds be steadily subjected to its conditions without elevation, deepened awe. To travel alone with the Primordial cannot but be solemn. The moon is of the hue of the glow-worm; and Night of the sepulchre. Nux bore not less Thanatos than Hupnos, and the bitter tears of Isis redundulate to a flood. At three, if a cab rolls by, the sound has the augustness of thunder. Once, at two, near a corner, I came upon a priest, seated, dead, leering, his legs bent. One arm, supported on a knee, pointed with rigid accusing forefinger obliquely upward. By exact observation, I found that he indicated Betelgeux, the star 'a' which shoulders the wet sword of Orion. He was hideously swollen, having perished of dropsy. Thus in all Supremes is a *grotesquerie*; and one of the sons of Night is — Buffo.

In a London square deserted, I should imagine, even in the day, I was aware of the metallic, silvery-clinking approach of little shoes. It was three in a heavy morning of winter, a day after my rediscovery of Cosmo. I had stood by the railing, regarding the clouds sail as under the sea-legged pilotage of a moon wrapped in cloaks of inclemency. Turning, I saw a little lady, very gloriously dressed. She had walked straight to me. Her head was bare, and crisped with the amber stream which rolled lax to a globe, kneaded thick with jewels, at her nape. In the redundance of her décolleté development, she resembled Parvati, mound-hipped love-goddess of the luscious fancy of the Brahmin.

She addressed to me the question:

'What are you doing there, darling?'

Her loveliness stirred me, and Night is *bon camarade*. I replied:

'Sunning myself by means of the moon.'

'All that is borrowed lustre,' she returned, 'you have got it from old Drummond's *Flowers of Sion*.'

Looking back, I cannot remember that this reply astonished me, though it should — of course — have done so. I said:

'On my soul, no; but you?'

'You might guess whence *I* come!'

'You are dazzling. You come from Paz.'

'Oh, farther than that, my son! Say a subscription ball in Soho.'

'Yes? . . . and alone? in the cold? on foot . . . ?'

'Why, I am old, and a philosopher. I can pick you out riding Andromeda yonder from the ridden Ram. They are in error, M'sieur, who suppose an atmosphere on the broad side of the moon. I have reason to believe that on Mars dwells a race whose lids are transparent like glass; so that the eyes are visible during sleep; and every varying dream moves imaged forth to the beholder in tiny panorama on the limpid iris. You cannot imagine me a mere *fille*! To be escorted is to admit yourself a woman, and that is improper in Nowhere. Young Eos drives an *equipage à quatre*, but Artemis "walks" alone. Get out of my borrowed light in the name of Diogenes! I am going home.'

'Far?'

'Near Piccadilly.'

'But a cab?'

'No cabs for *me*, thank you. The distance is a mere nothing. Come.'

We walked forward. My companion at once put an interval between us, quoting from the *Spanish Curate* that the open is an enemy to love. The Talmudists, she twice insisted, rightly held the hand the sacredest part of the person, and at that point also contact was for the moment interdict. Her walk was extremely rapid. I followed. Not a cat was anywhere visible. We reached at length the door of a mansion in St. James's. There was no light. It seemed tenantless, the windows all uncurtained, pasted across, some of them, with the words, To Let. My companion, however, flitted up the steps, and, beckoning, passed inward. I, following, slammed the door, and was in darkness. I heard her ascend, and presently a region of glimmer above revealed a stairway of marble, curving broadly up. On the floor where I stood was no carpet, nor furniture: the dust was very thick. I had begun to mount when, to my surprise, she stood by my side, returned; and whispered:

'To the very top, darling.'

She soared nimbly up, anticipating me. Higher, I could no longer doubt that the house was empty but for us. All was a vacuum full of dust and echoes. But at the top, light streamed from a door, and I entered a good-sized oval saloon, at about the centre of the house. I was completely dazzled by the sudden resplendence of the apartment. In the midst was a spread table, square, opulent with gold plate, fruit, dishes; three ponderous chandeliers of electric light above; and I noticed also (what was very *bizarre*) one little candlestick of common tin containing an old soiled curve of tallow, on the table. The impression of the whole chamber was one of gorgeousness not less than Assyrian. An ivory couch at the far end was made sun-like by a head-piece of chalcedony forming a sea for the sport of emerald ichthyotauri. Copper hangings, panelled with mirrors in iasperated crystal, corresponded with a dome of flame and copper; yet this latter, I now remember, produced upon my glance an impression of actual grime. My companion reclined on a small Sigma couch, raised high to the table-level in the Semitic manner, visible to her saffron slippers of satin. She pointed me a seat opposite. The incongruity of its presence in the middle of this arrogance of pomp so tickled me, that no power could have kept me from a smile: it was a grimy chair, mean, all wood, nor was I long in discovering one leg somewhat shorter than its fellows.

She indicated wine in a black glass bottle, and a tumbler, but herself made no pretence of drinking or eating. She lay on hip and elbow, *petite*, resplendent, and looked gravely upward. I, however, drank.

'You are tired,' I said, 'one sees that.'

'It is precious little that *you* see!' she returned, dreamy, hardly glancing.

'How! your mood is changed, then? You are morose.'

'You never, I think, saw a Norse passage-grave?'

'And abrupt.'

'Never?'

'A passage-grave? No.'

'It is worth a journey! They are circular or oblong chambers of stone, covered by great earth-mounds, with a "passage" of slabs connecting them with the outer air. All round the chamber the dead sit with head resting upon the bent knees, and consult together in silence.'

'Drink wine with me, and be less Tartarean.'

'You certainly seem to be a fool,' she replied with perfect sardonic iciness. 'Is it not, then, highly romantic? They belong, you know, to the Neolithic age. As the teeth fall, one by one, from the lipless mouths — they are caught by the lap. When the lap thins — they roll to the floor of stone. Thereafter, every tooth that drops all round the chamber sharply breaks the silence.'

'Ha! ha! ha!'

'Yes. It is like a century-slow, circularly-successive dripping of slime in some cavern of the far subterrene.'

'Ha! ha! This wine seems heady! They express themselves in a dialect largely dental.'

'The Ape, on the other hand, in a language wholly guttural.'

A town-clock tolled four. Our talk was holed with silences, and heavy-paced. The wine's yeasty exhalation reached my brain. I saw her through mist, dilating large, uncertain, shrinking again to dainty compactness. But amorousness had died within me.

'Do you know,' she asked, 'what has been discovered in one of the *Danish Kjökkenmöddings* by a little boy? It was ghastly. The skeleton of a huge fish with human ——'

'You are most unhappy.'

'Be silent.'

'You are full of care.'

'I think you a great fool.'

'You are racked with misery.'

'You are a child. You have not even an instinct of the meaning of the word.'

'How! Am I not a man? I, too, miserable, careful?'

'You are not, really, *anything* — until you can create.'

'Create what?'

'Matter.'

'That is foppish. Matter cannot be created, nor destroyed.'

'Truly, then, you must be a creature of unusually weak intellect, I see that now. Matter does not exist, then, there is no such thing, really, — it is an appearance, a spectrum — every writer not imbecile from Plato to Fichte has, voluntary or involuntary, proved that for your good. To create it is to produce an impression of its reality upon the senses of others; to destroy it is to wipe a wet rag across a scribbled slate.'

'Perhaps. I do not care. Since no one can do it.'

'No one? You are mere embryo ——'

'Who then?'

'*Anyone*, whose power of Will is equivalent to the gravitating force of a star of the First Magnitude.'

'Ha! ha! ha!' By heaven, you choose to be facetious. Are there then wills of such equivalence?'

'There have been three, the founders of religions. There was a fourth: a cobbler of Herculaneum, whose mere volition induced the cataclysm of Vesuvius in 79, in direct opposition to the gravity of Sirius. There are more fames than *you* have ever sung, you know. The greater number of disembodied spirits, too, I feel certain ——'

'By heaven, I cannot but think you full of sorrow! Poor wight! come, drink with me. The wine is thick and boon. Is it not Setian? It makes you sway and swell before me, I swear, like a purple cloud of evening ——'

'But you are mere clayey ponderance! — I did not know that! — you are no companion! your little interest revolves round the lowest centres.'

'Come — forget your agonies ——'

'What, think you, is the portion of the buried body first sought by the worm?'

'The eyes! the eyes!'
'You are *hideously* wrong — you are so *utterly* at sea ——'
'My God!'

She had bent forward with such rage of contradiction as to approach me closely. A loose gown of amber silk, wide-sleeved, had replaced her ball attire, though at what opportunity I could not guess; wondering, I noticed it as she now placed her palms far forth upon the table. A sudden wafture as of spice and orange-flowers, mingled with the abhorrent faint odour of mortality over-ready for the tomb, greeted my sense. A chill crept upon my flesh.

'You are so *hopelessly* at fault ——'
'For God's sake ——'
'You are so *miserably* deluded! Not the eyes *at all*!'
'Then, in Heaven's name, what?'
Five tolled from a clock.

'*The Uvula*! the soft drop of mucous flesh, you know, suspended from the palate above the glottis. They eat through the face-cloth and cheek, or crawl by the lips through a broken tooth, filling the mouth. They make straight for it. It is the *delicioe* of the vault.'

At her horror of interest I grew sick, at her odour, and her words. Some unspeakable sense of insignificance, of debility, held me dumb.

'You say I am full of sorrows. You say I am racked with woe; that I gnash with anguish. Well, you are a mere child in intellect. You use words without realisation of meaning like those minds in what Leibnitz calls "symbolical consciousness". But suppose it were so ——'

'It is so.'
'You know nothing.'
'I see you twist and grind. Your eyes are very pale. I thought they were hazel. They are of the faint bluishness of phosphorus shimmerings seen in darkness.'

'That proves nothing.'
'But the "white" of the sclerotic is dyed to yellow. And you look inward. Why do you look so palely inward, so woe-worn, upon your soul? Why can you speak of nothing but the sepulchre, and its rottenness? Your eyes seem to me wan with centuries of vigil, with mysteries and millenniums of pain.'

'Pain! but you know so *little* of it! you are wind and words! of its philosophy and *rationale* nothing!'

'Who knows?'

'I will give you a hint. It is the sub-consciousness in conscious creatures of Eternity, and of eternal loss. The least prick of a pin not Paean and Aesculapius and the powers of heaven and hell can utterly heal. Of an ever-lasting loss of pristine wholeness the conscious body is sub-conscious, and "pain" is its sigh at the tragedy. So with all pain — greater, the greater the loss. The hugest of losses is, of course, the loss of Time. If you lose that, any of it, you plunge at once into the transcendentalisms, the infinitudes, of Loss; if you lose *all of it* ——'

'But you so wildly exaggerate! Ha! ha! You rant, I tell you, of common-places with the woe ——'

'Hell is where a clear, untrammelled Spirit is sub-conscious of lost Time; where it boils and writhes with envy of the living world; *hating* it for ever, and all the sons of Life!'

'But curb yourself! Drink — I implore — I *implore* — for God's sake — but *once* ——'

'To *hasten* to the snare — *that* is woe! to drive your ship upon the *lighthouse* rock — that is Marah! To wake, and feel it irrevocably true that you went after her — *and the dead were there* — and her guests were in the depths of hell — *and you did not know it!* — though you *might* have. Look out upon the houses of the city this dawning day: not one, I tell you, but in it haunts some soul — walking up and down the old theatre of its little Day — goading imagination by a thousand childish tricks, vraisemblances — elaborately duping itself into the momentary fantasy *that it still lives*, that the chance of life is not for ever and for ever lost — yet riving all the time with under-memories of the wasted Summer, the lapsed brief light between the two eternal glooms — riving I say and shriek to you! — riving, *Mérimée, you destroying fiend* ——'

She had sprung — *tall* now, she seemed to me — between couch and table.

'Mérimée!' I screamed, —— '*my* name, harlot, in your maniac mouth! By God, woman, you terrify me to death!'

I too sprang, the hairs of my head catching stiff horror from my fancies.

'Your name? Can you imagine me ignorant of your name, or anything concerning you? Mérimée! Why, did you not sit yesterday and read of me in a letter of Cosmo's?'

'Ah-h . . . ,' hysteria bursting high in sob and laughter from my arid lips — 'Ah! ha! ha! Xélucha! My memory grows palsied and grey, Xélucha! pity me — my walk is in the very valley of shadow! — senile and sere!

— observe my hair, Xélucha, its grizzled growth — trepidant, Xélucha, clouded — I am not the man you knew, Xélucha, in the palaces — of Cosmo! You are Xélucha!'

'You rave, poor worm!' she cried, her face contorted by a species of malicious contempt. 'Xélucha died of cholera ten years ago at Antioch. I wiped the froth from her lips. Her nose underwent a green decay before burial. So far sunken into the brain was the left eye ——'

'You are — *you are Xélucha!*' I shrieked; 'voices now of thunder howl it within my consciousness — and by the holy God, Xélucha, though you blight me with the breath of the hell you are, I shall clasp you, — living or damned ——'

I rushed toward her. The word 'Madman!' hissed as by the tongues of ten thousand serpents through the chamber, I heard; a belch of pestilent corruption puffed poisonous upon the putrid air; for a moment to my wildered eyes there seemed to rear itself, swelling high to the roof, a formless tower of ragged cloud, and before my projected arms had closed upon the very emptiness of inanity, I was tossed by the operation of some Behemoth potency far-circling backward to the utmost circumference of the oval, where, my head colliding, I fell, shocked, into insensibility.

. . . . . .

When the sun was low toward night, I lay awake, and listlessly observed the grimy roof, and the sordid chair, and the candlestick of tin, and the bottle of which I had drunk. The table was small, filthy, of common deal, uncovered. All bore the appearance of having stood there for years. But for them, the room was void, the vision of luxury thinned to air. Sudden memory flashed upon me. I scrambled to my feet, and plunged and tottered, bawling, through the twilight into the street.

The Death of Peter Waydelin

Arthur Symons

'The Death of Peter Waydelin' is the perfect example of a condensed *Künstlerroman* as it concerns a painter and his sacrifice for art. The topoi of the self-destructive genius, Symbolist vision, avant-gardism and bohemianism, are all present in this story which is a most vivid ecapsulation of the culture of the 1890s. The triumph of style over content is at its core; as Waydelin says, all art 'is a way of seeing'. Symons himself provides a succinct commentary on his story and the models on which Waydelin is based, in the unpublished typescript, 'The Genesis of Spiritual Adventures':

> 'The Death of Peter Waydelin' which is a morbid analysis of diseased nerves and of a depraved imagination, had no other basis than my recollections of Toulouse-Lautrec and Aubrey Beardsley. It was conceived cruelly; and it seems to me the only one of the stories which is realistic. I made it out of many curious and sinister incidents I had seen in the East End and in Soho and in a certain house such as those I have described in Islington; a house in one of those hideous streets capable of giving anyone who has returned from abroad what even the French call 'spleen'. Waydelin accepted his fate, because his existence had turned back upon him, in the invariable way of those who have failed in achieving what they had set their hearts on young. And there is Clara, who has had her part in his ruin, passionless and painted. I give here my own impressions of Sada Yacco and of those of Waydelin: near the end of this he refers to Lautrec without mentioning his name.

Prior to its appearance in *Spiritual Adventures* (1905), the story was published in *Lippincott's Monthly* with the title 'Peter Waydelin's Experiment' (1904). The story indeed recounts the artist's experiment in immersing himself in the animalistic, corroding life of music halls, in order to remain true to his artistic vision. The central conundrum of Decadence – Art versus Life – is probed at the heart of the tale, as artifice and nature, and the artistic framing of nature are woven together.

Peter Waydelin, the painter of those mysterious, brutal pictures, who died last year at the age of twenty-four, spent a week with me at Bognor, trying to get better, a little while before it was quite certainly too late; and we had long talks of a very intimate kind as we lay and lounged about the sand from Selsey to Blake's Felpham, along that exquisite coast. To him, if he were to be believed, all that meant very little; he hated nature, he was always assuring you; but at Bognor nature deals with its material so much in the manner of art that he can hardly have been sincere in not feeling the colour-sense of those arrangements of sand, water, and sky which were perpetually changing before him. One of our conversations that I remembered best, because he seemed to put more of himself into it than usual, took place one afternoon in June as we lay on the sand about half-way towards Selsey, beyond the last of those troublesome groins, and I remember that as I listened to him, and heard him defining so sincerely his own ideas of art, I was conscious all the time of a magnificent silent refutation of some of those ideas, as nature, quietly expressing herself before us, transformed the whole earth gradually into a new and luminous world of air. He did not seem to see the sunset; now and then he would pick up a pebble and throw it vehemently, almost angrily, into the water. We were talking of art. He began to explain to me what art meant to him, and what it was he wanted to do with his own art. I remember almost the very words he used, sometimes so serious, sometimes so petulant and boyish. I was interested in his ideas, and the man too interested me; so young and so experienced, so mature already and so enthusiastic under his cynicism. He puzzled me: it was as if there were a clue wanting; I could not get further with him than a certain point, frank, self-explanatory even, as he seemed to be. Of himself he never spoke, only of his ideas. I knew vaguely that he had been in Paris, and I supposed that he had been living there for some time. I had met him in London, in the street, quite casually, and he had looked so ill that I had asked him there and then to come with me to Bognor, where I was going. He agreed willingly, and was at the station with his bag the next day. I never ask people about their private affairs, and his talk was entirely about pictures, his own chiefly, and about ideas. As he talked I tried to piece together the man and his words. What was it in this man, who was so much a gentleman, that drew him instinctively, whenever he took up a brush or a pencil, towards gross things, things that he painted as if he hated them, but painted always? Was it a theory or an enslavement? and had he, in order to interpret with so cruel a fidelity so much that was factitious and dishonourable in life, sunk to the level of what he painted? I could not tell. He was not obviously the man of his pictures, nor was he obviously the reverse. I felt in those pictures, and I felt equally, but differently, in the man, a fundamental sincerity; after that came I know not how much of pose, perhaps merely the defiant pose of youth. He was a problem to me, which I wanted to think out; and I listened very attentively to everything that he said on that afternoon when he was so much more communicative than usual.

'All art, of course,' he said, 'is a way of seeing, and I have my way. I did not get to it at once. Like everybody else, I began by seeing too much. Gradually I gave up seeing things in shades, in subdivisions; I saw them in masses, each single. It takes more choice than you think, and more technical skill, to set one plain colour against another, unshaded, like a great, raw morsel, or a solid lump of the earth. The art of the painter, you observe, consists in seeing in a new, summarising way, getting rid of everything but the essentials; in seeing by patterns. You know how a child draws a house? Well, that is how the average man thinks he sees it, even at a distance. You have to train your eye not to see. Whistler sees nothing but the fine shades, which unite into a picture in an almost bodiless way, as Verlaine writes songs almost literally "without words". You can see, if you like, in just the opposite way: leaving in only the hard outlines, leaving out everything that lies between. To me that is the best way of summarising, the most abbreviated way. You get rid of all that molle, sticky way of work which squashes pictures into cakes and puddings, and of that stringy way of work which draws them out into tapes and ribbons. It is a way of seeing square, and painting like hits from the shoulder.

'I wonder,' he went on, after a moment, 'how many people think that I paint ugly pictures, as they call them, because I am unable to paint pretty ones? Perhaps even you have never seen any of my quite early work: Madonnas for Christmas cards and hallelujah angels for stained-glass windows. They were the prettiest things imaginable, immensely popular, and they brought me in several pounds. I take them out and show them to people who complain that I have no sense of beauty, and they always ask me pityingly why I have not gone on turning out these confectionaries.

'I contend that I have never done anything which is without beauty, because I have never done anything which is without life, and life is the source and sap of beauty. I tell you that there is not one of those grimacing masks, those horribly pale or horribly red faces, plastered white or red, leering professionally across a gulf of footlights, or a café-table, that does not live, live to the roots of the eyes, somewhere in the soul, I think! And if beauty is not the visible spirit of all that infamous flesh, when I have sabred it like that along my canvas, with all my hatred and all my admiration of its foolish energy, I at least am unable to conjecture where beauty has gone to live in the world.'

He looked at me almost indignantly, as if he took me for one of his critics. I said nothing, and he went on:

'I have done nothing, believe me, without being sure that I was doing a beautiful thing. People don't see it, it seems. How should they, when we do our best to train them up within the prison walls of a Raphael aesthetics, when we send them to the Apollo Belvedere, instead of to the marbles of Aegina? Our academies shut out nine parts of beauty and imprison us with the poor tenth, which we have never even the space to frequent casually and grow familiar with. How much of the world itself do you think exists as a thing of beauty for the average man? Why, he has to know if the most exquisite leaf in the world, the thing I came upon just now in the lane, belongs to a flower or a weed before he can tell whether he ought to commend it for existing. I hate nature, because fools prostrate themselves before sunsets; as if there is not much better drawing in that leaf than in all the Turners of the sky. You see, one has to quote Turner to apologise for a sunset!'

He laughed, really without malice, waving his hand towards the sky with a youthful impertinence. For a little while he was silent, and then, in a different tone, he said:

'I wonder if it is possible to paint what one doesn't like, to take one's models as models, and only know them for the hours during which they sit to you in this attitude or that. I don't believe that it is. Much of our bad painting comes from respectable people thinking that they can soil their hands with paint and not let the dye sink into their innermost selves. Do you know that you are the only man of my own world that I ever see, or have seen for years now? People call me eccentric; I am only logical. You can't paint the things I paint, and live in a Hampstead villa. You must come and see me some day: will you take the address? – 3 Somervell Street, Islington. It's not much like a studio. However, there's "Collins's" at hand, and I live there a good deal, you know. I lived in the Hampstead Road for some time on account of the "Bedford". But "Collins's" suits me and my models better.'

He broke off with an ambiguous laugh, flung his last stone into the water, and jumped up, as if to end the conversation. Something in the way he spoke made me feel vaguely uneasy, but I was used to his exaggerations, his way of inventing as he went along. Was I, after all, any nearer to his secret, to himself as he really was?

Waydelin went back to London and I to Russia, which I shall always remember, after that terrible summer under the gold and green domes of Moscow, as the hottest country in which I have ever been. When I came back to London I thought of Waydelin, made plan after plan to visit him, when one evening in November I received a brief note in his handwriting, asking me if I would come and see him at once, as he was very ill, and wanted to see me on a matter of business. I started immediately after dinner and got to Islington a little after nine. The street was one of those drab, hopeless streets to which a Russian observer has lately attributed the 'spleen' from which all Englishmen are thought to suffer. There was a row of houses on each side of the way, every house exactly like every other house, each with its three steps leading to the door, its bow window on one side, its strip of dingy earth in which there were a few dusty stalks between the lowest step and the railing, the paint for the most part peeling off the door, the bell-handle generally hanging out from its hole in the wall. I rang at No. 3. I had to wait for some time, and then the door was opened by an impudent-looking servant girl in a very untidy dress. I asked for Waydelin. 'Mrs. Waydelin, did you say?' said the girl, leering at me; then, calling over my head to the driver of a four-wheeler which just then drew up at the door, 'Wait five minutes, will you?' she turned to me again: 'Mr. Waydelin? I don't know if you can see him.' I told her impatiently that I had come by appointment, and she held the door open for me to come in. She knocked at a room on the first floor. 'Come in,' said a shrill voice that I did not know, and I went in.

It was a bedroom; a woman, with her bodice off, was making-up in front of the glass, and in a corner, with the clothes drawn up to his chin, a man lay in bed. The cheeks were covered by a three days' beard; they were ridged into deep hollows; large eyes, very wide open, looked out under a mass of uncombed hair, and as the face turned round on the pillow and looked at me without any change of expression I recognised Peter Waydelin. The woman, seeing me in the glass, nodded at my reflection, and said, as she drew a black pencil through her eyelashes: 'You'll excuse me, won't you? I have to be at the hall in ten minutes. Don't stand on ceremony; there's Peter. He'll be glad to see you, poor dear!' She spoke in a common and affected voice, and I thought her a deplorable person, with her carefully curled yellow hair, her rouged and powdered cheeks, her mouth glistening with lip salve, her big, empty blue eyes with their blackened under-lids, her fat arms and shoulders, the tawdry finery of her costume, half on and half off her body. I moved towards the bed, and Waydelin looked up at me with a queer, mournful smile.

'It was good of you to come,' he said, stretching out a long, thin hand to me; 'Clara has to go out, and we can have a talk. How do you like the last thing I've done?'

I lifted the drawing which was lying on the bed. It was a portrait of the woman before the glass, just as she looked now, one of the most powerful of his drawings, crueller even than usual in its insistence on the brutality of facts: the crude contrasts of bone and fat, the vulgar jaw, the brassy eyes, the reckless, conscious attitude. Every line seemed to have been drawn with hatred. I looked at Mrs. Waydelin. She had finished dressing, and she came up to the bedside to say good-bye to Peter. 'Horrid thing,' she said, nodding her head at the drawing; 'not a bit like me, is it? I assure you none of them like it at the hall. They say it doesn't do me justice. I'm sure I hope not.' I bowed and murmured something. 'Good-bye, Peter,' she said, smiling down at him in a kindly, hurried way, 'I'll come back as soon as I can,' and with a nod to me she was out of the room.

Peter drew himself slowly up in the bed, pointed to a shawl, which I wrapped round his shoulders, and then, looking at me a little defiantly, said: 'My theory, do you remember? of living the life of my models! She is a very nice woman and an excellent model, and they appreciate her very much at "Collins's"; but it appears that I have no gift for domesticity.'

I scarcely knew what to say. While I hesitated he went on: 'Don't suppose I have any illusions, or, indeed, ever had. I married that woman because I couldn't help doing it, but I knew what I was doing all the time. Have you ever been in Belgium? There is stuff they give you there to drink called Advokat, which you begin by hating, but after a time you can't get on without it. She is like Advokat.'

'You are ill, Waydelin,' I said, 'and you speak bitterly. I don't like to hear you speak like that about your wife.'

Waydelin stared at me curiously. 'So you are going to defend her against my brutality,' he said. 'I will give you every opportunity. Did you know I was married?'

I shook my head.

'I have been married three years,' he said, 'and I never told even you. I know you did not take me at my word when I talked about how one had to live in order to paint as I painted, but I did not tell you half. I have been living, if you like to call it so, systematically, not as a stranger in a foreign country which he stares at over his Baedeker, but as like a native as I could, and with no return ticket in my pocket. Why shouldn't one be as thorough in one's life as in one's drawing? Is it possible for one to be otherwise, if one is really in earnest in either? And the odd thing is, as you will say, I didn't live in that way because I wanted to do it for my art, but something deeper than my art, a profound, low instinct, drew me to these people, to this life, without my own will having anything to do with it. My work has been much more sincere than any one suspected. It used to amuse me when the papers classed me with the Decadents of a moment, and said that I was probably living in a suburban villa, with a creeper on the front wall. I have never cared for anything but London, or in London for anything but here, or the Hampstead Road, or about the Docks. I never really chose the music-halls or the public-houses; they chose me. I made the music-halls my clubs; I lived in them, for the mere delight of the thing; I liked the glitter, false, barbarous, intoxicating, the violent animality of the whole spectacle, with its imbecile words, faces, gestures, the very heat and odour, like some concentrated odour of the human crowd, the irritant music, the audience! I went there, as I went to public-houses, as I walked about the streets at night, as I kept company with vagabonds, because there was a craving in me that I could not quiet. I fitted in theories with my facts; and that is how I came to paint my pictures.'

As he spoke, with bitter ardour, I looked at him as if I were seeing him for the first time. The room, the woman, that angry drawing on the bed, and the dishevelled man dying there, just at the moment when he had learnt everything that such experiences could teach him, fell of a sudden into a revealing relation with each other. I did not know whether to feel that the man had been heroic or a fool; there had been, it was clear to me, some obscure martyrdom going on, not the less for art's sake because it came out of the mere necessity of things. A great pity came over me, and all I could say was, 'But, my dear friend, you have been very unhappy!'

'I never wanted to be happy,' said Waydelin; 'I wanted to live my own life and do my own work; and if I die to-morrow (as likely enough I may), I shall have done both things. My work satisfies me, and, because of that, so does my life.'

'Are you very ill?' I asked.

'Dead, relatively speaking,' he said in his jaunty way, which death itself could not check in him; 'I'm only waiting on some celestial order of precedence in these matters, which, I confess, I don't understand. So it was good of you to come; I would like to arrange with you about what is to be done with my work, presently, when they will have to accept me. I always said that I had only to die in order to be appreciated.'

I had a long talk with him, and I promised to carry out his wishes. All the money that his pictures brought in was to go to his wife, but, as he said, she would not know what to do with them if they were left in her own hands, not even how to turn them into money. He was quite certain that they would sell; he knew exactly the value of what he had done, and he knew how and when work finds its own level.

I sat beside the bed, talking, for more than two hours. He could no longer do much work, he said, and he hated being alone when he was not working. But it amused him to talk, for a change. 'Clara talks when she is here,' he said, with one of his queer smiles. I promised to come back and see him again. 'Come soon,' he said, 'if you want to be sure of finding me.'

I went back two days afterwards, a little later in the evening so that I need not meet Mrs. Waydelin, and he seemed better. He had shaved, his hair was brushed and combed, and he was sitting up in bed, with the shawl thrown lightly about his shoulders.

'Would you like to know,' he began, almost at once, 'how I came to paint in what we will call, if you please, my final manner? One day, at the theatre, I saw Sada Yacco. She taught me art.'

'What do you mean?' I said.

'Look here,' he went on, 'they say everything has been done in art. But no, there is at least one thing that remains for us. Have you ever seen Sada Yacco? When I saw her for the first time I said to myself, "I have found out the secret of Japanese art." I had never been able to understand how it was that the Japanese, who can imitate natural things, a bird, a flower, the rain, so perfectly, have chosen to give us, instead of a woman's face, that blind oval, in which the eyes, nose, and mouth seem to have been made to fit a pattern. When I saw Sada Yacco I realised that the Japanese painters had followed nature as closely in their women's faces as in their birds and flowers, but that they had studied them from the women of the Green Houses, the women who make up, and that Japanese women, made up for the stage or for the factitious life of the Green Houses, look exactly like these elegant, unnatural images of the painters. What a new kind of reality that opened up to me, as if a window had suddenly opened in a wall! Here, I said to myself, is something that the painters of Europe have never done; it remains for me to do it. I will study nature under the paint by which woman, after all, makes herself more woman; the ensign of her trade, her flag as the enemy. I will get at the nature of this artificial thing, at the skin underneath it, and the soul under the skin. Watteau and the Court painters have given us the dainty, exterior charm of the masquerade, woman when she plays at being woman, among "lyres and flutes". Degas, of course, has done something of what I want to do, but only a part, and with other elements in his pure design, the drawing of Ingres, setting itself new tasks, exercising its technique upon shapeless bodies in tubs, and the strained muscles of the dancer's leg as she does "side-practice". What I am going to do is to take all the ugliness, gross artifice, crafty mechanism, of sex disguising itself for its own ends: that new nature which vice and custom make out of the honest curves and colours of natural things.

'Well, I have tried to do that; in all my best work, my work of the last two or three years, I have done it. I am sure that what I have done is a new thing, and I think it is the one new thing left to us Western painters.'

'I am beginning to understand you,' I said, 'and I have not always found it easy. When I admire you, it has so often seemed to me irrational. I am gradually finding out your logic. Do you remember those talks we used to have at Bognor, one in particular, when you told me about your way of seeing?'

'Yes, yes,' he said, 'I remember, but there was one thing I am almost sure I did not tell you, and it is curious. I don't understand it myself. Do you know what it is to be haunted by colours? There is something like a temptation of the devil, to me, in the colour green. I know it is the commonest colour in nature, it is a good, honest colour, it is the grass, the trees, the leaves, very often the sea. But no, it isn't like that that it comes to me. To me it is an aniline dye, poisoning nature. I adore and hate it. I can never get away from it. If I paint a group outside a café at Montmartre by gas-light or electric light, I paint a green shadow on the faces, and I suppose the green shadow isn't there; yet I paint it. Some tinge of green finds its way invariably into my flesh-colour; I see something green in rouged cheeks, in peroxide-of-hydrogen hair; green lays hold of this poor, unhappy flesh that I paint, as if anticipating the colour-scheme of the grave. I know it, and yet I can't help doing it; I can't explain to you how it is that I at once see and don't see a thing; but so it is.

'And it grew upon me too like an obsession. I always wanted to keep my eyes perfectly clear, so that I could make my own arrangements of things for myself, deliberately; but this, in some unpleasant way, seemed horribly like "nature taking the pen out of one's hand and writing", as somebody once said about a poet. I would rather do all the writing myself; the more so, as I have to translate as I go.'

He broke off suddenly, as if a wave of exhaustion had come over him. His eyes, which had been very bright, had gone dull again, and he let his head droop till the chin rested on his breast.

'I have tired you,' I said; 'you must not talk any more. Try to go to sleep now, and I will come back another day.'

'To-morrow?' he said, looking at me sleepily.

I promised. When I went back the next day he was weaker, but he insisted on sitting up and talking. He spoke of his wife, without affection and without bitterness; he spoke of death, with so little apprehension, or even curiosity, that I was startled. His art was still a much more realisable thing to him.

'Do you believe in God, religion, and all that?' he said. 'To tell you the honest truth, I have never been able to take a vital interest in those or any other abstract matters: I am so well content with this world, if it would only go on existing, and I don't in the least care how it came into being, or what is going to happen to it after I have moved on. I suppose one ought to feel some sort of reverence for something, for an unknown power, at least, which has certainly worked to good purpose. Well, I can't. I don't know what reverence is. If I were quite healthy, I should be a pagan, and choose, well! Dionysus Zagreus, a Bacchus who has been in hell, to worship after my fashion, in some religious kind of "orgie on the mountains". That is how somebody explains the origin of religion, or was it of religious hymns? I forget; but, you see, having had this rickety sort of body to drag about with me, I have never been able to follow any of my practical impulses of that sort, and I have had to be no more than an unemployed atheist, ready to gibe at the gods he doesn't understand.

'I am afraid even in art,' he went on, as if leaving unimportant things for the one thing important, 'I don't find it easy to look up to anybody, at least in a way that anybody can be imagined as liking. I have never gone very much to the National Gallery, not because I don't think Venetian and Florentine pictures quite splendid, painted when they were, but because I can get nothing out of them that is any good for me, now in this all but twentieth century. You won't expect me, of all people, to prate about progress, but, all the same, it's no use going to Botticelli for hints about modern painting. We have different things to look at, and see them differently. A man must be of his time, else why try to put his time on the canvas? There are people, of course, who don't, if you call them painters: Watts, Burne-Jones, Moreau, that sort of hermit-crab. But I am talking about painting life and making it live. If it comes to making pictures for churches and curiosity shops!'

He spoke eagerly, but in a voice which grew more and more tired, and with long pauses. I was going to try to get him to rest when the front door opened noisily and I heard Mrs. Waydelin's voice in the hall. I heard other voices, men's and women's, feet coming up the stairs. I looked apprehensively at Waydelin. He showed no surprise. I heard a door open on the landing; then, a moment after, it was shut, and Mrs. Waydelin came into the bedroom, flushed and perspiring through the paint, and ran up to the bed.

'I have brought a few friends in to supper,' she said. 'They won't disturb you, you know, and I couldn't very well get out of it.'

She would have entered into explanations, but Waydelin cut her short.

'I have not the least objection,' he said. 'I must only ask you to apologise to them for my absence. I am hardly entertaining at present.'

She stared at him, as if wondering what he meant; then she asked me if I would join her at supper, and I declined; then went to the dressing-table, took up a pot of vaseline and looked at her eyelashes in the glass; then put it down again, came back to the bed, told Peter Waydelin to cheer up, and bounced out of the room.

I could see that Waydelin was now very tired and in need of sleep. I got up to go. The partition between the two rooms must have been very thin, for I could hear a champagne-cork drawn, the shrill laughter of women, men talking loudly, and chairs being moved about the floor. 'I don't mind,' he said, seeing what I was thinking, 'so long as they don't sing. But they won't begin to sing for two hours yet, and I can get some sleep. Goodnight. Perhaps I shall not see you again.'

'May I come again?' I said.

'I always like seeing you,' he said, smiling, and thereupon turned over on the pillow, just as he was, and fell asleep.

I looked at his face as he lay there, with the shawl about his shoulders and his hands outside the bedclothes. The jaw hung loose, the cheeks were pinched with exhaustion, sweat stood out about the eyes. The sudden collapse into sleep alarmed me. I could not leave him in such a state, and with no one at hand but those people supping in the next room. I sat down in a corner near the bed and waited.

As I sat there listening to the exuberant voices, I wondered by what casual or quixotic impulse Waydelin had been led to marry the woman, and whether the woman was really heartless because she sat drinking champagne with her friends of the music-hall while her husband, a man of genius in his way, lay dying in the next room. I forced myself to acknowledge that she had probably no suspicion of how near she was to being a widow, that Waydelin would deceive her to the end in this matter, and the last thing in the world he would desire would be to see Mrs. Waydelin in tears at the foot of the bed.

As time went on the supper-party got merrier, but Waydelin did not stir, and I sat still in my corner. It was probably in about two hours, as he had foreseen, that a chord was struck on the piano, and a man began to sing a music-hall song in a rough, facile voice. At the sound Waydelin shivered through his whole body and woke up. In a very weak voice he asked me for water. I brought him a glass of water and held it to his lips. He drank a little and then pushed it away and began shivering again. 'Let me send for a doctor,' I said, but he seized my hand, and said violently that he would see no doctor. In the next room the piano rattled and all the voices joined in the chorus. I distinguished the voice of Mrs. Waydelin. He seemed to be listening to it, and I said, 'Let me call her in.' 'Poor Clara may as well amuse herself,' he said, with his odd smile. 'What is the use? I feel very much as if I am going to die. Will it bother you: being here, I mean?' His voice seemed to grow weaker as he spoke, and his eyes stared. I left him and went hastily into the other room. The singer stopped abruptly, and the girl at the piano turned round. I saw the remains of supper on the table, the empty glasses and bottles, the chairs tilted back, the cigars, tobacco-smoke, the flushed faces, rings, artificial curls; and then Mrs. Waydelin came to me out of the midst of them, looking almost frightened, and said, 'What's the matter?' 'Get rid of these people at once,' I said in a low voice, 'and send for a doctor.' Her face sobered instantly, she took one step to the bell, was about to ring it, then turned and said to one of the men, 'Go for a doctor, Jim,' and to the others, 'You'll go, all of you, quietly?' and then she came with me into the bedroom.

Waydelin lay shivering and quaking on the bed; he seemed very conscious and wholly preoccupied with himself. He never looked at the woman as she flung herself on the floor by the bedside and began to cry out to him and kiss his hand. The tears ran down over her cheeks, leaving ghastly furrows in the wet powder, which clotted and caked under them. The curl was beginning to come out of her too yellow hair, which straggled in wisps about her ears. She sobbed in gulps, and entreated him to look at her and forgive her. At that he looked, and as he looked life seemed to revive in his eyes. He motioned to me to lift him up. I lifted him against the pillows, and in a very weak voice he asked me for drawing-paper and a pencil. 'Don't move,' he said to his wife, who knelt there struck into rigid astonishment, with terror and incomprehension in her eyes. The pose, its grotesque horror, were finer than the finest of his inventions. He made a few scrawls on the paper, trying to fix that last and best pose of his model. But he could no longer guide the pencil, and he let it drop out of his hand with a look of helplessness, almost of despair, and sank down in the bed and shut his eyes. He did not open them again. The doctor came, and tried all means to revive him, but without success. Something in him seemed consciously to refuse to come back to life. He lay for some time, dying slowly, with his eyes fast shut, and it was only when the doctor had felt his heart and found no movement that we knew he was dead.

Appendices

APPENDIX I: PARODIES

A Misunderstood Artist

H. G. Wells

With attention to the interrelation of incompatible artistic media, 'A Misunderstood Artist' is a parody of 'art for art's sake', and in particular, Whistler's 'Ten O'Clock Lecture' (1885). The story is not a vicious mockery of the Aesthetes but a whimsical and light-hearted burlesquing; it also pokes fun at the narrow-mindedness of the Philistine middle class, in overheard conversations on a train. Wells's inventiveness is in applying Whistler's tonal arrangements of colour to the culinary art of the kitchen. He plays with the idea that even the basic biological function of sustenance through food can be a beautiful and 'useless' art form.

※

The gentleman with the Jovian coiffure began to speak as the train moved. "Tis the utmost degradation of art,' he said. He had apparently fallen into conversation with his companion upon the platform.

'I don't see it,' said this companion, a prosperous-looking gentleman with a gold watch-chain. 'This art for art's sake – I don't believe in it, I tell you. Art should have an aim. If it don't do you good, if it ain't moral, I'd as soon not have it. What good is it? I believe in Ruskin. I tell you ———'

'*Bah!*' said the gentleman in the corner, with almost explosive violence. He fired it like a big gun across the path of the incipient argument and slew the prosperous-looking gentleman at once. He met our eyes, as we turned to him, with a complacent smile on his large white, clean-shaven face. He was a corpulent person, dressed in black, and with something of the quality of a second-hand bishop in his appearance. The demolished owner of the watch-chain made some beginnings of a posthumous speech.

'*Bah!*' said the gentleman in the corner, with even more force than before, and so finished him.

'These people will never understand,' he said, after a momentary pause, addressing the gentleman with the Jovian coiffure, and indicating the remains of the prosperous gentleman by a wave of a large white hand. 'Why do you argue? Art is ever for the few.'

'I did not argue,' said the gentleman with the hair. 'I was interrupted.'

The owner of the watch-chain, who had been sitting struggling with his breath, now began to sob out his indignation. 'What do you *mean*, sir? Saying *Bah!* sir, when I am talking ———'

The gentleman with the large face held up a soothing hand. 'Peace, peace,' he said. 'I did not interrupt you. I annihilated you. Why did you presume to talk to artists about art? Go away, or I shall have to say Bah! again. Go and have a fit. Leave us — two rare souls who may not meet again — to our talking.'

'Did you ever see such abominable *rudeness*, sir?' said the gentleman with the watch-chain, appealing to me. There were tears in his eyes. At the same time the young man with the aureole made some remark to the corpulent gentleman that I failed to catch.

'These artists,' said I, 'are unaccountable, irresponsible. You must ———'

'Take it from whence it comes,' said the insulted one, very loudly, and bitterly glaring at his opponent. But the two artists were conversing serenely. I felt the undignified quality of our conversation. 'Have you seen *Punch*?' said I, thrusting it into his hand.

He looked at the paper for a moment in a puzzled way; then understood, thanked me, and began to read with a thunderous scowl, every now and then shooting murderous glances at his antagonist in the opposite corner, or coughing in an aggressive manner.

'You do your best,' the gentleman with the long hair was saying; 'and they say, "What is it for?" "It is for itself," you say. Like the stars.'

'But these people,' said the stout gentleman, 'think the stars were made to set their clocks by. They lack the magnanimity to drop the personal reference. A friend, a *confrère*, saw a party of these horrible Extension people at Rome before that exquisite Venus of Titian. "And now, Mr. Something-or-other," said one of the young ladies, addressing the pedagogue in command, "what is *this* to teach us?"'

'I have had the same experience,' said the young gentleman with the hair. 'A man sent to me only a week ago to ask what my sonnet "The Scarlet Thread" *meant?*'

The stout person shook his head as though such things passed all belief.

'Gur-r-r-r,' said the gentleman with *Punch*, and scraped with his foot on the floor of the carriage.

'I gave him answer,' said the poet. 'It was a sonnet, not a symbol.'

'Precisely,' said the stout gentleman.

''Tis the fate of all art to be misunderstood. I am always grossly misunderstood — by every one. They call me fantastic, whereas I am but inevitably new; indecent, because I am unfettered by mere trivial personal restrictions; unwholesome.'

'It is what they say to me. They are always trying to pull me to earth. "Is it wholesome?" they say; "nutritious?" I say to them, "I do not know. I am an artist. I do not care. It is beautiful."'

'You rhyme?' said the poet.

'No. My work is — more plastic. I cook.'

For a moment, perhaps, the poet was disconcerted. 'A noble art,' he said, recovering.

'The noblest,' said the cook. 'But sorely misunderstood; degraded to utilitarian ends; tested by impossible standards. I have been seriously asked to render oily food palatable to a delicate patient. Seriously!'

'He said, "Bah!" Bah! to *me!*' mumbled the defunct gentleman with *Punch*, apparently addressing the cartoon. 'A cook! Good *Lord!*'

'I resigned. "Cookery," I said, "is an art. I am not a fattener of human cattle. Think: Is it Art to write a book with an object, to paint a picture for strategy?" "Are we," I said, "in the sixties or the nineties? Here, in your kitchen, I am inspired with beautiful dinners and I produce them. It is your place to gather together, from this place one, and from that one, the few precious souls who can appreciate that rare and wonderful thing, a dinner, graceful, harmonious, exquisite, perfect." And he argued I must study his guests!'

'No artist is of any worth,' said the poet, 'who primarily studies what the public needs.'

'As I told him. But the next man was worse — hygienic. While with this creature I read Poe for the first time, and I was singularly fascinated by some of his grotesques. I tried — it was an altogether new development, I believe, in culinary art — the Bizarre. I made some curious arrangements in pork and strawberries, with a sauce containing beer. Quite by accident I mentioned my design to him on the evening of the festival. All the Philistine was aroused in him. "It will ruin my digestion." "My friend," I said, "I am not your doctor; I have nothing to do with your digestion. Only here is a beautiful Japanese thing, a quaint, queer, almost eerie dinner, that is in my humble opinion worth many digestions. You may take it or leave it, but 'tis the last dinner I cook for you." . . . I knew I was wasted upon him.

'Then I produced some Nocturnes in imitation of Mr. Whistler, with mushrooms, truffles, grilled meat, pickled walnuts, black pudding, French plums, porter — a dinner in soft velvety black, eaten in a starlight of small scattered candles. That, too, led to a resignation: Art will ever demand its martyrs.'

The poet made sympathetic noises.

'Always. The awful many will never understand. Their conception of my skill is altogether on a level with their conceptions of music, of literature, of painting. For wall decorations they love autotypes; for literature, harmless volumes of twaddle that leave no vivid impressions on the mind; for dinners, harmless dishes that are forgotten as they are eaten. *My* dinners stick in the memory. I cannot study these people — my genius is all too imperative. If I needed a flavour of almonds and had nothing else to hand, I would use prussic acid. Do right, I say, as your art instinct commands, and take no heed of the consequences. Our function is to make the beautiful gastronomic thing, not to pander to gluttony, not to be the Jesuits of hygiene. My friend, you should see some of my compositions. At home I have books and books in manuscript, Symphonies, Picnics, Fantasies, *Etudes* . . .'

The train was now entering Clapham Junction. The gentleman with the gold watch-chain returned my *Punch*. 'A cook,' he said in a whisper; 'just a common cook!' He lifted his eyebrows and shook his head at me, and proceeded to extricate himself and his umbrella from the carriage. 'Out of a situation, too!' he said — a little louder — as I prepared to follow him.

'Mere dripping!' said the artist in cookery, with a regal wave of the hand.

Had I felt sure I was included, I should of course have resented the phrase.

Incurable

Lionel Johnson

Johnson's parodic tale 'Incurable' takes many clichés of the Decadent, artistic mindset, lampooning them through exaggeration. However it also works in a serious manner as it dwells on ideas of genius, posterity, and spiritual and creative angst. Johnson's narrator clearly keeps a distance from the overly sentimental and unexceptional poet, as the latter chases notoriety through his work, and even suicide. He mocks the poet's futile actions by contrasting him with his practical-minded musician friend who compares him with the most anti-Decadent character, Dickens's Pickwick.

Mist hung grey along the river, and upon the fields. From the cottage, little and lonely, shone candlelight, that looked sad to the wanderer without in the autumnal dark: he turned and faced the fields, and the dim river. And the music, the triumphing music, the rich voices of the violin, came sounding down the garden from the cottage. His mood, his mind, were those of the Flemish poet, who murmurs in sighing verse:

> Et je suis dans la nuit . . . . Oh! c'est si bon la nuit!
> Ne rien faire . . . se taire . . . et bercer son ennui,
> Au rhythme agonisant de lointaine musique ....

For this was the last evening of his life; he felt sure of that; and, foolish martyr to his own weakness that he was, he fell to meditating upon the sad scenery and circumstance of his death. The grey mist upon river and field, the acrid odours of autumn flowers in the garden, the solitariness of melancholy twilight, these were right and fitting; but there, in the cottage behind him, was his best friend, speaking with him through music, giving him his *Ave atque Vale* upon the violin. A choice incident! And instinctively he began to find phrases for it, plangent, mournful, suitable to the elegiac sonnet. True, his friend was not all that he could have wished: an excellent musician of common sense, well dressed and healthy, with nothing of Chopin about him, nothing of Paganini. But the sonnet need not mention the musician, only his music. So he looked at the dim river and the misty fields, and thought of long, alliterative, melancholy words. Immemorial, irrevocable, visionary, marmoreal . . . .

The *Lyceum* was responsible for this. That classic journal, reviewing his last book of verses, had told him that though he should vivisect his soul in public for evermore, he would find there nothing worth revealing, and nothing to compensate the spectators for their painful and pitying emotions. He had thought it a clumsy sarcasm, ponderous no less than rude; but he could not deny its truth. Tenderly opening his book, he lighted upon these lines:

> Ah, day by swift malignant day,
> Life vanishes in vanity:
> Whilst I, life's phantom victim, play
> The music of my misery.
> Draw near, ah dear delaying Death!
> Draw near, and silence my sad breath.

The lines touched him; yet he could not think them a valuable utterance; nor did he discover much fine gold in his sonnet, which began:

> Along each melancholy London street,
> Beneath the heartless stars, the indifferent moon,
> I walk with sorrow, and I know that soon
> Despair and I will walk with friendly feet.

It was good, but Shakespeare and Keats, little as he could comprehend why, had done better. He sat in his Temple chambers, nursing these dreary cogitations, for many hours of an October day, until the musician came to interrupt him; and to the violinist the versifier confessed.

'I am just thirty,' he began, 'and quite useless. I have a good education, and a little money. I must do something; and poetry is what I want to do. I have published three volumes, and they are entirely futile. They are not even bad enough to be interesting. I have not written one verse that any one can remember. I have tried a great many styles, and I cannot write anything really good and fine in any one of them.' He turned over the leaves with a hasty and irritated hand. 'There, for instance! This is an attempt at the sensuous love-lyric: listen!

> Sometimes, in very joy of shame,
> Our flesh becomes one living flame:
> And she and I
> Are no more separate, but the same.
>
> Ardour and agony unite;
> Desire, delirium, delight:
> And I and she
> Faint in the fierce and fevered night.
>
> Her body music is: and ah,
> The accords of lute and viola,
> When she and I
> Play on live limbs love's opera!

It's a lie, of course; but even if it were true, could any one care to read it? Then why should I want to write it? And why can't I write better? I know what imagination is, and poetry, and all the rest of it. I go on contemplating my own emotions, or inventing them, and nothing comes of it but this. And yet I'm not a perfect fool.' 'That,' said the musician, 'is true, though it is not your fault; but you soon will be, if you go on maundering like this by yourself. Come down to my cottage by the river, and invent a new profession.' And they went.

But the country is dangerous to persons of weak mind, who examine much the state of their emotions; they indulge there in delicious luxuries of introspection. The unhappy poet brooded upon his futility, with occasional desperate efforts to write something like the *Ode to Duty* or the *Scholar Gypsy*: dust and ashes! dust and ashes! Suddenly the horror of a long life spent in following the will-o'-the-wisp, or in questing for Sangrails and Eldorados, fell upon him: he refused to become an elderly mooncalf. The river haunted him with its facilities for death, and he regretted that there were no water-lilies on it: still, it was cold and swift and deep, overhung by alders, and edged by whispering reeds. Why not? He was of no use: if he went out to the colonies, or upon the stock exchange, he would continue to write quantities of average and uninteresting verse. It was his destiny; and the word pleased him. There was a certain distinction in having a destiny, and in defeating it by death. He had but a listless care for life, few ties that he would grieve to break, no prospects and ambitions within his reach. Upon this fourth evening, then, he went down to the end of the garden, and looked towards the river.

The sonnet was done at last, and he smiled to find himself admiring it. In all honesty, he fancied that death has inspired him well. He had read, surely he had read, worse sestets.

> I shall not hear what any morrow saith:
> I only hear this my last twilight say
> *Cease thee from sighing and from bitter breath,*
> *For all thy life with autumn mist is grey!*
> Dirged by loud music, down to silent death
> I pass, and on the waters pass away.

A pity that it should be lost; but to leave it upon the bank would be almost an affectation. Besides, there was pathos in dying with his best verses upon his lips; verses that only he and the twilight should hear. Night fell fast and very gloomy, with scarce a star. Leaning upon the gate, he tried to remember the names of modern poets who have killed themselves: Chatterton, Gérard de Nerval. They, at least, could write poetry, and their failure was not in art. Yet he could live his poetry, as Milton and Carlyle, he thought, had recommended: live it by dying, because he could not write it. 'What Cato did and Addison approved' had its poetical side; and no one without a passion for poetry would die in despair at failure in it. The violin sent dancing into the night an exhilarating courtly measure of Rameau: 'The Dance of Death!' said the poet, and was promptly ashamed of so obvious and hackneyed a sentiment. At the same time, there was something strange and rare in drowning yourself by night to the dance-music of your unconscious friend.

The bitter smell of aster and chrysanthemum was heavy on the air; 'balms and rich spices for the sad year's death', as he had once written; and he fancied, though he could not be sure, that he caught a bat's thin cry. The 'pathetic fallacy' was extremely strong upon him, and he pitied himself greatly. To die so futile and so young! A minor Hamlet with Ophelia's death! And at that, his mind turned to Shakespeare, and to a famous modern picture, and to the Lady of Shalott. He imagined himself floating down and down to some mystical mediaeval city, its torchlights flashing across his white face. But for that, he should be dressed differently; in something Florentine perhaps; certainly not in a comfortable smoking-coat by a London tailor. And at that, he was reminded that a last cigarette would not be out of place: he lighted one, and presently fell to wondering whether he was mad or no. He thought not: he was sane enough to know that he would never write great poetry, and to die sooner than waste life in the misery of vain efforts. The last wreath of smoke gone upon the night, not without a comparison between the wreath and himself, he opened the garden gate, and walked gently down the little field, at the end of which ran the river. He went through the long grass, heavy with dew, looking up at the starless sky, and into the impenetrable darkness. Of a sudden, with the most vivid surprise of his life, he fell forward, with a flashing sensation of icy water bubbling round his face, blinding and choking him; of being swirled and carried along; of river weeds clinging round his head; of living in a series of glimpses and visions. Mechanically striking out across stream, he reached the bank, steadied and rested himself for an instant by the branch of an overhanging alder, then climbed ashore. There he lay and shivered; then, despite the cold, tingled with shame, and blushed; then laughed; lastly, got up and shouted. The shout rose discordantly above the musician's harmonies, and he heard some one call his name. 'It's that moon-struck poet of mine,' said he, and went down to the gate. 'Is that you?' he cried, 'and where are you?' And out of the darkness beyond came the confused and feeble answer – 'I – fell into the river – and I'm – on the wrong side.' The practical man wasted no words, but made for the boathouse, where he kept his punt; and in a few minutes the shivering poet dimly descried his rescuer in mid-stream. The lumbering craft grounded, and the drowned man, with stiff and awkward movement, got himself on board. 'What do you mean,' said the musician, 'by making me play Charon on this ghostly river at such an hour?' 'I was – thinking of things,' said the poet, 'and it was pitch dark – and I fell in.' They landed; and the dewy field, the autumnal garden, the rich night air, seemed to be mocking him. His teeth chattered, and he shook, and still he mumbled bits of verse. Said the musician, as they entered the little cottage: 'The first thing for you to do is to take off those things, and have hot drinks in bed, like Mr. Pickwick.' Said the doomed man, quaking like an aspen: 'Yes, but I must write out a sonnet first, before I forget it.' He did.

APPENDIX 2: BACKGROUND SOURCES

From Charles Baudelaire, 'Notes Nouvelles sur Edgar Poe' (1857)

Selected Writings on Art and Literature, P. E. Charvet (trans. and intro.), [1972] (London: Penguin, 2006), pp. 188–9, 199–200. [Within the same article on Poe, Baudelaire delivers his characteristic eloquent definition of Decadence as well as capitalising on the 'intensity' of Poe's short story form: the conceptual affinities between and simultaneous genesis of the short story and Decadence emerge here.]

The phrase 'a literature of decadence' implies that there is a scale of literatures, a literature in infancy, a literature in childhood, in adolescence, etc. I mean that the term presupposes an inevitable and providential process, like some inescapable decree; and what then could be more unjust than to reproach us for accomplishing the mysterious law? All the meaning I can extract from this academic pronouncement is that we ought, somehow, to feel ashamed of obeying this law with pleasure, and that we are guilty of rejoicing in our destiny. That sun which a few hours ago was crushing everything beneath the weight of its vertical, white light will soon be flooding the western horizon with varied colours. In the changing splendours of this dying sun, some poetic minds will find new joys; they will discover dazzling colonnades, cascades of molten metal, a paradise of fire, a melancholy splendour, nostalgic raptures, all the magic of dreams, all the memories of opium. And the sunset will then appear to them as the marvellous allegory of a soul, imbued with life, going down beyond the horizon, with a magnificent wealth of thoughts and dreams.
[. . . .]
   In the domains of literature, where imagination can achieve the most interesting results, can reap, not the richest nor the most precious treasures (these belong to poetry), but the most numerous and the most varied, one was particularly dear to Poe: the short story. The short story has one immense advantage over the novel, with its large canvas, namely that its brevity adds to the intensity of its effect. Reading a short story, which can be accomplished at a sitting, leaves a far sharper imprint on the mind than an episodic reading, a reading often interrupted by the worries of business and the care of mundane interests. The unity of impression, the totality of impact, is an immense advantage that may give this type of composition a very special superiority, to the extent that a story that is too short (which is no doubt a weakness) is still worth more than a story that is too long. If skilful, the artist will not adapt his ideas to the incidents; but, having conceived, in leisured deliberation, an effect he intends to produce, he will then invent the incidents, link up a series of events, best suited to bring about the effect desired.

From Walter Pater, 'Conclusion', *The Renaissance: Studies in Art and Poetry* (1873)

The Renaissance, Adam Phillips (ed.) (Oxford: Oxford University Press, 1998), pp. 152–3. [After *The Renaissance*'s main text, this 'Conclusion' exhorts readers to live the 'Greek' life themselves. Following Pater's chapters 'Leonardo' and 'Winckelmann' it could be read as a powerful advocation of homosexuality, concerns over which led to its exclusion from the second edition. Nevertheless, this philosophy influenced a generation of writers and artists, both creatively and personally.]

To burn always with this hard, gem-like flame, to maintain this ecstasy, is success in life. In a sense it might even be said that our failure is to form habits: for, after all, habit is relative to a stereotyped world, and meantime it is only the roughness of the eye that makes any two persons, things, situations, seem alike. While all melts under our feet, we may well grasp at any exquisite passion, or any contribution to knowledge that seems by a lifted horizon to set the spirit free for a moment, or any stirring of the senses, strange dyes, strange colours, and curious odours, or work of the artist's hands, or the face of one's friend. Not to discriminate every moment some passionate attitude in those about us, and in the very brilliancy of their gifts some tragic dividing of forces on their ways, is, on this short day of frost and sun, to sleep before evening. With this sense of the splendour of our experience and of its awful brevity, gathering all we are into one desperate effort to see and touch, we shall hardly have time to make theories about the things we see and touch.

[. . . .]

For our one chance lies in expanding that interval, in getting as many pulsations as possible into the given time. Great passions may give us this quickened sense of life, ecstasy and sorrow of love, the various forms of enthusiastic activity, disinterested or otherwise, which come naturally to many of us. Only be sure it is passion – that it does yield you this fruit of a quickened, multiplied consciousness. Of such wisdom, the poetic passion, the desire of beauty, the love of art for its own sake, has most. For art comes to you proposing frankly to give nothing but the highest quality to your moments as they pass, and simply for those moments' sake.

From Brander Matthews, 'The Philosophy of the Short Story' (1885)

Brander Matthews, *The Philosophy of the Short-story* (New York: Longmans, 1901), pp. 15–17, 22–3, 36–7. It appeared in *Lippincott's Magazine* (October 1885), expanded from *Saturday Review* in 1884. [In the 1880s Brander Matthews theorised the short story form, clarified its principles based on Poe's ideas, and situated it within the landscape of other literary forms and genres. Here, apart from giving the generic traits of the short story, he employs a remarkable Darwinian metaphor.]

A true Short-story differs from the Novel chiefly in its essential unity of impression. In a far more exact and precise use of the word, a Short-story has unity as a Novel cannot have it. Often, it may be noted by the way, the Short-story fulfils the three false unities of the French classic drama: it shows one action, in one place, on one day. A Short-story deals with a single character, a single event, a single emotion, or the series of emotions called forth by a single situation. Poe's paradox that a poem cannot greatly exceed a hundred lines in length under penalty of ceasing to be one poem and breaking into a string of poems, may serve to suggest the precise difference between the Short-story and the Novel. The Short-story is the single effect, complete and self-contained, while the Novel is of necessity broken into a series of episodes. Thus the Short-story has, what the Novel cannot have, the effect of 'totality', as Poe called it, the unity of impression [. . .] The Short-story is not only not a chapter out of a Novel, or an incident or an episode extracted from a longer tale, but at its best it impresses the reader with the belief that it would be spoiled if it were made larger, or if it were incorporated into a more elaborate work.
[. . . .]
The writer of Short-stories must be concise, and compression, a vigorous compression, is essential. For him, more than for any one else, the half is more than the whole. Again, the novelist may be commonplace, he may bend his best energies to the photographic reproduction of the actual; if he show us a cross-section of real life we are content; but the writer of Short-stories must have originality and ingenuity. If to compression, originality, and ingenuity he add also a touch of fantasy, so much the better [. . .] It may be said that no one has ever succeeded as a writer of Short-stories who had not ingenuity, originality, and compression; and that most of those who have succeeded in this line had also the touch of fantasy.

[. . . .]

The fact is, that the Short-story and the Sketch, the Novel and the Romance, melt and merge one into the other, and no man may mete the boundaries of each, though their extremes lie far apart. With the more complete understanding of the principle of development and evolution in literary art, as in physical nature, we see the futility of a strict and rigid classification into precisely defined genera and species. All that it is needful for us to remark now is that the Short-story has limitless possibilities: it may be as realistic as the most prosaic novel, or as fantastic as the most ethereal romance.

From J.-K. Huysmans, *À Rebours* (1884)

Against Nature, Robert Baldick (ed. and trans.) (London: Penguin, 1959), pp. 163–4, 193. [Huysmans is cited as being the 'First Decadent', and *À Rebours* is often seen as a prototype for later Decadent novels, most notably *The Picture of Dorian Gray*. These segments are from longer analyses where Des Esseintes appreciates the stylistic and subjective effects of short fiction by Barbey d'Aurevilly and Villiers de l'Isle-Adam.]

The extraordinary book that contained this tale was Des Esseintes' delight; he had therefore had printed for him in bishop's-purple ink, within a border of cardinal red, on a genuine parchment blessed by the Auditors of the Rota, a copy of *Les Diaboliques* set up in those *lettres de civilité* whose peculiar hooks and flourishes, curling up or down, assume a satanic appearance.
[. . . .]
With Barbey d'Aurevilly, the series of religious writers came to an end. To tell the truth, this pariah belonged more, from every point of view, to secular literature than to that other literature in which he claimed a place that was denied him. His wild romantic style, for instance, full of twisted expressions, outlandish turns of phrase, and far-fetched similes, whipped up his sentences as they galloped across the page, farting and jangling their bells. In short, Barbey looked like a stallion among the geldings that filled the ultramontane stables.

Such were Des Esseintes' reflections as he dipped into the book, re-reading a passage here and there; and then, comparing the author's vigorous and varied style with the lymphatic, stereotyped style of his fellow writers, he was led to consider that evolution of language so accurately described by Darwin.

[. . . .]
[T]he *Contes cruels* [was] a collection of stories of indisputable talent which also included *Véra*, a tale Des Esseintes regarded as a little masterpiece.

Here the hallucination was endowed with an exquisite tenderness; there was nothing here of the American author's gloomy mirages, but a well-nigh heavenly vision of sweetness and warmth, which in an identical style formed the antithesis of Poe's Beatrices and Ligeias, those pale, unhappy phantoms engendered by the inexorable nightmare of black opium.

This story too brought into play the operations of the will, but it no longer showed it undermined and brought low by fear; on the contrary, it studied its intoxications under the influence of a conviction which had become an obsession, and it also demonstrated its power, which was so great that it could saturate the atmosphere and impose its beliefs on surrounding objects.

From John Gray, 'Les Goncourt' (1889)

The Dial 1 (1889): pp. 9–13. [Although beginning rather close to Nordau, Gray links the idea of abnormality to the Paterian ideas of the individual personality of the artist, and the importance of personal experience. As his argument develops, his anti-English and pro-French rhetoric is typical of many critical pieces that opposed the British Matron and her followers.]

The artist is always an abnormal creature, a being with an overdeveloped brain, or diseased nerves, as some express it. As specially distinguished from the literary grocer, he cannot choose but give his own personality in his work. His greatness is in the insight that discovers new motives, and in the earnestness with which he carries them out. It is quite the rule that the really great only gain their place after fierce struggling; for apart from the actual work, they have to create a taste for it, a task generally tedious in proportion to its worth.
[. . . .]
Documentary fiction is now accepted. The real thing, and variously pretentious imitations of it, are even fashionable. The realist, as we sometimes call him, is sent out to tell us what he sees and hears and feels, but the commission includes authority to select at his discretion. Now the peculiar temperament of the Goncourt personality, its passion for the choice, the rare, makes it produce results too strange. Though they believed strongly in the far superior value of the actually seen and felt, their particular

predilections sometimes came in to defeat the immediate purpose, when they reproduced what they, and but a very few similar temperaments, feel and see. I do not mean to say that they exaggerate. Where there is unusual insistence over trivialities, it is merely nature seen by two exceptional organisms of peculiarly rare culture. What they give us is, as a rule, intelligible to any sentient being, which is enough; for writings all of nerve are not for readers made all of gristle.

[. . . .]

How they manage their still life! The whole art with which they arranged backgrounds and accessories was largely their own invention. True, the revolt against conventional artistic surroundings was already begun elsewhere. Some of the best English art, for instance (the Preraphaelite work affords a notable example), had been strongly characterised by its freedom from the trammels of tradition. At the present moment, alas! the movement seems to have died down in our midst, and when it returns it will be through France. In moments of supreme emotion, a trivial or irrelevant fact, a strange shape, an unexpected sound, have a value the artist cannot afford to neglect. If the Goncourts were not the first to discover this principle, at all events no one hitherto has so thoroughly understood and consciously applied it as they.

[. . . .]

To more intelligent people in England they give the same impression as, now, to the corresponding class in France; except perhaps that the English aversion to the exotic is stronger than the French. The concentration, the devotion to the subject, that enables the Goncourts to impart to the reader's nerves the smart of the pain they describe, is condemned, because it is 'unpleasant', with more persistence here than there. For the French can certainly claim a higher average artistic intelligence than we, in that at least some appreciable proportion of them understand the phrase 'art for art's sake'.

From Lionel Johnson, 'A Note upon the Practice and Theory of Verse at the Present Time Obtaining in France' (1891)

The Century Guild Hobby Horse 6 (1891): pp. 61–6: p. 64. [By the time of this article, French Decadence in Britain was at its apogee and in vogue. Here Johnson masters a concise, perceptive and rather dispassionate definition of the term, even before Arthur Symons's illustrious, lengthy manifesto of 1893.]

In English, *décadence* and the literature thereof, mean this: the period, at which passion, or romance, or tragedy, or sorrow, or any other form of activity or of emotion, must be refined upon, and curiously considered, for literary treatment: an age of afterthought, of reflection. Hence come one great virtue, and one great vice: the virtue of much and careful meditation upon life, its emotions and its incidents: the vice of over subtilty and of affectation, when thought thinks upon itself, and when emotions become entangled with the consciousness of them.

From Oscar Wilde, *The Critic as Artist* (1891)

In Josephine M. Guy (ed.), *Criticism: Historical Criticism, Intentions, The Soul of Man*, vol. 4 of *The Complete Works of Oscar Wilde* (Oxford: Oxford University Press, 2007), pp. 199–200. [In this passage from 'The Critic as Artist' (Part 2), Wilde mocks Kipling's journalistic, Realist fiction with eloquence and biting wit. He goes on to claim that the psychology of fiction is not 'morbid enough', as he discusses the variety and novelty of subjective modes.]

He who would stir us now by fiction must either give us an entirely new background, or reveal to us the soul of man in its innermost workings. The first is for the moment being done for us by Mr. Rudyard Kipling. As one turns over the pages of his *Plain Tales from the Hills*, one feels as if one were seated under a palm-tree reading life by superb flashes of vulgarity. The bright colours of the bazaars dazzle one's eyes. The jaded, second-rate Anglo-Indians are in exquisite incongruity with their surroundings. The mere lack of style in the story-teller gives an odd journalistic realism to what he tells us. From the point of view of literature Mr. Kipling is a genius who drops his aspirates. From the point of view of life, he is a reporter who knows vulgarity better than any one has ever known it. Dickens knew its clothes and its comedy. Mr. Kipling knows its essence and its seriousness. He is our first authority on the second-rate, and has seen marvellous things through keyholes, and his backgrounds are real works of art. As for the second condition, we have had Browning, and Meredith is with us. But there is still much to be done in the sphere of introspection. People sometimes say that fiction is getting too morbid. As far as psychology is concerned, it has never been morbid enough. We have merely touched the surface of the soul, that is all. In one single ivory cell of the brain there are stored away things more marvellous and more terrible than even they have dreamed of, who, like the author of *Le Rouge et le Noir*, have sought to track the soul into its most secret places, and to make life confess its dearest sins. Still, there is a limit even to the number of untried backgrounds, and it is possible that a further development of the habit of introspection may prove fatal to that creative faculty to which it seeks to supply fresh material. I myself am inclined to think that creation is doomed. It springs from too primitive, too natural an impulse. However this may be, it is certain that the subject-matter at the disposal of creation is always diminishing, while the subject-matter of criticism increases daily. There are always new attitudes for the mind, and new points of view. The duty of imposing form upon chaos does not grow less as the world advances. There was never a time when Criticism was more needed than it is now. It is only by its means that Humanity can become conscious of the point at which it has arrived.

From Arthur Symons, 'The Decadent Movement in Literature' (1893)

Harper's New Monthly Magazine 87 (1893): pp. 858–67: pp. 858, 860, 866–7. [This article by Symons is probably the most quoted and referred to declaration of Decadence in Britain. Apart from giving Symons's definition of the term, these excerpts comment on French prose by discussing the Goncourts, and on English prose with the example of Walter Pater.]

After a fashion it is no doubt a decadence; it has all the qualities that mark the end of great periods, the qualities that we find in the Greek, the Latin, decadence: an intense self-consciousness, a restless curiosity in research, an over-subtilising refinement upon refinement, a spiritual and moral perversity. If what we call the classic is indeed the supreme art – those qualities of perfect simplicity, perfect sanity, perfect proportion, the supreme qualities – then this representative literature of to-day, interesting, beautiful, novel as it is, is really a new and beautiful and interesting disease.
[. . . .]
    An opera-glass – a special, unique way of seeing things – that is what the Goncourts have brought to bear upon the common things about us; and it is here that they have done the 'something new', here more than anywhere. They have never sought 'to see life steadily, and see it whole': their vision has always been somewhat feverish, with the diseased sharpness of over-excited nerves. 'We do not hide from ourselves that we have been passionate, nervous creatures, unhealthily impressionable,' confesses

the *Journal*. But it is this morbid intensity in seeing and seizing things that has helped to form that marvellous style – 'a style perhaps too ambitious of impossibilities', as they admit – a style which inherits some of its colour from Gautier, some of its fine outline from Flaubert, but which has brought light and shadow into the colour, which has softened outline in the magic of atmosphere. With them words are not merely colour and sound, they live. That search after 'l'image peinte', 'l'épithète rare', is not (as with Flaubert) a search after harmony of phrase for its own sake; it is a desperate endeavour to give sensation, to flash the impression of the moment, to preserve the very heat and motion of life. And so, in analysis as in description, they have found out a way of noting the fine shades; they have broken the outline of the conventional novel in chapters, with its continuous story, in order to indicate – sometimes in a chapter of half a page – this and that revealing moment, this or that significant attitude or accident or sensation. For the placid traditions of French prose they have had but little respect; their aim has been but one, that of having (as M. Edmund de Goncourt tells us in the preface to *Chérie*) 'une langue rendant nos idées, nos sensations, nos figurations des hommes et des choses, d'une façon distincte de celui-ci ou de celui-là, une langue personnelle, une langue portant notre signature'.

[. . . .]

Mr. Pater's prose is the most beautiful English prose which is now being written; and, unlike the prose of Goncourt, it has done no violence to language, it has sought after no vivid effects, it has found a large part of mastery in reticence, in knowing what to omit. But how far away from the classic ideals of style is this style in which words have their colour, their music, their perfume, in which there is 'some strangeness in the proportion' of every beauty! The *Studies in the Renaissance* have made of criticism a new art – have raised criticism almost to the art of creation. And *Marius the Epicurean*, in its study of 'sensations and ideas' (the conjunction was Goncourt's before it was Mr. Pater's), and the *Imaginary Portraits*, in their evocations of the Middle Ages, the age of Watteau – have they not that morbid subtlety of analysis, that morbid curiosity of form, that we have found in the works of the French Decadents? A fastidiousness equal to that of Flaubert has limited Mr. Pater's work to six volumes, but in these six volumes there is not a page that is not perfectly finished, with a conscious art of perfection. In its minute elaboration it can be compared only with goldsmith's work – so fine, so delicate is the handling of so delicate, so precious a material.

From Arthur Waugh, 'Reticence in Literature' (1894)

The Yellow Book 1 (April 1894): pp. 201–19: pp. 210–11, 217. [The *Yellow Book* was a far broader publication than popularly perceived, as is demonstrated by this early piece of in-house self-criticism, voicing the conservative opinions of Arthur Waugh (father of Evelyn). His charges of 'effeminacy' are similar to Nordau's conclusions, and were, no doubt, included by the editor to provoke a response from the defenders of the modern.]

Art, we say, claims every subject for her own; life is open to her ken; she may fairly gather her subjects where she will. Most true. But there is all the difference in the world between drawing life as we find it, sternly and relentlessly, surveying it all the while from outside with the calm, unflinching gaze of criticism, and, on the other hand, yielding ourselves to the warmth and colour of its excesses, losing our judgement in the ecstasies of the joy of life, becoming, in a word, effeminate.

The man lives by ideas; the woman by sensations; and while the man remains an artist so long as he holds true to his own view of life, the woman becomes one as soon as she throws off the habit of her sex, and learns to rely upon her judgement, and not upon her senses. It is only when we regard life with the untrammelled view of the impartial spectator, when we pierce below the substance for its animating idea, that we approximate to the artistic temperament. It is unmanly, it is effeminate, it is inartistic to gloat over pleasure, to revel in immoderation, to become passion's slave; and literature demands as much calmness of judgement, as much reticence, as life itself. The man who loses reticence loses self-respect, and the man who has no respect for himself will scarcely find others to venerate him. After all, the world generally takes us at our own valuation.

[. . . .]

The two developments of realism of which we have been speaking seem to me to typify the two excesses into which frankness is inclined to fall; on the one hand, the excess prompted by effeminacy – that is to say, by the want of restraints which starts from enervated sensation; and on the other, the excess which results from a certain brutal virility, which proceeds from coarse familiarity with indulgence. The one whispers, the other shouts; the one is the language of the courtesan, the other of the bargee. What we miss in both alike is that true frankness which springs from the artistic and moral temperament; the episodes are no part of a whole in unity with itself; the impression they leave upon the reader is not the impression of Hogarth's pictures; in one form they employ all their art to render vice attractive, in the other, with absolutely no art at all, they merely reproduce, with the fidelity of the kodak, scenes and situations the existence of which we all acknowledge, while taste prefers to forget them.

But the latest development of literary frankness is, I think, the most insidious and fraught with the greatest danger to art. A new school has arisen which combines the characteristics of effeminacy and brutality. In its effeminate aspect it plays with the subtler emotions of sensual pleasure, on its brutal side it has developed into that class of fiction which for want of a better word I must call chirurgical.

From Hubert Crackanthorpe, 'Reticence in Literature: Some Roundabout Remarks' (1894)

The Yellow Book 2 (July 1894): pp. 259–69: pp. 260–1, 266. [Crackanthorpe's response to Waugh highlights the problem of using labels, such as 'Decadence'. However, his argument develops into a powerful vindication of progressive art. Once more, the individual personality is posited as the key to artistic development, but Crackanthorpe's anti-conservative rhetoric owes much to Darwin as well as Pater.]

Art is not invested with the futile function of perpetually striving after imitation or reproduction of Nature; she endeavours to produce, through the adaptation of a restricted number of natural facts, an harmonious and satisfactory whole. Indeed, in this very process of adaptation and blending together, lies the main and greater task of the artist. And the novel, the short story, even the impression of a mere incident, convey each of them, the imprint of the temper in which their creator has achieved this process of adaptation and blending together of his material. They are inevitably stamped with the hall-mark of his personality. A work of art can never be more than a corner of Nature, seen through the temperament of a single man. Thus, all literature is, must be, essentially subjective; for style is but the power of individual expression. The disparity which separates literature from the reporter's transcript is ineradicable. There is a quality of ultimate suggestiveness to be achieved; for the business of art is, not to explain or to describe, but to suggest. That attitude of objectivity, or of impersonality towards his subject, consciously or unconsciously, assumed by the artist, and which nowadays provokes so considerable an admiration, can be attained only in a limited degree. Every piece of imaginative work must be a kind of autobiography of its creator – significant, if not of the actual facts of his existence, at least of the inner working of his soul. We are each of us conscious, not of the whole world, but of our own world; not of naked reality, but of that aspect of reality which our peculiar temperament enables us to appropriate. Thus, every narrative of an external circumstance is never anything else than the transcript of the impression produced upon ourselves by that circumstance, and, invariably, a degree of individual interpretation is insinuated into every picture, real or imaginary, however objective it may be. So then, the disparity between the so-called idealist and the so-called realist is a matter, not of aesthetic philosophy, but of individual temperament. Each is at work, according to the especial bent of his genius, within precisely the same limits. Realism, as a creed, is as ridiculous as any other literary creed.

[. . . .]

Sometimes, to listen to him you would imagine that pessimism and regular meals were incompatible; that the world is only ameliorated by those whom it completely satisfies, that good predominates over evil, that the problem of our destiny had been solved long ago. You begin to doubt whether any good thing can come out of this miserable, inadequate age of ours, unless it be a doctored survival of the vocabulary of a past century. The language of the coster and cadger resound in our midst, and, though Velasquez tried to paint like Whistler, Rudyard Kipling cannot write like Pope. And a weird word has been invented to explain the whole business. Decadence, decadence: you are all decadent nowadays. Ibsen, Degas, and the New English Art Club; Zola, Oscar Wilde, and the Second Mrs. Tanqueray. Mr. Richard Le Gallienne is hoist with his own petard; even the British playwright has not escaped the taint. Ah, what a hideous spectacle. All whirling along towards one common end. And the elegant voice of the artistic objector floating behind: '*Après vous le déluge.*' A wholesale abusing of the tendencies of the age has ever proved, for the superior mind, an inexhaustible source of relief. Few things breed such inward comfort as the contemplation of one's own pessimism – few things produce such discomfort as the remembrance of our neighbour's optimism.

From Max Nordau, *Degeneration* (1892; first English trans. 1895)

George L. Mosse (trans.), [1968] (Lincoln and London: University of Nebraska Press, 1993), pp. 317, 318, 319. [Nordau's assessment of the nature of Decadence begins with a scant examination of the artistic tradition, but then rapidly descends into a pseudo-scientific diagnosis of aberrations in the pathology of the artist in question. Almost comic today, *Degeneration* was a bestseller in 1895, and after Wilde's conviction, Nordau appeared to have been prophetic. The book's more chilling notoriety, however, comes from its role as one of the major 'scientific' arguments that underpinned Nazi ideology.]

Decadentism has not been confined to France alone; it has also established a school in England. We have already mentioned, in the preceding book, one of the earliest and most servile imitators of Baudelaire – Swinburne. I had to class him among the mystics, for the degenerative stigma of mysticism predominates in all his works. He has, it is true, been train-bearer to so many models that he may be ranked among the domestic servants of a great number of masters; but, finally, he will be assigned a place where he has served longest, and that is among the pre-Raphaelites. From Baudelaire he has borrowed principally diabolism and Sadism, unnatural depravity, and a predilection for suffering, disease and crime. The ego-mania of decadentism, its love of the artificial, its aversion to nature, and to all forms of activity and movement, its megalomaniacal contempt for men and its exaggeration of the importance of art, have found their English representative among the 'Aesthetes', the chief of whom is Oscar Wilde.
[. . . .]

The predilection for strange costume is a pathological aberration of a racial instinct. The adornment of the exterior has its origin in the strong desire to be admired by others – primarily by the opposite sex – to be recognised by them as especially well-shaped, handsome, youthful, or rich and powerful, or as preeminent through rank or merit. It is practised, then, with the object of producing a favourable impression on others, and is a result of thought about others, of preoccupation with the race. If, now, this adornment be, not through mis-judgement but purposely, of a character to cause irritation to others, or lend itself to ridicule – in other words, if it excites disapproval instead of approbation – it then runs exactly counter to the object of the art of dress, and evinces a perversion of the instinct of vanity.
[. . . .]

When, therefore, an Oscar Wilde goes about in 'aesthetic costume' among gazing Philistines, exciting either their ridicule or their wrath, it is no indication of independence of character, but rather from a purely anti-socialistic, ego-maniacal recklessness and hysterical longing to make a sensation, justified by no exalted aim; nor is it from a strong desire for beauty, but from a malevolent mania for contradiction.

From Vincent O'Sullivan, 'On the Kind of Fiction Called Morbid' (1896)

The Savoy 2 (April 1896): pp. 167–70. [Like much of the criticism in *The Savoy*, this essay is in many ways a response to Nordau and his followers in the press. Breaking down the barriers of literary eras, O'Sullivan shows the common bonds between the modern and the classic. His argument of how Shakespeare would be received were he a new writer of the day is indeed accurate, as the popularity of Thomas Bowdler's heavily expurgated *The Family Shakespeare* (1807) among Victorian readers stands testament.]

No; it is certain that abnormal nerves are not understood or thought proper in the suburban villa: and they are not tolerated by the Press, which is almost the same thing. Even editors, those cocks that show how the popular wind blows, if they have no kicks, have few ha'pence for the writer of stories which are not sops to our pleasure. The thought of death is not pleasant! (folk may be imagined to exclaim); to escape that we laugh at sorry farces and the works of Mr. Mark Twain; and yet, here is a zany with a hatful of dun thoughts formed to make one meditate on one's tomb for a week!

Still, for him, poor devil! life is not all (as they say) beer and skittles. With an impatience of facility, he sets to work sedulously on a branch of art which he is pleased to consider difficult; it cannot be pleasant work, since it progresses with shudders and cold sweats; it cannot be easy, since it is acknowledged to be no easy thing to turn the blood from men's faces. He is even charmed by the fancy that he is driving his pen to a very high measure. He may (by chance) be right; he is possibly wrong; but I am glad to say I have yet to hear that Banquo's ghost at the feast, and Caesar's ghost in the tent, are deemed infamous, or (as the cant goes) immoral. And, talking of Shakespeare, has it ever occurred to you how the critics would waggle their heads at 'Romeo and Juliet', if it were presented to-day as a new piece by William Shakespeare, Esq.? [He quotes *Romeo and Juliet* IV, iii, ll. 40–55.] Methinks I see the words: 'exotic', 'morbid', 'unhealthy', ready-made for that! Ah! how, then, can my modern writer expect to be suffered, any more than we suffer an undertaker to send out cards setting forth the excellence of his wares. When he takes to the road, he must know that he is in for a weary and footsore journey: comely persons, in beautiful garments, with eyes full of invitation look down from bordering windows and jeer at his sober parade; he sees cool, shaded by-lanes which are never for him; others pass him on the road singing blithe, gamesome songs, and he is left to loiter. And be sure he travels in glum company: the stiff-featured dead, with their thin hands and strange smile, fall into step with him and tell him their dream-like tales.

From John M. Robertson, 'Concerning Preciosity' (1897)

The Yellow Book 13 (April 1897): pp. 79–106: pp. 84–5. ['Préciosité' originates from the cultivated, refined style and mannerism of seventeenth-century France; its British equivalent, reappraised by Walter Pater, is 'euphuism'. By taking a universal, academic approach, Robertson provides insights to stylistic refinement in a social and cultural context and in regard to Decadence. The following extract is a description of the 'common element or symptom' among 'preciosities' in different epochs and cultures.]

Clearly, as we said before, the explanation is never that of vulgar absurdity; in all, we are dealing, it may be, with egoism, with unbalanced judgement, with juvenility of intelligence, with lopsidedness, with certain faults of character; but in none with raw fatuity. Rather we are struck everywhere with a special sort of sensibility, a curious cleverness, an incapacity for commonplace – to say nothing of higher qualities in any one instance. Preciosity, in fact, is a misdirection of capacity, not at all a proof of incapacity for better things. And we have to look, finally, for the special conditions under which the misdirection tends most to take place. In terms of our previous conclusion, they will amount in general to some defect of regulative influence, some overbalance of the forces of individual self-will and literary sectarianism. Such defect and overbalance, it is easy to see, may arise either in a time of novelty and enterprise or in a time of dissolution, since in both there are likely to be movements of thought and fancy ill-related to the general development of judgement and knowledge. Of all the social forces which regulate the play of speech and literature, the healthiest are those of a vigorous all-round culture; and an all-round culture is just what is lacking, in the terms of the case, alike in an epoch of decadence and in an epoch of novelty. Decadence means a lack of healthy relation among the social forces, an elevation or excessive enrichment of some elements and a degradation of others. In imperial Rome certain prior forms of intellectual and civic energy were absolutely interdicted: hence an overplus or overbalance in other forms, of which factitious literature was one. Energies repressed and regulated in one sphere could play lawlessly in another, where formerly the force of regulation had been a general discipline of common sense, now lacking. The former rule of old and middle-age over youth was dissolved under a *régime* which put age and youth equally in tutelage; and the faults of youth, of which injudicious and overstrained style is one, would have a new freedom of scope. A factitious literature, an art for art's sake, would tend to flourish just as superstition flourished; only, inasmuch as bad intellectual conditions tend ultimately to kill literature altogether, that soon passed from morbid luxuriance to inanition, while superstition in the same soil grew from strength to strength.

From Henry Harland, 'Concerning the Short Story' (1897)

The Academy, 5 June 1897: pp. 6–7. [Harland here discusses the process by which the author 'dissects' the 'impression' in order to render it into the form of the short story. Hence, not only does he extend the short story's artfulness to the mental realm of its inception, but he also suggests links between the short story and subjective experience.]

You start with an impression. But an impression is never a simple thing, which can be conveyed in two minutes' conversation. It is never an obvious thing. It is always a complex thing, it is always elusive. It is a thing of shades and niceties and fine distinctions. It is a thing in its very nature intensely personal; it is an intimate thing. And the artist who wishes to incarnate his impression in the form of a short story has a task of infinite delicacy before him. He has already felt his impression, but now he must understand it. He must study it, analyse it, dissect it, until he knows exactly of what elements it is made, exactly what elements they are that give it its peculiarity, that differentiate it from other impressions. He must dissect it, and study it, and understand it; and then he must put it together again. He must vivisect it, indeed; and then he must heal it, and see that it is still alive and whole. All this he must do before he begins to write. And now, when he does begin to write, his pre-occupation must be — the precise opposite of the manufacturer's pre-occupation. The manufacturer's difficulty was to make a small 'idea', by dilution and adulteration, fill a large vessel. The artist's difficulty will be, by distilling and purifying his impression, to present it to us in a phial.

From Havelock Ellis, *Affirmations* (1898)

(London: Walter Scott, 1898), pp. 175–6. [The following excerpt is from a chapter on Huysmans. With a focus on the relationship between 'part' and 'whole', Ellis develops the definition of Decadence from Paul Bourget's prominent idea of the independence of the linguistic unit expressed in *Essais de Psychologie Contemporaine* (1883–6).]

Technically, a decadent style is only such in relation to a classic style. It is simply a further development of a classic style, a further specialisation, the homogeneous, in Spencerian phraseology, having become heterogeneous. The first is beautiful because the parts are subordinated to the whole; the second is beautiful because the whole is subordinated to the parts. Among our own early prose-writers Sir Thomas Browne represents the type of decadence in style. Swift's prose is classic, Pater's decadent. Hume and Gibbon are classic, Emerson and Carlyle decadent. In architecture, which is the key to all the arts, we see the distinction between the classic and the decadent visibly demonstrated; Roman architecture is classic, to become in its Byzantine developments completely decadent, and St. Mark's is the perfected type of decadence in art; pure early Gothic, again, is strictly classic in the highest degree because it shows an absolute subordination of detail to the bold harmonies of structure, while later Gothic, grown weary of the commonplaces of structure and predominantly interested in beauty of detail, is again decadent. In each case the earlier and classic manner – for the classic manner, being more closely related to the ends of utility, must always be earlier – subordinates the parts to the whole, and strives after those virtues which the whole may best express; the later manner depreciates the importance of the whole for the benefit of its parts, and strives after the virtues of individualism. All art is the rising and falling of the slopes of a rhythmic curve between these two classic and decadent extremes.

From Frederick Wedmore, 'The Short Story' (1898)

The Nineteenth Century: A Monthly Review 43 (March 1898): pp. 406–16: pp. 407, 414. [Wedmore's essay is one of the most perceptive understandings of the 1890s short story. Partly influenced by Brander Matthews's formal, reductionist theorising of the short story, Wedmore's refreshing reflections demonstrate an acute awareness of the short story as a distinct genre that entails high craftsmanship and consciousness of style.]

A short story – I mean a short imaginative work in the difficult medium of prose; for plot, or story proper, is no essential part of it, though in work like Conan Doyle's or Rudyard Kipling's it may be a very delightful part – a short story may be any one of the things that have been named, or it may be something besides; but one thing it can never be – it can never be 'a novel in a nutshell'. That is a favourite definition, but not a definition that holds. It is a definition for the kind of public that asks for a convenient inexactness, and resents the subtlety which is inseparable from precise truth. Writers and serious readers know that a good short story cannot possibly be a precise *précis*, a synopsis, a *scenario*, as it were, of a novel. It is a separate thing – as separate, almost, as the Sonnet is from the Epic – it involves the exercise almost of a different art.

[. . . .]

Among the better writers, one tendency of the day is to devote a greater care to the art of expression – to an unbroken continuity of excellent and varied style. The short story, much more than the long one, makes this thing possible to men who may not claim to be geniuses, but who, if we are to respect them at all, must claim to be artists. And yet, in face of the indifference of so much of our public here, to anything we can call Style – in face, actually, of a strange insensibility to it – the attempt, wherever made, is a courageous one. This insensibility – how does it come about?

From G. K. Chesterton, *Charles Dickens* (1906)

11th edn (London: Methuen, 1917), p. 69. [In these musings, Chesterton suggests a particularly pertinent summary of the characteristics that tether short fiction with Decadence: slightness, Impressionism, hallucinatory experiences. The Aesthetic idea of life-as-art is here formulated as life-as-short-story.]

Our modern attraction to short stories is not an accident of form; it is the sign of a real sense of fleetingness and fragility; it means that existence is only an impression, and, perhaps, only an illusion. A short story of to-day has the air of a dream; it has the irrevocable beauty of a falsehood; we get a glimpse of grey streets of London or red plains of India, as in an opium vision; we see people – arresting people with fiery and appealing faces. But when the story is ended, the people are ended. We have no instinct of anything ultimate and enduring behind the episodes. The moderns, in a word, describe life in short stories because they are possessed with the sentiment that life itself is an uncommonly short story, and perhaps not a true one.

Arthur Machen, ['The Amber Statuette'] (1907)

From *The Hill of Dreams* [written 1895–7] (Boston: Dana Estes, 1907), pp. 298–301. [The following excerpt from Machen's unparalleled Decadent novel does not only function as an allegory of the nonconformist Aesthete short-storyist of the 1890s, but also stands alone as an independent Decadent short story, one that is thematically akin to a Gautierian fantasy. The struggling author's opulent hallucination inspires him to write a story of entrancing artifice. The disparaging of the 'story' by the Philistine critics captures the culture wars of the time quite succinctly.]

But on that bright morning neither the dreadful street nor those who moved about it appalled him. He returned joyously to his den, and reverently laid out the paper on his desk. The world about him was but a grey shadow hovering on a shining wall; its noises were faint as the rustling of trees in a distant wood. The lovely and exquisite forms of those who served the Amber Venus were his distinct, clear, and manifest visions, and for one amongst them who came to him in a fire of bronze hair his heart stirred with the adoration of love. She it was who stood forth from all the rest and fell down prostrate before the radiant form in amber, drawing out her pins in curious gold, her glowing brooches of enamel, and pouring from a silver box all her treasures of jewels and precious stones, chrysoberyl and sardonyx, opal and diamond, topaz and pearl. And then she stripped from her body her precious robes and stood before the goddess in the glowing mist of her hair, praying that to her who had given all and came naked to the shrine, love might be given, and the grace of Venus. And when at last, after strange adventures, her prayer was granted, then when the sweet light came from the sea, and her lover turned at dawn to that bronze glory, he saw beside him a little statuette of amber. And in the shrine, far in Britain where the black rains stained the marble, they found the splendid and sumptuous statue of the Golden Venus, the last fine robe of silk that the lady had dedicated falling from her fingers, and the jewels lying at her feet. And her face was like the lady's face when the sun had brightened it on that day of her devotion.

 The bronze mist glimmered before Lucian's eyes; he felt as though the soft floating hair touched his forehead and his lips and his hands. The fume of burning bricks, the reek of cabbage water, never reached his nostrils that were filled with the perfume of rare unguents, with the breath of the violet sea in Italy. His pleasure was an inebriation, an ecstasy of joy that destroyed all the vile Hottentot kraals and mud avenues as with one white lightning flash, and through the hours of that day he sat enthralled, not contriving a story with patient art, but rapt into another time, and entranced by the urgent gleam in the lady's eyes.

The little tale of *The Amber Statuette* had at last issued from a humble office in the spring after his father's death. The author was utterly unknown; the author's Murray was a wholesale stationer and printer in process of development, so that Lucian was astonished when the book became a moderate success. The reviewers had been sadly irritated, and even now he recollected with cheerfulness an article in an influential daily paper, an article pleasantly headed: 'Where are the disinfectants?'

APPENDIX 3: FURTHER READING: A TIMELINE

This timeline focuses selectively on British and a few continental short-story collections, and Little Magazines of, or related to, Aestheticism and Decadence. It also includes relevant literary milestones, key facts and events (it does not include poetry).

1840
Edgar Allan Poe, *Tales of the Grotesque and Arabesque*
  See also *The Prose Romances of Edgar A. Poe* (1843) and *Tales* (1845).

1849
Dante Gabriel Rossetti, 'Hand and Soul'
  This is both a manifesto of Aestheticism and the archetypal Aesthetic short story and 'imaginary portrait'.

1850
The Germ, issues 1–4
  Edited by William Michael Rossetti and ran from January to April.

1857
Obscene Publications Act
  Lord Chief Justice Campbell's original definition of obscenity, defined by the intent of the writer.

1859
Charles Darwin, *On the Origin of Species*

1863
Théophile Gautier, *Romans et Contes*
  See also Gautier, *Nouvelles*

1864
Algernon Charles Swinburne, 'Dead Love'
  This remarkably morbid tale both anticipates and even outdoes 1890s Decadent fiction.

1868
Court trial: Regina v. Hicklin. Henry Scott's pamphlet entitled 'The Confessional Unmasked: shewing the depravity of the Romish priesthood, the iniquity of the Confessional, and the questions put to females in confession' banned under Obscene Publications Act as pornography.
Amendment to the OPA. Chief Justice Cockburn changed the definition of obscenity from the intent of the writer, to the effect it has on the reader.

1869
Charles Baudelaire, *Le Spleen de Paris*
  These prose poems can be read as short stories.

1874
The term 'Impressionism' is coined by Louis Leroy in his scathing review of Claude Monet's *Impression, soleil levant* at the First Impressionist Exhibition in Paris.
Jules Barbey d'Aurevilly, *Les Diaboliques* (*The She-Devils*)

1876
Camillo Boito, *Storielle Vane* (*Vain Tales*)
  See also *Senso: Nuove Storielle Vane* (*Senso: New Vain Tales*) 1883.

1877
William Hurrell Mallock, *The New Republic or Culture, Faith and Philosophy in an English Country House*.
  Originally a satire on the Oxford of Wilde, Pater and Benjamin Jowett,

Mallock's book was so accurate, it became a handbook for Aesthetes of the 1920s.

1880
J.-K. Huysmans, *Croquis Parisiens*

1882
Arthur Heygate Mackmurdo, Herbert Horne and Selwyn Image establish the Century Guild of Artists.
Robert Louis Stevenson, *New Arabian Nights*
This was a pivotal work in the development of the British short story.

1883
Villiers de l'Isle-Adam, *Contes Cruels* (*Cruel Tales*)
See also *Nouveaux Contes Cruels* (*New Cruel Tales*) 1888.

1884
The Century Guild Hobby Horse. First 'trial' issue (No.1), published by the Guild.
J.-K. Huysmans, *À Rebours* (*Against Nature*)

1885
Le Scapin (1885–6)
French Little Magazine edited by E.-G. Raymond and André Bucquet.
Richard Francis Burton, *The Book of the Thousand Nights and a Night* (10 vols)
Expanded to 16 vols: *The Supplemental Nights to the Thousand Nights and a Night* (1886–8).
John Calcott Horsely, 'A Woman's Plea: To the Editor of *The Times*'. *The Times* letters, Wednesday, 20 May 1885
The first of several 'British Matron' letters objecting to the Nude in art.

1886
The Century Guild Hobby Horse relaunch (vol. 1; numbers 1–4)
Le Décadent (1886–9)
French Little Magazine edited by Anatole Baju.
La Décadence (October)
The only three issues of this magazine were edited by René Ghil, E.-G. Raymond and André Bucquet.
Robert Louis Stevenson, *The Strange Case of Dr Jekyll and Mr Hyde*

1887
The Century Guild Hobby Horse (vol. 2; numbers 5–8)
Walter Pater, *Imaginary Portraits*

1888
The Century Guild Hobby Horse (vol. 3; numbers 9–12)
Oscar Wilde, *The Happy Prince and Other Stories*
Richard Garnett, *The Twilight of the Gods and Other Tales*.
   Expanded ed. 1903.
Leonard Smithers and Harry Sidney Nichols launch the pornographic imprint 'The Erotika Biblion Society'.
   The project ended in 1909. One of the publications was the notorious novella *Teleny, or The Reverse of the Medal* (1893) whose anonymous co-authors most likely included Oscar Wilde.

1889
The Dial 1
The Century Guild Hobby Horse (vol. 4; numbers 13–16)

1890
The Century Guild Hobby Horse (vol. 5; numbers 17–20)
Vernon Lee, *Hauntings. Fantastic Stories*
Oscar Wilde, *The Picture of Dorian Gray*
   Revised and expanded in 1891.

1891
The Century Guild Hobby Horse (vol. 6; numbers 21–4)
Oscar Wilde, *House of Pomegranates*
Oscar Wilde, *Lord Arthur Savile's Crime and Other Stories*
Oscar Wilde, *Salomé*
Jean Lorrain, *Sonyeuse*
Marcel Schwob, *Coeur Double* (*Double Heart*)
   Dedicated to R. L. Stevenson.
William Morris inaugurates the eclectic Kelmscott Press.

1892
The Dial 2
The Century Guild Hobby Horse (vol. 7; numbers 25–8)
The Pagan Review (August)

Vernon Lee, *Vanitas: Polite Stories*
Marcel Schwob, *Le Roi au masque d'or* (*The King in the Golden Mask*)

1893
The Dial 3
The Hobby Horse, New Series (Bodley Head) numbers 1 and 2
M. P. Shiel, *Prince Zaleski*
Hubert Crackanthorpe, *Wreckage: Seven Studies*
George Egerton, *Keynotes*
   This volume inaugurates John Lane's 'Keynote Series'.
E. Nesbit, *Grim Tales*
Frederick Wedmore, *Renunciations*
H. B. Marriott Watson, *Diogenes of London*
Jean Lorrain, *Buveurs d'âmes*
Arthur Symons, 'The Decadent Movement in Literature'

1894
The Yellow Book, vols 1–3.
The Chameleon
The Hobby Horse, New Series (Elkin Mathews) number 3. (Final).
The Chap-Book (1894–8)
   American Little Magazine edited by Herbert Stuart Stone.
R. Murray Gilchrist, *The Stone Dragon and Other Tragic Romances*
Count Eric Stenbock, *Studies of Death: Romantic Tales*
George Egerton, *Discords*
Arthur Machen, *The Great God Pan and the Inmost Light*
   The Great God Pan was first published in the little magazine *The Whirlwind* (1890).
Remy de Gourmont, *Histoires Magiques et Autres Récits*

1895
The Yellow Book, vols 4–7.
M'lle New York (1895–6; 1898–9)
   American Little Magazine edited by Vance Thompson.
Ernest Dowson, *Dilemmas: Stories and Studies in Sentiment*
Ella D'Arcy, *Monochromes*
Robert W. Chambers, *The King in Yellow*
Arthur Machen, *The Three Impostors*
George Moore, *Celibates*

Henry Harland, *Grey Roses*
H. G. Wells, *The Stolen Bacillus and Other Incidents*
H. G. Wells, *The Time Machine*
Thomas Hardy, *Jude the Obscure*
Pierre Louÿs, *Aphrodite*
   This was the yellow-covered book that Wilde had 'under his arm' when arrested, popularly mistaken for a copy of *The Yellow Book*.
Jean Lorrain, *Sensations et souvenirs*
After three trials Oscar Wilde is convicted at the Old Bailey, London, to two years' labour for homosexual practices.
Max Nordau, *Degeneration*
   Originally published as *Entartung* in Germany in 1892.

1896
The Savoy, vols 1–8.
The Pageant, vol. 1.
The Yellow Book, vols 8–11.
The Dial 4
M. P. Shiel, *Shapes in the Fire*
Una Ashworth Taylor, *Nets for the Wind*
Vincent O'Sullivan, *A Book of Bargains*
Hubert Crackanthorpe, *Vignettes*
Frederick Wedmore, *Orgeas and Miradou with Other Pieces*
Mabel E. Wotton, *Day-Books*

1897
The Pageant, vol. 2
The Yellow Book, vols 12–13.
The Dial 5
The Dome (1897–1900)
   Edited by Ernest J. Oldmeadow.

1898
Baron Corvo [Frederick William Rolfe], *Stories Toto Told Me*
   It was expanded and republished as *In His Own Image* (1901).
Henry Harland, *Comedies and Errors*

1899
Maurice Hewlett, *Little Novels of Italy*

Joseph Conrad, *Heart of Darkness*
Arthur Symons, *The Symbolist Movement in Literature*

1900
Jean Lorrain, *Histoires de Masques*

1902
Jean Lorrain, *Princesses d'ivoire et d'ivresse*

1903
Pierre Louÿs, *Sanguines*

1904
Vernon Lee, *Pope Jacynth and More Supernatural Tales: Excursions into Fantasy*

1905
Arthur Symons, *Spiritual Adventures*
Vernon Lee, *For Maurice: Five Unlikely Stories*

Notes

Selwyn Image 'A Bundle of Letters'

The Century Guild Hobby Horse 3:12 (1888): pp. 121–33.
Ref.: Matthew Brinton Tildesley, 'The Sketches of Dorian Gray: Oscar Wilde and *The Century Guild Hobby Horse*', *The Wildean* 37 (July 2010): pp. 65–82.
Mr. Ruskin: The majority of the *Hobby Horse*'s editors, chief contributors and readers were Oxford men, many of whom studied under John Ruskin (1819–1900).
At-Home: Image is referring to a party or reception at a fashionable residence in London. Basil Hallward's description of 'crush at Lady Brandon's' in *The Picture of Dorian Gray* is strikingly similar to Image's work, from the event itself to the narrator's distaste at having to attend.
'A Scrap of Paper': English version of Victorien Sardou's French play, *Les Pattes de mouche* (1860). Sardou's opera, *La Tosca* (1887) was the principal influence on Giacomo Puccini's *Tosca* of 1900.
Catullus: Roman poet, known for his erotic and homoerotic content. Image's remarks that the book might 'fall into some much less appreciative hands' echo the famous 1868 amendment to the Obscene Publications Act, adding to the titillation for cognisant readers.
Confessio Poetae: (Lat.) A Poet's Confession.
'Lay of the Last Minstrel': Long narrative poem (1805) by Walter Scott (1771–1882).
Simeon Solomon: English Pre-Raphaelite painter (1840–1905).

The late Bishop . . . book: John Jackson's (1811–1886) *The Sinfulness of Little Sins: A Course of Sermons* (1855).
Ars Artium: (Lat.) The Art of Arts.
Turner: Joseph Mallord William Turner (1775–1851) was a British painter of the Romantic period.
Michelangelo and Leonardo: Michelangelo di Lodovico Buonarroti Simoni (1475–1564) and Leonardo di ser Piero da Vinci (1452–1519) are the most important artists and polymaths of the High Renaissance.
Milton's metrical version of the Psalms: The English poet John Milton (1608–74) reworked several of the Biblical Psalms in 1648 and 1653. Image considers that these are below his usual standard of work.
Μηδὲν ἄγαν: (Grk) Nothing in excess.

Ernest Dowson 'A Case of Conscience' (1891)

The Century Guild Hobby Horse 6:21 (1891): pp. 2–13. Collected in *Dilemmas: Stories and Studies in Sentiment* (1895).
Ref.: 'Short Stories', *The Athenaeum* (3 August 1895): pp. 158–9.
Ploumariel: Dowson appears to have invented the name of this French village.
absinthes: A drink popular in nineteenth-century France with a very high volume of alcohol, flavoured with wormwood (*Artemisia absinthium*) and other herbs such as anise and fennel. It is green and, when served with iced water and sugar, becomes cloudy. It is the signature drink of the Decadents and bohemians, and is historically rumoured to have hallucinogenic effects. Famous absinthe drinkers include Baudelaire, Verlaine, Arthur Rimbaud, Henri de Toulouse-Lautrec, Wilde, Ernest Hemingway and Vincent van Gogh.
linsey: Coarse fabric woven from linen and wool or cotton and wool.
oraison: (Fre.) Prayer.
Aves: (Lat.) Hail Mary (Ave Maria); a form of Roman Catholic hymn, or devotional chant.
Curé: (Fre.) Priest.
Angelus bell: The sound signalling the evening recital of the triple Hail Mary.
Ite! missa est! (Lat.) 'Go! Mass concluded!' from the Catholic Mass.

Ernest Dowson 'The Statute of Limitations' (1893)

New Series *Hobby Horse* 1 (1893), pp. 2–8. It was collected in *Dilemmas* (1895) where Dowson opted for sparser punctuation and slightly different paragraph breaking, without changing the language.
Refs: R. K. R. Thornton and Monica Borg (eds), *Ernest Dowson: Collected Shorter Fiction* (Birmingham: Birmingham University Press, 2003), p. 156; Jad Adams, *Madder Music, Stronger Wine: The Life of Ernest Dowson, Poet and Decadent* (London: Tauris, 2000); Matthew Brinton Tildesley, 'Seeds of Darkness: Joseph Conrad and Ernest Dowson', *Postgraduate English* 17 (March 2008), <http://www.dur.ac.uk/postgraduate.english/Issue 17/Tildesley on Conrad (17).htm>
Statute of Limitations: A type of law which restricts the time period within which legal action can commence.
Chili: Chile. For the setting of his short story Dowson must have chanced upon Maturin Murray Ballou's *Equatorial America: Descriptive of Visit to St. Thomas, Martinique, Barbados, and the Principal Capitals of South America* (1892).
fluctuating course of nitrates: The Chilean nitrate industry was the world's most developed.
Southern Cross: A constellation of the night sky visible in the southern hemisphere.
quinine: Painkilling, anti-inflammatory drug.
mantilla: Spanish veil for women, often of lace, worn over the head and shoulders.
faro: A gambling game in which players guess the order of cards from a deck.
reck: To have caution.
Agnas Blancas: (Spa.) A fictional place. 'Agnas' is Dowson's creative variation of the female name 'Agnes' which means chaste or pure. 'Blancas' is Spanish for 'white'. Agnas Blancas is symbolic of the image of preserved purity of the girl betrothed to Michael Garth.
Horace: Quintus Horatius Flaccus (65–8 BC) was a famous Roman poet of the Augustan period, early Roman Empire. He is a major influence on Dowson. The Latin titles of some of Dowson's most famous poems such as 'Non Sum Qualis eram Bonae Sub Regno Cynarae' (1891) and 'Vitae Summa Brevis' (1896) are lines from Horace.
Tauchnitz: A German publishing firm which pioneered the cheap, mass-market paperback.

comme on ne l'est plus: (Fre.) 'as one is no longer'. Cf. Dowson, *A Comedy of Masks: A Novel* (1893), Chap. 19: 'Did I not say that he was tenacious – *comme on ne l'est plus?*'

les absents ont toujours tort: (Fre.) saying for 'the absent are always wrong'.

the 'Prince's Progress' of Miss Rossetti: Christina Rossetti (1830–94) was a Pre-Raphaelite poet. Published in *The Prince's Progress and Other Poems* (1866), 'The Prince's Progress' is a narrative poem about a prince on his way to meet his bride. His journey is slowed down by a series of enchanting encounters and temptations; his arrival is delayed and, as a result of her frustration, the waiting bride dies. The stanza quoted by Dowson (ll. 485–90) is part of the dirge about the dead bride. The poem's theme of the idealised lady, and the perpetual deferral of love's fulfilment, is resonant not only as regards to this story, but to Dowson's work in general.

taffrail: The outer railing around the stern of a ship, often made in ornate fashion.

Helen: Helen of Troy, the icon of feminine beauty.

Charles Ricketts 'The Cup of Happiness' (1889)

The Dial 1 (1889): pp. 27–33.

Refs: J. P. G. Delany, *Charles Ricketts: A Biography* (Oxford: Clarendon Press, 1990); see esp. pp. 44–5; William Gaunt, *The Aesthetic Adventure* (Oxford: Cape, 1945), p. 201.

Madam Thalia: Thalia was a common name in Greek mythology, and here Ricketts seems to be playing on both the secondary goddess of vegetation and the Muse of Comedy, both named Thalia.

La Comédie Humaine: Although Ricketts is referring to a statue, its name, *La Comédie Humaine* (Fre. 'the human comedy') refers to the multi-volume work of inter-related novels by Honoré de Balzac (1799–1850).

Schumann: Robert Schumann (1810–56) was a German composer, pianist and music critic of the Romantic era.

Warum: (Ger.) Literally 'why', 'Warum' is part of Schumann's *Fantasiestücke*, op. 12 (1837).

Venus: Roman goddess of love, sex, fertility, beauty and prosperity.

Aphrodite Anadyomene: (Grk) Aphrodite is the Greek counterpart to Venus, and Aphrodite Anadyomene refers to Venus/Aphrodite rising from the sea. A common scene for artists from the ancient to modern eras, Botticelli's *Nascita di Venera* (*The Birth of Venus*, 1486) is the most iconic.

Cnydos: A location in ancient Greece, noted for the sculptures *The Lion Tomb* and the *Statue of Demeter* both represented in fragments at the British Museum, London.

Byzantine: Usually referring to the ancient city of Byzantium; when used as an adjective, Byzantine can mean complex and devious behaviour.

Cardinal Virtues: Of Classical and Christian literature, the four Cardinal Virtues are Prudence, Justice, Temperance and Courage.

Bon mots: (Fre.) Literally, 'good words'; clever remarks or wit.

National Gallery: Founded in 1824, the National Gallery is a publicly owned art gallery in Trafalgar Square, London, and one of the five most visited galleries in the world.

Lohengrin: Opera by the German composer Richard Wagner (1813–83). Although not as highly regarded in the Victorian age as later, Wagner was extremely popular in Victorian Decadent circles.

Colophium: 'Colophium' refers to the resin or rosin used for lubricating stringed bows. In this context, it is possibly a misprint for 'colophum' meaning 'to give a blow' in eighteenth-century English. Another possibility would be the Latinised Greek word 'colophon' which can mean 'summit', 'top' or 'finishing touch'. Thus Ricketts could be using it to mean 'enough' or 'desist'.

I was painted by an Academician: Member of the Royal Academy of Arts of London, usually indicated by the suffix 'R.A.' to the artist's name.

tipsy-cake: Sweet dessert cake, with sponges soaked in sherry and brandy.

Renaissance arabesques: Based on both traditional Islamic ('Arab') and ancient Roman designs, arabesques are intricate decorative patterns usually consisting of scrolling and interweaving foliage or abstract designs. Arabesques have been popular in European design from the Renaissance era onwards.

sotto voce: (Ita.) Literally, 'under voice'; as a theatrical direction it means, 'aside' and/or 'softly'.

jessamine: Variant of Jasmine.

lourd: (Fre.) Heavy, clumsy.

flosh petal: Flosh refers to a hopper, or bucket shaped box in which mined ore is held. The petal is therefore cup-like.

List!: Listen.

Lilith: (Heb.) In Jewish mythology, Lilith was the Biblical Adam's first wife, created from the dust, as he was, in contrast to Eve who was formed from Adam's rib.

lyres: (Lat.) From the ancient Greek, meaning a small, curved stringed instrument, similar to a harp.
Solomon's idolatry: Biblical King of Israel who reigned c. 970–31 BC; builder of the First Temple, Solomon is said to have had seven hundred wives and three hundred concubines, and was punished by God for his idolatry.
Beryls: Hexagonal crystals.

Anon. [Charles Ricketts] 'Sensations' (1889)

The Dial 1 (1889): pp. 34–6. The author is presumed Charles Ricketts.
Ref.: Maureen Watry, 'At the Sign of the Dial: Charles Ricketts and the Vale Press 1896–1903', 2004, *University of Liverpool Library*, 17 October 2007, <http://liv.ac.uk/library/sca/exhibs/ValePress.html> (last accessed 15 February 2014).
Bach: Johann Sebastian Bach (1685–1750) German composer and musician of the Baroque period.
Monsieur, vous . . . frappe: (Fre.) 'Has anything happened to you, sir? The house was hit!'
ET CUM SPIRITU TUO: (Lat.) 'And with your spirit', response to the Roman Catholic Dominus Vobiscum ('The Lord be with you').
Solemn High Mass: Full ceremonial Catholic Mass, in Latin, including the use of incense.
nuque: Nape of the neck (from French).
Saint Jerome: (c. 347–420) Latin priest, theologian and historian, famed for translating the Bible into Latin (the Vulgate Bible). Most artistic representations of Jerome show him as an old man, bald and with a long grey beard.
redowa: Dance of Czech origin, being a leaping version of the waltz. It was popular in European ballrooms during the nineteenth century.

Charles Haslewood Shannon 'A Simple Story' (1889)

The Dial 1 (1889): pp. 5–8.
Ref.: Matthew Brinton Tildesley, '*The Century Guild Hobby Horse* and Oscar Wilde: A Study of British Little Magazines, 1884–1897', PhD Dissertation, Durham University, 2008, p. 232.
Seven Isles: This probably refers to the Greek Ionian Islands, also known as The Heliades.

Hilarion: Fourth-century Greek saint, disciple of St Anthony. The Temptation of Saint Hilarion was a source of inspiration for many singularly erotic paintings of the nineteenth century, most notably that by Dominique Papety (1815–49).

W. S. Fanshawe [William Sharp] 'The Black Madonna' (1892)

The Pagan Review 1 (15 August 1892): pp. 5–18. It is collected in *Vistas* (1894).
Refs: Koenraad Claes, 'Towards the Total Work of Art: Supplements and Other Paratext to Little Magazines of the 1890s', PhD Dissertation, 2011, University of Ghent, p. 176; Dennis Denisoff and Loarraine Janzen Kooistra (eds), '*The Pagan Review*', *The Yellow Nineties Online*, 2010, <http://www.1890s.ca/HTML.aspx?s=PRV1_Intro.html> (last accessed 17 February 2014).
Titans: An old race of Greek gods and goddesses spawned by Gaia and Uranus. They were overthrown by the Olympians.
Nubians: An ethnic group from the area between Egypt and Sudan.
yestereve: The evening of yesterday.
Ashtaroth: Related to Astarte, an ancient Canaanite deity and Semitic demon, associated with sexual vitality and temple prostitution.
burnous: A long hooded, usually woollen, cloak worn by Arabs.
fulgurant: Stupendously bright, like a flash of lightning.

Anon. [John Francis Bloxam] 'The Priest and the Acolyte' (1894)

The Chameleon (December 1894): pp. 29–47.
Honi soit qui mal y pense: Anglo-Norman phrase meaning 'shame on him who thinks ill of it.' In Britain, it is the motto of the Order of the Garter.
St. Anselm's: Bloxam's parish of St Anselm's is fictional. However, St Anselm was Archbishop of Canterbury in the eleventh and twelfth centuries. He was exiled twice; first by William II for his attempts to reform the Church, and subsequently by Henry I for his role in the Investiture Controversy, a significant medieval conflict between Church and State. He also wrote theological philosophy, including analysis of the relationship between sin and free will.
jerry-built: Built cheaply and shoddily.
'And whosoever ... to powder': Matthew 21: 44 (KJV).

cassock: Ankle-length clerical clothing of the Roman Catholic faith (in this instance), usually black.

cotta: Ecclesiastical over-garment; a surplice or tunic, usually white linen or cotton, reaching to the knees or ankles, and with wide sleeves.

'The Blood of ... everlasting life': From the Holy Eucharist, or Communion, where Christians drink wine representing the blood of Christ.

George Egerton 'A Lost Masterpiece: A City Mood, Aug. '93' (1894)

The Yellow Book 1 (1894): pp. 189–96.

gamin: (Fre.) An often homeless boy who wanders in the city.

Cockney sparrow: A skinny, underfed child, usually female.

Elysian Fields: In Greek mythology it is an afterlife for heroes and those associated with gods.

Soll und Haben ... Freytag: (Ger.) *Debit and Credit* (1855), by Gustav Freytag; a popular social multi-volume novel.

Whitman: Walt Whitman (1819–92): American poet, essayist and journalist.

Canaletti and Guadi: Giovanni Antonio Canal or Canaletto (1697–1768) and Francesco Guardi (1712–93) were landscape painters of the Venetian School.

Thomas Haynes Baily: Bayly (1797–1839); English songwriter and author.

Miss La Creevy: A character in Dickens's *Nicholas Nickleby* (1838–9).

Jagersfontein diamond: The Excelsior Diamond was mined in Jagersfontein in 1893 and was the largest in the world.

Jouvence: La fontaine de Jouvence (Fre.), the Fountain of Youth, in the eponymous French town in Saône-et-Loire.

kohol-tinted: kohol or kohl is an ancient form of black eye-liner, used in many Asian and Middle Eastern countries.

Je suis ... pompier: (Fre.) 'I am the true fireman / the only fireman'. L'art pompier (Fireman Art) was a derisive term to describe late nineteenth-century paintings usually about historical and mythological subjects that were academic, grandiose and pompous. The term is also extended to the 'fireman author'.

la mióla: Probably Egerton's neologism, the female equivalent of 'miolo' (Por.) which means 'crumb, core, or brain'. It likely refers to the inventions of the protagonist's mind (core).

Corcovado: A mountain range in Rio de Janeiro, Brazil.

Home Rule, Bimetallism, or the Woman Question: Irish Independence from Britain, the Gold Standard or the 'New Woman'.

Hubert Crackanthorpe 'Modern Melodrama' (1894)

The Yellow Book 1 (1894): pp. 223–32. Collected in *Sentimental Studies and a Set of Village Tales* (1895).
Refs: William Greenslade, 'Naturalism and Decadence: The Case of Hubert Crackanthorpe', in J. D. Hall and Alex Murray (eds), *Decadent Poetics* (Basingstoke: Palgrave, 2013): pp. 163–80: p. 176; Nicholas Freeman, *Conceiving the City: London, Literature, and Art 1870–1914* (Oxford: Oxford University Press, 2007), p. 67; Jad Adams, 'The Drowning of Hubert Crackanthorpe and the Persecution of Leila Macdonald', *English Literature in Transition, 1880–1920*, 52.1 (2009): pp. 6–34: pp. 14–15.

Charlotte M. Mew, 'Passed' (1894)

The Yellow Book 2 (1894): pp. 121–41.
Refs: Joseph Bristow, 'Charlotte Mew's Aftereffects', *Modernism/Modernity* 16 (2009): pp. 255–80: p. 265; Penelope Fitzgerald, *Charlotte Mew and Her Friends* (London: Collins, 1984), p. 62.
Hawkers: Costermongers, street merchants.
muffin-bell: Hand-held bell in two halves, with a wooden handle.
alley-tors . . . suckers: An assortment of children's toys.
chromo: Chromolithograph: a method of producing colour prints, widely used in the nineteenth century.
'The realm . . . grave': From a letter by George Eliot (1819–80) to Georgiana Burne-Jones (1840–1920).
Day of Account: Judgement Day.
plagal cadence: In church music this cadence finishes a hymn; usually sung to 'A-men'.
hideous English of their fate: From George Meredith's *The Egoist* (1879), Chap. 37.

Lionel Johnson 'Tobacco Clouds' (1894)

The Yellow Book 3 (1894): pp. 143–52.
'a spirit in my feet', *as Shelley and Catullus have it*: Johnson quotes

from Percy Bysshe Shelley's 'The Indian Serenade' (1822), and a very similar line is found in Catullus XLVI, l. 8.

Lucretius: Titus Lucretius Carus (c. 99–55 BC), Roman poet, philosopher and Epicurean.

'with Milton ... early Italy': Here Johnson is referring to antiquarian *belles lettres*, namely the 1759 edition of Milton's *Paradise Lost* (1667), printed by John Baskerville, and Lucretius's only surviving work, *De Rerum Natura* (*'The Nature of Things'*), most probably the 1512 'Juntine', Florence edition, edited by Pietro Candido.

sedulous: Diligent, hard working.

occultis de rebus quo referam: (Lat.) literally, 'relevant matters, that are hidden' or 'veiled answers'.

Milton, in his evil days: In Book Seven of Milton's *Paradise Lost*, the poet invokes Urania, the Muse of Astronomy to help him, saying:

> More safe I sing with mortal voice, unchanged
> To hoarse or mute, though fallen on evil days,
> On evil days though fallen, and evil tongues;
> In darkness, and with dangers compassed round. (7, ll. 24–7)

cigarette: It is worthy of note that cigarettes were a relatively new concept in late-Victorian society, and still had an air of the avant-garde about them. Oscar Wilde praises the cigarette in many of his works, and they represent the final twist in Pierre Louÿs's time-travelling, erotic tale, 'A New Sensation' (*Sanguines*, 1903).

Nichomachean Ethics: This is the title given to Aristotle's most famous work concerning ethics.

Whence have we sago?: Sago is a starch extracted from the pith of palm trees.

Proesentia temnis: (Lat.) Misspelling of 'Praesentia temnis'– 'one despises what one currently has', from Lucretius III, l. 957.

Civitas Dei: (Lat.) City of God.

Regnum Hominis: (Lat.) Kingdom of Man.

Stuart king: King James VI of Scotland and I of England, opposed smoking most vehemently, and published *A Counterblaste to Tobacco* in 1604.

dames of Thessaly: In classical Greece, the moon was said to be controlled by Thessalian witches.

'of Propertius ... Golden': All of these ancient writers' works include tales about witches.

Sadducismus triumphatus: *Saducismus Triumphatus* is the title of Joseph Glanvill's book on witchcraft, published in England in 1681. The book is said to have influenced Cotton Mather, and the Salem Witch Trials.
Nox, et noctis . . . volantes: (Lat.) Misspelling of 'nox et noctis signa severa noctivagaeque faces caeli flammaeque volantes' – 'night, and the stern stars of night, and heaven's torches wandering through the night, and the flying meteors' from Lucretius V, ll. 1190–1.
'faery elves . . . Sits arbitress': From Book One of *Paradise Lost*.
Smiter of the Firstborn: Alluding to the Biblical tale of the smiting of the firstborn child of all Egyptians in Exodus 12: 12, and the origins of the Jewish ritual of Passover.
otia dia: (Lat.) Lucretius V, l. 1387, 'abodes of unearthly calm'.
sa musique, sa flame: (Fre.) Literally, 'his music, his passion'.
the Compleat Angler . . . Walton: The English writer, Izaak Walton (1594–1683) is best known for his book *The Compleat Angler* (1653) in which he expostulates on the art and spirit of fishing, through prose and poetry. The River Lea, which runs through Amwell and Ware in Hertfordshire, was a favourite haunt of Walton's.
'Addison, rather than Steele': Joseph Addison and Richard Steele were co-founders of *The Spectator* magazine in 1711. In the early years, the two men were the sole contributors to the magazine.
Will Wimble . . . Sir Roger's woods: Here Johnson reveals that he will not be reading the *current* edition of *The Spectator*, but a tale by Addison, relating to fishing, from number 108, 4 July 1711.
Giuntine: ('Juntine') 1512 Florentine edition of Lucretius mentioned above.
It ver et Venus: (Lat.) 'Youth and Venus', a common phrase in ancient Roman poetry, including the works of Lucretius.
L'Allegro: Pastoral poem of 1645 by John Milton.

'C. S.' [presumed Henry Harland] 'To Every Man a Damsel or Two' (1894)

The Yellow Book 3 (1894): pp. 155–7.
Ref.: Barry J. Faulk, *Music Hall and Modernity: The Late-Victorian Discovery of Popular Culture* (Athens, OH: Ohio University Press, 2004), p. 102.
Gainsborough: Very large hat, often decorated with feathers or flowers, named after those depicted in the works of the English painter Thomas Gainsborough (1727–88).

florin: British two-shilling, or twenty-four pennies coin, minted between 1849 and 1967.

Victoria Cross 'Theodora: A Fragment' (1895)

The Yellow Book 4 (1895): pp. 156–88.
Refs: Charlotte Mitchell (ed.), *Victoria Cross (1868–1952): A Bibliography* ([Brisbane]: Victorian Fiction Research Unit, University of Queensland, 2002), pp. 3–4, 16–17; Nicolas Freeman, *1895: Drama, Disaster and Disgrace in Late Victorian Britain* (Edinburgh: Edinburgh University Press, 2011), pp. 39–40.
dum casta manet: (Lat.) 'while one remains chaste'.
Schopenhauer's theory . . . the ends of Nature: See 'The Metaphysics of the Love of the Sexes' (1844). Arthur Schopenhauer (1788–1860) was an influential German atheist philosopher whose most famous idea is that suffering is the result of the quenchless striving of what he calls 'Will'.
Turkish fez: Short, box-like, truncated conical hat usually made of red felt, with a tassle.
Ranees: Plural of ranee or rani (Hin.); Indian queen or rajah's wife.
Mohammedan: Muslim (follower of the Prophet Mohammed).
Sikh: Follower of Sikhism, a sixteenth-century, monotheistic religion of the Punjab.
Astarte: An ancient Mesopotamian goddess.
Shiva: The Destroyer, one of the major Hindu gods.
The fate of Hippolitus . . . Bacchus: *Hippolytus* (428 BC) and *The Bacchae* (405 BC) respectively, tragedies by Athenian playwright Euripides (c. 480–406 BC).
zouave: A woman's short, open-fronted embroidered jacket inspired by that of the zouave uniform (the zouaves were light infantrymen serving in the French army in North Africa).
Taj: The Taj Mahal mausoleum at Agra, India.
Herod with your daughter of Herodias: In this Biblical myth that fascinated Decadent and Symbolist artists and authors alike – the most famous instance being Wilde's monodrama *Salomé* (1891) – after Salome, the daughter of Herodias, dances in front of King Herod, the last is so entranced that he promises to grant anything she asks. Salome asks for John the Baptist's head on a platter, the only thing Herod dithers to grant. The resonance of this allusion to the story is obvious.

R. Murray Gilchrist 'The Crimson Weaver' (1895)

The Yellow Book 6 (1895): pp. 269–77.
Refs: 'The Hectic and the Morbid in the 1890's', *Studies in Short Fiction* 6:1 (1968): pp. 90–2: pp. 90–1; 'Mr. R. Murray Gilchrist', *The Academy* (9 December 1899): pp. 689–90: p. 690.
tenour: The course or general sense of meaning.
Diana: The Roman goddess of hunting, of lunar associations.
Actaeon: A Greek mythological hunter. For spying on Artemis's, or Diana's, bathing, naked body, the goddess turned him into a stag which was eventually torn to pieces by Actaeon's own men.
columbary: Dovecote or pigeon-house.
corse: Corpse.
eld: Archaic for olden times.
riband: A narrow strip of fabric; anything resembling a ribbon.
chrysolite: It refers to a variety of gems in the spectrum of green.
bartizan: A turret projecting or overhanging from a top corner of a medieval castle.
Nepenthe: A drug that heals sorrow and sadness by inducing forgetfulness.

Mrs Ernest [Ada] Leverson 'The Quest of Sorrow' (1896)

The Yellow Book 8 (1896): pp. 325–35.
Ref.: Dennis Denisoff, 'Decadence and Aestheticism', in Gail Marshal (ed.), *The Cambridge Companion to the Fin de Siècle* (Cambridge: Cambridge University Press, 2007): pp. 31–52: p. 51.
Philistine: In the Hebrew Bible, the Philistines were the enemies of Israel, and Matthew Arnold used the term to describe the English middle classes in his seminal work *Culture and Anarchy* (1867–8).
Lys de la Vallée: (Fre.) Lily of the Valley.
epicurism: More commonly 'epicureanism'; pertaining to Epicurus's teachings (c. 307 BC) of pleasure as the highest good. Epicureanism is partnered with Aestheticism and Decadence, as evinced by Walter Pater's *Marius the Epicurean* (1885).
mashed: Amorously attracted.
Chopin's nocturnes, and photographs by Mendelssohn: Frédéric Chopin (1810–1849), Polish composer of the Romantic era, wrote many, popular 'nocturnes' – melodic, song-like piano pieces. Jakob Ludwig Felix Mendelssohn Bartholdy (1809–1847) was a German Romantic composer.

Leverson's linking of Mendelssohn with photography seems to be an instance of her penchant for obfuscation.
beau role: (Fre.) the leading part in a performance.
boutade: (Fre.) thrust, outburst.

Ella D'Arcy, 'The Death Mask' (1896)

The Yellow Book 10 (1896): pp. 265–85. Collected in *Modern Instances* (1898).
Ref.: 'Modern Instances by Ella D'Arcy', *The Bookman* (August 1898): p. 41.
mouleurs: (Fre.) Moulders, dye-workers.
Simian: Anthropoid; ape, monkey, or human.
ouvrière class: (Fre.) Working class.
inches and muscle: Possibly ribald penis reference, implicitly about the worship of the body over intellect.
gamins and filles: (Fre.) Boys and girls.
caryatides: (Grk) Ancient Greek pillars of a building in the form of women; the most famous ones are in the Erechtheion on the Acropolis, Athens.
entablatures: The structures above the capitals of columns.
échorché: (Fre.) A painted or sculpted skinless figure, with the body's muscular tissues exposed.
creux: (Fre.) The term 'pensée en creux' in sculpture terms means to 'see something in relief', for example, the mould from which a statue is to be cast.
microcephalous: (Grk) Literally 'of a small head', disproportionate to the body. Microcephaly is an abnormal genetic condition.
absinthe: See p. 428.
Silemus-like . . . Bacchantes: Suggestive of Dionysian figures associated with debauchery, lewdness and drunkenness.

Rudolph Dircks 'Ellen' (1896)

The Savoy 1 (1896): pp. 103–8.
Ref.: Matthew Brinton Tildesley, 'The Shadow of Oscar Wilde: A Study of Subversive and Clandestine Sexuality in Four Novellas from *The Savoy*', *Short Story Criticism* 152 (March 2011): pp. 302–11 (Gale Cengage Learning).

Frederick Wedmore 'To Nancy' (1896)

The Savoy 1 (1896): pp. 31–40. Collected in *Orgeas and Miradou with Other Pieces* (1896).
Ref.: Tildesley, 'The Shadow of Oscar Wilde'.
cobotin: Sham actor, or poseur.
Weymouth: A seaside town in the southern English county of Dorset. It is significant that Nancy's innocent beginnings are set in provincial England, whereas her later fall from grace occurs in cosmopolitan London.
John of Bologna: (1529–1608) A Renaissance sculptor, born in Flanders, heavily influenced by Michaelangelo.
Sylvia Grey: (1866–1958) An English burlesque dancer on the Victorian stage, and in the nineteen twenties, an actress in French cinema.
Voltaire's Sylvia [and] the Camargo: Marie Anne de Cupis de Camargo ('La Camargo') was a celebrated eighteenth-century French dancer. Voltaire, La Camargo and the actress Silvia Baletti (also known as Flaminia) all appear in the section 'Paris' in the memoirs of Cassanova.
Ingres: Jean Auguste Dominique Ingres (1780–1867) was a French neo-classical and Romantic painter. His *Grande Odelisque* (1814) is a reclining nude, famous for being a slim, elongated and romanticised view of the female form, departing from anatomical realism.
Erard: Sébastian Érard (1752–1831) was a French maker of pianos and harps.
Quakeress: The Quakers, or Society of Friends, are a Protestant Christian denomination, historically renowned for temperance, pacifism and plain dress.
hundred Earls: 'The daughter of a hundred Earls' is a line from Alfred, Lord Tennyson's poem 'Lady Clara Vere de Vere', and refers to members of the British aristocracy.
tant bien que mal: (Fre.) 'More or less'.
carmine: Bright red.
forelock: Literally, the foremost lock of hair. To seize Time by the forelock is to act with urgency.
Noblesse oblige: (Fre.) Literally, 'nobility obliges'. To act in accordance with one's position or rank.

Frederick Wedmore 'The Deterioration of Nancy' (1896)

The Savoy 2 (1896): pp. 99–108.
Refs: Tildesley, 'The Shadow of Oscar Wilde'; Ronald Pearsall, *The Worm in the Bud: The World of Victorian Sexuality*, 2nd edn [1969] (Harmondsworth: Pelican-Penguin, 1971), pp. 430–46.
dénouement: (Fre.) Final part, or resolution to a story.
Variety Stage: Theatrical show with varied content, such as songs, dancing, juggling, comic turns, etc., presided over by a theatrical host.
Bedford Camden Town: The Old Bedford Music Hall in Camden, London.
Gatti's, Westminster Bridge Road: 'Gatti's-in-the-road' Music Hall, Westminster Bridge Road, London, named after its owner, Carlo Gatti the Swiss entrepreneur.
'notices': Favourable reviews, used in advertising and press reports.
Shylock's . . . Portia: In Shakespeare's *The Merchant of Venice* (c. 1596–8), the character Shylock is the archetypal Jewish moneylender, and Portia the young heroine.
the dickens: Euphemism for the devil, as in Shakespeare's *Merry Wives of Windsor* III, ii, 1327: 'I cannot tell what the dickens his name is.'
Sisters of Charity: Phrase commonly linked to Christian missionaries or nuns.
He sang of love . . . the song for me!: The closing lines of William Wordsworth's poem, 'Oh Nightingale! Thou Surely Art', 1807.

Arthur Symons, 'Pages from the Life of Lucy Newcome' (1896)

The Savoy 2 (1896): pp. 146–60.
Refs: Tildesley, 'The Shadow of Oscar Wilde'; Ian Fletcher, *Rediscovering Herbert Horne: Poet, Architect, Typographer, Art Historian* (Greensboro, NC: ELT Press, 1990), pp. 12, 16, 118; Alan P. Johnson, 'Arthur Symons' "Novel àla Goncourt"' [sic.], *Journal of Modern Literature* 9.1 (1981–2): pp. 50–64.
acid-drops: Boiled sweets with a strong acidic flavour.
gauferer: Most probably this is a misspelling of gaufrier (Fre.), meaning a waffle iron, or hinged, two-plated iron.
crowner's quest: Corruption of 'coroner's inquest'.

Theodore Wratislaw, 'Mutability' (1896)

The Savoy 5 (1896): pp. 39–51.
south-wester: Wind blowing from a south-westerly direction.
foot of the down: A down is a small hill, often composed of chalk, in southern England, and in this case close to the coast. The 'foot' signifies the base of the hill.
vieux-rose-colour: (Fre.) Literally 'old' rose colour – a darker shade of pink.
Ascot: Ascot Racecourse is a horseracing venue in Berkshire, England, closely associated with the British Royal family.
beating a tattoo: A tattoo is a military drum performance; that is, fast-beating.
no Elizabeth to forgive Tannhauser: Richard Wagner's opera *Tannhäuser* (1845) is an extravagant exploration of love, both sacred and profane. The character Elizabeth represents holy, self-sacrificing love in the tale, and is Tannhäuser's salvation.

Joseph Conrad 'The Idiots' (1896)

In *The Savoy* 6 (1896): pp. 11–30.
Refs: Tildesley, 'Seeds of Darkness'; Robert Louis Stevenson, *The Strange Case of Dr Jekyll and Mr Hyde and Other Tales of Terror*, ed. Robert Mighall (London: Penguin, 2002); Arthur Symons, *Notes on Joseph Conrad: With Some Unpublished Letters* (London: Myers, 1925).
Treguier . . . Ploumar [etc.]: Akin to many of Ernest Dowson's short stories, the action here takes place in rural Brittany, north-western France.
biniou: Binioù (Fre.). Small Breton instrument similar to bagpipes.
Sabots: (Fre.) Wooden shoes or 'clogs'.
ma chère amie: (Fre.) 'My dear friend'.
soutane: (Fre.) Priest's cassock.
Allez! Houp! (Fre.) 'Go on! Jump!'
Malheur: (Fre.) Literally 'bad hour'. Misfortune.
sibillation: To speak with a hissing sound.
Lotharios: Seducers of women or 'womanisers'; from the character Lothario in Miguel de Cervantes' *Don Quixote* (1605 and 1615).
gendarmes: French military force, charged with police duties.
declivity: Downward slope.

John Gray 'Light' (1897)

The Pageant (1897): pp. 113–34.
Ref.: G. A. Cevasco, *John Gray* (Boston: Twayne, 1982), pp. 8–14, 25–35.
belles lettres: (Fre.) The literal translation is 'beautiful writing' or 'letters'. However, the phrase was popular in the literary world of the 1890s; it reflected the fetish for small-run, artistically designed books, printed on handmade paper. The early years of the Bodley Head, presided over by Elkin Mathews and John Lane, typified the style.
Martin biblical subjects: John Martin (1789–1854), British, Romantic painter, engraver and illustrator.
daguerreotype: (Fre.) Early form of photography whereby images were superimposed upon a highly polished silver surface, later protected under glass. Introduced in 1839, the daguerreotype was the most popular form of photograph until the 1860s.
Parsees: Indian people descending from Persian Zoroastrians.
Tierra del Fuegians: The Chilean and Argentinian islands of Tierra del Fuego were a target for British Anglican missionaries from 1855.
Calvary: The hill upon which Christ was said to have been crucified.
Except a man ... God: A fundamental condition of much Protestant dogma. It represents a conscious decision to accept the Christian faith.
Jacopone da Todi: (c. 1230–1306) Italian Franciscan Friar, poet and pioneer of early Italian theatre.
Apollyon: (Grk) Biblical angel, whose name means destroyer. The Biblical Hebrew equivalent 'Abbadon' refers to a place of destruction, the bottomless pit and the land of the dead.
genetrix: (Lat.) Mother or literally, female creator.
Johann Scheffler: (1624–77) A German priest, physician, mystic and poet. After converting to Catholicism in 1653, he adopted the name Angelus Silesius.
Friedrich Spe: Friedrich Spee (1591–1635) was a German Jesuit and poet, famed for speaking out against the use of torture, and a notable opponent of witchcraft trials.
Crashaw's poem on the circumcision: Richard Crashaw (1613–49) was an English Metaphysical poet whose work includes verses in the sub-genre of Christian literature known as Circumcision poetry. Such poems focus on the physical, human and 'fleshly' nature of Christ. Other writers of Circumcision poetry include John Donne (1572–1631) and John Milton.

Max Beerbohm, 'Yai and the Moon' (1897)

The Pageant 2 (1897): pp. 143–55. It was collected in *A Variety of Things* (1928).
Refs: John N. Hall, *Max Beerbohm: A Kind of life* (Yale: Yale University Press, 2002); J. G. Riewald, 'Max Beerbohm and Oscar Wilde', in J. G. Riewald (ed.), *The Surprise of Excellence: Modern Essays on Max Beerbohm* (Hamden, CT: Archon, 1974), pp. 47–64.
Yai: Although this is a Thai name, in Beerbohm's story it is a corrupted version of Yae, a Japanese feminine forename, which also means 'double-' or 'multi-layered'. A likely candidate for the inspiration of 'Yai and the Moon' is A. B. Mitford's *Tales of Old Japan* (1871).
Bay of Yedo: Former/poetic name for Tokyo Bay.
treillage of convolvulus: Treillage refers to a trellis, the lattice-work formed by climbing (scandent) ornamental plants such as vines. Convolvulus is the flowering plant belonging to the same family as morning glory and bindweed.
fandangles: Excessive and useless ornaments.
ipso facto: (Lat.) 'By the fact itself'.
Moon: It is likely that Beerbohm drew his scientific knowledge about the moon from Edmund Neison's *The Moon and the Condition and Configuration of its Surface* (1876).
selenography: The cartographical description of the surface of the Moon.
Lick Observatory: Astronomical observatory near San Jose, California. It was built under the patronage of James Lick and completed in 1887.
Neuromania: A post-Darwinian pseudo-science, typified by the desire to give all human experience and behaviour a scientific explanation, rooted in the chemical processes in the brain.
Echolalia: (Grk) William James defines 'echolalia' as the '[a]utomatic repetition of every sound heard' (*The Principles of Psychology* [1890], vol. 2, Chap. 27 titled 'Hypnotism').
always spying . . . telescope: Compare with 'Shall I, the last Endymion, lose all hope / Because rude eyes peer at my mistress through a telescope!' (Oscar Wilde, 'The Garden of Eros', ll. 227–8, in *Poems* [1881]).

Villiers de l'Isle-Adam 'Queen Ysabeau' (1897)

The Pageant 2 (1897): pp. 222–31.
[Epigraph]: Manethon, or Manetho, author of *Aegyptiaka* (*History of*

Egypt), was an ancient Egyptian historian and priest who lived in the 3rd century BC, during the Ptolemaic period. Queen Nitocris is a questionable historical figure, purportedly the last Pharaoh of the Sixth Dynasty, and of great beauty. Her cold, revenge plot is resonant with Villiers's tale of Queen Ysabeau.

gore: An archaic term referring to a triangular piece of cloth, inserted into a garment to widen its girth.

gabels: In old English law a gabel is a rent, service, tribute, custom, tax, duty; an excise.

John of Nevers: John the Fearless (1371–1419) from the House of Valois-Burgundy was for a period regent of France for King Charles VI, his mentally disabled first cousin.

Tenzons [and] *Virelays*: A Provençal poem in the form of a dialogue or *tension* between two competing troubadours, and a fourteenth-century French verse form, respectively.

Louis of Orleans: (1372–1407) brother of King Charles VI and allegedly a secret lover of Isabeau. He was assassinated by order of John the Fearless.

tocsin: A bell sounding an alarm or a warning.

breaks you upon the wheel: The breaking wheel was a medieval torture and execution device used until the eighteenth century. The victim was placed upon a wheel where he had his bones broken by bludgeoning; death was usually slow.

Oscar Wilde 'The Nightingale and the Rose' (1888)

The Happy Prince and Other Tales (London: Nutt, 1888), pp. 27–41.
Ref.: Jarlath Killeen, *The Fairy Tales of Oscar Wilde* (Aldershot: Ashgate, 2007), pp. 41–59; esp. pp. 50–2.
A collocation from Edward FitzGerald's *The Rubáiyát of Omar Khayyám* (1859) curiously captures the central image of the story: '"Red Wine!" – the Nightingale cries to the Rose / That yellow Cheek of hers to incarnadine' (stanza 6). Analogues of Wilde's story are found in Ovid, John Keats and Hans Christian Andersen.

Vernon Lee 'The Legend of Madame Krasinska' (1890)

The Fortnightly Review 47.279 (March 1890): pp. 377–96. It was collected in *Vanitas: Polite Stories* (1892).
Refs: Ruth Robbins, 'Vernon Lee: Decadent Woman', in John Stoke (ed.),

Fin de Siecle/Fin du Globe: Fears and Fantasies of the Late Nineteenth Century (London: Macmillan, 1992), pp. 139–61: p. 152; Catherine Maxwell and Patricia Pulham, *Vernon Lee: Decadence, Ethics, Aesthetics* (Basingstoke: Palgrave, 2006), pp. 9–11.
Little Sisters of the Poor: Catholic order founded in mid-nineteenth-century France.
Lucretia Borgia: (1480–1519) Italian daughter of the future Pope Alexander VI and iconic *femme fatale*. The Borgia family was notorious for its political corruption and debauchery.
crâne: (Fre.) skull, suggestive of 'cerebral'.
Deadly Nightshade [and] Belladonna Atropa: Poisonous flowers.
Volunteers in '59 . . . Solferino: The Battle of Solferino, Italy, June 1859 was fought between the Austrian Army and Napoleon III's French Army, allied with Sardinia (the victors).
With baby obligato: (Ita.) With obligatory baby. 'Obbligato' means musical accompaniment.
Chanoiness: Chanoinesse (Fre.) Female canon.
volume of Gyp: GYP is the pseudonym of French essayst and novelist Sibylle Aimée Marie-Antoinette Gabrielle de Riquetti de Mirabeau, Comtesse de Martel de Janville (1849–1932).
variosities: Possibly an unorthodox way of saying a multitude of different things.
Addio, mia bella, addio: (Ita.) 'Farewell, my lovely, farewell.'
cloisonné: Decorative coating of objects with compartments of vitreous enamel.
Garibaldi's hymn: 'All Forward!' (1862); a patriotic lyric (1862) by Giuseppe Garibaldi (1807–82).
Faites votre jeu, messieurs: (Fre.) 'Place your bets, gentlemen.'
Rien ne . . . manque: (Fre.) 'End of bets – twenty-three – red, odd, and fail' (roulette jargon).
tresette: (Ita.) Literally, 'three-sevens'; an Italian trick-taking card game.
moreen: A worsted, ribbed drapery used for furnishings.
Montepulciano: From the red Italian wine grape variety.
S. Bonifazio: A reference to the painting *La sala delle agitate al San Bonifazio* (*Ward of Madwomen at San Bonifazio in Florence*) (1865) by Telemaco Signorini (1835–1901).
the Aeneid, translated by Caro: A lyrical translation of Virgil's epic *Aeneid* by Italian author Annibale Caro (1507–66).

Mongibello: (Ita.) 'Beautiful mountain'. In Sicily, Etna is known as Mongibello.

Casta Diva: A renowned aria in Act I of Vincenzo Bellini's (1801–35) opera *Norma* (1831).

Ghibelline nobles: A faction based in central and northern Italy supporting the Holy Roman Emperor during the thirteenth to sixteenth centuries.

in the days of Dante's grandfather: Bellincione Alighieri, Dante's paternal grandfather. Lee alludes perhaps to the early 1200s.

pipkins: Small pots, usually ceramic.

niello: A black metallic alloy.

Pater noster qui es in caelo: (Lat.) 'Our Father who art in Heaven'.

Oscar Wilde 'The Sphinx without a Secret' (1891)

Lord Arthur Savile's Crime and Other Stories (London: James Osgood, 1891): pp. 75–87. Previously published as 'Lady Alroy', *The World*, 25 May 1887.

Ref.: Wilde, *The Picture of Dorian Gray*, Joseph Bristow and Ian Small (eds), p. 423.

Café de la Paix: A famous Parisian café near the Boulevard des Capucines, next to the Opéra, which attracted artists, authors and bohemians.

Pentateuch: The first five books of the Old Testament.

House of Peers: The House of Lords, being the second chamber of the British government, after the House of Commons.

Gioconda in sables: Possibly a parodic reference to the enigmatic quality of the *Mona Lisa*. Sable is a type of animal fur used to make fur coats. In this sense, the Sphinx without a Secret is a bathetic modern rendition of the Mona Lisa. 'Sable' hairs are also what are used to make very fine painters' brushes.

ma belle inconnue: (Fre.) 'My beautiful stranger' (feminine).

E. Nesbit 'The Ebony Frame' (1891)

Longman's Magazine 18.108 (October 1891): pp. 605–15. Collected in *Grim Tales* (1893).

Refs: Emma Liggins, 'Gendering the Spectral Encounter at the *Fin de Siecle*: Unspeakability in Vernon Lee's Supernatural Stories', *Gothic Studies* 15.2 (2013): pp. 37–52: p. 38; Nick Freeman, 'E. Nesbit's New

Woman Gothic', *Women's Writing* 15.3 (2008): pp. 454–69: p. 458.

The Trial of Lord William Russell: A painting (1825) by Sir George Hayter (1792–1871). Baron Russell (1639–83) was a politician caught in the Rye House Plot against King Charles II, wishing the ascendance of a Catholic ruler (James II). He was not directly involved in the plot and was executed for treason.

chimley-back: The soot that comes down from sweeping a chimney.

This was a woman ... papers and pens: Nesbit is possibly giving the impression of a Pre-Raphaelite 'type' that is often referred to in literature of the late Victorian period in a generic way. The description here suggests the Rossettian 'stunner' in paintings like *La Donna della Finestra, La Ghirlandata, Sibylla Palmifera, Veronica Veronese* or Burne-Jones's *Cupid and Psyche*. The specific symbolic details in the story pertain to the lady as a learned witch.

after long grief... Round me once again: From Alfred Lord Tennyson's (1809–92) *Maud* (1855), Part II.

Eric Stenbock 'The True Story of a Vampire' (1894)

Studies of Death: Romantic Tales (London: David Nutt, 1894), pp. 120–47. Reprinted in Ian Fletcher and John Stokes (eds), *The Shadow of Death; Studies of Death*, Degeneration and Regeneration: Texts of the Premodern Era (New York; London: Garland Publishing, 1984).

Refs: John Adlard, *Stenbock, Yeats and the Nineties*, with an hitherto unpublished essay on Stenbock by Arthur Symons and a bibliography by Timothy d'Arch Smith (London: Cecil and Amelia Woolf, 1969), pp. 83, 91; W. B. Yeats (ed.), *The Oxford Book of Modern Verse, 1892–1935* (Oxford: Oxford University Press, 1936), p. x.

'en arc d'amour': (Fre.) 'In an amorous curve'.

Grace is ... eternally: See Psalms 45:2 (KJV).

csardas: A traditional folk dance from Hungary.

relâche: (Fre.) Halt, stoppage, interlude, respite.

Nie umiem ... kocham: (Pol) 'I cannot express how much I love you.'

extreme unction: In Catholicism it is the last sacrament of a dying person in which the organs of the five senses are anointed.

H. G. Wells 'The Flowering of the Strange Orchid' (1894, 1895)

The Stolen Bacillus and Other Incidents (Methuen: London, 1895): pp. 17–35. The story first appeared in *Pall Mall Budget* 2 (1894). It is collected in *The Country of the Blind and Other Stories* (1911).
Ref.: Yoonjoung Choi, 'The Wonderful Visit and the Wilde Trial', *The Wellsian* 31 (2008): pp. 43–55.
diatoms: Unicellular micro-organisms, an order of algae.
vandas [and] *Dendrobe*: Genii of usually epiphytal orchids cultivated for their beauty.
Chlorodyne: A nineteenth-century concocted narcotic medicine.
Darwin: Wells refers to Darwin's *Fertilisation of Orchids* (1862).
Cypripediums: A genus of northern-hemisphere orchids known as Lady's Slipper.
Palaeonophis Lowii: Wells means Phaleonopsis Lowii, a species of orchid found in Burma and western Thailand.

Una Ashworth Taylor 'The Truce of God' (1896)

Nets for the Wind (Boston: Roberts; London: Lane, 1896), pp. 156–72.
Ref.: Talia Schaffer, *The Forgotten Female Aesthetes: Literary Culture in Late-Victorian England* (Charlottesville: University Press of Virginia, 2008), pp. 54–5.
There is a legend … bondsman: This is probably an allusion to William Morris's tale of 'The Ring Given to Venus' from *The Earthly Paradise* (1868–70), developed from information in Sabine Baring-Gould's *Curious Myths of the Middle Ages* (1865) and based on William of Malmesbury's (c. 1095/96–c. 1143) *De Gestis Regum Anglorum*. See also a variant of the tale in Prosper Mérimée's (1803–70) short story 'La Vénus d'Ille' (1837).

Vincent O'Sullivan 'Original Sin' (1896)

A Book of Bargains (London: Smithers, 1896): pp. 113–25.
Refs: Holbrook Jackson, *The Eighteen Nineties* [1913] (London: Grant Richards, 1922), p. 222; Jessica Amanda Salmonson (intro.), 'A Fallen Master of the Macabre', in Vincent O'Sullivan, *Master of Fallen Years: The Complete Supernatural Stories of Vincent O'Sullivan* (London: The Ghost Story Press, 1995).

[Epigraph]: This is the first quatrain of Baudelaire's sonnet 'La Destruction' ('Destruction') from *Les Fleurs du Mal* (1857):

The Fiend is at my side without a rest;
He swirls around me like a subtle breeze;
I swallow him, and burning fills my breast,
And calls me to desire's shameful needs.

in Jonathan Culler (ed.) and James McGowan (trans.), *The Flowers of Evil* (Oxford: Oxford University Press, 1993; 1998), p. 229.
L'Ennemi des Lois: (Fre.) *The Enemy of the Laws* (1893), a political novel by Symbolist author Auguste-Maurice Barrès.
Charité, Monsieur!: (Fre.) 'Charity, sir!'
bonne: (Fre.) Housemaid.

M. P. Shiel 'Xélucha' (1896)

Shapes in the Fire (London: Lane; Boston: Roberts, 1896): pp. 1–17.
Refs: William L. Svitavsky, 'From Decadence to Racial Antagonism: M. P. Shiel at the Turn of the Century', *Science Fiction Studies* 31:1 (2004): pp. 1–24: pp. 10–12; Susan J. Navarrette, *The Shape of Fear: Horror and the Fin de Siècle Culture of Decadence* (Lexington: The University Press of Kentucky, 1998), pp. 153–4.
'He goeth after her . . . and knoweth not . . .': Compare with Proverbs 7:22–3 (KJV).
petit mal: (Fre.) A little illness. A staring or absence spell lasting for a few seconds due to anomalous electrical brain activity.
cista: (Lat.) Literally 'chest'. A Classical casket.
Sybarites: Pursuers of sensual and luxurious pleasures.
the Priap of the détraqués: 'Détraqué' (Fre.) means someone who is dangerously deranged; a madman, a psychopath. In Greek mythology, Priapus or Priapos was a minor rustic fertility god. Priapus is marked by a grotesquely oversized, permanent erection, which gave rise to the medical term priapism.
choragus: Leader or sponsor of an ancient Greek drama chorus.
I will not say of Paphos, but of Chemos! and Baal-Peor!: Paphos is a coastal area of Cyprus and birthplace of goddess of love Aphrodite. Chemosh and Baal-Peor are degenerate deities of the Moabites who lead the Israelites to depraved idolatry.

Here Lucy Hill . . . wholly: The way Shiel spins these fancies is strongly evocative of Wilde's erudite, purple prose.

Mérimée: The name of the main character alludes to French writer Prosper Mérimée whose novella *Carmen* (1845) is based on Georges Bizet's eponymous opera. He also wrote the influential horror story 'La Vénus d'Ille' (1837).

elle dérangera l'Enfer: (Fre.) 'She will disturb Hell.'

She will introduce the pas de tarantule into Tophet: The (Galician) 'passion of the tarantula' into 'Tophet', a Biblical place; proverbially it refers to an extremely unpleasant or painful condition or place; hell.

manat rara meas lacrima per genas: (Lat.) 'Does a rare tear fall down my cheek' (our translation). Horace, *Odes*, IV, I, l. 34. This is the same poem from which Dowson's 'Cynara', the most celebrated lyric of *fin-de-siècle* Decadence, takes its title.

expert as Thargelia; cultured as Aspatia; purple as Semiramis: An Ionian hetaera (courtesan) in ancient Greece, a Milesian hetaera (c. 470 BC–400 BC), and Queen of Babylon respectively. The epithets Shiel attributes to these 'splendid harlots of history' are historically congruent.

Tarare: (Ita.) Calibrate.

constellation: Cygnus.

Begum: (Tur.) The feminine version of Beg, a high class rank.

thulite tint: Pinkish colour.

cap-à-pie: (Fre.) 'From head to foot'.

The barren plains . . . wagons light: John Milton, *Paradise Lost*, Book 3, ll. 437–9.

Sabaeans: An ancient people from what today is Yemen.

Aristotle's quintessential light: Quintessentian light, or ether, is the fifth element posited by Aristotle.

Ourania Hierarchia: In transliterated Greek it means Hierarchy of the Heavens.

balneum: (Lat.) Bath.

Tadmor . . . Palmyra: Ancient city in central Syria.

Nux bore not less Thanatos than Hupnos: 'The night bore not less Death than Sleep' – in a variant spelling of transliterated Greek.

redundulate: Flowing or rippling, akin to the movement of water.

Buffo: (Ita.) Buffoon; a comic opera actor or singer.

Parvati . . . Brahmin: In Hinduism Parvati is a powerful goddess associated with the Himalayas and the wife of Shiva. Brahmin refers to Hindu castes.

bon camarade: (Fre.) 'Good comrade'.
Drummond's Flowers of Sion: (1623) A book of poetry by Scottish poet William Drummond of Hawthornden (1585–1649).
Paz: Or Faz; a village in eastern Iran.
Andromeda yonder from the ridden Ram: Reference to constellations.
Nowhere: Probably an allusion to William Morris's utopian novel *News from Nowhere* (1890).
Eos drives an equipage à quatre: The Greek goddess of dawn, driving a four-horse-drawn chariot.
Spanish Curate: A late Jacobean comedy (performed in 1622 and published in 1647) written by John Fletcher (1579–1625) and Philip Massinger (1583–1640).
ichthyotauri: Shiel probably means ichthyosauri, plural for ichthyosaurus (from the Greek for fish-lizard), a marine animal that lived between the Triassic and Jurassic periods.
Sigma couch: A semi-circular Roman couch, resembling the letter 'C'.
Danish Kjökkenmöddings: (Dan.) Kitchen-middens; prehistoric mounds of debris found in Denmark and other northern European regions.
Herculaneum ... 79: Mount Vesuvius erupted in August AD 79, totally destroying the cities of Herculaneum and Pompeii.
wight: Living creature.
Setian: Probably a reference to the Roman Gnostic sect Sethians.
delicioe: (Lat.) 'Delicious'.
Leibnitz: Gottfried Wilhelm von Leibnitz (1646–1716). German philosopher and mathematician.
Paean and Aesculapius: Classical gods of medicine and healing, usually synonymous.
Marah: Hebrew for 'bitter' waters, a place through which the Israelites travelled during the Exodus.

Arthur Symons 'The Death of Peter Waydelin' (1905)

Spiritual Adventures (New York: Dutton, 1905): pp. 147–74. First published as 'Peter Waydelin's Experiment', *Lippincott's Monthly Magazine* 73.434 (February 1904): pp. 219–29.
Refs: 'The Genesis of Spiritual Adventures', Unpublished TS, 'Arthur Symons Papers', Rare Books and Special Collections Department, Princeton University Library; John M. Munro, *Arthur Symons* (New York: Twayne, 1969), pp. 105–8.

Toulouse-Lautrec: Henri Marie Raymond de Toulouse-Lautrec-Monfa (1864–1901), French Postimpressionist painter.
Bognor ... Selsey to Blake's Felpham: Coastal area in West Sussex.
Whistler: James Abbott McNeill Whistler (1834–1903) was a British painter of American birth who advocated 'art for art's sake' and was famous for his tonal compositions.
Verlaine ... 'without words': Paul Verlaine (1844–96) was a famous Decadent poet and friend of Symons. Waydelin refers to Verlaine's poetry collection *Romances sans paroles* (*Songs without Words*, 1874).
molle: (Fre.) 'Soft'.
Raphael aesthetics: Raffaello Sanzio da Urbino (1483–1520) was an Italian Renaissance painter who inspired the entire Pre-Raphaelite movement in Victorian Britain.
Apollo Belvedere: A well-known Classical statue originally by Greek sculptor Leochares.
marbles of Aegina: A group of Classical sculptures from the Temple of Aphaia on the Greek island of Aegina. They were shipped to Munich in 1811.
Turner: Joseph Mallord William Turner (1775–1851) was a famous English landscape painter.
Advokat: Or advocaat (Dch) is a custard-like cream liqueur containing egg yolks, aromatic spirits such as brandy, and sugar.
Sada Yacco: Kawakami Sadayakko (1871–1946) was a Japanese geisha, dancer and actress who performed in America and Europe. Pablo Picasso painted her several times.
women of the Green Houses: Courtesans residing in brothels in the pleasure district of Yoshiwara, Japan.
Watteau: French painter Jean-Antoine Watteau (1684–1721), credited for inventing the *fête galante* genre.
Degas: Edgar Degas (1834–1917) was a French Impressionist painter who often depicted dancers.
green: Besides yellow, a signature colour of the Decadents and a favourite of Wilde (see for example 'Pen, Pencil, and Poison' (1891) subtitled 'A Study in Green'). The green carnation was a symbol of artificiality. Green was also used to denote homosexuality.
aniline dye: The first synthetic dye (indigo) based on an organic base, obtained in 1826.
peroxide-of-hydrogen hair: Hydrogen peroxide was (and still is) used to achieve blond hair by bleaching.
Dionysus Zagreus ... 'orgie on the mountains': the author is fusing two

versions of the ancient god associated with wine, feasting and sexual indulgence: the Greek god Dionysus Zagreus and the Roman Bacchus. The resulting image is one of unbridled debauchery.
Watts, Burne-Jones, Moreau: George Frederic Watts (1817–1904) was a British Symbolist painter; Edward Burne-Jones (1833–98) was a British Pre-Raphaelite painter; and Gustave Moreau (1826–98) was a French Symbolist painter who, with his luxurious and bejewelled manner, inspired the Decadent writers.

PARODIES

H. G. Wells 'A Misunderstood Artist' (1894)

Pall Mall Gazette, 29 October 1894: p. 3.
Jovian coiffure: Hairstyle of the Roman god Jove; in the Romantic era, 'Roman'-style hair cuts were very popular in Britain among the upper classes.
Ruskin: in Volume 2 of *Modern Painters* (1846/56) John Ruskin argues for the moral dimension of Beauty.
Venus of Titian: *Venus of Urbino* (1538) is an oil painting by the Italian painter Titian (c. 1488/90–1576), depicting a nude reclining Venus.
Nocturnes . . . scattered candles: Wells possibly has in mind Whistler's *Nocturne in Black and Gold – The Falling Rocket* (1875). Ruskin criticised this painting; as a result, Whistler filed a lawsuit against Ruskin in 1877. The harmonious arrangement of black-coloured food alludes to Des Esseintes's funereal 'black' dinner in Chapter 1 of *À Rebours*.

Lionel Johnson 'Incurable' (1896)

The Pageant (1896): pp. 131–9.
et je suis . . . lointaine musique: (Fre.) 'And I am in the night . . . oh, the night is so beautiful . . . / Do nothing . . . be quiet . . . and be rocked by ennui, / the dying rhythm of ancient music' (our translation).
Ave atque Vale: (Lat.) 'Hail and farewell.'
Paganini: Nicolò Paganini (1782–1840), Italian violinist and composer.
Sometimes, in very . . . love's opera!: Here Johnson pokes fun at Arthur Symons's sensual poetry and poetic rhythms: compare with 'Music and Memory', 'To a Dancer' and 'Stella Maris'.

Ode to Duty or the Scholar Gypsy: Poems by William Wordsworth and Matthew Arnold, published in 1807 and 1853 respectively.
will-o'-the-wisp: A pure fantasy or illusion.
Sangrails and Eldorados: Referring to the unattainable Holy Grail and Eldorado, the legendary city of gold.
Chatterton, Gérard de Nerval . . . in art: Thomas Chatterton (1752–70) was an English poet and literary forger, and a favourite of Oscar Wilde (and the Hobby Horsers). Gérard de Nerval (1808–55) was a French Romantic poet, admired by Symons. Those two poets committed suicide.
Carlyle: Scottish thinker Thomas Carlyle (1795–1881).
Cato [and] Addison: A reference to Roman orator Cato the Younger (95 BC–46 BC) and English physician Thomas Addison (1793–1860), both of whom committed suicide.
Rameau: Jean-Philippe Rameau (1683–1764) was an influential composer of Baroque music, who extensively used the harpsichord.
Lady of Shalott: (1833, 1842) A ballad by Alfred Tennyson and common theme for Pre-Raphaelite painters. The poem contains Aestheticist ideas and paradoxes regarding the role of the artist.
Charon: In Greek mythology the ferryman who carries the souls of the departed to Hades through the rivers Styx and Acheron.
Mr. Pickwick: A character from Charles Dickens's first novel, *The Pickwick Papers* (1836).

BACKGROUND SOURCES (SELECTIVE NOTES)

Genera and species: Darwin's classification and sub-classification of living things.
Ultramontane: Literally, 'beyond the mountain', this phrase refers to other peoples, or specifically to those who hold Papal authority above national premiership.
Lymphatic: In this instance, lacking physical or mental energy.
Véra: One of Villiers de l'Isle-Adam's *contes cruels*.
Poe's Beatrices and Ligeias: Huysmans probably has in mind Poe's tales 'Berenice' (1835) and 'Ligeia' (1838), although the protagonist of 'The Visionary' (1832) is named Beatrice.
The Goncourts: Edmond (1822–96) and Jules de Goncourt (1830–70) were French Naturalist novelists and famous journal writers. Symons and other British writers were influenced by them.
Plain Tales from the Hills: (1888) A book of humorous short stories

recounting the lives and loves of colonial ex-pats in India, by Rudyard Kipling (1865–1936).
Browning: Robert Browning (1812–99) English poet, known in particular for his dramatic monologues.
Meredith: George Meredith (1828–1909) English poet and novelist.
Author of Le Rouge et le Noir: Marie-Henri Beyle, known as Stendhal (1783–1842), author of the realist novel *Le Rouge et le Noir* (*The Red and the Black*, 1830).
'une langue rendant . . . notre signature': (Fre.) 'A language making our ideas, our feelings, our representations of men and things, a distinct way of this or that one, a personal language, one bearing our signature' (our translation).
Flaubert: Gustave Flaubert (1821–80), French novelist.
Hogarth's pictures: William Hogarth (1697–1764), English painter, printmaker, satirist, critic and cartoonist, famous for painting scenes which include ribald behaviour and risqué or grotesque imagery.
chirurgical: Surgical.
Velasquez: Diego Rodríguez de Silva y Velasquez (1599–1660), Spanish painter.
Pope: Alexander Pope (1688–1744), English poet.
Ibsen: Henrik Ibsen (1828–1906), Norwegian playwright, director and poet.
The New English Art Club: Formed in 1866, with members such as Walter Sickert (1860–1942) and Philip Wilson Steer (1860–1942). The Club was greatly influenced by contemporary French art, in particular Impressionism.
The Second Mrs Tanqueray: A play (performed in 1893) by Arthur Wing Pinero (1855–1934).
Richard le Gallienne: (1866–1947) English author and poet, often thought of as counter-Decadent.
Banquo's ghost: From Shakespeare's *Macbeth*.
Caesar's ghost: From Shakespeare's *Julius Caesar*.
Spencerian: This refers to an idea by biologist, sociologist and philosopher Herbert Spencer (1820–1903).
Sir Thomas Browne: (1605–82), English polymath and author.
Hume: David Hume (1711–76), Scottish philosopher, historian and economist.
Gibbon: Edward Gibbon (1737–94), English historian and Member of Parliament, famous for *The History of the Decline and Fall of the Roman Empire* (1776–8).

Emerson: Ralph Waldo Emerson (1803–88), American essayist, lecturer and poet, and leader of the Transcendentalist movement.

Select Bibliography

ANTHOLOGIES

Baldick, Chris, and Jane Desmarais (eds) (2013), *Decadence, From Petronius to Proust: An Annotated Anthology*, Manchester: Manchester University Press.

Beckson, Karl (ed.) [1966] (2011), *Aesthetes and Decadents of the 1890s: An Anthology of British Poetry and Prose*, Chicago: Academy Chicago.

Denissof, Dennis (ed.) (2004), *The Broadview Anthology of Victorian Short Stories*, Peterborough: Broadview.

Gerber, Helmut E. (ed.) (1967), *The English Short Story in Transition 1880–1920*, New York: Pegasus.

Harrison, Frazer (ed.) (1974), *The Yellow Book: An Illustrated Quarterly: An Anthology*, Woodbridge: Boydell.

Luckhurst, Roger (ed.) (2009), *Late Victorian Gothic Tales*, Oxford: Oxford University Press.

Nassaar, Christopher S. (ed.) (1999), *The English Literary Decadence: An Anthology*, Lanham: University Press of America.

Richardson, Angelique (ed.) (2002), *Women Who Did: Stories by Men and Women, 1890–1914*, London: Penguin.

Romer, Stephen (ed.) (2013), *French Decadent Tales*, Oxford: Oxford University Press.

Schaffer, Talia (ed.) (2007), *Literature and Culture at the Fin de Siècle*, New York: Longman.

Showalter, Elaine (ed.) (1993), *Daughters of Decadence: Women Writers of the Fin-de-Siècle*, New Brunswick: Rutgers University Press.

Standford, Derek (ed.) (1968), *Short Stories of the 'Nineties: A Biographical Anthology*, London: John Baker.

Willsher, James (ed.) (2004), *The Dedalus Book of English Decadence: Vile Emperors and Elegant Degenerates*, Sawtry: Dedalus.

CRITICISM

Brake, Laurel (2001), *Print in Transition, 1850–1910: Studies in Media and Book History*, London: Palgrave.
Brooker, Peter and Andrew Thacker (eds) (2009), *The Oxford Critical and Cultural History of Modernist Magazines*, Oxford: Oxford University Press.
Chan, Winnie (2007), *The Economy of the Short Story in British Periodicals of the 1890s*, New York: Routledge.
Claes, Koenraad and Marysa Demoor (2010), 'The Little Magazine in the 1890s: Towards a Total Work of Art', *English Studies* 91.2, pp. 133–49.
Clark, Petra (2013), 'Bitextuality, Sexuality, and the Male Aesthete in *The Dial*: "Not through an orthodox channel"', *English Literature in Transition, 1880–1920* 56.1, pp. 33–50.
Dowling, Linda (1979), 'The Decadent and the New Woman in the 1890's', *Nineteenth-Century Fiction* 33.4, pp. 433–53.
Dowling, Linda (1986), *Language and Decadence in the Victorian Fin de Siècle*, Princeton: Princeton University Press.
Ellmann, Richard (1987), *Oscar Wilde*, London: Penguin.
Fletcher, Ian (ed.) (1980), *Decadence and the 1890s*, Stratford-upon-Avon Studies 17, New York: Holmes.
Freeman, Nick (2011), *1895: Drama, Disaster and Disgrace in Late Victorian Britain*, Edinburgh: Edinburgh University Press.
Garbáty, Thomas J. (1960), 'The French Coterie of the *Savoy* 1896', *PMLA* 75.5, pp. 609–15.
Gordon, Jan B. (1972), '"The Wilde Child": Structure and Origin in the *Fin-de-Siècle* Short Story', *English Literature in Transition, 1880–1920* 15.4, pp. 277–90.
Hall, Jason David and Alex Murray (eds) (2013), *Decadent Poetics: Literature and Form at the British Fin de Siècle*, Basingstoke: Palgrave Macmillan.
Hanson, Ellis (1997), *Decadence and Catholicism*, Cambridge: Harvard University Press, 1997.
Harris, Wendell V. (1962), 'Identifying the Decadent Fiction of the Eighteen-Nineties', *English Literature in Transition, 1880–1920* 5.5, pp. 1–13.
Harris, Wendell V. (1968a), 'The Hectic and the Morbid in the 1890's', *Studies in Short Fiction* 6.1, pp. 90–2.
Harris, Wendell V. (1968b), 'John Lane's Keynotes Series and the Fiction of the 1890s', *PMLA* 83.5, pp. 1407–13.
Hunter, Adrian (2007), *The Cambridge Introduction to the Short Story in English*, Cambridge: Cambridge University Press.
Jackson, Holbrook (1913), *The Eighteen Nineties: A Review of Art and Ideas at the Close of the Nineteenth Century*, London: Richards.
Kingcaid, Renée A. (1992), *Neurosis and Narrative: The Decadent Short Fiction of Proust, Lorrain, and Rachilde*, Carbondale and Edwardsville: Southern Illinois University Press.
Ledger, S. (2007), 'Wilde Women and *The Yellow Book*: The Sexual Politics of Aestheticism and Decadence', *English Literature in Transition* 50.1, pp. 5–26.

MacLeod, Kirsten (2005), '"Art for America's Sake": Decadence and the Making of American Literary Culture in the Little Magazines of the 1890s', *Prospects* 30, pp. 309–38.
MacLeod, Kirsten (2006), *Fictions of British Decadence: High Art, Popular Writing and the Fin de Siècle*, Basingstoke: Palgrave.
Marshall, Gail (ed.) (2007), *The Cambridge Companion to the Fin de Siècle*, Cambridge: Cambridge University Press.
May, J. Lewis (1936), *John Lane and the Nineties*, London: The Bodley Head.
Mix, Katherine L. (1960), *A Study in Yellow: The Yellow Book and its Contributors*, Lawrence: University of Kansas Press.
Navarette, Susan J. (1998), *The Shape of Fear: Horror and the Fin de Siècle Culture of Decadence*, Lexington: University Press of Kentucky.
Pittock, Murray (1993), *G. H. Spectrum of Decadence: The Literature of the 1890s*, London: Routledge.
Pondrom, Cyrena N. (1968), 'A Note on the Little Magazines of the English Decadence', *Victorian Periodicals Newsletter* 1.1, pp. 30–1.
Praz, Mario [1933] (1978), *Romantic Agony*, Oxford: Oxford University Press.
Reed, John R. (1982–3), 'Decadent Style and the Short Story', *Victorians Institute Journal*, pp. 1–12.
Reed, John R. (1985), *Decadent Style*, Athens: Ohio University Press.
Schaffer, Talia (2000), *The Forgotten Female Aesthetes: Literary Culture in Late-Victorian England*, Charlottesville: University Press of Virginia.
Shaw, Valerie (1983), *The Short Story: A Critical Introduction*, Harlow: Longman.
Stableford, Brian (1998), *Glorious Perversity: The Decline and Fall of Literary Decadence*, Rockville: Wildside Press.
Sturgis, Matthew (1995), *Passionate Attitudes: The English Decadence of the 1890s*, London: Macmillan.
Sullivan, Alvin (ed.) (1984), *British Literary Magazines: The Victorian and Edwardian Age, 1837–1913*, West Port: Greenwood Press.
Thornton, R. K. R. (1983), *The Decadent Dilemma*, London: Edward Arnold.
Weir, David (1995), *Decadence and the Making of Modernism*, Amherst: University of Massachusetts Press.

Index

absinthe, 39, 41, 175, 179, 428n
Aestheticism (-ic), 1, 3, 12, 13, 14, 15, 16, 18, 94–5, 99, 166, 174, 272, 305, 350, 357–8, 413, 418, 456n
Affliction of Childhood, The (De Quincey), 65
Alhambra, the, 4, 206, 263
Aristotle, 6, 372
Arnold, Matthew, 439n
art for art's sake (appearances in the stories and excerpts), 386, 392, 406, 416
Arts and Crafts, 9
Athenaeum, The, 38

Balzac, Honoré de, 18
Baudelaire, Charles, 15, 281, 413
  'La Destruction', 451n
  'Éloge du maquillage', 272
  Les Fleurs du Mal, 160, 366
  'Notes Nouvelles sur Edgar Poe', 400–1
  Petits Poèmes en Prose, 15
Beardsley, Aubrey, 8, 10, 13, 160, 166, 272, 297, 305, 350, 365, 366, 380
Beerbohm, Max, 11, 166
  'A Defence of Cosmetics', 272
  'Enoch Soames', 21
  'The Happy Hypocrite', 15–16
  'Yai and the Moon', 18, 272–3, 445n
Bloxam, John Francis, 'The Priest and the Acolyte', 9–10, 19, 86–7, 433n
Bodley Head, The, 98, 444n
Bristow, Joseph, 112
British Imperialism (-al, -ists), 7, 20, 49
British Matron, The, 3–5, 20, 65, 405
Broadbent, Muriel, 206
Burton, Sir Richard Francis, 136

Carlyle, Thomas, 357, 399, 417
Catholicism (-ic), 5–6, 9, 17, 19, 38, 39, 45, 46, 48, 65, 68, 86–7, 126, 134, 253–4, 299, 342; *see also* Mass
Catullus, 30, 427n
Century Guild Hobby Horse, The, 8–9, 10, 11, 27, 28, 29, 49, 126, 206, 456n
Chambers, Robert W., 370
Chameleon, The, 9–10, 86
Chap-Book, The, 8
Chat Noir, Le, 8
Chekhov, Anton, 24n
Chesterton, G. K., 418–19
cigarettes, 19, 67, 111, 127–33, 156, 316, 436n
Classicism (-ic, -al), 1, 9, 11, 56, 127, 292, 408–9, 417
Confession, 5, 39, 87–8, 90, 96, 408
Confessional Unmasked, The, 6
Conrad, Joseph, 18, 233
  Heart of Darkness, 22, 49
  'The Idiots', 20, 22, 233–4, 443–4n
conte cruel, 13, 19, 281
Corvo, Baron, 20
Cosmopolis, 233
Crackanthorpe, Hubert, 15, 22, 104–5
  'Modern Melodrama', 20, 105, 435n
  'Reticence in Literature: Some Roundabout Remarks', 2, 4, 411
Crashaw, Richard, 269, 444n
Cross, Victoria, 10, 136
  Six Chapters of a Man's Life, 136
  'Theodora: A Fragment', 19, 136–7, 438n
cross-dressing (*and* transvestism), 19, 136–7, 156
  genre cross-dressing, 16

D'Arcy, Ella, 10, 15, 112, 174
'The Death Mask', 18, 174–5, 440n
Modern Instances, 175
Monochromes, 174
'The Pleasure-Pilgrim', 15, 20
d'Aurevilly, Jules Barbey, 13, 404
dandy, 18, 19, 136, 166, 281, 299, 305
Darwin, Charles (-ian), 234, 350, 354–5, 403, 404, 411, 450n
Davidson, John, 365
Decadence (-nt, -ism) (appearances in the stories and excerpts), 385, 401, 407, 408–9, 412, 413, 415, 417
Décadence, La, 8
Décadent, Le, 8
democratisation and elitism, 7, 10–11
Dial, The, 7, 8, 9, 11, 21, 56, 65, 68, 254
'Apology', 65, 67–8
Dickens, Charles, 396, 407
Dircks, Rudolph, 181–2
'Ellen', 20, 182, 440n
doppelganger (also doubles and split personality), 14, 19, 20, 207, 305, 327, 366
Douglas, Alfred (Bosie), 9, 126
Dowling, Linda, 17, 24n
Dowson, Ernest, 5, 10–11, 13, 19, 22, 38, 220, 233
'A Case of Conscience', 18, 38–9, 428n
Dilemmas, 16
'Souvenirs of an Egoist', 17
'The Statute of Limitations', 18, 48–9, 429–30n
poems, 49
Doyle, Arthur Conan, 418
'The Case of Lady Sannox', 13
Dracula (Stoker), 343
Duffy, J. J., 'Facts for Men on Moral Purity and Health', 21
Dyer, A. S., 4

Education Act (1870), 7
Egerton, George, 15, 98
'A Cross Line', 20
'A Lost Masterpiece', 17, 98–9, 434–5n
Ellis, Havelock, 10, 332
Affirmations, 417
Empire, the, 4, 134, 187
entropy (-ic), 22, 87, 220, 234, 350, 358
epicureanism (-ean, epicurism), 28, 127, 169, 439n
erotica, 6, 15; *see also* pornography
expurgation (-ed), 6, 27, 414

Fatal Woman, 18, 19, 72, 160, 281, 350, 370
'Field, Michael', 65

Firbank, Ronald, 5
flâneuse (-eur, -eurie), 16, 17, 98, 112, 305
Flaubert, Gustave, 409
Fletcher, Ian, 7, 8
Foltinowicz, Adelaide 'Missie', 38, 49
fragmentation (-ent, -ed, -ary), 6, 8, 14, 15, 17, 20, 21, 22, 49, 56, 105, 206, 358
French sensibility and influence (France, Francophilia), 8, 12, 13, 16, 18, 19, 39, 65, 186, 234, 281, 324, 380

Galton, Arthur, 9
Gautier, Théophile, (-ian), 137, 281, 332, 409, 419
Genre, 8, 12–16
  camouflage, 6, 15–16
  hybrids, 15–16
  specialisation, 14–15
Germ, The, 16
Gesamtkunstwerk, 8; *see also* Total Art
Gilchrist, R. Murray, 159–60, 370
'The Crimson Weaver', 19, 160, 296, 439n
The Stone Dragon, 13
Gissing, George, 112
Gordon, Jan, 8, 14
Gothic, 17, 19, 21, 159, 234, 281, 332, 370
Gray, John, 5, 9, 19, 253–4
'Les Goncourt', 405
'Light', 18, 254, 444n
Silverpoints, 254
Greek sensibility (Greece, Hellenism), 9, 68, 154, 402, 408
green, 41, 388, 454n
Grundy, Mrs, 11

Hardy, Thomas, 112, 207
Harland, Henry, 10, 12, 13, 112, 134, 136, 174
'Concerning the Short Story', 416
'The Invisible Prince', 19
'To Every Man a Damsel or Two', 20, 134, 437–8n
Harris, Wendell V., 13, 14
Hegelian, 14
Hemingway, Ernest, 22
Henley, W. E., 159
Hermetic Order of the Golden Dawn, The, 71
Herodias, 158, 438n
Holmes, Sherlock (Doyle), 8
homoeroticism (-ic), 8, 9, 17, 254, 295, 342, 427n
homosexuality (-al), 9, 19, 86, 126, 288, 299, 342–3, 402, 454n
Horace, influence on Dowson, 51, 429n, 452n

Horne, Herbert Percy, 9, 27, 49, 206
Horsley, John Callcott, 3
Huysmans, Joris Karl, 18, 21, 417
   À Rebours (*or* Des Esseintes), 12, 17, 65, 99, 220, 281, 350, 404–5, 455n
hysteria (-ics), 18, 20, 258, 272–3, 305, 370, 378, 413; *see also* lunacy; madness

Image, Selwyn, 5, 9, 11, 23n, 27, 206
   'A Bundle of Letters, 16, 27–8, 127, 187, 427n
   'On the Representation of the Nude in Art', 5
Impressionism (-ist), 15, 17, 49, 112, 418, 421, 457n
l'Isle Adam, Auguste Villiers de, 13, 160, 281, 404
   'Queen Ysabeau', 19, 281, 446n
   'Véra', 405

Jackson, Holbrook, 15–16, 365
James, Henry, 12, 105
   'Death of a Lion', 21
Japanophilia (Japan, Japanese influence), 272, 296, 387, 395
Johnson, Lionel Pigot, 9, 126
   'Incurable', 21, 396, 456n
   'A Note', 406
   'Tobacco Clouds', 15, 17, 127, 435n
Joyce, James, *Ulysses*, *Dubliners*, and *Finnegan's Wake*, 21

Keats, John (-ian), 160, 272, 397, 446n
Kelmscott Press, The, 9
Kipling, Rudyard, 407, 412, 418
Künstlerroman, 17, 21, 379

Lane, John, 7, 10, 13, 98, 136, 160
Lautrec, Henri de Toulouse, 380
Le Gallienne, Richard, 2, 457n
   The Worshipper of the Image, 18
Lee, Vernon, 305
   'Dionea', 18, 20
   'An Eighteenth Century Singer', 16
   'The Legend of Madame Krasinska', 19–20, 305, 446n
   'A Wicked Voice', 17
   other works, 20, 305
Lesbianism, 112, 305
letter-writing (epistolary form), 6, 27–9, 32, 37, 38, 187, 196
Leverson, Ada, 166
   'An Afternoon Party', 166
   'The Quest of Sorrow', 18, 166–7, 327, 439n

'Suggestion', 12, 20, 166
'Tooraloora: A Fragment', 137
life as art, 34–6
Lippincott's Monthly Magazine, 380
literacy, 7
little girls, cult of, 49, 196
Little Magazines, 1, 5, 7–11, 20
London County Council, 4
Louÿs, Pierre
   Aphrodite, 288, 425
   'A New Sensation', 436n
Lucretius and Milton (in 'Tobacco Clouds'), 127, 128, 133, 436–7n
lunacy (-ic; and insanity), 112, 234, 273, 308, 313; *see also* hysteria; madness

M'lle New York, 8
Machen, Arthur, 370
   ['The Amber Statuette'], 21, 419
   The Great God Pan, 19, 98
   The Hill of Dreams, 17, 28
   'The Novel of the White Powder', 21
   'The White People', 20
Mackmurdo, Arthur Heygate, 27
madness, 52, 82, 84, 119, 121, 234, 254, 278; *see also* hysteria; lunacy
marivaudage, 19
Mass, 65, 66, 87, 91, 97, 240, 241, 345, 428n; *see also* Catholicism
mass market periodical, 7–8, 168–9
Mathews, Elkin, 13, 98, 444n
Matthews, Brander, 14, 403, 417
Mattos, Alexander Texeira de, 281
Melodrama, 22, 49, 182, 206
Mew, Charlotte, 112
   'Passed', 112, 435n
Milton, John (notable use of), 37, 128–9, 131, 372, 399, 428n, 436n
Mirbeau, Octave, 13
Modernism (proto-, -ist), 1, 9, 10, 21–2, 49, 56, 65, 68, 112
Moore, Arthur, 38
Moore, George, 5, 166
Moore, Thomas Sturge, 9, 11
morbidity (-id) (appearances in the stories and excerpts), 12, 20, 40, 53, 182, 366, 380, 407, 409, 414, 416
Moreau, Gustave, 298, 389, 455n
Morris, William, (-ian), 8, 9
Morrison, Arthur, 112
music halls, 4, 5, 20, 27, 134, 135, 187, 196, 202, 206, 320, 380, 386

National Gallery, The, 36–7, 58, 389, 431n
National Observer, The, 159

Naturalism (-ist), 14, 17, 21, 105, 112, 456n
Navarette, Susan, 370
Nesbit, E., 332
   'The Ebony Frame', 18, 332, 448n
   'Man-Size in Marble', 332
New Realism, 13, 105; see also Realism
New Woman (Woman Question), 14, 19–20, 24n, 98, 104, 136, 174, 370–1
Nietzsche, Friedrich, (-ean), 10, 370
Nordau, Max, 10, 112, 273, 405, 410, 414
   Degeneration, 2, 12, 13, 412–13
'La Nuit' (de Maupassant), 18

O'Sullivan, Vincent, 365–6
   A Book of Bargains, 15, 366
   'On the Kind of Fiction Called Morbid', 414
   'Original Sin', 15, 19, 366, 450n
   'A Study of Murder', 366
Obscene Publications Act, 5–6, 427n
orientalism (-al), 11, 130, 137, 148–57, 262, 263, 272, 348, 350
Ormiston Chant, Laura 'Mrs', 4
orphans, 87, 182, 206
Oxford, The, 4
Oxford University, 9, 27, 86, 272, 299, 328

paederasty (-ic), 9, 86, 343
Pagan Review, The, 11, 72
paganism, 11, 71–2
Pageant, The, 8, 11
Paget, Violet see Lee, Vernon
Pall Mall Gazette, 342, 350
Pall Mall Magazine, 112
parody (self-, -ies, -ic), 14, 21, 99, 166–7, 169, 305, 327, 342, 343, 392, 396
Pater, Walter, (-ian), 16, 17, 22, 370, 405, 408, 409, 417
   euphuism, 12, 415
   his general influence, 9, 28, 71, 305, 358, 411
   'The Child in the House', 16
   'Conclusion', 11, 28, 127, 402
   Imaginary Portraits, 15, 16, 409
   Marcus the Epicurean, 409, 439n
   The Renaissance, 27–8, 127, 409
   'Style', 12
periodicals, 7
philistinism (-ine(s)), 12, 168, 392, 395, 413, 419, 439n
Pissarro, Lucien, 11
Poe, Edgar Allan, 13, 160, 281, 395, 400–1, 403
   'The Mask of the Red Death', 305
   'The Oval Portrait', 332

'The Philosophy of Composition', 12
pornography (-ic), 5, 6, 87
Pre-Raphaelites, 8, 9, 11, 16, 298, 332, 335, 406, 413, 449n, 454n
prostitution (-ute(s)), 3–5, 20, 112, 115, 134, 206, 212, 299, 387, 454n
Protestant Electoral Union, 6
Protestantism (-ant), 5–6, 10, 19, 39, 68, 254, 444n
Punch, 393, 394, 395
Puritanism (-an(s)), 2–5, 45, 160, 195
Purity Societies, 4, 56

Realism (-ist), 14, 23n, 404, 405, 407, 410, 412, 457n; see also New Realism
Reed, John R., 14, 16, 18
Richards, Grant, 104
Ricketts, Charles, 9, 11, 56
   'The Cup of Happiness', 15, 17, 21, 56, 430n
   'Sensations', 17, 22, 65, 432n
Robertson, M. John, 'Concerning Preciosity', 415
Rossetti, Christina, 'The Prince's Progress', 49, 54, 430n
Rossetti, Dante Gabriel, 72, 335, 449n
   'Hand and Soul', 16, 17
Royal Academy, The, 3, 10, 196
Ruskin, John, 28, 392, 427n, 455n

Sade, Marquis de, 281
sadism (-istic), 13, 413
Sassoon, Siegfried, 112
Saturday Review, The, 72, 350
Savoy, The, 8, 10–11, 13, 104, 181–2, 366, 414
Schopenhauer, Arthur, 147
Schwob, Marcel, Vies imaginaires, 16
Scofield, Martin, 22
Shakespeare, William, (-ean) (appearances in the stories and excerpts), 131, 179, 180, 200, 397, 399, 414
Shannon, Charles Haslewood, 9, 11, 56, 65, 68
   'A Simple Story', 17, 68, 432n
Sharp, William ('Fiona Macleod'), 11, 71–2
   'The Black Madonna', 15, 18, 72, 433n
Shaw, George Bernard, 10, 56, 332
Shaw, Valerie, 15
Shiel, M. P., 14, 98, 160, 370
   Shapes in the Fire, 14–15, 370
   'Xélucha', 19, 21, 370–1, 451n
   other works, 370
Sickert, Walter, 15, 457n

The Sin (Stuck), 19
Sinclair, May, 112
Smithers, Leonard, 10, 13, 104, 136, 365
Solomon, Simeon, 34
Song of Solomon, 34, 63, 293, 432n
Spe, Friedrich, 269, 444n
Spectator, The, 133, 437n
Spirit Lamp, The, 9
Stanford, Derek, 13–14, 16
Steer, Wilson, 294
Stenbock, Eric, 342
   'The True Story of a Vampire', 19, 343, 449n
Stevenson, Robert Louis
   Jekyll and Hyde, 366
   'Olalla', 234
Strand Magazine, The, 8
Swinburne, Algernon Charles, (-ian), 19, 72, 413
   'Dead Love', 421
   poems, 72
Symbolism (-ist), 8, 17, 58, 272, 281, 299, 379, 438n
Symons, Arthur, 1, 10–11, 18, 20, 21, 23n, 134, 166, 206, 220, 233–4, 281, 342, 343, 365, 456n
   'The Death of Peter Waydelin', 17, 379–80, 453n
   'The Decadent Movement in Literature', 408
   'Esther Kahn' *and* 'Christian Trevalga', 16
   Lucy Newcome Stories, 20, 206–7, 442n
   Notes on Joseph Conrad, 233–4
   Spiritual Adventures, 16
   travel memoirs/essays, 16

Taylor, Una Ashworth, 357–8
   'The Seed of the Sun', 358
   'The Truce of God', 18, 358, 450n
   other works, 358
Temple Bar, 112
Tennyson, Alfred Lord, 31–2, 357, 456n
'Thy Heart's Desire' (Syrett), 20
Times, The, 3, 4
Todi, Jacopone da, 265, 444n
Total Art, 9; *see also Gesamtkunstwerk*

vampirism (-ires, -ic), 19, 234, 299, 343, 345, 350
Venus di Milo, 6, 178

Verlaine, Paul, 18, 175, 382
'A Village Decadent' (Byng), 10

Wagner, Richard, (-ian), 8, 10, 17, 431n
Waugh, Arthur, 'Reticence in Literature', 410, 411
Wedmore, Frederick, 12, 13, 22, 23n, 186–7
   'The Deterioration of Nancy', 196, 442n
   'The Short Story', 417
   'To Nancy', 20, 187, 294, 441n
Wells, Herbert George, 7, 332, 350
   'The Flowering of the Strange Orchid', 18, 350, 450n
   'A Misunderstood Artist', 21, 392, 455n
   his Scientific Romances, 350
Whistler, James Abbott McNeill, 14, 15, 272, 382, 395, 412, 454n, 455n
   'Ten O'Clock Lecture', 392
Wilde, Lily, 281
Wilde, Oscar, 4–6, 9, 12, 13, 14, 17, 56, 65, 86–7, 126, 166, 253, 272, 299, 350, 365, 370, 412, 413, 423, 425
   trial / conviction, 6, 10, 27, 86–7, 160, 413
Wildean, 105, 272, 342, 350, 358
   'The Critic as Artist', 407
   The Importance of Being Ernest, 221
   'A Modern Millionaire', 327
   'The Nightingale and the Rose', 17, 299–300, 446n
   The Picture of Dorian Gray, 2–3, 5, 15, 18, 22, 28, 56, 127, 166, 174, 220, 253, 272, 305, 327, 358, 404, 427n
   Salomé, 272, 281, 438n
   'The Sphinx without a Secret', 20, 327–8, 448n
Wilson, Patten, 160, 296
Woman's World, 7
Woolf, Virginia, 21–2, 112
   Monday or Tuesday, 21
   To the Lighthouse, 21
Wratislaw, Theodore, 220
   'Mutability', 19, 220–1, 443n
   his poetry books, 220, 350

Yacco, Sada, 380, 387, 454n
Yeats, William Butler, 71, 342
   'Rosa Alchemica', 11
Yellow Book, The, 7, 8, 10, 11, 13, 15, 20, 98, 134, 136, 160, 174, 187, 305, 410, 425

Zola, Emile, (-esque), 2, 10, 65, 234